EAGLE TACTICAL COLLECTION

WILLOW FOX

Eagle Tactical Collection

Willow Fox

Published by Slow Burn Publishing

Cover design by GetCovers

V3

EXPOSE: JAXSON

EAGLE TACTICAL BOOK ONE

CHAPTER ONE

ARIELLA

I ran for my life, and it was all *his* fault. Secrets had brought me over a thousand miles from home. I fled with only one thought in mind: a second chance. Starting over was my only option for survival.

I squinted through my sunglasses, shucking them to the empty passenger seat, finding it difficult to see. My vision adjusted, but the night was setting in fast as daylight fell over the horizon.

I struggled to see the narrow, snow-covered road ahead.

The streets at the bottom of the mountain had been freshly plowed and salted. The headlights on my five-speed were angled at odd intervals, casting shadows over the road covered in potholes beneath the slush.

The car jolted and bounced with my foot on the gas, splashing my scalding, stale coffee from the cup holder.

My eyes burned and welled.

"Shit!"

Tears threatened the surface, but I wouldn't cry. It wasn't the sting of blistering liquid that hurt. I'd done this to myself. I blamed him, but it was as much my fault.

Secrets surrounded my past. Benjamin Ryan had been part of those secrets, but there was more than even he knew. There were secrets I could never tell him, even as he was whisked away in handcuffs.

I packed my car with my possessions and hurried out of the state of New York. Of course, not before finding a small log cabin in the woods that I could afford in cash, sight unseen.

I also lined up a job interview at a nearby resort, but there was no guarantee of landing a position right away. My last one had ruined my life, and I couldn't even put it on my resume.

I'd have to be frugal with the few dollars left to my name, which consisted of a few ones in my wallet.

Was I bitter?

Sure as shit, but I moved on, started over, and prayed for a second chance. A fresh start is what I did, what I craved, and the only way to get that was to move.

I went back to using my maiden name: Ariella Cole. I wasn't in hiding per se. After all, I had done nothing wrong or criminal.

I couldn't say the same for him.

I didn't want to get mixed up in his illegal affairs.

I had planned on arriving at my new home before dark, but the interview had been in the afternoon at Blue Sky Resort, a ski lodge just outside of Breckenridge, Montana.

It was for a position covering other worker's shifts, everything from waitressing at the restaurant to doing housekeeping tasks and handling the ski rental equipment. I'd take whatever I could get.

The interview had seemed to go well, and they had asked to run a background check. I wasn't keen on it but I didn't have a choice, so they'd see that my ex-husband, Ben, had run up our credit. They couldn't deny me a job because of that, right?

He was serving time in federal prison for several felonies. That couldn't count against me, right?

When I'd left the resort, with my piping hot, burnt coffee, it had grown dark. The front desk attendant had given me directions since my phone died, and GPS was sketchy as to whether it worked in the mountains.

I headed for my new house, weary, tired, and worn after a lengthy interview and an even longer drive across the country. I wanted to discover my new home, climb into bed under the warm covers and sleep for a week.

The interviewer informed me they'd run my references, and I had to submit to a background check.

It sounded all good, and while I hoped the job was mine, there were no guarantees. They hadn't offered me anything yet.

I downshifted my car, but I struggled to get up the mountain.

The bald tires spun as I white-knuckled the steering wheel. The back of the vehicle fishtailed.

I downshifted again and stomped on the gas to climb the godforsaken beast of a mountain when the car slipped and slid backward downhill.

"Shit!" I screamed and stomped on the brakes hard, which only had me doing donuts as I spun and slid down the icy path of the mountain. I would have braced for impact if I had known how, but I just wanted to survive. I needed to survive.

My stomach ached with dread. My palms were sweaty, and I clung to the steering wheel, attempting to maneuver my car out of danger.

I had no control over the vehicle, like it had a mind of its own.

The car spun and smacked into a tree. The window smashed. It wasn't enough to stop the momentum from sliding down the mountain, and the back wheels skidded off the road.

By some miracle, the vehicle came to a halt. The back wheels teetered off the edge of a ravine.

The car's front appeared stable, but would it propel me downward and into oblivion if I made any sudden movements?

I glanced in the rearview mirror.

It grew darker by the minute, and I couldn't ascertain how far down the ditch went, but given the fact the entire drive up the mountain was switchbacks and dangerous, without a doubt, it was deadly.

Exhaling a soft, slow breath, I couldn't stay in the car. I needed to get help.

I hadn't seen a car on the road since I attempted to climb the damned mountain. Was there a reason for that? Did anyone live up in Breckenridge, or was I the only one crazy enough to head up there on the cusp of winter?

I probably should have traded my car in for a vehicle with all-wheel drive or a truck, but it wasn't like I could afford it.

I was strapped for cash. I spent every dime on getting to Breckenridge and paying cash for the cabin I found on one of the realtor sites online.

The place looked like a gem, backed up to a gorgeous river, and within walking distance to a few local shops in town.

This had to mean I wasn't the only one in Breckenridge, but they were smart enough not to travel at night up the mountain.

My phone was dead, and even if it had any juice left, I knew without a doubt there would be no cell service around here.

There had been no service at the bottom of the mountain. That had been when my phone still had a tiny amount of battery power.

Not that I didn't have anyone to call. My sister would expect to hear from me, but we weren't on the best speaking terms. She was pissed that I moved to Breckenridge instead of staying in New York with her.

I couldn't stay. I had to get as far away from New York and the enemies we'd made.

I glanced behind me at my knapsack. I couldn't risk reaching for it. Not until I was out of the car.

With slow precision, I unlocked the door and eased the driver's side open. I made no sudden movements.

While I'd have preferred to stay in the confines of the car that offered shelter, it teetered on the edge of a ravine. I wasn't ready to meet death.

The car creaked and groaned as I was careful to shift my weight from one foot and then the other out from the vehicle.

The vehicle didn't launch off the cliff as I had first feared. I shivered and pulled my jacket tight.

I couldn't easily open the back door from my position. The snow was several inches thick, and I had stuffed my boots in the trunk.

There was no way I could maneuver myself to grab my warm and comfy shoes. My fancy heels would have to suffice because I wasn't going barefoot. That would be even stupider in this weather.

"Okay, I can do this," I said to myself.

There wasn't another soul on the road, and I didn't even want to consider what wild animals like bears or wolves come out at night. I hadn't the slightest idea if they were nocturnal. I hoped I didn't run into any creatures because I had nothing but my hands to protect me, and well, I may as well just lie down and play dead.

Okay, so getting my bag from the backseat wasn't as easy as I thought. I exhaled a nervous breath, my stomach in knots as I climbed back into the driver's seat, reached for my knapsack in the back, along with my purse on the passenger seat.

I didn't make any sudden movements, and I backed away from the car, shut the car door, shoved my purse into the bag, and swung it over my shoulder.

My hands shook from the cold and the adrenaline coursing through my veins. I dug into my pockets, retrieving a pair of leather driving gloves. They would have to suffice.

With daylight nearly gone, I headed for the main road of the mountain.

I kept to the center of the snow-covered path. I'd probably hear something long before I'd see anything, but I wasn't holding my breath.

The moon offered the faintest bit of light to illuminate the snow-covered road.

I had no flashlight, and the darkness of night seeped in, which reminded me there wasn't a town for miles because there were no city lights nearby.

I glanced up at the heavens, the frigid night air offering way to a sparkle of stars peppering the night sky. It would be a beautiful sight if it wasn't so cold and I didn't worry about freezing to death.

My lungs hurt from the cold. With each breath inward, a thousand knives were stabbing at my lungs.

With my jacket zipped up tight, I leaned my head down toward my coat. I needed to find shelter. With sundown, the night would only grow colder.

My hands trembled even with the warmth of my gloves. The edge of the road was difficult to see with no light. It seemed even more impossible to determine if there was any evidence of shelter.

I kept walking up the mountain. The only way I could tell I was headed in the correct direction was because the wind assaulted my face, and my footprints were evidence of where I'd been.

I could no longer see my car in the distance. The broken windows may have offered little shelter from the wind, but I could have been warmer had I stayed inside the vehicle. I could also have been catapulted down the ravine had I so much as shifted the car's weight.

There was no use second-guessing my decision. I just hoped that the main road would lead off to a driveway, a house, a cabin, or some sign of civilization.

The chill of the cold brought tears to my eyes, freezing my eyelashes, stinging my cheeks. My hands were numb, and my knapsack offered no clothes. Frozen inside and out.

I stumbled over my feet.

My toes burned from the frigid air that assaulted every inch of my body. The sensation went beyond numb and tingling.

I tripped and braced myself as I hit hard-packed snow on the road, eating a mouthful. I spit out the contents as best I could.

My lips were numb, along with my cheeks.

I shivered and curled up in the fetal position in the middle of the snow-covered road. I buried my face away from the chill.

Shielding my cheeks from the cold, getting an ounce of warmth and a reprieve from the elements. I pulled my bag closer to protect me from the wind. I shut my eyes.

My body trembled, but I wasn't cold. Not like I had been earlier. Numb. Nothing but emptiness, a cold and lonely existence stabbing at me.

CHAPTER TWO

JAXSON

I turned the satellite radio up. It was the only channels that came in within a hundred miles of Breckenridge.

We were literally in the middle of nowhere. Just the way I liked it. I've lived in Montana all my life, grew up in a small town a few hours from Breckenridge.

I cranked the music, letting it blare and taking a few minutes to myself after a long day visiting the next town over, I drove the main pass through to Breckenridge.

It was late. The road was not well-traveled, let alone between storms. While it wasn't currently snowing, there were a few inches from the most recent storm.

I had no trouble with my truck getting up the mountain, and I had chains for my tires when the weather gave off a real bite.

I slowed on the main road, the mountain pass.

Catching sight of a small car tinkering on the edge of the ravine, I put my truck in park and left the engine to idle and the lights on.

I reached for a flashlight and stepped out. I pulled my coat on and zipped it, as the night air was chilly.

If someone needed my help, I wanted to be prepared.

"Hello? Anyone in there?" I called out toward the vehicle. The windows were smashed, and the lights were off. There weren't any hazards flashing.

I shined my flashlight into the car. There was no sign of anyone inside. It was likely someone stopped by and picked up the driver.

Who in their right mind would drive that car up the mountain in winter?

It didn't have to be a snowstorm to know that you needed four-wheel drive and chains to make it through the snow. That didn't even consider when the rain washed out, the road or the ice storms made the road impassable.

I pointed my flashlight toward the ground.

There was a set of tracks, female footprints based on the heels and shoe size, and they headed for the main road. I shined the light farther down. The impressions continued, but my flashlight couldn't be seen after the turn in the road, a switchback.

Sighing, I headed to the truck, climbed back in, and was grateful for the warmth of shelter. Hopefully, whoever broke down was already picked up and on their way to town.

I put the truck in drive and shined my brights.

With my foot on the gas, I crept my vehicle up the mountain pass, my eyes on the main road and on the footprints buried in the snow, following them up the mountain. I didn't want to get distracted and miss if the person went off-trail.

Thankfully, she was smart enough to stay in the middle of the road.

I picked up speed a little, both antsy and worried. The last thing I wanted was someone to freeze to death because I took my time.

Another mile north and a figure lay in the road, dark, curled up, and not moving.

I left the car running.

It was a person, though I couldn't tell from the distance if she was alive. I assumed it was a woman based on the shoes.

I stepped closer.

She lay shivering on the snow-packed road. The woman was

curled up, a gray-green knapsack and her purple coat blocking any evidence of an actual person as she attempted to bury herself to keep warm.

I cleared my throat, not wanting to startle the woman.

She didn't budge on my approach. That wasn't a good sign.

"Hello," I said and bent down, resting a hand on her back.

At least she was alive. Her body trembled against my hand. She was as cold as ice, and it was no wonder why.

I heard her try to speak, but I couldn't make out her words.

"I'm Jaxson," I said to her, trying to reassure the young woman that I didn't intend to cause her any harm. "Can you stand?"

Her words were mumbled and incomprehensible.

"I'm going to pick you up and carry you to my truck," I said.

She nodded slightly, and I breathed a sigh of relief that she was at least responsive, even if she was too cold to speak.

I scooped her up into my arms and carried her to my truck.

It only took a minute for me to open the passenger side door while holding her. I maneuvered her inside and hurried around to the driver's side door. I climbed into the truck and blasted even more heat on her. I cranked the temperature up to thaw the poor woman.

She shivered in the front of my truck. She'd been careless abandoning her car, walking at night in the cold, alone.

I reached into the backseat for an extra blanket I kept on hand for emergencies. This qualified as an emergency.

I unfolded the thick blanket and covered her body to help her get warm.

We were too far from the nearest hospital for her to be evaluated for frostbite. That was a solid two-hour drive in pleasant weather, and it meant passing the other side of the mountain where the weather was unpredictable.

"How long were you out there?" I asked.

I unzipped my coat and pulled it off my shoulders. The car was already warm and too hot for me.

She didn't seem to be overheated, so I left the thermostat alone and tried my best to make myself comfortable.

"A while," she said.

It was the first time I could understand the words coming past her lips. The tremble in her voice had vanished. She was quiet, and her hands shook as she held them in front of the heater.

I was afraid to suggest for her to remove her gloves, concerned about frostbite.

"I'm Jaxson Monroe," I said as I introduced myself to her again. She may not have heard me outside, or she did but didn't respond.

"Ariella Cole."

She smiled a bright and wide grin. Her cheeks were red, but at least they weren't bruised or discolored from the cold.

It could have been colder outside had it been the thick of winter. She was lucky.

"How are you feeling?" I asked.

I had a million questions, and the longer I stared at her, the more I realized how beautiful she was, in a very much girl-next-door kind of way.

Except there were no girls next door, and the number of women in Breckenridge was too few for my liking.

Honestly, I only needed one woman to care for, cherish, and take care of for the rest of my life. Of course, it wasn't that simple, nothing ever was.

Was it that I'd saved her made me want to protect her? No, I needed to protect her. I couldn't explain the all-encompassing feeling.

"A little warmer," she said as she glanced at me and gave me a faint smile. Her cheeks' red flame appeared to be from a soft blush instead of the cold this time.

I couldn't help but wonder why.

"Good. I'm glad I can get you a little warmer. If you can buckle yourself in, I'll get us back on the road and to town in no time."

I wasn't going anywhere without both of us being belted into the truck. Even with only a few inches of snow on the road, it was still dangerous. There were wild animals that could tear across the road at a moment's notice.

Ariella nodded, and her hands trembled, but she secured the seatbelt. I did the same and put the truck in drive.

We headed up toward Breckenridge.

I didn't ask her if that's where she was heading. If she stayed anywhere else, I'd find her a room for the night and deal with her situation tomorrow.

"To town," she said, her voice barely above a whisper.

"Yes, Breckenridge. Please tell me that's where you were heading." I hated to think she made a wrong turn and didn't have to travel up the dangerous mountain.

"It is. I just bought a place along the river. Though I imagine this time of year it's probably frozen."

"Any chance you bought it from Mason Reid?" I asked.

"Yes, how did you know?" Ariella asked.

"He's one of my former military buddies, my brother," I said. "I know exactly where you're staying. It's a nice place, small, and was gutted and renovated by yours truly. Well, Aiden and me."

"Who's Aiden?" Her eyes crinkled as she stared at me.

"Another one of my military buddies. Declan, Mason, Aiden, and I started a security firm, Eagle Tactical, a few years back."

I couldn't explain why I was so open to this woman, willing to divulge any secret if she asked. There was something about her. Was it the fact she was fresh meat, and I hadn't had a taste of her yet?

"All of you served together?" Ariella asked. She grinned and stared at me.

My heart fluttered in my chest, demanding to be set free. It had been a long time since anyone looked at me in that rare way.

I laughed, hoping for her not to notice the sexual tension brewing in the truck. As much as I wanted to act on it, I had some measure of self-control. We had just met. "We were all Special Forces with the Army."

With wide eyes, she grimaced as she removed her gloves. "Wow, a town of heroes."

I glanced at her long, thin fingers. They looked okay, albeit a little red, but there was no evidence of frostbite, which was good news.

"That is our motto," I said joking with her.

I returned my attention to the snow-covered road as we headed farther north and made the turn off for Breckenridge. "We don't have too much farther to go."

"Okay," she said. "That's good. Is there any place local to grab dinner? I'm starving, and I won't be able to go grocery shopping until my car gets pulled out of the ditch." Her voice was soft, wistful almost.

"I can take you over to Lumberjack Shack. They've got great food."

They were also the only place we could get in at nearly eight o'clock. It was late for the town, the bar was the only place open, and they didn't serve a decent dinner.

"Lumberjack Shack? I hope the food is better than the name."

"My buddy owns the place."

"Shit. I'm sorry," she said, quick to apologize. "That would be wonderful right now," she said.

She seemed to relax in the front seat and removed the blanket nestled around her body.

"Warm?" I asked.

That was a good sign after how cold and out of it she'd been earlier.

"Yes. Do you mind turning down the heat a bit?"

I adjusted the thermostat in the truck, hoping to make her a little more comfortable.

It was hot. Warm enough to make me want to strip down to my boxers and nothing else. I couldn't do that, not while driving and with a young lady in the truck.

"Thank you."

I pulled the truck down a gravel road and through the thick forest of trees before we slowed down to a crawl. "We're almost there," I said.

She reached for her bag and unzipped it to retrieve her purse.

I parked out front. The restaurant would ordinarily be closed on a Monday night, but I had a key. I helped Lincoln out from time to time, not with the cooking but tending the bar. Lincoln lived upstairs above the restaurant. He'd help me out, and well, if he didn't, I'm sure I could whip up something for her to eat.

"The place looks closed," she said.

The lights inside were dim, and there weren't any other vehicles parked around the front.

"It's after nine. Everything is closed at this hour. I have a key that can get us inside. Don't worry. It's not like there's an alarm system or anything to hack."

"Good, because I wasn't looking forward to spending my first night in Breckenridge in lockup," Ariella said.

"Come on." I climbed out from the truck and headed up the porch stairs and inside. I tried the door first, and it was locked. Pulling out my key for this very occasion and unlocking the door, I led her inside. "Ladies first."

She gave me a look, a cocked eyebrow, and a quirked grin. A beat later, she shrugged and stepped inside.

"It's beautiful," she said, having a look at the décor. "I'm sorry about what I said earlier. I get cranky when I'm hungry."

I bit my tongue to keep from commenting.

"I love the fact this place is a log cabin. It fits the bill of being a lumberjack shack."

It was apparent she was trying to make up for the insult she'd thrown out in the car. "I get a real Paul Bunyan vibe from this place. I'll bet the food is amazing too."

"It is some of the best in Montana. A real home-cooked meal from one of the top chefs in the area. If he didn't own the place, I'd worry someone else would steal him away," I said.

Truthfully, I'd been trying to steal him away to come work with the boys at Eagle Tactical full-time, but he wouldn't do it. He loved cooking too much to be back in the field permanently.

Heavy footsteps hit the stairs, and a moment later, Lincoln stepped into the restaurant.

"Jaxson, what are you doing here?" Lincoln asked.

While I may have been hungry, the look on Ariella's face told me she was starving.

"Grabbing some dinner. We haven't eaten yet, and I was hoping you'd make us something in the kitchen."

"The kitchen's closed, but for you and the pretty lady, I can make an exception," Lincoln said and grinned. "Where's Isabella? Shouldn't you be getting home to her? It's late."

Was he trying to kill any shot I had with Ariella? I didn't have a shot in hell, but I liked to think I did.

"At home, asleep." I didn't further elaborate. Why did my egg-headed military brother have to bring up Isabella?

"Do you have a menu?" Ariella asked Lincoln.

The way her eyes scoured over his body made my heart thump wildly in my chest.

I wanted her to look at me like that, not him.

Was I the jealous type? I never thought about it much, considering there weren't that many women to fawn over in town.

Lincoln smirked and rolled his eyes. "You're not one of those vegetarian types, are you?" He leaned in closer and whispered, "I can make one hell of a salad, but the bear around here is mighty tasty and to die for."

Her eyes widened in horror, and I tried not to laugh at Lincoln's joke. He usually wasn't quite so funny, but it seemed Ariella definitely wasn't from this side of the woods or even the state.

"I will have a salad," Ariella whispered. She sounded parched.

I couldn't help but stare at her, completely taken back by her beauty. Under the warm amber glow from the restaurant lighting, I finally got a good long look at her rosy complexion and freckles dusting her nose and cheeks. Her hair was dark and she had olive eyes that took my breath away.

She was gorgeous and not just because she was the newest resident of Breckenridge, and we didn't get a lot of ladies in town, let alone single ones.

However, I guessed that she was single. I had no idea.

I was just hoping she wasn't taken, given that she wasn't wearing a wedding band. That didn't mean anything, though. She could have been getting it sized.

Then again, if she was married, where was the bastard who let her drive to Breckenridge in that shitty car that couldn't make it up the mountain in winter? I'd kill him if he ever so much as hurt a hair on Ariella's head.

I exhaled a heavy sigh, not realizing how protective I'd become over a stranger. That's all she was, a young woman I'd rescued out in the cold. The thing was I wanted to know more about her. I wanted to discover who she was, why she was here, and well, if she was single and looking for a warm bed to crawl into.

I couldn't throw caution to the wind and sleep with her just because I had needs. No. Those days were over.

"Lincoln's just joking about eating bear. He makes a mean sandwich, and his stew is to die for."

"Stew. That sounds delicious," Ariella said. She rested her hands on the wooden table as we sat down. She removed her coat and hung it on the chair behind her.

"Okay, good. I'll fix you up something in the kitchen. Just sit tight and try not to fall victim to this one's lame attempts at flirting," Lincoln said, pointing at me.

I wanted to slug him.

"What brings you to Breckenridge?" I asked, watching her while my heart pitter-pattered in my chest.

While I knew she'd bought a cabin along the river, I didn't know why. Mason had said little other than he'd sold the place to an out-of-towner.

"Fresh start. I enjoy camping and thought what better place to live than the middle of nowhere."

I laughed, and while I doubted that was the entire story, if she didn't want to tell me, I wouldn't push the issue, either. "You picked the farthest corner of the world, didn't you?" I teased her. "Where are you from, Ariella?"

"New York, but I grew up in Nebraska," she said and held up a hand. "No Cornhusker jokes, please."

"I'm not sure I know of any." It was clear she wasn't a fan of Nebraska, not that I could blame her. I probably wouldn't like it much, either. I loved Breckenridge, though, and while winter could be brutal, it was also beautiful up here.

"Good," she said and laughed. Her eyes met the table before glancing back up at mine. "Can I ask you a question?"

I shrugged. "Go for it."

"Is Isabella your wife or girlfriend?"

She glanced down at my hand on the table.

I wasn't wearing a wedding ring, either, and it was obvious she was taking a long, hard look.

"No, she's my daughter."

CHAPTER THREE

ARIELLA

I'd wanted to ask him who Isabella was since the moment Lincoln brought up her name. I wasn't sure how to ask without completely prying or seeming nosey.

It had to be that he'd rescued me out in the cold, and I already had a sense of attachment to him. Wasn't there a name for that?

"You have a daughter?" That took me by surprise. It shouldn't have, as he was old enough to have kids. So was I.

"Yes, she's three years old." His expression seemed pained. His eyes crinkled just slightly before continuing to speak. "Her mom wanted to give her up for adoption and came to me, needing my signature to give up my rights as a father. I couldn't do it. I refused." His breathing deepened, and his ears reddened as he spoke.

I nodded as I listened to him tell me what happened.

"My options were full custody or give her up completely."

Lincoln brought two glasses of water to the table, giving Jaxson a look. "Dinner will be out soon," Lincoln said.

"Thank you," I said, glancing up at Lincoln before turning my attention back to Jaxson. "She's at home now, Isabella?"

"Yes. I have to depend on my brothers far more than I want to with raising Isabella, but they don't seem to mind." He laughed under his breath.

Had I missed the punchline? I didn't see what was so funny. "What's that?"

He smiled, shaking his head. "Forget it. It's not important."

I didn't quite understand what he wanted me to forget since I didn't know what he was talking about.

"Okay," I said, relieved that Lincoln was carrying our food over to the table. The delicious smell of stew wafted into the air as he brought two large bowls to the table, one for each of us. "Thank you."

"Anything else I can get for you?" Lincoln asked, staring directly at me.

Did he recognize me? The air had been sucked out of my lungs.

Jaxson opened his mouth. "We could use spoons."

"I'll get the lady a spoon. You can get yourself your silverware." He pointed at Jaxson. "Don't let this guy boss you around."

I feigned a smile. It had probably been my imagination. "Oh, I won't. Thanks for the tip," I said.

Lincoln headed toward the kitchen, grabbed two sets of silverware, and brought it over to the table.

"Thank you," Jaxson said before I could even voice the same sentiment.

"Let me know if you need anything else," Lincoln said before disappearing back into the kitchen.

"He knows how to make himself scarce," I said.

I reached for the spoon as the steam wafted from the bowl of soup. I took a sip, and my eyes closed. I relished the taste, the warmth, the fact it was a meal in my stomach.

I couldn't remember the last time I'd eaten today. The burnt coffee I picked up at the resort was stale and didn't count as a meal.

"Yeah. Lincoln's a good guy. Rough around the edges, and Isabella used to be terrified of him, but now they're best buds. Declan comes in a close second to Lincoln, which is funny because he spends more time with her. I swear he's ready to be a dad and settle down."

I took another bite of stew, grateful for the warm and comforting meal after a disastrous evening earlier. "Is Declan watching her now?"

Jaxson nodded between bites. "Yes. My brothers all take turns watching her when she's not at daycare. They're amazing. I couldn't do it without them." He sipped his water and glanced up at me. "So, you moved out here to get away, a change of scenery."

I nodded, not giving anything else away.

He couldn't know why I came to Breckenridge. I couldn't risk endangering him or his little girl.

"Any kids?" he asked.

"Not that I know of," I said, staring at him, trying hard not to laugh.

He grinned first and nodded. "Good one. You know what I do for a living. What about you?"

"Is this twenty questions?" I asked, trying to relax, but it wasn't the easiest task under his gaze. I couldn't tell him what I did for a living, or rather what I used to do.

Currently, I was unemployed. I knew he wasn't trying to be rude. This was probably how small-town people made small talk.

The thing of it was I might have been from New York, but my job took me all over the world. There were dangers in him knowing who I worked for and what I did. Hell, even Benjamin, my ex-husband, had no clue who he was married to.

I lived with secrets, slept with them, and recognized they were mine and mine alone.

"Sorry. Between my brothers and a toddler, I don't get a lot of opportunities to engage with a beautiful young woman."

The room grew warmer. Was I blushing? I glanced at the bowl of soup and pushed a strand of hair behind my ear. "I'll bet you're used to being a flirt. You are former military, and it shows."

He was no doubt gorgeous, with thick muscles behind his shirt. I'd worked with a few guys who had quite the physique, but the way he stared at me, it was clear I held his attention. It was flattering.

"Believe it or not, most of the town is married or one of my brothers."

"That can't be true." There were nearly nine hundred residents of Breckenridge, at least according to the internet.

I had researched the town thoroughly before moving here.

"You'll see," he said with a knowing grin.

I laughed under my breath.

I hoped there were more prospects in this town, not that Jaxson wasn't gorgeous on the eyes and had an incredible physique, but I also didn't want to throw myself at the first nice guy I met.

It had been a long time since I'd met any nice guys.

Ben, my ex-husband, was a bastard. The thought of marriage was like spoiled milk. I didn't want to go near it. I wasn't here looking to hook up or marry.

I never wanted to marry again. Once was enough. I wasn't even interested in dating, but with his gaze on me, my stomach in knots, I had to push those thoughts aside.

We finished our stew, and Lincoln came out of the kitchen to clean up the dishes. "How was it?" he asked me.

"Delicious! Do you always cook everything?" I asked. He may have owned the restaurant, but that didn't mean he ran the kitchen.

"Yes," Lincoln said, a glint in his eye. He appeared pleased by the compliment.

"I'll take the bill when you're ready," I said, not wanting to keep Jaxson out any later, especially knowing he had a daughter at home and a brother watching over her.

I intended to pick up his share of the meal too. After all, he'd saved my life earlier today. While I may not have been able to afford it, I'd figure it out.

"Your money's no good here."

"What?" I asked, confused.

Lincoln smiled. "It's on the house. Any friend of Jaxson eats free. At least for the first time. After that, we'll see what happens."

"Come on. Let me pay. This guy saved my life tonight. I can't leave knowing I owe both of you for your kindness."

Jaxson covered his mouth with his hand. He was grinning like an idiot, trying to hold back his laughter.

"What?" I asked, staring pointedly at Jaxson.

"You will not change his mind. Lincoln is the most stubborn of them all. Just say thank you and be done with it, or we'll never leave."

I glanced from Jaxson to Lincoln, staring up at him from where I sat at the table. He towered above. "Thank you," I said with genuine appreciation.

Lincoln gave a curt nod. "I'm sure I'll see you around. Jaxson, lock up the place on your way out. I'm going to clean up the kitchen and then head on upstairs."

"Will do, boss," Jaxson said, putting his hand back down on the table, grinning. "Are you ready to get out of here?"

I stood and grabbed my coat. No doubt I would need it back outside.

Pulling my jacket back on, I zipped up the teeth and then shoved my hands into my gloves.

I wasn't looking forward to the icy wind or the chill in the air outside, but it wouldn't be for long. We'd be in Jaxson's truck soon enough and then at the cabin.

Jaxson led me outside, his hand on the small of my back. I tried to hide the smile that shined right through me. Could he see it too? Was it that obvious that being around him made me at ease and free?

He walked me to his truck's passenger door and opened the door for me, offering me a hand inside. The truck was far taller than I was and reaching the running boards took a bit of a jump at my height. "Thank you."

"It's my pleasure," Jaxson said.

He waited for me to buckle before he shut the door and came around the truck to climb into the driver's side. He turned on the engine.

A welcoming blast of warm air hit my face. I pushed the vents away, grateful the truck hadn't cooled off since we stopped for dinner.

He pulled out of the lot and away from the restaurant. "Do you need to stop and pick up the key for the cabin?"

I'd already forgotten about the keys.

"Yes! The owner mentioned he left the keys in the mailbox but that it was at the end of the driveway. He made it sound rather far, like I'd need to drive down to get it."

"We'll grab it on the way up to the cabin," Jaxson said.

"Thank you. You think of everything, don't you?"

He smiled and laughed under his breath. His hands remained on the steering wheel, and his focus on the road.

He took his time as we headed farther north up the face of the mountain.

I gripped the side of the door as the switchbacks grew steeper and more challenging to see with each turn.

The headlights on the truck bounced back as a thin layer of fog hung in the air.

"Relax. I've got it. I take this route every day," he said, glancing at me.

"I know." I hadn't known, but I didn't want him to see through the fact that I was scared to death. Had it been obvious?

"Okay, stalker," he joked, smiling as he reached out, resting a hand on my arm. "I've driven through worse. Don't worry. You'll get the hang of it. Especially when you trade in your car for something a little more practical."

"Trade in my car? Do you think I totaled it?" I'd done a number on it, smashing the windows and denting the body when I had crashed into the tree.

He was right, and I needed to think about a more reliable vehicle for Breckenridge's roads, but how would I afford it?

Jaxson guided his hand back to the steering wheel. "Even if you got it fixed up, it still won't get you up the mountain in a blizzard."

"What about if my car had those metal things on the wheels?" I asked, trying to remember what they were called.

"Chains?"

"Yes, those." I hoped I could buy a set of chains and fix the car, and put off making payments on a new vehicle.

My income was tight. I'd spent every dime on that property and driving across the country to Montana. I didn't have a job lined up, and my wallet was near empty.

He lamented before answering. "I've never seen a car like yours around here."

I stared out the window, mesmerized by the beauty of the night.

We cleared the fog, which seemed strange since we'd traveled higher, but it appeared only to be a small patch along one section of the mountain.

In the distance, lights twinkled at the base of the mountain. A small town clustered together. "It's beautiful out here," I said as he slowed on the approach and turned off the road.

Jaxson rolled down his window as he came up to the mailbox and retrieved a set of house keys. "Here you go," he said, handing me the cold metal.

"Thank you." I took the keys with my gloved hands. As quick as he had opened the window, Jaxson shut it and put the truck in drive, heading down the narrow gravel road and through the forest.

I couldn't see anything except a few feet in front of us from the headlights. There was no sign of a cabin. "How much farther?" I asked.

"Another mile or two."

Snow crunched beneath the tires as we finally slowed on the approach. The lights were off, the cabin dark as night.

"I guess no one left the porch light on."

He laughed under his breath.

"What's so funny?" I asked, not seeing anything worth joking about.

From the outside, the wood exterior looked nice, well-kept, and rustic. It was indeed a log cabin, single-story and small, but the perfect size for one person. I didn't need anything big or pricy.

Besides, I couldn't afford anything else.

He shut off the engine of his truck and stepped outside in the cold air.

Jaxson didn't answer me. I climbed out from the truck, my shoes hitting the fresh snow piling up that hadn't been shoveled.

His vehicle had driven through it with ease, but I trampled through the slush and up the porch steps covered in ice.

"Be careful," Jaxson warned, his breath on my neck as he followed me up the steps, a hand on my lower back.

Was he trying to make sure I didn't fall, or was the proximity something else far more intimate?

Already, I enjoyed being around him, but that was dangerous. I barely knew the guy, and he had a kid.

Talk about complicated.

That didn't even include the fact that there was a bounty on my head.

There were several people who wanted me dead. Living in the middle of nowhere was supposed to protect me, but would it?

"Do you have the key?"

"Yes," I said, trying the front door key that Jaxson had retrieved earlier from the mailbox. It slid into the lock easily and turned.

I pushed open the door, expecting it to be warm and inviting. It certainly wasn't warm.

I shivered and reached for the wall, looking for a light switch. Nothing. "It's freezing."

"The cabin uses a wood-burning stove to heat the place." He stalked right for the stove and bent down. He grabbed a few logs kept dry out of the snow and worked on the fire. Jaxson stacked the wood and struck a match, and it slowly caught ablaze.

"You know your stuff," I said, watching him with curiosity.

It had been years since I'd lit a fire like that. The last house had a gas fireplace that involved flipping a switch. I wasn't so lucky out here. However, the wood-burning stove would be a lot warmer. "What about the lights?"

He headed toward the bed, just a few feet away from the fire that roared to life.

The open floor plan offered no real privacy, but I hoped it would help heat the space evenly.

The cabin had come fully furnished, which was nice since I had little with me. Most of it had been sold in New York. Everything else of mine was stuffed into the trunk of my car.

"Here you go." Jaxson grabbed a flashlight style lantern and handed it to me. "Keep a few extra sets of batteries on hand."

The smile fell from my face. "You're joking." He had to be kidding with me.

The cabin had electricity, right?

I had wanted to live off grid, but I hadn't actually intended to live primitively.

"About what?"

"There's seriously no electric in this place?" I couldn't believe it! How could his buddy sell me a house that didn't have electricity? It hadn't been mentioned—one way or the other—on the listing online.

"You bought a cabin in the woods. You're lucky it has indoor plumbing."

CHAPTER FOUR

JAXSON

I may not have known Ariella that well, but it didn't take a mind reader to see she was pissed.

Her hands were balled up at her sides, her jaw tight and brow furrowed. She breathed heavily and loudly, although that could have been from the fact it was cold in the cabin, and she was chilled.

While I needed to get home to Isabella, I also didn't want to leave Ariella alone, in the cold and dark. If I'd have known earlier in the day that she was arriving, I'd have stopped by and started the fire in the stove.

The cabin was frigid, and it would take hours to warm it up to a decent temperature.

"I can't believe this," she said, pacing the length of the room, her feet heavy on the wooden floorboards. "I would never have moved here if I knew there wasn't electricity. How am I supposed to survive without a refrigerator?"

I wanted to tell her to relax. Was that the wrong answer? I hated when the guys told me to chill out.

"I'll bring my generator over, and we can hook it up to a

refrigerator. We'll have to go into town in the morning and pick one out. I can drive it back and sent it up for you."

She groaned.

"You didn't notice the lack of a fridge in the pictures?"

Her lips pursed, and her eyes narrowed. "I may have been in a rush to buy considering the price. Now I see why it was affordable."

She rubbed at her forehead and slowly removed her gloves.

"Listen, why don't you come back with me tonight? Stay over at my place for a few hours until your cabin gets toasty. Then I can drive you back, or you can walk home. It's not far between our properties. There's a bridge that goes over the river. I live just on the other side of it."

She exhaled a heavy breath, and her tongue darted out, licking her lips. "We're neighbors."

"That's right," I said. "What do you say? I can bring by the generator in the morning, and we can go into town and pick up a new fridge."

She stalled and shifted her weight on her feet.

Was there another option that I wasn't considering? I didn't know of anyone giving away a free refrigerator, and the nearest thrift shop was hours away and never carried appliances. It was unlikely anyone had a spare refrigerator, though freezers were easier to come by since many of the townies were hunters and stored meat in the freezers.

"I'll be fine tonight. It's been a long day. I should probably just crawl up under the blankets and head to bed."

"If you're sure." I didn't want to push her. "There are extra blankets in the closet if you're cold. Do you have a phone? I can give you my number in case you need anything."

She slowly unzipped her coat. "It's dead. I need to charge it, but that seems an impossible task." Ariella yawned and brought her hand up to her lips as if she could hide the gesture.

"I'll bring you a solar charger in the morning. I have a spare." I stepped back toward the door, not wanting to overstay my welcome.

It was late. My daughter was at home and needed me.

"Thank you."

I headed for the door. “If you need anything, I'm just over the bridge. It's not too far a walk.”

“I'll be fine, but I appreciate it.”

“Lock up after I leave. Most people don't lock their doors in Breckenridge, but you shouldn't make that a habit.” I'd seen too much in my day to leave a door unlocked.

She quirked an eyebrow. “Is there something I should know?”

Her eyes were bright and wide, a deep olive that matched her sweater. I wanted to step closer, lean in to touch her shoulder, and reassure her she would be fine, but we barely knew one another, and I wasn't one to make empty promises.

“It's just better to be safe than sorry,” I said.

It wasn't anything specific or anyone who caused trouble.

In the middle of nowhere, being in the woods led to a few individuals with dark pasts hiding out and keeping off-grid. While they never bothered me, I couldn't say the same for a pretty young girl, all alone.

I'd have to keep an eye on her and make sure she was safe.

“I'll see you tomorrow.” I headed outside and waited until I heard the click of the lock before hurrying down the porch stairs and to my truck.

Fresh snow fell, and I climbed into my truck and headed back the way I came, on the same narrow road that led to her house. I would have to travel back to the main road, then head another mile or so north before the next turnoff. While our houses were close, the distance and drive to get there was a lot longer than by foot.

The higher north I traveled, the more snow seemed to fall. It was blustery cold the moment I stepped out of the truck.

I hurried inside my house, a two-story log cabin, and removed my coat and shoes. The hearth was lit, offering warmth and an ambient glow to the living room where Declan lay asleep.

He snored softly. A checkered flannel blanket covered him. He had stretched out on the sofa, taking up the entire length.

I didn't have the heart to wake him.

Declan was a good friend, helping me out with Isabella. While he didn't have any kids of his own, it was obvious he wanted them and would make a great father one day.

With the lights already off, I locked up the house and quietly headed up the stairs to check on Izzie.

Curled up in her bed, she stirred as I entered the room.

I held my breath, not wanting to awaken my baby girl. I watched over her for a long moment before finally tiptoeing out of her room and into mine.

Exhausted, I collapsed onto the mattress, not bothering to undress further.

At least my shoes were downstairs by the front door. There was no way I could do much else.

I shut my eyes, prepared to let sleep win when a loud crash vibrated through the house. It came from downstairs.

"Declan?"

On high alert, I hurried out of bed and grabbed my gun from the safe.

I'd do whatever was necessary to protect my little girl.

Quietly, I headed down the stairs, one step at a time, to make sure the intruder couldn't hear me.

Gun drawn, I kept my back to the wall of the stairwell.

Coming around the corner, Declan gasped and held up his hands in surrender. "Careful, Jax. Don't shoot."

"What the hell was that?" I asked, lowering the barrel of the gun as I turned on the safety.

"Avalanche. Earthquake. Who the hell knows?" Declan said. He rubbed at his eyes and ran a hand through his short-cropped, dark hair. "Woke my ass up, and clearly, it did yours as well."

I doubted it was an avalanche or earthquake based on the sound. "I wasn't asleep."

"You came home late," Declan said.

"Did you get my text from the restaurant?"

"Yes. Lincoln called and told me all about the pretty girl you were having dinner with. So, who is she?"

Declan headed for the fridge and grabbed himself a beer,

bringing it to the sofa to have a seat. He was awake and expecting to converse.

I wasn't in the mood for a drink.

I put the gun on the coffee table and sat down on the sofa with my brother. "Ariella. She's the new buyer of the cabin on the river, my next-door neighbor."

Declan smiled, and his grin widened. "Is she as hot as Lincoln made her out to be?"

I tried my best not to grin, but it was hard not to reveal at first glance how she made me feel. Being around her made my heart soar like a balloon high above the clouds.

"You're smitten," Declan said and laughed under his breath.

I didn't need my friends ganging up on me and teasing me about Ariella. It was likely that I'd see her again, and not just tomorrow morning.

"I was just being friendly and helping a neighbor out," I said, trying my best to change the subject. "By the way, she had no idea the cabin didn't have electric."

"Damn," Declan said. He sipped his beer. "I'll bet she was pissed when she found out."

That was an understatement.

"Yeah. I offered her my generator, and I was going to go into town with her in the morning and bring back a fridge. She's going to need to do something if she plans on living here year round."

"You don't have to take care of her, Jax. She's a grown woman," Declan said.

I knew that, but I didn't care. In part, it was my responsibility. I always seemed to clean up after my buddies made a mess of things.

I was the responsible one.

"I realize that," I said and stood.

I didn't need a lecture from Declan. He was younger than me, only by a year, but it still irked me when he tried to give me advice.

"Who'd you think was going to buy the place?" Declan asked.

"Honestly, I thought it'd be some rich folks from California.

Some lavish city people who wanted a second home in seclusion, off-grid, where they could spend a few weeks a year in the outdoors."

"That was wishful thinking. No one comes out here for just the summer. Well, almost no one."

I sighed and stood.

The unspoken name he was referring to was the mother of my baby girl.

Emma was a summer fling, a woman who had come to Breckenridge to get away from her wild city life and unwind for the summer.

She'd done more than relax. She'd found her way into my bed and ended up pregnant.

"Sorry, I didn't mean to bring her up," Declan said.

He knew I hated talking about her. It wasn't that I was in love with the woman; it had no doubt been a summer fling for both of us, but I hadn't been too fond of hearing she planned on giving up Isabella for adoption. Showing up on my doorstep, it hadn't been to tell me she was pregnant or ask about my involvement.

No.

She'd shown up that day to ask me to sign my parental rights away, something I refused to do.

"I'm going to head out, get a few hours of sleep before work," Declan said. "Do you need me for anything else before I go?"

"Tomorrow, on your way down the mountain pass, Ariella's car ended up in a ditch. Can you pull it out and tow it over to the shop? I'm not sure it's in mountain weather shape, but she's going to need something to get her around town. Also, find her a pair of used chains she can put on her tires to get her up the mountain. Let me know what they cost and I'll cover it."

"You got it." Declan owned the tow shop in town.

When we decided to start Eagle Tactical, he hired out help, bringing in a mechanic and a crew to support him.

"You're welcome to stay and crash on the couch. It's snowing out there, but I know that's never stopped you before."

It was late, and while the snow had just started coming down within the past hour, it likely hadn't lightened up any.

Declan grabbed his beanie and jacket, pulling the thick material over his shoulders before zipping his coat. He slipped on a pair of boots and then donned his gloves.

"Have fun tomorrow with the new girl." He winked at me.

"Her name is Ariella," I said, correcting him.

"Whatever. I hear from Lincoln she's cute, and the blush on your ears gives it away that you like her. I can't wait to meet her. If you don't sink your teeth into her, I might have to."

"It's time for you to go." I ushered him out the door and shut it behind him. I ran a hand through my hair, gasping for breath.

Just the thought of Declan trying to steal her away pained me.

Why was that?

She wasn't mine. She wasn't anyone's, well, as far as I knew. She hadn't exactly told me her story, why she was in Breckenridge, and whether or not she was single—not that I was looking.

I was a father, which came first and foremost.

I took the gun back upstairs and secured it in the safe before stripping down to my boxers for bed.

I climbed under the covers; morning would come soon enough, and my little girl would wake me at the crack of dawn.

For a few scant hours, I could dream of Ariella, of her smile and laugh, and let the nightmares that haunt me vanish in the night.

CHAPTER FIVE

ARIELLA

I had trouble sleeping. At first, it had been the cold air and being in an unfamiliar place. While it might have been my home, it wasn't warm and cozy.

My fingers and toes were chilled beneath the thick blankets, and I'd dug out every extra comforter and quilt that I could find in the linen closet.

Halfway through the night, I threw the rest of the wood into the fire, stoking it to keep the cabin warm.

Sometime later, I no longer needed the blankets and had fallen asleep to the blazing hearth.

I stirred awake, hearing the crunch of tires outside and an engine idle. What time was it?

"Ariella." He knocked briskly.

"Just a second," I said from the bed. The covers were tangled, and half of the blankets were on the floor. The room was stuffy.

I pushed myself out of bed and didn't flinch like I'd expected as my bare feet touched the wood floor. The cabin was warmer than the previous night.

I unlocked the door and pulled it open. A blast of cold air smacked me in the face and forced me to take a step back.

"Holy hell, it's hot in here," Jaxson said.

He hurried toward the wood-burning stove and pointed at the bare spot where firewood had been stacked the previous night.

"Did you burn the entire lot?"

"Was I not supposed to?" We were in the forest and there had to be more lying around.

"It has got to be a hundred degrees in here."

Sweat licked his forehead, and he removed his hat and gloves. His eyes moved over my body, reminding me I had slept in my clothes from the previous night.

I didn't have any extra clothes in my knapsack. My belongings were in the car's trunk, abandoned halfway down the mountain.

He had to be exaggerating. "It's not that hot."

He stepped farther inside the cabin, pointing at a thermometer gauge affixed to the wall. "Look at this," Jaxson said.

I didn't want to look at it and see that he was right. "It's hard to tell, given there's no electricity."

Jaxson snorted under his breath and stalked toward the front window and yanked open the curtains. "Now you can see, and you don't need a flashlight."

He was getting under my skin. It hadn't been his fault about the cabin, but it didn't help my mood.

I slipped on my heels, not the most sensible in this weather, but my boots were back in the vehicle. Grumbling under my breath, I grabbed my coat from the hook near the door.

"I want you to take me to your buddy, the one who sold me the cabin." I grabbed my keys and purse and yanked the door open and turned back. "What are you waiting for?" I asked.

He let out a heavy sigh before following me out the door.

I stomped through the snow, partially because I was wearing heels and also because I was pissed. My feet were freezing.

I pulled my jacket closed so that he wouldn't see my discomfort.

Suckered into thinking I'd gotten a great deal on a home when, in reality, I'd been played like a fool. I was going to give it to his friend, the lashing that he deserved!

I waited outside his truck. The engine was on, but the doors were locked.

Another minute, and he was at the truck, unlocking the doors and letting me inside. "Thanks," I said, climbing inside the warmth of the cabin.

"Hi," a small voice squeaked from the backseat. My eyes widened and I spun around to see who was in the truck.

"See, Daddy didn't take too long," Jaxson said to the toddler in the backseat. "Ariella, I'd like you to meet my daughter, Isabella."

"Hi, Isabella," I said, giving her a forced smile. She was cute, with her daddy's eyes and deep mahogany hair.

I didn't want to smile. I wasn't happy. Anger bubbled through me as I attempted to buckle my seatbelt. My hands trembled.

Isabella's smile beamed, oblivious to the tension in the truck between us.

"Are you taking me to Mason's house?" I asked.

"He's at work right now," Jaxson said. He rested his hands on the steering wheel but didn't put the truck into reverse.

We sat in the driveway, in front of the cabin, awkwardly.

I knew why I was pissed. It had everything to do with his friend. But why did Jaxson seem unsettled? "So, take me to his work."

That was the easiest solution. I'd give him a piece of my mind, and perhaps I could get the house stuff sorted.

Though I wasn't sure how it would get fixed. Even if he gave me back the money and took possession of the property, I had nowhere else to live. A hotel would be costly, and another property at that price was unheard of.

I should have known the price was too good to be true, but I was eager to move and optimistic.

I was a sucker.

Isabella made clicking sounds with her tongue in the truck's backseat. Her feet swung, and every so often, the tips of her toes would hit my seat.

Jaxson spun around, his hand falling onto her leg. "No kicking the seat, Izzie." He was gentle but firm with his daughter. The way he paid her attention warmed my heart.

Inwardly, I groaned. I didn't want to notice him in that way.

Yes, he was gorgeous and probably had an impressive body under his jacket and jeans, but I was newly divorced. I wasn't looking for love or even a fling.

Besides, he had a daughter which no doubt complicated matters further, not to mention my past.

He huffed under his breath before he finally put the truck into reverse. "Fine. If you want me to take you to Mason, I'll drive you there."

"That's all I'm asking," I said. I sat quietly, staring out the side window and paying attention to the route. I did not know where anything was located, and as Jaxson drove us down from the direction we came, he turned off the road a few miles down.

If I remembered correctly, we traveled in the restaurant's opposite direction, but it was nearby.

Jaxson pulled up outside a large brick complex.

Smoke billowed in waves from the chimney. He put the truck in park and glanced back at his daughter.

"Daddy will be right back." He left the engine running and locked the doors, shoving his keys into his pocket.

I was envious of his keyless entry and remote start. My vehicle was crap compared to the massive truck that he drove.

"Okay. Let's go," I said as I stalked up the stairs of the small building. A sign just outside the door read Eagle Tactical.

So, this was where Jaxson worked.

I opened the door and stepped inside the building. A young woman sat at a desk near the front of the entryway.

"Can I help you?" she asked, her tone bubbly and wearing a plastered smile. She looked every bit fake.

"I'm here to speak with Mason," I said. I didn't elaborate on the reason for my visit.

She frowned, flipping open her scheduling calendar. She

glanced over the individual slots and pages. I hadn't given her my name. Was she looking for a name she didn't recognize on the calendar?

Jaxson came up from behind. She mustn't have seen him when he first entered the building.

“Good morning, Lucy.”

"Mr. Monroe, I didn't see you come in," Lucy said. "How is little Isabella doing?"

"She's good. Thank you. Is Mason in his office? Ariella would like a word with him."

Lucy stood and sauntered off down the hallway. She knocked before opening a door and poking her head in, presumably giving him the message.

I shifted on my feet, the snow dripping down and making a mess on the wood floor. I didn't wipe my feet very well when I came inside.

She cleared her throat and gestured us to follow her down the hall.

I went first, my feet clicking hard against the wooden floor with each step. Jaxson was just a few feet behind me on my heel.

The hallway was freshly painted toasted oatmeal, but the boards beneath were wood. The building looked updated recently.

"Can I help you?" Mason asked. He sat behind his desk, buried behind a mess of paperwork, his attention on his computer and not the least bit on me.

"I'm Ariella Cole. You sold me the cabin just up the road." I assumed he knew the address and that he wasn't making it a habit of buying and selling shady properties.

"That's right, a real gem." His brow furrowed, and he glanced past me. "Good morning, Jaxson." He pushed the chair back from the desk and stood.

"The property you sold me was misrepresented. It doesn't have electricity, and you failed to make that apparent before signing the papers."

I stepped farther into the small, overcrowded office. An ugly green, dented file cabinet sat nestled beneath the window. Above it was another stack of manila folders waiting to be filed.

"Jaxson, do you want to give me a hand?" Mason asked, gesturing at me.

"Excuse me?" I asked.

I didn't need to be handled.

"I'm not the problem," I said, my hands in fists at my side. I needed to control the anger raging inside of me before I did something I'd regret. "Your listing neglected to point out that there was no electricity and no heat on the property."

Mason took a step closer toward me. "Now hold on right there, Missy. The cabin has heat. If you don't know how to chop firewood or bring in logs and need a man to do it for you, that's not my problem."

I pulled back my fist to land a blow to Mason's cheek, but Jaxson grabbed my arm and guided it back down to my side forcefully. "Get off me," I said, shrugging out of his grasp. I didn't need to be manhandled.

"You need to take your girlfriend and go," Mason said. He pointed at the door.

How dare he!

"I'm not his girlfriend." I didn't need to explain to Mason how we met.

Besides, they were colleagues and military brothers. He'd probably find out soon enough.

Weren't small towns full of gossip?

"You owe me for misrepresenting the cabin." I stood my ground, my feet planted in front of him. I wasn't leaving.

"I don't owe you a damned thing, lady," Mason said. "The listing called the place 'quiet, rustic living'. There's no lie in that phrase, and the fact you neglected to see if it had electricity is not my fault. Many cabins in the woods out here are used as a second property for a weekend getaway. Besides, if anyone is to blame, Jaxson dealt with the listing. I only approved it."

"Excuse me?" That caught me off guard. What did he mean, Jaxson dealt with the listing?

Was he a realtor too? Didn't he work here, at Eagle Tactical?

"You always did like to throw me to the wolves," Jaxson said. He folded his arms across his chest, his eyes narrow as he glared at Mason.

I scoffed and spun around on my heel, mouth agape as I stared up at Jaxson. "Are you calling me a wolf?"

"If the shoe fits, honey," Mason said from behind me.

I wanted to kill that smug bastard. I ignored Mason for a second and tried to regain my composure.

Jaxson towered above me. His eyes locked on mine, and I realized he never answered the question. He was avoiding it.

Hell, I probably would be too if I were standing in his shoes. "Are you responsible for the listing?"

He cleared his throat, but he didn't answer me, only stared into my eyes. I swallowed the lump that formed in my throat.

"We should get back out to the car. I left Izzie in there, and it's been long enough," Jaxson said and hurried down the hall like a hurricane, leaving me standing there with Mason.

Was he trying to get away from me or avoid answering the question? Perhaps he was inclined to do both. I groaned and heard Mason chuckling behind me. "You'd better go catch him before he leaves you in the cold and dust. I know I would."

"God, you're an ass," I muttered on my way out of his office and rushed to the car.

Jaxson sat in the truck's cabin waiting for me. I climbed into the passenger side and buckled up. I shot him a look that said, 'fuck you.'

I was no longer in the mood to talk. It didn't help that his adorable little girl was seated behind us, singing Disney princess songs.

"You're mad. Let me explain," Jaxson said.

"Can you? Do you mean it wasn't intentional?" I found it difficult to believe that he just forgot to include that little tidbit in the listing.

While he seemed like a nice guy, he was a jerk just like Mason.

He answered me calmly as he turned to face me, the truck still in park. "I offered to help Mason list the cabin. That was my mistake, and the few dollars he gave me for helping, I swear it's all yours."

Was he trying to make me feel bad? I was short on cash, like really short, where my bank account was drained and all I had was a couple of ones left in my wallet.

I still needed to fix my car and now install electricity in the cabin. That had to cost a fortune! I wasn't rich, and this wasn't my second home.

"I don't want your money." I could use it, but I wasn't about to tell him that minor fact.

He had a daughter, and kids were expensive. I would not take his money.

That jerk Mason, I would have gladly snatched from his greedy little palms, but that didn't seem a likely scenario.

Jaxson stared at me, his gaze unwavering. "Okay. How about I take you into town and buy you a fridge and generator?"

"Are you serious? I don't need handouts." It was precisely what I needed to survive and live in that rustic cabin, but I didn't want to seem desperate.

CHAPTER SIX

JAXSON

She hated me, not that I blamed her. I'd been completely incompetent in listing the cabin.

Ariella was right.

I had neglected to put that it didn't have electricity but only because it never crossed my mind. I needed to make it up to her, and the most logical way was to help her with the fridge and generator.

While I intended to loan her one for the short term, the truth was she needed one until the place was hooked up to the grid.

"I promise what I'm offering isn't a handout. It's just me doing something neighborly," I said, trying to reason with her. "We are neighbors, Ariella. I'm going to be seeing a lot more of you whether you like it or not."

She groaned and ran a hand through her long brunette hair.

I kept my attention on the road as I drove us down the mountain and into town. It would be an all-day event, and I didn't even bother asking if she had other plans. I assumed she didn't, other than getting her car towed out of the ravine and fixed up.

Ariella stared out the window, her voice soft and barely audible over Isabella's loud singing. "Thank you," she whispered.

"Of course," I said. I wanted to keep her talking, to learn about her, what she was doing in Breckenridge. "I hope I'm not keeping you from other plans you might have had for today."

"Just some unpacking and retrieving my car. I need to call a tow truck, but my phone is still dead," she said. "There isn't a phone in the house, so I'm going to need another favor."

"Another favor?" I joked with her. "You're going to owe me pretty soon."

She groaned under her breath.

"It's not that bad," I said. "Besides, I talked to Declan last night when I got home. He should have it in the shop later this afternoon."

"Thank you."

She'd never been here before and was probably trying to escape something or someone.

Most people who ventured to the middle of nowhere did so because they had secrets to hide.

I was overthinking it.

I'd been in the military in my younger years and had seen a lot that left a lasting impression.

In my day-to-day work for Eagle Tactical, I dealt with all of it, everything from kidnappings and ransom drops to human trafficking. We work closely with the local police department and county sheriff.

"You never told me what you do for a living." I wasn't trying to pry, but I was curious all the same. It came with the job, digging into people's lives.

"Yeah, I guess you could say I'm unemployed at the moment. I had an interview yesterday afternoon at Blue Sky Resort, but I'm not sure when I'll hear anything back. Any chance Lincoln is looking to hire a waitress?"

Lincoln kept the overhead on his restaurant as low as possible, which meant he wasn't usually open to new hires. "I can ask him, but you'd have better luck at Blue Sky, especially this time of year."

"Any chance you know the owner?" she asked. "Maybe you could put in a good word for me?"

"Daddy, I'm hungry," Isabella whined from the backseat.

I glanced back at Isabella over my shoulder and then at Ariella. "Can you open the glove box?"

"Yeah, sure." She leaned forward and unclasped the glove box, revealing a bag of pretzels. "How old are these?" Ariella laughed and pulled the baggie out.

"A week or two, max. It's fine." I snatched the baggie from Ariella, opened it, and handed it back to Isabella. "Here you go. We'll get lunch in a bit, Izzie."

She munched loudly as she ate her pretzels in the backseat. Her feet were kicking but just missing the seat.

I glanced back at her. No doubt she was bored with being in the truck and needed time to run around.

"We'll be there soon," I said, trying to assure her it wouldn't be too much longer in the truck.

Ariella glanced out the side window, quiet and lost in her thoughts.

"I'm sorry. You were saying?" I hated how quickly I could get distracted.

Ariella shifted in her seat, staring at me, her undivided attention entirely focused on me. "I was just wondering if you knew the owners of Blue Sky Resort. I *really* need a job."

The emphasis on *really* made my stomach clench.

How bad off was she?

I hadn't seen her belongings, and I assumed everything she owned was in her car since she bought the cabin fully furnished.

Another reason I had believed the owner was looking for a second house, a temporary getaway for a vacation.

"I don't, but if they don't hire you, let me know, and I will ask around."

She wouldn't be without a job for long. The community of Breckenridge was small but tight-knit and helped one another out.

"Thank you."

"Daddy, I'm bored," Isabella said. She tossed the empty bag on the floor of the truck, the crumbs spilling out with it.

"I know, baby girl." I pulled up to the front of the big box hardware store and parked the truck before I helped Izzie out of her car seat and carried her on my hip. Together, the three of us headed inside and out of the cold.

"They sell refrigerators here?" Ariella asked, following beside me. I could tell she was hurrying to keep up.

"All major appliances," I said, leading her down an aisle and toward the back of the store. "It shouldn't take too long, and then we can grab lunch and head back home."

"You know your way around this place."

"We do enough shopping here to keep this location open," I joked, walking her toward the appliance section. It wasn't difficult to find the refrigerators, and we walked up and down the aisle twice. "See anything you like?"

She shuffled her feet, and every time we walked past one nicer than the next, her eyes widened as she balked at the sticker. "I could buy a new car at this price!"

I tried not to laugh.

I understood her predicament. She was out of work and concerned about the financial aspect of buying a new household appliance. There was no way she could buy a decent vehicle that would get her up the mountain and safely around town for the cost of a refrigerator.

I held my tongue, trying to think of another store, a different place that might be more affordable, with fewer bells and whistles, so to speak.

She paced the aisle once, twice, and by the third time, she stopped in front of a mini fridge.

"I can probably afford this one," she said. "If I put it on my credit card." She seemed to talk to herself, or she was talking to me, but her voice had dropped so much that I'd barely heard her remark, but I had heard it.

I came up beside her, Izzie growing restless on my hip. Reluctant to put her down, I didn't want her running off and tearing through the store, getting into trouble. She was fast and spritely.

"Listen," I said to Ariella. "I offered to cover the cost of your refrigerator, and I meant it."

"You shouldn't have to do that," she said, folding her arms across her chest. "It's not your fault I fucked up."

"Fucked. Fucked. Fucked," Izzie repeated what Ariella said.

Ariella's olive eyes widened in horror. "Oh, my gosh! I'm so sorry," she said, quick to apologize.

It was clear she wasn't used to being around kids.

"You shouldn't say that, Isabella." Ariella looked horrified, and for a good reason, but I let out a loud sigh.

"She's heard worse from the guys." However, I gave them hell when they cursed in front of my little girl.

I didn't have it in me to do the same to her.

"That's no excuse," she said. "Again, I'm so sorry."

"Apology accepted."

I didn't want her stressing over what she'd done. Mistakes happened. We'd all made them, and Izzie was bound to hear far worse things in her lifetime.

"Back to the refrigerator," I said, nodding toward the appliances. "Do you want to pick one out, or should I do it for you?"

She chewed her bottom lip, her eyes filled with trepidation. What was she worried about?

I had offered to pay and was intending on making good on my promise. Mason may have sold her the cabin, but I should have been more careful in its listing. She should have realized there wasn't a fridge, but I had neglected to include details about electricity. Had the roles been reversed, I'd have flipped out too.

"Sure, if you want to buy me a fridge, you can buy me this one," she said, pointing at the mini fridge that couldn't even hold a case of water. It was cheap, certainly within my budget too, but it wouldn't do her any good at home to store her groceries.

I headed down the aisle, glancing at the appliances once more before stopping at the end cap and examining a floor model.

Its bright yellow sticker was an affordable price and offered a 60-day warranty. Hopefully, that would be sufficient.

"What about this one?" It was still more than her mini fridge, but she more than likely could afford it if she wouldn't let me pay. Though I fully intended on purchasing the fridge for her.

"That'll do." We found a cashier and had them ring up the item.

I pulled out my credit card, handing it to the cashier before Ariella could offer her own form of payment.

"Thank you," she said to me as we loaded it into the bed of the truck, tied it down, and then headed into town for lunch.

Izzie behaved incredibly well for the afternoon. I knew how bored she was, but she seemed quite mesmerized by Ariella.

Izzie sat beside me in the booth. While we waited for our food to come, she climbed under the table and snuck over to sit next to Ariella.

"Hey there," Ariella said, smiling at Isabella. "Do you want to keep me company?"

Izzie shook her head, her eyes bright and wide.

She climbed onto the seat, sitting on her knees, so she had a little extra height. Her hands reached out, playing with Ariella's hair, touching her.

"Izzie," I said, warning her to behave. Not everyone liked to be touched by a toddler.

"She's okay," Ariella said with a grin, glancing at me. She didn't seem to mind, or if she did, she pretended it didn't bother her. "How old are you?" she asked Izzie, although I'd already told her yesterday.

"Three," she said, holding out three fingers proudly to announce her age. "How old are you?"

"Izzie." I laughed, trying to scold her, but it was difficult when she had that adorable look in her eyes, that twinkle of both mischievous and delight that made her even more loveable. "We don't ask grownups their age."

"Okay," Izzie said and rolled her eyes.

"Oh, my gosh. She's already a teenager," I said.

I couldn't believe the eye roll. She had to have learned it from someone, but I wasn't sure where she'd picked it up. She'd spent quite a bit of time with Declan, and he had a few nasty habits, but I hadn't witnessed that one previously.

Izzie scrunched her nose while smiling. "Do you have a boyfriend?" she asked Ariella.

"I do not have a boyfriend," she said, matter of factly, before I could even tell Izzie to cool it. "What about you?" Ariella asked, teasing Isabella. "Do you have a boyfriend?"

Izzie violently shook her head. "Gross! Boys are icky!"

I laughed under my breath. At least that answer settled my nerves. "Good, keep saying that."

I didn't want her thinking about boys and boyfriends, or girlfriends. She was much too young to be thinking about crushes and what came along with that.

"What about you?" Ariella asked, scrunching her nose up and smiling just like Izzie had done a moment earlier. "Do you have a girlfriend?" she asked me.

While I knew she was playing games and entertaining my daughter, which I was grateful for, was she also asking because she was interested, or was I reading into it? I wanted her to be asking because she liked me, not because she was just putting me on the spot. Though, why did I care how she felt? We barely knew one another.

"Do you want to be his girlfriend?" Izzie asked.

"I don't think it quite works like that," I said, glaring at Izzie. She didn't seem to take the hint. Her mouth opened about to say something else that would inevitably embarrass me further.

"Sure, it does," Ariella said. She was wearing a 100-watt smile, her eyes shining as she didn't seem to take her gaze off of me.

Lincoln brought out three plates from the kitchen, interrupting the moment. I wasn't sure whether to kiss him or kill him.

Izzie snuck back under the table and climbed onto the seat beside me to eat. I cut up her lunch into small, bite-sized pieces and watched as she grabbed each bite with her hands, foregoing a fork. We'd have to work on that at some point.

"Saved by the bell," Ariella said, the smile more subdued, but she seemed at ease, happier, carefree. Her shoulders relaxed, and the tension seemed to slip out of her body as she ate her salad.

I helped Izzie with her meal before digging in on my burger. I hadn't realized how hungry I'd been or how late the afternoon had gotten.

It was any wonder Izzie hadn't melted down.

When the bill came, I wouldn't let Ariella pay, although she offered. Knowing she didn't have a job, whatever money she had, she probably needed far more than I did right now. "You'll pay after you get hired at the lodge," I said. I hoped the job came through for her.

"Fine, but then you're buying the drinks. You said there's a bar around town, right?"

It had been ages since I'd gone out on a date. However, she hadn't exactly called us going out a date. I was reading too much into her intentions. We were friends, neighbors, and I was supposed to be helping her out, not trying to get in her pants.

"Jaxson?"

"Oh, sorry." I hadn't heard what she'd said after asking about a bar.

"It's fine," she said and waved her hand dismissively. "We should head back to the cabin and hook up the fridge to your generator. Assuming you don't mind me borrowing it. I promise it's just until I get a job and can buy my own."

My cell phone buzzed in my pocket. I reached into my pants and grabbed my phone, holding out a finger to her to wait a second. It was Declan. "Hey, what's up?" I asked.

He had promised to tow her car for me, and while he was supposed to be at Eagle Tactical this afternoon, I hadn't heard about any big calls or operations coming through.

Usually, the team texted me if something important was going on, a big client, or a dangerous mission if I wasn't at the office.

"I pulled your girl's car from the ravine. Her tires are completely bald. The window was smashed, and the bumper dented. The bumper isn't a big deal, but the trunk was crushed and the latch is broken and won't be fixable. It'll cost her a few grand to make the car drivable, and that doesn't include getting it in shape for Breckenridge winter. What do you want me to do?"

I exhaled a heavy sigh. Ariella would not be happy about the news. Already, the smile fell from her face as I stared at her, like she already knew.

"Let me call you back," I said to Declan before hanging up. "Do you have full liability on your car?" I asked Ariella.

Wordlessly, she shook her head. I already suspected that was the case. "Declan says it'll be several grand, and that doesn't get your car into safe shape for getting up the mountain. We can find you a set of used chains, but I'm not crazy about you driving up in that car. You need four-wheel drive or at least all-wheel drive on a vehicle if you're going to be working in another town and having to travel up and down the mountain pass daily."

"Shit," she said under her breath.

"Shit. Shit. Shit," Isabella repeated, staring at Ariella.

CHAPTER SEVEN

ARIELLA

I couldn't afford several grand in repairs on my car, let alone a new fridge. "Any chance there's a bus that'll take me to town?"

Should I just abandon the car? That's all it was good for anyhow.

Besides, my past was tied to that vehicle. Wasn't it better if I left it and every part of New York behind?

"There aren't any buses in Breckenridge, but I'm sure we can find you someone who can give you a lift who lives in town and works in the city."

"You guys consider where we were today a city?"

The population had been less than 10,000 people. It is hardly classified as a city.

We headed out of the booth at Lumberjack Shack and back to Jaxson's truck. He had started the engine and warmed up the vehicle for us before we got back inside.

I climbed into the passenger side and waited while he secured Isabella into the car seat.

He seemed like a pro, knowing exactly what to do in the least amount of time possible so that he could climb into the truck quickly. "You're good at that," I said.

It was a stupid comment to make, but I was impressed. My sister had two kids, and when she was pregnant with the second and in labor at the hospital, I was delegated to watching the littlest boy. It had taken me an hour to get him in his car seat, and even then, I wasn't comfortable with how it had been latched. It didn't seem secure.

"Thanks," he said as he climbed into the driver's seat.

Slamming the door shut, he put the truck into reverse before pulling out of the parking lot and onto the main road.

"Next stop, your house, to drop off the fridge. You're going to need groceries too, but that can wait."

"It can?" I was almost relieved by his suggestion to wait.

"Yes. We're going to need to chop up firewood before nightfall. Remember, you burned up everything dry and in the house."

"Can't I order some and have it delivered?"

"Sure, but it's not cheap," Jaxson said.

I knew that, but I was not an outdoorsy girl who chopped firewood.

I didn't know the next thing about splitting wood, and I wasn't incredibly strong, either. I wasn't expecting Jaxson to do it for me. I just thought the house wouldn't require firewood to keep warm.

I needed to stop blaming Mason for the listing. I should have come to Breckenridge and visited the cabin before paying for it with every dollar to my name.

"Daddy!" Isabella squealed from the backseat.

"Yes, sweetie?"

"I'm bored," she announced, whining and groaning as she tried to free herself from her car seat. Thankfully, it appeared too tight for her to unbuckle herself.

I turned around and offered her my undivided attention while Jaxson focused on the narrow, snow-covered road. It seemed the roads stayed covered with snow all winter, and it wasn't even the coldest months of the year.

"What's your favorite color?" I quizzed her, trying to keep her preoccupied for the rest of the drive.

"Purple," she squealed with delight and grinned proudly, her nose scrunched up. Her hands stalled on her buckle, already forgetting what she had been attempting to do. "You?"

"That's a tough one," I said. "I'd have to go with turquoise that shimmers, like a mermaid's tail."

"You're very specific," Jaxson said while he kept his focus on the road.

While I was turned to face Isabella, the car veered off the main road and up the long narrow driveway to my house. We were almost back.

"I like mermaids too!" Isabella squealed and clapped her hands together.

"You do?" It had been fairly obvious with her mermaid shirt, hairbow, and sneakers. "I never would have guessed it."

He pulled up to the front of the cabin and parked the truck. "Thank you." He kept his voice low and soft, and I wasn't sure if he was trying to keep Isabella from hearing or it was supposed to be a private moment between us.

I shifted in the front seat and brushed against his coat. "It's my pleasure," I said. After all, he'd done to help me, and we barely knew one another, it was the least I could do.

He shut off the truck and stepped out into the cold before unbuckling Isabella and carrying her on his hip.

I hurried to the front door, unlocked the entrance and gestured for him to bring his daughter inside. While it wasn't nearly as warm as it had been that morning, the house was still considerably comfortable.

The temperature would drop tonight. Leaving the door open to bring in the refrigerator would also cool the place.

"Izzie, you stay in here," he said, plopping her down on the sofa.

"But, Daddy, I want to be with you and Ella," she said, struggling to pronounce my name. It was sweet, endearing, really.

He bent down, crouched at her level, unbuttoning her jacket and sliding it off her shoulders. "Ariella," Jaxson said, correcting her as he slowly annunciated my name for her to repeat.

The little girl rolled her eyes at her daddy. "Ella. 'Tis what I said."

"It's all right," I said, resting a gentle hand on Jaxson's shoulder.

He stood and I took a step back, making room. There wasn't much space between the sofa and the coffee table for the two of us with Isabella on the couch. "Izzie, I need you to stay on the sofa, okay?"

"Yes, bossy Daddy," Isabella said.

"I'm telling you, I'm raising a teenage daughter already." Jaxson gestured for me to follow him outside. "Do you think you can give me a hand with the fridge, or is it too much for you to do?"

I may not have been as strong as Jaxson, but I didn't want to be forced to sit on the couch and watch. "I can help."

"Okay, good." He undid the ropes, and together we guided the fridge out of the truck and into the house.

Jaxson did most of the lifting and heavy work. I guided the fridge and made sure it didn't crush him.

Twenty minutes from start to finish, the fridge was in the kitchen, and the electric cord was left accessible for when the generator was brought over.

"Thank you again for everything." I hated being in his debt, but twice, he'd helped me, and I would not forget it.

"Don't mention it. I'm going to wheel the generator over. Can you stay here and keep an eye on Izzie?"

"Sure." I didn't know the first thing about kids.

She sat on the couch, her feet kicking the air, probably trying to reach the coffee table, but her legs were too short. He wouldn't be gone that long.

He slipped out the front door and left his truck. I frowned, watching from the window, curious why he didn't bring his vehicle with him.

"Where did Daddy go?" Isabella asked.

"He'll be right back." My stomach tensed. I could not deal with a crying toddler.

I dashed over to the sofa to sit beside her, attempting another distraction to keep her from growing upset. While I wanted to know if there was a girlfriend or partner in the picture, I wasn't sure how to delicately ask a three-year-old that question.

"What's your favorite thing to do with your Daddy?"

"Tickle fight!" she proclaimed and stood on my sofa, lifting her shirt to show me her belly.

"Do you want me to tickle you?" I asked her.

Isabella grinned and vigorously nodded her head. My fingers pretended to tickle her, but I didn't even come close to touch her before she squealed and giggled, jumping back.

"Oh, come on. That didn't tickle!" She'd make a superb actress someday. Jaxson was right about her practically being a teenager, being melodramatic.

"Tickle!" she squealed and tried to tickle my neck. Her fingers were chilly and wiggling, but it wasn't the least bit causing me to laugh.

I pretended to giggle and tickled her hips, and she squirmed with actual fits of giggles. Her legs kicked, and her chin bent downward as she squealed with delight.

I let go for a second, allowing her to catch her breath. I didn't want her in tears or upset.

"More!" she leaped into my arms. "Tickle more!"

I tickled her a little more, watching her thrash as she giggled, her cheeks rosy.

"Does your daddy have a girlfriend?" I asked, not entirely sure she could answer between her fits of laughter. I probably shouldn't have been asking about him, but I couldn't stop myself, the curiosity getting the better of me.

"Daddy likes to play with the boys." She giggled and slipped from my grasp. My hands paused.

"Oh." That wasn't what I expected to hear. While I shouldn't have been disappointed, my heart sunk like an anvil in the sea.

Jaxson stalked into the house, an extra pair of boots in hand. "What's that you're telling about me, Izzie?"

She snuck away from me, climbed off the sofa, and ran toward her daddy. "You like to play with Declan and Aiden."

CHAPTER EIGHT

JAXSON

Shit.

Was my daughter telling Ariella I was gay?

I was pretty confident Izzie didn't even know what that meant, let alone what she was saying. I liked women a lot.

While I didn't bring women around because of Izzie, that didn't mean I didn't enjoy their company.

I put the winter boots down on the ground and bent down to Izzie's level, hugging her. "I work with Declan and Aiden, Izzie. I don't think the right term is playing with them."

Isabella's brow furrowed. She had no idea what I was saying, and it didn't matter.

I glanced back at Ariella on the sofa and hoped she understood.

"I brought you these," I said, showing her the fur-lined boots.

They'd been a gift I hadn't given that sat in the back of my closet, unopened and unworn.

"I hope they'll fit, I'm not sure what size you are, and I don't have a lot of spare women's boots lying around."

I handed her the shoes, and she slipped them on to see how well they fit.

"I must be Cinderella," she joked and wiggled her feet. "These are super comfy. I will not ask why they were at your house. I honestly don't care. I'm just glad to have a warm pair of boots again, and I promise to return them as soon as I get mine from the car."

"Don't worry about it. They won't be missed," I said.

"Where's the generator?" Ariella asked.

I pointed toward the window on the opposite side of the cabin.

"Around back. It needs to stay outside, but I'm going to hook up an extension cord and run it out the back door. I'll tape the cord down if I need to, to make sure you can shut the door tight."

"Thank you," she said and stood, coming toward me. "Can I help with anything?"

"You've helped enough." I didn't intend to come across as harsh, but it was clear she was asking Izzie about me. Why else was my daughter telling her I liked to play with boys?

I scratched the back of my neck and headed over to the fridge, hooking up the extension cord before taking it outside.

Ariella stood in the hallway watching me.

"I'm sorry if I was out of line." She kept her voice down so that only I could hear her, which I appreciated immensely. I didn't want Izzie to have a plethora of questions later.

"Next time, if you want to know something, just ask me."

"Right. I'll do that," she said and pursed her lips.

Already, I could tell she wanted to ask me something, but I wasn't sure what it was. Had she asked Izzie while I'd been outside and hadn't gotten the answer she hoped for? Why was she asking twenty questions about me?

"You're staring," I said as I stepped outside. She hung in the doorframe, keeping the back door open while watching me hook up the generator outside and start the engine on it.

"Just watching you work," Ariella said.

There was more to it than that, but I wasn't sure what she was getting at. "Listen, I like women. I just try to keep my daughter away from anyone I date."

Why was I telling her this? She hadn't asked. She was probably just being friendly with Izzie, and I got the wrong impression from what I'd heard when coming into the cabin.

"Is Isabella's mom in the picture?" she asked, leaning against the doorframe.

She wrapped her arms around herself, her jacket abandoned inside the house.

Ariella had to be freezing. I hurried up with the generator and ushered her back inside, where it was warmer.

"No, she's not. It's just the two of us." I didn't elaborate, not because I didn't want to, but because we were back inside, and Izzie was within earshot.

I didn't want her to overhear the conversation.

"I'm happy to talk about it with you, but it would be better if we had that discussion when it's just the two of us."

"Of course," she said.

I shut the door and locked it, the electric cord pushed to the side. "I'll secure the cord next time I come by."

I could tape it down, but I needed to get some tape and didn't have any on hand with me at the moment. I knew what was in the cabin, and I hadn't left any behind.

"I'm sure it'll be fine. Thank you again for all your help today, and I will pay you back for everything," Ariella said.

I wasn't worried about the money, whether she was good for it. That was beside the point. It was clear she was in a bind and needed help.

I hadn't made her life any easier with the property listing, and guilt weighed heavily on me. Even though it hadn't been intentional, it still was clear that she struggled to make ends meet.

I dug my hand into my coat pocket, almost forgetting the other device I'd brought over from my house.

"For your cell phone," I said, retrieving a small solar powered charging device. "It doesn't need outside light. You can put it on a windowsill."

I took a few steps into the kitchen and set up the device with the solar panel facing the window, keeping it on the ledge inside above the sink.

"Do you have your phone handy?" I wanted to make sure it was set up before I left.

She headed toward her bed and retrieved her knapsack that sat on the bottom shelf of the end table. Crouched down, she dug through the bag for a moment before finding her cell phone.

I hadn't seen a flip phone in ages, especially with the craze for smartphones.

"Wow. You keep it old school," I said, taking the device from her before plugging it into the solar charger.

"I'm all about practicality and what I need. Well, that or you can consider me cheap." She flashed me a wide grin.

She was hiding something, but I couldn't be certain what it was.

"Thank you for the charger. I should call my sister once my phone is charged. I'm sure she's wondering if I made it here safely."

Everyone I knew had a smartphone, and anyone with a burner style flip phone in my line of business usually had secrets. I tried not to let the nagging suspicion cloud my judgment.

"You're welcome to use my phone," I said, pulling it out from my pants pocket.

"That isn't necessary." She waved her hand dismissively. "It can wait until tonight. I'm sure the phone will have enough of a charge before nightfall. I hope, anyway."

It would take a few hours to charge the battery, but it would be usable within the hour. The solar charger was top of the line commercial grade used by our team. It wasn't something you could pick up off the shelf of a store. I had used it countless times on Eagle Tactical missions when I was in the field and didn't have easy access to an accessible outlet.

"Use my phone," I insisted and pushed my phone at her.

She glanced over at the device. Her tongue darted out to the corner of her lips.

Was she debating whether to call her sister in front of me? Had she wanted the call to be private, and I had overstepped her boundaries? She didn't say a word, just held the phone in her hand.

"I can sit with Izzie and give you some privacy."

There wasn't a ton of privacy in the cabin. It was one large room, like a studio style setup.

"It's not that. I don't have her phone number memorized," she said, her cheeks red.

Was she embarrassed about not knowing the number offhand? I could recant every phone number for my military buddies, they were like family to me.

Had her sister's number recently changed, and she hadn't had time to memorize it?

She handed me back my cell phone. "I'm sure she can wait a few more hours. It's only been a day." Ariella didn't sound the least bit concerned about calling her sister later.

I held my tongue, not wanting to make a scene. If she didn't remember the number, there were ways I could help, I had resources and connections through Eagle Tactical, but I wasn't sure that was what she wanted. I didn't want to push her and make her uncomfortable.

"If it were someone I cared about and hadn't heard from them, I'd be concerned," I said.

I didn't elaborate that I'd probably have unleashed the entire task force of Eagle Tactical to go looking for that person. We were different. She had moved to the middle of nowhere, with no connections. Was it possible she and her sister weren't close?

"Daddy, I have to go potty!" Izzie squealed from the sofa and stood on the couch cushions.

I shot her a look of warning that she'd better sit her butt down or stand on the floor. Isabella knew that jumping on beds and couches was not allowed.

The little tyrant did whatever she damned well pleased half the time, though. Being a single dad wasn't easy.

"I think that's my cue to take her home," I said.

"She can use the bathroom here," Ariella offered. "I have indoor plumbing."

"You're welcome for that," I half-joked. I had been responsible, along with my military buddies, for setting up indoor plumbing. While we hooked up the indoor plumbing and PVC inside and under the floorboards, we'd also hired a licensed plumber who doubled as an excavator to hook up to the sewer line.

"I'm going to take her back home, let her use the little kid potty, and then put her down for a nap."

"No nap!" Izzie exclaimed, jumping on the sofa.

"Sit your butt down!" I scolded her. She knew better and was testing my limits or showing off for Ariella. Perhaps it was a bit of both.

Pretty soon, she'd meltdown without an afternoon nap. It was only a matter of time. She'd done well today, but I couldn't depend on her lasting through dinner.

Izzie went from a standing position on the sofa to jumping into a sitting position. "Potty, Daddy!"

"Do you mind if we use your bathroom?"

Izzie followed me to the small private bathroom, and I helped her before she climbed off the toilet and ran past me with her pants down.

"Oh, my gosh. You, child, will be the death of me," I muttered, flushing the toilet before washing my hands.

I stepped out of the bathroom, and Ariella was bent down to Izzie's level, helping her pull her pants back up. *Thank you*, I mouthed to her.

She smiled and nodded.

"Come on, Izzie." I grabbed her coat and helped her get her arms into the sleeves while she thrashed about, not wanting to go home.

"No nap!" she squealed.

I groaned and tried to control my temper. Isabella was tired, and I hadn't kept to her routine. It was my fault she was behaving like a rambunctious toddler. "We need to leave Ariella here. Say goodbye."

I slid one arm into her sleeve and worked on the other one before she slid her arm back out.

"I don't mean to interrupt. I'm sure you have this handled, but she could nap on my bed," Ariella offered.

I shot a glance at her over my shoulder.

"I mean, I need to learn to chop firewood. If you don't mind giving me a hand, she could stay inside and nap in my bed," she repeated.

It wasn't the worst idea, and Izzie seemed to go for it, nodding vigorously with bright, wide, doe-like eyes.

"That still means you need a nap, little miss," I said, pointing at Izzie.

She slipped her coat off, scooted past me, and ran for the queen-sized mattress. I tucked her under the covers while Ariella closed the curtains, making the cabin darker. Quietly, I headed to the front door and waited for Ariella to put her coat and shoes on.

A few minutes later, we were outside, just the two of us.

"I'm sorry if I overstepped," Ariella said, quick to apologize. "I know you have a routine, and I just thought I might help." She looked flustered and nervous. Was she worried I'd yell at her?

I exhaled a long, heavy breath I hadn't realized I'd been holding. "It's fine. Izzie tends to meltdown when she doesn't get her afternoon nap, and half the time, she fights with me about lying down. If she doesn't rest, she's crabby for dinner and sometimes falls asleep before she eats. It's just a vicious cycle. Thank you for offering her your bed. She likes you."

"I like her too. She's a good kid."

It was obvious Izzie had already grown attached to Ariella. It had only been a day together, and I had seen the sparkle in Izzie's eye, the smile that adorned her face when she looked at Ariella.

There hadn't been a female figure in Isabella's life. That had been my fault. The guys were great, helping look after her and support me, but it wasn't a woman figure.

One day, she'd need someone to come to and talk with about things that she didn't want to discuss with her dad. I had thought I had another ten years, but that glint in Izzie's eyes told me more than her words at this point could ever do.

I slid my gloves on as we stood outside on the porch. "You have a shed around back," I said, changing the subject. "There's an ax inside to chop wood, and around back is a stump where you can do the chopping."

"Great." Her voice dripped with sarcasm. Her tongue darted out past her cherry red lips before chewing on her bottom lip. "Any chance I can find wood in the forest and skip the chopping part?"

"Wouldn't that be nice? There are probably some logs, and I'm not suggesting you go all lumberjack style and chop down a tree, but you might come across logs that are too big to fit into your wood-burning stove. You'll need to know how to size those logs properly, which involves using an ax," I said.

She followed me as I headed around to the shed and opened the doors. I retrieved an ax from inside, sheltered from the snow, and then shut the doors when I was done, to keep the contents inside dry.

"There's an ATV in the shed. It's old and dated, but it works. It should help you get around the woods and into town if you follow the trail with the orange triangles." I pointed toward the entrance to the trail on her property. It followed along the riverbed and was a shortcut to town.

"That's great. Thanks," she said.

Ariella watched as I grabbed a log and placed it on the large stump, preparing to split it.

I pulled back the ax and swung; it split cleanly into two pieces. I wasn't sure how to explain the action. It was easier to show her. "Piece of cake. Your turn," I said, handing her the handle of the ax, the blade toward the ground.

"Right." She took the ax, and I grabbed a log and situated it on the stump before I took a step back to give her space. She gripped the handle with two hands and swung back before following through, going forward in one swift motion.

She got the ax's blade a few inches into the piece of wood before it got stuck. "It won't budge. I think I broke it."

"It's not broken. You just have to dislodge it," I said, taking the ax and lifting the blade, hitting it sideways against the stump. It took a half swing, nothing too forceful to break it free.

"Are you sure I can't just gather firewood in the forest?" she asked with a half-hearted laugh. The smile on her face was gone, and the glint in her eyes had faded. "I think I may have oversold the idea of living in a small town in the mountains."

"You'll get the hang of it," I said, hoping to boost her confidence.

I didn't imagine it was easy for her, moving out into the middle of nowhere. While I was curious about her reasons, I wasn't one to push.

I certainly could have done a little research with the tools and resources from Eagle Tactical, but it didn't feel right. She wasn't Izzie's babysitter. Had that been the case, I would have run her name through the database and dug through her past to make sure Izzie was safe.

"Hopefully before summer," she said with a hearty laugh.

My phone buzzed in my pocket, and I pulled out my cell phone and removed my gloves so I could answer. "Eagle Tactical, this is Jaxson," I said, taking a step back from the stump to allow for a little privacy. I could tell from the caller I.D. that someone was calling about the business, and it wasn't a personal call.

"Hi, Jaxson. This is Bridget Sanders from the Blue Sky Resort. We wanted to get a background check run for a new hire. Is that something you guys can do for us this week?"

"Yes. If you want to email me the form with the employee's name and information, I can have one of our guys run the background check and get it back to you shortly."

I gave her my email address before I hung up the phone and headed back toward Ariella as she split another piece of wood in half.

I hoped she was the new hire the background check was for. Knowing that I'd be the one running the information on her past and digging up all her dirty little secrets, I was covered in filth.

CHAPTER NINE

ARIELLA

"Everything okay?" I asked.

He'd gotten a work call, and while he'd taken a step away to answer it privately, I couldn't help but wonder who it was or what he might need to do.

Eagle Tactical.

He'd mentioned the name of the company.

While I hadn't heard of them before arriving in Breckenridge, the fact he worked there had me curious, especially when he'd told me former military soldiers owned the company.

"Just a work thing," he said and shoved his phone back into his pocket.

Was he hiding something? Could he not talk about work? A part of me was curious about what he did for a living, how he coped with danger.

"Do you need to go to work?" I asked. I didn't know what his hours were. Just because I didn't have a job, didn't mean he didn't have to work.

"No, I have the day off," Jaxson said, matter of factly.

He stepped closer toward me and took a breath, a pause before coming up from behind. His hand rested on my hip. I expelled a soft, nervous breath when he rested his hands over mine to help guide me with the ax.

The moment was intimate, and had it not been so cold outside, I might have been warmer, but the truth was my fingers were numb, and my face tingled. Even with my gloves, hat, boots, and thick winter coat, I was still cold.

"You're freezing," Jaxson said, his breath against my cheek.

I didn't hide it from him. "Yes. I hate the cold."

He laughed and pulled me closer, the ax fumbling from our hands to the ground. "Careful," he warned me. "You could get hurt dropping a blade so carelessly."

We'd both dropped it without thinking, but I didn't want to point that out.

I spun around in his embrace, our jackets thick and keeping me from really feeling his body against mine like I wanted.

He reached for my hat and pulled it down a little farther on my head to cover me a little better. "We should go inside and warm up," Jaxson said.

"I don't want to wake Izzie."

"That kid will sleep through anything," Jaxson said, his breath warm against my frozen cheeks. He took my gloved hand and led me back into the cabin. The warmth of the house immediately put me at ease, and while it wasn't as toasty as it had been earlier, Jaxson brought a few logs inside and brought the fire roaring back to life. "Do you know how to start a fire?" he asked.

I removed my cold, damp outdoor clothes—my hat, gloves, shoes, and jacket—leaving them by the fire to dry.

"If I have lighter fluid and a long lighter, I can figure it out."

"You are not using lighter fluid in your wood-burning stove. Is that clear?" His tone forceful and his eyebrows raised in alarm, he didn't seem the least bit amused in my humor.

"That was a joke." It was mostly a joke. I'd had bonfires outside and knew how to start those types of fires.

He loaded the wood into the stove, and the hot ashes at the

bottom caught right away. Another few minutes and the fire roared back to life.

I sat quietly on the sofa, and Jaxson came over once he seemed satisfied with the fire, sitting beside me. We'd only known one another two days. I wasn't ready for a relationship, even with the most handsome man I'd ever met.

If there hadn't been a kid involved, I would have let my guard down further and allowed myself to indulge in a fantasy involving him, but that was out of the question. We couldn't, and besides, I wasn't exactly sure what was going on with Izzie's mother.

"You're quiet," Jaxson said, sitting back relaxing on the sofa.

"Just thinking," I said, avoiding his stare as he kept watching me.

"About?"

"It's been a long time since I've been around another man." I wasn't sure I should have brought up my ex-husband or the divorce, but it was the truth.

I wasn't used to dating or sex with anyone but the bastard I'd been married to for way too long. There was more to it, a place I didn't want to go or drudge up. Not that he would have known.

Jaxson sighed, running a hand through his hair. "I know the feeling. Well, maybe not another man." Chuckling, he nudged me. "Have you ever been married?"

"Yes." I glanced at Jaxson, exhaling a heavy breath. "We're not together anymore. He's a distant memory, one I wish I could erase."

"Divorced or separated?" he asked.

"Divorced. What about you?" I held my tongue on the fact he was in prison. I wasn't ready to talk about that with anyone.

"I've never been married. After I took full custody of Izzie, she's been my entire life."

I brushed a strand of hair behind my ear. The way he stared at me sent a shiver through my body and made my insides toasty.

"I can see that. It's clear you're a good father."

"Thank you," Jaxson said, his eyes shining.

"It's true." I shifted on the sofa and our legs touched briefly.

"I have to ask, and I hope you don't mind, but many people who come out to the mountains, a small town in the middle of nowhere, are running from something or someone. Are you running, Ariella?"

The way he said my name made me shiver.

Could he know my secrets? Did he know who I was and what I'd been accused of doing?

I hadn't changed my first name, and Ariella wasn't the most common name, like Mary or Jennifer. I assumed hiding in plain sight had been to my advantage, but I was wrong.

CHAPTER TEN

JAXSON

"No," she whispered, her gaze meeting mine, our eyes locked.

I tried reading her expression, watching her face and body language to determine if she was lying to me. I'd been around enough interrogations in the military on both sides of them that I could see right through a liar.

What was she hiding?

Did it have more to do with her past and ex-husband than anything else? I didn't want to hound her with questions or run a background check on her solely out of my curiosity. It was wrong, and I didn't want to be that person, questioning her every move, not trusting her.

Though I had to remember, we barely knew one another.

I wanted to get to know her.

There weren't many women who were single in Breckenridge, and the ones who were, I knew all of them. Some had approached me, asked me out, or pursued me countless times. I had turned them down, and it had grown easier once Izzie was in the picture.

"You're just starting over?" I offered in the way of an explanation.

"That's right," she said as relief flooded her features. Her shoulders relaxed, and her eyes were no longer doe-like.

She was hiding something. I should have afforded Ariella her privacy and secrets, but I couldn't protect her if I didn't know what was going on.

Was I overreacting because of my line of work and she didn't need protection?

I'd seen it all before, women in abusive marriages fleeing their husbands. That had been my first fleeting thought when she'd told me she'd been married and had come out here to live. I suspected there was more to it than that.

"Well, I'm glad you picked this cabin," I said, stretching my arms before turning my gaze toward the ceiling and then back to her. "It's nice to have a neighbor who isn't Mason."

"No kidding," she laughed under her breath. "How do you work with him?"

"He's a good guy," I said. "Albeit a pain in the ass, but he's got his heart in the right place, and he always has my back."

The longer I stared at her, the more I wanted to kiss her.

It had been three years of focusing on Izzie and not allowing myself the opportunity to indulge in my desires. I didn't want to ruin a perfectly good friendship that we'd already established, but was it worth it?

My heart constricted, but my body leaned forward, my lips closing in but pausing, waiting for her to make the next move to lean into me.

Her breath hovered over my lips, the warmth of her mouth teasing me, making my body ache for her touch.

My heart pounded against my ribcage as my lips parted slightly. I shifted closer if that was possible, without pulling her into my lap.

Her eyes lowered to my lips. The cabin warmed as I slid my hand to the back of her neck. My fingers played with her hair, letting the moment drag on, our lips not quite touching yet.

Ariella's lips parted, and a jolt of electricity coursed through my body as she leaned in, brushing her lips against mine.

Starving for her touch, I pulled her closer, one hand at the back of her neck, the other on her lower back. I wanted our bodies to melt together, to become one.

She moaned, and I took the opportunity as an encouragement to continue.

I pulled her into my lap, her hips against mine, our lips fused with a heated passion. I wanted nothing more than to strip her naked and drive myself into her, but I couldn't do that. I wouldn't do that, not with Izzie in the room.

This would have to satisfy the urgent need building within my body.

"Jaxson," she gasped and pulled back, her breath ragged. Her forehead rested against mine, and she was panting hard.

My eyes shut, enjoying the moment and the intimacy between us. I hadn't realized how much I missed being this close to someone.

"We need to take things slow," Ariella said.

I knew she was right, we'd just met, and I had my daughter to think of foremost. "Yes, slow is good." I didn't want to lie, but kissing her had unleashed a flurry of emotions pent up for the past three years.

I wanted to carry her to my bed and ravish her, but she was right.

"Slow is overrated," she whispered and pressed her lips firmly against mine.

I moaned, my body responding to her touch, her kisses, the way she whispered. Everything inside me was on fire. Her hips shifted and thrust against me.

I groaned; she was killing me. I wouldn't be able to keep any measure of self-control if she continued the ministrations against my crotch.

"Ariella," I rasped, trying to regain my strength to stop what we'd both started before it was too late. "Slow," I said, trying to remind her of her earlier words. It was hard to say more than one word at a time.

My brain wasn't working, my body fueled with a desire for her.

"Sorry," she whispered and climbed off my body. Had she

realized what she'd done to me? Could she feel the evidence of my desire for her?

She sat on the sofa, turned to face me. Her fingers rested on her thighs.

"I think we should go slow. You have a daughter who needs your undivided attention, and I—"

"You, what?" I asked, wanting her to be honest and open with me. I pushed an errant strand of hair behind her ear and waited for her to answer my question.

"I'm not ready to trust again, to be in a relationship. I have a feeling you're not looking for a one-night stand, and that's all I can offer you."

My stomach knotted, and I scooted back. Her words burned my heart.

Is that what she wanted?

I wasn't interested in sleeping with random women or even a friends-with-benefits scenario. I had a daughter, and anyone I brought around, I wanted for the long run, not for one night.

While I didn't know how long she'd been divorced, we had just met. I needed to give her time. She was right. We needed to slow down, take a break from whatever was happening between us.

"You're right, I'm not interested in an empty fuck," I said and stood.

Staying the afternoon, letting Izzie have a nap, it was all a mistake.

I laced my boots and grabbed my coat. I didn't want to wake Isabella, but I could quietly put her jacket on her and put her into the car seat. If I was lucky, the short drive back to the cabin would lull her to sleep, and she could finish her nap at home.

CHAPTER ELEVEN

ARIELLA

My lips still tingled from the recent kiss.

When I'd told him I wanted to go slow, he seemed onboard with the idea. I hadn't intended to hurt him, but I needed to be honest.

I wasn't ready for a commitment, and I suspected he wanted a wife. He had a daughter and was probably looking to finish his family.

I wasn't sure I could be that for him, ever.

I sat on the sofa, lost and flustered as he gathered his coat and boots. "You don't have to go."

"Yes, I do." He zipped his jacket, put his beanie back on, and then secured Isabella's jacket around her little body before carrying her to the door. "I'll call Declan and have him give you a ride to pick up your car when it's done at the shop."

Great.

Now he didn't want to see me again.

"Okay. Thank you." I stood and headed toward the kitchen to check my cell phone that sat on the windowsill. The battery had just about fully charged.

I unplugged his solar charger. "Here, take this." He wouldn't be back for it, and I wasn't sure I wanted to face him again, either.

"I'll give you my number. Text me, so I have your number, and I can forward it to Declan."

"Okay." I punched in his digits and texted him. *It's Ariella*. I didn't send anything special. I didn't know what to say. The heated moment between us had turned as cold as ice.

I'd really screwed up.

"I'll see you around," Jaxson said and headed with Izzie to the truck.

I watched from the door. I stood awkwardly with my arms crossed in front of me. The chilly wind made me numb.

He backed out of the driveway, and I shut the door.

How was I going to make this right? Could I fix what I'd done?

He didn't know my secrets, that Ben had stolen millions from investors in a Ponzi scheme, and we both had been charged with dozens of crimes. He'd been convicted of several felonies. I'd stood trial, and while I'd gotten off with no convictions, I had been threatened countless times back in New York. That had been one reason why I'd left.

I wanted what happened to be forever in the past, buried. I had done nothing wrong. I didn't know what he'd done, but my name had been on the company papers because we were married.

I'd signed forms I didn't understand, and that made me an accessory. I should have been more careful, but I trusted him. I wasn't involved with the company. I never saw the financial records or accounts. That had been how I'd been able to get off without a single conviction.

I truly was clueless.

"I'm sorry," I whispered to the chilly afternoon air as Jaxson had already pulled away and down the road out of sight. I hadn't meant to hurt him. I didn't want him to think less of me or blame me, like every one of Ben's investors had.

While I hadn't been convicted, I still held the weight of guilt, dirty of his crimes. I should have known what was going on.

My eyes burned with tears.

The only person I'd gotten close to since my divorce and the trial, and he knew nothing of my past. I'd ruined my clean slate without him even knowing the truth.

Should I have leaped in heart first and taken a chance with Jaxson?

I couldn't lie to him. After everything he'd done for me, I would not hurt him. At least that hadn't been my intention.

With a resigned sigh, I dialed my sister, Delphine. I wasn't expecting a warm greeting, but she had insisted I call her when I got settled in my new home.

"Hello?" Delphine's soft voice resounded through the phone.

"Hey, Delphine, it's me, Ariella." I paused, unsure what to say. We hadn't been close in years.

She blamed me for what happened with Ben.

When I was charged and searching for a lawyer, she'd shut me out and told me she wanted nothing to do with me. I wasn't looking for a handout or a free pass. I just needed help, and she turned her back on me.

She was a paralegal and knew plenty of defense attorneys but didn't want any association with me. I hated her for that year, but then I saw her at the trial when I was put on the stand. She'd been in the back row.

That had been the beginning of our reconciliation.

"Hey," her voice was soft, and her single word of greeting sounded hesitant.

"Is this a bad time?" I asked. I collapsed onto the sofa and stretched out my feet to rest on the coffee table.

"It's never a great time," Delphine said.

"Right." Why was I bothering to call her when she wanted nothing to do with me? "Well, you said to let you know when I got my feet planted in Breckenridge. I'm here. Everything is great." I gritted my teeth.

When we were younger, she could see right through my lies. Had that changed?

"Good. Listen, Marcus is home. I can't talk right now." She kept her voice low, hardly above a whisper. Marcus hated me, and she wasn't telling him I called. I'd have done the same had the situation been reversed.

Marcus was her husband of ten years. He was the king of assholes, well, maybe the prince. He narrowly was behind Benjamin, and while Marcus hadn't cheated on Delphine or stolen millions from his clients, he was more than just a bit of a snob. He acted like he was untouchable and could do no wrong.

"Okay. Bye," I said and hung up the phone. I don't know why I bothered. While I was expecting a frosty greeting, a part of me hoped we could reconnect. I couldn't have been more wrong.

Ending the call, I glanced down at the missed voicemail and hit play.

"Hi, Ms. Cole, this is Bridget Sanders with Blue Sky Resort. We met yesterday at my office. We'd like to formally offer you the flex position. We wanted to let you know that we've started the background check, and assuming everything goes smoothly, we'd like you to start first thing Monday morning. Please call us back if you have any questions. Otherwise, we'll be in touch with you later this week."

I hung up the phone, my stomach in knots, waiting to hear if I'd cleared the background check.

I texted Jaxson.

He probably didn't want to hear from me, but I didn't want him worrying about me and getting food for dinner or groceries.

If the ATV in the shed could get me into town, I could take my backpack and get some food for the house. While I had little money, I had a credit card that would have to suffice.

Thanks for the help today and for everything. Taking the ATV out to the store. I texted.

Remember to stay on the orange triangle trail. Be careful.

CHAPTER TWELVE

JAXSON

Early the next morning, I headed into Eagle Tactical after I dropped Izzie off at daycare. I had avoided my work emails, which meant I needed to open up the correspondence from Blue Sky Resort.

Lucy sat at the front desk, a cup of coffee in hand.

"Good morning," I said as I passed her desk and headed for my office.

"Fridays are wonderful," Lucy said, sipping her coffee.

Sitting down, I jiggled the mouse and waited for the screen to light up. It was time to find out if Ariella got the job.

I shouldn't have cared one way or the other, but I did. I wanted her to be happy, and while I wasn't strapped for cash, I would eventually need my generator back, which meant she needed to purchase one.

I opened my emails and walked away from my desk long enough to grab myself a coffee while I let all the emails file into my inbox.

"Morning," Mason said. "How did things go with the spitfire?"

I grunted under my breath.

That was certainly one way to describe Ariella. I didn't think she was trouble other than the possibility that she very well might break my heart.

Spending the rest of the day apart yesterday had been a wise decision. I didn't want to get emotionally involved with someone who couldn't meet my needs.

I'd learned that about Emma. She had only been interested in one thing, sex, and while that had been fun, she wasn't interested in being a mother to our little girl.

"That good?" Mason asked. He stood by the coffeepot and poured himself a drink. I waited until he was done to do the same.

I didn't want to kiss and tell or speak ill of her. I had no reason to, and she had done nothing wrong. "Everything's fine. I dropped her off yesterday after loaning her my generator."

I didn't go into detail with Mason about purchasing her a fridge or teaching her to chop firewood. He'd give me crap, and I'd never hear the end.

His eyes narrowed as he studied me.

"You have the hots for the new girl," Mason crooned.

"Oh, shut it." I would not listen to his insistent teasing. Nothing happened as far as he knew.

I poured myself a cup of coffee and took it to my desk. I sat down and sipped my hot beverage, the blackness of the coffee fitting my mood.

Mason put down his coffee on the corner of my desk. He folded his arms across his chest and watched me.

"What is it?" I asked. Mason lingered until he got what he wanted, but there was nothing to tell. At least nothing I planned on sharing.

"Bridget Sanders called this morning and left two messages. She's anxious about the two new hires and getting backgrounds run ASAP."

I groaned and ran a hand through my hair. Background checks and research weren't the most exciting aspects of our job.

It was simple work, easy pay, and I should have been grateful for the extra income it brought into Eagle Tactical, but I preferred being out in the field.

"She called me yesterday on my day off. I told her to email me the paperwork, and I'd get to it as soon as I could." Bridget could wait a day or two for the background checks to come back.

Mason shifted to sit at the edge of my desk. "I think Bridget has a crush on you. Why else would she call your cell phone when she could have submitted the requests through regular channels?"

"You're crazy," I said. The woman was in her mid-sixties. She was nice, but she wasn't my type. I was pushing forty and preferred women closer to my age. "She's always been impatient, wanting results before she even sends over the employees' names."

"True." Mason pushed himself off my desk and retrieved his cup of coffee. "She copied me on the two hires. Did you see the names yet?"

Had that been why Mason was hanging around my desk and pestering me? "Let me guess, one of them is Ariella." I already knew she'd applied for the position at Blue Sky Resort. That would mean she should get the job, which was good news.

"Yes, and the other one is your least favorite person."

I had no clue who that could be. "My mother?" I joked.

"Wow. I'll remember to tell her that at the next holiday dinner I'm invited to," Mason said, his lips curved upwards. He nudged my shoulder. "Have a look."

I rolled my eyes before I found the email and opened up the application to read the individuals' names. The first application was Ariella Cole, that hadn't been a surprise. At least she'd get the job. I opened the second application and coughed, practically choking on air.

Mason smacked my back. "Don't die over it."

"Emma Foster." I read the name aloud. "What's she doing in Breckenridge?" I asked Mason, not that I should have expected him to know the answer.

My daughter's birth mother had returned.

"Beats me," Mason said. "I thought she lived in Los Angeles."

"So did I." That's where she lived three years ago when Izzie was born.

Mason sipped his coffee, his eyes on me the entire time. "You're pissed. I can see it all over your face."

"Well, I'm not happy that she's suddenly back in town. She gave up her rights to Izzie."

I hoped Emma hadn't changed her mind and now wanted to be part of the equation. That wasn't a possibility, not for me. I didn't want to confuse Isabella, either.

What if Emma left again? I had to protect my little girl, and if it meant keeping Emma away from Izzie, I would do whatever was necessary.

"You could make sure she doesn't get the job at Blue Sky Resort," Mason said. His eyes crinkled with a grin that lit up his face.

"You're absolutely mad if you think I'm going to manipulate the results of the background check."

That wasn't something I could do. Even if I didn't want Emma around, I would not destroy her life or her future. I reached for my coffee, taking another sip.

"Do you want me to do it?" Mason asked.

A part of me wanted him to do whatever was necessary to keep Emma away and Izzie safe, but I would never condone such an action or be involved in any part of it.

"You know I can't say yes." Even though a small piece of me wanted to ensure that Emma was gone from our lives.

"You should confront her head-on, not avoid the situation. If she's going to be working at Blue Sky Resort, go visit her," Mason said.

He stepped back from my desk and stalked toward the door.

"That's what I would do. Make it clear you want nothing to do with her, and if she plans on sticking around town, it won't be for Isabella or you."

I exhaled a heavy breath. Mason was right.

"Yeah, I can do that." I also had her temporary address on her background check application.

I glanced over the information. I recognized the address as a rental unit, a small cabin outside of town not too far from the resort. I could visit her and give her a heads up before investing any more time and energy into our community.

Whatever regrets she had about Izzie, it was too late. I would not let her hurt my daughter.

"Can you run the backgrounds while I stop over at Emma's house?"

"Sure thing," Mason said. "You know how much I love digging into people's lives and uncovering their dirt."

I drove toward the Blue Sky Resort. Just across the street were log cabin rental properties. I pulled up out front of cabin #218 and climbed out of my truck.

Exhaling a heavy breath, my stomach in knots, I gave a forceful knock on the door. I didn't want to be here, but it had to be done. I would not let her interfere with my daughter.

The door creaked open sluggishly and in no rush. Standing in her silken negligee, one hand on the door, she glanced me over from head to toe. "Jaxson, I wasn't expecting to see you."

"Seriously? That's where you want to start."

I couldn't believe the nerve of her! I stomped past her front door, letting myself into the rental property. The cabin was small, much smaller than the place Ariella had purchased.

"What are you doing in town?" I asked, my voice booming. I didn't pretend to be thrilled to see her because I wasn't the least bit happy about her return.

Emma shut the door behind her and scampered into the room. "I'm applying for a job. By the looks of it, you already deduced that much. They must have asked Eagle Tactical to do the background check, am I right?"

"You shouldn't be here, Emma. You signed away your rights as Izzie's mother." I would not let her come running back into our lives and ruin everything.

She wrung her hands together in front of her. "I know, and I shouldn't have done that," she said, staring at me with her piercing brown eyes. "I wasn't ready to be a mother back then, but I am now."

"No." My answer was firm. "You planned on putting her up for adoption. Signing away your parental right to me is no different. You don't get to run off and then decide to come back and play parent when you feel like it."

Emma's eyes welled up. "Jaxson, please."

"No. I won't stand in the way of you taking this job, but you are not to have contact with my daughter." I headed for the door.

"Our daughter," she whispered.

My cell phone buzzed, and I took the moment as an opportunity to leave. I grabbed my phone and stepped outside of the cabin, shutting the door behind myself. I didn't want Emma hearing the conversation or her chasing after me. "Hey, Mason. What's up?" I recognized his number.

"You will not believe this, but Ariella Cole, she was married to Benjamin Ryan."

"The same Benjamin Ryan who went to prison for stealing millions from investors?"

This day just went from bad to worse.

My stomach dropped as my legs failed to cooperate, as though they were encased in lead. I approached my truck and climbed inside, sitting in the front seat, trying to regroup.

My head spun.

I knew a woman like Ariella didn't move out into the mountains in a small town in the middle of nowhere because she liked the outdoors. She wanted to get off-grid.

Had she played me for a fool with not having electricity? I'd have bet anything she didn't want electricity. She didn't want to be found.

"That's right. Her married name, Ariella Ryan, came up when I searched, but her records were expunged. I did a little further digging when I recognized her name and the name of her ex-husband. She was arrested and charged but acquitted in a court of law," Mason said. "As far as her past is concerned, she's clean enough to get the job, but I thought you might want to know."

"Fuck."

I'd lost a pretty penny with her husband. The money that I believed I'd invested into real estate had instead been used in a Ponzi scheme, using my cash to pay other investors, until he'd gotten caught.

My entire life savings had vanished one day, and while Benjamin had gone to prison, I didn't believe Ariella was as innocent as she pretended to be.

CHAPTER THIRTEEN

ARIELLA

A loud, forceful knock pounded against my front door. I wasn't expecting visitors.

"Just a sec!" I called, coming to the door. I pulled it open, surprised to see Jaxson on the opposite side. "I wasn't expecting to see you today," I said.

He'd left yesterday in a huff after the few kisses we'd shared.

"You lied to me about who you are. Your actual name is Ariella Ryan."

His eyes narrowed, and his hands bunched in fists at his sides. He looked beyond pissed. The tips of his ears were red, and they matched his cheeks.

I took a step back as he entered my house. I kept space between us, even though I didn't sense I was in physical danger.

"That was my married name. I've taken my maiden name, and I am legally Ariella Cole. I never lied to you."

"The hell you didn't!" His voice thundered.

I shivered and jumped from the intensity of his rage. "I was acquitted. I didn't know what my ex-husband was involved in," I said.

Didn't he believe me? I wasn't a thief or a monster. I wasn't the one behind bars doing jail time for stealing millions.

"The hell you didn't! You owned a yacht, a mansion, and had a vacation home in the South Pacific!"

"I didn't know about those purchases," I said. It was the truth.

I didn't know about the additional bank account or luxuries that Benjamin had indulged in. While we were married, he had signed my name and forged it to further involve me in his illegal affairs.

He stalked closer, hovering within my personal space. "I don't believe you," he seethed.

"I'm telling the truth," I whispered, staring up at him and into his icy blue stare. "I knew the business had done well, but I didn't know where the money came from. I was naïve, and I trusted a man who took advantage of me." I took a step back, the heat radiating off his body and onto mine.

"Where's the money you stole?" He followed me, my back against the wall with nowhere to go.

"I didn't steal anything," I said and stood my ground. "I'm not a thief. My ex-husband was responsible, and he's in prison for what he did."

One hand came up against the wall, trapping me. His body was inches from mine. "I was one of your ex-husband's clients," Jaxson said, his breath hot against my cheek.

"I'm sorry," I said, quick to apologize. "I don't know what you want me to do." My voice was barely above a whisper, staring into his icy gaze.

It didn't take a genius to see he was angry, but it wasn't my fault. Didn't he realize that?

"The government froze all our accounts. They took the money that he'd stolen and redistributed it." At least that's what I thought happened.

His nostrils flared as he huffed. He was still pissed at me, but didn't he realize that's why I left? He wasn't too fond of me getting a fresh start. "Tell me why that's my problem."

I opened my mouth and quickly shut it. I had to tread carefully so as not to further antagonize him.

"It's not your problem. It's mine. I will get you the money for the refrigerator. I swear I will pay you back."

As soon as I landed a job, the first thing I would do was return him the money that he'd loaned me.

He pulled back, pacing the length of the cabin. "It's not about the money for the stupid refrigerator. It's the fact you lied to me, Ariella. Do you not see how that makes me look? I had to hear about it from Mason that you're a liar."

"I'm not a liar." I had neglected to give him information on my history, but we'd just met. Why would he think I'd have confided in him about my past?

I pushed myself away from the wall and folded my arms across my chest, coming to sit at the edge of the mattress.

"You're an asshole," I said, glaring at him.

"Excuse me?"

"You heard me." My hands trembled, but I shoved them farther into the arms of my shirt so that he wouldn't notice.

Anger raged through me. How dare he not believe me? Was he planning on interfering with me getting the job at Blue Sky Resort? That had to have been how he'd found out, through the background check.

Shit.

Was that reason enough for it to disqualify me for the position?

"All I did for you, and I'm the asshole." His jaw was tight, and he headed for the door. He pulled the door open and allowed a cold gust of wind to blow into the cabin.

I refrained from shivering, not wanting him to see my discomfort.

"Good luck at your new job and your new life," he shouted and slammed the door shut on his way out.

"Fuck!" I screamed and stood in the middle of the cabin, infuriated. I could see him outside, hurrying into his truck and speeding off down the road.

I couldn't keep running, no matter how hard it got.

I started my new job and orientation at Blue Sky Resort on Monday morning. While Jaxson knew about my past and my history, my employer hadn't been made aware.

I couldn't help but wonder if he had something to do with that or the fact my record had truly been expunged since I was exonerated.

I wasn't the only new employee, which was a relief. Emma and I spent the first month getting to know the routine and shared lunch every afternoon. It was nice to have someone to talk to, and who didn't know about my past.

"Do you want to grab drinks after work?" Emma asked. She worked behind the front desk while I had spent most of the first month handing out ski and snowboard equipment. It wasn't too bad, except for the occasional smelly boots that were returned and needed to be sprayed with disinfectant.

While I had little money, it was also payday, which meant I could afford to splurge on a drink. I needed to make friends and wanted to spend time some place other than my cabin or the resort.

"That would be fantastic," I said. "Do you know of any good bars around town?" It was already nearing the end of our workday, and I was antsy to get out.

"Well, it's not a bar, but they have great food and serve drinks. It's just up the road, Lumberjack Shack."

I groaned. Why did she have to suggest the one place Jaxson had taken me on my first night in Breckenridge? Lincoln owned the place, and Jaxson was friends with him, which meant we could run into each other.

"Oh, is something wrong with that place?"

I hadn't realized she'd heard my sound of discontent. "No."

I didn't have a good excuse and wasn't ready to confide in her about my past or that I was formerly Ariella Ryan. She didn't need to know about my ex-husband or the crimes he had committed in both of our names. I also wasn't ready to talk about Jaxson with anyone yet.

"Okay, good." Emma's brow furrowed. "I don't know too many places in town. I'm still new here too."

Was it that obvious that I wasn't from Breckenridge or even Montana? "Where did you move from?" I asked. I hadn't realized she was new to town. At least we had something else in common other than our employer.

"I'm from California. Lived on the west coast my entire life, in Los Angeles."

"Tired of the city life?" I guessed. Why would anyone leave sunny weather to come here? Unless she had a secret of her own?

"I used to come out here with my family—my sister and her kids —for vacation."

Well, at least she was familiar with the area if she used to vacation in or around Breckenridge. "Did you come to the resort with your family?"

"We didn't stay at Blue Sky, but they snowboarded down the slopes while I took in some other sights." Emma winked at me. Her brown eyes glinted in the light before she glanced at her watch. "If you know the way to Lumberjack Shack, I'll meet you there."

"Sounds good." I grabbed my purse and headed to my car.

I was grateful Declan had managed a few minimal repairs and offered me a set of tire chains. He showed me how to put the chains on my tires and made it clear that I wasn't to drive with them on all the time, only when I drove on the snow covered terrain, specifically up the mountain.

I wouldn't get stuck again. Hopefully.

Declan had picked me up in his tow truck before work on my first day, early. I'd squared up with him on the payment and driven to the resort for orientation, making it just in time.

My credit card was nearly maxed, and since I didn't have full liability on the car, I wouldn't get a cent from insurance to help pay for the damages. Declan had been quiet on the drive to get my car, and I was grateful he hadn't mentioned Jaxson's name once.

Unlocking the door of my car, goose-pimples formed on my arms, and a chill ran down my spine. Someone watched me. I just knew it. I spun around, keys in hand to use as a weapon if I was in danger.

No one was behind me.

There were a few people in the parking lot. Still, I didn't recognize any of them: a family with their trunk open retrieving ski equipment, a woman buckling her young daughter into a car seat, and a gentleman wearing a baseball cap and a light jacket standing by his vehicle.

The guy alone, with the thin leather, seemed out of place. The baseball cap could have been a ruse, so I wouldn't recognize him. I tried not to stare.

My mind played tricks on me. I'd been concerned that someone would discover who I was, Ariella Ryan, and would come after me for the money my ex-husband stole. It had happened before when we lived in New York.

I climbed into my car and took off out of the parking lot and for the main road into town. The resort was about forty miles south of where I lived. The winter had been surprisingly mild and the snow that had fallen began to melt, making the road sludgy and wet. Declan had put a new set of tires on my car, and while they'd been previously used, they still had more life than my bald ones that hadn't given me anything but a headache.

There wasn't any music on the radio, the channels too far from where we lived. My car didn't have satellite radio, so I had to resort to popping in a CD for tunes. I traveled up the mountain, the slush recently plowed to the side, probably from one of the townspeople.

The sun began to set, but not before I pulled up in front of Lincoln's restaurant.

I didn't see any sign of Emma's car yet, but I'd left a little ahead of her. I glanced at my cell phone. She hadn't called, which at least was good news. She wasn't canceling on me.

I headed for the front entrance, the wooden door heavy as I swung it open. There wasn't a hostess, and no one took reservations even in season during the busiest months.

A sign by the front entrance read 'seat yourself,' so I grabbed a seat at the bar and put my coat down on the second stool to save Emma a seat.

The bartender's back was to me. His tight jeans and dark black t-shirt hung to his curves. I licked my dry lips and glanced him over. His butt looked pretty damned good.

I hadn't even had a man to fantasize about in ages. My ex-husband hadn't been dynamite in the sack. His needs had always come first, and then when he was done, so was I.

"Can I get a leg spreader?" I asked cheekily.

The bartender spun around and faced me.

The smile on my face fell to the floor. My stomach tensed. "Jaxson," I whispered and cleared my throat. His eyes locked on mine. "What are you doing here?"

I tried to sound confident in my question, like seeing him didn't tear apart my heart after the fight we'd had at my house.

"Don't you work at Eagle Tactical?" I asked. Had he changed careers recently? Did something happen between him and his military buddies? He'd been hostile toward me. Was there more to it I didn't know?

He grabbed a rag and wiped the wooden counter, his eyes avoiding me. "Just helping Lincoln out. Friday nights are always busy here, and I got off work early."

"Right." I glanced over my shoulder, hoping Emma would be here soon. I could use her support right now. I wasn't sure how much more I could take of Jaxson, talking with him, pretending like everything was okay, because it wasn't.

"I'll make you a special drink," he said and grabbed a shot glass from beneath the counter.

I wordlessly watched as he sliced a jalapeno pepper in half and placed it into the shot glass.

My stomach somersaulted. I wasn't keen on spicy drinks or foods. Then he poured tequila and several dashes of hot sauce into the glass before sliding the concoction across the bar.

"Your Anus Burner. Enjoy." His eyes twinkled with mirth before he headed across the bar to help another patron.

"I guess I deserved that," I muttered under my breath.

"What's that?" Emma asked.

I spun around on my chair and removed my coat. "I saved you a seat."

"I saw you met the bartender." She sat down and leaned against the bar, waving at Jaxson to get his attention. "Jaxson!"

He ignored Emma because she was with me. "My apologies in advance if he makes you a shitty drink. We're not on the best-speaking terms."

"Wait, you know my boyfriend?" Emma shifted to face me.

My eyes widened, and I sipped the drink so that I didn't have to say anything, momentarily forgetting about the hot and disgusting concoction until it touched my lips.

I coughed and tried not to gag.

"We're neighbors," I said, not wanting to confide anything else. How long had they been together? Jaxson hadn't mentioned it when we'd first met, but that had been over a month ago.

CHAPTER FOURTEEN

JAXSON

What the hell was she doing at the bar? It wasn't bad enough that Ariella had shown up for drinks, but now Emma joined her.

Were they seriously friends?

I wanted to go outside and shoot something.

"Jaxson!" Emma's voice echoed across the bar, but I ignored her. Was there any chance she'd just go away?

I could see her waving to me, leaning across the bar, trying to get my attention.

I exhaled a heavy breath. I couldn't ignore her forever, even if I wanted to.

It wasn't bad enough dealing with Ariella, but now I had to face the mother of my child, the woman who had stomped on my heart and given up Izzie. I'd already confronted her and hoped that she'd have gone back to California, but it seemed I wasn't that lucky.

Swallowing the bile rising in my throat, I put on a fake smile, all cheer.

"Isn't he great?" Emma said with a thousand-watt grin. She was putting on all the charm. Two could play at that game.

"Yeah," Ariella said. She nursed her shot glass but had barely touched it. She shifted on the stool, looking mighty uncomfortable.

Was it from the Anus Burner or the fact she wasn't expecting to see me? I wasn't too pleased to run into her, either.

"What do you want, Emma?"

Emma batted her eyelashes, smiling up at me with a smug grin. "Aside from you?"

"That's not part of the menu," I said, trying to keep it professional.

Did Ariella know Emma was Isabella's mother? They'd both been hired by Blue Sky Resort.

Were they now friends? I didn't want to ask because I wasn't prepared for the answer.

Ariella sipped her drink and grimaced.

"You're going to swallow it all down, every last drop," I said, staring at Ariella.

God, I was turned on right now, watching her fingers stroke the rim of the shot glass.

How long had it been since I'd been with a woman? The fact I couldn't remember meant it was too damned long.

She lifted the glass to her lips, mouth parted, and drank the disgusting concoction that I'd had the displeasure of trying many years ago, thanks to my military buddies.

Ariella's eyes slammed shut and winced as she swallowed the drink, slamming the empty shot glass against the wooden bar top. "I want a Screwdriver," Ariella said, matter of factly.

Emma glanced from Ariella to me, her brow furrowed. "Make me a Sex on the Beach."

"You'll get what I give you," I said. We weren't done by any stretch.

I grabbed a shaker and mixed ice, vodka, orange juice, lemon juice, and triple sec. Then I strained it over ice and topped it with ginger ale.

I handed the drink to Emma.

"Well, at least it's not what you had," Emma said to Ariella.

"Enjoy your Golden Shower." I grabbed another glass from beneath the bar to make Ariella a drink.

Emma stared at the liquor, a look of disgust on her face. "Why do you have to be such an ass?"

"That's what I said," Ariella chimed in. "Well, I don't remember if I said it aloud, but I thought it," she muttered.

"Don't worry, your drink is next," I said. "I didn't forget you." As much as I despised Emma, Ariella frustrated me, but I didn't hate her.

Not really.

I'd had a month to sit on the news that she'd lied and didn't tell me who she was. It had hurt, but we weren't together. She didn't owe me anything.

I didn't want to point out that I'd been harsh, and I sure as shit would not apologize, but I had to do something.

"I'm not sure I'm thirsty," Ariella said, glancing at Emma's drink.

I grabbed another shaker and mixed it with ice, vodka, peach schnapps, orange juice, and cranberry juice. I'd had this concoction and had rather enjoyed it, even with its name.

I served her drink over ice, sliding the glass to Ariella. "Enjoy your Tight Snatch," I said, staring at her, refusing to back down.

"Why couldn't you have made me that?" Emma said, reaching for Ariella's drink.

Ariella whisked it out of Emma's reach and brought the glass to her lips, a faint smile on her face. "You know just what I like."

Was she trying to flirt with me?

I'd been an ass to her tonight and was she trying to reconnect with me? Was it the alcohol talking?

I'd cut her off with the second drink. I didn't need her getting into an accident on her way home tonight.

"Hey, ladies," Declan said, coming over to the bar. He put one arm around Ariella and the other around Emma.

"Declan!" Emma squealed, her eyes widening. "Can you please tell this grump to make me a drink that I'd like?"

Declan snorted and pointed at the yellow-tinged drink. "What'd he make you?" he asked.

"A Golden Shower," I said and grinned. "We all know she deserves it."

"Ouch," Declan said and stepped away from the ladies.

He came around to the other side, going behind the bar. He turned to face me, keeping his voice low so that only I could hear him. "Take the night off. You're not doing Lincoln any favors antagonizing the customers."

I wasn't one to walk away or back down. "Lincoln asked for my help."

"Yeah, but I don't think he's going to appreciate when his customers don't come back because you're giving them disgusting drinks."

"My Tight Snatch is pretty good," Ariella said. They could hear our private conversation. She sipped her drink, offering me a warm smile.

Declan grabbed me by the arm and dragged me around to the back room, out of earshot of any customers. "What the hell is going on?"

"Emma is now friends with Ariella!" I couldn't just let it go.

It wasn't bad enough Emma had returned, but now she was making friends around town. To me, that meant she wasn't planning on leaving soon.

"Oh, the horror," Declan said with a laugh and rolled his eyes. "I've seen you face down, far worse and not break a sweat. These two women have you in a tizzy, Jaxson. Go home, clear your head."

"I can't do that." I wouldn't leave. Lincoln needed me, and I hadn't seen Ariella in a month.

As angry as I was with her, I was glad to see her. It meant she was still in Breckenridge and hadn't left because of me.

"Shit, man. You're smitten. I'm just not sure for which one."

I folded my arms across my chest, my face neutral. "You're confused."

"I think you're the one who is confused," Declan said. "I know you're upset with Emma, but she told you about Izzie. You could give her a second chance."

Emma?

Did he think I had feelings for Emma still? "Emma's the mother of my child, but that's it. I can't even look at her in that way, knowing she wanted to give up Izzie, my daughter, to a stranger."

"Well, she did the right thing. She didn't lie about not knowing who the father was, and she came to you. That couldn't have been easy."

He was right. It wasn't easy for either of them. "This isn't about Emma."

"Of course, it's not." Declan's eyes narrowed. "So, it's about Ariella?"

"No," I said, answering a little too quickly and forcefully.

Declan grinned. "Okay, good. I know she's got a past, but she's hot. If you're not going to ask her out or pursue her, I will."

"Don't you dare!" The thought of Declan taking Ariella home boiled my blood.

Smirking, he walked backward out of the hall and approached the bar. "Never took you for the jealous type."

"Fuck," I muttered under my breath as I headed back out to help bartend. "Me either."

At first glance, I didn't see Ariella or Emma. They'd both gotten up and were now dancing to the music that had been cranked up louder.

Drink in hand, Ariella swayed to the music. Her hips were doing things that made my body respond in ways I wasn't prepared for tonight.

I found it difficult to focus on anything but her as I stood behind the bar.

Ariella locked eyes with me and smiled. Whether it was the drinks or the fact she was having fun, I couldn't tell.

She nodded in my direction, acknowledging me.

I tore my gaze away from her. She'd lied to me, fooled me into believing she needed help and money, and I'd been the sucker to buy her a damned refrigerator.

I hated myself for it, but even more so, I hated Ariella for how she made me feel.

A gentleman I didn't recognize sauntered over to her, dancing up against her, coming between Ariella and Emma.

The younger man was shorter than I am and a few pounds heavier, but not in muscle.

I didn't have to worry about him stealing her interest, right? He wasn't that attractive.

Ariella laughed and feigned a smile.

Was she talking to him? I couldn't believe he'd earned her time. I stared down at the counter, grabbed a rag, scrubbed at the wood, and rubbed at it hard as if that would take away the anger and pain that radiated through my chest.

I refused to lift my gaze upward.

I didn't want to witness another man flirting with Ariella. Even if I was pissed at her, she was off-limits to anyone else.

My hands bunched into fists, and I threw the rag on the floor. My feet slammed against the tile as I came around from behind the bar.

Her blue eyes widened on my approach, and she shifted awkwardly, holding up a hand to tell the gentleman to back off. "Please back off," Ariella said.

Her voice was soft, tentative, not the least bit threatening.

"Come on, now," the man groaned and stepped closer. His lips hovered by her ear as he whispered something to her.

I hurried across the dance floor, wanting to make sure she was all right.

I stepped between him and Ariella and threw my arm around her. "Sorry I'm late, babe," I said and planted my lips on hers.

I was saving her ass or about to get sucker punched.

CHAPTER FIFTEEN

ARIELLA

Out of nowhere, he kissed me.

I opened my mouth to ask Jaxson what the hell he was doing when his tongue glided into my mouth, which only made me further speechless.

Sweat trickled down my forehead, and my heart raced as I stopped moving on the dance floor.

My body responded to his tongue in my mouth and his hands around my hips, pulling me closer, tighter, harder. He was nestled up against my thigh.

I swallowed the lump in my throat and slowly pulled back.

Jaxson stared at me. His fingers moved over my lower back and slid beneath my shirt.

I shivered from his touch.

My insides melted and made my knees tremble.

"Looks like he's gone," Jaxson said, though his eyes never seemed to leave my gaze.

"What? Oh, right." Was that why he had kissed me intimately, to ward off the drunk loser who wouldn't take no for an answer?

I'd been handling it.

Then he swooped in and locked lips with me. I leaned closer, and my breath caressed his ear with a whisper. "I guess I should thank you for coming to my rescue."

Emma hadn't been the least bit helpful. She was nowhere in sight, and I'd just been dancing with her a moment earlier. "Where'd Emma go?" I untangled from Jaxson's embrace.

"She probably left when I started kissing you."

"Emma likes you," I said.

I didn't want to come between them if they were involved.

His hands didn't untangle from mine, his fingers caressing my lower back against my bare skin in soothing motions. His touch had a way of being hypnotic, lulling me closer to him.

"What Emma and I had ended long before you got here," Jaxson said.

Did Emma know that?

She'd called him her boyfriend when they'd first gotten to the bar. Did she just want it to be true?

"I work with Emma. She's one of the few friends I've made in town." She was the only friend I had anywhere.

I had alienated everyone back home, and I didn't want to do that here.

This was my second chance, a fresh start where almost no one knew my past.

"Did she tell you she's Izzie's birth mother?" Jaxson asked.

"What?" I took a step back, the news hitting me like a knife to my chest. The bar was steamy, suffocating.

I slipped from Jaxson's embrace and down the hall, needing to find the door outside.

I needed air.

I needed to cool off before I got sick from the news.

Stumbling through the throes of customers, I found my way down the hallway and out a back exit, into the frosty night air.

Darkness enveloped the sky. The new moon offered no light, and while stars had been abundant, it didn't help me see so much as my hands in front of me.

I leaned forward, taking several deep breaths. I didn't need to see to know that I was on the verge of throwing up.

It probably had more to do with the adrenaline spiking through my system than anything else, but I was worn and exhausted.

"Ariella," Jaxson said, hurrying outside after me. He rested a warm and reassuring hand on my back.

I wanted to pull away from him, to tell him not to touch me, that I didn't belong with him, but I couldn't do it.

The words didn't come.

My body was too tired to speak, too exhausted to explain my racing thoughts. I could never make him happy, not in the way Emma could.

"Just breathe," he said, rubbing my back over my sweater.

It was frigid outside without a coat, and only now had I felt anything but the heat of an inferno raging inside of me.

"You're shivering. Do you think you can make it back inside? I can find us a quiet place to sit down."

Nodding, I didn't speak. I forgot that he probably couldn't see much in the darkness. "Yes," I said.

He led me back into the bar, through the crowd of guests, both locals and out-of-towners vacationing and staying at the resort. Jaxson took my hand and wordlessly led me up the back staircase.

"Where are we going?" I finally asked, fatigued from the adrenaline rush earlier.

Some people found the fight-or-flight reflex stimulating. I found it exhausting.

I never understood people who liked bungee jumping or throwing themselves out of an airplane with a parachute. I preferred a far less exciting lifestyle.

"Lincoln has a place upstairs. We can crash there for a little while. It beats outside, and when you're feeling better, I can drive you home."

He probably thought I couldn't hold my liquor, and while I was a lightweight, one had nothing to do with the other.

Jaxson unlocked the door, flipped on the light, and led me inside, a hand on my lower back as he guided me to sit down on the sofa. "Thank you," I whispered, staring up at him.

He seemed to be on a mission, opening the fridge, helping himself to something. Apparently, Lincoln wouldn't mind.

"Drink this," he said, bringing me a bottle of water. "Do you need crackers too?" He handed me the water and then, before I could answer, started tearing apart the cabinets searching, presumably, for crackers.

"This will be fine. Thank you." My hands trembled as I sat on the couch. I struggled to open the stupid bottle of water.

Most people never noticed the tremor, but when my adrenaline beat me at my game of trying to be tough, it became pretty obvious.

"How many drinks did you have tonight? Did that jerk come anywhere near your drink?" Jaxson frowned. His brow furrowed as he came to sit beside me on the sofa. "Shit."

"What?" I asked. Had he just now noticed the tremor? "No, I didn't let anyone but you near my drinks tonight. I only had two. It's not that big of a deal."

I shoved the plastic water bottle and my hands between my legs, hoping to stop the shaking, but it wasn't just my hands trembling. My legs were bouncing too.

Fuck, I hated my body. It betrayed me whenever I had a surge of emotions that made my heart race.

Sitting down had helped immensely, and while the tremors hadn't settled, I no longer had the pit of my stomach heavy like I was going to throw up or pass out.

He took notice of the bottle unopened in my grasp and took it from me, loosening the lid before he handed it back. "Is this my fault?"

Why was he jumping to that conclusion?

How could it possibly be his fault? "Jaxson, you're not making any sense." I sipped the water, using two hands to keep from spilling the contents all over me. The damned tremor wasn't helping me, either.

Why couldn't I live a normal life like everyone else?

Why did I have to be unfortunate enough to be in my mid-thirties with an autonomic nervous system that hated me? I had dealt with it on my own for years, but it freaked out new people.

"The drink I made for you," he said, staring at my hands, watching as I brought the water bottle to my lips for another sip. "I was an asshole."

"You were mad," I said, having forgiven him. He'd rescued me on the dance floor. That searing, passionate kiss also helped. I'd be thinking about it for the next month. "I can assure you the disgusting drink you made didn't do this."

"Do I need to call a doctor? Your face is flushed."

"My heart is racing too," I said and laughed. I was used to the symptoms, and I just hated when they took over my life. "Relax. Just sit with me." I liked his company, though I wasn't sure I was ready to confess that much to him yet.

"Okay," he said and sat back on the sofa. He didn't look the least bit relaxed. Jaxson shifted one leg over the other. Then put his foot down, rearranging his position on the sofa before putting two feet down.

I sat there, not moving, watching him literally squirm in his seat. "Do you have ants in your pants?"

"I'm glad you're feeling up to making a joke and finding all of this funny."

"I wouldn't go that far," I said, bringing the water bottle to my lips for another swig. "I guess I'm just used to this, and while it's not fun, I usually can sense the spiral before the downfall."

"Does this happen a lot?" Jaxson asked. He leaned forward, his hands folded together in his lap, his eyes never leaving mine.

I wasn't used to talking about my health issues with anyone other than my physician back home. I needed to find a new doctor in Breckenridge, though a neurologist who specialized in autonomic disorders would not be easy to come by.

"It happens from time to time." I didn't elaborate. I wasn't sure I wanted to confide in him. Everyone I trusted always betrayed me.

"We don't have to talk about it if it's making you uncomfortable," Jaxson said.

Exhaling a loud sigh, I leaned back on the couch, letting the leather sofa cradle my body as much as possible. It was far more comfortable than my sofa at home. Eventually, I'd want to get new furniture, but I had bills to pay. "Where's Izzie?" I asked.

"She's at home with my sister, who is in town for the week."

"Why aren't you home with your family?" That surprised me, though. I didn't know that much about him. We hadn't been on speaking terms until today.

Jaxson stretched out, his arm falling around my shoulders on the back of the couch.

I glanced at him, and he shot me a coy smile before refocusing his attention on the wall. "She's a handful."

"Your sister or Izzie?"

"Both." Jaxson snorted with a laugh under his breath. "Izzie has been testing my patience like all three-year-olds do, and my sister, Skylar, is just about as annoying as Izzie."

I held my tongue, smiling as I stared at Jaxson. "Does she live far away?" I asked.

"She's about a four-hour drive, which means she's not planning on leaving tonight."

"That's too bad. I was hoping you'd show me your bedroom, but I guess if you have a houseguest," I said, teasing him.

He groaned. "You're killing me."

"Somehow, I doubt that," I said, shifting to face him. I rested my hand on his chest and patted his shirt reassuringly. "I think you can handle a little family time. You're a tough guy. I mean, you do that Eagle Tactical stuff for a living."

I didn't know all that it entailed, but it was a high-adrenaline job, something I could never do.

While I had previously held a high-profile job, my responsibilities had never held the same type of risk. I'd been assigned surveillance from a computer, often behind a desk in an office somewhere around the globe. Another secret.

He grabbed my wrist, his fingers interlocking with mine. "Are you always a tease?" Jaxson asked and leaned closer.

One hand held mine. The other that had snaked around the sofa was now tangled in my hair. He pulled me closer and onto his lap.

Startled, I spilled the open bottle of water all over his shirt and pants.

He shrieked from the cold, and I leaped off his body like I'd just mutilated him.

My hand rested over my heart, realizing what happened. "You're going to give me a heart attack."

"Well, at least you don't look like you came in your pants."

I snickered under my breath. While I tried not to grin, it seemed an impossible task. "You could have peed yourself?"

"Right, because that is so much better."

"Snarky is not your color," I said.

He grabbed a hand towel from the kitchen and patted down his pants to dry them off in a lame attempt.

"Do you need a hand?" I sat on the sofa, watching him, waiting for him to settle down.

He kept blotting at his soaking wet crotch, his shirt damp forgotten.

That didn't seem to bother him.

"No one's going to see. It's just you and me up here." I reminded him we were alone. "There's probably a dryer around here. You can take off your clothes and shove them in the dryer. Turn it on for a few minutes."

"You would like that, wouldn't you? Was that your plan all along?" He removed his shirt first, balling it up and throwing it at me on the sofa.

His hands went to the button on his jeans, unclasping it before sliding the zipper down.

Time stood still as I held my breath, waiting for him to finish undressing.

"Yes, you caught me. I wanted to get you naked in Lincoln's house," I said and covered my enormous smile that seemed impossible to hide.

Jaxson slid his jeans down and tossed the denim at me.

"Are you expecting me to do your laundry? In case you haven't realized, this isn't the 1950s." I couldn't take my eyes off of him.

Shirtless, he had an impressive body. He didn't need a tan to show off his muscles.

My eyes fell over his body, examining every inch that I could see, his boxers getting in the way of anything more exciting.

"Lucky for you," Jaxson said. He stalked toward me, leaning forward, half-naked.

I exhaled a heavy breath.

My body responded in kind, wanting to touch him, taste him, and explore everything he had to offer. I struggled to keep my eyes open, his body hovering, teasing me.

I shifted closer as he leaned in, wanting a kiss, a taste of what he offered. One kiss hadn't been enough earlier in the bar.

I craved more.

Being around him, half-naked, was stirring my insides and making me restless beneath him. He hovered above me, his eyes boring into mine.

Jaxson snatched his wet clothes from my grasp, leaving me breathless and panting.

"Such a tease," I muttered under my breath.

A voice by the door cleared his throat, albeit rather loudly, to get our attention.

Jaxson took a step back, wet clothes in hand, as he spun around to see who had come inside the apartment.

"You two couldn't make it back to Jaxson's place?" Lincoln asked. He shut the door behind himself and stalked into the kitchen, his footsteps heavy against the floor.

It wasn't a rhetorical question.

"Please do me a favor and don't do anything on that sofa. I like it and would hate to have to throw it out or burn it after Jaxson's ass gets all over the leather."

Lincoln had a sense of humor. I laughed and covered my lips. "We were just coming up here to rest." It was a lame excuse, but I didn't want to tell him the real reason and face his pity.

"Of course, you were." He glanced at Jaxson as he stood in nothing but his boxers and a smile.

"Believe it or not, she spilled water on me, and I was just about to put my clothes in your dryer," Jaxson said.

"That's a new excuse, and I don't buy it," Lincoln said.

Jaxson stared at me, waiting for my input. "Give me a hand here."

I took another sip of the near-empty water bottle. "You're doing just fine."

It was fun to see him flustered and being teased by his friend.

Lincoln didn't appear mad, and while he probably wasn't thrilled to walk in on guests in his home, he wasn't kicking us out yet, either.

Lincoln pointed at Jaxson. "Is this guy trying to take advantage of you, because if he is, I'll kick his ass?" He approached Jaxson, holding out his hand for the wet clothes.

Was he checking to see if I'd spilled water on him?

"He's quite the gentleman," I said.

Lincoln grunted under his breath, satisfied with the wet clothes. "I'll throw this into the dryer. You can borrow something of mine from the dresser. I'd rather not have you half-naked in my living room."

"Aw," I whined in protest. "I was enjoying the show."

Lincoln thudded with heavy footsteps down the hall, wet clothes in hand. "Well, I wasn't, and I live here."

"Fair enough." I finished the last of my water, already feeling much better. Perhaps it was the banter, the fact both men had taken my mind off everything else that had been bothering me.

I hadn't realized Jaxson had disappeared down the hall until he returned to the living room wearing a pair of gray sweats and a black t-shirt.

"Now, where were we?" Jaxson asked, approaching the sofa. He stood in front of me, hovered above as I stared up at him. His legs straddled mine, teasing me without so much as touching me.

I whimpered in protest. Being in his proximity, having seen him half-undressed moments earlier, had made me crave him even more.

As if the kiss hadn't been my initial undoing.

"You were just about to tell me why you don't have a girlfriend," I said.

CHAPTER SIXTEEN

JAXSON

"I can answer that," Lincoln interrupted as he stomped back into the living room.

"I'd rather you didn't," I shot out, hoping he would mind his own business.

I glared at Lincoln, warning him to shut the hell up.

He had no trouble finding dates with the ladies. He'd always been able to pick up any girl he wanted in a bar and bring her home. It didn't hurt that the restaurant he worked and owned had a bar and a bedroom upstairs.

I didn't want to think about all the women he'd had on the couch where Ariella sat.

She stared up at me with dark, soulful eyes, her cheeks still red but not as flushed as she'd been earlier when I brought her upstairs to rest. "Don't you have meals to make and guests to tend to?" I asked.

"I came upstairs to find out why you weren't manning the bar. Imagine my surprise when I found you and Ariella up in my place, already undressed."

"It really was because I spilled water on him," Ariella said, her voice soft and timid. Was she afraid of Lincoln? He was a big guy, same as I was, same as the rest of our band of brothers who served.

"Just don't leave a stain on the couch. I don't want to have to replace that sofa," he quipped before retreating out the door and back down the stairs.

"I hope I didn't get you into any trouble," Ariella said as her eyes fell toward her lap.

I reached down, my thumb guiding her chin up to face me. I wanted to stare into her eyes, see the truth, know what she was thinking.

It was dangerous, investing my time and energy into a woman who might never want to commit. That was the easy part.

She'd lied to me, and I still couldn't let that go, the nagging suspicion that there might still have been more she wasn't telling me.

My body had betrayed me, kissing her on the dance floor, and while I usually kept a level head, I couldn't seem to do that around her.

I released my grip on her chin, unable to tear my gaze away from her, transfixed.

"You never answered my question," Ariella whispered, staring up at me.

I let out a heavy sigh, unsure how to answer. It was far more complicated than just not having a girlfriend. She knew about Izzie. "Isabella is a lifelong commitment. Let's just say not everyone feels the same way."

"I don't believe that," Ariella whispered. She reached for my hand and nodded beside her at the empty seat on the sofa.

I collapsed onto the leather, the material sinking around my body comfortable after a long day. "I don't want to waste my time with a woman who isn't interested in being around for the long run."

"What about Emma?" she asked. "Why aren't you with her?"

I ran a hand through my hair, ruffling it. She sure knew how to ask the hard questions. "I don't love her."

Could the answer be as simple as that?

It was the truth.

We hadn't ever been in love.

"Oh," Ariella said, her voice soft as her mouth formed a little "o" shape.

"She came to town a few years ago for a family vacation with her sister and her kids. While they went snowboarding, she came to the bar for drinks. That's how we met. We both got trashed and ended up at my place."

It was literally as simple as it sounded. I left out the part where I had gotten hammered after my sister had come for a visit and just left. The house was quiet, empty, and I needed to dull my heart from her nagging and blaming me for our father's death.

"Well, it's obvious to me that she wants you back." She shifted on the sofa, pulling slightly away, dragging her legs up onto the leather and to the side, tucking them under herself.

I'd seen how Emma had acted today, and I couldn't say I was surprised.

I'd been shocked when I discovered she had moved to Breckenridge for a job.

After the initial anger, the disgust had worn off. She had a right to live wherever she wanted, but that didn't mean I had to give her custody or let her see Isabella. That wasn't a conversation I needed to have with Ariella.

"Wanting someone back implies they were theirs to have originally. That was never the case. We were never friends or lovers. We had one drunken afternoon together, and it had been a poor lapse in judgment." It had been the only time I'd engaged in a one-night stand and look where it got me.

"She didn't tell me that."

I wouldn't have expected her to. While I didn't know Emma incredibly well, I also didn't think she would be forthright with information, even if she and Ariella were friends.

"I'm not surprised. It didn't work to her advantage. She thinks we're more than we are, especially after Izzie."

I didn't want Emma.

I wasn't sure I even wanted to risk my heart with Ariella, but I would regret not trying. There was something about her that captivated me.

"What about you? Any more secrets that I should know about?" I asked.

She pursed her lips, her eyes tightening. "I'm literally an open book on the internet. Search my name, and you can find every detail of my life."

Was it that simple? "Is that why you didn't tell me your real name?" I asked.

Was she worried I couldn't handle knowing who she was? It hadn't been my best day, learning that her ex-husband had been responsible for stealing investors' money.

I no longer blamed her for any involvement. She'd been prosecuted and acquitted. While I hadn't followed her case as closely as I'd followed her ex-husband's, I had done a little research after I'd discovered that she'd lied to me.

"I wanted a second chance to start over. There had been threats made against my life when I was married to that scum-sucking bastard. Bricks were thrown through our windows, and someone sprayed graffiti on the siding and doors. For months, I had been afraid to go home, sleeping in my car where I worked. That didn't last. I got fired, and while I had been acquitted, it wasn't like they were offering me my job back. They told me I was bad publicity and too much of a risk."

I could sense her frustration.

Her tone had grown louder, more determined as she spoke. She sat up straighter and pushed a strand of her dark hair behind her ear.

"I thought no publicity was bad publicity," I said. I guess that wasn't true.

"That's a lie," Ariella said.

I tried to keep a level head, remain calm.

Hearing her life had been in danger worried me. I'd dealt with some unhinged people in my line of work. "Have the threats stopped since moving here?" I asked. She'd tell me if she was in danger, wouldn't she?

Slowly, she nodded. "No one seems to know who I am. As long as that continues, I should be fine. I just keep hoping that with time it'll all blow over." She twirled the edge of her long dark hair. "I'm not sure if you know this, but I was blonde when it all happened—the trial, the threats, the news media. Having long dark hair has made it so no one recognizes me."

I liked her hair.

Hell, I liked almost everything about her.

I wasn't too happy about her past, but I accepted it. Letting out a soft breath, my fingers tangling in her curls.

I leaned forward. I wanted to kiss her, to take away her pain and the difficulty of her past. "I like your dark hair. I think it looks sexy," I whispered.

Everything about her was sexy, from her pouty bottom lip to the bounce in her step.

Her eyes slowly closed, and she leaned forward, our lips colliding as I pulled her closer. As I brought her onto my lap, the kiss deepened.

She shifted against my hips, making my insides roar to life with the sweet sounds she made of a soft moan from the back of her throat.

I wanted to devour her and taste every inch of her body, but we couldn't do it here, not in Lincoln's place above the bar.

I pulled back with all the strength I had, and my forehead pressed against hers. Listening to the soft, heavy gasps for air as she caught her breath, I stole one more kiss. "I should get you home and to bed," I whispered.

"I'd like that very much."

I led Ariella downstairs and quickly dropped off her car key with Lincoln.

He agreed to drive her car and drop it off later with Declan following and giving him a ride back home.

We scooted out the side door for privacy.

I kept her close, with one hand at her lower back, keeping her at my side in the darkness. I'd always had decent night vision, adjusting quicker than most.

I opened the passenger side door and helped her into the truck. I waited for her to buckle before I shut the door and came around to my side.

I wanted to follow her inside, take her home and ravish every ounce of her skin.

Would she invite me inside? I didn't want to be forceful or take advantage of the situation.

She had two drinks, but that had been quite a while ago. While she could have probably driven herself home, I didn't want to lose the opportunity to take care of her.

The ride was short and quick. I pulled up out front and hustled to the passenger door. Leading her to the dark cabin, I wanted to make sure she got inside safely, especially without a porch light.

"You should install solar lights outside," I said. I doubted she'd do much until the spring thaw. It was too cold to dig up the yard.

"I'll add that to my to-do list," Ariella said. She stood outside, keys in hand, fidgeting with them but not making any attempt to unlock the door.

I had no intention of leaving until she went inside. I shoved my hands into my coat pocket to keep warm and shuffled my feet. "I hope you're feeling better."

"I am. Thank you for that tonight. Do you want to come in? I can offer you coffee, a drink, or something else?" She chewed her bottom lip.

Ariella looked nervous.

I couldn't tell if she was hesitant or just worried I'd turn her down.

"I'd love that something else," I said, teasing her.

Her cheeks reddened, and I waited for her to unlock the door before I followed her inside. After a minute, she turned on the lantern and lit a few candles. It made for a nice, ambient glow.

"Can I get you something to drink?" Ariella offered. She removed her coat and boots. I did the same, keeping mine by the door.

"I'll have whatever you're having," I said as I approached the wood-burning stove.

I bent down and grabbed the handle to open the door. The hinge squeaked in protest. I made a mental note to fix that the next time I came over.

"I'm going to throw some wood on the fire." While I looked forward to climbing under the covers with Ariella, I also didn't want the cabin to be frigid.

However, it would give me an excuse to cuddle up against her and make her hot and sweaty.

Stoking the fire, bringing it roaring back to life, I tossed in a piece of wood and then another. Her gaze never left me. "See something you like?"

"Actually, yes," she said and sauntered over toward me.

With two bottles of beer in hand, she put them down on the coffee table and tugged on her bottom lip, pulling it between her teeth.

Was it a nervous habit or something else? I hadn't been around her enough to take note.

"What's that?" I asked, cocking a grin at her.

She gestured at my clothes. "You have too much on. I liked what I saw earlier tonight. Too bad Lincoln walked in."

"It was too bad, wasn't it?" I'd have to get my clothes tomorrow and return Lincoln's sweats.

I stalked toward her and pulled her into my arms, her body nestled tight against mine, a perfect fit. "Seems only fair, though, to see you in nothing but your underwear."

CHAPTER SEVENTEEN

ARIELLA

I swallowed the lump that formed in my throat.

Did he want to see me in my underwear?

Of course, he did, I had invited him into my house. I didn't think he only wanted a drink, did I?

"You first," I said, my lips almost touching his.

His body pressed tight against mine, his fingers caressed my lower back, just as he had earlier, inching my shirt up. His warm hands stroked my bare skin, but he didn't remove my shirt, just teased me.

Jaxson took a half step back, pulling his shirt up and over his head, letting it hit the floor with a thud. "Your turn."

Goosebumps from the chill in the air pebbled my arms, but my breathing came out louder, ragged, and heavy as warmth flooded my senses.

The room temperature hadn't changed. It was me, and I was the one getting hot and bothered by looking at Jaxson shirtless.

Could I let this happen?

There was still one more secret, a big one that he didn't know. I should have told him earlier tonight, when he asked, but I'd held onto that last piece and guarded it along with my heart.

When I didn't budge from my position, his fingers grazing my skin slid my shirt up, inch by inch, taking his time—lifting my arms into the air, letting him undress me if that's what he wanted to do.

He fell to his knees, his lips on my stomach, his breath warm and inviting, making my body unsteady.

"I need to tell you something."

His hands held my hips, keeping me against him as he kissed a warm path up my stomach and across my bra. Jaxson's fingers grazed over my breast, teasing me, tasting me with soft kisses as he pulled my shirt up and over my head, discarding it to the floor.

"Is it about your health?" he asked, pausing briefly, his gaze latched on mine.

I shook my head. "The doctor gives all clear," I said, forcing a smile along with my joke.

Sex, I could do. There were no rules against engaging in intimate physical activity.

While I wanted to tell him the truth about what I did for a living before I was fired, now didn't feel the right time.

"Then that's all that matters." He grinned, his eyes dark with want. He captured my lips in a searing, heated kiss, his fingers tangling in my hair, pulling me closer and tighter against his body.

"You still have too many clothes on. You weren't wearing sweats earlier," I reminded him as my hands went to his hips, caressing the waistband of the soft, stretchy material.

"Go ahead," he told me, giving me permission to undress him.

I hooked my fingers in both his sweats and his boxers, bringing it all down in one motion, bending down to guide his pants off. My eyes raked over his naked body, every inch of him.

I wanted to take him in my mouth, taste him, touch him, caress him in every way I knew how.

How long had it been since a woman dropped to her knees for him?

He cleared his throat, and that seemed to gather my attention as my gaze stared up at him.

"You're killing me," he groaned between gritted teeth. Jaxson hoisted me from the floor and planted my feet firmly on the ground, not allowing me to be on my knees.

I giggled unceremoniously, licking my bottom lip, wanting to taste him.

Jaxson lunged forward. His tongue swiped against my lips, and pushed into my mouth in haste.

With one hand on my hip, the other in my hair, he pulled me harder against him.

I still had my pants and bra on, and he stood naked. It seemed like a dream come true for me. I'd imagined what he looked like, what his skin was like under my touch, but I never thought I'd experience a night with him.

He pulled back, each breath heavy, his eyes narrowed. "Every time you stick that tongue out or chew that bottom lip, I'm going to kiss you, hard."

"Is that a threat?" I liked what he had in mind.

"Only you would take that as a challenge, Freckles," Jaxson growled out as he spoke.

I didn't want to admit how he drove me wild and my body flushed at the nickname he'd given me.

My insides were warm, and my heart pounded against my ribcage like a prisoner trying to break free. Heat burned over my skin and inside, waiting for sweet release.

My tongue darted out and dared him to kiss me hard. I wanted to experience what he had to offer. I liked this dance, the way we played, the not soft and sweet.

He grabbed my hips, yanked me toward him, and his mouth descended hard on mine. His tongue stroked my lips and pushed its way into my mouth.

I opened my lips and granted him access, allowing him whatever he wanted. I was at his mercy, willing to do anything and everything.

All he had to do was to take command.

He lifted me into his arms, and I wrapped my legs around his body. Jaxson carried me to the bed, our lips fused in passionate kisses, neither of us untangling first.

In haste, we hurried to the mattress, Jaxson's body covering mine, crawling above me, releasing my grip on his hips. I kept my mouth with his, fire fueled kisses never seeming to cease.

His hands pushed at my pants, and I offered help, lifting my hips so he could slide the material off. I moaned in protest when he pulled back from my lips. Sliding my slacks down my hips and kissing a trail between my thighs, he continued teasing me.

I grew restless, desiring more. "Please," I panted, already quite breathless. I lay on my back at his mercy, allowing him to do with me as he pleased.

"Please, what?" Jaxson asked, raising an eyebrow at me.

I wasn't sure what he wanted to hear. I wasn't above begging, but I was already doing that when his fingers teased against my panties, and he bent down, blowing softly over my center.

My insides throbbed to be touched, pleased, and satisfied. Was he going to tease me to oblivion? "Please, Sir?"

"Not what I was looking for, but I do like the sound of that," Jaxson crooned. "I never would have taken you for a submissive."

"I'm not," I countered defensively.

"There's nothing wrong if you are, Freckles," Jaxson said with a grin. His fingers grazed my heated core through my panties, but he hadn't removed my last two shreds of clothes yet, my panties or bra.

Growing restless, I shifted slightly, undoing my bra and letting the material hit the bed, not caring quite where it landed. "That's better," I exhaled a soft sigh.

"That it is," Jaxson said, pleased with my decision. His tongue teased me through my panties, finding that sweet spot to make my toes curl.

My eyes slipped shut, my fingers tugged on the bedsheets, curling between my digits as his fingers took their sweet time to glide my last remaining bit of clothing off. His lips and tongue danced over my skin on a warm path down my thigh, inch by inch, until I wore nothing.

I tried to sit up, pulling at him to come closer. What happened to the hard and frantic pace that we'd started? I wanted that, and he'd gone slow and sweet, savoring his time with me.

"You're going to kill me," I muttered, my back arching off the mattress as his kisses trailed higher toward his intended destination.

His breath lingered for a moment before crawling back up my body while his fingers slid down between my thighs, finding my wetness. "Not kill you, just bring you toward the brink multiple times," Jaxson whispered before his lips landed on mine once again.

Warm fingers caressed my body, exciting and arousing me while he guided my legs farther apart, climbing above me. My hand moved down his skin, wanting to take him in, touch him, stroke him before guiding him inside of me.

Slowly, his warmth, his body, became one with mine. I lifted my hips and wrapped my legs around him, guiding him farther and deeper, my back arching off the mattress. Everything fit perfectly.

I clung to him and a flood of warmth tingled within my body. My toes curled, and my insides spasmed.

"I'm going to—"

I didn't let him go, our bodies one. It was too good, too intense, and I didn't have to worry. "You'd better," I muttered into his ear, nipping the lobe before finally letting go, collapsing against the mattress, gasping for air.

He shuddered and grunted the last few strokes, falling against me before rolling onto his side, catching his breath.

A long silence fell over us, our breathing hard, hearts racing in unison.

My eyes fell shut, and the comfort from a warm blanket pulled up and draped over my naked form lulled me toward sleep.

I wanted to say something, but the words didn't come.

Sleep cocooned me, and after the exhausting day earlier, I was out cold.

I rolled over in bed, my arm snaked out, finding the mattress beside me cold. I was alone.

"Jaxson?" I mumbled and rubbed the sleep from my tired eyes.

He didn't answer me. No one answered.

Irritated, I sat up in bed, discovering I was indeed naked and hadn't dreamed the previous night.

Sighing, I didn't know why he left, but it didn't matter. If he wanted this to be nothing more than a one-night stand, I could handle that responsibility. I had told him from the beginning that I wasn't looking for a commitment or a relationship.

Begrudgingly, I pushed myself out of bed.

"Shit!" I cursed, glancing at the battery-operated clock on my bedside table. My alarm hadn't gone off.

If I didn't high-tail my ass out of the house soon, I would be late for work. I stumbled through the house, half asleep, pulling a fresh change of clothes on and skipping coffee. There would be coffee at the resort, and I could grab a hot cup when I got to work.

Tossing clothes on, sliding into the warm boots Jaxson gave me, I was hurrying out the door.

I couldn't afford to get a mark on my attendance record or get sacked from my job. The pay wasn't spectacular, but I'd made ends meet over the past month.

My foot was like lead on the gas, swerving down the mountain at a pace I wasn't even comfortable with, and I'd become accustomed to driving back and forth daily.

Every so often, I glanced at the clock, willing time to stop. I knew that was an impossibility, but I hoped that I'd picked up a few minutes on my swift attempt down the mountain.

The only way faster would have been skiing down the slopes, and that wouldn't have ended well for my car or me.

White knuckles gripped the steering wheel. I tried not to think about Jaxson, the heat of his kisses, the taste of his lips, the warmth of his body above mine, overpowering me.

Last night had been amazing, and he'd disappeared after, without a trace.

I'd glanced at my phone before flying off into the car. He hadn't texted. There were no missed calls. I shouldn't have been pissed, but I had the right to feel something.

He'd opened the door to my heart. Trusting didn't come easy, and he bailed the minute after he got what he wanted. Sex.

"Damn him!" I shouted, slamming my hand against the steering wheel.

My heart thudded against my chest. I shifted on the fabric of the seat, hurrying to get to work and anxious for a variety of reasons.

I had to keep what we did a secret. I couldn't tell anyone, least of all Emma.

Hurrying into the parking lot, I slammed on the brakes, the car jolting forward as I came to an abrupt halt. I threw myself out of the car, locked the doors, and with a brisk pace, rushed inside the resort.

The front desk was around the corner, and I barreled inside. Just as I was around the corner, I froze.

I recognized the gentleman from the other day, the one with the leather jacket and baseball hat, an odd combination for the current weather.

Everyone in Breckenridge had thick down jackets, ski coats, or heavy parkas. The black leather didn't look the least bit warm and had to be made for spring.

"I'm sorry, sir. We can't give out information about our guests at the resort," Emma said.

She stood behind the front desk, a plastered smile on her face. Her brow furrowed as she tilted her head slightly to the side.

"I'm not looking for a guest. I believe the woman is an employee and her name is Ariella Ryan."

CHAPTER EIGHTEEN

JAXSON

Last night had been amazing, fantastic, the best night of my life.

No, I wasn't going overboard.

Being with Ariella reminded me how great it was to share the comfort of another and a warm bed.

I hadn't wanted to leave, but my sister, Skylar, had been watching Izzie. Ariella hadn't budged when I kissed her goodbye after throwing my clothes back on. I had scribbled a quick note and left it on her brand-new fridge.

Have to go home to Izzie. I wish I could stay all night with you. Text me if you want me to bring you breakfast. -Jaxson

I had expected she'd text or call. Something to let me know she didn't regret what happened between us and it meant more than a one-night stand to her. I hadn't wanted to seem overzealous with the note or scare her away either.

My phone buzzed on my desk, and I reached out, hopeful that Ariella had answered me.

What time does Izzie go down for a nap?

It was just Skylar.

She had come and visited me unannounced and stayed for the

week. I couldn't just bail on my job, and vacation time was usually planned out.

Besides, spending time with my sister was hardly classified as a vacation. At least it kept Izzie from having to go to daycare for the week, which wasn't a bad tradeoff. The daycare always closed by six o'clock, and I was shit for getting there on time. One of the guys would often pick Izzie up if I was stuck in the field on an assignment for a client.

I ignored my sister's text. Izzie would not go down easily for Skylar. She hated naps, and it wasn't even noon yet.

Skylar would have to entertain her all day, not just for a few hours. That was the price for coming to visit.

I was an ass, but if she wanted to spend time with her niece, she needed to act like she wanted to be there.

There were still no messages from Ariella.

Exhaling a heavy sigh, Declan trotted into my office. "We need to have a meeting," Declan said, his arms folded across his chest, his brow tight.

"Sure. What about?"

"Come with me," Declan said, gesturing for me to follow him. His heavy boots trampled on the floor as he led me to the conference room where the rest of the Eagle Tactical team had been situated around the table.

"What's going on? Is there a new assignment?" I asked. Usually, I was consulted with first, but I had been preoccupied lately. Lincoln sat at the table with Declan, Aiden, and Mason.

Lincoln cleared his throat. His expression was grim. "We're worried about your involvement with the new girl." I hadn't expected to see him at Eagle Tactical today.

He was a contractor for us, worked specific assignments when we needed his expertise, but he wasn't a full-time employee because of his restaurant.

Steam shot off my body, and I clenched my fists, my short nails digging into my palm. "My personal life is no one else's business."

I couldn't believe the guys! Were they trying to stage an

intervention? They knew I didn't sleep around. I had a daughter to worry about and look after.

Mason leaned back in his chair, all too relaxed for the occasion. "You're getting too close to her, Jaxson. That girl is trouble, forty-two million dollars' worth of trouble."

That had been precisely how much money she'd been charged with stealing. "She's not that girl," I said, defending her. "What her ex-husband did doesn't define her. Besides, don't we all deserve a second chance?"

They'd been through hell.

We all had. We'd carried each other through good times and bad. None of us were free of our burdens and the mistakes that we'd made in the past.

"Listen, I don't know her that well," Lincoln said, "but I saw you two getting pretty cozy in my apartment, and that's not like you. You don't jump headfirst into fucking the hottie next door. That's Aiden's M.O."

My jaw tightened. "You don't know what you're talking about." It was none of their business that we had sex. It wasn't like they could tell!

"I know you're a respectable man," Lincoln said, "but what you were doing wasn't respectable. She'd been drinking. Declan told me you'd been serving her piss-ass drinks at the bar."

It seemed Lincoln hadn't believed me when he'd stumbled into us last night. "I brought her upstairs to have some water, sit down away from the crowd, and calm down. I gave her two drinks earlier that night, and I thought she was having a panic attack after I said something to her downstairs while we were dancing. She has some other medical thing. It doesn't matter," I said, dismissing my rationale.

They didn't need to know about her medical history or what she'd been going through in minute detail.

"Right." Mason didn't believe me.

"I swear she spilled water on my clothes. Nothing happened at your place, Lincoln." I wasn't sleazy like that.

While I may have wanted to rip off her clothes and listen to her scream out my name, I wouldn't have done that on his couch and in his home.

"But something happened?" Lincoln asked.

It wasn't any of their business what transpired between us. We were grown adults, allowed to behave however we chose.

She hadn't been inebriated. It had been two drinks and more time elapsed between her alcohol consumption and when I'd fallen into bed with her—something that none of them needed to know about.

Aiden sat quietly, his hands folded together on the table. I'd never known him to be so silent. "Do you have anything to add?" I asked.

"I haven't met her," Aiden said. "I've read her file, the one our client asked us to retrieve on her. I rarely agree with mixing business and pleasure, but I've never seen you so happy. Despite that, I don't know her. I only know what's on paper, and the girl has secrets. Did you know what she used to do for a living before her life blew up?"

I hadn't asked her, and after I'd seen the name 'Ariella Ryan' and had realized the connection, there had been no reason for me to continue searching for information. "No, I guess I don't know what she did for a living. Does it matter?"

I hadn't asked her. I should have. I didn't think it mattered.

"Before she was fired, Ariella Ryan was an agent for the C.I.A. She did remote surveillance internationally for several years before she married and settled down in New York City, working at a field office and pretending to be the curator for a small museum."

I held Declan's stare.

Was he serious?

The woman had many secrets but a C.I.A. operative? I couldn't even imagine it was the truth.

She was small, fragile, and while I didn't consider her helpless, I'd seen how she reacted last night and doubted her ability to do any field work.

"You're skeptical," Mason said. "I was too, especially after meeting her, but it makes sense. Why else would she want to live off-grid?"

I shook my head. I didn't believe it.

She'd been upset when she found out the cabin didn't have electricity, angry in fact.

Had she played me?

Declan slid a manila folder across the table at me.

I forced the file open and sifted through the pages quickly to see what was true and what wasn't. "Why didn't this come up when I searched for her name?"

"She goes deep," Mason said. "Her cover was nearly blown by her ex-husband when he was arrested. After that, the details get a little fuzzy, but we suspect her marriage may have been a cover. She went deep, a little too deep, and when the government went after her husband, someone put a target on her back and went after her too."

I ran a hand through my hair. "This all sounds crazy." I had trouble wrapping my head around what they told me, but staring at the file, it was all in there. A copy of her identification and a scan of her C.I.A. credentials, including her badge. "Are you sure this is her?"

"It gets worse," Mason said. "We've been doing a lot of digging into her past. From what we can surmise, her husband may not have been responsible for the Ponzi scheme he went to prison for last year. She's still being hunted by the same men who set up her husband. From what I found on the dark web, there's a hit for Ariella Ryan, aka Ariella Cole."

Fear crept into my chest, suffocating me. She was in danger.

"The good news is her exact location hasn't been discovered yet," Aiden said. "We still have time to help her if that's what you want."

I stood, the file open but forgotten on the conference table. "Of course, it's what I want. She needs our help. If she's C.I.A., then she's practically one of us."

"I'm not sure I'd go that far," Lincoln retorted, his tone sharp, his eyes tight. He didn't seem on board with helping her.

Even if she weren't C.I.A. and had just been a girl with a self-destructive past, I still would have helped her.

I wasn't keen on the fact she'd lied to me, kept the truth from me, but she needed my help.

I wasn't going to abandon her when shit got tough.

My phone buzzed in my pocket. "I swear if it's Skylar again," I grunted under my breath and withdrew my cell phone.

I held up a finger to tell the guys to hold on a minute. "It's Ariella," I said.

My stomach twisted like a vine, worry evident on my face. I swallowed the rising lump in my throat and planted my feet firm on the floor to ground myself. I had plenty of practice in the field, not letting my emotions overcome me. Today was no different.

I needed to be strong for Ariella, and as pissed as I was that she lied to me, I also needed to keep a level head. I didn't want her turning her back on me now, not after what we shared last night.

"Go on, answer it." Mason gestured to my phone.

The guys would not give me an ounce of privacy, but I deserved that after having my head shoved in the sand, unaware of the truth of her past and the danger that surrounded all of us.

"Hello?" I didn't get another word out before her words poured out of her in a whisper.

"It's Ariella. I need your help. There's someone at the resort looking for me, and they're using my married name. Can you pull surveillance from the hotel and find out who it is?"

She certainly knew a lot about what we could do, Eagle Tactical's capabilities, without a warrant.

A typical citizen wouldn't have been so knowledgeable, but a C.I.A. agent would know our skills and abilities to do what she asked.

"Are you in danger?" I asked, not answering her question.

She still didn't know that I was aware of her previous career, her life before she was married, the secret she'd kept from me.

Was I mad at her for deceiving me? Yes, but I would not let that cloud my judgment when she needed my help.

"I don't know," she whispered. "Possibly. I'm hoping it's just someone after me because of what Benjamin stole."

"Ariella, we need to talk, clear the air about some things." I stood, unable to just sit and listen to what she said. I put the phone on speaker.

"I know," she stammered. "Shit. He's coming this direction."

"Describe him to me." I muted her call. "She's at Blue Sky Resort. We need immediate access to the surveillance footage. I recall that we set up their system and it's all backed up to the cloud."

Declan pushed himself up, the chair squeaking as he stood. "I'll work on getting backdoor access. As soon as I get his name, I'll have Mason run a background on the guy."

"I want to know if he so much as has a parking ticket in his name," I said.

"Of course," Declan said.

Mason's expression remained grim, but he didn't speak.

I unmuted the call and tried to catch up with what Ariella had said about the man's description.

Lincoln had jotted it all down while we'd talked amongst each other, and I glanced over the list describing his height, weight, hair color, and clothes.

"I found it odd he was wearing a leather jacket when there was snow on the ground. It caught my attention, but I didn't recognize him," Ariella said. "He was outside in the parking lot when I left work yesterday evening. I almost walked by him at the front desk when he spoke to Emma."

"Mason and Declan are giving me a hand with getting access to the surveillance footage and running background on this mystery man. I'm going to head out to the resort with Lincoln and pick you up. Can you lie low, find someplace to hide? We will text you when we're at the resort."

A muffled gasp erupted from the opposite end of the line.

My heart dropped into my stomach.

I snatched my phone from the conference table and shrugged my coat on as I rushed out to my truck.

Heavy steps followed me with Lincoln on my heels while he tried to catch up. I hadn't exactly announced I was leaving right now, but with the sound of a struggle, I couldn't wait another moment.

"Ariella?" I pulled the keys from my pocket, started the engine, and rushed outside into the brisk chill.

Evidence of a struggle, a gasp, a clack, something had fallen.

Was it the phone?

The line went dead.

CHAPTER NINETEEN

ARIELLA

Sweaty, rough hands snatched me from the hiding space in the hallway.

My phone fell to the ground, and the assailant stepped down with his boots, smashing my device to pieces, crunching the screen under his steel-toed boots.

I hadn't expected anyone to come from behind, not when the man with the baseball cap had been just a few feet away, around the corner, in front of me.

I had kept hidden.

Little good it did me. My defensive tactical training kicked in.

My years at the C.I.A. had involved hands-on combat training even though I was practically a desk clerk with a background in technology, science, and profiling. The only fieldwork I had done was surveillance assignments, a side effect of my health issues that had occurred early in my career but after passing all required training and tests. Lucky me.

He restrained my neck in a headlock, keeping me from breathing, I had seconds before I would go unconscious.

I slammed my elbow into the assailant's groin, smashed my head back into his nose, and spun around to escape his grip around my neck.

Gasping hard, trying to drink in all the oxygen that I could, my heart screamed for help, but the words never left my lips.

I didn't recognize the blond, beady-eyed man. His thick muscles protruded from his t-shirt.

"Connor. She's over here!"

Connor?

He must have been the one with that stupid baseball cap who was asking about me. I didn't recognize the man's name, and the beady-eyed attacker was a stranger to me as well.

Connor, the man with the baseball cap, strolled around the corner. His footsteps were thudding against the tile floor, coming toward me, blocking off my exit out of the hallway.

"What do you want?" Had it been the money Benjamin stole, or were they after me because I had once worked for the C.I.A.?

Had my identity been leaked by my previous employer or someone else?

I had no access to state secrets, no special privileges as a former agent. I was a disgrace to the agency, and they'd make that clear when I had been forced to resign.

Yanking on my long dark hair, the beady-eyed man took a fistful into his palm, gripping the strands. He tugged hard.

I screamed from the pain while he dragged me out the back hall to the exit.

Screaming for help, I kicked and dug my toes into the stone road, but it didn't help.

I tried twisting to break free, but he moved fast, my hair tangled in his grip.

Connor was in front of me, a switchblade in his hand. The cold steel grazed my cheek. "Scared yet?" he seethed between crooked teeth as his partner held me captive.

"Let me go!" I struggled against him and fought back with every ounce of strength I could muster.

My elbow jammed into his stomach.

He chucked me against the icy brick exterior of the building.

My head smacked the rough texture before my legs buckled beneath me.

"We know who you are," Connor said, kicking my chest, knocking the wind out of me again. "We want our investment returned to us. All two million dollars, and since we're generous, we'll only tack on another two million in interest. You'll get it to us by sundown tonight."

I snorted under my breath. It had to be dirty money.

What the hell had Benjamin been thinking when he'd taken their money to invest and steal? Two million wasn't a small amount, and they wanted four million by sundown?

Beady-eyed man held me down, his weight pinning me to the ground, his arms overpowering me, while Connor brought the blade against my skin.

Laughing, he tore at my coat, ripping my warmth to shreds. The edge scratched my skin and tore at my clothes.

A fire burned over my arms and chest. I fought back with my forearms, struggling to get up, and while I tried to roll him over, having two men made it an impossible match.

The longer I stayed down, the easier it was for them to continue to attack me.

My fingers grazed over the stone pavement. I slipped a rock into my palm, prepared to use it to defend myself.

Connor released his grip, closed the switchblade, and shoved it into his back pocket.

A heavy snort left beady-eye's lips, and with only one man and no weapon against my skin, I swung my hips and thrust my body around, using my legs to kick his legs out from under him, forcing him onto his back as I pinned him down and smacked him with the rock.

"Never touch me again," I snarled, breathing, heavy anger chilling me along with the cold.

Connor reached down, offering a hand to his buddy to help him up. "Four million, or you'll be digging a grave for the little girl and her daddy."

How did they know about Jaxson and Izzie?

I held my breath for a few seconds before exhaling a slow and even lungful.

How long had they been watching me? Since the day I moved into the cabin?

I hadn't seen Izzie in over a month. Jaxson and I hadn't been close again until last night.

The world spun around me. I leaned back against the cold, rough brick of the building and let it support my weight and my shaky legs.

"I'll get you the money." I gritted my teeth, and a toughness washed over me.

I didn't know how I would save them.

I didn't have four million dollars, but I would let nothing happen to either of them. "Where is the drop?" I asked.

I stood outside with a torn jacket, shivering by the front entrance.

I walked from the back exit, where I'd been threatened and beaten, to the main doors. I threw away my shredded coat, the bloodstains a reminder of my weakness.

I didn't even know where I bled from. Everything ached, and the cuts where the blade had gashed my skin burned, but I hadn't seen any significant injuries.

Waiting for Jaxson, time appeared to stand still.

Shivering, I stood in my torn pale pink sweater. It was too thin for winter, and my jacket was worthless, as was the sweater I wore, but that wasn't hitting the trash until I got home.

His dark blue truck tore into the parking lot and came to an abrupt halt in front of the resort.

Jaxson left the truck running before he leaped out of the vehicle.

Lincoln sat in the passenger seat, his expression gruff. He didn't look pleased to see me or to have his day interrupted.

Jaxson hurried around to me, removing his coat and pulling it on my shoulders.

He opened the back door and helped me into his truck. The warmth of his jacket and the heat surrounded me.

"Thanks," I said. My shoulders trembled as I shivered in the truck.

Jaxson scooted into the backseat beside me and shut the truck door.

There was nowhere to move, with our proximity tight, and his knees brushed up against my legs. His warm hand grazed my cheek, and the other tangled in my hair, glancing me over from head to toe.

Unlike the men who had attacked me, Jaxson's touch was gentle yet firm.

I grimaced. My head ached from when I'd been slammed into the brick wall.

"I'll drive us to the hospital," Lincoln said and scooted over to the driver's side.

"That's unnecessary." I didn't want to go to the hospital.

There would be too many questions, and the police would have me file a report, and an investigation would be underway. "I can't go to the hospital. Isn't it two hours from here?"

"A little less than that," Jaxson answered.

He leaned forward and retrieved a tin box labeled 'first aid' from beneath the passenger seat.

"I'm all right," I said as he tended to the wound on my head.

He took a penlight from his kit and had me follow the light with my eyes.

"Since when did you become a medic?" I asked.

His expression remained blank, and he shut off the light. "She doesn't appear to have a concussion. Why don't you drive us back to Eagle Tactical?" Jaxson asked. He turned his attention back to me. "Since when did you become a C.I.A. operative?" he retorted.

I winced and swallowed the lump in my throat. "How did you know?"

No one was supposed to find that out. I had been assured that my identity and past with the agency had been scrubbed clean.

Jaxson didn't answer my question. "What happened in there?"

I rubbed the back of my neck and shrugged off his coat.

Was it warm in the truck or was I feverish under his scrutiny?

He pulled his coat tighter around my shoulders. The coat was warm around my shoulders, and I slipped my arms into the sleeves. Jaxson fastened the zipper, pulling it to the top. "You're freezing, Freckles. You need this more than I do."

Hearing the name he'd given me made me warm and toasty. "I don't feel cold," I whispered. My eyes fell to his lap.

He opened an alcohol wipe and swiped it against the abrasion on my forehead.

I hissed from the sting that radiated through my head. "Tell me you have drugs in there."

While I appreciated him taking care of me, I didn't like the burning sensation that the alcohol caused.

"There might be a few ibuprofen," Jaxson said. He tended to the gash on my head, cleaning it before using butterfly bandages to close the wound. "There's nothing any stronger if that's what you're asking."

He leaned forward and kissed my injury when he was done.

Lincoln's eyes were on us as he drove, every so often glancing in the rearview mirror. I did not know what he thought of me. I wasn't sure I wanted to know. The look of loathing was enough to send my heart plummeting.

I told Jaxson everything about Connor and the man with the baseball cap, how they'd attacked me and demanded four million dollars by sunset. While I hadn't wanted to tell him the rest, he deserved to know the truth and hear it from me.

"They'd been watching me, probably since the day I came to town. They knew about you and Izzie," I said.

Jaxson closed up the first aid kit and shoved it back under the seat.

His hand latched onto mine. While I'd always known his hands were large, the warmth eased my anxiety a little.

"They threatened you," he said, matter of fact, like my life hadn't just been torn apart and blown up in one afternoon.

I winced when I attempted a nod. "Yes. I'm so sorry." I didn't want him to hate me.

While I wasn't keen on Lincoln's intolerable glare, I didn't want to experience that from Jaxson.

He lifted his hips and retrieved his phone from his pocket. "Skylar, it's Jaxson. I need you to make sure the doors are locked and keep Izzie inside and away from any windows. Arm the alarm and then take her into the playroom. Don't answer the door for anyone, is that clear?"

He hung up his phone and shoved the device back into his pocket. "Head straight for my place," Jaxson said.

"Affirmative," Lincoln said.

Lincoln had downshifted the truck and rolled out the gears, he hurried up the mountain pass to get to Jaxson's house quicker. The pace quickened as trees whizzed by the windows on our way up.

I didn't know what we would do about the men or the money that they wanted, but they were becoming two thoughts furthest from my mind.

I was worried about Izzie. Jaxson's hands gave mine a tentative squeeze.

He was concerned too.

"I'm sorry," I said, keeping my voice low, so the conversation was between the two of us.

A stony stare from Lincoln made my heart skip a beat, and I met his gaze in the rearview mirror.

Jaxson's jaw remained tight, his shoulders square. "I have to ask you something and you owe me the respect of answering honestly."

I wanted to tell him I'd always been honest, and while I'd kept secrets, I hadn't lied to him, not outright.

My stomach bubbled with fear and dread.

What was he going to ask now?

I gave him the best smile I could muster to ease any worries that he had and squeezed his hands in mine. "Of course. What is it?"

"When you moved into the cabin the very first night, you told me you were shocked about not having electricity. Did you lie to me? The more I play that night over in my head. I keep thinking that you genuinely seemed surprised but knowing what I do, that you wanted to move off-grid, go somewhere that you wouldn't be exposed, it makes sense that you would have intended not to have electric."

Jaxson unclasped his hold from me and dug out his phone again. He pulled up the original listing on the cabin. He showed me the listing, holding his phone for me to see.

Off-grid. Quiet, rustic living at its finest either year-round or the perfect getaway cabin with hundreds of miles of trails all around.

"I hadn't taken off-grid to mean no electricity."

"Well, you should have," Lincoln added sharply from the driver's seat.

I pursed my lips, considering the right words. Why was he pissed at me?

Was it because I had worked for the agency or because he was defending his friend? "Yes, off-grid could mean no electric, but it can also mean a small town in the middle of nowhere which is precisely what the cabin is and where it's located."

I'd spent a great deal of time looking into small towns, but most I hadn't been capable of affording, and getting a loan would have been too risky. I needed to keep a low profile, little good that had done.

I'd still been found, and I wasn't sure where I'd messed up, except my credit card. While it had been assigned to my maiden name, the name I'd legally taken, it was possible some asshat had figured that out and exposed me.

Now they were hunting me down.

"Shit."

"What?" Jaxson asked.

He shoved his phone back into his pocket. We turned off the road, onto the last trail up to his house in the woods.

"I just realized how they found me. I've been stupid. I thought that if I kept a low profile, everything would blow over, but it's clear that was a mistake."

"You've made a lot of mistakes," Lincoln muttered from the front seat.

"What's that?" I shot back and turned to face him, letting go of any trace of Jaxson against me.

The truck came to an abrupt halt. "We're here," Lincoln said, putting the truck in park.

"Stay in the truck. Keep the doors locked."

Lincoln shut off the engine and took the keys with him. They locked the truck and hurried inside.

"How am I supposed to stay warm?" I asked.

No one could hear me. Both men were already outside rushing to get into the house and make sure Izzie was all right.

A red hatchback sat in the driveway in front of the house. I didn't recognize the car, but I hadn't been to his house. I shifted closer to the door but kept inside the vehicle.

The truck's engine roared to life, and I jumped in my seat, realizing Jaxson had turned on the auto start. At least I wouldn't freeze to death.

Part of me wanted to help. I didn't enjoy sitting around, watching events unfold and not being involved. I also knew I was no good if I was injured, and I didn't have the luxury of acting like an agent, gun drawn, running around with body armor.

The reality was I never had a traditional field assignment unless you called stakeouts and surveillance operations exciting. It wasn't a thrilling job, but it was essential in catching the bad guys.

I missed being able to use my skills. The resort hadn't been the most exciting job, but I thought it would have given me a fresh start. Instead, it paid barely above minimum wage, and I'd been tracked down. That wasn't anyone at the resort's fault.

I was prone to keeping secrets. That's all I'd ever known but look what good it had done.

I had lied to Jaxson, the one guy I liked and had a chance with, all because telling the truth was too hard and too risky. I was worried about being exposed and look where that got me.

I hated myself.

BOOM!

BOOM!

A loud explosion rattled the truck and blew out the windows.

I covered my ears and my head on instinct, but I heard nothing but a slight ringing sensation and beyond that, silence.

CHAPTER TWENTY

JAXSON

Jogging into the house, key in hand, I threw open the door and unarmed the alarm, leaving the door wide open behind me for Lincoln to follow.

I didn't turn around to see where he was. I didn't wait for him.

"Skylar! Izzie!" I shouted and hurried through the house, upstairs to the playroom, where I told them to go.

I threw open the door and lunged inside, only to find it empty.

"Skylar! Izzie!" I tried again, hoping they would answer me, needing to know they were both all right.

Isabella was my world, and while Skylar wasn't my favorite person, I trusted her to look after Izzie and make sure she was safe.

Silence filled the house as I flung each door open, searching high and low for both of them.

I fled down the stairs and to the basement, discovering Izzie in a laundry bin atop a mound of bedsheets.

Skylar had the lid of the dryer open doing a load of darks. The washing machine tumbled and thudded, probably making it difficult to hear, besides the basement's soundproofing. I had set it up as a training facility before we invested in the building that we have now for Eagle Tactical.

I exhaled a sigh of relief, throwing my arms around Izzie, pulling her tight and spinning her around, comforted that she was safe.

"Sorry, I didn't hear you guys come in." Skylar glanced at me over her shoulder and pointed at Lincoln. "We haven't met," she said, smiling and putting out her hand for an introduction.

"I'm Lincoln Taylor." He offered his hand. "It's a pleasure to meet you." Lincoln smiled charmingly at my sister and brought her hand to his lips.

Skylar grinned and giggled. It didn't take a genius to see what was happening between the two of them.

"She's off-limits." I wanted it made clear that he wasn't to date Skylar.

If they dated, then I'd have to see more of her. That was the last thing I wanted, for Skylar to find another reason to hang around Breckenridge.

There were other reasons, too.

She was far too juvenile to handle Lincoln.

She liked to play the field and go out partying. I was lucky she hadn't done that in town, coming home after the bar closed, trashed, and stumbling through the front door.

I wouldn't tolerate that type of behavior, certainly not around Izzie.

BOOM!

The house vibrated from a nearby explosion. I clutched Izzie to my chest, covering her, uncertain what was happening around us.

Lincoln met my stare. I handed Izzie back to Skylar. "Stay down here." My boots smacked the stairs hard on the way up, running out the front door to check on Ariella.

The truck's window had been shattered. I ran through the snow to the truck, my feet slipping under me, but I caught myself before falling. "Ariella?"

Her head poked up, her eyes wide and her body trembling.

"I was just sitting here when the windows blew. It sounded like an explosion nearby."

No one could have missed the deafening roar.

"Do you smell that?" she asked.

I spun around, glancing over my shoulder toward the bridge between our houses. Smoke billowed into the sky.

Ariella unlatched the door and yanked it open. I took a step back, getting out of the way for her. Her feet sunk into the snow with each quick step she took toward the bridge.

Unlike at the house, where I'd shoveled and it had slightly iced over, the bridge's path was thick with recent wet snow.

"Stay with Skylar," I shouted at Lincoln as he stood on the porch, his brow furrowed and phone in his hand. He pointed in the smoke's direction. He saw it now, too.

"I'm calling the fire department," Lincoln said.

I followed Ariella through the forest and across the bridge, along the trail between our properties. It was much shorter and a quicker route than by truck.

Thick, black smoke rose into the chilly air. The heat of the fire roared and whipped with the wind against the cabin. There was no chance of saving it or anything inside.

"No!" Ariella shouted, rushing toward the cabin.

I hurried after her, grabbing her by the waist, restraining her as she tried to break free, twisting and turning to pull herself from my grasp.

"Please! I have to get inside!"

"You can't," I whispered against her ear, clinging to her body, holding her back, willing her to stay with me.

Didn't she understand the danger?

The fire bellowed and boomed, the sound deafening as it ate away at the structure, fire soaring outside through the windows and where the roof had been moments earlier.

Her body went limp in my arms, and I scooped her up and carried her back to my house.

"Put me down!" She tried to pry out of my embrace and

eventually gave in when I didn't let her go. Her head rested against my chest, her arms around my neck.

"Is she okay?" Lincoln opened the front door for me as I brought her inside and gently guided her onto the sofa to lie down.

"I'm fine," Ariella said, sitting up, her feet dangling off the sofa instead of stretched out like I'd laid her. She unzipped my coat and pulled it off, handing it to me.

"What was so important in that house that you felt it necessary to run into burning flames? I know you don't have a pet, and no one else lives there." I'd been there the night before, and it had just been the two of us, alone, exploring each other's bodies.

Already, it seemed like a lifetime ago.

She hadn't even acknowledged my letter that I'd left her on the fridge. All that would have to wait. There were more pressing matters at hand. Besides, I wasn't even sure I could forgive her yet and be with someone who had deceived me.

I pushed the memories from last night away. I had to compartmentalize what happened between us.

"In my knapsack, there were some photos." Her eyes were cast down toward the floor.

I stepped closer and bent down. "What kind of photos?"

I wasn't able to ignore the knot in my stomach. She found it necessary to lie to me again.

What had she hidden away in the cabin that was worth risking her life over?

"You wouldn't understand." Her piercing green eyes glanced up at me.

"Try me, Freckles." I kept her trapped against the sofa. My legs straddled hers.

She swallowed, and her tongue darted out, licking her lips. Silence enveloped the room.

"I'm going to check on Skylar and Isabella," Lincoln said. He hustled out of the room and down the basement stairs.

Each thud was louder than the previous against the wooden steps.

Ariella gnawed on her bottom lip, tugging the cherry pink edge between her teeth. Her eyes fell to the floor.

"You *will* answer me, Freckles." I lifted her chin with my thumb, my fingers grazing her tender skin.

"What was the question?" Her lips pouted, her brow furrowed, and she tilted her head to the side.

"You are the queen of avoidance, aren't you?" I could see it written all over her face. "Don't play me." I didn't like games, and I would not engage in them with her. "The photographs in your cabin. What are they? Family photos? Something else? It's just you and me. You owe me an honest answer, Ariella. Especially after you lied to me about why you came to Breckenridge."

A soft puff of air escaped her lips with a sigh. She gently pushed against my chest. When I didn't move out of her way, she rolled her eyes and folded her arms against her chest. "It wasn't a lie. I've never told anyone who I used to work for, even when they employed me."

"You mean the C.I.A.," I said. Even now, she avoided using the agency's name.

Ariella shifted against the sofa but couldn't move farther than her butt allowed without sweeping her legs away from me, which she didn't do.

I reached out and guided her arms from their folded position. Taking her hands in mine, I could feel that her fingers were frigid from the outside temperature. Her cheeks also had a slight blush which I assumed had been from the cold. It could have also resulted from the stress of her home burning down to the ground.

"You're freezing. Why didn't you say anything?"

"It didn't seem important," she whispered, meeting my stare.

On the back of the leather sofa rested a throw blanket.

I stood and pulled the warm blanket down and unfolded the Sherpa, covering her with it. Her shoulders slumped, and her demeanor seemed to relax once she was tight under the blanket. I sat beside her, my legs brushing against hers, sitting atop the blanket.

"You need to take better care of yourself. I understand you're upset about the fire, but whatever was destroyed, it wasn't worth dying over."

"You don't know that," Ariella said, her eyes wide. She turned to face me. Her hands clutched the blanket around her small frame.

"Then explain it to me." I didn't enjoy being left in the dark. She continually gave me pieces of a puzzle, one at a time. "I don't like being strung along or having to drag secrets out of someone."

She trembled beneath the blanket, and I couldn't tell if it resulted from her being chilled or the adrenaline issues that she'd had the previous day.

Was this a daily occurrence regarding her health? Another question that I wanted answers to but wasn't expecting all of it explained tonight. Foremost, was the lie about her past, the fact she'd worked for the C.I.A., and whatever had her risking her life to go back inside for that stupid knapsack.

"About four years ago, I was pregnant," Ariella said.

Pacing the length of the living room, I could have easily worn a hole through the floor. Restless energy poured out of me until I heard her faint answer.

That took me by surprise. I swallowed the lump in the back of my throat. "I didn't know." I didn't want to overwhelm her. Approaching her, I towered above. "What happened?"

She stared down at the blanket. "Noah was born prematurely, at twenty-eight weeks. There were complications for both the baby and for me. He was a fighter, lived two weeks in NICU but in the end, it was just too much."

I sat down beside her, my hand falling on her thigh, giving her a reassuring squeeze. "I'm so sorry."

My heart ached.

Her son would have been around the same age as Izzie. It broke my heart to imagine what she went through and experienced.

She pressed her lips tight. "Me too. The fire took the last and only picture I had of my son."

Heaviness weighed over me.

Her eyes glistened with tears and she breathed in, sniffling, but the wetness didn't fall from her eyes.

Her strength surpassed mine.

"I don't want to talk about it anymore. It hurts too much to think about. I miss him every day, but his hospital bracelet and photo were inside my knapsack."

I pulled her into my lap, my embrace crushing her, keeping her tight to me.

Her body trembled. Her breaths were shallow and short.

"Let me take your pain away," I whispered into her ear.

Her cheeks were flushed. Her hands came up to my neck, icy cold. She ran her fingers through my hair. "You can't. No one can."

My forehead pressed firmly against hers. I wouldn't take that as an answer. I wanted to lay her down on the sofa and kiss her pain away.

"I don't know how I would have raised Noah with Benjamin in prison, on my own." Ariella winced. "I'm sorry."

"About what?" Why was she apologizing to me?

She kissed my cheek before she moved her head to rest on my shoulder. "I don't know how you do it." She paused for a beat, exhaling a heavy sigh. "Raise a daughter by yourself. It's impressive to me that you're a single father and you work full-time."

"Maybe it will comfort you to know that we believe you and your ex-husband were set up," I said.

She pulled back from my embrace. I thought hearing that would have made her happy. "What?"

"Blue Sky Resort requested that we run a background check on you before you were hired. I didn't dig too deep. Once I connected you were married to Benjamin Ryan, I'll admit, I lost my shit."

"Is that an apology?" Ariella asked, tilting her head before climbing off my lap. I didn't want her to pull away.

"It might be," I said. "Mason kept digging and discovered your previous employer. There were a number of questionable transactions that were traced back to the C.I.A.. Mason brought up that someone might have set you and Benjamin up."

"Who would set him up? Unless they were also setting me up, but why? Could there be a mole in the organization, someone who set me up to take the fall?" Rubbing her temples, she leaned forward, her head in her hands.

I hoped she wasn't about to get sick. I wanted to take her back with me to Eagle Tactical, but I wasn't sure she'd be willing to go.

The anger quelled and dissipated as her body relaxed. "I never thought I would want to thank Mason," she said.

"You'll have your chance."

"Benjamin wasn't guilty?" Her voice was soft, reflective of the news. "He's serving a 150-year term in federal prison for securities fraud, wire fraud, money laundering, the list goes on. Gosh, I'm such an asshole." She pulled away from my touch. "I told him I hated him, that I never wanted to see him or talk to him again."

I hadn't considered the fact she might still have harbored feelings for her ex-husband. If he wasn't guilty, what chance did I have that she'd even want to be with me?

I ran a hand through my short hair and needed to change the subject fast. The whole thought of Ariella feeling guilty and wanting to be with him again made bile rise into my throat.

"That aside," I said and cleared my throat. "We have more pressing matters. You mentioned earlier that the thugs who attacked you demanded four million dollars."

"That's right. I don't have that kind of money. If I did, do you think I'd be living in the woods without electricity or accessible heat?"

She had accessible heat. It may not have been the easiest method to warm the place, but the cabin still could be kept plenty warm. I held my tongue. There was no sense fighting over a cabin that had burned to the ground. The fire department would take at least twenty minutes to climb the mountain, and whatever water the truck had would be all they could use.

Twenty minutes was too long to save the cabin, but it would stop the destruction from spreading and turning the forest into a giant tinder box.

The wail of sirens on their approach echoed outside and through the canopy of trees.

"I don't have that kind of money, either, but I think there's another way." I headed for the window, staring outside at the heavy blackness, like clouds that billowed to the sky, for a moment before turning around to give her my attention.

Ariella stood slowly, folding the blanket back to its original shape, each corner perfectly lined up to match. "I would love nothing more than never to lay eyes on those men again, but I know if we don't stop them, next time will be worse."

She placed the Sherpa blanket over the back of the sofa where I'd grabbed it from earlier. "Do you think they're somehow responsible for the fire?" she asked.

Ariella walked ever so quietly. Her footsteps were silent to the ear. Had I not been watching from the corner of my eye, I never would have known she stood beside me.

I turned and watched the plume of smoke.

"Can we go outside and watch?" Her voice was soft and tentative. Was she afraid I'd tell her no?

While I wasn't keen on taking her with me, I wanted to survey the scene and determine if evidence had been left behind out in the open. If the firemen hadn't arrived yet, maybe we could spot tire tracks or footprints.

Years of tactical and military training told me this wasn't an accident. It was risky but I wasn't going to let anything happen to Ariella.

"Take this," I said and offered her my coat, the same one she'd worn earlier. I grabbed another jacket to put on.

"Wait here. Let me tell Lincoln what we're doing so he doesn't worry." I hurried down the basement steps, informed Lincoln and Skylar that we would check out the fire next door and see if anything suspicious stood out.

"That was fast."

I had little to tell them, and I didn't want Ariella going alone. I opened the front door and led her outside. "It's hard to say, but if I trust my gut, they won't be too far from here."

If someone had intentionally started the fire, they'd have stuck around watching the damage they caused.

With my hand on the small of her back, I led her through the forest and across the bridge.

Smiling, she still wore the boots I'd given her. I bought them as a gift for my sister when she visited and never brought sensible shoes. The box had been shucked in the back of my closet and now had finally seen the light of day.

We crossed the bridge. Through the tree line, red lights flickered and flashed from the fire engine pulling into the driveway of her property.

She grumbled under her breath. "Would you look at that? The damned shed survived."

The structure had been on its last legs. It was any wonder the thick smoke hadn't knocked the building over.

"I guess I know where I'll be living from now on," she muttered and shoved her hands into her coat pockets.

There was no chance in hell I'd let her live in that crooked shed. "What about insurance money for the cabin?"

Insurance would pay to rebuild the house and her living expenses up to a certain amount, depending on her coverage.

The firefighters unlatched the hose and used the reservoir of water available. There weren't any fire hydrants nearby.

Water blasted the fire, causing a thicket of smoke to flood the area. I reached out, grabbing Ariella against me, and ducked my head into my jacket to breathe.

The outside air burned my lungs.

She coughed on the plumes as the wind shifted direction toward us while we stood behind the property. "I don't have insurance," she choked out.

The flames had been suffocated by water, smothering us in the process as the breeze picked up.

The gust of air brought the charred remnants ablaze, ash in the air, embers floating like fireflies gliding in the wind. My eyes burned, and Ariella continued to cough on the smoke.

We needed to turn around. This had been stupid and dangerous. I'd thrown her right into danger.

The heaviness of the air filled with dark smoke turned me around. The bridge wasn't visible. With one arm around her waist, I pulled her through the dense fog of smoke. I couldn't even see my own hands in front of me.

I held my breath and pulled her tight against me so that she wouldn't get lost and wander into further danger. Smoke burned my eyes. My nose tickled from the ash. This was my fault.

The breeze picked up, and I gasped, needing a drink of air into my lungs. Ariella coughed and wheezed, the smoke bothering her far worse. The air caught beneath the charred remnants of the cabin, and the fire blazed back to life as we grew too close in the smoke to see.

Heat sizzled against my cheeks.

I cursed and yanked Ariella closer, pulling her behind me. "Keep your arms around my waist," I demanded.

I needed my hands to feel my way through the trees and while I didn't want to get burned, I wanted even less for her to be the one to discover the wild flames.

Skirting the fire, a blast of wetness smothered the flames momentarily. More smoke charged into the air.

I coughed and stumbled forward.

My eyes burned.

Through the heat and warmth that had been nearby, still simmering on the foundation, I led us around the property. Sweat coated my cheeks and brow while my back pebbled with goosebumps from the chill.

Bringing her with me around the fire and away from the smoke, escaping harm's way, I sensed the brightness before seeing anything clear. My vision blurred from the smoke, but one foot smacked the ground in front of the other.

Panting hard, I collapsed forward, away from the plumes of

smoke, my knees on the icy cold snow, breathing in the fresh air—the smoke behind us.

I heard the shouts of firefighters. I was no good to Ariella.

My hands clutched the earth, gasping hard for each breath of oxygen that I could.

With blurred eyes, a man towered above me.

A mask covered my lips and my vision wavered and blurred before the world went black.

CHAPTER TWENTY-ONE

ARIELLA

"Jaxson?" He'd stumbled forward, one foot and then another until he'd fallen onto his knees.

I crouched down, keeping him close.

"Help!" I shouted for the firefighters, hoping there was a paramedic nearby. My hands clutched his jacket, and my fingers stroked his hair. I didn't see any burn marks, no evidence of injuries.

Unless it was something I couldn't see, perhaps smoke inhalation. Could it be something else that I didn't know about? "Please, help him!"

The smack of boots against the snow forced a shiver down my spine and my hair to stand on end. It reminded me of glass crunching underfoot. A team of paramedics rushed over to help.

Jaxson's body went slack, but my hands caught him before he hit his face into the snow, guiding him down as gracefully as I could.

I coughed and gasped. Waves of dizziness washed over me, but I ignored the spinning sensation.

Jaxson needed help.

I could wait. I would wait because he was in need. He had a

daughter, and if something happened to him because of my carelessness, I would never forgive myself.

One paramedic gently guided me away, informing me they needed space. I didn't want to let go of his hand; I didn't want to lose the only connection I had with someone. Letting go was not an answer I would accept.

"No," I shook my head repeatedly, trembling, although I wasn't cold.

Nausea attacked my stomach, and I pushed a wayward lock of hair behind my ear, exhaling through my mouth. Anything to keep from spilling my lunch. Except, I couldn't remember the last time I ate.

My head throbbed, my heart pounded, and my stomach coiled. "I won't leave him," I said, clutching his hand tight. "He didn't leave me."

"We need to look you over," the gentleman said, his eyes studying the bump I sustained earlier. "You should get checked out too."

"I'm not going anywhere without Jaxson." I refused to release my grip on his hand. No one would separate us.

The paramedic grumbled and gave a resigned sigh. "Well, would you at least have a seat so I can check you out too? I'm worried about the injury to your head."

He hadn't even seen all the cuts and bruises, the scrapes that covered me from earlier.

"I'm fine," I insisted, pointing at the bandage on my head. "This is unrelated." I squatted with my knees bent, keeping a close eye on Jaxson, ignoring the attention that the paramedic paid to me.

"Yes, and you're bleeding right through your bandage," the paramedic said. He grabbed a few pads of gauze in a nearby bag with gloved hands and rested it against my forehead.

I winced from the initial sting of contact. There were droplets of fresh blood in the snow—my blood.

My butt slumped into the cold, slushy snow.

My gloved hand rubbed over the evidence of my blood, burying it from anyone else's watchful gaze.

"Why don't you come with me? Sit in the back of the ambulance bay so I can patch up your head," the paramedic said.

Another paramedic tended to Jaxson, covering his face with an oxygen mask against his mouth and nose.

"Will he be all right?"

The paramedic escorted me through the snow and wet sludge to the bay of the ambulance. He yanked open the double doors and offered me a hand, helping me inside.

"Have a seat." He pointed to the gurney.

I'd have rather stood, but I did as I was told. I sat at the edge of the hard cot, my lips tight and hands dug into the side of the bed.

He slammed the doors shut from the outside.

"Hey!" I screamed and jumped off the gurney, trying the door handle. He'd locked me inside. "Help!"

Everything outside the ambulance sounded muffled. Could they hear my cries for help?

"Help! Let me out!" My hands pounded hard against the metal doors.

A door slammed, and the engine of the ambulance purred to life.

"Shit," I muttered. "Help! I'm locked in!" I tried again, but no one answered.

The ambulance jolted forward, and my feet fumbled until I gripped the nearby wall to steady myself. I had no phone, and Jaxson hadn't been in the best shape when I'd stupidly gone into the ambulance. He wasn't a paramedic, but how had he fooled the others unless none of them were paramedics?

Hadn't Jaxson mentioned that the hospital was a two-hour drive?

I couldn't worry about Jaxson right now. I hoped Lincoln would find him.

I needed to escape.

The door would not open from the inside. I opened the nearest cabinet. Three shelves sat empty, but on the bottom shelf a small black duffel sat alone.

Bending down to reach for the duffel, I unzipped the bag to find a few supplies, nothing of any use to me: gauze, bandages, and medical tape. It held the same items that he'd used earlier for my forehead to appear as a paramedic without actually being one.

I hustled to the opposite side of the ambulance, checking the other cabinet. There were several vials, unlabeled but no syringes that I could see.

"Drugs?"

What were they doing with those? I smashed the vials against the floor. I would not chance that he'd try to use those on me.

The ambulance picked up speed as we traveled down the mountain, fleeing past the town.

While I couldn't see out any windows, with the heavy descent, the rush of the weight of the ambulance, I could hear the squeak of the brakes at every turn.

I slammed my fists against the thick partition between the driver and myself.

The driver ignored me. He sat alone in the front seat.

At least I only had one person to fight off when he eventually stopped and opened the door. He couldn't leave me in here forever.

"What do you want?" I shouted. My hands bunched together in fists as I pounded against the glass. "Let me go!"

The glass was dirty, thick, and had a goopy-dried coating around the edges. The window was made to open and slide, but someone had made sure that would not happen.

"Fuck!" Had he been involved in burning down my cabin? It seemed probable. "Who are you?"

Several vehicles sat in the middle of the mountain pass, blocking traffic.

"What the hell," he grumbled.

His voice, though muffled, I could hear, which meant he heard me just fine.

He slammed hard on the brakes, sending my body flinging through the back of the ambulance bay, smacking into the wall, the gurney slamming my knees.

I grimaced and swallowed back a groan from the pain. I didn't want him to get any ideas.

The tires squealed as he revved the engine.

A single-seat was positioned by the interior window, and I sat facing the front of the ambulance on my knees, clutching the seatback so that I could watch through the glass.

Several vehicles had blocked the main pass of the mountain. Had there been an accident?

Through the dirty opening, I spotted a familiar truck. My heart fluttered in my chest.

Could Jaxson be there?

No, I had to be delirious.

He was at the top of the mountain at home, lying unconscious on the snow outside of my burned-down cabin. More than one person owned that type of vehicle.

I could see figures outside their trucks, on the side of the road, but couldn't make out anyone's face. The glass was too dirty and distorted. Everyone appeared blurry.

"Help!" I screamed. Could anyone hear me?

He slammed the gas to the floor as the ambulance lurched forward, head on for the multitude of vehicles waiting below.

"Shit," I clutched the seat and reached for the buckle to spin around and secure the seatbelt, but it had been sliced in two. It was worthless.

The ambulance driver refused to slow down as the vehicle plowed down the mountain road, slamming into the trucks, SUVs, and police cruisers that had been sitting in the middle of the road.

I clung to the seat, the impact throwing me from the bench chair to the floor. "Help!" I shrieked.

Could the men outside hear me?

The crunch of metal drowned out their voices.

My head throbbed, and the ambulance's engine roared. The back of the vehicle fishtailed on what I could only surmise had been ice and snow.

The vehicle spun and catapulted down a ravine, throwing me around the back of the ambulance until darkness won over.

Every part of me, inside and out, ached like fire dripping over my skin.

I groaned, and my eyelids fluttered open, the brightness forcing the pounding in my head to intensify and offering a warmth that made me imagine it was the sun.

"Looks like she's awake," a gruff voice echoed.

It took all my strength to focus, to stay awake and alert.

My fingers grazed the cold stone surface of where I curled up.

I wasn't in a bed.

There weren't any beeps of machines or sign that I'd been transported to a hospital. The last memory I had was of the accident, which meant that I hadn't escaped yet.

I exhaled a heavy breath and winced.

It hurt to breathe. That wasn't a good sign.

I rolled over on the hard floor and forced myself to sit, my back pressed up against a cold slab of cement.

The bright light that warmed me earlier had been the flicker of a single bulb in a darkened room.

Was I being held in someone's basement?

There was no sign of the ambulance or the forest floor.

The room smelled old, musty, and tickled my nose. I scrunched my face to keep from sneezing, glancing up at the dimly lit bulb.

Two men with long, thick beards sat on stools in the dark, knives in their hands, watching me.

I strummed my fingers over the cold stone floor. I was injured, but I could move. My fingers and toes wiggled. The men hadn't restrained me. There were no binds keeping me from moving.

"What do you want?" I asked, my voice hoarse, my mouth parched.

One man used his knife to whittle a stick, the end sharp.

Did he intend to use that on me?

I bit down on my tongue, the intense pain helping wake me from the foggy disconnect that surrounded my head. Had I not been in an accident, I would have surmised I had been drugged. Was it possible that both had happened?

The second man picked at the edge of his fingernails with his knife and then used it to clean between his teeth. With squinty eyes, he stood and towered from above. "Turns out there's a price on your head. We're just collecting the bounty. Sit tight."

That was the last thing I was prepared to do, sit and wait for my death.

What happened with Jaxson? Was he all right?

I didn't want these men to know that he meant anything to me, not if they'd use that against me too.

"How much am I worth?" If they were after money, I could convince them I had a bucket of wealth offshore. All they had to do was let me live.

Did they know who I was, what my ex-husband had been convicted of, or was this bounty because of my work with the agency?

The younger of the two men, the one whittling a long, sharp stick, pulled out his cell phone. "Buyer says she's worth the same dead or alive."

"Lucky for us," the second man said, his eyes lighting up with the prospect of my death.

"Whatever he's willing to give you, I can double it!" Would they see my bluff?

The man who stood above me tilted his head to the side and leaned down, knife in hand. The blade scratched my cheek. His putrid breath smelled of stale coffee.

"Yes, but I enjoy listening to the screams of a helpless woman when I stab her repeatedly. What fun is it for me if I let you live? This way, I get the money and my fun." He winked at me.

I leaned forward, coughing up bile.

His fingers yanked at my hair, pulling me to stand. He did nothing to help the throbbing sensation in my head except make it worse.

I clutched my forehead with one hand and the wall behind me

with the other to keep from losing my balance. “Let me go.” I would not be helpless.

I kicked him in the groin. He was swift, the blade of the knife pressed on my neck, my body tight against the cold cement wall.

“Are you sure you want to do that?” he asked, leaning in, his sick breath against my cheeks.

The hairs on my arms stood on end, and a chill ran down my spine.

I’d had plenty of practice fighting at the agency with a dummy knife, but under pressure, everything was different.

Fight or flight, and I froze.

CHAPTER TWENTY-TWO

JAXSON

Her faint scream brought me back and focused. I lifted my gloved hand, latching on to the mask around my face and yanking it off.

"You need to lie back down," the paramedic said as he hovered over me.

"The hell I do." I coughed as I pushed him away and stood, watching the ambulance tires spin on ice and snow before flying down the mountain road.

"You're not… where are you taking her?" I took several deep breaths, in through my nose and out through my mouth.

Already, I was doing better, more alert, less cloudy.

Whatever had been in that canister, it wasn't oxygen. They'd tried to drug me.

Two firefighters were dousing the smoking remnants of the cabin, keeping it from lighting ablaze again. They were chatting amongst one another; I couldn't hear them over the rush of water pounding the rubble.

The paramedic had to know something. He must have been involved. He didn't seem the least bit stressed or surprised that his vehicle had just been stolen with a woman in the back, screaming for help.

I landed a forceful blow to his face, wrestling him to the ground, pinning him down and keeping his hands far from his medical bag just a few feet away. I didn't know what he had in there, whether it was a gun or a sedative, but I would not let him touch me.

Another firefighter came up from behind the paramedic with a spotlight. He turned on the light, the brightness forcing the paramedic to shield his eyes, blinding him as I kept him pinned to the snow.

"Get off me!" the paramedic shrieked. "You're crazy."

"You ain't seen crazy," I spat.

"What the hell is going on?" the firefighter asked. "You're not local EMS. You okay, sir?" He kept the spotlight on the paramedic, but his attention was now trained on me.

He tossed me a set of zip ties from his pocket. He recognized something was amiss as well.

There was only one ambulance in all of Breckenridge. The Adams family ran the EMS unit, and being a member of Eagle Tactical, I knew every one of the Adamses.

"I will be." I rolled the assailant around onto his stomach and tied his hands together before I stood. "What do you want with Ariella?" I yanked him around, making him sit in the cold, mushy snow.

"There's a bounty on her head. She's just a payday."

How many people were after her?

I pulled my phone from my pocket, dialed Lincoln and the rest of the Eagle Tactical team. I patched them through on a conference call together.

"Hey, what's going on, man?" Lincoln asked.

I'd left him at my house, just a few yards away, and he didn't know what had just transpired.

"Yeah, where are you?" Mason asked.

"Ariella's house burned down. We got caught up in the smoke and someone posing as a paramedic forced her into the back of the ambulance and took off with her down the mountain pass," I said. I further went into detail, demanding for them to call the local Breckenridge sheriff's office and block off the road.

"I'm on it," Declan answered.

"I also need a sheriff's unit brought up to the old cabin, the one Ariella purchased. One guy pretending to be a paramedic is in zip ties."

I didn't have cuffs handy, and while I could have easily dragged his ass down to the station, I needed to get to Ariella and protect her.

"You going to question him?" Lincoln asked.

I wanted to strap him down and interrogate him, shove the barrel of my gun against his bare skin. That would take time, and it wasn't something I had a lot of right now.

"I'm leaving that up to the sheriff." There were too many witnesses with the fire department standing just a few feet away.

The type of interrogation I wanted to do would be off the books and highly illegal.

I rushed back between the tree line and over the bridge, skirting the house. The smoke had diminished. Lincoln approached the car. "I'm driving," he said.

I started the engine with my key fob and climbed into the passenger seat.

Lincoln didn't miss a beat, hurrying into the driver's side. The moment he shut the door, he had the vehicle in reverse and whisked us away from the house.

I yanked the seatbelt, securing it while Lincoln rushed us down the mountain pass, the road slick and wet from ice and snow. My stomach sank at the danger that lurked ahead.

"We'll get to her in time, don't worry." Lincoln's hands were tight on the steering wheel.

My foot tapped against the floor mats, anxiety creeping in, making the drive seem longer. "Were Izzie and Skylar okay?" I hadn't forgotten about them back at the house.

"They're fine. Izzie went down for a nap. Skylar was reading a book when I left her."

"Okay." I let out an anxious breath I hadn't realized that I'd been holding.

Lincoln flew down the mountain pass, a pro at taking the switchbacks in haste. He slowed as we drew near. A mess of vehicles were smashed and driven through, the ambulance already having left its wake.

"Look there!" Lincoln pointed at the tire tracks off the road and the ambulance down at the bottom of the ravine on its side. He pulled off the road and hit the brakes.

I threw open the truck door and hurried down the ravine, my boots skidding down the side of the mountain along with me. I didn't care if I landed on my ass, as long as I found her.

Mason and Aiden were already down by the ambulance with the sheriff and several other townsfolk conversing.

"Ariella!"

Mason spotted me first and shook his head no.

My stomach sank.

I didn't know if that meant she wasn't there, or if worse, she didn't make it. I refused to accept that she'd died. There wasn't a body as far as I could see. Unless she was in the back of the ambulance?

"Where is she?" I shouted, sliding down, my feet slipping under me, but I caught my balance. My arms out, I steadied myself before running the last leg of distance toward my buddies.

"She's not here," Mason said, his eyes filled with sorrow. He didn't want to be the one to convey bad news, but someone had to tell me what happened.

That wasn't enough of an answer for me. I needed more. "Where is she?"

Lincoln came up from behind, having followed me down the slope of the ravine. He poked his head into the ambulance bay, examining the scene and any evidence left behind.

I exhaled a loud breath, my heart hammering in my chest. "Any leads?" I wouldn't abandon Ariella. She needed me more than ever.

"Declan is back at Eagle Tactical, running surveillance and scouring the dark web for leads. Although he pulled down the bounty earlier from the net, it's clear someone saw it and acted on it while the information was still fresh," Mason said.

Lincoln shoved his hands into his coat pocket. "There's not much to go on other than the ambulance was definitely not used for medical purposes. The equipment is pretty scarce in there, which means there likely wasn't anything she could have used as a weapon, either."

"She's smart." She worked for the C.I.A. at one point, and I trusted that she'd do everything in her power to stay alive.

She just needed to survive long enough until we found her.

Shoving my fingers into my coat, I kept my head down, examining broken branches and a single set of footprints that appeared to be a size 12 men's that were farther from the group.

I followed the trail, not sure what to expect. "Look, there's one set of prints."

The footprints sunk into the ground, potential evidence that she'd been carried and unable to walk. There didn't appear to be a second set of prints coming back, either, which meant it couldn't have been the sheriff or anyone else helping with the search party.

"The mountain pass runs just south of here. They could have gone down the road to another pickup point. There's no way they planned on keeping the ambulance and not being seen," Mason said.

"Maybe, but south is that direction." I pointed south and then continued to follow the footprints that led west. "They didn't go to the road. It's possible they got turned around."

If we were lucky, they were still in the forest. I held up my hand, signaling to wait.

Crouching down, I examined droplets of fresh blood on the snow. "She was here." I'd never been more certain in my life.

I hurried, following the trail of footprints and droplets of blood that were mixed and mottled, difficult to find with branches strewn everywhere.

Lincoln, Mason, and Aiden followed at my heel as we scoured the forest, making sure we weren't being played and the tracks had been a diversion. That didn't appear to be the case.

I wanted to scream out for her, but if we were close along with the assailant, I didn't want to further put her life in danger.

In the distance, a cabin sat nestled in the woods, four black SUVs in the driveway. "Any chance you guys brought a gun?" I didn't want to go in outnumbered and unarmed.

"Did we come armed?" Lincoln laughed under his breath.

He lifted his shirt, showing me his gun. He then reached for his ankle holster, retrieving his spare weapon and handing it to me. "Looks like I'm saving your ass again, Monroe."

"Just like old times," I joked, "where you think you're saving me, but in actuality, I'm rescuing you."

With his gun drawn, he moved behind a tree as we grew closer. "Keep thinking that," Lincoln said.

Aiden crouched down, pulling a switchblade from his pocket. "I'll slash their tires and keep them from getting away."

"Good thinking." We didn't want them taking Ariella off the property. I gestured for us to fan out. We needed to surround the cabin, find out what awaited us inside.

The car door of the SUV slammed shut. I snuck behind a tree, doing my best to camouflage. When I woke up this morning, I hadn't thought this was how my day would go. I bet Ariella didn't think the same, either.

Slow and even breaths. The cold sucked the air out of my lungs and burned, but I ignored the pain in my chest.

Our footprints were fresh, but that didn't worry me as much as the sound of branches cracking under our boots. My foot came down slow and cautious as I moved from one tree with my sight on another to use as a minimal form of protection.

Aiden needed to be careful with the men outside by the SUV.

I held my breath.

He stabbed one tire before moving around the vehicle to hit another.

The men stood outside and talked, oblivious to what happened around them. That was good. It meant they were distracted.

We just needed to keep them that way while we found and rescued Ariella.

I took another step closer, coming up to the cabin. I crouched beside the window and peered in, careful not to be seen. There were gruff voices, but no one in the room faced the window.

A loud, feminine, ear-piercing scream echoed through the house.

I didn't wait any longer; I rushed toward the nearest entrance and barreled in through the back door, gun drawn with Lincoln and Mason right behind me.

They had heard her cry for help too.

CHAPTER TWENTY-THREE

ARIELLA

Fear drenched me to the core of my existence.

I trembled under the blade of his knife. The smirking bastard with breath old and putrid nicked my neck, reminding me he was in charge.

I could do this.

I had to do this. I talked myself up, my hands in fists at my sides, gathering strength.

I stomped on his toes, his boots thin, then shoved my knee hard up into his groin.

He doubled over in pain to grab his family jewels when the knife clanked to the floor. I yanked my knee hard up again, this time into his face, before ramming him headfirst into the wall.

He fell like a ton of bricks.

I bent down and snatched his knife. The handle trembled in my hands. It was my only line of defense to get out of the cellar.

"Nice one. You know if you kill him, it means more money for me," said the second man who had sat on his stool whittling his stick. He stood, the sharp instrument in his grip.

I stepped over the imbecile, keeping my back to the wall for protection.

There were no windows in the basement. The small space closed in on me like a coffin.

My fingers grazed the cement, reminding me it wasn't moving. The dizziness was all in my head.

The room was constrictive, and as car doors slammed, beads of sweat trickled down my forehead.

"Let me go," I said with as much conviction as I could muster. "I told you I have money. I can give you far more than anyone else will for killing me."

I'd tell a million lies if it would save my life. Would he fall for it?

"Unlike Carter, I don't want to kill you. I prefer to play with the merchandise." He snickered and unfastened his belt.

My eyes widened, and my stomach somersaulted. I gripped the handle of the knife until my knuckles turned white.

"Come here, girly," he said, stalking toward me.

I screamed loud and hard. My lungs burned from the pain. My throat would be hoarse tomorrow, but I didn't care if it meant that I lived to see another sunrise.

I screamed again, hoping to bring the men from outside down to the cellar. They wanted me dead, and while I didn't want to end up six feet under, I also wasn't about to get raped by a madman after a payday.

I skirted the wall, my gaze finding nothing, the only weapon in my defense a blade that was smaller and meant getting closer than his sharpened stick.

"We could play a game," he whispered. He was grabbing my arm and pinning it back above my head, forcing the damned weapon to fall. At least he didn't have his shaft.

It took all the courage I had to muster the words he wanted to hear. Could I convince him to let me go? "I like games," I said and swallowed the lump that formed in my throat.

His decrepit hand stroked my cheek, and I turned my head away, refusing to look at him. He grabbed me by the chin and forced my face to look at him. "Doesn't look like you enjoy this game very much," he said.

He leaned closer to me, his body just inches from mine.

The room spun.

Had the thermostat been suddenly turned up? Sweat licked my skin and my stomach recoiled.

I stomped his foot, but he wore steel-toed boots, offering him protection and only making the bottoms of my feet throb.

I winced but didn't let him see my discomfort or surprise that the maneuver hadn't worked.

His hand that had been on my chin fell to my knee. "Don't even think about fighting this, girly. You know you want it." He leaned toward me.

"I could never want anyone like you!" I spat in his face and squirmed to escape his grasp.

The knife lay on the floor out of my reach with my hands pinned above my head.

He kept me trapped, and though I attempted to use the force of my entire body to fight him, he was taller than I was, heftier, and had me restrained.

"I do like a girl who fights," he said and snickered.

The other man who had attacked me earlier and had been lying on the ground stirred awake.

He grabbed my legs, keeping me from kicking either of them again.

I screamed again, and the bastard who had me pinned to the wall and my hands clamped above my head shoved his hand over my mouth.

I bit down on his fingers, unwilling to give in to his demands or temptations.

"You bitch!" he snarled and threw his hand back, smacking me hard across the face. "I'll show you," he said, unzipping his pants.

Heavy footsteps pounded against the ceiling of the cellar. "Help!" I screamed, thrashing as I tried to break free of both men.

"Ariella!" Jaxson's voice was music to my ears, the sweetest symphony I'd ever heard in my life.

His boots slammed against the stairs. He and his buddies came tearing down the basement to help.

"What the hell?" The man spun around, pants at his ankles.

The other man on the floor released his grasp from my legs and grabbed the switchblade to defend himself.

"I'll kill you!" Jaxson screamed, slamming his fist into the first man's face, the guy with bloody fingers. I hadn't realized how deep I'd bitten down. Seeing the blood made me gag.

Lincoln and Mason tore down the dimly lit stairs with Jaxson, disarming both men, knocking them momentarily unconscious.

I threw myself into Jaxson's embrace.

Lincoln pulled out a pair of zip ties and secured both attacker's hands to ensure they were no longer a threat.

Being wrapped in Jaxson's strong, warm arms made me relax. I rubbed my cheek against his chest and closed my eyes, drinking in his strength.

Lincoln cleared his throat. "Sorry to break up the reunion, but there's still a bunch of guys out front with Aiden. We need to get out of here, now."

Lincoln headed up the stairwell first, gun drawn.

"Stay behind me," Jaxson said, leading me up the stairs. Like his shadow, I clung to him.

The men gave one another signals. He nodded for me to follow.

Each step they took was silent, absent as if they never were here.

Shouts from the basement erupted. The two men downstairs had woken up.

"We need to move, now!" Jaxson grabbed my arm and pulled me to run with him as he led me out the back door and into the forest.

"Where's your truck?" I'd heard a car door earlier, not long before Jaxson had come down and rescued me.

We kept running through the forest with no end in sight. I glanced over my shoulder. Men in black suits with guns were trailing behind us.

"Way too far." His hand clutched mine, a lifeline.

He pulled me through the forest.

I wasn't out of shape. Ordinarily, I could have run miles without a hitch, but I'd been assaulted twice today and survived an accident in an ambulance.

It wasn't my best day.

He pulled me tight against a tree, his body pressed against mine, protecting me.

Bullets whizzed by our heads. I froze, frightened. The sound of a gunshot rippled through my body, forcing the adrenaline to rear its ugly head.

I trembled but found solace in the warmth of Jaxson's body pressing me tight against the rough bark.

His embrace was firm, protective, and warm. His touch was strong while his attention was entirely on keeping me safe.

Lincoln found a tree for cover.

Mason did the same.

"We can't keep running," Jaxson said. He wasn't talking to me.

Lincoln, Mason, and Jaxson began firing their weapons at the men in suits with guns.

"Who are they?" They didn't look like the C.I.A.. They weren't the same grungy bastard types who had attacked me at the resort or burned down my cabin and abducted me for money.

"Bounty hunters," Jaxson said.

My hands pulled him closer, willing him to do whatever he needed to do to save me. He wasn't joking.

These were men on a mission to kill.

"Since when do bounty hunters wear suits?" I tried to make a joke. Probably bad timing as he pressed himself entirely against me, his face in mine, taking cover as bullets rained around us.

His forehead leaned against mine. My fingers tugged at his jacket. I shivered, the coat he loaned me long since discarded.

"You're freezing, shit." Jaxson tried making himself as small as possible, not to let his limbs extend from beyond the cover of the tree trunk.

He slipped off his coat and put it around my shoulders. "You need this more than I do." His eyes twinkled with that charm that only Jaxson had.

He was a hero in every sense of the word.

"You're going to be cold," I said, attempting to reason with him why I shouldn't take his spare coat since I'd already taken possession of his last jacket, and that hadn't ended well for his clothes.

Lincoln and Mason fired off shots at the men. The sound of gunfire coming at us seemed to diminish. Were the men dead, injured, or out of bullets?

"I'll be fine," he scoffed. "Now, stay here. Don't move." Jaxson raised his gun again, firing off several more shots before silence ensued.

Was it over?

I trembled against the trunk of the tree, warmer as I slid my arms into his coat but unable to move, too afraid the men played dead.

What if they were waiting for us to move, to sneak out from hiding and shoot me?

"All clear!" Aiden shouted from where the bullets had been flying from earlier.

"Don't move," Jaxson said.

Wordlessly, I nodded. I could handle not moving. I was good at that, especially right now when my body wasn't cooperating. Even if I wanted to walk, I didn't think myself capable.

The trunk of the tree held me up. My weight pressed tight. I let my fingers graze over the wood, memorizing every detail, the texture against the pads of my fingertips—anything to take my mind off what had just transpired.

Jaxson poked his head out, his hands on my hips as Mason, Lincoln, and Aiden tracked through the forest back toward the cabin from where the gunshots had gone off.

"All clear," Mason said.

Jaxson didn't so much as release his hold or move away like I thought he might. He held me, kept me protected. Was he worried it wasn't over? Did he think I couldn't look after myself?

His jaw was tight, square, and clenched. "We left those two goons tied up. It probably won't be long until they want their revenge. Boys like that don't appreciate losing."

"Great," I muttered under my breath.

"They got their revenge and then some. They need a body bag," Aiden said, pointing at both men lying in a pool of their own blood on the snow-covered ground.

I shivered.

"It's over," Jaxson said. His shoulders relaxed. The tension slipped out of him.

The warmth of the sun began to fade as it set. I wasn't quite at ease. "Is it?" I whispered.

The men from the resort, the thugs who attacked me earlier in the day, were expecting four million dollars, and I didn't have a cent.

Jaxson held me tight. His hand latched around mine. We waited outside the front of the cabin, the one where I'd been dragged and nearly raped, for the police to arrive.

I wasn't looking forward to giving my statement. I didn't want to relive the trauma over again.

All I wanted was to go home and soak in a warm bath.

Except I didn't have a bath anymore. Hell, I didn't have a house anymore.

The police finally came along, taking their sweet time. The Eagle Tactical guys had to answer questions of their own about the incident, as did I.

I didn't like being separated from them, especially Jaxson, but we were outside and only a few yards away. I could see him, but not being safe in his warm arms made it difficult.

Just as the last statements were given, Declan strolled up in his truck offering us a ride.

I climbed into the backseat sandwiched between Jaxson and Lincoln.

Aiden grabbed the front seat.

Mason cleared his throat.

"Sorry, man, there's no room," Lincoln joked with Mason.

"Looks like Mason's going to sit on Jaxson's lap," Aiden grinned.

Jaxson rolled his eyes.

"You're groaning because you know it's true," Aiden said.

Jaxson's gaze met mine. "You're going to have to sit on my lap for the ride back to Eagle Tactical."

"Okay," I answered a little too quickly. They didn't notice. Jaxson didn't budge from his position on the side, and I scooted onto his lap.

Lincoln scooted over, making room for Mason. He jogged around the back of the truck, and Declan started to take off, the door open, messing with him.

"Don't be an ass!" Mason chased after the truck before Declan softly came to a stroll, making Mason climb in while the vehicle was still moving. Albeit it wasn't moving fast, I couldn't hide the grin on my face. He deserved it, just a little.

Mason flung himself into the truck and slammed the door.

"Got everyone?" Declan glanced in the rearview mirror, taking a brief mental headcount before hitting the gas and hightailing it out of there.

The backseat was a little too cozy. I shifted on Jaxson's lap, my cheeks burning from the heat or his proximity.

All the men of Eagle Tactical were eye candy. To be thrust in the backseat on Jaxson's lap and practically sandwiched in with Lincoln, wasn't so bad. Mason was growing on me too. He saved my life, even after I'd been an ass to him. Whether it was well-deserved was still debatable.

"Thanks, you guys," I whispered, my hands trembling.

Jaxson's warm, strong embrace wrapped around my waist, his fingers against my hips. Every part of me burned like I was on fire, but my heart ached, conflicted with doubt. He'd left after we'd been intimate without so much as a word goodbye. How could I forgive that transgression?

Should I forgive him?

He saved my life. I owed him my life, but did I owe him my heart?

"All in a day's work," Mason said. He gave me a faint smile. Did he no longer hate me? That had to be good news, especially if I saw Jaxson again.

Conflicted was the understatement of the century. Everything about Jaxson was perfect, but I was a mess. He deserved better, someone who made him happy.

He had a daughter, and then there was Emma.

The guys laughed and joked on the rest of the ride back to Eagle Tactical. I sat quietly, lost in my thoughts and the heat of the moment between Jaxson and myself. His lap was warm, comfortable, his embrace even more magical.

I whimpered, disappointed when we arrived, and I needed to climb out of the truck. I had thought no one heard me, but Jaxson raised an inquisitive eyebrow.

I shut my lips fast and glanced away, humiliated.

The guys all piled out of the truck.

"I need a ride to my vehicle," Lincoln said.

"Ariella and I need a ride back to my house," Jaxson said, already deciding that I was going with him.

I wasn't sure where I was going or what would happen next. I didn't have a house. Everything had burned in the disaster. I still had a date with thugs who wanted four million dollars that I'd missed and a cell phone that had been smashed in the fight at the resort.

My life was a mess.

"Lincoln, I'll give you a ride if you're buying me dinner," Aiden joked.

"Fine. Never a dull moment or a day off," Lincoln said.

Declan hurried over toward Jaxson and me. He shoved his hand into his coat pocket, retrieving a smartphone. "A small present. You can thank Jaxson later," Declan said with a wink. He handed me the phone. My mouth practically hit the floor.

"What are you—I don't understand," I said. My fingers grazed over the crystal screen. It appeared brand new. There were no scratches or scuffs, pristine condition. It was better than my flip phone.

"When you mentioned your cell phone had been destroyed earlier, I texted and asked him to set you up with a new phone. He also made sure that no one else can trace your whereabouts. Other than us," Jaxson said. He laughed.

I wasn't sure if he was joking or not. I didn't care. "Thank you," I said to both men. They'd saved my life. If they wanted to implant a tracker on me or put one in my phone, I was at their mercy. I owed them.

Declan gestured at the phone in my hand. "We tied it to your recent phone plan. It's already active, and anyone who needs to get ahold of you will be able to."

Mason hurried over to us. "Do you still need a ride home?"

Jaxson pulled me tighter against him. The wind outside whipped through the air, stinging my cheeks, but his proximity warmed me. "Yes, we both could use a ride back to my place."

I shuffled my feet and shoved my hands into my coat pockets. Jaxson's scent surrounded me, especially on his coat. He had to be freezing, but he hid it rather well. Did he always pretend to be the tough guy?

"Follow me," Mason said, hurrying to his truck.

Jaxson grabbed my arm, linking ours together as he walked me to Mason's truck and opened the back door for me.

I slid into the backseat, the leather chilly against my bottom, forcing an unwanted shiver. I had no home to return to, but if Jaxson insisted I go back with him, I would not say no.

I didn't want to be alone. Not until I knew I wasn't in any further danger.

Jaxson shut the door for me and climbed into the front seat. Mason started the truck and pulled out of the lot.

"Drop off Ariella at my house, then I want to make a stop, just you and me," Jaxson said.

Where did they plan to go after dropping me off? I relaxed in the backseat, staring out the window as we headed up the mountain pass. I pulled the new phone from my pocket, my finger scrolling through the contents he'd been able to retrieve off the cloud, including my contacts.

I had several missed calls and a few text messages from Emma asking me where I was and if everything was okay. I'd call her back tonight when I had a few minutes alone.

I checked my voice messages, my stomach in knots when I heard my boss, Bridget Sanders from the Blue Sky Resort, fire me. "Shit."

"What's that?" Mason asked. He glanced at me in the rearview mirror.

My cheeks burned. Jaxson wasn't happy when I'd cursed in front of Izzie. It was a nasty habit I had trouble breaking.

"I just got fired from my job." I deleted the message and shut off the screen for my phone, pushing the button on the side to put it into silent mode. I didn't want to hear from anyone else. My mood turned sour.

"I can't believe they fired you," Jaxson said.

Mason's gaze met mine again, his focus back on the road a moment later. "Wait. They likely don't know what happened, that you were kidnapped and unable to get to work. You can't fault them for being in the dark. I'm sure if you talk with your boss, you can have your old job back."

I didn't even care about that stupid place or the job. The money was crap pay, but it was employment. "Doubtful. They fired me because, according to them, I lied on my resume since I didn't disclose my married name or my previous employer." I ran my fingers through my unkempt hair, tugging at the strands with a groan. "In her words, I'm too much of a liability."

Mason and Jaxson exchanged a silent glance.

"It never ends," I seethed. My fingers dug into the leather seat. As if that was the worst of my problems. "Those men will be looking for their money." I'd never made the drop at sundown.

Jaxson shifted in the passenger seat and turned around to face me. "You're under our protection. We plan on making that clear."

CHAPTER TWENTY-FOUR

JAXSON

My blood boiled from hearing that Ariella had been fired from the resort.

She was too good for them, overqualified to be cleaning toilets and changing bed sheets.

"I'm under your protection?" Ariella's soft whisper caught in her throat. I almost couldn't hear her, but I strained to listen to every word.

"Of course." Didn't she realize how much she meant to me already? I cared deeply for a woman who held a closet of secrets. Would she ever let me inside?

Declan had texted Lincoln and me the information he'd pulled from the resort. The surveillance he acquired had taken no time to identify the two men who had attacked Ariella at the resort.

They were commonly referred to as 'off-gridders' living on the outskirts of town together in a commune.

I knew a few of them through my work with Eagle Tactical. They were usually harmless, feared authority, and were reclusive individuals who avoided anyone who wasn't one of them.

In the simplest of terms, they were shady.

Why had they gone after Ariella?

Had they been victims in the Ponzi scheme as well?

We still didn't have all the answers, and while it looked like her ex-husband may not have been rightfully convicted, the evidence still pointed to him.

Had the C.I.A. set him up? Had they intended to set up Ariella as well, and she'd got away with a decent lawyer?

Mason turned down the road for my house. "I'm going to walk her inside," I said. Mason left the engine running as I hopped out from the truck the moment he pulled to a standstill.

I opened the back door of the truck for Ariella and offered her my hand. Her eyes fell on the snow and slush as she climbed out of the truck.

I held her close and could smell the smoke from the fire on her clothes and skin. It tickled my nose. I probably needed a shower too.

"Come on inside." I ushered her to my front door, unlocked the deadbolt, disarmed the alarm, and led her inside.

She slipped off her winter boots first and then my jacket, handing it to me. "Thank you for this," she said.

The energy I'd harbored had me forgetting how cold it had been outside, how my fingers were numb. I slipped on the coat, smelling a mix of her womanly scent and smoke mingled together.

Skylar hurried down the stairs and stopped midway, her hand hovering on the railing. "Is everything okay?"

"Yes. Thank you for keeping an eye on Izzie. Ariella will be staying with us." I didn't elaborate for how long. It wasn't something we'd discussed, but the obvious fact her house was a pile of ash showed it wouldn't be a few short days. "Can you show her to my bedroom for a fresh change of clothes? She may want to shower and get cleaned up. I'm sure you're familiar with where the linens are located."

Skylar had stayed over enough times that she knew her way around my house.

"I'll show her around," Skylar said.

"Thank you," Ariella said. With quiet steps, she approached the bottom stair and turned around, glancing over her shoulder at me. "I'll be here when you get back."

"I expect nothing less. I'll set the alarm. Don't open the door for anyone, is that understood?"

"Yes," they both said in unison.

I wanted to pull Ariella into my arms, kiss the pain away, the worry and doubt she had etched to her face. Instead, I armed the alarm and rushed out the front door, locking it with my key.

Mason sat in the truck, his fingers strumming the steering wheel. The bone-tingling chill licked my spine. I shivered and jogged to the truck.

"Ready to kick some ass?"

"Let's hope it doesn't come to that."

Mason reversed our course and headed back to the mountain pass.

We headed another mile north, and then we took a sharp left on a snow-covered trail, a bit too narrow for the truck.

Thin branches walloped the truck while we drove through the thicket of trees. Mason didn't seem the least bit annoyed by it. Had it been my truck, I'd have preferred a walk in the cold over scratching the paint on the exterior.

Mason shot me a look as we climbed out. It was just the two of us. We didn't come for a fight; we came with a warning.

With my hand on my holster and Mason at my side, we walked along the snow-covered stone driveway.

My boots crunched the snow, the slush packed down from multiple vehicles that drove over the area.

The commune housed more families than I probably was aware of. I knew of at least six who lived in the complex, but there were far more whom I didn't know.

The outside structure was made of wood, and from first glance, the building appeared large and stylish, a lodge in the middle of the forest. It had probably been built for a wealthy family several generations ago. It had been stripped down to its bare essentials, which didn't include running water, heat, or electricity.

Ariella had thought her cabin was sparse.

While the off-gridders had a large plot of land and shelter over their heads, there wasn't much inside. It was as basic as it could be.

I'd been inside occasionally and hoped today wasn't one of the times. The interior always smelled musty and foul, like tent city in the summer, wreaking of urine.

By the front entrance, which was always wide open, the door abandoned, probably destroyed and never replaced, stood a guard with a shotgun.

"It's Jayden," I said, keeping my voice down.

"How do you want to play this?" Mason asked, glancing at me out of the corner of his eye.

"Tight, but cautious. He's not the same man he was back in the old days."

We'd served in the military with Jayden. He'd been a buddy of ours, but somewhere along the way after the war, we'd lost contact. He had guarded the compound. I always thought he'd be on the right side of the law, but he refused an invitation to come work with us at Eagle Tactical.

We never understood why.

I approached Jayden first with Mason right at my hip, defending me.

Jayden didn't budge from his position at the door, standing guard. "What brings the Eagle Tactical guys out here today?" His eyes raked over me, landing on my holster. "You came armed?"

"Don't I always?" I didn't go anywhere without packing heat. "We're here to speak to Ian Connor and Seth Rogers."

One glance at the surveillance footage sent to my phone, and I knew these men. They were scumbags, but they weren't blackmailers or extortionists. The fact they roughed up a girl, Ariella, wasn't their typical M.O..

Jayden shifted his weight on his feet. I took that as a sign of discomfort, although his face appeared blank and emotionless. "What about?"

"Your guys threatened and assaulted one of mine," I seethed

between clenched teeth. Stepping closer, one hand balled into a fist, with the other I pulled my weapon and shoved it into Jayden's face.

"You'll let me inside." I was tired of his childish games and antics.

Mason cleared his throat and rested a hand on my arm. "Jaxson." His tone warned me to cool off or calm down.

We weren't going in for a firefight, but I damn well would bring them one if they so much as looked at Ariella again.

"Is this official Eagle Tactical business?" Jayden asked.

I lowered my gun, shoved my shoulder into Jayden's chest, and knocked him backward and into the doorjamb.

I didn't wait for an invitation. I plowed through the front entrance. "Ian Connor! Seth Rogers!" I shouted, letting the bastards know I had come for them.

Mason was at my side. "You sure you want to do that?" he whispered.

I wouldn't let anything happen to *my* girl. We would be quick, in and out, and then we could go home and call it a night. I'd throw myself in the shower, let the scalding water rush down my body, and wipe away my sins—every one of them.

Ian strolled around the corner, his hands shoved into his jeans, shoulders slumped. "What brings you boys to my neck of the woods?" he asked. He edged closer, just out of my reach, taking his sweet ass time.

My eyes narrowed like a hawk, my focus solely on Ian. "The fact you haven't learned how to treat a lady with respect," I said.

I shoved my gun into its holster on my hip and grabbed him by the shoulders, his t-shirt, thin and threadbare, torn. Forcing his knees to the ground, I shoved my leg hard upwards. My knee caught his chin as I barreled into him. As I pinned him to the floor, he wrestled to get away from me.

"Get off me!" Ian scurried to escape my clutches.

"What? Don't enjoy being manhandled? You should keep your filthy paws off my girl," I growled at him. He kicked me, sweeping his feet out to knock me on my ass. "Bastard."

"Me? You come to my home," he said, gasping for breath, "and attack me!"

I ignored the throes of people standing around watching us in the center fighting like wild animals.

He deserved a good ass-kicking for what he did to Ariella. I wanted him to remember the pain.

"You need a hand?" Mason asked. He folded his arms across his chest and towered above.

He seemed to enjoy the show. "Just keep an eye out for the other asshole," I muttered.

"Already watching him," Mason said. His eyes were on him, and I glanced across the large room and laid eyes on Seth. Mason stalked across the room, and I didn't have to watch to know he'd take care of him in the same way I was looking after Ian.

I pulled back my fist, landing a blow to Ian's face, stunning him momentarily. Standing up, I would not lie around when a man's ass needed kicking.

"What girl would ever want the likes of you?" Ian asked, getting to his feet. He lunged for me, headfirst into my stomach, knocking me backward. I tripped over someone who stuck out their foot, giving Ian a hand.

"Fucking bastards," I growled and planted my hands on the floor to stand when I realized my hip was ice cold, my gun gone.

I glanced over my shoulder to find the barrel of my weapon staring back at me, in the hands of Emma Foster, my daughter's biological mother. The same woman I told to leave town.

What the fuck was she doing here?

"Get up." Emma held my weapon. Her hands trembled as she pointed it at me.

Slowly and cautiously, I stood, careful not to make any sudden movements. "Give me the gun." I held out my hand, waiting for her to relinquish control over the weapon.

The brunette with brown eyes who had charmed me once would not do it ever again.

"No." She refused to lower the barrel of my gun.

So be it. I would not stand there and wait for her to shoot me, accident or otherwise. On second thought, it might not be an accident if she had returned to Breckenridge to get Izzie back.

"Last chance, Emma, or I'm about to break your finger." No one said I didn't warn her.

She huffed under her breath. "I have the gun, Jaxson," she said, reminding me she thought she was in power.

I had military and survival training. With a sloth grip, four fingers, and not using my thumb, I slammed my right hand against her wrist. With my left hand, I spun the gun from her palm and turned it toward her.

"Motherfucker!" she screamed, her thumb on the trigger forcing her digit to break.

"I warned you."

Behind me, Jayden's overpowering presence resonated, his footfalls not the least bit silent. "Back off!" I shouted.

Jayden held up his hands. "Just checking on the girl." He wrapped an arm around her shoulders, walking her away from the crowd to take care of her.

Anger soared within me. What was Emma doing at the commune? Did she live here now?

"You know Emma?" Ian asked, a smile on his face, laughing under his breath and wincing after getting the shit kicked out of him. "Of course, you do. We all do. The girl gives magnificent head."

I rammed into him headfirst, tossing him to the ground, scuffling on the floor. My fists slammed against his chest, one punch after another.

I wasn't happy with Emma, but I liked even less the way Ian spoke about her. "You will learn to respect women."

"I respect them. I respect letting them ride me," he said and sneered.

Ian knew just what to say to get under my skin. He slammed his forehead upward against mine, knocking me back for a moment and landing a blow to my left cheek.

I hadn't expected him to make a good play.

Fuck, that hurt.

Snickering, he pushed me off him.

I stumbled backward. My head throbbed, and while I was prepared to kick his scrawny ass until he bled to death, that wasn't why we came.

We were here with a warning and a firm message that she was under our protection. "Ariella is off-limits. You and your buddies stay away, or you're going to deal with Eagle Tactical." I made my voice loud and clear for all the off-gridders in the complex to know that if they messed with her, they messed with all of us.

"Fine, keep your tight little Ariella. We've got Emma for a good time," Ian said and winked. He was trying to get a rise out of me.

I threw another punch and landed on his chest. I slammed my knee upwards into his groin and watched him double over, collapsing onto the ground. I stared down, waiting for him to get up.

He groaned and cried like a little baby. He was definitely alive, just discovering the burn of a good ass-kicking.

Mason had Seth in a headlock, the off-gridder on his knees. "How'd you find out who Ariella was?"

Seth's hands flailed and Mason loosened his grip to let him answer.

He coughed and gasped for air, bent forward, his hands on his knees. "At Lumberjack Shack, Ian and I overheard two guys talking about her, how she was loaded. Emma mentioned getting drinks with her friend Ariella. We put two and two together. How many Ariellas could there possibly be in Breckenridge? A google search turned up the rest of the information. We thought it'd be an easy payday and a fresh start for all of us."

Mason slowly eased up and let go, tossing the thug on the ground.

I took the opportunity to step forward and crouched down, fisting his shirt in my hand, snarling at him. I ignored his stench, the smell of piss and filth that burned my nostrils. "Ariella is under our protection. You so much as look at her the wrong way and you'll find yourself in an unmarked grave."

"You've been warned," Mason said, standing beside me. "Next time we won't be so nice." He patted me on the back, a silent message that we were done and to let the asshole go.

The crowd dispersed, no longer interested if a fight wasn't ensuing. I didn't see Emma. Jayden probably was tending to her wounds.

With our message made loud and clear, we left the compound and headed for the truck.

"Listen," I said, climbing into the vehicle. "With what happened tonight, the fact Emma was at the compound, do me a favor, and let's not say anything to Ariella. The two of them are friends, and I don't want to further complicate matters."

Ariella was delicate, and while she'd been through hell, I didn't want her questioning Emma's motives for being her friend. That would be my job to deal with, not hers.

Mason started the engine and stomped on the gas. "It's not like I have coffee with her every morning. Speaking of which, I'm surprised you didn't bring up that we could use someone like her on our team, ex-C.I.A., surveillance skills, and she needs a job."

"It had crossed my mind." I wasn't sure the guys would go for it. We were always looking for talent and people we could trust.

"I'll talk to the others, but I think we could make it work under one condition."

There it was, the catch that made my stomach sink. "Which is?"

Deep down, I already knew the answer. We were equal owners, the guys and I, in Eagle Tactical. She would be our employee.

"You two have to keep it professional. If she works for us, then you're her boss. You can't sleep with her and not expect matters to get more complicated than they already are at the moment," Mason said.

My jaw tightened. I didn't like his stupid rules, but he was sensible. I needed to think about the team and Ariella, what was best for them, not myself. "Just friends."

Could I let her go because it was in her best interest? The thought tore me up inside. But a relationship was far more dangerous. She would be in the office, I would be in the field, and we couldn't let our feelings impede our missions.

Mistakes can cost lives.

Distractions were deadly.

"Right." Mason shot me a look as we turned down the road for my house. "Can you keep in it your pants while the two of you are living together?"

CHAPTER TWENTY-FIVE

ARIELLA

Every inch of the house smelled of Jaxson, musky and intense. It tickled my nose.

The giant glass windows overlooked the forest, and as night fell, there wasn't much to see.

Could anyone who traveled up the mountain see us?

Jaxson hadn't warned me to close the curtains or shut off the lights. He'd set the alarm for the house. We would be safe. I had to believe that, or I would never be able to settle down.

"Come on," Skylar said, stomping up the stairs.

"Daddy?" Izzie came around the corner. Her eyes lit up when they landed on me. She squealed and jumped, her eyes wide and cheeks rosy. As she threw her arms in the air for me to hold her, I bent down, hugging her to my chest.

"Your daddy will be home soon," I said. She squeezed me tight, my body melting under her innocence.

Her world was protected because of Jaxson. She had no idea the dangers of evil and what horrors men were capable of.

"Play with me?" Her hand latched tight onto mine, dragging me toward her room. I needed to shower, get dressed, and clean up, but I couldn't say no to her.

Skylar stepped between us, breaking Izzie's hold on my hand. "Isabella, I'm sure Ariel has better things to do with her time."

"Are you the Little Mermaid?" Izzie began jumping up and down, clapping her hands together. "Can you sing? Do you have a tail?"

Great. Now I had to disappoint a toddler. My singing voice was atrocious, and I definitely did not have a mermaid's tail, or any tail, for that matter. "I don't sing as beautifully as Ariel," I said. I turned to Skylar. "My name is Ariella."

"Sure, whatever." She shrugged and shot me a look. "That's what I said."

"It's not." I pinched the bridge of my nose, too exhausted to argue. Dropping my hand, I folded my arms across my chest.

What was her problem?

The glint in Izzie's eyes was enough to settle my nerves and soothe my boiling blood. I bent down to Isabella's level, making eye contact with her. "I would love to see your room."

Izzie snatched my hand and dragged me down the hall. She rushed inside her bedroom and stood waiting for me to join her.

I flipped on the light and was met with an abundance of mermaids all over her bedroom. I covered my mouth with my hand to keep the giddy grin from my lips and tried not to burst out laughing.

The girl was obsessed with mermaids.

The walls were painted cerulean with white and pink foam bubbles. Near the window, a mermaid's tail sparkled and shined, with glittery hues of teal and a thin silver outline. "Did your dad paint your bedroom?"

Impressive would have been an understatement. Someone with a lot of artistic talent made her bedroom come to life.

"Look up!" Izzie pointed at the stars, and she smacked off the lights, revealing they glowed in the dark along with the outline of the mermaid's tail.

"Wow."

Skylar hit the light switch and stood in the doorway. "It is something else," she said. "A bit too girly for my taste."

"Then I guess it's a good thing it isn't your bedroom." I probably should have held my tongue, but I was not too fond of the way Skylar spoke about Izzie, let alone behaved as if she couldn't understand. Isabella may have been three, but kids were smart. They picked up on everything.

"You ready for the tour?" Skylar picked at her nails, staring down at her hands.

"I'll be back," I said to Izzie and followed Skylar down the hall for the briefest tour possible. She opened Jaxson's door to his bedroom. "Dresser is in the corner. The bathroom door is next to it. I'll grab you a towel."

"Thank you."

She brushed past me and knocked into my shoulder. I bit back a yelp of pain.

The woman didn't know what I'd been through, and I wasn't about to confide in her.

She hated me. I wasn't sure why.

Was it because I slept with Jaxson? Did she know? Why did she care?

The bedroom dark, I flipped on the light, and a warm ambient glow cast from the ceiling fan and light overhead.

His king-sized mattress was pressed against the wall near the window, the bed made, the comforter perfectly centered with the pillows fluffed. I wanted to lie down, curl up under the sheets, but I couldn't invite myself into his bed.

He'd offered for me to stay at his house, not in his bedroom.

My teeth tugged on my bottom lip. Why had Jaxson run off without so much as a goodbye last night?

No note. No phone call or text. I couldn't think about that right now.

My eyelids drooped, exhausted from the day's events.

I tugged on the dresser's handle, the oak, heavy, robust. The rails glided open, and the top drawer revealed to me his boxers and socks.

This felt far too intimate after one night together that hadn't resulted in even waking up alongside one another. I slammed the drawer and tried the second one down, grabbing a dark red university t-shirt with the words *Montana Grizzlies*.

With my fist tight on the shirt, I brought it to my face. The soft material caressed my cheek as I drank in *his* scent. Although his room smelled uniquely of him, the t-shirt was muskier, stronger, and I clung to it.

Skylar strolled down the hall, and with the sound of her footsteps approaching, I lowered the soft tee.

She threw a fluffy mint bath towel at me.

"Thanks." I seized the linen, surprised she didn't bring me a hand towel or washcloth instead and tell me that's all there was clean.

With the softness of the towel in my palm, my grip tight on his tee, the dam nearly broke. No one would see my downfall, certainly not a girl I hadn't spent over five minutes with who wanted nothing to do with me.

I yanked open a second drawer with two pairs of sweatpants and grabbed the ones on top before fleeing to the master bathroom. I flipped the light and slammed the door shut behind me.

My chest seized and clenched tight. It was like I was drowning, the air not finding its way fast enough inside my lungs.

I stripped down, my clothes in a pile, and stumbled to the bathtub. The room spun, my feet unsteady beneath me. The wall held me up, my back to it, my breathing long yet shallow, gasping for air.

Blinding dots peppered my vision. I reached my arm into the tub, pushed past the curtain, and started the shower.

The only thing that mattered was getting every speck of dirt and grime from those bastards off my body.

I rubbed at my arms, scrubbing with my hands outside of the tub. The water was tepid. I cranked it hotter.

I needed to erase everything, destroy the filth burned to my flesh.

With my palm up, I tested the water, pleased that it was hot.

Steam covered the mirror, and I stepped into the tub. The shower rained down.

With white knuckles, I snatched the bar of soap, scrubbing it over my skin. I needed to rid myself of their filth. I repeatedly washed—the heat from the shower leaving a blush over my body.

It wasn't enough. The dirt wouldn't disappear. The steam in the bathroom clouded my vision as it swirled in the air. Smoke.

The soap skidded out of my grasp to the tub. I dove for the slippery bar, my knees embracing the tub, the scorching water pouring over my head, gliding down my back.

My hands trembled. Tears flooded and broke free, the shower mixed with my defeat slipping down the drain. I pulled my knees to my chest. The water pounded against me, hot rain against my body.

The smell of smoke wafted in with an icy gust. I shuddered and buried my face into my bent knees.

A cool rush of air caressed my skin, causing goosebumps to cover me under the spray of water. I felt a shadow, a body standing above me. The sobs racked my body.

"Freckles." While I could hear his voice, I didn't move.

The shower shut off and a warm, fluffy towel wrapped around my shoulders.

I turned my head slightly to see him, to acknowledge he was real, and I wasn't hallucinating.

"Let's get you out of the shower," he whispered. His strong voice echoed in the bathroom but didn't pull me from being locked up inside my head. "The water is freezing."

I hadn't noticed when the temperature grew cool. My teeth chattered.

Drained of energy, I couldn't speak. I had no ability to move other than the tremors that I had no control over.

Tears wept from my soul and slid down my cheeks. The warm towel no longer offered as much comfort as the heat from the shower dissipated.

Jaxson scooped me up and lifted me into his arms.

I wanted to wrap my arms around his neck but that required

more strength than I had in me. My eyelids drooped as I rested my wet head against his shirt.

He smelled of smoke and it tickled my nose as I breathed in his scent.

"I need to dry you off."

He held me tight in his embrace and gently guided me to stand in front of him, my feet on the warm, shaggy bath rug. I stared at the maroon which matched the color of my skin. Bruised, battered, beaten.

His touch was light and gentle, and he steadied me as I swayed. One hand remained planted on my hip, the other drying me off with the mint-colored towel.

I wanted to ask why he had green towels and red rugs. It felt odd but the words didn't reach my lips. I was stuck inside my head.

Each stroke of the towel and I swayed. "Okay, we're almost done. I'm going to put this on you and then tuck you into bed," Jaxson said, explaining everything he did.

He sat at the edge of the toilet and brought me closer. Each step I took seemed to take minutes in my head, tunnel vision, a nasty side effect I'd experienced time and time again.

Nudging me closer to the toilet, his legs straddled me, keeping me upright while he guided his university t-shirt over my arms and head, letting it fall around my waist. "I think pants are too much for you right now." He stared at me.

What was he thinking?

Was he repulsed by my inability to do anything but collapse?

CHAPTER TWENTY-SIX

JAXSON

I lifted Ariella into my arms and carried her from the bathroom to my bed. With a gentle finesse, I laid her down on the mattress and helped guide her under the warm downy blankets.

"Freckles?" My stomach clenched, concern in my tone. "Are you all right?"

She wasn't all right. Only an idiot would have asked such a stupid question.

I climbed atop the covers. My body nestled tight beside hers. She lay calm, motionless on her back, cocooned under the comforter and bedsheets.

I breathed in her scent and shut my eyes, smiling and torn up inside.

How was I going to handle letting her live under my roof but keeping things platonic? I never intended for last night to be a one-night stand but if we couldn't be together—I didn't want to finish that thought.

I kissed her cheek and stood.

Quiet as a mouse, I slipped out of the bedroom, grabbed a towel from the linen closet and hurried back to avoid Skylar.

I didn't want to deal with her tonight. I didn't have it in me to answer her questions or see the disapproving look cross her face.

I withdrew my phone from my pocket. A group text popped up for me on the main screen.

My vision glazed over the display, the letters blurring together. I'd read it later.

I stripped down and tossed my filthy clothes into the hamper. Doing my best to keep the noise down, I meandered into the bathroom and left the door slightly ajar. If she needed me, I wanted to hear her. I started the shower and was pleased the water had heated again.

Scrubbing the smoke, blood, and dried remnants of grime down the drain, I let the water immerse me as if nothing else existed.

One hand rested against the cold tile as water pounded my face, my chest, soaking me inside and out. My eyes burned and I shoved my face back under the hot spray. I rubbed my eyes and finished my shower.

When I was done, I slipped on a pair of boxers and sat at the edge of the mattress and reached for my phone.

I wouldn't be able to sleep without knowing what was sent.

Lincoln had sent a new text: *If you can keep it in your pants, she's hired. No fraternizing with the subordinate.*

The text had been sent to all of Eagle Tactical. Obviously, the guys had discussed hiring her. I assumed Mason had been behind it after our discussion in the truck earlier.

Relief should have washed over me, but it didn't.

Conflicted, hurt, the desire pent up inside of me would have to be squashed. We had to keep things platonic.

They were right, it would be for the best. If she would be living under my roof, we couldn't start a relationship and work together, not if I was her boss.

This was about *her*. What was in her best interest. Ariella came first.

I climbed under the covers beside her. It would be the last night we could share a bed.

Tomorrow, I would have to show her to the guest room, but tonight, I would savor the warmth of her body and the sweet smell of her scent on my pillow.

When I wrapped an arm around her waist, Ariella didn't stir. She was serene in slumber and I hoped her dreams offered her peace.

"Daddy!" Izzie's squeal brought me out of dreamland.

Sunlight poured in through the curtains. I buried my face in the pillow. Dawn broke. I wasn't ready to face the day, but my little munchkin made sure I was made aware of the hour.

I rubbed the sleep from my eyes and realized Ariella lay asleep beside me in bed. I held up my finger to my lips to indicate to Isabella to be quiet.

Climbing out of bed, the cold floor caused a shiver to run down my spine.

Izzie's eyes were wide and bright. I followed her out of the bedroom and closed the door, holding one hand on the wood to keep it from banging shut, steadying it.

She grasped onto my hand and I lifted my little munchkin into my arms, carrying her down the stairs.

"Breakfast?"

"Yes, I will make you breakfast," I rasped.

I tried to keep quiet not to wake Skylar, either.

When did she plan on leaving?

Izzie squirmed out of my arms and I sat her on the counter. "Pancakes, Daddy?"

Opening the pantry, I pulled out the pancake mix along with a bowl. "Yes, I can make pancakes for you this morning." I kissed her cheek.

Soft footsteps trampled down the back stairs. If I knew Skylar, she would sleep all afternoon. While she'd been up early yesterday to help with Izzie, if she didn't have to, she wouldn't.

"Good morning," Ariella's soft voice greeted. It was music to my ears.

I could get used to this, but things had to change. "Morning," I said. My tone came out gruffer than I intended.

She quirked an eyebrow and I offered her a smile, not wanting to alarm her.

"You look better."

Her gaze fell to the floor, a blush spread across her cheeks. Ariella nibbled on her bottom lip, avoiding my stare.

I wanted to reach out and guide her chin up to see her stare.

The guys were right, I had to keep things platonic between us. "I have some good news. Do you want to take a seat?"

She perched herself on the stool at the counter, seated near Izzie. She emitted a soft sigh before meeting my gaze.

I measured the pancake mix, pouring it into the bowl and then measured out the water.

"Sure," she said, making herself comfortable. When I didn't press about last night and her curled up in the shower, she seemed to relax.

Yanking the drawer open, I fished out a spoon and placed it on the counter. "I spoke with the guys last night." I had technically spoken with Mason, and Lincoln had responded on behalf of the team, but I didn't feel the need to elaborate.

"Oh?" She wiped her palms on her bare legs.

My tee shirt swept down to her knees much like a nightgown. She swam in my shirt and realizing there were no panties underneath made my heart race.

The kitchen seemed warmer than usual. I had Ariella to thank for that; my body responded to her sexiness and all she did was sit there innocently on the stool, listening to me.

"Yes. We'd like to invite you to work for Eagle Tactical," I said.

Ariella's eyes lit up. "Really?"

"Yes."

Isabella snatched the spoon from my grasp before I could stir the ingredients. She wanted to help.

"There are a few things we need to discuss, though, regarding your employment."

I let Izzie keep the spoon and pushed the bowl toward her. If she wanted to help, so be it. I could use all the help I could get, my stomach tensed.

My heart wouldn't stop pounding against my ribcage. Is that what Ariella felt every single day?

Her tongue swiped her top lip, and she rolled her lips tight between her mouth. "Yes?" The softest, most timid sound came from her mouth. Ariella sounded angelic and while I recognized that she had been with the C.I.A., I also understood she wasn't a field agent. Her responsibility with our team would be in the office, where she would be safe.

"I would like you to stay here, under my roof, at least until you get things settled." I didn't want her thinking that I was kicking her out or making her feel unwelcome with what I had to say next.

Her gaze went from me to Izzie. "Okay." After a beat, she glanced back at me. "Is that it?"

I wished that was all I had to say, but the guys were right. In order to protect Ariella, I had to put her first. "We need to keep things platonic between us. I'll be your boss at Eagle Tactical."

A rush of air expelled from her lips. Her face went ghostly pale. "Oh." She smiled, her lips tight, her eyes narrow. "Of course. That's fine. I wouldn't expect special treatment. It wouldn't be fair to your other employees."

She pushed herself off the stool and ran a hand through her unkempt hair.

"I should probably find something to wear. It's not appropriate for me to only be wearing a tee in front of my boss."

I didn't mind it, in fact I liked it a lot, but I had to let her go. "Feel free to borrow whatever you need from my dresser. We can go into town later today and go shopping for new clothes."

She rubbed her eyes.

I prayed she wasn't about to cry.

Shuffling her feet, she pointed behind herself at the stairs where she'd come down from minutes earlier. "I'll grab something from your dresser and then get out of your hair."

Ariella spun around to run away from me, but I wouldn't have it.

I stepped away from the counter and grabbed her by the waist. Turning her around to face me, one hand poised on her hip, the other in her hair.

I wanted to kiss her, to pull her body tight against mine and slide my knee between her thighs. Staring into her eyes, our breathing matched, heavy and deep.

"I thought we were going to keep things professional?" Ariella whispered, breathless.

I hated the guys. How easily I let them come between the woman I yearned for and my job. They were doing this to protect all of us, but why did it feel like hell?

Why did I have to choose? I could have both, just not in the way I desired.

Need poured through me, overtook every ounce of power inside of me.

I leaned down, demanding one last taste, a kiss, a rough fuck if she let me have her.

Ariella guided a hand to my chest. My heart pounded against her palm. "We can't do this. I need the job, I want to work for Eagle Tactical," she said, staring up at me with those powerful olive eyes. "It's a dream come true."

I wanted to be part of her dreams, the dirty kind that involved having my way with her on my desk. "You're always the sensible one," I said, unable to break my gaze away from her.

Somewhere between finding her on the road and saving her life, I'd fallen for her, hard.

BONUS TEASER FOR STEALTH: MASON

Hazel

Had I known what this morning would bring, I would have run.

"Come with me." Nikolai yanked me by the arm, his grip marking my skin, leaving behind a lasting bruise.

"No." I shrugged out of his grasp. "Get off me. I'm not going anywhere with you." Just because we were bound by blood didn't mean I had to abide by *his* rules.

Nikolai Agron, the head of the Russian mob, was my jerk of a stepbrother.

"The deal has already been made. He'll take care of you and you'll give him children."

"I'm not marrying anyone because you arranged it." What century did he think we lived in? Had he lost his mind?

"You will do as you're told, Hazel." The way he said my name sent a shiver down my spine.

He towered above me and gripped my hair. Yanking my long curls, he brought my face to his. "You will marry Franco Ivanov and you will obey him."

I scoffed at his idea of marriage and the moment he loosened his grip on my hair, I spat in his face. "I'm not yours to give away or sell." He backhanded me across the face.

"I own you! Don't you ever forget that, little sister."

STEALTH: MASON

EAGLE TACTICAL BOOK TWO

CHAPTER ONE

Hazel

I didn't dare gaze into the eyes of the man who bought me. Thanks to my stepbrother, Nikolai, I belonged to Franco, his second in command in the mafia.

"Next week, you'll be my bride," Franco said, his teeth yellowing and crooked.

He grabbed my jaw and yanked my face closer to his for a kiss. His breath smelled of vomit. My stomach recoiled.

We stood outside his black sedan, the door open.

I was to go with him. I'd sooner starve myself to death. That was still a possibility after I went with the man to whom I was engaged to marry.

Bile rose to my throat, and I swallowed the burning acid as it slid back down. I kept my mouth sealed shut, but it didn't stop him from planting his thick, dry lips against mine. His tongue pushed at my mouth, rough and forceful, but I refused to grant him access.

The scum-sucking vermin could kiss the soles of my feet.

I wanted to kill my stepbrother but not before I took out Franco.

Franco's thick hand palmed my hair, his fingers tangled in my locks before he yanked hard, bringing my face to his. "Other girls should be as lucky as you."

My stepbrother was nowhere to be found. Typical. Sell me and move on, like I meant nothing to him. I was a piece of property. That was it.

Franco shoved me toward the back door of his sedan.

Oh hell, no. I had the upper hand now, with only Franco and his driver.

If I made it to his house, who knew the danger that awaited, how many men I'd be forced to fight or what other security measures would exist.

"Get off me!" I slammed my elbow into his stomach and stomped on his toes before kneeing him in the crotch.

His driver lifted his gun, pointing it at my head.

"Please, you'd be doing me a favor," I said. I'd sooner die than marry *him.*

"Don't shoot her!" Franco pushed the gun away from the driver, lowering the barrel.

I pulled back my fist, landing another blow, this one to Franco's face before his hand yanked my hair and slammed my head into the side of the car.

The world spun and nausea swept over me.

He shoved my body into the back of the vehicle, slammed the door shut, and stomped around to the front passenger side.

"Don't puke on the interior, bitch."

The car engine started.

My vision blurred, but I felt for the door handle and gave it a hard pull. Damn child safety locks. It didn't open.

Roar.

I flew back against the seat as the driver slammed on the gas. The tires squealed, and my nose tickled with the scent of burning rubber.

The skyline grew smaller in the distance as we tore out of the city.

Where the hell were we going? Where did Franco live?

"Where are you taking me?" I rubbed my eyes, confused and

tired. The blurred vision was getting better, but I still felt like I'd been run over by a car.

"Home sweet home, darling. We're going to Russia."

Russia wasn't my home.

I'd never been out of the country.

My fingers stroked the white gold locket against my neck, the only token of my mother that I had left, a gift from my deceased father.

I wasn't going to Russia or any other country with Franco.

I shoved my hand into my pocket and retrieved my cell phone. I turned it on silent and sent out a text requesting help.

I didn't know how long I had until the flight or until they searched me. I'd been foolish not to bring a knife or, at the very least, mace, some kind of weapon to defend myself.

I had memorized Mason's number, having stalked him online. It had been years since we'd seen each other.

We'd gone to boarding school together. He had joined the army after high school, and I had been sent to live with my father.

It was no secret he worked for the security firm Eagle Tactical. I couldn't call them. It would be too risky.

I hoped that their business line could receive texts. I didn't have Mason's personal number; it appeared to be unlisted.

Mason, I need your help. Please track my phone and come for me. I wouldn't ask if this wasn't life or death—my death. Hazel

It was short and to the point. It was all I could do. I hoped it would go through and he'd come for me.

CHAPTER TWO

ARIELLA

Sunlight filtered in through the skylight casting the kitchen in a warm golden tone.

The aroma of coffee filled the room, and I hurried to the pot, grabbed a cup, and poured myself a drink.

Izzie sat at the kitchen table eating a bowl of cereal. It was the quietest I'd ever seen her, except when she napped.

Jaxson clomped down the stairs, dressed and ready to go.

I still needed to shower, but I'd be quick. "Are we driving into work together?" I asked.

"No." His response was short, his tone cold, emotionless.

Had I done something to piss him off?

We hadn't talked about that night when he'd found me in the shower, curled up with water pounding over me. I'd been unable to move, shaken to the core. He'd dressed me, carried me to bed, and slept beside me.

It was the only night I'd slept in that bedroom. I was now delegated to the guest room, which I guess made sense.

We agreed that if he was going to be my boss, we had to keep things platonic.

That wasn't what I wanted, but I had mixed feelings. He hadn't stuck around after the one night we shared at my place before the fire burned my house to the ground. We also hadn't spoken about it, and now it seemed pointless to rehash a relationship that couldn't ever be.

I stared at him, the cup of coffee poised at my lips, two hands on my mug.

The tremors were under control, and while my house had burned down, I was able to get a prescription from the local doctor for the medications I needed for my battle with autonomic dysfunction. I was managing for the most part.

His cell phone rang and he grabbed it off the kitchen counter.

"Morning, Declan. What's up?" He waltzed into the living room for privacy, at least some semblance of it.

I sipped my coffee and sat down at the kitchen table across from Izzie. "Is that good?" I asked, trying to make polite conversation with a three-year-old.

It was my first week on the job, and Jaxson was buried in his office.

I wasn't sure if he was ignoring me or giving me space and not preferential treatment.

Lucy hadn't so much as acknowledged my existence or the fact that Eagle Tactical now employed me. While she was at the front desk at the building entrance, I was shoved at the breakroom table with my laptop plugged into the nearest outlet.

It was clear they had made room for me to join them, and I'd take what I could get, office or not. I probably was lucky I even had a computer to work on; the keyboard was faded and worn.

The hallway was fine, it was a place to work.

I could almost see Jaxson if I leaned back in my desk chair, which I kept doing, the chair squeaking.

Lucy glanced over her shoulder at me, glaring with narrow eyes and a sharp jaw.

So maybe we weren't going to be friends like Emma and I had become.

I was okay with that, as long as she didn't bury me under paperwork.

A message popped up on the screen.

Mason, I need your help. Please track my phone and come for me. I wouldn't ask if this wasn't life or death—my death. Hazel

Who was Hazel, and why was I getting her message?

I still wasn't that friendly with Mason. We'd come to an understanding, or maybe it was the fact my cabin burned down that I had forgiven him.

It wasn't his fault for the fire, and the anger that I held toward him for selling me that crappy place seemed stupid now. Plus, he hadn't kept me from getting employed and helped Jaxson with the off-gridders who had threatened me.

We were almost friends. Well, not quite. He didn't hate me, and I didn't despise him, at least not anymore.

I stood, and the chair squeaked.

Lucy spun around in her seat, eyes wide. "Do you mind? Some of us are trying to get work done!" she snapped.

I didn't have a ton to do, granted it was my first week, and no one had assigned me any surveillance or backgrounds to research. I held my tongue.

I didn't need a new enemy. I had enough of them from my past.

My boots clunked over the tile floor, and I sauntered over to Mason's office. I knocked on the open door, not wanting to barge in unannounced.

"Yes, Ariella?" Mason glanced up from his computer. "What can I do for you?"

He didn't sound thrilled that I was bothering him, but I needed to make sure the message wasn't a joke, and it was real.

"I need you to see something that popped up on my computer," I said. I didn't want to elaborate. I wasn't sure who Hazel was to him, if anyone at all, and the doors were all open. The guys could all hear our conversation. I was trying to be discreet, for his sake.

His attention that had been on me briefly returned to his computer, his right hand clicking and scrolling with the mouse. "Declan can help you if you're having computer troubles."

"You need to see this," I said. When he didn't glance up or get up, I tried again. I guess I did need to spell it out for him. "Do you know someone by the name of Hazel? It sounds like she's in trouble."

He leaped out of the chair like it was on fire and followed me to my desk. He hunched forward, reading the message that remained on my screen.

"So?" I asked.

He studied the message for longer than necessary before he folded his arms across his chest. "Track her phone from the text. You can do that, can't you?"

Apparently, it was rhetorical. Before I could answer, he gave off orders.

"Send me her coordinates. If she's near Chicago, like I think she is, then I'll call one of my buddies with the U.S. Marshal's office, Colton. He'll lend us a hand."

"Will do." I sat back down at the desk and opened up a new window as I started a backend trace from the phone number where the text originated. Once I finished that, I was able to ping its location off the cell towers. Sure enough, Chicago.

I texted Mason the information from within our private network.

"Send her a text back. Let her know to go along with it."

I had no idea what Mason was talking about, but I relayed the message via text. I opened up a second window as I accessed the surveillance cameras along the highway. The vehicle they were in was headed for O'Hare International Airport.

"Where are you going?" I said to myself as I watched the screen.

Footsteps thumped inside Mason's office, and then the door slammed abruptly. Had I been that loud? I opened my mouth to apologize, but it didn't happen.

Mason was on the phone with someone. I could hear his muffled, gruff voice through the wall. He was talking to someone, perhaps this person Colton whom he had mentioned earlier.

How would the U.S. Marshals be able to help?

What had Hazel gotten herself into?

Hopefully, it wasn't a hoax, but the look that crossed Mason's face when he'd read the message on my laptop—it had to be authentic and she was in danger.

I wanted to do more. I couldn't let it go. I opened up the text message window for Hazel and sent another reply.

Can you tell me what's going on?

Maybe I could offer more help if we had more information. They were heading to the airport. If I knew what flight, perhaps I could hack into the ticketing system and put them on the no-fly list.

Mason?

I swallowed the lump in my throat.

Yes.

I texted back a little too quickly. Hopefully, he wouldn't be upset that I lied. She wouldn't ever have to know. And if I could help, why shouldn't I try?

What's my favorite color?

Shit. How was I supposed to know that? Was this a trick question? Radio silence. I didn't answer. She didn't respond. I screwed up.

Mason swung open the office door and stepped into the hallway. "Quit sending texts to Hazel. I can see everything on your monitor."

My stomach tanked.

Shit.

From where he stood, he couldn't see my computer screen. The only explanation was that he decided to hack my computer. When had he done that, after Hazel sent me the first message?

Mason threw on his coat and headed down the hall toward the front entrance. "Answer her. Tell her rainbow," Mason shouted to me over his shoulder.

Rainbow.

I breathed a sigh of relief. My fingers drummed against the desk. I waited for her to answer while I kept an eye on the monitor.

There were several surveillance cameras outside the airport. The black sedan she was in passed through the last one with no further exits. I linked into one of the satellite feeds, narrowed in on her coordinates. I needed to be with her, to see what was going on.

Where the hell had Mason gone? Didn't he want to watch?

I shifted uncomfortably in the seat, and Lucy glanced back over her shoulder at me, another death glare.

I grimaced but shrugged in response. I wasn't apologizing for my concern for Hazel or the squeakiness of the chair.

Two black SUVs swerved toward the sedan, forcing the vehicle to come to an abrupt halt.

I held my breath and watched as four men jumped out with guns draw and yanked open the back door.

The feed turned snowy and went dead.

CHAPTER THREE

Hazel

With my head bent down, I'd been quietly texting on my cell phone, when Franco spun around in his seat and yanked the phone from my grasp.

"Hey! Give that back!" From the backseat, I lurched forward.

Franco rolled down the window with the touch of a button and tossed my cell phone out onto the highway.

"You bastard!"

"You don't need a phone in Russia," Franco said. He rolled the window back up.

From the side mirror, I could see the smug look cross his face, pleased with his actions toward me.

I wasn't going to Russia, but time was running out.

We passed the last exit and drew closer to the airport's departures and arrivals. He didn't seem the kind of guy who would have us fly commercial, but it was a long flight.

If he forced me into the airport, I'd kick, fight, and threaten that I have a bomb, anything to keep me from going with him.

Why did he want me to go to Russia? Was that where he lived? Did my brother even care that Franco was taking me out of the country?

Two SUVs pulled up alongside us before one trapped the car at the front and the other around the back. The driver slammed on the brakes to keep from colliding with the SUVs. The sedan would have been no match.

Four men in street clothes, guns drawn, rushed at our vehicle.

One of them yanked the back door open—my saving grace.

"Hazel Agron, you're under arrest. You have the right to remain silent."

What the hell?

I thought they were helping me?

Go along with it. The words played over in my mind. Was this Mason's idea of a joke?

The man nearest to me dragged me out of the sedan and pushed me down onto the asphalt, face first. He held my hands behind my back, incapacitating me as he handcuffed me and read me my rights.

"Don't say anything!" Franco shouted at me.

Was he worried about himself or me? I doubted that he cared about what happened to me. He could buy a new bride. He'd find someone else to replace me, and I was fine with that.

The metal cuffs dug into my wrists as the man searched me for weapons before hoisting me to my feet. He escorted me to the back of his SUV and shoved me inside, handcuffs still on, my hands secured behind my back.

The man who had snapped on the cuffs was the first to speak. "Mason sent us." He shut the door and walked around to the opposite side before he climbed in beside me. "Sorry about the theatrics, but we had to make it look convincing."

"Can you get these off me?"

The SUV lurched forward, and he undid the cuffs. My wrists hurt from the metal. I rubbed the marks, hoping they'd vanish.

We circled the airport before heading for the highway. "I'm Colton Carr with the U.S. Marshals. We don't usually kidnap people from thugs."

"Maybe you should," I said and laughed softly. "Thanks for saving my life."

"Don't thank us yet. Those guys won't just go away. I've worked all my life to put guys like that behind bars," Colton said.

"Yeah." I glanced out the window as we pulled onto the interstate. What was the plan? Where would I go? "What happens now?"

I couldn't go home. Nikolai would hand me right back to Franco.

"We're taking you to a safe location."

"Like witness protection?" I asked. I could handle not talking to my brother ever again.

"We'll get papers for you and set you up with a new identity. Agent Stanford and Blakely will drive you across the country. It's too risky to put you on an airplane right now, and I spoke with Mason. We both agree it's best if you're far from Chicago."

I'd fallen asleep.

Big mistake.

The screech of tires woke me.

A strong and heavy scent of smoke filled the car, as I ducked in the backseat of the black SUV. I averted my stare.

Gunfire erupted from every side.

The driver, U.S. Marshal Stanford, who had been rather quiet for the past several hours, bled profusely from the chest, gasping and moaning, struggling to breathe.

I couldn't do much from the backseat.

The second agent, U.S. Marshal Blakely, who had been seated on the passenger side of the vehicle, was now slumped over from a bullet to the head.

The dark-haired driver gasped for breath. "Hold on," he shouted, his foot stomping on the gas as he steered us into the men with guns blazing, ramming into one of the black SUVs before backing up and doing it again.

My body jolted around in the SUV. My heart hammered in my chest.

The driver hit the vehicle's gas hard in reverse. I glanced over my shoulder out the broken back window as we catapulted past the men, the vehicles, and kept going away from the men who wanted me dead.

The pounding in my heart hadn't ceased. The moment of agony stretching onward.

I wanted to escape, to reach for the door and throw myself outside into the unknown and pray that I could outrun the bastards.

Nearly twenty hours ago, they'd wanted me in their possession like property, and Franco wanted to marry me.

Now bullets were spraying all around me. It seemed he changed his mind about the arranged marriage.

While I wanted to be brave, I was terrified. Shaking profusely in the back of the vehicle, I crawled onto the floor in a ball, sobbing as the SUV continued its course in reverse. U.S. Marshal Stanford no longer gasped for breath. He too was slumped over like U.S. Marshal Blakely, not offering me the least bit of protection.

I needed to get my shit together. I hadn't come this far, escaped the Russian mafia, only to wind up dead in the middle of nowhere.

My arm stretched out in an attempt to unfasten the U.S. Marshal's weapon. He no longer had any use for it. My fingers stretched, fiddling with the holster from my position on the floor, the vehicle still hauling backward toward who the hell knew what.

With a hard thud, the vehicle jolted and bounced, the suspension making me feel like we were on a springboard.

What the hell did they hit? I didn't dare glance up. The men and their gunshots sounded farther in the distance, faded and forgotten. Except they wouldn't have given up unless he'd injured them and forced them unable to follow when he hit the vehicles.

I couldn't quite remember how many impacts I had felt, at least three. Had there been four collisions? My body still jarred, my neck sore, and my stomach ached, but that had more to do with terror than anything else.

I carefully peered up, glancing out the back window.

Shit. We were heading toward a ravine.

"Stop! You have to stop the truck!" I didn't know why I screamed it at Stanford. He was dead. He couldn't help me. His foot remained like lead on the pedal, refusing to lighten up.

I couldn't tell how far the drop was, but the grass was gone, and there were mountains in the distance. It didn't look promising.

Forgoing the gun, I was out of time. I reached for the handle of the back door and popped it open.

The grass rushed by, the crisp winter air hit my cheeks. I had to do this if I wanted a chance at survival, and I did, more than anything.

I wanted a second chance at life.

I climbed with haste from the floor to position myself on the seat. I took two quick breaths before flinging myself out of the vehicle, hearing the crunch of metal down below.

I rolled as best I could out of the truck. My cheeks burned, my knees ached, and I had a terrible headache, but I was alive.

Gasping for breath, I lay staring up at the sky, grateful to still be alive.

After several seconds, I pulled myself from my reverie and stalked toward the ravine, staring down at the ledge where the vehicle had gone.

Down below, the SUV lay on its ceiling, crushed.

A part of me wanted to go down and make sure both U.S. Marshals were dead, but I already knew the answer. They'd died saving my life.

CHAPTER FOUR

MASON

It was the middle of the night. My phone buzzed, breaking me of sleep and comfort.

"What?" I wasn't a morning person, let alone a middle of the night wake my ass kind of guy.

"It's Colton. We've got a problem."

My stomach felt like it fell out. I ran a hand over my tired eyes and jumped out of bed. In the dark, I grabbed clothes and rushed into the bathroom.

"Shit." I flipped on the light, the brightness blinding. "What is it?" I wasn't ready for whatever he was about to spring on me.

Hazel was supposed to be on her way to Eagle Tactical for our protection. I had requested the best in Chicago, and that was Colton Carr.

"The U.S. Marshals were hit sometime in the past two hours. They didn't call in like they were supposed to, and their vehicle isn't moving. I've got GPS coordinates. I need you to go check it out."

"Why didn't you escort her?" I put my phone on speaker, yanked off my boxers, and threw them at the wall. He should have been in the vehicle. "I called you, Colton. I wasn't asking for the next best agents to help."

"Stanford and Blakely are two of the best the Marshals service has to offer. Do you want me to call the sheriff's office? You should know the mafia is involved, the Russian mob. They're going to keep trying to track her down."

I tugged on a clean pair of boxers and jeans, then threw on a sweater. I grabbed the phone and hurried with socks in my hand to fetch my shoes.

I didn't have a second to spare. Hazel's life was in danger. "I know that."

"Let me know what you find," Colton said.

"Yeah." I hung up the call with Colton, grabbed my car keys, and slipped on my socks and boots before I headed for my truck. "Fucking bastard," I muttered under my breath.

I asked him to do one thing, why couldn't he have listened?

The darkness of night enveloped the vast expanse of land, across the mountains and down the valley. The night sky was speckled with stars, a beautiful sight if I wasn't in a rush to find Hazel.

I slowed as I approached the coordinates and pulled over to the side of the road. I left the engine idle and the headlights on, unlocking the door.

I stepped out onto the street.

There was not another vehicle in sight for miles. Where the hell was the missing SUV? Had it been picked up already by a tow truck? That didn't seem right or likely on a Friday night. Especially if the vehicle had just recently been located.

I grabbed a flashlight from the truck and headed out into the field. Shining the light ahead of me, searching for any sign of Hazel seemed an impossible task.

She could have been anywhere by now.

She'd never been to Breckenridge. She wouldn't know how to find me.

My flashlight flickered, going out in the darkness.

"Damnit!" I threw the stupid flashlight into the distance but didn't hear the thud I expected.

Instead of a soft landing on the grass and field, there was a clank on metal in the distance.

I grabbed my phone from my pocket and used the flashlight feature to get a better look at the sound that I'd heard: a smashed-up vehicle in the ravine, crushed.

"Hazel!" I shouted and practically held my breath, listening for a response.

There were no noises from below. Darkness surrounded the vehicle.

I carefully catapulted down the side of the ravine, scaling the mountain. My boots slid under my feet, forcing me to lose my balance, but I caught myself before landing on my ass.

I'd made it to the bottom of the ditch. I glanced up the mountainside. It would be hell to climb back up but I could do it.

"Hazel?" I called out into the night.

No response.

I approached the smashed vehicle; bullet holes covered the body of the SUV. "What the hell happened?"

I crouched down, finding two male bodies. I checked them each for a pulse; neither were alive. There was no sign of Hazel.

That had to be good news. It meant she survived the crash, right?

Unless she'd been ejected out the windshield.

No, that was a horrible thought.

She had to be alive. Hazel was a fighter.

I dialed Aiden. He would know what to do. I didn't want to wake Jaxson. He had a kid at home, and Lincoln had the restaurant. Declan would be useful in the office, so I patched Aiden and Declan in on a conference call.

"What's up?" Aiden asked. He didn't sound as tired as I felt.

"Aren't you just peachy?" Declan yawned. "What's going on?"

"I need help. It's regarding an off-the-books assignment." I didn't wait for them to answer. I headed back to my truck. Standing out in the field, searching for her wasn't doing a lick of good.

"You have my attention," Aiden said.

I hadn't wanted to involve them. I had hoped it could stay a private matter, but now it was extending into Eagle Tactical business. "A friend of mine is in trouble. She lives in Chicago, her father recently died, and it turns out her brother is head of the Russian mob."

"Shit. Drop it on us light, why don't you?" Aiden joked.

I ignored his attempt at humor. I wasn't laughing.

Hazel was out there, and men hunted her if they hadn't found her already. "I contacted Colton Carr yesterday afternoon when I received a message sent to our encrypted phone number. According to Colton, Hazel was sold as part of an arranged marriage set up by her brother." Bile rose in my throat just thinking about it. "Colton pulled her out of danger and put her en route to us when the U.S. Marshals were run off the road and attacked."

"Shit," Declan muttered. "Do you think whoever was after her picked her up? Is this a recovery mission?"

I ran a hand through my hair. "I hope not." I tugged on the strands before dropping my hand to my lap. "If we're lucky, she's still out there, hiding, waiting for our help."

"Tell me what you need," Declan said.

The phone connected to the car's Bluetooth.

I buckled myself and headed back onto the road.

Hazel wasn't just any girl; she was the first girl I loved. I still was in love with her, and everyone I had been with, I always compared to her.

"Aside from finding Hazel?" I gripped the steering wheel and did a U-turn, heading toward my house. "I'm going back to my house."

"Woke us up to tell us you were heading back to bed?" Declan snorted. "Gee, thanks."

"I've got night vision equipment and thermal detectors that I can use to find her. She's on foot, no more than two hours ahead of us. She would likely follow the road which would lead to town, but it means she has to navigate the mountain."

"We should be grateful it's not snowing. Hopefully, she has warm clothes and doesn't die of exposure," Aiden said.

Great.

Way to ruin my good mood. I hit the gas harder, needing to get home. If I were lucky, I'd find her first before the men who wanted her dead.

It worried me that the only abandoned vehicle had been the one she'd ridden inside. Lined with bullet holes, the other vehicle, or vehicles for that matter, were still out there. They hadn't been run off the road and down in the ravine. Which meant the men were at large, stalking Hazel like she was their prey.

"I'll rendezvous with you at your place," Aidan said. "Declan, head to the office. Maybe you can pull up something that'll help us figure out what the hell is going on."

If I found the men who were after Hazel first, I'd kill them with my bare hands.

CHAPTER FIVE

JAXSON

I'd found it difficult to sleep, tossing and turning through all hours of the night.

Usually, I was dead to the world when I slept, but the smell of Ariella's sweet scent mingled on my pillow and forced my mind to play over the night we shared.

Regret burned a hole in my stomach.

I drowned in her spicy aroma, and while the sheets didn't reek of sex, unfortunately, it still smelled blissfully of *her*. I buried my head beneath the thick blanket.

I hated that I hadn't told Ariella what she meant to me that night we shared, but now it felt a lifetime ago.

Funny how a few days could change your life.

My cell phone buzzed on the nightstand. I pushed the blanket down and grumbled.

I was not ready to be awake for work. My phone screen lit up the pitch-black bedroom.

With an exhausted gaze, I felt for the phone and hit answer. Shoving it against my ear, I shut my eyes, attempting to wake up, which seemed counterproductive.

"Eagle Tactical," I said. The call coming in wasn't one of the guys, and at this disgusting hour, it had to be a client. "This is Jaxson Monroe. Can I help you?"

"I certainly hope so," a deep gruff voice said. The man had a thick accent, Ukrainian or Russian. It was difficult to tell them apart. He cleared his throat. "I'd like to hire you to find my wife."

I sat up in bed and turned on the bedside lamp. "We don't typically handle domestic matters," I said.

I scooted to sit at the edge of the bed. My feet were planted firmly on the floor. The ground was cold, and the air outside of the warm blankets gave me goosebumps.

With the phone to my ear, I stood and headed straight for my dresser.

"This isn't a domestic matter. She was arrested yesterday morning. When I contacted the authorities to have her bond posted and released, she was never brought in for booking."

He had my attention. "Do you believe the authorities are involved in her disappearance?" That sounded a tad wild, even by my standards.

"No, that would be preposterous."

I opened the drawer to my dresser, grabbed a fresh set of clothes, and tossed the items to the bed. "It likely wasn't the authorities who picked up your wife."

"That is precisely my concern. I have many enemies. I would hate to think they came after my most prized possession. I can assure you that I will pay handsomely for her return to me."

While that was nice to know, it wasn't the only factor we considered. "Send me a photograph of your wife, along with her name and any distinguishing attributes—body piercings, scars, or tattoos, so that we can easily identify her."

I gave the gentleman my email address to send the information to me.

"I'd also like to meet you." It was a requirement. Anyone I hired as a client, I needed to know they were clean and not thwarting an active investigation.

"Of course. How does noon sound?"

I gave him Eagle Tactical's address and took his name and phone number before I hung up.

I showered and dressed in a hurry, shoved my phone into my back pocket, and shut off the lights to my bedroom.

Coming down the back stairwell directly to the kitchen, I put on a pot of coffee. I was going to need the extra jolt to stay awake today.

My body was sluggish, and I couldn't afford my mind to feel the same.

I stared at the coffeemaker, waiting for it to drip into the pot, the hiss of the water heating filling my foggy head.

"Who would kidnap a woman, pretend to be the authorities, and arrest her?" I said to myself. I leaned on the counter.

It didn't make sense. My gut instinct had me second-guess everything the man had said over the phone.

As soon as I received communication with him, I could track his phone, run a background check, and make sure he had nothing to hide.

It was what we did with all our clients that involved missing persons or abductions. In most cases, a spouse was involved or if it was a child, the parents. We didn't inform the parents or spouse that we looked into their financial, background, and past transgressions.

Soft footsteps pattered down the back stairwell. I straightened up and expelled a heavy breath. I could feel her presence, smell her sweet scent from across the room. Ariella had awoken.

"Did I wake you?" I hadn't intended the question to come out sharp and rough, but lack of sleep had done me in.

I wasn't a morning person without a solid six hours of sleep. I'd had far less, especially during training involving sleep deprivation and combat situations. This was neither of those, thankfully.

"No. I couldn't sleep. Is the coffee ready?" she asked.

I grabbed two mugs from the cabinet, flipping them over and placing them right side up. "Almost."

The coffee maker brewed and gurgled. Steam wafted from the back of the unit. It wasn't high tech or fancy, but it made a mean cup of coffee in a pretty decent amount of time. I hated to be kept waiting for my morning brew.

The last of the coffee dripped into the pot, and I poured two cups. I turned around and handed her a mug.

"Thank you," she whispered, staring at me.

I tried not to stare at her in the baggy flannel bottoms or the white t-shirt that clung to her breasts and revealed her nipples through her shirt. I failed miserably.

Her eyes widened, and she adjusted her shirt, one arm over her ample breasts, the other hand bringing the mug to her lips for her coffee.

I wanted to apologize; I knew I should have said something.

Instead, I glanced away, ran a hand through my morning hair, and pointed at the fridge. "Help yourself. I have to leave early this morning and get a head start on a new client."

"Oh. Anything I can help with?" Her eyes were full of promise and hope.

"No. There's no sense in you coming into work early. I'll run the background check this morning. When you get into the office, we'll see what we can have you work on."

She sipped her coffee, holding the mug to her lips as she took a long, slow gulp. "I don't mind coming in early."

"That's not a good idea." The two of us alone together, at the office, I had wild thoughts that involved bending her over my desk, lifting her skirt, and having my way with her.

Down, boy. I needed to cool it before she witnessed my arousal.

Her brow furrowed and her bottom lip jutted out. "Well, maybe it's not up to you." She put her coffee mug down hard and splashed remnants of what remained in her cup.

She got my attention. "Excuse me?" I stepped closer and stared down into those intense green eyes, an olive hue that sucked me in every time.

"I work for Eagle Tactical, not just you," she said. Her lips were firm and her jaw tight.

Desire made me want to lean down, wrap an arm around her waist and pull her tight against my skin.

I imagined lifting her jaw with my thumb, guiding her lips to mine. We were just inches apart.

Could she feel the heat radiate off my body and onto hers?

I ran a hand along the back of my neck and took a step back to recover from the fantasy. It couldn't happen. It shouldn't happen.

She was my employee, and while I had feelings for her, we'd made a commitment that we wouldn't act on those desires. I needed to respect that. I could use a cold shower.

"Did I do something to piss you off?" Ariella asked.

"Yes."

CHAPTER SIX

Hazel

The sky had grown dark, the distant sound of wild animals rustling through the grass. I kept in the meadow, the road just a few feet away, but I wouldn't walk on the paved surface.

Every time a car drove by, I stopped and ducked, lying against the grass, hiding from the men who were out searching for me, the same men who killed the U.S. Marshals.

Was it Franco or one of his goons? Either way, I wasn't safe.

My feet hurt and were blistered. I couldn't remove my shoes, though. That would be even more painful and stupid.

I hadn't anticipated that the U.S. Marshals would end up dead. This was all my fault.

I wrapped my arms around myself, the steep incline up the mountain difficult on my city girl calves.

I was not in shape, at least not for a hike of this magnitude. I was out of breath.

The higher I climbed, the more snow that covered the route.

The sound of tires on gravel and sludge forced me to freeze.

Someone was coming. Was it Franco?

I ducked down and held completely still, the forest surrounding me, allowing the vehicle to pass by as I went unnoticed by the driver.

The truck sped along the slushy snow and gravel road up the mountain. In the distance, through the forest, a porch light flickered.

I went off the road and through the brush, branches crunching under my feet.

I needed to take the shortcut. It was the only way to get out of the cold as fast as possible.

From my crouched position, I watched with fascination as a man stepped out from his truck and stood outside the building. It was too big to be a house.

It wasn't possible for him to see me. I took several more steps forward.

He couldn't know I was out here, right? My stomach flopped, and I wiped the sweat from my palms on my jeans.

He was nothing more than a silhouette, a handsome one at that from what I could tell, but it was dark, and within a few short moments, he had gone inside.

I hovered near the forest entrance and stepped into the slick, snowy muck. My shoes sunk into the dampness as I approached the building with a darkened sign that read 'Lumberjack Shack.'

Outside, two vehicles were parked. Was it the owner and a staff member? It didn't look open, but it was also very late or incredibly early, depending on how you looked at it.

I hurried toward the entrance and tried the door, curious if they kept it locked.

It didn't budge. I peered into the window; the chairs were situated upside down on the tables. The place was closed for the night.

Would they be opening soon? The sun might not come up for a few more hours, but if they served coffee and breakfast, then they would open.

The front door flung open, and I jumped, startled. It wasn't one of the men after me.

One glance at the gentleman, and he looked every bit a mountain man, with his thick beard and flannel shirt. "You almost gave me a heart attack!" I said.

"Me? You're the one peeking in through my windows." He studied me before glancing at the near-empty parking lot. "No car?"

There was no point in lying to him. "I walked." I wrapped my arms around myself, feeling tiny compared to his size and stance.

He could easily overpower me, but his eyes shone with mirth.

He didn't look scary, not like Franco.

"Come in, out of the cold," he said.

I didn't wait for him to ask twice or second guess himself. I followed on his heel and joined him inside. I exhaled a loud, long breath, the warmth of the building already soothing my aching and tender muscles.

The restaurant was dimly lit, and he fixed that right away, making my eyes hurt. I shielded my gaze until I adjusted to the brightness.

"You look like you could use a meal and maybe a shower," he said.

Yeah, I wasn't taking my clothes off. Fat chance of that, buddy. "Coffee sounds good." I needed caffeine to keep me awake.

I'd slept maybe an hour or two max in the car on the ride across the country. Had I known what would have gone down, I'd have tried sleeping more.

"I'm Lincoln," he said, introducing himself.

I stared at him, debating on whether I should give my name or lie. "Ashley Sinclair." The lie slipped out before I could even stop myself if I wanted to.

"It's nice to meet you, Ashley Sinclair." His eyes were tight, narrow as he headed behind the counter to put on a pot of coffee.

I followed, my feet leaving a mess of snow and ice on the inside of the restaurant floor. Lincoln would hate me. He'd hate me more when he realized I couldn't pay for the coffee. "Actually, I could just use a glass of water."

I didn't even have a dollar to my name. My wallet and possessions were back with Franco.

Everything I owned had been left behind.

"You look like you've been through a lot today. Coffee is on the house," Lincoln said.

"Really?" I couldn't believe he was nice just to be kind. People in Chicago weren't genuinely nice unless they wanted something and it was to their benefit.

"You remind me of someone," he said.

I climbed onto the stool to sit at the counter. "Well, I can assure you we've never met. I've never been to—where am I exactly?"

I'd been on my way to Mason at Eagle Tactical, but all I remembered was that it was somewhere in Montana.

"You really are in trouble if you don't know what town you're in," Lincoln said. He grabbed a mug and poured me a cup of coffee. "Cream and sugar?"

"Yes, please." He grabbed a handful of prepackaged creamers and sugar from under the counter.

"Thank you." I opened and dumped in two creamers before adding four packets of sugar.

"Holy cow, you have a sweet tooth." He laughed and ran a hand along his jaw. "Not sure I've ever seen someone use that much sugar in a single cup of coffee."

Had that been rude of me to do that without trying his coffee first? Wasn't all coffee the same, bitter and strong?

His cell phone buzzed, and he reached into his pants pocket. His brow furrowed as he answered a text message.

"Girlfriend?" I asked. He looked puzzled. Maybe she was mad that he wasn't in bed at this hour?

"No. Uh, my second job."

"Oh." I held the warm cup between both my hands, blowing on it softly before bringing the steaming mug to my lips. I inhaled the heat before letting my lips graze the porcelain. "So, you work here part-time?"

"I own the place," Lincoln said. He put his phone away, shoving it back into his pocket. "You said your name was Ashley?"

"Yeah, that's right." I took another swig of my coffee to keep myself preoccupied.

It was easier to lie when I didn't have to face the man who had whisked me out of the cold and warmed me up.

"Did you get separated from someone?" Lincoln asked. He poured himself a cup of coffee, black. "I can't fathom why you'd be out in the cold without a car."

"I live just down the road."

Lincoln smiled. "Of course. You probably come here all the time. I just have a terrible memory. A side effect of serving in the war."

I took another sip, my stomach grumbling from hunger.

"How do you like your eggs?" Lincoln asked.

"What's that?" Had he heard my obnoxious stomach growl too?

"I'm going to make you something to eat, and while I'd ordinarily offer pancakes, I'm betting you could use the extra protein. You look like you walked for miles outside. Am I right?"

Was it that obvious that I was in trouble? I covered my face with my hand. "I just got a little turned around coming from my house."

Another lie. How easily they slipped out.

"Right. How do you like those eggs? I'm going to make mine scrambled."

My mouth watered at the thought of food. It wasn't even being prepared yet, and already, my senses could imagine the taste. "That sounds delicious."

"I'll be right back," Lincoln said, heading to the kitchen.

I turned in my seat, keeping an eye on the door. I wanted to be alert and prepared in case the men who had run us off the road and shot at the SUV came back for me. I hadn't seen them since I had escaped out of the vehicle and jumped out before the SUV plunged down into the ravine. Did they presume I was dead?

Did Mason think I was dead?

As much as I'd stalked him online, I hadn't been able to find out if he was single or had ever married. There wasn't much about him outside of the obvious fact that he'd served in the army special forces and now was part owner of Eagle Tactical. It was almost like he wanted people to know that about him, and that was it.

I sipped the last of my coffee, desperate for another cup. I slid off the stool and came around behind the counter. Lincoln was busy in the kitchen. Hopefully, he wouldn't mind me intruding for a second cup.

The bell on the door rang as someone opened the door and headed inside.

I ducked behind the counter and snapped my mouth shut.

"Hello?" a thick Russian accent reverberated through the restaurant. His voice boomed and echoed with each heavy step he took.

Fuck!

A second set of steps separate from the man who spoke approached the counter.

"Can we get some service?" another Russian said.

He smacked the top of the counter and lifted the cup that I'd just poured.

CHAPTER SEVEN

MASON

I pulled up in the parking lot after hearing back from Lincoln that a strange girl had shown up at the restaurant.

It had to be Hazel.

Who else would have wandered there on foot in the middle of the night? His text had been brief but detailed enough to indicate the girl was in trouble.

I needed to catch him up to speed, but that would wait. I parked next to an unfamiliar SUV and stepped out of my truck.

Bullet holes lined the outside body of the SUV. I grabbed my gun and hurried around to the back of the restaurant, through the door that had been left unlocked for deliveries.

The sun hadn't risen yet, but the delivery trucks usually came before the restaurant opened with customers.

I tore inside, gun drawn, through the kitchen, meeting Lincoln.

"Where is she?"

"Can we get some service?" a thick Russian accent echoed from the other side of the door.

"Out there," Lincoln said. He reached beneath the kitchen

counter and grabbed his spare gun. "I left her for five minutes to make breakfast, I swear—"

I held up a hand for him to be quiet. They mustn't have seen her, or they'd have taken her and left already.

I grabbed a serving tray and used it to hide my gun. Lincoln followed directly behind me so they wouldn't see his weapon, either.

"Can I help you gentleman?" I asked, stepping out from the kitchen.

I tried to ignore the bright auburn hair nestled in the crook of the counter, hidden out of sight. She trembled on the floor, her body tight like a peanut, like in one of those drills we learned back in elementary school.

"Kitchen isn't open yet. We can get you coffee to go."

The men exchanged wayward glances. "What kind of restaurant isn't open for breakfast?"

"The kind that doesn't serve—breakfast," Lincoln said between gritted teeth.

His hands were clenched at his sides as he came around my side to block the entrance to the kitchen and behind the counter where Hazel had stashed herself.

Had she seen the men coming? How had she known to hide?

"Know where I might find a bed?" the man with thinning black hair asked. His muscles protruded from his shirt.

Why the hell wasn't he wearing a coat? What idiot ran around in winter without a jacket?

"There's no vacancy this side of the mountain," I said. I didn't want either man staying in town.

"Right." They exchanged a quick, cursory glance before lifting their weapons.

Guns drawn toward us, bullets flew through the air.

I ducked by the counter and scooted behind it with Hazel. Her eyes met mine.

I gestured for her to stay down.

Lincoln fired off a round of shots, and I stood from behind the counter, doing the same, landing several blows to their chests and then a final kill shot to the heads.

"Shit," Lincoln muttered, coming around to kick the guns away from their hands.

He felt their pulses, a habit of never being too careful, just to make sure they were as dead as they looked. "Do you think insurance covers the damage?"

I laughed under my breath. That was his biggest concern?

I helped Hazel stand. She trembled in my arms, her eyes wide, full of terror. "It's okay. You're safe now," I said. "They can't hurt you."

"I'm not worried about them," Hazel whispered. "It's Franco I'm afraid of."

"Get her out of here," Lincoln said. "Take her to Eagle Tactical. I'll clean up this mess and phone the local sheriff."

"He's going to want all of our statements." While I wanted to protect Hazel, I wasn't going to break the law for her, either.

We had killed two men in self-defense, but she was a witness and the reason the men had been in the restaurant. We couldn't leave her out of the story.

Besides, the sheriff and I had a good relationship. We consulted for the local police department from time to time and helped them when they needed assistance.

It would be wise to let them know what they were in for. It was possible that this wasn't anywhere close to being over.

"Yes, I know." Lincoln shooed us out of the restaurant. "I'll tell him to come by your office. Just get her out of here and keep her out of danger."

I glanced out the window, making sure there weren't any other vehicles or men loitering outside before I opened the door and led her out to my truck.

"Thanks for saving my life," Hazel said.

I tried not to stare at her, but damn, it was hard. I hadn't seen her in over a decade.

I grinned like a damned idiot and opened the truck door. "Hop in."

Gosh, it was good to see her again. Though I'd have preferred it to be under different circumstances.

I offered her a hand as she struggled with making it up on the running board. Once inside the truck, I shut the door and hurried around to the driver's side.

I climbed in, pulled out of the lot, and kept my attention on the road. I made sure that no one followed us.

"How have you been? Well, I mean minus all this," I said.

What a stupid question. Since when did I become a bumbling fool around the ladies?

Hazel had captured my interest and my heart in high school. We'd gone to boarding school together in Chicago. While my parents had lived in Montana, I'd gotten into a mountain of trouble, and they'd sent me to live with my grandma in Chicago.

That hadn't lasted.

Two weeks with her, and I had the option of attending military school or boarding school.

Hazel sighed long and loud. Her stare was on me the entire time.

"Do I have something on my face?" I asked. I rubbed at my forehead.

"No. It's just, I haven't seen you in so long. I want to hug you and then hit you for breaking my heart," Hazel said.

What? When had I broken her heart?

I tried mulling it over, but my attention was quickly diverted when a black town car headed north up the road.

On instinct, I reached out and guided her head down so that as the vehicle passed up, they wouldn't see her face.

"More Russians?" Hazel's voice trembled.

They didn't look like the goons from earlier, but it was still peculiar to see anyone who wasn't a local at this hour.

I waited until the vehicle passed to answer. "I don't think they were with the guys back there at the restaurant."

There were guests who stayed at the resort and came up to the restaurant or hiked on the local trails, but that didn't happen until daylight.

Something felt amiss, but I didn't want to worry her.

The sun was almost about to peek from the horizon. I stomped on the gas.

It would be easier to move in the dark.

Daylight would make Hazel stand out with that fiery auburn hair. I'd have to send Ariella to the store to pick up hair dye and probably a few other necessities.

One thing at a time. The first, was making sure she survived.

I pulled up out front of Eagle Tactical and rushed her inside the building, securing the deadbolt the moment we were inside. "Come with me."

I led her down the hallway and to my office. I didn't want her anywhere near the entrance, and while there was a back door, it wasn't easily accessible with the snow and ice along the path leading up to it. No one ever shoveled the back walk.

She followed me into my office, her footsteps soft and invisible against the tile while my strides were loud and forceful as I announced my presence.

Aiden and Declan poked their heads out of their respective offices. "Good morning," they said in unison.

"This is Hazel. Hazel, meet Aiden and Declan," I said, introducing them.

"Glad you made it in time to the restaurant," Declan said. "Lincoln texted us the firefight was over, or we'd have sprinted over to help."

"We had it handled." We weren't outmatched or outgunned. I'd been through worse, countless times. "I'm going to take Hazel into my office, chat with her in private for a few minutes. The sheriff will come by in a bit for our statements. Let him in, would you? Also, keep the door locked. We can't be too careful."

I didn't wait for their answer. I shut the office door almost in their faces. They took a knowing step back; I was in charge since this was my case.

Hazel was a priority, *my* priority.

"Have a seat," I said, offering her the sofa in the corner. I approached the storage cabinet and fumbled through a few trinkets before landing on one that would have to do.

"What are you looking for?" she asked.

I showed her the golden bangle, sliding it on past her hand, letting it dangle on her wrist.

"I'm more of a silver kind of girl," Hazel said.

"Keep that on until everything is resolved with Franco. Okay?" We didn't have much in terms of tracking devices upstairs.

The basement housed our surveillance equipment, specialty gadgets, and a high-end server with a faraday cage to keep hackers out while we were able to infiltrate even the toughest security. We also had weapons locked away, but we'd made an agreement early on that only those of us who worked for Eagle Tactical would be the only ones to know about the basement or what was down there.

I wasn't ready to leave Hazel unattended, even to go downstairs and search for a different style of tracking device. The bangle would suffice, and it looked good on her.

She stared at the bracelet on her wrist. A faint smile played at the corner of her lips. "If I'd have known you were going to give me jewelry, I'd have visited you a lot sooner."

I turned the desk chair around and slunk into the leather, facing her. "It's a tracking device. As long as you're wearing it, you'll be safe."

"Isn't it rather obvious?" She thrust her arm at me, the bracelet swinging on her wrist. "It's not very discreet."

We had discreet high-tech trackers, but the fact was I wasn't letting her out of my sight. It was a formality, just in case something happened.

"It doesn't have to be. I'm not letting Franco anywhere near you." I sat across from her, clasping my hands together in my lap. "I want to know everything about the bastard. Lay it on me, all of it."

Her fingers played with the bracelet as she spoke. "I don't know much about him. My brother, the new head of the Russian mafia, sold me to his second in command."

"He sold you?" My fists clenched, and I stood, disgusted with any man who thought a woman was his property. I couldn't sit still; my legs wouldn't allow it. I paced the length of my office, practically wearing a hole in the tile. "Keep going."

I needed more details.

As much as it sickened me to hear it, I wanted to know *everything*.

"Nikolai thought it was high time I married and arranged the purchase to Franco Ivanov."

I stopped pacing when I recognized the withdrawn and hesitant look cross her face.

I bent down, clasping her one hand in mine, and with my other hand, I brought my fingers into her bright red tresses, guiding her chin to meet my stare.

"I will not let anything happen to you. I promise you, Hazel, you're safe with me."

"I'll never be safe again," she rasped. "Franco won't stop looking for me."

Her hands trembled, and she pulled away to wipe the salty tears that glistened at the corners of her eyes.

"I mean, maybe he will, but if that's the case, it's only because he wants me dead. They killed two U.S. Marshals, Mason. Men like that don't stop. They'll never give up searching for me. I wouldn't be surprised if Franco demands his men return me—dead or alive."

I wouldn't let that happen to Hazel. She meant too much to me, and besides, it was my job to protect those who couldn't protect themselves. "First, you're going to have to speak with the sheriff. When you're done, I'm going to have you relocated and a protective detail with you at all times."

"I thought I was staying here." Hazel patted the sofa. "I can sleep here. It's really no big deal."

Was she ridiculous? While we had decent security at Eagle Tactical, it was a prime location for Franco to search for her.

We couldn't house her with one of our Eagle Tactical members, which was against protocol, and she had indirectly hired me when she reached out requesting help.

Besides, I couldn't watch her twenty-four-seven. It would be better, for her sake, to have the entire team helping her.

Jaxson swung the door open, oblivious to what was happening. He hadn't been kept in the loop, and that was my fault.

His brow furrowed, pointing at Hazel.

"We have a new client," Jaxson said. "He called this morning and hired us for our services to find his missing wife. I'm sorry. We haven't met. I'm Jaxson Monroe."

"Ashley Sinclair," Hazel said with a forced grin as she held out her hand.

CHAPTER EIGHT

JAXSON

"How nice to meet you, Ms. Sinclair," I said and stepped closer, offering out my hand.

One glance at her, and without a doubt, I recognized her from the picture on my phone as Hazel Agron.

What was Mason doing with her? "Can I have a word with you, alone?" I asked Mason.

"Sure. I'll just be a sec," he said to the woman seated on the sofa in his office.

I stepped out into the hallway and gestured for him to come into my office.

I forced the door closed harder than intended. It slammed.

"Something on your mind?" Mason asked. It was just the two of us.

"That girl you think you're protecting, she's not who she says she is."

Why was Hazel in his office lying about her identity? Did Mason realize that he'd been deceived?

I wanted to be reasonable. I was still running background on

Nikolai as well as Hazel. The information had been squeaky clean for both of them. Not so much as a parking ticket.

Mason's eyes shined and the corners of his lips curved upward. "I know that, but how do you know that?" he asked.

I slumped into my plush office chair and slid it around to face Mason. "Have a seat." I gestured to the empty seat in my office.

He exhaled loudly through his nose and sat down. "What's going on, Jaxson?"

"I received a call early this morning from a new client requesting our help in locating his missing wife."

"Missing wife? Tell me you didn't hire him." Mason leaned forward on his knees, his head in his hands. "Did you miss what happened with your girlfriend yesterday morning?"

My jaw clenched and my hands bunched at my side into fists. "She's not my girlfriend, and no, I was busy running background checks for Blue Sky Resort, again. I'm surprised they hired us after the last time, with Ariella."

Hunched forward, his elbows on his knees, he ran a hand through his short, cropped hair. "Please tell me we didn't take the Russian mob on as a client," Mason said.

What the hell was he talking about? "She's with the Russian mafia?"

I'd done preliminary searches, and everything had come back squeaky clean.

My specialty was in the field. I wasn't a hacker. I didn't know how to access what wasn't easily accessible. Declan was the go-to guy for that, and Ariella, I had a feeling she could probably keep up with him, with her former C.I.A. training.

I shouldn't have turned Ariella's offer down earlier that morning. I'd been foolish and self-indulgent.

"She's not willingly with the Russian mafia," Mason said and cleared his throat. "Hazel's brother is the head of the mob in Chicago. I'm guessing you already know that's her real name."

We didn't keep secrets from one another. "Why didn't you tell me you accepted her call for help?"

I didn't like the position that this put our team in; hiring both sides wasn't advisable. We weren't mediators, and this was the mafia we were dealing with, not a messy divorce.

"Aiden and Declan already know," Mason said. He held out his hands, palms upward. "Lincoln knows too."

"Lincoln?" I stood, the chair squeaking as it slid behind me. "Why am I the last to know?"

"Because you have your head so far up your ass, Monroe. You buried yourself in your office to avoid the hottie out there," Mason said, pointing at the door. "If you spent five minutes not being narcissistic, then you would have seen what's right under your nose."

It was a good thing Mason wasn't my employee and we were equals or I'd have fired his ass and thrown him out the front door.

"You're out of line, Reid." If he was going to call me by my last name, two could play at that game.

A soft knock rapped at the door. "What?" I shouted and yanked the office door open.

Ariella stood on the other side, her eyes wide as she averted her stare from me to Mason.

"Don't shoot the messenger," she said, "but the sheriff is here for your statement, Mason."

"Your statement? What the hell, Mason?" How much had I missed?

Mason stood and brushed past me without another word. He led Sheriff Nelson into his office and shut the door behind himself.

"What the hell is going on?" I asked.

Declan and Aiden had disappeared down the hall, and Ariella slunk into the seat at her desk, attempting to look small and invisible.

"Ariella?" I wanted someone to tell me what the hell I'd missed. It seemed she knew about Hazel. What else did she know?

"Yes?" her voice squeaked as she met my stare.

"My office, now." I stomped into my office and didn't turn around.

I could hear her soft footsteps as they fell against the floor.

She left the office door open and probably hoped Declan or Aiden might save her ass.

"What can I do for you?" Ariella asked. She stood with her arms tight against her side, her shoulders slumped.

"Have a seat."

"Are you firing me?"

"What?" I laughed under my breath at the absurdity of her question. "Do I have a reason to fire you?"

Had she done something that I wasn't aware of yet?

She didn't move from her position on the floor just a few feet away. Her body was practically a statue, except for the slight tremble.

"I don't believe so," she stammered.

"Good." I pinched the bridge of my nose. Five seconds, and she was giving me a headache. Maybe I was blaming her for something that wasn't her fault. She didn't know the mess I'd gotten Eagle Tactical involved in by accepting Franco as a client. Shit. Franco. He planned on coming to the office around noon. "I need your help."

She nodded but didn't say a word.

"The minute the sheriff is done with his interview, I need you to take Hazel to the resort."

"Blue Sky Resort?" Ariella asked. Dread crossed her face. She looked like she might be sick.

"You can do that, can't you? I need you to rent a room. No one will think anything of it since no one knows you work for us." It would be an easy solution for the time being. I needed to get Hazel out of the office and some place safe.

"I—yeah, I can do that." She rolled her lips tight between her teeth.

I didn't imagine it would be easy for her to step foot back in the resort that had fired her and where she'd been assaulted. The job itself wasn't easy.

"I don't think Mason is going to want to leave her side," Ariella said. "They have some type of past connection, history together."

"They do?" She knew more about Hazel than I did. "What else do you know?"

She appeared to relax under my scrutiny. Ariella took another step and came to sit down in the chair that Mason had vacated a few minutes prior. "Hazel reached out to him for help," Ariella said. "Maybe I should start from the beginning."

"That would be good." I perched myself at the edge of the wooden desk and listened to her recant how she'd received a message on her laptop and that Mason had been involved in contacting the U.S. Marshal's office, someone by the name of Colton, to help extract her.

I knew Colton. We'd served in the military together.

"Stay here," I said and headed out into the hallway and to Aiden's office for the safe stashed in the wall, hidden away in the closet.

Aiden and Declan went silent the minute I stepped into their office. "Don't mind me," I said and went right for the safe.

"Something we can help you with?" Declan asked.

"Yes. I need to get Ariella a credit card to get a room and check-in early at the resort," I said.

I opened the safe and flipped through the materials that were available.

"And you don't think whoever runs the check-in desk will notice she's using a fake name?" Declan grinned. "Are you trying to set her up to get arrested?"

Shit. "No." The hotel would require a credit card for incidentals when checking in. "I'll book the room online and have her check-in and use her own card."

Aiden shook his head. "You're getting sloppy."

It was the lack of sleep. I didn't do my best work after being up all night. "I didn't sleep well last night."

Declan and Aiden exchanged a glance.

"What?" I growled at the two of them.

"Your sexual frustration is killing all of us. Please, go home. Shower, sleep, bluff the squirrel," Declan said.

I choked out a laugh, embarrassed.

I couldn't believe what they suggested. My glance shot out toward the open door and Ariella, who had stepped out into the hallway.

Fuck me.

I'd pretend she didn't hear what Declan said because I wished I hadn't heard it.

Her footsteps grew louder as she knocked on the open door.

"I thought I told you to stay in my office?" I threw my arms up into the air. "Why does no one listen to me around here?" I stomped past Ariella on the way out of Declan's office.

Ariella didn't move.

"Are you coming?" I shouted over my shoulder.

"Do I have to?" I heard her mutter under her breath. My cell phone buzzed in my pocket. I grunted and held up a finger to tell her to hold on a second while I checked the caller ID. It was Skylar.

It was like she knew when I was busy and had to call and pester me.

What now? I couldn't deal with her. I rejected her call and took a long, slow breath to regroup.

I turned around to yell at Ariella to hurry up when I discovered she had already followed, silent and practically invisible on my heel.

I stopped abruptly when I turned around to face her, and she nearly slammed into my chest. Her reflexes were fast and she caught herself before we collided.

I almost wished she had knocked into me. It would have given me an excuse to touch her.

"I'm going to pay for your room in advance over the internet. If anyone asks, including Emma, tell her that you're staying at the resort until insurance is figured out with your house," I said.

She needed to be prepared for questions, especially returning to Blue Sky Resort.

"I've got it handled. Don't worry," she said, giving me a reassuring smile. She reached out and rested a hand on my arm. "Are you okay?" Her voice was soft and sweet, like honey.

I wanted to pull her against me, touch her, taste her, and let the agony that filled my heart disappear.

"Just tired," I said. Her touch was soft yet firm. I pulled away. We couldn't do that or be that for each other.

She shuffled her feet. It was the most I'd seen her move all morning. "I didn't hear Izzie last night. Did she keep you up? I must have slept through it."

"It wasn't Izzie."

I didn't elaborate.

How could I?

The smell of her scent on my pillow kept me awake all night.

She'd think I was crazy if I told her the truth. Maybe I was going slowly insane, needing my next fix of *her*.

I hadn't ever felt the desire as strong as I did now, a deep ache that tore away at me every second that I couldn't touch her or be with her.

We'd only shared one night together.

It had been wonderful, but I had to push it out of my head. Exhaustion had crept over me and made me desperate.

CHAPTER NINE

ARIELLA

Why hadn't Jaxson been able to sleep? If it wasn't Izzie, what had kept him up all night?

I'd slept great. The guest room hadn't been as cozy as the first night that I had curled up under his sheets and he'd held me, but neither of us spoke about that incident. He'd been there to look after me, that was all.

"I promise I'll be out of your house soon," I said.

"Good," he said, his tone gruff. He rubbed at his jaw, not able to meet my stare.

"Did I do something to piss you off? Because if I remember correctly, I should be mad at you. Not the other way around."

That caught his attention. His gaze fell down to my eyes and then my lips.

Had the heat come on? The room was several degrees warmer than it had been just a few minutes earlier.

Jaxson didn't answer me. He didn't say a word. He didn't have to. His brow furrowed, and his eyes looked tired.

"I shouldn't have said anything," I muttered under my breath. I'd probably just gone and made things a lot worse for the two of us.

"No," he said, his voice hoarse. He grabbed my arm and pulled me closer, invading my personal space.

I struggled not to meet his stern gaze that studied me.

What was he thinking? My breathing came out in soft, shallow breaths.

His proximity was all it took to further heighten my senses.

A simple touch of his hand sent a spark of lightning through my body, warming me, creating an ache of need that I'd squashed down to nothingness.

"I want you to talk to me, Freckles."

Hearing him use the nickname he'd given me was my undoing.

I couldn't stand there in front of him and pretend that everything would be all right. It wasn't fine.

My heart ached beyond measure. He'd left in the middle of the night after our first intimate night together.

There'd been no note, no discussion later of it.

"Was I just a girl you wanted to get into bed?" I hadn't intended the question to come out quite so harshly.

Jaxson took a step back like I'd slapped him. His eyes widened, and he ran a hand through his hair. "Come with me," he commanded.

"Are you always this grumpy?" I snipped, irritated that every second I spent time with him, he'd grown to be a different person. Was this what he was like at work? How did the guys stand it?

He quirked an eyebrow, not looking the least bit amused by my question. "I'm not the grumpy one," he retorted.

He grabbed my hand, tugged me into his office, and shut the door abruptly at my heels, his hands letting go of mine.

I tried not to jump when he'd startled me, but I wasn't great at hiding my emotions or reactions, apparently. "What are you doing?" I didn't feel in danger or threatened, but Jaxson also hadn't been himself, at least what I knew of him.

"We need to talk." He gestured for me to come closer while he perched himself at the edge of his desk.

I stood, arms folded, staring at him. I wouldn't sit down. "Whatever you need to say, say it."

I was tired of his antics. Jaxson had been warm, protective, and kind when I'd gotten to know him, but every minute that I was in his presence, it seemed like I could do nothing right. It had only been a few days at work, and maybe I needed to give us time to figure it out.

He exhaled a heavy sigh and folded his arms across his chest, mirroring my position. "I think it would be best if you stayed with Hazel at the resort. I'll make sure when I book the reservation that I request a room with two queen beds."

"Excuse me?" I didn't back down, challenging him. "You brought me in here, shut the door, to tell me to what, get out of your house?"

Was he not man enough to do it in front of his buddies?

"No. That's not—" he groaned when his phone buzzed.

Skylar's name popped up on the screen. "Fuck." He rejected her call.

It seemed he wasn't only avoiding me. Had his change in mood been a result of Skylar coming to visit? "You should take that call; it might be important," I said.

"It's not," Jaxson said.

I stared at him, surprised he hadn't taken the opportunity as an excuse to end the awkwardness between us.

"You think I'm a jerk for not answering Skylar."

That wasn't what crossed my mind. "No. You're a jerk for not saying goodbye, texting me, or leaving a note after we slept together. You're a grumpy bosshole at the office and lately at home. If I had realized how much my presence irritated you, I wouldn't have accepted the job."

I didn't wait for his response. I jetted out of his office in time as the local sheriff was on his way out the main door.

"Hi, Hazel, I'm Ariella," I said, offering her my hand as I introduced myself to her. "I'm going to take you someplace safe."

Hazel glanced from me to Mason. He gave her a warm smile and a nod. "I'll be right behind you in my truck. We just need to make sure that no one knows we're together."

I hadn't been back to the Blue Sky Resort since the attack.

I still needed to pick up my paycheck for the time that I'd worked there but hadn't wanted to step foot in that place again.

I pulled into the parking lot.

The building loomed over us.

Mason was just a few minutes behind. He didn't intend on coming in the main entrance. He'd let himself in via the back and then take the elevator up to our floor.

Hazel didn't have anything with her. No bags. No clothes. She wore Mason's sweatshirt and a baggy pair of sweats, the hood over her head.

She kept her face down, her hands shoved into her pockets, and tried to appear inconspicuous.

I could do this. It was an easy assignment. All I had to do was check into the hotel lobby, get the key card and take Hazel up to the room, which would be our room.

I hadn't broken the news to her that I'd be rooming with her indefinitely.

"Everything okay? Are you going to be sick?" Hazel asked.

Emma stood behind the registration desk. We were friends, and while I was glad to see her, I hadn't spoken with her since before I'd been fired. She hadn't known about the assault and abduction.

Had she known why I'd been fired, that I had another name, or that I'd previously been employed by the C.I.A.?

"Ariella," Emma said, a dutiful smile on her face. It was the same gleeful expression that she gave all the guests at the resort.

Hazel glanced from Emma to me. I could tell she had questions, but thankfully she didn't start asking them.

"I have a reservation," I said, digging out my wallet from my purse.

"Under which name?" Emma asked. The smile disappeared from her sunny disposition.

She knew. "Ariella Cole." It was my legal name and maiden name.

I'd changed it after the divorce. I was formerly Ariella Ryan, the wife of Benjamin Ryan. He'd been convicted of several felonies for embezzlement, money laundering, the list went on. And now she knew.

Emma stood behind her desk. Her fingers tapped away at the keyboard as she stared at the screen.

Did she see the reservation? Was she just trying to take her time and fluster me? I thought we were friends, but the cold shoulder she gave me was my answer.

"Do you have a credit card, Ms. Cole?" Emma asked. "I will need one with the name Ariella Cole on it."

I handed over my credit card. "Of course. Do you need to see my government-issued identification too?" I flashed my driver's license at her, and I was ready to pull it out of my wallet from behind the plastic screen if she wanted to see it.

She tapped away at the keyboard. "No need." Another minute, and she retrieved two room keys, running them through the scanner as she assigned us a hotel room. "I've got two queen beds on the third floor. Can I help you with anything else?"

She handed us the keycards and wrote down our room number.

"I'm sure you can find your way to the elevator."

"Thank you," I forced out, snatched the keycards, and stalked away from the registration desk with Hazel at my side.

"Wow. Did you steal her boyfriend?" Hazel joked.

I pushed the elevator button to go up. "Something like that." I hadn't even considered that she might have been pissed about Jaxson.

Hazel didn't need to know about my past. My job was to look after her and get her to the hotel room.

Mason would be joining us anytime now.

We stepped into the elevator, just the two of us. I pushed the button to the third floor and hit the 'close doors' button repeatedly as a gentleman rushed toward the elevator.

I didn't want to be trapped with him, just in case he was after Hazel.

The doors slammed shut and the elevator ascended up to the third floor. I breathed a sigh of relief. I was probably making something out of nothing. He was probably just a guest at the resort.

Hazel remained quiet, and I stepped out of the elevator first when the doors opened. Mason was already in the hallway and stood outside our assigned room.

They worked at lightning speed. Declan must have provided him with the room number by hacking into the resort's system.

I opened the door with the room key, and Mason went in first, flipped on the light, and checked the bathroom and closet.

"Are you sure it's safe?" she asked, glancing around the room with a frightful gaze as she followed Mason in.

I shut the door behind myself and locked it, using the deadbolt.

"Yes. Keep the curtains shut. Someone will be with you at all times." Mason sat in a chair in the corner of the room that faced the door, his back to the wall.

"I'll be staying the night," I blurted out. "Jaxson uninvited me to stay with him."

I was pretty much homeless. With no insurance on my house and the fire that had destroyed the property, I had nothing.

"Wow," Mason said. He ran a hand through his short, cropped hair. "You do know why he's been an ass lately, don't you?"

I didn't answer his question. I wasn't sure. I assumed it had to do with me and he regretted that Eagle Tactical had hired me.

"Jaxson's sexually frustrated. I see the way he looks at you," Mason said.

"Like he wants to kill me?" I laughed.

"The man needs to get laid. He stares at you like you're the prize he wants at the fair."

It was absurd. "That can't be it." I didn't want to believe that he'd treated me like crap and kicked me out of his house because he wanted to have sex with me. "Oh my gosh! I'm an idiot. Jaxson's probably upset that he can't bring another woman over with me living in one bedroom and his sister in another."

"I'm pretty sure he doesn't want anyone else," Mason said, spelling it out for me.

Was that true? "I don't know, Mason. You didn't see him this morning in the office or when we're at his house. He can barely look at me."

"I'd have the same problem if I was living under the same roof as the woman I love and can't have," Mason said.

His gaze moved from me and locked on Hazel.

I could feel the sexual tension brewing between them with just a simple look. I cleared my throat and backed up toward the door.

"I need to head to the store and pick up a few things for Hazel. She's going to need clothes, toiletries, anything else?" I asked.

"Get her hair dye and sheering scissors," Mason said. "We can't take a chance that she'll be easily spotted by Franco or his buddies. Ariella, I want you to know you're welcome to stay in the extra bed. One of us will be here keeping watch over Hazel, protecting her, but you don't have to go back to Jaxson's if you don't feel comfortable."

"Thanks."

I wasn't sure what I was going to do, but having the option to stay at the hotel eased my mind more than I thought it would. I'd need to pick up my clothes, the few belongings I'd purchased after moving in with Jaxson.

"Do you need anything else?" I asked Hazel.

"Chocolate and maybe a box of condoms." She grinned, casting a glance at Mason.

Mason groaned. "Woman, you are going to make my job difficult. I can see it now."

"You haven't seen anything yet." Hazel winked at Mason.

I took that as my hint to leave.

CHAPTER TEN

Hazel

"She seemed nice," I said the minute the hotel room door closed.

Mason secured the lock before sitting back down on the chair.

"Ariella? Yeah, we haven't worked together long," Mason said. He didn't elaborate.

Okay. So maybe talking about Ariella wasn't the best conversation starter.

I turned off the television. It had been years since we'd seen one another. I didn't want to watch T.V. or pretend like what we were doing was normal.

I wanted to catch up with Mason, discover every flaw, and see how much he'd changed since high school when we were practically kids and inseparable.

"I've missed you," I said and stood from the bed. I toed off my shoes and sauntered across the room toward Mason.

"Hard to tell since you never called." His voice was gruff, his expression hard. There was so much he didn't know, and I didn't know how to tell him.

"Neither did you," I said.

We were both at fault for letting our lives go separate ways.

He'd gone into the army, and I was supposed to attend college in California. I had promised to write to him and he had every right to be angry. I'd broken that promise.

"I'd ask how you've been, but I can see that's not a story with a happy ending," Mason said.

"It could be," I said. I towered above him and straddled his legs before sitting down on his lap, facing him.

I wanted to jump back in time, have him take me with him, far from Chicago. It was too late to change the past, but I wanted to forget the time spent apart.

"Tell me you don't have a girlfriend or are married." I reached for his left hand, bringing his digits up to my face.

My lips latched onto his empty ring finger, grateful he appeared to be single.

"Hazel," his tone warned me to stop.

I didn't listen. I never listen.

I rolled my hips, teasing him, practically giving him a lap dance. With my fingers in his hair, I leaned forward, pushing my breasts against his chest.

I wanted him more than I wanted anyone in my life. I'd loved him since we were fourteen. He was the one who had gotten away.

"Promise you'll protect me."

I needed him like I needed air to breathe. He had no idea what I'd done to survive.

His forehead rested against mine. His warm, strong palm rested at my lower back. "You have my word. I won't let anything happen to you," Mason said.

I tangled my fingers in his hair.

His eyes shut.

My breath caressed against his lips. I wanted to kiss him. I needed to feel alive as I craved that connection with him.

He was my chance at freedom from Franco, at the prospect of a normal life, not one where I was forced to marry a man I didn't know and shipped off to another continent.

"I want you, Mason." My lips crashed down hard on his, not waiting for him to stop me or tell me how this was a terrible idea.

I didn't care that we'd barely talked or reconnected. Right now, in that very moment, I needed to feel safe. Mason was my safety net. He would catch me if I fell.

His mouth opened in kind, responding to the kiss, his hand pulling me tighter against his body. Warm, strong hands slid beneath my thick sweatshirt. His gentle touch grazed my bare skin.

I shuddered as he caressed my back, need outweighing everything else.

"Are you sure this is what you want?" Mason asked between feverish kisses.

"Yes," I said, staring deep into his gaze.

He lifted me into his arms and carried me to the bed, laying me down. He crawled up the mattress, straddled me, and hovered above my body. In haste, I tugged at his shirt, pulling it up and over his head.

Mason leaned down, whispering into my ear. "Do you realize you could get me fired doing this with a client?"

Staring up at him, I wrapped my legs around him, pulling him down, needing to feel his weight crush me, protect me, and make me whole—need outweighing everything else. I had no good answer other than I wanted him.

Was that enough? My fingers fumbled at the button on his jeans, and my hands trembled as I struggled to undo the metal.

"Hazel?" His fingers held mine in his hands. He sat on my hips, straddling me, before pinning my arms to the sides.

"I just—I need you, Mason." I sounded desperate. He'd probably call in one of his buddies to take over and never want to see me again.

"Maybe we should slow down." He pulled back and climbed off my body.

I whimpered before I realized the sound that slipped out past my throat. He'd done that to me, made me feel things I thought were impossible.

I didn't want to slow down or stop. Breathing hard, gasping for air, I lay staring up at the ceiling.

Mason climbed off the mattress, fixing his jeans button which I had managed to unclasp but not unzip. He grabbed his shirt from the bed and put his top back on.

Mason cleared his throat. "Ariella will be back soon, and we can't be caught in a compromising position."

Was that his concern, that we'd be caught by his colleagues?

I sat up and hurried to the bathroom, slamming the door shut on my heel. I slid down along the door, my back against the cold wood as I sat on the floor, my knees pulled up to my chest.

Regret filled my heart. I'd been foolish to think we could pick up where we'd left off.

Time seemed to trickle by like sand in an hourglass, one grain at a time.

Without my phone handy or a clock nearby, I didn't know how long I spent on the floor.

A firm knock vibrated through the wooden door. "You all right in there?" Mason asked.

"Fine." I would be after all of this was over and Franco left me alone. I didn't know how that would ever be possible unless I was put into witness protection or given a new identity—the types of arrangements that were made in movies for innocent victims.

I wasn't innocent.

My hands were covered in blood, the same as Nikolai's.

CHAPTER ELEVEN

MASON

I'd never met anyone more confusing in my life.

Hazel had stolen my heart and my virginity in high school. We'd been each other's first and vowed to only love each other forever.

It had been a fantasy, an empty promise that neither of us kept after we had graduated high school.

I'd gone into the military. Hazel had gone across the country to college, somewhere out west.

When or why she returned to Chicago, I wasn't certain. In fact, I didn't even know with absolute certainty that she left Chicago as she had intended.

It would be a lie to say that I never thought about her. I found myself comparing other women to her constantly. She had been the one who got away—the woman I loved and let escape.

I hadn't chased her. Maybe I should have.

With time, I assumed we'd grown apart. We were two different people than when we knew each other back at boarding school.

She'd had that predatory look in her eyes when Ariella left the two of us alone.

I hadn't thought anything of it at first. I'd assumed she'd watch television, and I'd make sure that Franco didn't find out where she stayed.

I hadn't wanted to stop, with her pert little body tucked tight under my hips.

I could have spent hours memorizing every curve and tasting every inch of her skin. I wanted to discover her all over again, see if she was just the way I remembered her.

We couldn't let desire interfere and risk her life. I needed to be alert, keeping an eye on the room or anything suspicious happening nearby. It was hard to do that while my lips were locked with hers.

Her soft lips still sent tingles throughout my entire body.

I needed a cold shower, but that was out of the question.

Instead, I'd gotten the cold shoulder. She'd locked herself in the bathroom for nearly an hour.

Ariella would be back from the store any minute.

Did Hazel wait for Ariella to return so that she wouldn't have to be alone with me and face me after what happened?

I approached the bathroom door, my hand perched on the wood. I gave a soft rap. "You all right in there?" I asked.

I wasn't expecting her to have an issue with Franco or need me for anything that she couldn't handle on her own in the bathroom. I was just trying for a basic conversation starter, a way to get her to retreat from her hiding place.

"Fine."

Any woman who ever told me she was 'fine' was never all right. I'd learned repeatedly that 'fine' was a code word for 'leave me the fuck alone' or 'it's all your fault.'

I wasn't sure how this was my fault other than I'd stopped us from going any further. While we were two consenting adults, I also didn't think it was wise for Ariella to walk in on us hot and sweaty between the sheets.

I wasn't one to kiss and tell, let alone let the new girl at the office pay witness to our cravings.

I held up my hand to knock again, but that seemed

counterproductive. If she wanted to come out of the bathroom, she could join me.

I let my hand fall to my side and dug out my cell phone, glancing at the messages briefly before putting it on the table. There wasn't anything timely or important that came through.

I slumped back into the chair, my attention on the door as I waited for Ariella to return.

Hazel would undoubtedly come out of the bathroom when Ariella returned. Right?

Twenty minutes later, Ariella had arrived with several shopping bags of clothes and toiletries for Hazel.

Hazel wouldn't look at me as the two women sat perched on the bed, going through the contents of the bags.

I sat in the corner of the room, observing the two of them. It was almost as if I didn't exist.

Ariella glanced up at me and gave me a smile before returning her attention back to Hazel.

Well, I wasn't invisible at least.

"Do you want me to cut your hair and then color it?" Ariella asked.

Hazel looked distraught, her eyes wide and skin ghastly. "I knew I'd have to do this. I'm just not ready yet."

"I promise I'll make your hair look good, and no one will recognize you. We can chop off several inches, and with a bombshell blonde, no one will think twice it's you," Ariella said.

"I hope so."

"Come with me." Ariella brought the shearing scissors into the bathroom.

Hazel stalled for a long moment, her attention on the floor. She wouldn't so much as look at me.

When this was all over and Hazel was safe, the two of us needed to have a long talk.

"Are you coming?" Ariella asked.

Hazel meandered to the bathroom and then abruptly shut the door. I could hear chatter, and then the bathroom fan turned on, probably to drown out any discussion of me.

Had Ariella noticed the shift in mood with Hazel? I tried not to give any impression things had changed over the past hour while she'd been away.

The fire alarm emitted its ear-piercing squeal—the white light flashed inside the hotel room. I pulled out my gun, prepared for whatever happened next.

Stalking toward the bathroom and the room's exit, I gave a firm knock on the bathroom door.

"We hear it," Ariella said. She pulled open the bathroom door. It didn't appear that she'd started on cutting Hazel's hair. At least I didn't notice any recognizable difference.

"Put your hood back up," I commanded. With my gun drawn, I grabbed the handle to the door and carefully stepped out into the hallway.

Smoke filled the corridor.

"Stay close." I led the way with Ariella at the back and Hazel sandwiched between us.

My eyes burned with smoke, and I held my breath.

Fits of coughing erupted from behind. I couldn't turn around to see if it was Hazel or Ariella struggling to breathe.

"Keep moving. We're almost at the exit." I had studied the exit from our hotel room. We had to pass three doors before I reached the door to the stairwell.

Through the blinding smoke, my eyes burned and teared.

I felt for the door, swung it open, and was relieved the stairwell was smoke free.

"Come on!" I shouted for Ariella and Hazel. They were right at my feet, both of them hurrying down the stairs with me.

The floodlights to the stairs emitted a faint halogen glow. The bulbs flickered, spitting out enough light to illuminate the path.

I secured my gun, not wanting to alarm any of the guests as they poured out from each floor, the stairwell becoming more crowded as I kept Hazel behind Ariella and me tight to her back.

My boots trampled against the steps, and as I came to the first floor and followed the stream of guests out of the stairwell, my instincts took over.

Men with black ski masks and semi-automatic guns held hostages in the lobby.

"Turn that damned alarm off!" the man closest to me screamed. He waved the barrel aimlessly, threatening everyone but his buddies who had taken over the hotel.

"Get down!" another masked man shouted at us, his weapon poised at the guests coming down the stairwell. "On the ground, now!"

I gestured for Hazel and Ariella to get down.

"No secret signals." The masked man smashed the barrel of the weapon against my head, knocking me to my ass.

Blood dripped down my forehead. The gash burned, but not worse than my pride.

Doubled over, he searched me for a weapon, his semi-automatic pointed at my head. He shoved my gun into his dark black pants.

"Eagle Tactical, huh? You're coming with us."

CHAPTER TWELVE

ARIELLA

The smoke had been a diversion on the third floor to drive everyone out of their rooms and downstairs.

Who were the men with guns, and why had they assaulted Mason and taken him with them?

"I'll be fine," he said, glancing over his shoulder at us.

Crimson dripped to the linoleum floor, staining the hallway.

Mason was whisked out of the lobby.

I couldn't see where they took him. His hands were held up in the air, a sign of surrender. His weapon had been confiscated.

Did he have a backup gun?

Hazel's eyes glistened.

We lay on the floor near the stairwell, our hands on our heads. With my head turned, I faced Hazel, trying to convey that it would be okay.

The masked men, eight of them whom I had counted when we were first forced onto the ground, searched all of us as we lay on the floor, stealing away phones, keys, anything that could be used as a weapon or to call for help.

The fire alarm shut off.

Someone had pulled the fire alarm.

The fire department would be required to respond to the call and would notify the police when they saw what they were up against.

Thick metal chains secured the doors shut from the inside. We couldn't leave, not without someone escorting us out of the building.

My breathing hitched, and a wave of nausea coursed through my body. I needed to get ahold of my emotions and settle the fear that pumped into my veins.

I shut my eyes and counted to ten. I practiced my biofeedback breathing exercises to calm my heart rate, which would help settle my nerves too. I imagined a black nothingness with a single wave. With each breath, I followed the wave and inhaled slowly, held it, then exhaled at the same speed.

The tremor in my hand was minimal, but the exercise kept my entire body from shaking.

"Everyone, against the wall!" the masked man demanded of us. "Slowly! No sudden movements or we will shoot you."

He pointed the gun into the ceiling and blasted a round of bullets, instilling fear, reminding us that they were in charge and to do as instructed.

Hazel and I sat up and scooted back against the wall.

Where had they taken Mason?

Clearly, they'd known him. Which meant it had to be someone local, right?

Had they known Mason had been staying at the hotel? He hadn't checked in to the resort, so someone would have had to see him or his vehicle outside.

Unless it had nothing to do with Mason, and they just wanted to remove him out of the equation.

It was no secret that he was former military special forces and would lay his life on the line to protect everyone else.

Without him, what chance did we have to get out of this alive?

Of the eight masked men I'd noticed earlier, there were only six now. Where had the other two gone? One had taken Mason out of the room. Had I miscounted?

Hazel reached for my hand. I gave it a squeeze, wanting to reassure her that we would be okay. Her grip tightened against my palm. I glanced at her, frozen in fear, her eyes trained across the room at two men in suits on the floor held hostage with us.

"Them," she whispered so that only I could hear her.

"You know them?" I asked.

"That's Franco," Hazel whispered. She hung her head, letting the hoodie fall over her eyes.

Had the men recognized her? I didn't want to make it obvious that I'd spotted them.

Casually, I glanced around the room at everyone, mentally taking note of the number of hostages, how many were children, whether anyone was injured, and then let my gaze study the men who wanted Hazel.

They were talking amongst one another, their backs pressed against the wall. They looked like two giant thugs, dark hair, lots of muscle in dark suits.

They were too far away for me to hear what the two men said to one another. Maybe that was a good thing if they hadn't noticed Hazel nestled beside me.

I was her last chance of protection.

I didn't have a weapon, and there were masked men with guns watching our every move.

How were we going to get out of this alive?

CHAPTER THIRTEEN

MASON

Darkness surrounded my vision.

The man who had dragged me out of the hotel and into the back of a dark van shoved a hood over my head and bound my arms behind my back with zip ties.

He said nothing.

Was he concerned if he spoke again that I would recognize his voice?

He knew who I worked for, which meant he knew me.

The door slammed shut. I listened and waited for another door to slam. It didn't happen. The engine didn't hum to life, either.

A click from across the parking lot. Was it a door shutting? Had the offender gone back into the building?

I'd been alone in the white unmarked van that had been parked near the side exit of the resort. I needed to remove the binds from my wrists, and then I'd deal with the bastards who had taken over Blue Sky Resort.

What were they after, money? The hotel probably didn't have much cash on hand, as booking a hotel room always required using a credit card, but it was possible cash was exchanged for ski and snowboard rental equipment.

I'd seen eight men in masks, all in dark clothes and black pants, with matching black shoes.

They didn't want anyone to recognize them, but they knew me. Which meant I knew them. Whoever they were, they were amateurs.

I bent forward and used my body to create as much space as possible. I'd trained for this, and while I could have done the motion while in the hotel, I was outmanned and outgunned. I slammed down my arms, breaking the zip ties.

I yanked the hood off my head and tossed it to the floor before I opened the door of the truck and stepped out. That was too easy.

Sirens wailed in the distance, coming closer.

A fire engine and police car pulled into the parking lot.

An ambulance trailed in the distance.

The sheriff stopped in front of the building and stepped out, his lights left on but the siren silent. "I didn't expect to see you twice in one day, Reid. Can you tell me what's going on? The fire alarm went off, but no one is outside."

Even he recognized the huge red flag. "Hostage situation, eight offenders with semi-automatics. They're holed up in the lobby with hostages."

I reached for my phone in my pocket to discover it wasn't there. I'd left it on the table upstairs.

Shit.

I needed to contact the team.

"Did they tell you what they wanted? Any demands?" Sheriff Nelson asked.

"Nothing. They knew I was with Eagle Tactical. One of them coldcocked me with his gun, stole my weapon, and dragged my ass outside. He threw me in the back of the van. Lucky for me, he only had zip ties and not handcuffs." Handcuffs were a hell of a lot harder to break free from.

"Locals. Did you recognize any of their voices?" Sheriff Nelson asked.

"No." I wished I could have been of more help.

"Do you have any guys inside?"

"Two, but they're not my brothers. The new girl we hired and a client. Neither have special forces training like my buddies."

I wanted it clear that they were not in a position to stop what happened on the inside.

Sheriff Nelson called for backup and then contacted Eagle Tactical for their expertise.

This is what we trained for, and while we weren't always the ones charging into danger, with our combined years of experience, we were always available for consultations in the field.

Emma stepped outside the side door, a box of cigarettes in hand.

"Stop right there! Hands up!" Sheriff Nelson blasted into the loudspeaker attached to his squad car.

She dropped her lighter and box of cigarettes to the ground. Eyes wide, she held up her hands and took a slow step back, reached for the door, and flung herself back inside the building.

The door slammed shut behind her.

"Call Declan," I said. "Tell him to run everything he can on Emma Foster."

"Wait, you know her?" Sheriff Nelson asked. "Is she your client? The one who's inside with your new girl?"

"No. Emma recently moved to Breckenridge. We ran her background when she was hired by the resort as part of their hiring practice. She came up clean."

Why did she come back to Breckenridge? It was clear she was helping the men who had taken over the building. And the fact she'd been hanging out with the off-gridders and living with them, what the hell were they after?

Sheriff Nelson tossed me his cell phone. I called Declan at the office, relayed the information about Emma to him. As I hung up the phone, Jaxson and Aiden pulled into the parking lot.

"Looks like the rest of your team is here," the sheriff said.

Aiden climbed out of the truck and glanced me over. "How's your head? Do you need to get checked out by paramedics?"

"My head is fine." Since when had he taken on Jaxson's role of being the parent to the team? I expected it from Jaxson, especially since he was a father. "My ego got a little bruised, that's all."

Getting my ass dragged out in front of the town couldn't have helped our image at Eagle Tactical. I should have fought harder and knocked that guy with the gun on his ass.

"I'm sure you'll recover. Hazel and Ariella are inside?"

"Unfortunately. Where's Jaxson?" I asked.

"He'll be out in a minute. He's on the phone talking to our client's brother. It turns out he's requesting information since he can't get ahold of Franco."

My head spun. "What? He's trying to hire us now too?" What were the odds? It wasn't like we were located in Chicago and they both had searched for a private security firm.

"No. Franco had given our contact information to Nikolai in case he didn't check in with him," Aiden said. "Any chance these guys are the ones from the restaurant this morning?"

"The two deceased men were Alexander Petrov and Miko Romanoff," I said.

Jaxson slammed the door of the truck as he stomped over toward us, fuming.

Was his shitty mood a result of the phone call or the fact he'd been sexually frustrated the past few days working alongside Ariella? There wasn't much more I could take of his attitude. I shot a glance at Declan. He saw it too, didn't he?

Declan gave a faint nod and then rubbed at his jaw, glancing at the resort. "How many armed men did you see?" Declan asked.

"There were eight in the lobby, armed with semi-automatic weapons and wearing ski-masks. I didn't see any body armor, which is good news for us," I said.

Another officer brought over a map of the facility and spread it out over the hood of the squad car.

I pointed at the exit that Emma had come in and out of easily. "This appears to be the only point of an entrance that isn't locked." I had noticed metal chains on the doors before being pistol-whipped.

I'd tried to take in as much detail as possible. I was the only eyes the team had right now.

"SWAT is on their way. I'd like Eagle Tactical to assist," the sheriff said, "but we're in charge of the operation."

"Of course," I said. "We wouldn't have it any other way." We knew how procedure worked on these types of cases. There was often red tape involved, and they couldn't just hand over the reins for us to take the lead.

"Where are Ariella and Hazel?" Jaxson asked.

I swallowed the lump in my throat. Had they not gotten the news from the sheriff?

"They're inside the resort." I met his icy stare, unwilling to cower.

His gaze tightened. "I realize that. Where in the building were they last located?"

I pointed on the map where we had been. By now, it was likely they'd been moved someplace else. "Here."

"How many hostages were inside?" the sheriff asked.

I hadn't been able to count fast enough the total number. I could give a rough estimate. "Fifty hostages, maybe sixty-five." There hadn't been too many people who had filtered in down the stairs while I'd been getting my head smashed in by the barrel of a gun.

"We'll start with negotiations and see what they want," Jaxson said.

"There's something you should know, Jaxson." He glanced from the map of the building back up at me. "We believe Emma may be involved in the hostage takeover. She came outside to take a smoke."

"I don't get it. Why not just smoke inside the building if she's involved?" Jaxson's brow furrowed, his jaw tight.

I didn't have an answer or an explanation for him, at least not yet. Maybe I was wrong. Maybe she heard the fire alarm and had been locked in a bathroom and then stepped outside for a cigarette. Except why else would she have fled back inside the building at the first sign of the authorities?

She had to be hiding something.

Declan folded his arms across his chest. "Was she coming outside to see if anyone was coming to intervene? I don't know Emma, but this doesn't sound like what I know of her."

I snorted under my breath. "She was with the off-gridders just last week."

"That doesn't make her guilty of a crime," Declan said, "just poor taste in friends."

"It does when she has a gun trained on Jaxson." I'd kept Jaxson's secret from Ariella, but I hadn't even considered mentioning it to the team. Should I have said something sooner? I ran a hand through my hair. It was too late now to second guess that decision. I couldn't make another mistake, not with so many lives at risk.

"Ariella doesn't know Emma's involved with the off-gridders," Jaxson said. "Means they could be using her to get to us."

Would they go that far? "Did she call you or try to communicate with you?" I asked Jaxson. Those two had been close, and while right now there'd been an obvious tiff of sorts, she still would have gone to him if she was in trouble, right?

"No. I texted her, but she didn't respond. Declan pinged her phone and said it's turned off," Jaxson said.

"They probably took everyone's phones," I said. "Hostage takeover 101."

"Thank you for that." Jaxson shook his head and stormed toward the truck.

"Where are you going?" I followed him as he opened the trunk and retrieved our tactical equipment.

Jaxson retrieved a bulletproof vest and put it on over his shirt.

"I refuse to sit on my ass and wait for SWAT to tell us how to do our job, or worse, the town sheriff. Are you coming with me?"

CHAPTER FOURTEEN

ARIELLA

With my back pressed against the cold brick, I tucked my knees to my chest.

Hazel sat to my right, pressed tight against my body as we were crammed together in the lobby.

I'd trained with the C.I.A. on how to take out an assailant in a hostage takeover, but there wasn't a class that involved eight armed men versus a tech operative.

I'd never had any exciting field opportunities. I'd sat in hotel rooms in foreign countries listening with surveillance equipment. That had been the extent of my excitement.

This went beyond that, and quite honestly, I could have done without the thrill. I didn't like high-adrenaline adventures, and this one was making my heart hammer in my chest.

Having autonomic dysfunction sucked on a normal day. Today, it really wreaked havoc on me. It took every ounce of strength to force my body to stay calm, to not tremble even though the fight-or-flight reflex had taken over.

My breathing exercises sucked. Biofeedback was a great tool with the right equipment. Seated on the floor with masked men threatening us with guns was not the right time to use it.

I wished I would have had a weapon. Although what good would it have done? I wasn't likely capable of stopping eight men, maybe one or two on a good day. Six had stayed with us, and the other two who had disappeared returned, but Mason wasn't with them.

Where was he? Was he alive? Had they tortured him?

I tried to think of anything else. Puppies. Summer sunsets. Surfing at the beach. Jaxson. The last one brought a faint quirk to my lips and it made my stomach flop.

I hadn't wanted to think about him.

The man Hazel was afraid of cleared his throat. "How much longer are you going to keep us? Some of us have business to attend to."

He had a heavy accent, definitely Russian. I'd studied languages as part of my curriculum at the C.I.A..

The shortest of the masked men stormed over to the Russian and shoved the barrel of the gun into his chest, poised against his heart. "You'll shut up!" the masked man barked.

"Or what? You'll shoot me?" the Russian snorted a laugh, unfazed by the threat. However, he didn't physically fight back. "You don't scare me. I've killed cockroaches bigger than you."

"That's Franco," Hazel whispered into my ear.

She'd mentioned that earlier, but I hadn't known which one he was until now.

There were two greasy-haired thick men in suits who sat on the floor against the opposite wall.

If the bastard shot Franco, he'd be unknowingly doing all of us a favor.

"You may not be afraid of death, but what about if I kill your friend?" The masked man moved the barrel of the gun away from Franco's chest to the other man's head. "I'm itching to pull the trigger."

"Go ahead and do it," Franco said. He sounded bored.

Was it some form of reverse psychology?

I couldn't see the masked man's eyes from across the room. We all watched. A heaviness fell over the room. Several soft gasps of fear from hostages spilled out.

"Enough!" A larger man wearing a mask and waving a gun pushed the barrel away from the man's head.

He grabbed the shorter man by the arm and dragged him down the hallway.

"Coward!" Franco shouted.

My hands trembled as I expelled a nervous breath. The men holding us captive weren't murderers. At least not yet.

What were they doing taking hostages at the resort? What could they possibly hope to achieve?

One of the masked men whisked a woman, her hands bound behind her back, toward us. "Let me go!" her voice carried down the hallway.

Emma?

Her long brown hair covered her red, splotchy cheeks and eyes. Had she been crying?

"Leave me alone!" Emma slipped away from the masked man's grasp and landed her gaze on me.

She sniffled and collapsed onto the floor in a heap at my side.

"Did they hurt you?" I asked, my voice hardly above a whisper.

The masked man lifted the handle of his weapon and pointed it at my forehead. "Quiet!" he snarled.

Trembling, I lowered my gaze. I didn't want to appear threatening. The last thing we needed was garnering Franco's attention and him noticing Hazel beside me.

"Smart girl," he said with a laugh. I imagined a dark and sinister smile behind those icy blue eyes.

His voice sent a shiver down my spine. It was rough and thick. He snorted and lowered the gun but bent down to grab my arm.

"You're coming with me." He yanked me to my feet, his grip tight and hard, unforgiving.

"No!" I pulled back from his grasp.

I was safer with the other hostages. I didn't trust the masked man, what he might make me do with him.

"You don't tell me no," he seethed and jerked my hair, his fist tangling the strands as he pulled my neck back to face him.

Were all eyes on us? I couldn't look away, my neck twisted to stare only up at the man's face, the mask making it impossible for me to see him.

He hoisted me over his shoulder and, with his other hand, grabbed Hazel's arm. She at least had a thick sweatshirt to protect her from his tight grip.

"Let me go!" I fought with all my strength. My hands punched at his lower back, pounding into him. It was worthless. He wore a vest beneath his black shirt, thick, like Kevlar, concealable.

"Shut it or I put a bullet in both of your heads!"

CHAPTER FIFTEEN

JAXSON

Mason grabbed a pair of bolt cutters, and we breached the side entrance of the resort. Sitting around and waiting for SWAT to negotiate wasn't going to work.

I'd gotten a call from Nikolai Agron, the last person I wanted to deal with today.

If everything I'd heard was true, then I'd taken on a client I wasn't comfortable handling. I had dealt with men who were scumbags in the past, but this was different.

I usually had the upper hand.

I didn't like that Ariella and Hazel were being held hostage, and Franco was nowhere to be found. The actions at the resort didn't reflect the mafia's strategies. Had Franco known Hazel had booked a room, he would have undoubtedly snatched her or killed her, depending on his desires.

I wasn't sure which he had planned. While he'd wanted her as his wife, the fact he'd gunned the marshals down and hadn't thought twice about her safety made me suspect that he was prepared to kill her. Was it because she betrayed him?

I gestured at Mason to follow me down the hall. He gave a curt nod and covered me from behind. Guns were drawn; we hugged the wall as we came around the corner. In the distance, voices grew louder, more prominent. That meant we were close.

Her mousy brown hair had been chopped recently into a bob cut. Emma Foster, the birth mother of my daughter, stood just around the corner to another hallway with a vending machine.

Dressed in her black slacks and blue-collared resort shirt, she tapped her foot against the linoleum floor. “I don’t see why I couldn’t have worn a mask and dressed up with you guys,” Emma said.

Just on the other side of the vending machine, was a masked man. His gun poked out from behind the appliance as he stepped forward.

Dressed all in black, he was the same height and build as I was. I could easily take him, but not with Emma watching.

Emma was definitely involved.

Had she known what was going down? How big a part did she play? Did she orchestrate the entire situation? I had a plethora of questions, but they wouldn’t get answered if I approached her. That wasn’t how she worked, not with me. There was a history between us, a complicated one.

We weren’t friends. We weren’t even lovers. We’d spent one night together, technically one very long day, and that had been it.

The masked man leaned into Emma and whispered something into her ear before she stammered off down the hall.

I waited until Emma was out of sight and rounded the corner before the masked man could anticipate that anyone had been watching them. I rammed into his body, throwing him off balance.

He stumbled backward, tripping over his feet, his gun falling to the floor out of his grasp. I held my breath. Had Emma heard the ruckus? Would she come back and find the two of us fighting?

Mason stood guard, watching my back.

I snatched the weapon from the ground and pointed it at the masked man. “Take it off,” I seethed between clenched teeth. There was only one way in, and that was dressed like them.

"Bite me," the masked man said and smacked his forehead against mine.

Fuck, that hurt. I swallowed the pain as he struggled for the gun in my hands. No. I wouldn't give it to him. I stomped on his foot, elbowed his stomach, and kneed his groin.

Playing dirty was the only way to survive. We weren't in a boxing ring playing by a set of predetermined rules. This was life or death.

"Bastard," he grunted and lunged at me, slamming my back against the brick wall.

I gasped from the impact, and Mason hurried closer, gun drawn and poised on the masked man's forehead.

I thrust his mask off, shocked.

Jayden Scott. He'd been running with the off-gridders for too long.

"What the hell?" I couldn't believe what he'd gotten himself involved in. We'd served in the special forces together and were brothers. It felt like a lifetime ago when I stared back at his cold gaze.

Was his involvement because of Emma? They'd seemed pretty chummy together near the vending machines earlier. Had that been why he'd shown up?

I handed Mason the semi-automatic as he stood behind me. I didn't need Jayden getting his dirty claws on it again.

With one hand gripping Jayden's black shirt, I shoved my pistol against his head. "Give me one reason I shouldn't unload the magazine," I said between gritted teeth.

"You don't know anything," Jayden said.

"Why are you here? What do they want?" Men don't show up and take hostages for sport, certainly not these men, off-gridders.

What were they after? I shoved my face in his, the safety off—my index finger on the trigger. I was ready to shoot him, a man whose life I'd saved a decade ago.

He snorted and shrugged. Jayden didn't so much as sweat with the barrel against his skin. "You don't have it in you to shoot me, Monroe."

I hated how well he knew me. The truth was I wouldn't shoot an unarmed man unless my life was in mortal danger. It wasn't, at least not right now, but everyone else's lives were.

I had no other choice. I took the handle of the gun and slammed it against his head, knocking him unconscious. He fell to the ground in a heap.

"Help me get his clothes off him," I said.

Mason stood there, shouldering one gun while keeping the other pointed around the corner, prepared at a moment's notice to protect us. "Looks like you got it handled."

Sighing, I stripped Jayden down to his boxers. I didn't feel good about what I did, but what other choice was there?

Two of us against eight, with dozens of hostages, didn't bode well. At least it was seven now, except Emma was involved.

I needed to take her out of the equation.

I opened the nearest door, a janitorial supply closet, and dragged Jayden inside. I shut the door, and with Mason's help, we quickly dragged the vending machine in front to block Jayden from escaping. Just in case he woke up before my plan was complete.

Quick to don Jayden's clothes, I slid on the last part of the ensemble, the black ski mask, and held out my hand for the gun that Mason had been watching for me.

"You sure about this?" Mason asked. "You're a father. Maybe I should be the one risking my life."

It seemed he had second thoughts. I couldn't allow myself to second guess any decisions now or in the future. "I got this."

I needed to protect Ariella as well as Hazel. My job involved risking my life. It was part of the position.

On my belt, were a handful of zip ties that Jayden had worn on his pants. While I didn't intend on taking hostages, I also couldn't let Emma discover I wasn't Jayden.

Would she recognize my voice or my eyes through the mask? We may have only spent one night together, but she'd shown up at my door with Isabella, and I'd shown up at her door telling her to leave town a little over a month ago.

I gestured for Mason to follow me down the hallway. Emma

stayed away from the hostages. She leaned against the wall, her phone in hand, staring down at the device, oblivious to my presence.

Mason hung back, watching with his gun drawn in case I needed backup.

I snuck up without her so much as flinching.

Her focus was entirely on the game she was playing on her cell phone, which involved a series of colorful bubbles that made no sense to me.

I grabbed her arms and thrust them behind her back. Her phone fell to the floor.

Yanking a zip tie, I secured her wrists, binding them together.

"Jayden," Emma's voice held a hint of annoyance. "This isn't funny. Let me go."

I didn't answer her. I didn't want to speak yet, worried she might recognize my voice wasn't *his*.

I had to be careful. I may have had only one chance, and I didn't want to ruin it before I found Ariella and Hazel.

It took all my strength not to turn around and glance at Mason. I was used to sharing signals in the field. He had my back. I had to trust that he had it now, too, while I couldn't turn around.

"Fine. If you want to play cops and robbers, I guess I can play along." Emma almost sounded bored.

The mask was hot, stuffy. I breathed heavily through my nose, doing everything I could to keep my mouth shut. It was difficult. I wanted to tell her to shut up. To shake her and demand to know what the hell she'd gotten herself involved with and why.

What sane person would leave their life behind to live amongst the off-gridders? Their refuge was a hell hole, compromised of a commune with no running water or heat. They were basic, lived off the land, and depended on each other for survival.

It might have been a nice idea if they weren't men with sinister pasts.

I still had yet to grasp what they wanted, why they'd taken over the Blue Sky Resort. I couldn't flat out ask Emma. It would alert her that I wasn't Jayden.

I grabbed her elbow and escorted her with heavy footsteps toward the crowd of noise and commotion. Mostly, it involved tears and whispered pleas, some praying, others talking amongst one another.

The offenders hadn't demanded silence. Okay, so they weren't worried about being overthrown or the hostages working together to defeat them.

If the perpetrators were all off-gridders, then these weren't the brightest men. Some had military training, but not all. Most who had served would have been dishonorably discharged.

These weren't honorable men.

I led Emma down the hall and glanced from one person to the next until my gaze landed on Ariella.

She rocked slowly, her knees pressed tight to her chest, her arms wrapped around her legs. To her right, was a hostage with an oversized sweatshirt, hood up.

I'd recognize that hoodie anywhere. It belonged to Mason Reid. It must have been Hazel buried underneath, which was probably wise.

I briefly glanced at the hostages. A few were town folk, the owners of the resort, and several guests I didn't know. They'd have to wait. Hazel was my priority, and Ariella. I refused to leave her behind.

"Leave me alone!" Emma pulled away from me, sniffled, and fell to the ground beside Ariella. She knew how to play the part of the victim. How long had she been auditioning for that role?

"Did they hurt you?" Ariella whispered, falling for her performance.

I hated watching Ariella filled with fear, trembling against the wall, but I had to make it convincing if I wanted everyone to believe I was one of them.

I had no other choice. I lifted the handle of my gun and poised it at her forehead. "Quiet!" I barked out orders.

The shiver coursed through her body. Anyone could see the fear I had instilled in her.

No. I had to separate the two. I was only here to save her. These men had caused her trauma. "Smart girl," I said and tried my damnedest to laugh.

I needed to be convincing, or I'd put all of our lives in danger. I lowered my gun and bent down to grab her arm. "You're coming with me." I hoisted Ariella to her feet.

"No!"

She was a fighter; I'd give her that. "You don't tell me no," I seethed. I had no choice but to demand her to come, show force. These men wouldn't take no so easily.

I grabbed a fistful of her hair and jerked her head back to face me.

I stared into her eyes, filled with fright. Could she see me? Did she recognize my eyes through the ski mask?

I wanted to tell her to trust me, but I couldn't. Her fear is what made it believable to everyone who watched us.

I couldn't risk Ariella fighting me. I needed to demand Hazel to come with me too. It was the only way to save them. Hopefully, Ariella would understand and forgive me when she saw it was me beneath the mask.

I tossed her over my shoulder and grabbed Hazel's arm, thrusting her up onto her feet.

"Let me go!" Ariella shrieked.

She was strong for her tiny frame, her fists landing blow after blow at my lower back. Truthfully, it didn't hurt. The vest did a decent job of shielding me from her assault.

Had she discovered who was beneath the mask?

I needed to sound convincing. I had to get us past the other armed men. "Shut it, or I put a bullet in both of your heads!"

Hazel was the least of all to fight me. Her body was limp, but my grip on her arm made sure that she didn't slip from my grasp.

I stalked with them back the way we came, past the hostages, including two men on my right in suits, legs spread out, seated on the floor. Our eyes locked. *Franco Ivanov.*

I whisked the girls past the throes of people.

"Where are you taking them?" another male voice answered. He stood twenty feet away, masked and armed.

"Put me down," Ariella grunted. She continued to pound against my back, but her motions felt less forceful. Was it for show, or had she felt defeated?

"For some filthy fun. I thought I'd teach them each a lesson for disobeying us." Bile rose to my throat. I wanted to vomit.

The masked man scoffed and turned on his heel, not entirely interested in me or my plans.

I carried them down the hall, turned, and shoved Hazel into Mason's arms.

Mason held up a finger to his lips to be quiet. He grabbed Hazel's hand and whisked her down the corridor, out the direction we came in.

"I won't let you!" Ariella continued to fight me. With her head bent down, she'd failed to see Mason helping Hazel. "Fight him!" she shouted to Hazel.

I kept my pace, falling behind Mason and Hazel as they jogged down the hall for the entrance that we'd come in from.

I wanted to tell Ariella that it was me, but I couldn't risk anyone discovering us.

What if another masked man caught up with us, or worse, Jayden had freed himself?

CHAPTER SIXTEEN

ARIELLA

I squirmed against his shoulder, and while the masked man had kept an arm around my hips, I didn't stop my movements. He'd grow tired or be forced to put me down and I'd have the chance to fight back. It was just the two of us.

His grip loosened just slightly, and I used all my strength to roll hard against him, knocking him over and us onto the floor.

A male voice grunted, "Damnit, Freckles."

It couldn't be. Could it? "Jaxson?" I whispered.

I probably should have run. It was my opportunity, but I'd recognize that voice anywhere when it said my name.

He glanced over his shoulder as he stood up, dusted off his pants, and offered me a hand.

Those piercing blue eyes stole my heart. I clutched his hand, and we tore out of the building.

SWAT awaited our departure out of the building. Guns pointed at us.

I threw my arms into the air.

Jaxson did the same. The shotgun was slung over his shoulder. He fell to his knees, the mask still on as SWAT surrounded him.

"Don't shoot!" I screamed at the men. "He's with Eagle Tactical." I had assumed they'd sent him in as part of their operation.

"Even more reason to arrest his ass," a man with a SWAT jacket said.

He stepped out from behind the command center positioned across the parking lot. He must have been the leader of the operation.

"Jaxson?" What the hell was going on?

SWAT agents patted me down to make sure I wasn't harboring a weapon before they whisked me away from Jaxson.

"I want to see Jaxson," I demanded. Why were they keeping us apart? "He saved my life." I insisted that they know he rescued me.

Was it the fact he was dressed as one of *them* that they had to check out his story?

Had he broken the rules coming in to rescue Hazel and me? Where was Hazel? Worry flooded my face as I sat in a metal folding chair, a blanket around my shoulders.

"Relax," Mason said, coming to sit beside me. He handed me a bottle of water. "Jaxson said you might need this."

"Thank you."

Hazel stood behind him. She was small in comparison, and I hadn't even realized how easily she disappeared. He was her protector.

Had he been inside the resort too? I hadn't seen him, but that didn't mean anything. Eagle Tactical worked as a team.

I doubted Jaxson had gone in alone.

"Where is he?" I asked. I opened the bottle of water and took a sip. I used two hands to hold the bottle, doing my best to keep my hands from shaking. The blanket helped, even though I didn't feel cold. I didn't feel much of anything other than exhausted.

"Debriefing and dealing with the repercussions of what we did,"

Mason said. He wrapped an arm around Hazel, pulling her tight against his body.

"I don't understand. Is he in trouble?"

Mason smirked, chill. "No more than usual. I need to get Hazel someplace safe. She mentioned Franco was inside the resort. I can't risk waiting around for him to find us out here."

"Yes, that's right." She couldn't stay at the hotel anymore. I didn't dare ask where he'd take her. I wasn't sure I wanted to know. It was best to keep it a secret from everyone.

He rested a hand on my shoulder. "Are you sure you're all right? If I take you with us, Jaxson will lose his shit. He's just barely keeping it together," Mason said.

I sipped at my water and wiped my lips. "I'm fine. I doubt he wants to see me. He kicked me out of his place. I'm the last person he wants to deal with. Remember, I planned on staying at the hotel to get out of his hair."

"Talk to him," Mason said. He patted me on the back before leading Hazel out of the tent.

I wanted to leave. I didn't want to stay with the itchy blanket curled up over my shoulders, drinking a bottle of tepid water. I wanted to go home, slip into a hot bath, and let my troubles disappear.

Jaxson stormed into the tent, his shoulders heaving as he laid eyes on me. "Are you okay?"

He towered above me as I sat on the frigid metal chair. I pulled the blanket tighter, trying to ward off the cold. I shivered, but it was more from his proximity than the chill in the air.

I didn't answer, just stared up at him. Did he really care about how I was, or was this his protector mode that had him asking?

Earlier that morning, he didn't give a damn about me or my feelings. Why had that changed now?

"Just peachy," I said and gave the best smile I could muster.

He bent down. His knees flexed as he came to my eye level. "You're mad at me."

"What gave you that impression?" I shut my eyes and exhaled loudly before opening them again.

He didn't budge and continued to stare at me. "How about I drive you home? We're free to go."

Was he serious? He'd practically told me to find someplace else to live a few hours ago. Had he forgotten, or was he just feeling guilty that I'd been one of the victims?

"You don't have to feel sorry for me." I gently pushed at his chest to make him back up as I stood. "I'll be fine. I'm just going to find someplace else to stay." I wasn't sure what other options there were for accommodations, but I'd figure something out.

Maybe I could stay with Emma if she had a spare bedroom, or at least a couch I could crash on.

If not, maybe one of the other Eagle Tactical guys would suggest some place I could crash. I wasn't stupid enough to room with one of them. Jaxson would probably make their life hell.

"I don't feel sorry for you," he said and stood. He exhaled loudly and linked my arm with his. "I'm taking you home."

"Jaxson, I have my car. I can drive home." I wasn't really sure where I would go. Home didn't exist for me, not anymore.

"No." A single-word response.

He wasn't listening to me. Jaxson led me out of the tent and to his truck. He unlocked the door and helped me inside. I'd kept the blanket, putting it on my lap as I climbed into the front seat. "This isn't necessary. I'm capable of driving myself."

He waited until I buckled before he shut the door and jogged around to the opposite side. Jaxson climbed in, started the engine, and buckled his seatbelt. "I'm taking you home." His voice was firm and commanding.

Was he used to bossing people around? He'd been doing it the past few days at the office and mostly to me.

I took Mason's words into consideration that Jaxson was sexually frustrated, but that didn't even make sense. We'd had sex recently, and I was pretty sure he wasn't the kind of guy who slept around. He had a kid, and it had been obvious when we first met that he put her first.

I didn't answer, just stared out the side window as he drove us out of the parking lot and to the main thoroughfare, up to the mountain pass.

"I get it. You're mad at me," Jaxson said. The radio was off and the heat-blasted at full speed.

I glanced from the side window at Jaxson and then folded my arms across my chest.

"I'm sorry if I stepped over the line in there, but I couldn't let anything happen to you, Freckles."

"Don't!" I warned him. He didn't get to call me that name, not anymore.

We climbed the mountain, Jaxson downshifting the truck. The tires spun but just as quickly pulled us up the road.

His hands gripped the steering wheel hard. The roads didn't look that treacherous, but the higher we climbed in elevation, the more snow began to fall. At first, the flakes were thick and light and the road covered in a dusting, but it grew heavier with each passing minute.

"I didn't mean to hurt you," he said. "I had to look convincing that I was one of them."

I shifted in my seat and turned a bit to face him. "You think I'm mad about what happened in the resort?" He did what he needed to do so that he could get Hazel and me out of there.

He glanced briefly at me before returning his attention to the snow-covered terrain. "Aren't you?"

I laughed under my breath. "Gosh, you are clueless." Were all men this clueless?

"Gee, thanks," he muttered. He grumbled something incoherent under his breath.

I stared at him. "What was that?" I asked, daring him to say it aloud.

"I said, 'women, you all are the same.'"

"Who are you comparing me to, Emma?" I yanked at the blanket, my fingers tugging at the scratchy wool, clawing at it in fists. "You don't get to lump me in the same category as the woman who dropped off your kid and wanted nothing to do with her or you."

I grimaced after the words left my lips. That wasn't what I really thought of Emma but knowing what I did, the fact she'd never brought it up once, but Jaxson had told me, it nagged at me in the back of my mind.

Why was she here? Was she vying for his affection and attention?

I hadn't seen them together other than the one night at the bar, but maybe there was something I didn't know. I hadn't been in Breckenridge that long.

Had he been keeping his own secrets from me?

With one hand, he rubbed his forehead, and the other remained planted on the steering wheel. "I'm sorry."

"For what?" I didn't want him to apologize if he didn't mean it or he didn't know what for.

He stalled, not answering me right away.

"Here, I'll make it easy on you. You've been an ass to me, in fact, the biggest bosshole that I know of. Tell me I'm wrong," I said, staring at him.

He kept his focus on the road and every so often he glanced in my direction, but now he didn't look at me. He shifted under my gaze, clearly uncomfortable with what I'd said.

He wanted the truth. He deserved it.

His jaw was tight, his teeth clenched. His left hand came down on the steering wheel as he guided the truck onto the private driveway toward his residence.

"Yeah, that's what I thought. Don't worry. I'll be out of your hair as soon as I can find someplace to live. I had planned on staying at the resort, but it's under new management at the moment."

He huffed under his breath. "Do you think you're funny, cracking a joke like that? You could have gotten killed today."

"Well, I didn't. I'm sure you're disappointed that I'm still here, taking up residence under your roof." I hadn't intended to go so far, but the words slipped out. He didn't really wish me dead, right? He just hated me. Was there a difference? I pinched the bridge of my nose, feeling a headache coming on.

Maybe I should grab my blanket and steal a pillow and go sleep in the damned shed, the only piece of property I owned with a roof.

Well, it was that or my car, but my vehicle was down at the resort, which made sleeping in it hard. That would be my plan. I could easily live out of my car. I just needed to get back to the resort. It had to beat the death daggers Jaxson shot my way.

He shut off the vehicle and emitted a heavy sigh. I could feel the heat, the anger, the stress brooding in the truck. I didn't want to sit around and wait for him to erupt at me again.

I unlocked the truck door, thrust it open, and unbuckled myself. I spun my legs to the side to jump down when the blanket tangled around me.

Wrestling with it, I failed to notice Jaxson had hurried around the truck.

His body trapped mine, my legs tight, with him practically straddling me. His hands rested at each side of my hips against the truck's interior leather as he blocked me from escaping.

"We need to talk."

"There's nothing to talk about," I said and pushed at his chest to force him to move, but he was too strong.

His hands came up, clasping mine, crushing my hands against his chest, leaning closer.

"I don't think you mean that," Jaxson said.

I wouldn't look at him. I didn't want to give him any more of my time or attention. "I do," I said.

"I would never want anything to happen to you, Freckles." His right hand came up and stroked my jaw and guided my chin up to meet his stare. "I've been a jerk, but it's because I don't know how to do this," he said and gestured between us.

"Do what?"

"Be professional." He leaned his forehead against mine.

My eyes closed. I could smell the sweat against his skin mixed with the special scent that made him uniquely Jaxson.

His fingers tangled in the nape of my neck, bringing my lips closer. He held me in that position, not kissing me, just drinking in my breath, stealing my anger and pain as I felt need overtake us.

I wanted him, but I didn't want my heart broken. Not again. I couldn't handle it shattering into a million tiny pieces.

"This isn't professional," I whispered. My eyelids fluttered open, my gaze heavy. Each breath grew raspy and deep. I wanted him more than I had wanted anything in my life.

The worst of it was that I knew what I'd been missing. I'd had a taste of the forbidden fruit, and I wanted more.

"Screw professional." His lips latched onto mine, hard and forceful with need.

I clutched him tighter and pulled him to me, my fingers tangled in his hair as I drank him in. I wanted him, needed him, craved what only he could offer me.

"I'm sorry," he whispered, breaking the kiss, his lips, soft and warm, caressing my neck, sucking and nipping at the sensitive flesh.

I whimpered. He knew just what to do to make my knees weak. Thankfully, I was already seated. I dipped my head, and my fingers guided his lips back to mine, our tongues dueling for control, his body pressed tight against mine. I wanted him but was afraid to voice the words, not after what happened.

He pulled back slightly, and his lips trailed a warm, soft path to my ear. "I have something to tell you," he whispered.

"Don't want to talk," I said, dragging his mouth back down onto mine. Talking is what got us into trouble. It turned into fighting. This felt good, amazing, in fact, and made my head spin in a wonderful way.

Every fear that had flitted through my mind had vanished with his lips on mine.

"I left you a note the night I went home," he whispered, dropping soft butterfly kisses to my neck yet again.

I froze, my eyes wide, pulled from the sweet moment, and thrown back like a rubber band that snapped me to the reality of what happened.

"What?" I pulled back and put a hand between us to stop him. I needed to hear this, whatever he felt important enough to drop on me now.

"I didn't want to wake you when I left, so I scribbled you a note and stuck it to your new fridge. I'm guessing you never saw it." His eyes twinkled, and as I stared into the deep blue abyss, I could see he spoke the truth.

Jaxson wasn't a man who would lie to save himself.

I didn't have the slightest idea he'd left a note. I'd been so upset with him for leaving with not so much as saying goodbye or texting that I'd grown angrier at myself for trusting again.

"I didn't know that," I whispered, staring at him. I shut my eyes and rested my forehead against his.

I shivered. I hadn't felt cold, but the vehicle door had been open for quite some time, and we'd let out all the heat from the truck.

"We should get you inside where it's warm," Jaxson said.

I gave in, offering my hand for him to help me out of the truck.

My boots sunk in the fresh snow as I followed him wordlessly inside his house.

He shut off the alarm as we entered, and while I wanted to continue our festivities, Skylar rushed over to greet us.

"Are you okay? I heard on the news about the hostage takeover. Do you know what they wanted? Were you there? I heard Eagle Tactical was brought in," Skylar rambled on.

I couldn't deal with her. I glanced at Jaxson and pointed at the stairwell. "I'm going to take a shower." I needed to rid myself of the filth that covered my body.

I wanted him to join me. I hoped he'd sneak away from Skylar and find his way into the bathroom with me. Unlike the last time, when he'd rescued me from the cold water crashing down against me, this time, I wanted it to be different. I needed it to be different.

One look, that was all I could give him to convey what I desired. I had to watch every word spoken with Skylar in the room and Izzie nearby.

I didn't know where she was and couldn't risk her repeating something sultry that would slip out past my lips.

I sauntered to the stairs and glanced over my shoulder, giving him the best come hither look that I could muster, and nodded toward upstairs.

I wasn't used to giving off a sexy vibe.

Would he get the hint?

CHAPTER SEVENTEEN

JAXSON

Had Ariella just shot me a sultry glance to come join her in the shower?

Was I reading into her sad gaze because I wanted her to desire me as much as I craved her?

Skylar droned on with question after question, asking about the hostage ordeal. If anyone was hurt, what they wanted, why they'd taken hostages, if there were demands, the list continued on.

I hadn't stuck around to find out why the gunmen had taken hostages. It had been obvious they were after something.

My guess was money, but they weren't about to get a truckload of cash from their heist. SWAT was handling rescuing the other hostages.

I'd been told to go home and that our services were no longer wanted after the stunt I'd pulled to save Ariella and Hazel.

It wasn't good for our company, but the local sheriff didn't seem nearly as perturbed as the lead on the case. We hadn't tried to step on any toes or insult the big guys with badges, but we did what needed to be done to save our people, and I told them I'd have done it all over again.

That's what got my ass in trouble. I had no regrets, at least not with how it went down.

My only regret was that I'd hurt Ariella.

She'd be even more upset with me if I didn't join her in the shower, assuming that was her intent.

Maybe she wanted me to sneak upstairs so we could finish what we'd started? Or I could have been completely off, and she'd reem me the minute I invited myself into the shower unannounced.

Yeah, talk about sexual harassment in the workplace. That's one for the books, but let's face it, she was living with me, her boss.

We were bound to cross some lines a little more than others.

I wanted to cross the line that with her, the one that kept us strictly as friends and professionals. I was over being just her boss.

If she gave her consent, what was the harm in falling into bed again?

Skylar continued droning on about how worried she was, how every local station had the crisis on television, and that she didn't want Izzie to see it but that she felt it necessary to watch it herself.

I found myself nodding, agreeing with her, pretending to listen, just to make the conversation over and done with.

I was being an ass, I knew, but Skylar and I didn't get along. We hadn't in years, since Dad died. She blamed me. I blamed myself. It was a great situation, really.

"Do you smell that?" I asked and sniffed my shirt. "I need to get showered and cleaned up. I stink, and I'm sure no one wants to smell this body."

Anything to get her to leave me alone for twenty minutes, maybe an hour.

"We need to talk, Jaxson, when you're done." Skylar folded her arms across her chest.

I stripped out of my shoes and headed for the stairs. "Just say it." Skylar never beat around the bush. She was brazen, a little too much so at times. Since when did she wait for permission for anything?

"I'm staying in Breckenridge permanently. I applied for a job and got hired at the coffee shop in town," Skylar said.

"Great," I muttered, storming up the stairs.

"I thought you'd be happy that I was around more," Skylar said.

"I said great!" I shouted back down at her as I hurried upstairs. The guest bathroom light was off and the door open.

Sneaky.

She'd snuck into my private bathroom. I slipped into my bedroom and noticed the bathroom light was on and the door had been left ajar.

I stripped out my clothes, my shirt on the ground, my pants, my boxers, and lastly, my socks. I opened the bathroom door naked, hoping I hadn't misread her signal.

Did she want this?

Did she want me?

I yanked back the curtain and stepped into the shower with her. Unlike the last time, when she'd been curled up on the floor, this time, she was exactly as I would have imagined, standing under the spray dripping wet.

I climbed into the steamy shower and pulled her tight. My lips crushed hers. I needed to feel her all around me.

Frenzied, I lifted one of her legs and guided myself inside her warmth, burying inside of her.

Ariella moaned as I swiftly entered her. Her fingernails gripped my back, digging in, marking me.

Her head dipped back, skin flushed. Was she blushing from desire or the heat of the shower?

Steam surrounded us.

The sound of water pouring out the shower, I prayed hid the noises we made from listening ears.

"Harder," she grunted into my ear, her teeth tugging on the lobe.

I groaned and tried to concentrate on satisfying her and not ruining an incredible moment.

I lifted her hips, her legs wrapped around me as I backed her up against the shower wall. She shivered, with her back to the interior.

"God, that's cold," she muttered and pulled me tighter, deeper, squeezing down.

It took every amount of measurable self-control I had not to disappoint her. "Won't happen again."

"I hope it does." Her breath tickled my neck before I captured her lips again.

I tried to go slow, drag out the inevitable moment, but the thought of losing her had torn me apart inside. I'd broken every protocol today. None of it mattered, only that we were here now, together.

My pace frenzied, driving deeper inside of her, needing to become one with her.

Her insides tightened, and I felt her tremble against me.

It was all the encouragement I needed. All fury unleashed as I grunted, clinging tight against her body, drinking in everything about this moment from her sweet, sexy scent down to the soft noises she made as we came undone together.

I didn't want to forget any of it, ever.

I shut off the water and carried her to my bed, laying her down, crawling above her, staring down at her.

"You're all mine, Freckles." I wanted to claim her and mark her as mine forever. While I knew she was alive and well and safe in my arms, I had to keep telling myself that she was here with me and this was real.

Her thumb stroked my jaw, and I leaned down, brushing my lips against hers, crushing her with a bruising kiss. I'd never felt quite so helpless until today, hearing about the hostage situation and that she was inside because I'd sent her there.

Guilt weighed heavily over me.

I pulled back, my elbows propped up so I could stare down at her as I settled my hips over hers, pressing her down into the mattress, covering her with my body, shielding her from the outside world, protecting her.

Her bottom lip curled between her teeth. "What's wrong?" I whispered, refusing to glance away.

She had my undivided attention. I slid my thumb over her lip, her jaw relaxed as she released her hold over the sensitive skin. Had she even realized what she'd been doing?

"You're my boss." She stared up at me, unmoving. With one hand, she caressed the stubble on my jaw, and the other rested on my lower back. "Just a few days ago, you were pretty clear sex was off-limits, that we couldn't do this and work together."

I rolled off her body and lay on my back, staring up at the ceiling with a huff. "I can't work with you and pretend you mean nothing to me."

Ariella rolled onto her side, tugging the covers up around her waist. She chewed her bottom lip again.

I leaned in, needing another taste, wanting to know she didn't regret what we'd just done. I couldn't go back to pretending that we were nothing more than friends.

Having her at the office had been driving me crazy. I'd wanted to bend her over my desk.

This kiss was softer, fueled with longing and want, not solely need and pent-up desires.

"What does that mean?" Ariella asked. "I'd rather give up my job than give up you."

My hold on her tightened. The guys would inevitably kill me, but I wouldn't let her leave the business or leave me, and being professional had been too damned hard.

"You're not leaving the team. You're one of us now." She'd proven herself, especially today, protecting Hazel, keeping her out of the hands of the men who wanted her dead.

"What are you suggesting?" she asked, staring down at me. Her fingers tapped against my chest.

I pulled the covers up around us, burying her between me and the warmth of the blankets. I kissed her cheek, nose, and eyelids, teasing her. I didn't have a great suggestion. While I wanted to shout out to the world that she was mine, I had a feeling that was too much for her. I didn't want to push her away.

"We go slow, keep what's happening between us," I said. It wasn't anyone else's business.

"Do you really think you're capable of keeping this a secret?"

I'd kept a lot of secrets. It was part of the job. I knew Ariella could handle it because she'd been required to do the same with the C.I.A.. "Yes. Why? Are you having doubts?"

Her eyes shone with mirth, and she giggled as she maneuvered her hips over mine. Her hand slipped down between the sheets, waking me up inside, making me feel alive all over again. "Oh, I can handle it, but I'm not sure grumpy bosshole will be able to pull it off," Ariella said.

I snorted. "Is that a challenge, Freckles?" She made me feel like a teenager all over again, my body instantly responding to her touch.

I was under her control and at her mercy.

After staying up nearly all night satisfying each other, dawn broke. Ariella had just fallen to sleep, and I had to get up for work.

I didn't have the heart to wake her. I kissed her but also thought better of leaving a note. The last time everything had gone terribly wrong for us, and while I didn't think my house was about to burn down, I didn't need to chance some great catastrophe, either.

I kissed her softly on her cheek.

She stirred, eyes still closed, and reached out with her arm against the mattress searching for me. I stood dressed and ready to go.

"Sleep in. I'll swing by with lunch and bring you into the office around noon. Just this once, you can come in late, boss' orders."

Her eyes lazily opened. "Are you sure? I don't want special treatment."

"Really?" I stared down at her with a grin and leaned in, kissing her again. "That's not what you were moaning last night."

Her eyes lazily shut, but the smile never left her lips. She moaned softly. "Yeah, you're right. Just don't tell the guys, remember?"

"You have my word." I would keep our little secret between us, at least until I knew the guys wouldn't give Ariella a hard time.

I could handle them harassing me. What I didn't want was them pressuring me to end the relationship or to dismiss her from the job.

I planted one last kiss on her forehead before I quietly snuck out of the bedroom and shut the door. I hurried down to the kitchen, needing a strong cup of coffee to keep me awake.

"Morning," Skylar said. She sat at the kitchen table reading the newspaper.

I strode across the kitchen, grabbed a mug, and poured a steaming hot cup of coffee. Already, I could smell the pleasant aroma and wanted to taste it.

I craved that first cup to wake me up. The last thing I wanted was to drive off the road on my way to work.

Izzie had slept in, which was unusual but not unheard of when she'd had a tiring day.

I hadn't spent enough time with my daughter lately, and I'd be spending more time with Skylar if she was moving to Breckenridge.

"Are you two a thing now?" Skylar asked. "I heard you guys all night squeaking the damned bed. I had to put headphones on to drown out the noise."

I lifted my mug to my lips and took a long drag of my coffee.

I attempted to hide the smile that was plastered to my face. Maybe she'd move out of my house if we kept her up with loud, obnoxious sex.

"What?" I asked, pretending like I hadn't heard her. I wiped the smile away and put the mug down on the counter.

"You two were knocking boots all night," Skylar said. It wasn't a question.

"Daddy!" Izzie squealed, stomping down the last of the steps. Her hair was a wild mess of tangles, and her pajamas were still on, but she was a bundle of cuteness.

"Morning, baby girl." I lifted her into my arms and spun her around, giving her hugs and kisses. I'd missed her so much and had depended on Skylar more than I wanted to admit.

"Knocking boobs, Daddy. I wanna knock boobs."

Skylar's face turned crimson, and she hung her head, covering her face with her hands.

"Boots," I said, correcting Izzie. "And it's not a saying we use." She was smart enough to understand that it wasn't something nice to say if I was telling her that. I didn't need to elaborate; she was, after all, only three years old.

"Come on. Let's get you dressed." I put her down on the ground, and she grabbed my hand, tugging me to follow her upstairs.

I did my best to keep quiet, not wanting to wake Ariella.

Following Izzie to her bedroom, I flipped on the light and strode to the dresser in a hurry. I needed to get into the office and find out what was going on with Mason and Hazel.

Were they all right?

I was supposed to meet with Franco yesterday, but after he'd been held up at the resort, I suspected he might stop by today. We needed to drop them as a client. There was no way we would turn Hazel over, and while I'd been doing my due diligence on Franco, I hadn't expected to come up against the mafia.

We'd dealt with criminals in the past, domestic violence cases and delinquents, but the mafia, that was new. I wanted to discuss how we were going to handle it with the guys before Franco or his goons showed up at Eagle Tactical. We needed a plan. Telling them we weren't going to accept the job didn't seem like enough.

I opened the drawers of the dresser, retrieving an outfit for Izzie. While in the process of dressing her, my cell phone rang.

I answered the call and held it to my ear using my shoulder. "Hey, I'll be in the office soon," I said, having recognized Declan's number pop up on my phone.

"Did you see the news this morning?" Declan asked.

My stomach sunk. "No. Is everything okay? Did Mason check-in?" I asked. I hadn't spoken with him about where he was taking Hazel, but I assumed it was his uncle's property in North Dakota. The team had gathered for a retreat there on quite a few occasions.

"Mason's fine, as far as I know. This is about Ariella," Declan said.

I hurried as I dressed Izzie and glanced back at the bedroom across the hall. "What about her?"

Was there another secret she hadn't divulged that I was now going to be beaten down with?

How much more could I take?

"Do you remember Benjamin Ryan?"

"Yes, he's her ex-husband," I said. I knew of him. The bastard stole my life savings.

"The D.A. dropped the charges against him, and he's been released from prison," Declan said. "Turns out there's evidence that he couldn't have been involved since the digital trail leads to a connection in another state outside of New York. There's an interview on the news asking what he plans on doing next with his life."

I swallowed the lump in my throat. Izzie was dressed, but her clothes didn't match. I'd been too busy listening to Declan to realize until after I dressed her how much she clashed.

"Do you like leaving me hanging?" I grimaced and took her hand, leading her out of her bedroom and back down the stairwell.

"He's coming back to claim his wife, Ariella Ryan."

CHAPTER EIGHTEEN

Hazel

I had kept my head down and avoided glancing at Franco during the hostage takeover. I could still feel his putrid breath when he had kissed me before throwing me into the back of his car recently.

I had no idea where Mason and I were heading. We'd already been driving for hours, and I'd fallen asleep for a while. The comfort of the vehicle and the fact I could relax had been enough to make me succumb to sleep.

I rubbed my eyelids and stirred, shifting in the truck.

It was still dark outside. I glanced at the clock in the vehicle. It was just past midnight.

"How are you holding up?" Mason asked.

"Just tired, otherwise I'm all right," I said. My fingers played with the white gold necklace, tugging on the chain, twirling it on my index finger.

"We're almost there. As soon as we head inside, I'll make us something light to eat before bed."

"I'm not very hungry." Although my stomach grumbled otherwise, I didn't think I could eat much. The last two days' events had been exhausting, and without much sleep, the thought of food wasn't appealing.

He drove down a gravel road, kicking up dirt and dust in our wake. Where the hell had he taken me? Did they have a safe house?

Mason didn't say a word, kept his attention on the road the last couple of miles until we pulled up out front of a rustic home, two stories, on a farm.

"We're not in Montana anymore, are we?" I hadn't seen any mountains, but it was dark.

"North Dakota. My uncle owns the farm and acres of land out here. He has plenty of room, but he's not very kind to strangers. It'd be best if we pretended we were a couple."

I snorted. He couldn't be serious.

He shut off the engine and unlocked the truck's door.

"You're joking. Right?" I asked and climbed out of the vehicle, following him around to the front door.

I didn't have any clothes or possessions with me, except the clothes on my back. Everything Ariella had been kind enough to buy for me was back at the resort.

His hand fell to my lower back as he escorted me up the porch steps. "I'm serious. If we want to stay here, then we need to convince him we're serious about each other."

"Great," I muttered under my breath. It wasn't that I didn't still harbor feelings for Mason, quite the opposite.

I'd practically thrown myself at him earlier, and he'd turned me down because he was concerned with what, his reputation?

I shuffled my feet as I felt the weight of his hand against my lower back. His touch was firm and possessive, and in any other circumstance, I would have gladly pretended to be his girlfriend. I didn't have the heart to do it today or the stamina to be someone else.

Exhaustion swept over me, and I stumbled as I stood on unsteady footing.

Mason's arm wrapped around my waist. "Whoa. Are you okay?" He held me close.

I nodded and rubbed my eyes. "I guess I haven't fully woken back up."

It was a lie.

I suffered when I didn't sleep, and I hadn't gotten enough rest to classify as a decent night's sleep in two days.

"We'll get you into bed soon," Mason said.

His breath against my neck sent a shiver coursing through my body. I hoped he couldn't feel my response. He held me close against him as a dog on the opposite side of the door barked profusely and heavy footsteps stomped to unlock the door.

It had taken a while, and finally, he pulled open the wooden door, the storm door still shut and locked.

"Mason?" The man had thirty years on Mason, but they looked so much alike in the eyes, the jawline, even the build. They could have almost been brothers. "What are you doing here in the middle of the night?"

He unlocked the storm door.

The stranger glared at me but let us inside.

A brown and white mixed breed dog greeted me enthusiastically, jumping, tail wagging.

"Down, Bear!" he commanded.

Bear had to be eighty pounds of pure muscle, with beautiful coloring and brown freckles on her white face. Her nose was a golden brown that matched her fur. "She's beautiful," I said as I petted her head, and she leaned against me for more pets and cuddles.

Mason embraced his uncle in a hug. I whimpered, already missing Mason's touch and hold on me. He was quick with a hug before wrapping his arm back around my hip, pulling me tight.

Was he trying to convince his uncle that we were a couple?

"Bear sure likes you," his uncle said. "She doesn't like too many people."

I found that hard to believe with her disposition, but maybe there weren't too many people who came around to his farm.

"Uncle Jeb, this is my girlfriend Hazel," Mason said. "We planned on calling, but you know how the phone signal is out here."

Uncle Jeb waved his hand dismissively. "Better not to use the phones. You know those things are constantly being monitored. No one has any privacy anymore."

He shut and locked the front door behind us. There were several deadbolts attached to the door.

"You didn't tell me you had a girlfriend," Uncle Jeb said.

Mason held me close against him. His body heat radiated off of him and onto me. I leaned into his touch and strong embrace.

"We recently reconnected," Mason said. "We knew each other back at boarding school, dated when we were kids."

Uncle Jeb's eyes brightened. "I remember Hazel. She was the best thing that ever happened to you. Kept you out of trouble."

Was that what he said to his family when he spoke about me? I rested a hand on his chest. It wasn't difficult to fall into the role of his girlfriend. I wanted to be his. "Mason was the best thing that happened to me at boarding school, too," I said.

I wasn't trying to flatter Mason or his uncle. I only spoke the truth.

Mason shucked his coat and shoes, leaving them by the entryway of the house. I did the same, following his lead. "I hope you don't mind, but we haven't eaten anything. I was hoping to whip up something in the kitchen before bed," Mason said.

"Be my guest. My house is your house, son. I'll change the sheets in the guest room while you make your lady something to eat."

We hung our coats and placed our shoes on the mat by the door. Mason latched onto my hand and tugged for me to follow him down the hall and into the kitchen.

He flipped on the light switch, bathing the kitchen in a bright daylight glow from the lightbulbs overhead.

I grimaced and shut my eyes, trying to adjust. The foyer hadn't been overly bright, but the kitchen blinded me.

Mason flipped another switch, only lighting half the kitchen. "Better?"

"Thanks." I let go of his hand and sauntered over to the counter to sit down on one of the stools. "I'm not sure how much I can eat. Sleep, that I can do." I stifled a yawn. Just speaking about sleep, made me even more tired.

"I promise I will tuck you into bed as soon as we're done eating."

I brushed a strand of hair behind my ear. Mason stared at me, making my stomach flop. Was he really going to tuck me into bed, or was he saying that for his uncle's benefit?

His Uncle Jeb hadn't followed us into the kitchen, but that didn't mean that he wasn't listening. He'd been just a room away, down the hall. I didn't know where the guest room that he'd spoken of was located in the house. I hadn't heard footsteps travel up the stairs or down the hall.

Resting my elbows on the counter and my head in my hands, I tried to stay awake.

"You're going to fall asleep in your food just like Izzie, aren't you?" Mason said, a huge grin spread across his face.

I didn't know who Izzie was or what he was referring to. "What?"

"Jaxson's daughter." He shook his head, the smile never leaving his face. "You just remind me of someone when you're sleepy."

I mumbled, incapable of answering in full sentences. I just wanted to sleep. I shut my eyes for a brief second, just to relax, when I felt a warm arm on my back and jumped in my seat.

"Relax," Mason said. He wrapped an arm around my shoulder. "I made us a sandwich. I'd like you to eat something before we climb under the covers."

I swallowed the lump in my throat. Were we actually going to share a bed? Hours earlier, I'd wanted to, but he'd turned me down. Now we were stuck pretending that we were madly in love and together.

"Come on. You need to eat something." Mason had made a sandwich for himself. He sat on the stool beside me and took a bite of his peanut butter and jelly.

I glanced at the peanut butter and banana sandwich that he'd made for me. When we were kids, it had been my favorite. He remembered. I wasn't hungry, but I lifted the bread to my lips and took a bite to appease him.

It took forever for me to finish the sandwich. Time seemed to stand still because I was tired and ready for bed. With heavy eyes, I finished the last bite and swallowed down a glass of water.

"I promise, tomorrow, I'll make us both something a little more nutritious," Mason said. He cleaned up the dishes, washing both of our plates in the sink, rinsing, and then drying each item.

I stood, wobbling from lack of sleep. "I can help dry the dishes," I offered. I walked around the counter to the sink and grabbed a dishrag, drying the plates after he washed each one.

"Thanks," Mason said. "As soon as we're done, I'll take you upstairs and tuck you into bed."

I licked my lips. Was he planning on sharing a bed with me? I wasn't sure how traditional his uncle was, whether he'd encourage or be insulted if we stayed in the same bedroom.

"What?" he asked.

I shook my head, a tired smile on my face. "I didn't say anything."

"No, but you're thinking it."

"How do you know what I'm thinking? Since when are you a mind reader?" I asked.

He shut off the water as I dried the last plate and placed it on the drying rack. I didn't know where anything went to put the dishes away.

Mason took the dishrag, folded it, and then grabbed my hand and led me up the stairwell. Wordlessly, I followed him, willing to sleep wherever he put me.

We reached the top of the stairs, and he opened the second door on the right and flipped on the light, leading me inside.

A single queen-sized mattress was pressed up against the wall. A quilt was pulled back, and several pillows had been fluffed and positioned for guests.

"Where are you sleeping?" I asked.

He shut the bedroom door. "With you, of course," Mason said. He pulled his t-shirt over his head and then undid his belt buckle, pulling his belt free.

I stood there, frozen, watching him undress.

Were we really sharing a bed together? We'd slept beside one another dozens of nights, snuck into each other's dorms and risked expulsion, but the number of times we'd actually had sex, I could count on one hand.

He opened the dresser and tossed me a t-shirt. "You can wear this to bed if you want. It's mine. I left a few things here in case I pay Uncle Jeb a visit."

"Do you bring all your girlfriends here?" I asked. I hadn't intended to come across as jealous, but the way Mason had insisted his uncle wouldn't trust me unless we were together, I found it unsettling. "Turn around," I said.

"What?"

"I'm not undressing in front of you. Turn around."

Mason rolled his eyes and then turned around to face the door.

I quickly stripped out of my clothes, which happened to be Mason's sweats that I'd worn earlier so as not to attract attention to myself. I slipped into his t-shirt and left my panties on before crawling under the blankets.

"Okay, you can turn around," I said. He removed his jeans and folded his clothes, leaving his things on the dresser before shutting off the light and stalking to the bed in only a pair of boxers.

Did the room get warmer?

"You didn't answer my question," I said. My eyes never left his body. He looked hot half-naked, and he was incredibly good-looking with his clothes on. It was any wonder a woman hadn't already snatched him up.

"About the girlfriends? You're the only person I've brought here who's not one of my military buddies, the Eagle Tactical guys."

Mason climbed beneath the covers, leaving me plenty of space on my side of the bed.

He was a professional. Even while sharing a bed and pretending to be together, he was keeping his hands to himself.

I groaned and rolled around, restless in bed.

"What's wrong?" Mason's soft voice, I found incredibly soothing.

His hand reached out, grazing my breast before settling on my side. Had it been an accident in the darkness, or had he wanted to touch me intimately?

"Aside from the fact I'm exhausted?"

"Fair enough. Get some sleep," he said. His lips grazed my cheek and planted a soft, gentle kiss against my skin.

"You don't have to pretend in here. It's just you and me."

His uncle couldn't see us in the privacy of the bedroom. He didn't have to pretend that he wanted to be with me. He'd already rejected me once today. I wasn't going to throw myself at him again.

"I would never pretend. I mean outside of Uncle Jeb, but that's just because he's paranoid about the government and what I do for a living."

Sighing, I curled up on my side, my eyes shut. I wasn't sure how much longer I'd last awake. "He's not wrong. I mean about what you do, the danger that follows you around."

I was part of that danger, risking his life, calling him for help to deal with Franco.

Would I ever be able to live my life again in a normal way, or would I be forced to go into hiding or witness protection?

"I can defend myself," Mason said. "Besides, nothing is going to happen to you while I'm with you."

He was so confident in his answer. I found comfort in his words. I shifted on the bed, inching closer. While I didn't reach out to touch him, I brushed against him, and knowing he was next to me made me at ease.

"You trust Uncle Jeb?"

"With my life," Mason said. "He won't let anything happen to you, either. Get some sleep." His lips grazed my cheek once more before the bed shifted, and he pulled me into his arms, cradling me.

I opened my mouth to object, to point out this wasn't professional, but it took too much energy and stamina that I didn't have to fight with him. I let him hold me and protect me.

My legs tangled in his, pulling him closer, the heat of our bodies stirring desires that intensified within me. I couldn't have him. He wasn't mine. Not anymore.

I awoke with a start. Bear was barking profusely downstairs. My body froze, the lights were off, the sky still dark.

I didn't know what time it was, but I felt much better, more rested. I'd slept for a while.

I reached out for Mason, but he wasn't in bed with me. "Mason?" I whispered into the darkness, unable to see him.

He didn't respond. Maybe he was downstairs and he'd startled Bear?

The sound of gunfire erupted from the lower level.

CHAPTER NINETEEN

MASON

I'd been startled awake, but by what, I wasn't sure. Hazel slept soundly, curled up on her side.

I untangled from her grasp and quietly grabbed my gun on the dresser tucked beneath my pants.

I headed out of the bedroom, and Uncle Jeb was in the hallway, shotgun in hand.

His eyes, tight and narrow, focused on the same thing I was, listening for what had awoken both of us.

My uncle had served in the marines many years ago. I gave him hand signals, not wanting to make a sound.

Bear howled from down below, and I hurried, gun drawn as I tore down the stairs as quietly as possible.

I needed to protect Hazel, and the best way to do that was to keep her upstairs and out of harm's way.

Uncle Jeb followed just behind me with his shotgun.

I didn't want to tell him he'd need more firepower than that if the men who were after Hazel had shown up. How had they found her? I'd been careful, making sure that no one had tailed my truck.

Had there been a tracker on the vehicle or on Hazel?

I'd given her the bangle, but there was no way that they could have hacked into our tracker. I was confident in our equipment and the security measures that we'd taken to ensure her safety.

Bear growled and barked. The sweet dog had been trained to attack. She'd sensed danger as much as we had.

Uncle Jeb came up on my right side while I flanked left and headed down the hallway. We left the lights off, to our advantage. My uncle knew his house in the dark, and I'd spent enough summers visiting that I was familiar with the layout.

Gunfire erupted from all angles outside, firing into the farmhouse. I hit the ground for cover. There was nowhere else to go. I crawled on my stomach toward the window. When the firing ceased after several long rounds, I poked my head up to see what awaited us.

There were dozens of vehicles with their lights on and engines running just outside the house.

I needed more manpower.

Even if I gave Hazel a weapon, it wouldn't be enough. I hurried back up the stairs and threw the door open.

She stood in the middle of the bedroom, pulling on the sweatshirt, getting dressed. I grabbed her arm and dragged her to come with me. "We need to get you out of here. It's a bloodbath."

I wouldn't wait for them to come and take her.

Uncle Jeb shot off his weapon. With every shot, he had to reload, costing us precious time.

Bullets tore through the house, ripping apart the walls. The men outside didn't have shotguns or pistols. They had semi-automatic weapons and didn't have to reload as often.

The first round had burned through the first floor. After they reloaded, they were now aiming haphazardly upstairs, wrecking every inch of the property that they could, ensuring there were no survivors.

I sheltered Hazel, covered her with my body as I lay above her on the floor. Fragments of wood and glass sliced my skin.

My arms burned, and blood dripped from my cheek. I ignored the pain. All that mattered was getting her out of here alive.

The firing ceased, and I grabbed Hazel by the arm, hoisting her to her feet. She trembled in my grip.

"We need to move." I led her down the stairs, my hand in hers, as I pulled her with me and kept her close to my body.

The headlights from the vehicles outside shined inside the farmhouse through the bullet holes.

Uncle Jeb sat on the floor, slumped down. Blood trickled from his chest and neck as he gasped for breath. "Get her... out of here."

"Everyone inside! Sweep the place. I want her dead or alive," Franco shouted his orders to the men outside.

I dragged Hazel with me down to the laundry room. Beneath the floor, was a false door. I pulled the board and opened the hatch. "Get in."

She shook her head violently and folded her arms across her chest. She'd been trembling earlier, but now she was shaking even more wildly.

I ran a hand over her cheek. I hadn't seen any blood on her, except for a few cuts and scrapes from the bullet shrapnel.

"I can't."

"You have to." We were running out of time. I needed her to hide, and then I had to cover the trap door to protect her. I didn't have time to even consider how I'd handle the men as they charged inside the house.

"I'm claustrophobic," she said.

"Shit. Then you're going to have to run." I prayed the men were all coming in through the front and back entrance. I hurried toward the side of the house, away from the doors, and used my elbow to clear the fragments of glass that were not fully broken and fell in the firefight.

I didn't see any men, but I could hear them. I helped Hazel through the window along with Bear, hoping that she'd protect Hazel.

Men came stampeding through the house, guns drawn. I hurried out of the room, not wanting to give Hazel's whereabouts to any of the men searching for her.

A thick Russian accent permeated the room. "Where is she?"

Uncle Jeb coughed and wheezed. I could hear his struggle.

I skirted the corner of the room and hugged the wall, peeking out to see one man towering over my uncle.

Another man shoved his foot onto my uncle's chest, making it harder for him to breathe.

I lifted the barrel of my gun and fired several shots, hitting the men before I took off through the darkened house, hiding from them in the dining room.

Bullets blasted through the farmhouse, tearing into my arm and burning me like lava, scorching my flesh. I winced and bit my tongue to keep my groaning at bay. No one could know where I hid.

It wasn't my first bullet wound, but it didn't sting any less. Blood dripped down my arm, making it harder for me to use two hands to aim, and the bastard had shot my good arm.

"We've got her!" a voice echoed from outside.

I stumbled forward. Why hadn't she fought back? I didn't hear so much as a scream pass her lips.

Heavy boots retreated through the house, but not before sending off one last wave of bullets. I dove for cover. A second round slammed into my chest, knocking me to the floor, unable to move.

I tried to stand, to lift myself up from the ground and fight. Inch by inch, I dragged myself across the dining room floor and then into the hallway.

A streak of blood followed me across the wood flooring. I wouldn't let Hazel be dragged off with Franco.

Car doors slammed, and headlights faded as the sound of tires squealed, and vehicles tore away from the farmhouse.

She was gone, and I was to blame.

I hadn't been able to save her or protect her.

CHAPTER TWENTY

Hazel

I slipped out through the broken window.

Glass tore at my feet. My shoes were by the front door, and I had no way of getting them before fleeing the farmhouse.

I ran hard and fast, with Bear at my side, in the darkness outside through the field. Breathing hard, I stumbled over a rock, smashing my toe and landing face-first against the ground.

Dirt covered my face and filled my mouth. I spit and coughed.

Gunfire erupted from behind me inside the house. Bear took off, abandoning me in the open field.

"Mason," I whispered, staring at the battered farmhouse. It hadn't fallen yet. The structure looked unstable from the hundreds of bullet holes that littered the walls.

I needed to run, but my feet were sore and raw. My heart wanted to save Mason, but the only way to do that was to surrender to Franco. Even that didn't secure Mason's freedom.

A flashlight shined right on me.

"Freeze! Hold it right there!" a gruff voice shouted at me.

I ran, hoping the darkness would blanket me, but there was a full moon.

He shot off a warning. The bullet whizzed by my side.

"Stop! Next time, I won't miss."

I came to an abrupt halt, my arms in the air. "Don't shoot. I'll go with you. Just leave my friends alone." It wasn't a bargain I could make. I had no leverage. He had the gun on me, but I still said it anyhow.

He snorted, grabbed my arm and yanked me to follow before he let go and rammed the gun into my back.

"Move faster," he commanded. As we drew closer, he shouted at the others. "We got her!"

I glanced down at the golden bangle hidden on my arm beneath the sweatshirt. Mason would find me, assuming he was still alive.

I couldn't allow myself to think like that. He was a fighter, always had been, even at boarding school.

The men repeatedly fired on the farmhouse, another round of bullets showering the building and the two men inside.

Uncle Jeb hadn't looked in good shape when I'd come downstairs. We should have checked on him, helped him, put him into the hidden crawl space under the house.

My stomach ached, wretched with guilt.

Had I just married Franco, none of this would have happened.

"There's my little firecracker," Franco said as he stomped through the grass, coming right for me.

I wanted to flee, but I couldn't move. The gun was nestled against my spine. My feet throbbed, which made it difficult to walk.

He fisted my hair and tugged on the strands, jerking my head up and my gaze, to meet his stern expression. "No more running, Hazel. The chase is over."

He dragged me by the hair and shoved me into the back of his town car, sliding in beside me.

"Don't even try escaping. Child locks are an incredible feature." His knees were spread wide, taking up a seat and a half.

I scooted as close as I could to the opposite door, trying to make myself small.

"It's a shame you killed those men and the marshals," Franco said. "I never thought my wife would take part in the messy aspects of the business, but it seems you're as dirty as I am."

"I didn't kill anyone."

I wasn't the murderer.

He couldn't blame me for what he did.

Franco turned to face me. "You don't believe that. I know the way you think. You're more guilty than I am. You reached out to him and sealed his fate."

His finger grazed my collarbone and touched the white gold chain my father had given me, holding a heart locket with a picture of my deceased mother.

He ripped the necklace from my neck, rolled down the window, and tossed it outside as we drove.

"No!" I gasped, feeling both naked and broken without the chain. I hadn't taken it off in years. It had become a part of me. "Why?" my voice croaked. "That was from my father!" Tears threatened my vision. I hadn't cried with all that I'd experienced, but now stealing a piece of me and disposing of it like trash. I couldn't take much more.

"I know. How do you think I was able to find you?" he asked.

I didn't understand, frowning as he stared at me. I shook my head. Was he going to elaborate?

Franco stretched his arm and wrapped it around my shoulders. I swallowed the lump in my throat as he pulled me tight against him and his lips grazed my ear. "Your father wanted to make sure you were safe. How do you think I was able to find you?" he whispered.

I shivered and pulled away, untangling from his grasp. "There was a tracker in the necklace? Let me go."

I didn't want to believe it, but how else had Franco been able to find me? Mason hadn't called anyone when we'd left Breckenridge. We'd shown up unannounced in North Dakota on his uncle's farm.

"I'm never letting you go," Franco whispered into my ear.

The hair on my arms stood on end.

I shimmied away, but his grip on my shoulders tightened.

We drove through the night straight to Chicago. I kept as far from Franco as possible in the back of the car. After some time, his hand fell away from my shoulder, and I'd been able to relax and fall asleep in short bursts.

The vehicle came to a standstill, and I stirred awake.

Rubbing the sleep from my eyes, I recognized the gated house. It had been my father's home before he'd died and left it to Nikolai.

"What are we doing here?" I asked.

Franco didn't answer me.

The driver opened the window, punched in a code, and proceeded forward to the front entrance before he shut off the engine and stepped out.

He opened the door for Franco.

Franco climbed out of the car and reached in, grabbed my arm, he dragged me out with him.

"Get off me." I attempted to shrug out of his grasp, but he didn't let me free.

There was nowhere to run, even if I could manage to escape. The wrought-iron fence had arrows at the top, ensuring no one would climb in or out. Not to mention my feet were swollen and gashed from the glass I'd stepped on last night in my plight for freedom.

Victor, one of my father's oldest friends, stepped out through the front door and down the stairs. He had thinning white hair and was scrawny compared to Franco. "Nikolai isn't here," Victor said.

"Fine. We'll wait." Franco released his hold on me, and I pulled farther away to keep out of his grasp.

I rubbed my bruised arms and stepped off the cement to let my sore feet sink into the grass. I didn't care that it was winter. The cold breeze made me numb, helping relieve the pain that I felt all over my body, the burning sting against my raw skin.

"It could be a while until he's back. Nikolai went to Breckenridge when he couldn't get ahold of you," Victor said.

My arms nestled tight across my chest as I shivered and glanced back at the car. At least the shelter of the vehicle and the seat had provided comfort.

Was there any chance that the driver had left the keys unattended, and I could steal the car and flee?

It was wishful thinking.

"Come inside," Victor said. "I'll call Nikolai and let him know you both have arrived."

The driver climbed back into the vehicle and started the engine, leaving me to follow Franco and Victor inside. I still didn't know why we'd come, but I suspected Nikolai wouldn't be pleased to see me.

Dried blood coated my body, and under the morning light, there were bloodstains on my arms, hands, and feet.

I limped up the wooden stairs and into the foyer.

Franco leaned in and sniffed my neck.

I shuddered and winced, disgusted.

"Find yourself a bathroom. No wife of mine will look this filthy," he said and yanked me by the hips. He pulled me close and tight against his body. "Freshen up for me. I like a girl who smells good."

I wanted to puke.

"I'll call Nikolai. Franco, please have a seat. Make yourself at home," Victor said.

Relieved when Franco released his hold on me, I hurried out of his clutches and up the stairs. The pain tore at my feet, but I kept a quickened pace. I wanted to get away, and I wasn't capable of running with tiny shards of glass still embedded in the soles of my feet.

The house smelled musty and old. While the interior hadn't changed much since Nikolai took possession of the property, the stench wreaked of his filth.

How many men had he murdered inside his home?

I hobbled to my childhood bedroom and ripped open the door. I stumbled inside, my feet leaving a trail of fresh blood on the perfectly white carpet.

I ignored the stains and the mess as I approached my closet. I'd spent many nights in the bedroom, not just in my childhood years.

I retrieved a sweater dress and black leggings from the dresser, along with undergarments.

I hurried into the nearest bathroom. There were no locks on the doors, no real privacy, just a semblance of it. I'd have to trust that no one would invade my personal space. There was no furniture to slide in front of the door.

As a kid living in the giant house, it hadn't mattered. No one had barreled through the bathroom door, but now, knowing that Franco could force his way in on a whim, my stomach ached.

I stripped down and turned on the shower, letting the steam permeate the bathroom while I retrieved a pair of tweezers from the medicine cabinet.

I sat on the closed toilet lid, lifting one leg at a time to remove any glass or debris buried in the bottoms of my feet.

I breathed loudly through my mouth, exhaling and grimacing as I grabbed the splinters of wood and shards of glass that had snuck under my skin.

"One down," I said. I worked diligently on my other foot before I finally climbed under the hot spray of the shower.

Staring down at the water, the clear spray at my feet turned brown and red as I washed away the remnants of yesterday.

What didn't wash away was the pain, the concern for Mason and his uncle. I hadn't removed the bracelet, keeping it against my skin. I hoped it could get wet, but it was too late. I'd already left it on under the shower spray.

I couldn't remove it. What if Franco stormed into the bathroom and took my clothes and bracelet? We weren't staying at this home for more than a few hours, however long it took for Nikolai to return.

We had driven more than fourteen hours, but my brother had a private plane. I expected that he'd flown to Montana and then flown home.

Why had he come all the way to Breckenridge? What had he hoped to do, convince me to return with him?

My brother was the biggest asshole on the planet, with a God complex. He was also the reason I never ended up in California. My father had spent the money that was earmarked for my tuition on Nikolai. He'd also told me it was too dangerous for me to be outside of Chicago and kept me trapped, but I wasn't a prisoner, not completely.

I'd been given permission to come and go from the property. I'd believed I had freedom, but it was a sham. The necklace he'd given me had provided my whereabouts. I was never alone, even when I wanted to be.

My father had helped me land my first job straight out of high school. Most hires with only a high school diploma started out landing a gig in retail or low pay work, something entry-level and mundane.

The water washed over me, cleansing me of my sins. I opened the shampoo bottle and squeezed a dollop-sized amount into my hand before lathering my hair.

I'd never had a typical entry-level position. I had wanted to go to college for graphic design, and my father had told me to send my resume to West Marketing Firm. I'd done exactly what he asked and had been hired at my first interview as the marketing manager.

Two months later, I was promoted to marketing director when my boss mysteriously disappeared.

Looking back, it had all been suspect, the employees, the clients, they'd all been Nikolai's friends and family, business partners in some way or another. I hadn't known that when I was eighteen.

I'd been naïve and foolish into believing everything Daddy said was true.

My father had lied to me and had me believe that I held a job at a prestigious firm straight out of high school because I'd had raw talent.

I rinsed the suds from my hair and soaped every inch of my skin.

The bathroom door thrust open, and a cold gust of wind followed the intruder.

"Get out!" I shouted and pulled the curtain tight around myself, hiding both my body and my bracelet from sight.

Franco's dark laugh filled the bathroom. "No point in being shy with me. We're going to be husband and wife."

"Over my dead body," I snarled.

"That can be arranged." He stepped closer, invading my personal space, and grabbed my jaw, forcing me to stare into his dark, soulless eyes. "You've been in here long enough. Get dressed and come downstairs."

He released his hold on me.

I breathed a sigh of relief.

"You've got five minutes. Any longer, and I'll pull out the cane. You'll discover the beauty of discipline and submission."

"I'll never submit to you."

Franco backhanded me across the face.

My cheek stung, and my eyes shut from the initial shock and pain. No one had ever hit me before, certainly not my face.

"Never is a long time. We have the rest of our lives together," Franco said, reminding me that I was *his*.

His phone buzzed in his pants, and he took a step back.

I shut off the shower, gesturing for him to get out of the bathroom.

"Nikolai, yes, I've recovered your sister. She's been quite the little firecracker," Franco said into the phone and paused.

I didn't budge from my position in the bathtub, standing with the curtain around my body, waiting for him to get out of the bathroom so I could have some privacy.

"I see. Yes, that's right. Very well," he said and smiled. "I will see you in a bit." He hung up the phone and shoved it back into his pocket.

"Get out!" I pointed at the door.

His eyes narrowed as he leaned closer, his rotten breath hitting me in the face. "I don't take orders from you." He shoved his lips over mine, forcing his tongue into my mouth.

I kept my lips closed and tried to back away, but there wasn't much place for me to run to with the shower curtain attached.

He slid his hand down inside the curtain, groping my breast. "I should fully inspect the merchandise before purchase," Franco said with a crooked grin. "You've been irritating. I should make sure I'm getting exactly what I paid for."

CHAPTER TWENTY-ONE

JAXSON

"Morning," Declan said as he came into my office. He perched himself at the edge of my desk. "What are you working on?"

I hadn't so much as looked up when he'd come into the room.

I let out a heavy sigh and ran a hand through my hair. "Trying to get ahold of Mason. After the day we all had yesterday, I thought it would be a good idea to try the satellite phone."

"He didn't answer?" Declan asked, his brow tight as he stood and came around to see what I was doing on the computer.

"No, he hasn't answered. If he'd have picked up when I called, I wouldn't have been quite so concerned. I tried calling his uncle since I'm sure that's where he went, but he's not picking up, either."

"We're talking about Uncle Jeb. That's not a surprise. The man probably ripped out his phone line. You know how paranoid he is. You've met the guy."

I slid away from my desk and stood. "True."

I strode out of the office to the hallway where the coffeepot was situated. I needed a strong cup of coffee to get me through my day.

"I just have a bad feeling. Mason should have checked in with us.

I'm not happy that he took Hazel and left town without saying anything to us."

Aiden stepped into the hallway, his arms crossed as he leaned against his open door, listening and weighing in on what we said. "You could call the local sheriff's office and have them do a wellness check."

"That'll go over really well, especially with Uncle Jeb," I said.

Declan poured a cup of coffee and took it over to his desk. "I can hack into surveillance footage and see if anything looks suspicious."

That would at least be a start. It wasn't something that I was capable of doing. "Thank you," I said.

Five minutes behind the computer, and Declan had hacked the satellite footage and zoomed in on the farmhouse.

"Shit," I muttered under my breath as I stood over his shoulder. The exterior was in disarray. It was difficult to tell what extent of damage the farmhouse had sustained, but the structure didn't appear stable.

"I'll get us a ride via chopper," Aiden said as he hurried back to his office and started making phone calls.

Our connections with local and state authorities often came in handy. We had a few friends who were federal, and while we usually helped them, this time, we were reaching out for their assistance.

I reached out to the county sheriff's department where Mason and Uncle Jeb were located. They were sending a team to check on the situation while we arranged transportation to the scene.

Before our helicopter arrived, we received a call from the county sheriff's office in North Dakota, informing us that EMTs were being called and they had found two bodies. Mason was alive, but his uncle hadn't made it.

"Mason wants to talk to you," the sheriff said. He had called using Mason's phone and put on the video feed so that we could talk.

I stepped out of the room and into my office, leaving the door open.

"It's good to see you, Mason," I said. He looked like hell, pale, blue-tinged lips, but he was conscious and breathing.

He tried to speak, but I couldn't hear him. Mason was far too quiet for the phone to pick up what he said.

"I can't hear you, buddy. It'll be okay. Go with the EMTs and let them do their job." I tried to assure him that everything was fine.

He looked like hell. He was lucky to still be alive.

The sheriff leaned down to hear what Mason was trying to say to us. "Hazel has a tracker."

I sipped my coffee. "Yes, that makes sense. It's probably how they were able to find you guys."

Mason shook his head. That wasn't the message that he was trying to convey. He gestured the sheriff close again.

The video on the phone shifted, giving a glimpse of the blood and the damage to the property. Mason had lost a significant amount of blood, but he was breathing. His heart was beating. He was a fighter.

"Hazel has a bracelet you can track. He gave it to her to protect her," the sheriff said. He frowned, glancing from Mason to me. "Who exactly are you guys?"

"Eagle Tactical," I said. I'd already told his office that when I called and requested their assistance, but either he didn't get the memo or didn't know who we were. "Mason, we'll get Hazel back. You let the EMTs and the doctors look after you. Get better, okay?"

We'd pay him a visit when Hazel was safe and out of harm's way.

I hung up the phone and hurried into the office with Declan.

"I got all of that," Declan said before I could relay the message. "I'm already on the bracelet and tracking Hazel's whereabouts. Shit." He glanced away from his computer monitor at me. "She's back in Chicago."

"Get the address. I'll call Colton Carr and see if he can get to her with a team before we can get there." I grabbed my coat and gulped the last of my coffee.

"What about Izzie?" Declan asked. "Maybe we should send Aiden and Lincoln?"

"Lincoln's busy with the insurance adjuster after what the bastards did to his restaurant," Aiden said from across the hallway. His boots clunked on the floor as he hurried into the office with us. "I'll come with you. We need at least a two-man team."

I laughed under my breath. I doubted two of us and the U.S. marshal would be enough to take down the Russian mafia in Chicago and rescue Hazel. "Declan, you stay here and track Hazel. Aiden, call Lincoln and tell him we need him ASAP. Offer him full-time, again. We need his help. We need all the help we can get," I muttered under my breath.

Declan glanced at me. His voice was tentative. "We could call Jayden. I know it's not ideal, but we could use the manpower."

"Absolutely not." I wasn't inviting an off-gridder to our team. Jayden may have been one of us in the military, one of our unit and our team, but he'd chosen them over us. "They're responsible for the hostage takeover at the resort yesterday."

"You don't know that Jayden was part of that; everyone involved wore masks," Declan said.

"Why are you defending him?" I asked. "And not everyone involved wore a mask. Emma was there, and so was Jayden. I stripped his ass bare and stole his clothes."

"Shit. You didn't tell us that." Aiden laughed. "I would have liked to have seen that. Any chance you took a picture?"

I rolled my eyes and grabbed my truck keys on the desk. "I didn't have time. Too bad, right? I'm heading out to the hanger. I'll call Carr on the way. Are you coming, Aiden?" I asked.

"I wouldn't miss the opportunity to kick some ass. Let me call Lincoln while we're in the car."

"Shit. I need to call Ariella too. I told her I'd pick up lunch and bring her back with me to the office." That wasn't going to happen. Maybe she'd be able to get Skylar to drive her to the resort to pick up her car. If not, I'd give her a lift tomorrow or when I got home.

Lincoln, Aiden, and I teamed up in Chicago with Colton Carr and his team of U.S. Marshals along with the Federal Bureau of Investigation.

"She's still on the property," Declan said.

He forwarded her location to my phone.

Examining the screen on my cell phone, there was a tiny red dot that blinked as it appeared to pace back and forth.

I wasn't sure whether the position was approximate or she was in fact moving, but we had her whereabouts, as long as the bracelet was still on her.

"We've got a team ready to go," Agent Bishop said. He was dressed in a suit, his team in SWAT gear surrounding the perimeter.

We stood just outside of the command center, a vehicle set up on the side of the road around the block and out of sight.

A young woman with long blonde hair wearing a Kevlar vest stormed into the command post. "I've got eyes and ears on the place. You should be getting a signal any moment."

She sat down in front of a monitor and adjusted the frequency, picking up the video feed and audio of Hazel.

"That's her. That's our target to extract," I said, giving confirmation.

"SWAT goes in first," Agent Bishop said. He was tall and lanky. He'd probably never spent a day in the military, but he commanded with authority.

"Fine," Lincoln said. He stood behind me, arms folded across his chest. He hadn't moved an inch, not even to step out of the way as agents came and went, having to squeeze past him in the narrow hallway.

"Do we have a visual on Nikolai Agron?" I asked.

"Not yet," Agent Bishop said. "We have confirmation that Franco Ivanov is there, along with another man we're running through our database. There are also a number of support staff, but the key players for the mafia don't appear to be onsite."

"Other than Franco," I said. He was one of the key players, and while he may not have been the head of the mafia, he was second in command and the reason we were here.

Agent Bishop watched from the screen as he gave commands to his fellow agents. They entered the perimeter of the property and came up along the house. "Wait until I give all-clear to enter."

I stared at the screen from over his shoulder. They were waiting until Hazel would be out of immediate danger.

She wasn't near the foyer. It would take several seconds from the breach until they entered the room where she was located.

Enough time to shoot her or grab her as a hostage and threaten her life.

I hated watching on the screen, unable to be part of the action.

My hands bunched into fists.

Franco stepped out of the room, leaving Hazel with the unidentified man in the house.

"Now!" Agent Bishop commanded as the SWAT team broke down the front door and barreled inside, guns drawn, announcing their presence.

Gunfire erupted from every angle. I shivered and swallowed the bile rising in my throat. I was used to being in the field, not watching from a monitor. It was painful knowing there was nothing I could do to help.

I wanted to go outside, be part of the action, but that wasn't an option. Agent Bishop had made it clear that we were allowed in the command post as a courtesy of Colton Carr.

I paced the small length of the trailer, finding it impossible to stand still while I kept my gaze on the monitors and surveillance footage from around the property.

One camera lost visual footage, but the audio was still patched in, which felt almost worse with the sound of gunfire and gut-wrenching screams.

I pinched the bridge of my nose, pushing down memories of my time overseas in the military. The horrors were resurfacing at the sounds of men screaming.

There wasn't more I could do, and so I waited with Aiden and

Lincoln. SWAT apprehended Franco as well as several other individuals in the household before bringing Hazel outside.

I hurried out of the command post, with Lincoln and Aiden on my heels.

Her eyes were puffy and red, her cheeks flushed. She tore outside, hobbling away from the armed agents when she saw us. Her brow furrowed, and tears welled in her eyes. "Mason," she whispered.

A single word, and I understood all the fears that were likely flooding through her. "We got to him in time. He's at the hospital," I said.

We had called and checked on him the moment we arrived in Chicago to make sure that he hadn't declined.

"He's stable," I said, hoping that would ease her mind.

She exhaled a heavy sigh. "Thank you."

Agent Bishop came up from behind. "We have a few questions for Hazel," he said.

"Sure. I'll answer anything I can." Hazel wrapped her arms around her chest.

Aiden grabbed an emergency blanket from the command post and pulled it over Hazel's shoulders.

"Thanks," she said.

Agent Bishop nodded his appreciation to Aiden before returning his attention to Hazel. "Do you know where your brother Nikolai is right now? We know this is his property."

"We were waiting for him to fly home. He was in Breckenridge looking for me." She exhaled a heavy breath and stared at the ground. "He should have returned home by now."

I spun around on my heels, noting the road had been closed off. He'd probably been on his way home and saw our agents. "He didn't call or reach out to Franco while you were in the house?" I asked.

Hazel shook her head. "Franco was focused on me." She swiped the tears as quickly as they'd fallen down her cheek. "Victor had been the one to call him, not Franco, but they did talk on the phone. I don't know what was said, I was in the shower at the time. Can we be done? I want to go see Mason."

Agent Bishop jotted down the little information that Hazel was able to provide. “Yes, of course. I believe we should be putting you into protective custody. With your brother out there and running the mafia, it’s only a matter of time until he finds you.”

“She’ll stay in our protective custody,” I said. Hazel had reached out to us, and without a doubt, it was what Mason would want for her.

“Are you sure that’s what you want, Hazel?” Agent Bishop asked. “We have a safe house that we can transport you to, provide you with a new identity, and ensure your safety.”

She lifted her gaze and met Agent Bishop’s hardened expression. “As much as I appreciate your offer, the U.S. Marshals weren’t able to protect me. I doubt you can, either. I’ll take my chances with Eagle Tactical. Besides, I want to see Mason.”

“You do realize that is probably where Nikolai is heading, to the one person he knows you want to be with,” Agent Bishop said.

“You have the contact information for Eagle Tactical. If you need anything from me, you can reach out to them until I replace my cell phone,” Hazel said.

“Very well,” Agent Bishop said before he headed back to the command post, their operation complete.

Lincoln stepped closer to Hazel, lifting her chin. “We’ll bring you to Mason if that’s what you want, but your brother is still out there. Agent Bishop is right; we’re leading you right into danger if we take you to him. You need to be aware of the risks.”

My phone vibrated in my pocket. I reached into my jacket and grabbed my phone, glancing at the caller ID, recognizing Ariella’s phone number. “Hey, we’re just finishing up here in Chicago,” I said, answering the phone.

“Jaxson. You need to come home.” Ariella didn’t sound like herself.

“What’s wrong? Is Izzie all right?”

“It’s Nikolai. He’s here and—”

The phone went dead.

CHAPTER TWENTY-TWO

ARIELLA

"Izzie, do we have to play hide and seek again?" I asked, exasperated.

I adored Jaxson's daughter, but she was a constant bundle of energy, and she'd already hidden a dozen times. She didn't grasp taking turns, and she liked to hide in the same place every time.

The doorbell interrupted our game.

I headed to the front door and attempted to glance through the peephole, but it was too tall for me. It had clearly been drilled for Jaxson.

Pulling the door open, Emma stood on the opposite side trembling, covered in blood. Her hair was wet, her clothes muddy and torn.

Rain pelted outside, the weather a few degrees above freezing.

"Come inside," I said, ushering her into the house and disabling the alarm. Jaxson had given me a secondary code that I was to use while he was away.

Her teeth chattered, and she rubbed her arms in an attempt to warm up.

"What happened?" I locked the door behind her and armed the alarm. She looked like she could have been mauled by a bear.

I glanced her over from head to toe. Maybe it wasn't that bad. She still had her arms and legs, but she looked in bad shape.

"I was at my place and he started shooting."

"Who started shooting?" I pulled out my phone. "We need to call the police."

Her eyes were wide and frantic. "No police."

She put a hand on my phone, her wet fingers making a mess of my device. I wiped it down and shoved it back into my pocket for the moment.

"If someone broke into your house and started shooting people, we need to call the sheriff," I said.

"Ella?" Izzie said, attempting to say my name. It was cute and amusing, considering she could say 'Ariel' and 'Ella' but refused to put them together. Honestly, I didn't mind the nickname. It was endearing.

I picked Izzie up, holding her in my arms, protecting her from Emma.

Emma didn't look well, and the fact she wasn't letting me call for help had me worried she wasn't herself.

Emma stared at Isabella, transfixed by the little girl, her biological daughter.

When was the last time she'd seen her? Had it been when she'd dropped her off and left her with Jaxson?

I'd heard the story from Jaxson about how Emma had intended to give her up and asked him to sign away his parental rights, but I'd never heard her speak of it, ever.

The long, sad stare at Izzie had my stomach in knots. I gently put Izzie down on the sofa and grabbed Emma by the arm and dragged her into the kitchen. "What the hell is going on?" I asked. I stood so that Emma's back was to Izzie and I could keep an eye on the little girl.

"He came and killed everyone." Emma's normally porcelain skin was sickeningly pale. Sweat glistened her forehead.

I reached for a clean rag and dampened it in the sink, adding a touch of soap and suds, helping clean her abrasions on her forehead. She needed a shower, though, and a fresh change of clothes.

"Who came?" I asked, trying to get it out of her. I wanted to know what happened.

Was it the men who had been after Hazel? Why would they have gone to Emma's home? The two women didn't look anything alike. She shouldn't have been mistaken for Hazel.

"I fucked up, royally." Emma swiped at her nose. Her eyes were red and brimmed with tears.

I reached for her hand, giving it a reassuring squeeze. "Whatever you did, I'm sure it can be fixed."

"I don't think so. They're dead because of me."

While I didn't know Emma that well, I didn't believe she had it in her to kill anyone. We'd worked together for a short time at the resort and been friends. Although, lately, we hadn't seen much of one another, I couldn't believe she had done anything that terrible. She had to be overreacting, right?

"Who is dead?" I needed to get her to open up and confide in me.

She wiped the tears and I grabbed a paper towel, offering it to her to dry her eyes.

"Thanks," she said between sniffles. "All of them. At least, I think they all are. I ran out the back door while they shot up the compound."

I didn't understand what she was talking about. "The compound? Don't you live in one of the cabins near the resort?"

"I only had that place while I was interviewing for the job. I've been living with the guys up there," Emma said and gestured north on the mountain.

My voice caught in my throat. "The off-gridders?" Jaxson had warned me to steer clear of them and the entrance to their compound.

Emma dabbed at her eyes with the paper towel.

I pulled out my cell phone and dialed the local police, letting him know who I was, that I worked for Eagle Tactical, and what Emma had witnessed. If what Emma said was true, they needed a team to scout the compound for survivors.

Jaxson would have been called in along with the rest of the Eagle Tactical team if they'd have been in town. I'd call him later when things settled down for a bit. There was no reason to worry him. He was busy en route to Chicago.

The sheriff's department paid us a visit after checking out the compound. "Emma, I need to bring you in for your formal statement."

Emma reached for my hand. "Will you come with me?"

"Sure. Let me bundle Izzie up, and then we can follow you down to the station," I said. I couldn't say no. She was broken. I knew what that felt like, to have your world crumble apart all around you.

I grabbed a snack from the vending machine at the police station for Izzie while we went into a separate room. "Come with me." The sheriff opened the door to an adjoining room and flipped on the lights. "You'll be able to see and hear everything. Make yourself comfortable. Hopefully, this won't take long."

Did he usually let people watch when statements were given?

Had he given me special treatment because he knew that I worked for Eagle Tactical?

I let Izzie sit on a table with her back to the glass window as I watched through the one-way mirror.

The sheriff stepped into the room with Emma and shut the door. "Can I get you something to drink? Coffee? Water?"

"No, thank you." Emma sat with her hands on the metal table. She looked incredibly calm after all that had transpired, but she was probably just in shock. Right?

He retrieved a pad of paper and pen. "Can you tell me what happened today?"

Emma exhaled a heavy sigh. "Yes." She glanced from the table to the sheriff. "I was at home, at the compound, when two men came in with guns drawn and began shooting everyone in sight."

"Do you know either of these men?" the sheriff asked.

"I've never seen them before."

"Are you sure? Can you recall if you saw them at the resort?"

She shook her head. "No. I never saw them at the resort or anywhere before. They weren't locals."

He exhaled heavily out of his nostrils. "Interesting. Can you tell me anything else? Like what might have made two men, who have never been to the resort or possibly even this town, come up to your home and execute everyone?"

Emma didn't answer.

My mouth went dry, and my hands trembled. I wrapped my arms around Izzie's waist, holding her steady on the table, offering her a weak smile.

What was Emma hiding?

The sheriff retrieved his phone from his pocket and scrolled through it before placing it on the table for Emma to view.

"Do you know what's on the video?" the sheriff asked.

Emma shook her head. She shifted on the metal chair, her head bent down, staring at the phone screen.

The sheriff presumably pushed play. I couldn't see the video, and the dialogue was too quiet to hear.

My fingers braided Izzie's hair, trying to distract myself from the weight of what happened through the glass. Maybe Izzie and I should have left. Emma had wanted us to be there to support her, but if she was involved, I wasn't sure I wanted to know about it.

"That's you on the surveillance footage," the sheriff said. "You were part of the team who took over the resort and held seventy-three people hostage."

Emma pursed her lips and folded her arms across her chest. "I was a victim."

"That's not what I see. What about this video?" He tapped his phone, and a moment later another clip played in the interrogation room.

Again, I couldn't hear what was said, but my chest ached as I found it harder to breathe.

"Tell me exactly what happened," the sheriff said, "and maybe we won't charge you with murder."

Silence filled the room for several long, drawn-out seconds before she finally cleared her throat to answer. "I always worked the front desk at Blue Sky Resort. It was my job to check in clients and take reservations. Imagine my surprise when one of the scout managers from Hollywood had booked a suite. I didn't plan any of it. You have to believe me."

He scribbled down notes as she spoke. "How did you know the client was a scout manager?"

"I used to live in Los Angeles. I worked for the studio and was a personal assistant to Mr. Joseph Kensington. He was my boss," Emma said. She exhaled a heavy sigh. "He was also an asshole, I might add. He liked to flirt with all the employees, including me. He told me to come into his office one time when the door was shut. He had a private bathroom and was whacking off when I walked in."

"So, you thought it would be a good idea to hold him hostage along with the other guests at the resort?"

Emma rubbed her eyes. "That wasn't my idea." She rested her hands on the table, tapping her fingers over the metal. "I mentioned to Ian about what my boss had done and how I'd been let go from my job. He told me no one else would get hurt. That his buddies would make sure Kensington never bothered anyone else. They were going to rough him up a little and then rob his hotel room. We figured there was probably a couple of grand in cash that he brought. It wasn't supposed to be a big deal. Ian took things too far."

"Does Ian have a last name?"

Her tongue darted out, swiping her top lips. "Yes. Ian Connor."

The air felt like it'd been sucked out of my lungs. Had Emma been in on the hostage takeover? The room spun, and I stumbled into the chair to sit down.

"Ella?" Izzie whispered, staring at me. She poked my cheek, seated above me on the table.

I reached for Isabella's hand and gave it a kiss. I didn't want to worry her. I tried to ignore Emma's voice from across the room, but it was pointless. I heard everything she said, and the more she spoke, the less remorseful she sounded.

"That still doesn't get us to the part about the men who attacked the compound, but I believe there may have been a correlation." The sheriff grabbed his file and flipped through, revealing a series of photographs. "Do you recognize any of these men?"

She pushed the file farther away, toward the sheriff. "No. Should I?"

"These were all hostages at the resort. Someone who might have a vendetta against their captors. Two of the men are known to work with a crime syndicate in Chicago." He flipped through the photographs and slid the picture across the table. "Take another look."

Emma exhaled loudly through her nose. "Yeah. I saw these two at the resort. They were sitting across from me in the hallway when I was being held with the other hostages, but they aren't the men who stormed the compound today."

"Did you see who did the shooting?"

"I didn't recognize them, but I did get a good long look at them right before I tore out on foot. They could have been friends with those guys." She tapped the picture. "But it wasn't them. Did you check the security footage from the compound?"

The sheriff slid back his chair, the feet squeaking with his movements. "What security footage?"

"Jayden set up cameras along the perimeter. I thought it was stupid and a waste of money, but maybe it can help you catch the men who did this?"

His eyes tightened. "I'm going to have a sketch artist work with you to recreate a representation of the men who targeted and attacked the compound. Can you do that for us?"

"Yeah, sure." Emma twirled her hair with her finger. "Can I get a bottle of water, something to eat? I'm famished."

I stood, unable to take any more of Emma's antics.

I bundled up Izzie in her winter coat and carried her out of the police station and down to my car. Thankfully, I had picked it up earlier that afternoon when Skylar had gone in to work.

I opened the back door and put her into the car seat that I had installed. Jaxson had a spare one in the house which had come in handy. After she was buckled, I climbed into the front seat, started the engine, and texted Skylar.

I'm taking Izzie with me to visit Mason. He's in the hospital. Will be home late.

I didn't further elaborate. If she had any questions, she could call me. I looked up the hospital where Mason had been brought and called them to ensure that he was able to have visitors.

Apparently, he'd been airlifted and transported to Sanford Health, a level one trauma center, over ten hours away from Breckenridge.

"Fuck!"

Izzie repeated my curse. "Fuck. Fuck. Fuck."

I exhaled a long, heavy sigh. Crap. I couldn't get mad at her; she didn't understand what she was doing when she repeated me. Hopefully, she'd stop saying 'fuck' before Jaxson returned home.

When would he be back?

Starting the car, I pulled out from the police station parking lot and headed home with Izzie. "I guess it's just you and me." At least until Skylar came home. I had a distinct impression that she didn't like me, but I wasn't sure why.

We drove back to Jaxson's home. Every part of me was exhausted. I was ready for bed but still needed to make dinner. I carried Izzie up to the house and put her down on the porch while I fished out my keys. As I grabbed them from my purse, my gaze landed on the door.

Shit.

The front door was ajar. I hadn't left it open. I'd locked it when I left, and there wasn't any sign of Skylar. The alarm wasn't on, or at least it hadn't gone off from what I could surmise.

Had I remembered to turn it on when we left?

I hoisted Izzie into my arms and backed up, slamming into a man who had come up around the side of the house. I felt the barrel of his gun nestled in my back.

"Welcome home," he said, his voice calm and even, almost a little too friendly. Was it because I had Izzie in my arms?

"What do you want?" I guided Izzie down, planting her feet on the ground. I didn't want her to glance over my shoulder at the man pointing his weapon at me.

"Let's go inside and have a little chat."

Izzie stepped inside, and I slowly reached for the light, flipping it on. "Is that really necessary?" I asked, nodding toward the gun. "There's a child here. Do we absolutely need to give the girl nightmares?"

"Call the Eagle Tactical guy. What's his name?"

"I don't know what you're talking about," I said, playing dumb.

He stepped into the house behind me and shut the door. "Call your boss. Tell him Nikolai is here and wants a trade."

I slowly pulled out my phone and dialed Jaxson. "I don't know that he'll pick up the phone. He's out of town." I didn't want to elaborate on his flight or the details of the mission.

"Hey, we're just finishing up here in Chicago." His voice was cheery, carefree, and at ease. I wanted to ask if everything had gone well, but I couldn't, not with the stranger in the house.

I spoke slowly and clearly, doing my best not to panic. "Jaxson." At least the gun wasn't pointed at me anymore, which gave me the opportunity to fight back. The only problem was Izzie. I didn't want to risk her life. "You need to come home."

"What's wrong? Is Izzie all right?" Jaxson asked.

Nikolai hadn't laid so much as a hand on her, but it didn't mean he wouldn't. I'd protect her to the bitter end, but if I wasn't alive, what good was I to Izzie?

My gaze lifted from Izzie to the man holding us hostage in Jaxson's home. "It's Nikolai. He's here, and he wants a trade."

There was no answer.

"Jaxson?" I moved my phone from my ear to look at the screen. "Great," I muttered under my breath.

“What?” Nikolai asked as he stepped closer, brooding.

“The call dropped.” I showed Nikolai my phone. I hadn’t hung up, and I was confident Jaxson wouldn’t have hung up the call, either.

“Call him back.”

I had zero bars. “I don’t have a signal.”

Nikolai shoved his cell phone at me. “Call him,” he demanded.

I dialed Jaxson’s phone and breathed a sigh of relief when he picked up. “Ariella?”

“Yes. Nikolai is here. He has a message he wants me to give you.”

Nikolai ripped the phone from my fingers, having lost his patience with me. “I know you have possession of my sister, Hazel.”

He stared at me, his eyes raking over my body before glancing at Izzie.

“Bring her to me, or you’ll be picking out a coffin for the little girl.”

CHAPTER TWENTY-THREE

JAXSON

"I'll kill him!" I shouted, staring at my phone. The bastard threatened my daughter's life and then, like a coward, hung up.

Lincoln rested a hand on my arm. "We're not going to let anything happen to Izzie, and we know Ariella is with her. She'll protect her. What's the plan?"

I couldn't think straight. My heart slammed against the walls of my ribcage, trying to break free of its prison. I took off on foot for our car, parked on the other side of the blockade.

"Someone tipped Nikolai off," I said.

Lincoln, Hazel, and Aiden followed after me. Lincoln dug out the car keys for the rental car from his pocket, while Hazel kept up with my pace, walking alongside me.

"Do you think it was Franco?" Lincoln asked. He hit the button on the remote to unlock the doors.

I hustled to the car and climbed in.

"Doubtful," Hazel said. She opened the door and hopped into the backseat. "Franco was convinced that Nikolai had arranged a flight home when he found out I was back in Chicago. We were waiting for him to return home. I thought he was en route."

Lincoln and Aiden climbed into the car. Lincoln started the engine and tore out of the neighborhood for the airport.

"Who else knew you were in Chicago?" I asked and turned around so that I could face her. I didn't think she'd lie to me, but I also wasn't sure what the hell was going on anymore. Why the hell was Nikolai at my house threatening my daughter and Ariella?

"Does it matter?" Lincoln asked. "We need to come up with a plan. I'll call Declan and let him know what's going on. He can stake out your house. Maybe he'll be able to slip inside or at least know how many men we're up against."

"At least Nikolai and his driver, Sacha," Hazel said. "They go everywhere together. I'm surprised Nikolai didn't marry me off to him." She shifted in the back seat and stared out the window.

"Can you go any faster?" I asked, glaring at Lincoln. Traffic may not have been Lincoln's fault, but we definitely weren't taking the best route. I wasn't familiar with Chicago, but there had to be another way to get to the airport.

Driving to the airport had been tedious, but not as painstaking as the flight home. We had a private jet, but it didn't mean we arrived any quicker than flying commercial.

When we eventually landed, we texted Declan.

Flight landed. On our way. Please tell me you have good news.

I wanted the mission to be over with and Izzie and Ariella to be safe and the operation behind us. That was wishful thinking.

Declan didn't answer. We rushed off the plane and straight to my truck. I threw myself into the driver's side, not letting anyone else take the reins. It was hard not to crave control, especially when it was my own family on the line.

"Are you sure you don't want to call the sheriff and involve the local police?" Aiden asked from the backseat.

"No. We're doing this off the books."

In the backseat of Declan's truck, was a stash of weapons and supplies for us. It would keep us from having to make an extra stop at the Eagle Tactical office.

"Any word from Declan?" I asked. My phone was buried in my pocket, but I had group texted our message so that any of the guys could answer if he responded.

I glanced at Lincoln beside me in the front seat.

Lincoln pulled out his phone, viewed the texts, and then shook his head. "Nothing yet. Don't you have surveillance cameras with your security system?"

"They're disabled, along with the alarm system. I attempted to access the system while we were catching our flight, but I couldn't get into the Wi-Fi system."

"Do you think he cut the power?" Hazel asked.

"I don't know. There's a battery backup system, but he could have disabled that if he knew how to hack into the system. It looks like the system was disarmed and hacked."

I had hoped it was impenetrable, but Declan could have hacked it. I wasn't sure about Nikolai's abilities or the man who tagged along with him.

"My brother is a thug. He's good with a gun and having his men do his dirty work. Nikolai wouldn't know how to hack anything," Hazel said.

Maybe that should have made me feel better, but it didn't.

"Shit. I need to call Skylar and warn her not to come home right now." I didn't want to give Nikolai another hostage. He hadn't mentioned her, which meant she mustn't have been home.

I used voice dialing and waited for Skylar to answer. It went straight to voicemail. "Listen, don't come home right now. Something is going down at the house, and I need you to go to my office. There's a sofa. Crash there for the night."

I ended the call. My eyes narrowed as I focused on the road. I should have called Skylar earlier while I was in Chicago. If she was already home from work and I had given Nikolai a third hostage, I would never forgive myself.

We hurried up the mountain pass and down the gravel road for my house, closing in, drawing nearer. I cut the engine and shut the truck off a few yards away. I didn't want to alert Nikolai that we had arrived. We needed the upper hand.

With quiet precision, we snuck out of the truck and closed the doors, careful not to alert anyone inside of our arrival. I stalked past Nikolai's vehicle. The driver was slumped forward, dead.

Had Declan taken him out, or Nikolai? I'd find out later, right now I needed to get to our gear and rescue Izzie and Ariella.

Quietly, I pulled the door handle to Declan's vehicle and slid the equipment from the back seat and the floor, providing our team with guns and gear for the mission.

We needed to assume Nikolai was armed and prepared for our arrival. There was no chance that we were entering through the front door.

I took in my surroundings, listening for any signs of distress or other armed men who might have been watching. The river trickled to my east, but that was the only sound that reached my ears. With careful precision, we strode forward in silence, approaching the house.

Aiden followed behind me, with Lincoln in the rear. I wasn't crazy about Hazel coming with us, but if we didn't use her as bait, there was a higher chance that Nikolai would shoot my baby girl or Ariella. He wouldn't shoot Hazel; at least I was mostly confident he wouldn't hurt her.

There were no guarantees. He had sold her off to be married.

I held my breath on our approach, hugging the window as I listened for sounds inside and any indication of their whereabouts.

Aiden tapped me on the back, and I glanced over my shoulder. He pointed at the ground, the broken cell phone on the slushy packed snow that had begun to melt.

Declan's phone had been abandoned, the screen smashed. I tilted my head up to glance at the roof. Had he climbed atop and dropped his phone?

With a goofy grin, he waved down at us.

Bastard.

He was in position with his sniper rifle. While I appreciated that he made sure no other assholes were hidden in the forest and he had the upper hand, I also needed to get inside the house. Lying up on the roof wasn't going to help me rescue Izzie and Ariella.

We needed to find a way inside the house and not through the front door.

CHAPTER TWENTY-FOUR

ARIELLA

I had hours until Jaxson flew back from Chicago and arrived in Breckenridge. He wouldn't turn over Hazel to Nikolai in exchange for his daughter and my safety.

Nikolai wasn't an idiot. He had to suspect the same, which meant there had to be another power play he had. I just wasn't sure what he planned.

He had snatched my phone along with his cell phone, burying both in his pocket. Not that I was anticipating my captor would allow me another phone call.

"Why are you here?" I asked, staring him down. While he was quite a bit taller than I was, I didn't give the illusion that I was afraid of him.

Big mistake.

He smashed the barrel of the gun against my cheek and pushed me backward, stumbling over the toys on the living room floor.

I caught myself, but not before Nikolai lurched forward and shoved me onto the sofa.

"Sit," he commanded—a single word with the authority to send shivers down my spine.

Izzie came running toward me. His tone must have frightened her. "Come here," I said, holding out my arms as she climbed into my lap.

She clung tight against me, and while she hadn't been bothered earlier by the stranger, unaware of the danger, it seemed now she understood that we were in trouble.

Izzie's arms clung around my neck. I shifted her weight, having her sit on my lap, my arms wrapped around her, protective and comforting.

"Would you put that away?" I gestured toward the gun that he'd assaulted me with moments earlier. "All you're doing is scaring her." I didn't want to admit that I was scared too. He probably got off on frightening women.

Nikolai huffed under his breath and shoved the gun into the waistband of his pants. "Don't try anything stupid," he said. His eyes tightened, and he glanced Izzie and me over from head to toe.

I swallowed the bile rising in my throat, the fear pulsing through my veins, pumping like oxygen to my heart. He wasn't going to let us go, and given his history of bloodshed at the compound, I needed a plan.

Think.

I clung to Izzie, but that didn't settle the terror that rotted in my stomach like spoiled meat. A thin sheen of sweat coated my forehead. I wiped my brow and stared down at the floor. The last thing I wanted was to appear threatening.

Nikolai was in charge.

I needed to make myself small and insignificant. Not so much so that he'd kill me, but that he wouldn't find me threatening. What had all my training at the C.I.A. taught me?

I could disarm him, but that assumed there weren't others ready to shoot me the minute I opened the front door. Or worse, what if he discharged his gun and shot Izzie?

I couldn't live with myself if something happened to her. Jaxson would never forgive me, either.

Get inside his head.

What made him tick? What was his agenda? Without a doubt, he didn't just want to strut out with Hazel at his side and return to Chicago. No. He was a mobster with a thirst for blood.

If I asked him why he was doing this, he'd shut me out. I needed to dig deeper. I glanced at the clock. We had at least a few hours together. Could I get him to talk?

My mouth was dry, and my words came out raspy. "We're going to be here a while. Can I get up and grab a book to read to Izzie?" I asked. While I didn't budge from my position on the sofa, I pointed toward the bookshelf in the dining room, just behind us.

"You don't move," Nikolai said. He strode across the room in earnest and stood there for a fraction of a second before he yanked a book from the shelf. He shuffled back to the living room and towered above us. "Here." He tossed a soft lavender paperback book at me.

Alice's Adventures in Wonderland.

I was shocked that it was a children's book he found. He'd been so quick that I thought he had pulled the first book he'd found on the shelf.

"Thank you," I said and opened the book, starting with the first page. "Have you read this before?" I asked Izzie. Hopefully, it wasn't too old for her, but it was a classic.

She shook her head no.

"She'll like it." Nikolai paced the length of the room several times over before standing in the corner of the room, just a few feet away, watching us. He folded his arms across his chest. "Read it to her."

I flipped past the title page and opened to chapter one.

"Down the Rabbit-Hole," I said and read the heading for the first chapter, while Izzie wiggled her bottom and curled up in my arms.

Her body relaxed as I read, every word seeming to comfort her. Could it have been a simple fact that this was a distraction that made her feel better?

"Alice was beginning to get very tired of sitting by her sister on the bank and of having nothing to do; once or twice she had peeped into the book her sister was reading, but it had no pictures or conversations in it, 'and what is the use of a book,' thought Alice 'without pictures or conversations?'"

Izzie rested her hand against my chest, over my heart, as she closed her eyes. Envious that she could sleep through anything, including a mad man waving a gun at us. Well, for the moment, the gun was tucked into his pants, but it was within his reach.

I kept reading, page by page. Her body slumped as she fell asleep in my arms. A sigh of relief fell past my lips and spilled out as I finished the second chapter.

"Keep reading," Nikolai demanded of me.

I did as he said, only because he flashed his gun at me, threatening both of our lives if I didn't do as he commanded.

Every so often, I glanced up as I read in a soft, hushed whisper to find a strange semblance of something familiar cross Nikolai's face.

"You've read this before," I said. The only solution was to get him to open up and talk. If I could find a way that related to him, maybe he'd spare our lives.

"We're not talking," Nikolai said. His finger gestured for me to turn the page and continue reading.

Avoiding conflict, I didn't shut the book. However, I also didn't do what he wanted. I kept the page unturned, the book open, my eyes wide as I stared up at Nikolai. "Your sister, Hazel, is quite a bit younger than you."

While I didn't know how old Nikolai was, he had years weathered to his skin, his brow, his hands, and neck. Stress aged a person; so did murder.

He didn't stop me, but he also didn't comment on my observation.

"Did you read this book to Hazel when she was little?" I asked. Could I conjure the good memories, and he'd come to his senses?

He pushed himself away from the corner of the room, his arms still folded against his chest, protective in nature. At the moment, he wasn't trying to scare me or wake Izzie. He paced the length of the room, back and forth, his jaw tight.

Nikolai's hands fell to his sides, his hands bunched into fists. "I read that book to my sister, but it wasn't Hazel."

"You have another sister?" Had she too been sold and married off to another mobster? I held my tongue; it wasn't an appropriate question to ask if I wanted him to open up and find a way out of this disaster.

I needed to act with stealth. I had to be sneaky if I was going to interrogate him without him even realizing that's what I was doing.

His bottom lip jutted out, and his top lip tightened. A tic coursed through him once, forcing his eyes to soften. As quickly as it happened, he grunted and shuffled his feet, pacing louder.

Please don't wake Izzie.

He couldn't read my mind. Not that I expected him to, I just didn't want her to be frightened again. She deserved some peaceful slumber free of nightmares. I wasn't sure I'd be so lucky if I survived today.

"Yes, I had a baby sister before Hazel. Her name was Rebecca." Something flashed behind his gaze, a flicker that made me believe he wasn't always the monster he'd become.

"You used to read *Alice's Adventures in Wonderland* to her?" I needed to make him see the connection, the familiarity, and maybe then he wouldn't put Izzie in harm's way. If only he realized her innocence and that she was an innocent child.

He stopped pacing and hovered above us.

I shivered from his presence, from his brooding nature that made me feel tiny and insignificant.

Nikolai reached toward me, and I shuddered from fear.

He grabbed the throw blanket on the back of the sofa and unfolded it, placing it over Izzie as she slept.

The warmth comforted me too. Was he not the monster everyone believed him to be? I didn't know how I could ask him if he had shot everyone in the compound without him turning defensive and building up a wall.

"Thank you," I whispered, staring up at him.

He grunted and stepped back, his nostrils flaring as he breathed heavily in and out of his nose.

"Are you and Rebecca still close?" I asked. I had to keep asking questions to understand what he was doing and maybe find a way out.

Nikolai's gaze grew dark. "She's dead."

Not another word was spoken. He didn't elaborate on how she died or when.

"I'm sorry." I had meant it; whether he realized it or not, losing a sibling was hell. I hadn't lost my sister, not physically, but emotionally, we'd fallen apart. I'd lost a child, and that had been heart-wrenching.

He stared at me long and hard before giving a once-over nod. "Yeah. Me too. Cost of being in the family business," Nikolai said. He gave a shrug as if it didn't matter anymore and was all in the past.

"There doesn't have to be a cost. You don't have to keep killing people," I whispered.

His feet slammed against the floor as he whipped out his gun and pointed it at my head. "Shut it!"

I'd gone too far.

I closed my lips and let my gaze fall down to the floor. I held Izzie asleep in my arms. "Let me put her upstairs in bed."

"No."

I needed to protect her, but I couldn't do that with the barrel of a gun against my forehead.

If I died, who would protect Izzie? Jaxson would when he arrived, but how much longer until that happened? I couldn't let her get hurt. I wouldn't. Jaxson had been there for me, rescued me. I owed him my life. Now I was repaying the favor.

"She doesn't need to be involved in this, Nikolai. This is between you and me."

He rolled his eyes and cocked the safety off on the gun. "No."

A single word. That's all he said, and I could argue until my last breath. But what good would that do Izzie?

"Fine." I didn't argue. It wouldn't do any good. I needed to get him to continue to open up to me. He wasn't going to do that with his gun poised and ready to shoot. "I'm sorry," I said, apologizing. "You're in charge."

"Damn right, I'm in charge!" he growled.

I didn't move. I didn't flinch. I needed him to see that I wasn't a threat, and maybe then he'd put away the gun.

Silence enveloped the room.

My heart pounded against my chest. Could he hear the fear, the adrenaline coursing through my veins?

His breathing was heavy and loud, filling the quiet space.

After several minutes, he pulled his gun away from my forehead, put the safety back on, and shoved the weapon into the waistband of his pants.

My eyes shut, relieved he wasn't pointing his pistol at me. We still weren't done. I wasn't safe until he was in handcuffs and carted off to jail. Had Jaxson phoned the local sheriff?

I hadn't heard sirens, but maybe they were smart enough not to alert us of their presence?

My voice soft and timid, I needed answers. "What's going to happen to Hazel?"

Nikolai had made it clear that he wanted his sister returned to him. While I didn't think he'd let Izzie or me go, I wasn't sure what he planned to do with his sister.

"Why do you care?" He paced the length of the living room again, glancing every so often out the window. When he seemed satisfied that it was still just the three of us in the house, he returned his attention to me.

"I consider Hazel a friend."

The truth was I didn't have many friends. I'd alienated everyone in New York when my ex-husband had been convicted on multiple felony counts for embezzlement and fraud. Emma had been a friend, but that had been short-lived.

Nikolai strode over to the fireplace, examining the photographs on the mantle. "She doesn't have any friends."

I didn't know if that was true or not, but she seemed close to Mason, a secret I would take to my grave. There was no reason that Nikolai needed to know about him.

"I saved her life at the resort," I said.

"You were at the resort when those bastards came in and took hostages?" Nikolai rushed at me, the gun back out of his pants and now in his hand. He shoved it up under my jaw.

"I was a hostage, same as Hazel," I said. Did he think I was involved? Would he kill me because I spoke about the situation?

He appeared unhinged. Should I have been surprised?

"But you got her out?"

"It wasn't just me. I had help from the Eagle Tactical team." I didn't point out that I was employed by them. I wasn't sure whether he'd kiss me or kill me.

He snorted. "Those bastards betrayed me. When they show up with Hazel, they're dead. Every last one of them, including the little girl."

"No one is touching my little girl," Jaxson's voice echoed through the house, loud and clear.

I glanced over my shoulder for Jaxson.

I could have sworn he was behind me, but he wasn't in the house.

Nikolai backed away from me and glanced out the window, satisfied that Jaxson hadn't arrived yet. "Nice try!" he shouted.

His gun poised at the alarm speaker system, he fired off a round, blowing the plastic into tiny shards that shattered around the room.

CHAPTER TWENTY-FIVE

JAXSON

"I'm going in there with you," Hazel demanded as we breached the property.

I didn't have time to argue. While I wasn't keen on another hostage, she was also the bait. The one thing that Nikolai wanted, and the only way to ensure Izzie's safety along with Ariella's, was to dangle the carrot in front of the rabbit.

"Stay out of the way," I warned. We had climbed in through the back window in the bathroom, and Declan had hacked into the security system through the wiring outside to offer a distraction.

I snuck inside the house through the window.

Declan stayed on the roof, keeping a lookout while Aiden and Lincoln followed behind me.

Hazel was in the rear, with no weapons, but she did have a bulletproof vest on to protect her.

Nikolai wouldn't shoot his own sister, would he?

Declan played my recording that we'd made a few minutes earlier outside over the speaker system attached to the alarm.

While the alarm had been disabled, it hadn't been destroyed. "No one is touching my little girl." It was strange to hear my own voice and dangerous to alert him of our arrival, but we had to do something.

From the window, I'd seen the bastard with a gun positioned on Ariella's forehead.

I couldn't take the chance that he'd shoot her or Izzie.

I kept my head down; they'd be looking for the team and for me.

"Nice try!" Nikola's voice shouted through the downstairs of the house. A single shot rang out as Nikolai pointed the gun at the speaker and blew it away.

We came around from the kitchen, Ariella's back to me, the sofa pointed toward the front door.

"Freeze!" I shouted, my gun drawn and poised on Nikolai.

Aiden and Lincoln held their firearms up, three men versus one.

"Don't even think about it," Lincoln said. "Put your gun down slowly."

"Give me Hazel and I'll walk away. You'll never have to see me again," Nikolai said. He held up his gun in a surrender maneuver.

I didn't trust him. We'd heard from Declan that the sheriff had received a call about the compound being shot up by two mafia fellows. One was inside my house, the other, I assumed was the dead man in the vehicle out on my driveway.

"That's not how this works," I said. I kept my gun trained on him as he came around into the living room, blocking Izzie and Ariella.

Aiden pulled out his handcuffs that he'd attached to his belt. "Put the gun down slowly. Arms up."

Nikolai held one arm up in surrender and the other, he slowly guided down.

The front door handle jiggled open, grabbing our attention. Who the hell was on the other side of the door? Declan was supposed to be up on the roof still.

Skylar pulled the door open and stepped inside, coming face to face with Nikolai.

With his free hand, he reached for Skylar, yanked her against him and gripped her hair, shoving the barrel of the gun against her neck.

"Let me go!" Skylar screamed.

"Daddy!" Izzie shrieked in terror.

I couldn't turn around and look back at my little girl and assure her everything was all right. My focus had to be on the monster standing just a few feet away from me, with my sister as his hostage.

Skylar had no formal tactical training. She'd never been in the military or spent a day doing self-defense. I couldn't count on her to get out of his clutches.

"You don't have to do this, Nikolai," Hazel said. She trailed out from around the hallway and came up beside Lincoln and grabbed his spare gun from his holster at his hip. She pointed the gun at herself, lifting it to her temple.

"Hazel, what are you doing?" Nikolai's eyes grew wide, and his voice was frantic. "Think about what you're doing, sis."

"If you kill her," Hazel said, her voice quivered as she spoke, "you'll never see me again."

With my gun trained on Nikolai, I couldn't stop Hazel from doing something stupid. I didn't know her well enough to determine if she was bluffing, but I couldn't take the chance. "You don't want to do that, Hazel."

"Yes, I do." Hazel nodded, her hand trembling with the gun poised against her skin, the barrel flush with her body. She might have been wearing a bulletproof vest, but it wouldn't save her, not with what she had planned.

"Listen to your sister," Lincoln said. "She's willing to die because of what you did."

Skylar struggled against Nikolai, squirming in his grasp, trying to shrug away from him, but he wouldn't let her escape.

"Let me go," Skylar whispered, her eyes welled with tears. "Please. I don't even know what's going on. I won't tell anyone."

I wasn't going to let him disappear. Not after all that he'd done. "Tell Hazel what you did, Nikolai."

Nikolai shook his head, his dark, thick hair falling into his eyes. "Everything I've done was for you, Hazel. All I wanted was your happiness."

"My happiness?" Hazel scoffed and stepped forward, her own

gun still pointed at her head. "You sold me to Franco to be his bride! I'd sooner die than marry that disgusting pig."

Nikolai blinked several times over; his expression looked perplexed. "What?"

"You heard me!" Hazel shouted as she stepped closer, unafraid of her brother. "I'm tired of you running my life and ruining it. I know what you and Dad did. I know about the jobs, the fake agency I worked for, the boyfriends you and Dad paid off. I'm not an idiot, you know."

Nikolai released his grip on Skylar, and she hurried away from him as Lincoln grabbed her and dragged her behind him for protection.

"They weren't good enough for you," Nikolai said, his attention on Hazel. "It's my duty to protect you. You're my baby sister. Those men weren't deserving of you."

"You bastard, that was my decision to make!" Hazel shouted up at him. As she stared him down, the gun trembled in her grip, her finger on the trigger.

Nikolai lowered the gun in his hand and reached for Hazel's weapon. "If you die, I'll kill every last one of them."

"No, you won't," Hazel said and turned the gun, pulling the trigger, and shooting Nikolai in the chest.

CHAPTER TWENTY-SIX

Hazel

I'd done it for them, everyone he'd ever killed, tortured, or hurt.

I turned the gun from my own forehead to his chest. It'd been reckless, without thought or calculation. He could have easily shot me with his gun in retaliation. I wouldn't have blamed him if he had.

My finger squeezed the trigger. It was the only way to put an end to what he'd done.

I couldn't go home again. Nikolai would never stop hunting me down, demanding that I do as he wanted because we were blood.

Franco had been arrested, but with the head of the mafia dead, another leader would rise from the ashes, and I would be forgotten. At least I hoped I would be forgotten.

The room spun; the world felt like it was moving in slow motion.

Lincoln kicked the gun away from Nikolai as he lay on the floor, bleeding out.

I stumbled several steps backward before hitting a warm body. Jaxson removed the gun from my hands. I felt cold and empty, alone.

"I'm sorry," Jaxson said into my ear. The cold, rough metal of handcuffs clasped onto my wrists as he secured them behind my back.

"I understand." I expected nothing less. They'd cart me off to jail. I'd be going to prison for a long time.

"Are handcuffs really necessary?" Lincoln shot Jaxson a glance.

"It's just a formality," Jaxson said. "I need to know that my family is no longer in any danger. I'll call the sheriff and let him know what happened."

Aiden bent down to Nikolai lying on the floor.

Blood pooled around Nikolai, his skin pale, his eyes closed. I didn't have the courage to ask if he was still breathing.

I wanted to kill Nikolai after all he'd done to destroy my life, but I'd never believed myself to be a murderer. Guilt weighed heavily on me. I'd acted in self-defense, not only for my own life but of those around me.

Nikolai would never have let any of them go.

Jaxson made a quick phone call to the sheriff while I sat on the floor beside my brother. His skin looked cold, but I couldn't touch him, my hands behind my back.

Aiden pressed against the wound, attempting to stop the flow of blood oozing out of the wound. With his other hand, he felt for a pulse and shook his head. "He's dead."

I collapsed onto my knees, staring down at my brother. Stepbrother or not, he was still family. Blood was blood.

"You're with Rebecca now. It's better that way," I whispered, staring down at Nikolai. I had never met Rebecca, his biological sister. He'd spoken of her greatly when we were younger, how her life had been cut short, murdered by another gangster. It had driven our father to become the head of the mafia, to rise up in retaliation.

I wanted it to be over, all of it. The carnage. The slayings. The killing for blood.

I'd given my statement to the local sheriff. The team from Eagle Tactical had given their statements, as had Ariella. We had been taken individually into a room, questioned, and then asked to provide in writing what happened.

I confessed to shooting Nikolai.

It seemed Nikolai had also killed his driver, Sacha, though I had no answer as to why.

I had expected to spend the rest of my life in prison, but the handcuffs came off, and I was free to go.

The D.A. wasn't going to press charges.

Had Nikolai been alive, he would have been charged with multiple counts of murder after raiding the compound and killing dozens of men, women, and children.

I thought I might vomit when the sheriff informed me what my brother had done in retribution for the resort. It was all over.

I headed out of the police station, surprised to find Ariella waiting for me.

"I never did thank you properly," Ariella said. She leaned against her sedan, her hands in her jacket pockets. "If you hadn't offered yourself as you did, I don't know how we would have gotten out of that situation."

I shrugged. "It was nothing." I didn't want her to make a big deal of it. "Have you heard anything about Mason?"

I wanted to see him, to make sure he was all right, and thank him for saving my life. He was one of the reasons that I was still standing, alive, and breathing.

"We've already chartered a flight to Fargo to visit him in the hospital. Do you want to come with us?" Ariella asked.

"Yes. I need to see him and thank him for what he did for me."

I hurried down the hospital corridor.

Would Mason even want to see me? His Uncle Jeb died because of me.

If I wouldn't have requested his help, his uncle would still be alive, and Mason wouldn't have been shot.

The smell of antiseptic burned my nostrils. I paused in the empty waiting room.

"Do you mind staying here with Izzie?" Jaxson asked Ariella.

"Sure," she said as she smiled and took the toddler from her father's arms.

I opened my mouth to offer to watch the little girl for Jaxson but thought better of it. I wasn't great with kids, and I wanted to see Mason. I was worried he wouldn't be happy to see me.

Lincoln and Jaxson headed through the doors and down the corridor. I hesitated before following, several feet behind them. They talked amongst one another. I was the outsider, and while they hadn't tried to exclude me, I wasn't one of them.

What was I doing here? I felt out of place.

Lincoln and Jaxson headed into the private room without so much as a knock. I hung out in the hallway, trying to find the courage to enter.

I could handle shoving a gun against my own head, but stepping five feet forward into a hospital room was too much. That, apparently, was my limit.

"How's Hazel?" Mason's voice was raspy and rough.

He couldn't see me, as I was just right outside his room, but I could hear the sweet sound of his voice. It was filled with concern for me.

I hugged the wall, my back against the cold, white brick.

"She could tell you herself if she came in here," Lincoln said.

"She's here?" Mason asked. The sheets rustled and the hospital bed creaked. "Hazel?"

I shut my eyes. I couldn't hide forever. He'd know I was avoiding him if I didn't storm into his room and greet him right now.

"Hey." I mustered the best smile that I could as I stepped into his hospital room. "I was just out in the hallway looking for flowers I could steal for you."

Mason smiled and laughed, grimacing.

"Does it hurt to laugh?" I asked, worried about him. I came up alongside his bed.

"It's worth it," Mason said. He reached for my hand, our fingers intertwining. "Sit with me."

I didn't want to tell him there wasn't room. He was injured, but if he wanted my company, how could I say no? He'd only been shot because of me.

"How are you feeling?" I asked, sitting on the edge of the hospital bed by his side. "Any news when you will be released?"

"The doctor says that I can be discharged into someone's care at home, or else I have to go to a rehab facility." His eyes never left mine. "You owe me one, Hazel."

I laughed under my breath. "Don't beat around the bush." I couldn't believe he was playing the fact that I owed him.

Of course, I owed him, but I didn't think he was the kind of guy who would have collected on it.

"Please, will you stay with me?"

I hadn't thought about where I'd go now that Nikolai was dead and Franco was in prison. Mason needed me, though, and I genuinely liked him. I hadn't felt that way for anyone else, ever. It had always been him since we were teenagers.

"Well, since you asked nicely," I said and gave a weak smile. I wanted to stay, but I wanted it to be because he wanted me in his life, not just as his caretaker. Leaning down, I planted a soft, chaste kiss on his forehead.

"Is that all I get? What's a guy got to do to get a real kiss around here, die?"

My eyes widened in horror.

"Bad joke?" Mason smiled with that boyish grin that made my heart flutter and knees weak. I leaned in and brushed my lips over his.

The heart monitor started beeping faster.

Jaxson stood by the window of the room, a smile on his face. "Don't kill him. We still need him as part of our team. Speaking of the team, Lincoln, I'm going to offer you full time again. I know your restaurant will be undergoing renovations. Is there any way we can talk you into joining us? Don't make me beg."

"I'm not even dead yet and you're replacing me," Mason said. He laughed and grimaced.

I rested a gentle hand on his good arm, hoping to settle him back down. "I'm sure they're not replacing you," I said.

"I wouldn't be too sure," Lincoln said. "I'll do it, at least for now. It'll be a while until the check comes through from insurance, and then I'll have to decide what I'm going to do."

"I'm sorry about your restaurant," I said, smiling weakly at Lincoln. If I hadn't gone to his restaurant that morning, maybe the thugs who wanted me dead wouldn't have shot up the place.

Lincoln's jaw was tight, and he leaned against the wall near the foot of the hospital bed. "Don't mention it. These guys have been bugging me for the past several years to join Eagle Tactical. They're probably happy about what happened."

"Happy is a strong word," Mason said, "but ecstatic, yes."

Lincoln rolled his eyes.

Jaxson headed past Lincoln and gestured for him to follow out of the room. "We'll leave you two to talk. We'll be in the waiting room with Ariella and Izzie. Let us know if you need anything," Jaxson said.

"Thank you for coming. Hopefully, they'll spring me out of here soon," Mason said.

I waited until the other guys were gone and down the hall.

"Something on your mind?" Mason asked.

"I'm sorry for everything." I leaned down, planting my lips on his, hungrily taking a taste.

Having almost lost him, had torn me up inside. I'd already lost my brother at my own hands. I couldn't lose the man I'd loved since I was a teenager.

Mason reached out and his thumb stroked my cheek as my chin rested in his palm. "You have nothing to apologize for, but I do know one thing you could do to help me feel better after we get out of here."

"Anything," I said. "I'm all yours. Whatever you need, Mason, I'm here for you." I meant it too. I'd do whatever he needed me to do to care for him, whether it involved changing bandages or making him meals.

"Any chance you have a cute little nurse's outfit? As long as you're going to be taking care of me, I thought we could do a little fantasy roleplay."

CHAPTER TWENTY-SEVEN

ARIELLA

I sat with Izzie in the waiting room, letting her watch a video on my smartphone. We kept the audio down so that we wouldn't bother any hospital patients.

Having lost track of time, I hadn't seen Jaxson approach us.

"How are my two favorite ladies?" Jaxson asked.

"Daddy!" Izzie jumped down from my lap and held up her arms for her daddy to lift her up.

Jaxson picked her up and twirled her around before holding her on his hip. "We'll be leaving soon, hopefully. It sounds like Mason's going to get sprung out of here today, as long as he has someone at home."

"Oh?" I didn't know if he lived alone or had roommates. I hadn't heard him talk about dating anyone, but it was obvious he had the hots for Hazel. Anyone could see it.

"Hazel is going to stay and help him out," Jaxson said.

"That's good." I was happy for her, thrilled that maybe the two of them could figure out their relationship with time and wouldn't have to hide it from everyone. Albeit a little jealous too, but I would never admit it to anyone.

Lincoln stood a few feet away, at the vending machine making himself a cup of coffee.

"I was worried about you," Jaxson said and sat down beside me in the empty chair. He reached out and brushed a strand of hair behind my ear. "Still am worried if I'm to be honest."

I smiled weakly. I couldn't stop thinking about Nikolai.

What Hazel had done, the blood, the fact Nikolai had done everything to protect his sister. It had been messed up and sick, but it didn't detract from the fact he was dead. "I'm fine." I wanted to be fine, telling myself and saying it aloud.

Would it make it true?

"Are you sure?" he asked, his hand falling to my back.

I relaxed under his touch as he softly caressed my back in soothing motions. I wanted him to touch me, to kiss me, to make love to me.

Lincoln was in the room, and we were supposed to be keeping our relationship a secret if we were going to be together.

I shook my head no. "I'll probably have nightmares for a while, but it's nothing I can't handle."

Lincoln's heavy footsteps broke the spell and moment between the two of us. "Can I get you guys a coffee? The machine isn't working. I'm going to go down to the cafeteria. Want anything?"

"I'm good," I said.

"Me too," Jaxson said.

Lincoln headed down the hallway and the opposite direction of Mason's room for the elevator to the lobby where the cafeteria was located.

We had a few minutes, just the two of us, plus Izzie. Thankfully, she didn't seem to grasp what was going on between us.

Jaxson put Izzie on the seat beside him and played a video on his phone, letting her watch it. He stalked to the vending machine and gestured for me to come over to him.

I stood and stretched before I pointed at the machine. "Didn't you hear Lincoln? The coffee machine isn't working."

"I heard. I just wanted a little privacy." With Izzie's back to us, he pulled me against him, tight and hard.

My eyes widened as his lips descended onto mine, his fingers at the nape of my neck, keeping me close. It wasn't hard to melt into his kiss, my body falling easily under his spell.

He pulled back, one hand still on my neck, the other sliding under my shirt, teasing the waistband of my pants. "Jaxson," I said, smiling from the pleasure but warning him to stop. We couldn't be doing this in the hospital, let alone five feet away from his daughter.

"Lincoln will be a few minutes, and Hazel is preoccupied with Mason. I'll bet they're making out."

"Good for them," I said. That wasn't a reason that we should be doing that here and now. I gently rested a hand against his chest. "I want to be with you, but today was a lot."

"You know that I would never have let anything happen to you and Izzie?" Jaxson said.

"I know and I appreciate what you did today. It could have ended a lot differently," I said. The thoughts still flashed through my mind of Nikolai with his gun pressed against my forehead. I had to push those thoughts aside, or I wouldn't be able to breathe.

His lips came down hard on mine again, bruising, with a fierce intensity filled with want and need, not solely desire.

He shifted us around, my back against the wall as he pushed his knee between my thighs, hitting my center, my heat. I let him kiss me, and while I wanted to be more than just his secret girlfriend, I also was willing to accept whatever he gave.

My lips parted, drinking him in, pulling him tighter against me. Every thought from my mind disappeared as we kissed, and time seemed to stand still.

Someone cleared his throat rather loudly. Was he trying to get our attention?

I whimpered in protest when Jaxson pulled away, and we both glanced at the intruder, Lincoln.

He held his cup of coffee in his hand and took a long, slow sip.

"Why don't the three of you get out of here?" Lincoln said. "I'll drive with Mason and Hazel to pick up his truck."

"Are you sure?" Jaxson asked.

"You have a ten-hour drive home. Izzie doesn't need to be kept out any later than necessary. I'll probably end up renting a hotel for the night and driving back tomorrow if Mason doesn't get released soon," Lincoln said.

Jaxson's cell phone rang, and he hurried over to grab it from Izzie as she watched her movie.

I stood awkwardly, giving Lincoln a weak smile. He'd been good to me, I had no complaints, but I still wasn't happy that he knew our secret. "Listen, what you saw—"

"It's none of my business," Lincoln said. "You make him happy, and I can honestly say there aren't too many people other than Izzie who can do that."

"You won't say anything to the others?" I hoped he could keep it to himself and not mention it to his buddies.

"Again, it's not my place," Lincoln said. He stepped closer. "You don't have to worry, Ariella. I like having you around. You're good for Jaxson, and you make him happy. That's all that matters."

I breathed a sigh of relief. "Thank you."

Jaxson hung up the phone and shoved it into his pocket.

"Daddy, phone." Izzie reached for his pants, trying to retrieve his phone.

"Not right now," he said and lifted his little one into his arms, giving her kisses. He shot a look at Lincoln. "Can you give Mason a message?"

Lincoln sipped his coffee. "Sure, what's up? Is everything okay?"

"The sheriff called to let us know they found his uncle's dog, Bear. They're keeping her at the station until someone comes to pick her up. Thankfully, she was all right, with a few scratches but no significant injuries. I let him know Mason was being released soon, but we're in Fargo, so it probably won't be until tomorrow."

"He'll be relieved to know Bear is all right," Lincoln said. "Text me the sheriff's number, and I'll make sure we pick up Bear on the way home."

It was a long drive back to Breckenridge. Jaxson insisted on being the one to drive. Izzie had fallen asleep an hour into the ride. It was dark and late, which probably helped her fall right to sleep.

"What's going to happen to Hazel?" I asked.

"You heard the sheriff; they don't plan on charging her with any crime because they closed the investigation and ruled it self-defense," Jaxson said.

"That's not what I'm talking about. Franco is still out there."

"He's in prison," Jaxson said. He glanced at me and reached for my hand as he drove.

Our fingers intertwined together. I gave his hand a squeeze, trying to reassure myself as much as him that I was okay. I didn't feel like myself. I still felt disconnected, lost in the events of the day.

"You don't worry that he'll come after you and your family?" I asked.

"If I worried about that, I'd be worrying about every bad guy we deal with," Jaxson said. He kept his voice low, careful not to wake Izzie. "Declan is fixing the security system and finding out how Nikolai managed to disable it."

Hearing that from Jaxson, I wanted to feel at ease. I wanted Franco to leave Hazel alone along with the rest of us. I squeezed his hand. "I guess it's just been a long day. Emma came to the house this morning, barefoot and hysterical."

"Nikolai shot up the compound where she's been living," Jaxson said.

"You knew she was living there? How?" I asked.

He let out a soft sigh, his focus and attention on the road as he spoke. "When I paid Ian and Seth a visit for harassing you, I discovered that she was living there. I had hoped she'd move out and come to her senses."

"She was involved in the hostage takeover at the resort," I said.

"I know."

I pulled my hand back as though I'd been burned. "How the hell did you know that? How many secrets have you been keeping?"

He placed his hand back on the steering wheel, his jaw tight. "More than I care to admit."

"What does that mean, Jaxson?" I couldn't believe he'd been hiding from me that he knew Emma had been involved in the hostage ordeal at Blue Sky Resort.

He let out a heavy sigh and glanced in the rearview mirror. "Can we have this conversation later?"

"No. I want to have the conversation now."

He'd been pissed when I'd kept secrets from him. How come he could keep secrets from me?

CHAPTER TWENTY-EIGHT

JAXSON

I wasn't thrilled that I'd been keeping *him* a secret, and now that we'd unleashed the fact Emma had been an off-gridder and was involved in the grim situation at the resort, it was bound to come out.

"Are you just going to ignore me?" Ariella asked. Her tone was sharp. She was undoubtedly pissed at me.

Great.

I had several hours left until we got to Breckenridge and home. It wasn't like I could drop her off and not see her again until work; we lived together.

I ran a hand through my hair, frustrated. Ariella tended to bring me down to my knees. "I'm not ignoring you; I've just got a lot on my mind."

"That's an excuse," Ariella said. She was pissed. I could hear her heavy, labored breathing as she shifted in her seat. She'd never get comfortable at this rate.

"Fine. You want every secret I've been keeping?" My voice raised in the confines of the truck. "I heard from one of the guys, and guess who was released from prison. Benjamin Ryan."

Ariella was dead silent.

"What? Don't you have something to shout at me for keeping that a secret? He's out of prison, Ariella. Do you know why?"

I glanced at her to see her eyes wide. Her mouth hung agape. I didn't let it go. If she wanted to know my secrets, I'd reveal hers, ones she didn't even know she had in the back of her closet.

"His convictions were overturned, every last one of them," I said. From the look on her face, she had no idea.

"You mentioned that he might not have been guilty. I just couldn't believe it was true." She ran her palms over her pants.

"Well, true or not, he's been released, and it's not on a technicality. I don't know what that means in regard to the C.I.A., whether they set him up or someone else." The truth was I hadn't had time to dig deeper or look into the mess of her past. "He made a statement on television when he was released."

"He did?" Her voice caught in her throat.

"Said something in the interview about planning on finding you," I said, a bitter taste filling my mouth.

I didn't want to lose her to *him*, her husband, or technically ex-husband. They were divorced, but if it had been based on the fact she'd believed he'd been guilty, and he wasn't, where did I stand?

What chance did I have against a wealthy man who had won her heart?

She exhaled a loud breath. "Well, if you see him, tell him to stay the hell away from me."

That took me by surprise. "What?"

Was she over him?

Did I not need to worry that he'd come and sweep her off her feet?

I wasn't one to get jealous easily, but I also didn't like to worry that a man with whom she had a history could breeze back into her life.

"He may not be guilty of the financial crimes that he was originally convicted of, but he's not innocent, Jaxson. Far from it."

What other crimes had he done that he hadn't been convicted of?

"Are you going to elaborate?" I asked.

Ariella yawned in the front seat. It was well past two in the morning. I recognized that she was drained. I was too. “Not tonight. I’m tired, Jaxson. Can we just leave it alone for now?”

Exhausted, I drove into the night, not wanting to crash in some shitty motel with bedbugs.

I didn’t want to fight with her. I’d almost lost her and my daughter today. I rested my hand on her thigh. “I care about you, Freckles.” I wanted her to know how I felt. I didn’t say it often enough, and she deserved to hear it from me.

“I know,” she mumbled. Ariella rested her head against the side window, her eyes shut. Her breathing had lulled after several long seconds.

She mumbled something unintelligible. Had she just said *I love you?*

“Freckles?”

She’d fallen asleep.

Mason had once told me that he suspected her marriage might have been a cover, that she’d gone deep as a C.I.A. operative, too deep. If that was true, why had she been watching him, and what made her decide to marry him? If it hadn’t been love, what was the catalyst?

There were secrets between us, but I wasn’t willing to give her up, not without a fight.

Truth was that I loved her too.

Did I have the courage to tell her?

BONUS TEASER FOR CONCEAL: LINCOLN

HARPER

I needed my caffeine fix if I was going to survive in this small, podunk town for the next few weeks.

My flight was short but choppy in the air and the stewardess had spilled my drink all over the seat in front of me. The poor bastard wore my coffee but that didn't solve my problem. I never got my drink on the flight.

I headed straight from the airport to the nearest coffee shop in Breckenridge. I prayed that they had a cafe that served a decent latte.

I doubted anyone would even recognize me, which played to my advantage. Plus, the giant sunglasses didn't hurt. This way, I didn't have to worry about reporters stalking me or fans snapping photos with their cell phone cameras.

It was early, the sun had come up recently and I strolled in, my mood more chipper than even I was prepared for on this early Sunday morning.

"Tall latte with caramel and whipped cream." I was going all out this morning.

The girl behind the counter in her brown apron and matching

hat didn't so much as smile. "What's the name?" she asked. Her name tag read *Skylar*.

Did she really not recognize me? "Harper." I almost thought of giving her my real name or even a fake name, wouldn't that be fun?

She squinted slightly, as if she was deciding whether to believe me or not as I paid in cash.

"It'll be just a minute." Her tone was monotonous as she faked a smile.

"Next!" Skylar snapped, taking the order of the woman behind me.

I took a step back from the register and sat down at a nearby table. The place wasn't overly crowded and the longer I waited, the more impatient I became.

The woman behind me was given her coffee along with two other patrons after I had ordered. "What the hell?" I muttered under my breath. Had she forgotten about my order?

A handsome gentleman, tall with thick muscles and tattoos that peeked out from his sleeves, stole my attention for a minute as he ordered. He seemed to brighten Skylar's mood too.

I was going to change that. She'd ruined my mood and my good morning. "Excuse me," I said, interrupting the two of them. I'd had enough waiting. "I ordered a coffee ten minutes ago."

"It's been five," Skylar snapped. "And your drink is on the counter waiting for you to pick it up."

I glanced at the counter as she casually placed the cup in my view. It hadn't been waiting for me to grab it. She'd kept it hidden. That snotty brat!

"You didn't call my name."

She pointed at the cup and the name written on it. "Heather."

I swallowed the lump in my throat. There was no way she knew that was my real name. "It's Harper," I corrected her.

"Same difference. Do you want your coffee or not?"

Ten minutes. That coffee had to be cold and gross. I liked my coffee piping hot. I didn't pay nearly ten dollars for a shitty cup of coffee. “You need to make me another latte.” I wasn’t going to accept this kind of crappy treatment from an overpriced cafe.

A second barista on the other side of the counter poured a cup of steaming hot coffee and secured a lid. “Lincoln,” she called out.

Oh hell no. That was mine. I snatched the cup before Lincoln could get his monstrous bear claws on it. He was a big guy but I was fast.

I gave him a smile before high-tailing it out of the cafe, like I was stealing a piece of artwork, making a run for the getaway car.

CONCEAL: LINCOLN

EAGLE TACTICAL BOOK THREE

CHAPTER ONE

LINCOLN

Exhaustion didn't even begin to explain the weariness behind my gaze.

I stumbled into the town coffee shop.

The bell jingled on the door as I entered, and the aroma of coffee beans gave me my first fix of the morning like a drug.

I needed more.

"Next," the girl behind the counter snapped.

Without my morning cup of coffee yet, I hadn't had the jolt to wake me. I stammered forward up to the counter. "Hey, Skylar."

Since when did she work here? Last I heard, she came to visit her older brother in town.

Apparently, she wasn't leaving anytime soon.

"What can I get for you?" she asked.

She stood behind the counter wearing a brown apron and matching hat.

While I felt fatigued, her eyes softened, and the corners of her lips quirked up when she seemed to recognize me.

"Hey, Lincoln, right?"

"Yes," I said as my gaze glanced over the chalkboard behind her with the list of available drinks and specials.

The owner always liked to change it up, and there was never a plain black coffee on the menu.

"What do you recommend?" Making a decision took too much effort at this hour.

"Brewing your coffee at home," Skylar said. "The coffee here is way overpriced but don't tell my boss I said that, or I'll get fired."

I snorted under my breath. "Noted. I'll have whatever's strong and make it black."

I couldn't deal with sugar at this early hour.

The sun hadn't even come up yet, and while I should have been in bed, I still had another hour until I usually woke up.

I hadn't been able to sleep, and with the recent shooting at the restaurant, my coffee maker had been toast.

Sleep had eluded me, even on a Sunday morning when I should have been able to relax and take the day off.

Stress didn't typically bother me, but after two mobsters had gunned down the restaurant, I was on high alert, ready on a whim. It resulted from my time in the military that forced me to be up at a moment's notice.

Skylar tapped away at the register before I shoved my credit card into the chip reader to pay.

A blonde stepped forward with giant sunglasses on, the kind a woman wears to either hide a black eye or to try to conceal her identity. Both of those seemed plausible.

"Excuse me," she said. "I ordered a coffee ten minutes ago."

"It's been five," Skylar said, "and your drink is on the counter waiting for you to pick it up."

"You didn't call my name," the woman wearing sunglasses said.

"Heather."

"It's Harper," she said, correcting Skylar.

Skylar stepped to the side where the drink sat perched on the counter, waiting to be picked up. "Same difference. Do you want your coffee or not?"

Another barista worked on my drink while Harper stood, arms folded across her chest.

"You need to make me another latte," Harper said. She unfolded her arms long enough to slide her sunglasses back up as they began to slip down her face.

"I don't need to do anything, ma'am," Skylar said. She turned and faced the register. "Next!"

The barista preparing my coffee headed over with the piping hot liquid and secured a lid to the cup. "Lincoln."

Harper snatched the coffee before I could get my hands on it. "I'm going to be late."

She stole my drink and stormed out of the shop, hurrying to her car.

"I hope she likes it black," I muttered under my breath—what a perfect way to start my morning.

I should have stayed in bed.

I picked up lunch and drove over to Mason's house to check up on him. It'd been a few weeks since he'd been shot by the mafia protecting his high school sweetheart, Hazel Agron.

Arriving at his house, before I could even lift my hand to the door, Hazel pounced. She was faster than their dog, Bear, that they'd adopted after Mason's uncle passed.

Hazel yanked open the door and threw her arms around me. "Thank you for coming," she whispered into my ear.

"Of course. I brought lunch," I said and lifted the bag of Chinese food takeout to show what I'd fetched.

Hazel ushered me inside Mason's house and shut the door.

I handed over the bag of food while I shucked off my coat and boots.

"Smells good," Mason said with a grunt as he pushed himself up from the sofa. "What'd you bring?"

"Orange Beef, Sesame Chicken, Sweet and Sour Shrimp,

Mongolia Beef, and a few appetizers. I wasn't sure what everyone wanted, so I tried to get a variety," I said.

I hadn't wanted to come empty-handed, and Hazel had been busy looking after Mason. She deserved a meal she didn't have to cook.

"I'm famished," Mason said.

He sluggishly ambled toward the table, the injury of two bullets getting the better of him.

"How are the restaurant repairs coming?" Mason asked.

Hazel unveiled the contents of the brown paper bag with all the dishes while I rummaged through the drawers for silverware. There were already paper plates on the table and chopsticks along with plasticware for eating.

"Slow and practically non-existent," I said. "Can I get you something to drink?"

I'd visited Mason over the years enough to have memorized not only the layout, but also where he kept everything in the cabinets.

"Water is good."

I grabbed three glasses from the cabinet and filled each of them with water. "How have you been feeling?" I asked, turning to face Mason but still keeping an eye on the glass so that I didn't make a mess.

"Tired, sore, I feel like I've been shot, twice." Mason laughed and sat down with a gruffness that I hadn't seen cross his face in the past.

He winced, trying to hide his obvious discomfort. "I'm feeling better already and anxious to get back to business."

"Ready to kick me out of Eagle Tactical?" I asked, mildly joking with him. Jaxson, one of our other special force's brothers, kept insisting I join the guys. We were all military brothers and had served together.

On occasion, I had helped them out when they needed an extra set of hands for a case or an assignment in the field.

"No, you're staying. I just want to get back in the field with you again."

The truth was that I loved the restaurant that I'd worked hard to make a success, but getting back to work there would still be a few months.

The restaurant needed a lot of repairs. The dining room had been trashed by the dozens of bullets that had rained down on the interior. I had an insurance agent working with me for the repairs, but it would take time.

I brought two glasses of water to the table for Hazel and Mason. I filled the third glass and set that down in front of my plate, taking a seat at the kitchen table.

"You look like you're doing better," I said. Being shot took time to heal, physical therapy to get a range of motion back, among other things.

Hazel remained quiet as she dished out her lunch on the plate in front of her.

Mason grunted. "I'm ready to get out of this house. No offense to Hazel," he said and glanced at her. "You've done a wonderful job taking care of me. I'm just not used to having someone look after me."

Hazel smiled and patted his good arm. "No offense taken, and I understand. I'd love to go out and get a drink, socialize."

He'd always been independent, even with the ladies. I couldn't remember Mason ever having a girlfriend live with him. He'd kept his relationships pretty quiet, though I'd seen him take a woman home once or twice from the bar.

"We should do that tonight," Mason said.

"You're not supposed to be drinking," Hazel reminded him.

He grumbled under his breath.

"She's right," I said, stepping in to defend Hazel. "We all just want what's best for you. If you're on painkillers, you can't be drinking."

I took a sip of water and placed the glass back on the wooden table. "If you want to come out tonight for an hour, just to get out of the house, I can drive you home."

The bar wasn't that far from Mason's place. It was too long a distance for him to walk after his injuries, but it wouldn't take long for me to drop him off if he wanted to see the guys for an hour.

Anything longer, and I worried that he'd overdo it and tax himself. Mason wasn't good at asking for help.

Mason took a bite of lunch, his gaze on the food in front of him.

I couldn't tell if he was pleased with my suggestion or was going to ask me to leave.

"An hour's better than nothing."

"How about we all meet after dinner but a little on the early side?" Hazel asked. "That way, the bar won't be as crowded."

Her gaze met mine, and she didn't have to say the real reason she wanted to meet earlier.

I sensed it already.

Mason would be too exhausted later in the evening.

He had dark circles under his eyes. His hair was messy, but that was probably more because he hadn't showered today.

"That sounds good, and I'm sure the others will be on board with that too. I'll text them and let them know to meet us at the bar at seven tonight," I said.

I finished the last of my lunch.

Mason looked beat, and I didn't want him to feel that he had to entertain me or be kept awake.

"Take a nap. I'll see you tonight," I said. I helped Hazel put the rest of the food away and into the fridge.

Mason disappeared down the hall and into his room to rest.

"How have you been doing?" I asked, keeping my voice low.

I didn't want to disturb Mason or have him overhear our conversation.

"It's been a lot," Hazel said, her eyes trained on the kitchen table as she tossed the dirty paper plates into the trash bin.

I grabbed the few pieces of silverware and glasses and took the items to the sink to clean.

I didn't want to leave a mess for her to deal with. She already had enough to do to take care of Mason.

"He appreciates your help and you being here, whether he tells it to you or not," I said.

"I know," Hazel said. She wiped down the table.

Standing in front of the sink, I waited for the tap water to run hot before I filled up the sink to wash the dishes from lunch and quite a few in the sink that had been left from breakfast.

"You don't have to do the dishes."

"I know," I said. I didn't budge from in front of the sink. Once the water grew warm, I plugged the drain and let the empty side of the sink fill with water.

Hazel pointed under the sink. "Dish soap is down there."

"Thanks." I already knew where Mason kept the soap. I opened the cabinet and retrieved the liquid. I squeezed a few drops into the sink. Suds formed as water poured in and made bubbles. "How are things between you and Mason?"

"Fine." Hazel's eyes widened as she glanced up at me. "Why? Did he say something?"

Her brow furrowed, and she shuffled her feet while she stood in the kitchen and seemed uncomfortable with my question.

I hadn't meant to offend her or cause any drama between the two of them. "No, I just know that moving to a new city can be challenging, and the fact you don't know anyone and are stuck taking care of Mason, it's probably a lot to deal with on your own."

"What are you, a psychologist?" Hazel asked. She folded her arms across her chest.

"No, I'm just used to being an ear for a lot of the guys. Mason used to talk about you a lot."

Maybe I shouldn't have said anything, but I found it hard to ignore the obvious fact that they both liked each other a lot.

At least I knew Mason liked Hazel. I didn't want to see her push him away when he eventually could take care of himself again.

"He did?" Her voice caught in her throat. "About what?" She leaned against the kitchen counter, her gaze on me the entire time as I washed the dishes by hand.

"He always compared the girls he dated to you. He'd talk about how he was young and stupid and had let you go away to school."

"I never went to college."

"Oh." I didn't know what to say to that.

She was the girl he'd gone to boarding school with and compared every girl after to. While most of the guys hadn't talked as openly about their pasts, Mason had regretted letting her go.

"I was supposed to," Hazel said, "but it's a long story, and I'd rather change the subject."

"Sure."

"Mason's a good guy. It's just a lot right now, taking care of him and trying to make him comfortable. I won't even tell you how difficult it is to get him into the shower."

I chuckled under my breath. "Mason's a big guy." He was twice the size of Hazel. "You're not asking me to bathe him, are you?"

Hazel grinned. "Would you?"

"No." I assumed she'd been joking, but I wasn't taking any chances.

There were some lines we didn't cross.

She scrunched her nose and laughed. "Damn. It was worth a shot."

I finished the last of the dishes and left them on the drying rack, stacked to the brim. "Anything else you need help with around here? Other than bathing your boyfriend."

Hazel shook her head. "I've got it. I'll tidy up the place while Mason's napping. I am looking forward to going out tonight. Don't hold it against me if I get wasted."

"As long as you don't drive home."

Her eyes shined with a glint of happiness, something that I hadn't seen the entire time that I'd been over during lunch.

The thought of getting out and socializing seemed to have shifted her mood for the better. Hopefully, it would help Mason too.

I arrived early at the bar to make sure that I could grab a comfortable booth for all of us to sit together.

In the corner of the bar, there was a booth that would easily seat our crew.

I claimed it before anyone else could, and while I wanted a beer, I'd wait to step up to the bar until one of the other guys came and could watch our table.

"Jaxson!" I waved to him as he shuffled into the bar, glancing around for the rest of us.

"Where's Ariella?" I asked as he scooted into the booth seat across from me.

His eyes narrowed.

"What? It's just the two of us." I already knew they were sleeping together, but the rest of the office wasn't supposed to know.

He was her boss.

Technically, the entire Eagle Tactical team was Ariella's boss, but Jaxson was sleeping with her.

They were also living together, but that wasn't because they were involved. It had been a result of her house burning down months ago.

"I don't know. Ariella will be here soon." Jaxson rested his hands on the wood table. "We thought it'd be a good idea to show up separate."

"Everything okay in paradise?"

I hadn't noticed any drama, but they were good at hiding their relationship.

Which was ironic, since Jaxson had been testy and short-tempered for the brief time they'd worked together before they'd fallen into bed.

She made him happy, and if the other guys couldn't see it, they were blind.

Jaxson nodded toward the door where Declan came through, along with Mason and Hazel trailing behind.

I scooted out of the booth. "I'll get us drinks," I said.

Already, the bar had grown crowded, and patrons waited for their drinks. I leaned against the bar, my hands clasped together, awaiting my turn.

A soft voice cleared her throat beside me as she hurried up to the bar and perched herself on the empty stool.

The coffee thief.

I gestured the bartender over to me next, but he hadn't come and taken my drink order yet.

"You," I said, landing my gaze on the girl who had snatched my hot coffee and left me grumpy earlier that morning.

She laughed under her breath and avoided my stare. Her long hair covered part of her face, hiding from me.

Was it on purpose?

The bartender headed over to me. "What can I get for you?" he asked.

"Let me buy you a drink," Harper said, and she shifted on the barstool to face me.

I wanted to push the long strand of hair out of her eyes and behind her ear, but I kept my hands to myself. "I'll have a beer," I said to the bartender. "Whatever's on tap."

While I had come up to the bar to order drinks for the table, I found myself interested in the mysterious new girl who had shown up in Breckenridge.

Was she here on vacation like everyone else who didn't live in the small town?

Harper retrieved her credit card from her wallet and slid it across the bar's counter to the bartender. "It's on me. I'll have a screwdriver."

The bartender poured my beer first and then went to work on making Harper a screwdriver.

While I wasn't one to let a woman pay for my drinks or buy me dinner, Harper had gotten under my skin earlier that morning.

The least she could do was apologize, and since that wasn't happening, I'd settle with a beer on tap.

"Thank you," I said to her, sipping my beer. The barstool beside Harper was empty.

I glanced back at my friends. They were giving me a thumb's up gesture when they noticed I spoke with Harper.

"It's the least I can do after this morning," Harper said. "I'm dangerous before I've had my coffee."

I sat on the stool and shifted around to face her. "You and me both."

She wasn't the only one who dealt in danger, but I held my tongue.

She didn't need to know about my life, who I was, or what I did for a living. I liked the mysterious factor for once.

Harper knew nothing about me, and I could keep it that way.

The bartender handed Harper her screwdriver, and she sipped the orange liquid, her eyes wincing with each taste.

Was she not used to the drink being strong? She had ordered vodka and orange juice.

"What are you doing in Breckenridge?" I asked.

Most tourists came in winter to the resort for skiing and snowboarding. We attracted watersports like rafting and kayaking in the summer, but spring typically was quiet and calm with newcomers.

"I'm here to blow up the town."

CHAPTER TWO

HARPER

I'd seen him enter the bar, the handsome man whose coffee I'd swiped earlier that morning at the coffee shop.

I couldn't help the anger that sizzled through my veins while I waited for my caffeine fix.

It hadn't been bad enough that the girl behind the register had been rude and overcharged me, she had also gotten my name wrong.

Then he'd strode in and smiled at her. One look, and she was putty to him.

Were they a couple?

Gross.

I wanted to puke. I also wanted my coffee really bad.

The barista was already preparing whatever the hell concoction he ordered, but mine was nowhere to be seen, and they hadn't called my name to tell me it was ready.

I'd been a spoiled brat and snatched his hot coffee. I'd done it dozens of times on the studio set, but this wasn't a movie studio. I'd been stupid and rude.

And the coffee was awful. Bitter and black. I deserved it.

I'd spent the day in my motel room.

I hadn't rented a place at the resort where I'd read the accommodations had been far more luxurious.

My agent set me up at the shithole so no one would recognize me.

It sucked.

My day had gone from bad that morning with no coffee, to worse when I discovered that the studio executives had opted to hire a private security team to keep me out of trouble.

I liked trouble.

At least that's what the studio and the tabloids wrote.

I'd made a reputation for myself as *The Vixen*. It hadn't been hard, and my agent had told me that no publicity was bad publicity.

Was that true?

It had landed me quite a few new movie roles, and I'd been mentioned on all the entertainment shows and magazines on a semi-regular basis.

I was the girl your mother warned you about. The one who stole your boyfriend and slept with a man just to toy with him.

Except that wasn't the real me.

I could still count the number of men I'd slept with in my lifetime on one hand.

I was shy, introverted, and hated being alone.

The rest was an act. It was a good thing I was an actress and a damned good one.

I'd had the world fooled, and somewhere along the way I'd fooled myself into believing I'd been happy.

I sat at a lonely table, nursing a vodka and orange juice—a screwdriver.

I wanted to appear tough. I couldn't drink anything girly, even though it's what I'd have preferred.

At any moment, someone could recognize me and snap a picture of Harper Madison. It would be on all of social media in a matter of minutes. I had to tread carefully.

When I saw *him* stalk into the bar with a purpose, he strode over and sat down at the booth in the corner, the largest booth there was.

I couldn't help but stare at him, transfixed.

I wanted to go over, strike up a conversation and apologize for being a brat earlier, but I couldn't move from my position.

His name was Lincoln. At least that had been the name on his coffee cup unless the girl had gotten his name wrong too?

His friends showed up, and eventually, he headed to the bar for a drink. That was my excuse, my chance to talk to him, which led me to a bad joke and the concern that he might have me arrested.

He'd been polite, and I'd earned his attention after buying him a beer. It was the least I could do, and while I should have come out and apologized for my behavior that morning, I found it too difficult to voice the words.

"What are you doing in Breckenridge?" he asked.

"I'm here to blow up the town." It was a joke. A lame joke since I'd shown up to help film a movie.

"Excuse me?" Lincoln asked, his eyes wide and mouth agape.

My joke about being here to blow up the town hadn't gone over well.

He put his drink down hard on the bar, forceful.

"It was a joke."

He grabbed my wrist and pulled me off the stool. His eyes raked over my body, sending a shiver down my spine.

Did he recognize me?

I hadn't been in disguise, but the bar was dimly lit, and this was a small town.

"Do I need to call the sheriff?" Lincoln asked. His grip didn't loosen from my wrist.

Quickly, he could yank both of my arms behind my back and restrain me.

Is that what he wanted to do?

A small part of me wanted that from him, his dominance.

He was a good-looking guy, and his brooding nature sent a shiver down my spine and made me feel warm and tingly all over.

"It was a joke," I repeated and shrugged my arm in an attempt to unclasp myself from his clutches. "Would you let me go?"

His eyes were tight and narrow, his jaw sharp. Is this what it was like to piss him off?

I didn't want to witness his wrath when he was angry.

"There's nothing funny about threatening our town," Lincoln said.

He unlatched his hand from my wrist, and I pulled my arm away in a hurry. I rubbed my wrist where his hand had held me tight, but there was no mark.

"Why are you really here, Harper? Is that even your real name?"

I exhaled a heavy breath through my nose, staring at my wrist, surprised there wasn't a bruise, a red mark, any evidence that he'd touched me. "Yes. No." I could still feel his firm grip, even though his hands were nowhere near my body.

"Which is it?"

"It's complicated," I said.

Harper was my stage name, the name that everyone knew me by, but it wasn't the name I was given at birth. I didn't have many friends, and the few people who knew me called me Harper because they'd only come to know me after I'd made a name for myself. Except for the few people like my agent and the studio executives who called me whatever they wanted whenever they wanted.

His eyes softened. "What do you want me to call you?" he asked. His words were calm, soft, and his tone seemed genuine, like he cared about me.

Didn't he recognize me as Harper Madison?

Maybe he didn't watch chick flicks. Perhaps he'd never seen me before this morning in the coffee shop.

"Harper is fine." I couldn't hide who I was, even if I wanted to try.

A part of me wanted to hide, escape, and let no one know about my past.

Filming in a small town had its advantages, but living there, I wasn't sure I was cut out for it.

I was pretty sure I wasn't ready to settle down in a town with less than a thousand people. The studio where we filmed in Los Angeles had more people working on a set than the town of Breckenridge.

"You're Lincoln, right?" I asked.

His lips quirked upwards with a faint smile. "Yes, I am." He sipped his beer.

"Can we do this again, start over?" I asked and held out my hand to introduce myself. "I'm Harper."

"Lincoln," he said and shook my hand with a laugh. He tilted his head slightly to the side, staring at me. "You never did answer why you're in town."

"Oh, right." I laughed under my breath. I guess I wasn't getting out of it that easily. "I'm here filming something small for the studio."

It was a little white lie.

While I was here to film a movie for the studio, it wasn't small or insignificant. The budget alone was probably more than the town's worth.

Lincoln finished his beer and gestured the bartender over for a second.

Against my better judgment, I ordered a second screwdriver.

The drinks were strong, but I didn't want the night to end. It was still early, and the handsome stranger, Lincoln, I'd won his full, undivided attention, and it wasn't because of my celebrity status.

"I'll have another one too," I said.

Lincoln pulled out his credit card. "They're on me," he said to the bartender, handing over his credit card. "Start a tab."

"Are you here filming a commercial or something?" Lincoln asked. His fingers drummed against the bar counter as he sat facing me.

Our knees brushed against each other, and my body tingled at the thought of what he looked like undressed. "Something like that," I said.

Lincoln was albeit handsome but not my usual type. He was strong, muscular, and looked quite a bit like a lumberjack with his thick beard and outdoorsy attire.

I'd never met a lumberjack before.

The bartender brought us both our drinks and placed them on the counter.

Leaning in, I reached for my drink at the same time Lincoln did, breathing in his masculine scent.

I momentarily closed my eyes as the bar felt several degrees warmer.

Was my face flushed?

Could he sense my attraction? I barely knew him.

What had gotten into me?

I didn't drink that often because I was a feather when it came to alcohol.

No doubt I could easily get knocked on my ass, but that was the result of watching everything I ate for filming. My agent had been strict and in-my-face, reminding me to count calories because the camera was unapologetic.

Sipping my drink, I avoided his intense stare.

"We don't have to talk about work," Lincoln said.

I breathed a sigh of relief. Good.

"You know where I'm from. It seems you have me at a disadvantage. Where are you from? New York, Los Angeles, somewhere else?"

"Just outside of L.A.," I said. "Have you lived here all your life? Do you live in a cabin in the woods?" He looked like the type who avoided civilization.

Lincoln laughed and placed the half-empty glass of beer on the counter beside him. "I'm well-traveled, and I spent quite a bit of time in the military, but I've always called Montana home."

"You were in the military?" I repeated, surprised by his look. I always thought military guys kept their crew cuts, but it was a stereotype.

Lincoln's eyes softened as he spoke. "It's been a few years, but I was in the army, special forces."

"Wow. That's impressive." It was no wonder he was built like a statue, perfect in every possible way.

I finished the last of my screwdriver and reached out, my hand touching his bicep. He really was thick. "I wonder what else is thick," I said under my breath.

Lincoln stared at me.

"Your muscles are thick," I stammered.

Shit.

Could I blabber on any more and embarrass myself further?

"You're hot."

Apparently so.

I needed to shut up, but I didn't seem capable of it. The words just kept spilling out past my lips.

He took another swig of his beer, and I made sure every drop was gone from my screwdriver before I gestured over the bartender for another drink.

Lincoln shook his head no. "I think you've exceeded your limit."

"I don't usually drink," I said.

The room swayed a bit, but more than anything, my gaze was on him. It was as if he was the only one in existence, and nothing else mattered.

I pinched the bridge of my nose. "You may be right. I should probably go back to the hotel."

As much as I wanted him to join me, I wasn't comfortable inviting him over to my place.

I may have wanted to be *that* girl, but I wasn't her.

"How about I give you a lift home?" He gestured the bartender over to close our tabs and ring us out.

A sheepish grin crossed my face. "I don't think that's a good idea."

"You driving is an even worse one," Lincoln said.

He was right, but luckily my motel was across the street and didn't require me to get behind the wheel of a car. "I'm staying just over there," I said, motioning with my hand.

The bartender slid a receipt and pen to me to sign, along with my credit card. We both closed our tabs.

He mumbled something under his breath.

"What's that?" I asked.

I signed the receipt, my signature a bunch of curls and scribbles, illegible, and I shoved my credit card back into my wallet.

Was he grumbling over the cost of drinks or where I had booked a room?

"I'll walk you home," Lincoln said.

If he wanted to accompany me across the street in the dark, I'd accept that proposition, but that was all I was willing to accept. "Knock yourself out."

I wasn't inviting him into my room for drinks or other scandalous acts. It was dark outside and walking alone in a small town in the middle of nowhere probably wasn't a wise decision.

I slid off the stool, my feet planted firmly on the ground, but my body swayed. I'd had one too many screwdrivers: two.

"Whoa, there," Lincoln said. He was quick to put an arm around my waist to steady me.

While I enjoyed his touch, I also didn't want him to get the impression that I was interested in more, at least not right now.

I'd just met the guy.

Well, technically, I met him earlier that morning, but it was still the same damned day.

I exhaled a breath, trying to steady myself in the bar. "I'm okay," I said and glanced at him as he stood beside me, towering over me. "You don't have to hold me up. I won't fall."

He leaned in, his breath warm, which sent tingles through my body. "If you insist," Lincoln whispered. His tight grip around my waist loosened.

I slipped from his grasp and staggered out of the bar, one foot in front of the other. I didn't tip over or fall, but he was right, I could not get behind the wheel of any vehicle.

Stepping outside into the cool spring breeze, I wrapped my arms tight around myself.

Lincoln kept up with me as he strode right along my side. He shucked off his coat. "Hold up," he said and wrapped his jacket around my shoulders. "Here."

I slid my arms into the sleeves, already warmer. He had long sleeves on and had been smart in what he wore. "Thank you," I said and pulled the lightweight coat tighter.

I shouldn't have borrowed his jacket. The smell of his masculine scent was intoxicating as it enveloped my senses.

I took in a long, deep inhale, breathing his scent in, my body warm and tingling.

"Everything okay?" Lincoln asked with a raised eyebrow.

Shit.

Had he noticed what I'd done?

No. He couldn't have.

I shoved my hands into his coat pockets, my fingers warmer already. Together, we strode across the quiet road for the motel.

Why was the parking lot jam-packed with vehicles? The motel hadn't been crowded earlier when I'd checked into the place. Had the rooms all been booked over the past couple of hours?

A flash of bright light in the darkness blinded me.

I held up my arm to shield my face and my identity. "Fuck," I said with a groan and stopped walking.

I'd been caught.

CHAPTER THREE

JAXSON

"Nice of Lincoln to offer to get us drinks," I said. Our friend and newest member of the Eagle Tactical team had disappeared to the bar and hadn't returned.

I'd have worried if I hadn't noticed that he sat perched on a stool, talking up the cute little blonde.

I tended to be observant in nature. My military training factored into the equation, but I failed to notice the blonde on her approach. Only that she had sat on a stool beside him.

Had he offered to grab us drinks because he wanted to speak to her?

Or had she snuck up and spoken to him first?

Ariella sat across from me.

The giant booth felt cold and lonely. I wanted her on my lap, curled up against my body. That would have to wait until later.

Tonight.

In the privacy of my home.

It was complicated.

I was Ariella's boss, and we'd made a rule of no fraternizing.

Obviously, it hadn't lasted. It'd been too difficult for me to work around her and live with her. The living arrangements had happened before we were involved.

Well, kind of.

We had slept together, and then her house burned down.

Seeing as how I was her next-door neighbor, I offered to let her stay. One night turned into two.

She couldn't afford to live anywhere else, and she was great with my daughter Izzie.

Hiding our relationship from the guys, though, that was the hardest thing I've ever done.

But I didn't see another choice. Ariella needed the job, and I needed *her*.

Mason grumbled under his breath as he sat beside Hazel and me next to him.

"What's that?" I asked, glancing at Mason.

"I want a drink—a really stiff, hard shot of something. Anything," Mason said.

Hazel patted his good arm, the one that hadn't been shot recently.

Mason was still recovering; albeit he had been home from the hospital for six weeks, but it took time to heal and recuperate.

It seemed he was getting a little stir crazy, not that I could blame him. I didn't think I could handle being cooped up at my house for six weeks, either.

He nudged Hazel beside him. "Are you really going to tell me I can't have one drink?"

"That's right, tough guy." Her hand slipped onto his thigh, and I averted my gaze. "No alcohol until you get the all-clear from the doctor. You have an appointment tomorrow, and if he says you can drink like a fish, then I'll bring you all the liquor that you want."

"He's not going to say that," I said. There was no way his physician would make that statement.

Hazel ran a hand through Mason's hair, pushing the long dark strands out of his eyes. "How about I grab you something special from the bar, a sweet virgin treat?"

"Are you trying to tease me," Mason groaned.

Hazel planted a kiss on his cheek before she climbed over Ariella and headed out of the booth to the bar.

"I'll give her a hand," I offered and scooted out from the opposite side of the booth.

I followed Hazel to the bar, on the opposite side of where Lincoln and the pretty girl were situated.

She almost looked familiar, but I wasn't sure why.

Hazel leaned against the counter and gestured over the bartender. The bar was busy, crowded, which was unusual for a Sunday night.

A few locals sat at the bar, but most of the tables were unfamiliar faces, and for a small town, that was unusual, especially out of tourist season.

Was there an event happening at the Blue Sky Resort? On occasion, there'd been conferences held off-season that had booked out every room in the place and brought tourists to all the local spots.

"Do you recognize her?" Hazel asked, her eyes on the blonde Lincoln chatted up.

I exhaled a heavy sigh. "It's like she's familiar, but I'm not sure from where."

The bartender finally stepped over, and we ordered two pitchers of beer along with a virgin daiquiri for Mason.

I handed over my credit card to the bartender while he rang up the orders.

"Mason's going to kill you," I whispered into Hazel's ear. I'd never known the man to drink anything girly in my life, let alone non-alcoholic.

Hazel grinned as she turned to face me. "Why? I told him he'd get a sweet virgin treat. Obviously, it's not me."

My eyes widened, and I glanced back toward the bartender. "That was more information than I needed."

I should have ordered myself something stronger tonight than beer if I was going to have to listen to Hazel and Mason's flirtations.

"Oh, come on. I see the way you and Ariella gaze at each other. You should ask her to dance," Hazel said.

"We're colleagues. More importantly, I'm her boss."

Hazel didn't have the slightest notion that Ariella and I were involved.

Right?

The bartender handed me the receipt, and I signed the slip of paper before he handed me two pitchers of beer.

I brought the pitchers back to the table while Hazel carried the strawberry daiquiri to the table and placed it in front of Mason.

"You have got to be kidding me," Mason said. He didn't look the least bit thrilled with the slushy sitting on the table in front of him.

"If you don't drink it, I will," Hazel said.

Mason pushed the glass across the table to Hazel. "Have at it."

I headed back to the bar to grab a stack of clear plastic cups for the beer.

"Need a hand?" Ariella's soft, warm voice caught me off guard as she stood behind me.

I spun around and handed her a few cups while I carried the rest to the table. "Sure." I appreciated her help. "Thank you."

It was painstakingly hard to sit across from her for a fun night out and not touch her, taste her, feel her body nestled up against mine—pure torture.

I planted the plastic cups on the table and grabbed Ariella's hand before she could sit back down.

Ariella had already dropped the cups on the table, and Hazel started handing them out and pouring beer into each one.

"Dance with me," I said, taking Hazel's advice. If she didn't think it was a big deal, then maybe the guys wouldn't, either.

Ariella's eyes widened. "Jaxson," she whispered, keeping her voice low and quiet.

It was difficult to hear her over the loud pulsating sound of music that played overhead on the speaker system.

"It's not karaoke night. I'm not asking you to sing with me."

"If you do, I'll kill you," Ariella said. "Even Izzie knows I don't sing."

I laughed under my breath. She'd heard me sing Izzie to bed a few times, and while I wasn't anything special in the vocals department, I could carry a tune—mostly.

"Then dance with me," I said and gave her hand a firm squeeze.

It was just a dance.

Everyone at Eagle Tactical knew there was chemistry between us.

There was no harm in dancing.

I'd found it hard enough to keep my hands to myself at the office, but there hadn't been another choice. Bending her over my desk and taking her the way I wanted was hardly classified as professional.

I yanked her closer.

She groaned and let me pull her tight against my body.

"Am I going to have to dance with all my work colleagues?" Ariella asked. "Because I'm not comfortable getting that intimate with Declan, Aiden, Mason, or Lincoln."

Laughing, I pulled her close and tight against my body. "Just me."

"Good, because I don't want to feel any of them bump up against me," Ariella whispered into my ear.

She wrapped her arms around my neck, her fingers warm against my skin.

Staring into her eyes, I wanted to kiss her, but I couldn't, not with the others watching.

There wasn't a corner, a hallway to sneak in and steal her away for a few kisses and intimate moments together.

"I want to take you home, have my way with you, Freckles." Every ounce of strength within me was focused on controlling my impulses.

I had to break my gaze and glance away. The temptation of *her* was just too damned much.

Her scent.

The feel of her warm body pressed tight against me.

I needed her.

Lincoln stood and helped the young blonde to her feet.

I guess he wasn't joining us tonight. That was fine with me. I wasn't sure how much longer I'd want to stay out at the bar and keep my hands to myself.

"Do you want to get out of here?" I whispered into her ear.

Freckles smiled and laughed at me, pulling back only slightly. "I do, but we can't. Lincoln has bailed, and Mason needs a friend, so does Hazel."

"They've got Aiden and Declan." Those guys were still single, as far as I knew. If they were dating anyone recently, they hadn't mentioned it.

"You're going to suggest we leave Hazel with the three of them? That poor girl has been tending to Mason for a month."

"Longer," I said.

"What?"

"It's been longer than a month. Six weeks that she's played nurse to his injuries." Mason hadn't been one to divulge any dirty details about what did or didn't happen between the two of them.

"Playing nurse?" Ariella let her hands slide down my back, holding me close as we danced intimately. "This is the first I'm hearing about it."

"Would she tell you?"

"Probably not," Ariella said, a bright smile on her face. She squinted up at me. "We should probably head back to the table. You should offer to dance with Hazel."

"Why?" It was Hazel's idea that I dance with Ariella, not that I hadn't thought about it, but I wasn't sure it was a good idea.

She untangled from around me, and the room felt several degrees chillier.

Ariella sauntered back to the booth and scooted back in to sit.

I sat down beside Mason and reached for the beer on the table that hadn't been touched.

Hazel cleared her throat, a huge grin plastered to her face. "You're not going to ask me to dance? I could use some of that bump and grind action."

I nearly spit my beer out of my mouth, coughing at her words.

My phone buzzed in my pocket, and I dug in and reached for it to answer. Anything to get out of that conversation with Hazel. Next, she'd probably ask me if Ariella and I were sleeping together.

"Eagle Tactical?" I answered the caller and stood, taking the phone with me as I headed outside, where it was quiet, and I could hear what was being said.

"Hi, yes. I'd like to inquire about your security services. We are looking to contract out security for our on-location production shoot in your area, beginning tomorrow."

"You do realize we're in Breckenridge, Montana." I hadn't heard about any film production taking place in our town.

News like that would have traveled fast.

"Yes, our studio manager was supposed to contact you, but it appears he neglected to do so. I apologize for the late notice, but we need a full team of security to staff us during filming, and our insurance policy requires that our feature star have a bodyguard."

I exhaled a heavy sigh. "How many security personnel do you require onsite during filming?" I asked.

"A team of four or five should be adequate in addition to someone who will babysit Harper Madison. I'll text you over her picture along with the location for production, which begins tomorrow morning. I should warn you. Miss Madison does not—how do I put this kindly—appreciate the length that the studio goes to ensure her safety. It is required that she is not aware of your services."

"That isn't how we work," I said.

We couldn't protect her if she didn't want us around.

"I'm not asking, sir. The contract will stipulate that Miss Madison is not to be made aware of her protective detail by any party within or employed by your company."

"And if I say no?"

"That isn't an option."

CHAPTER FOUR

LINCOLN

I'd never seen the motel parking lot crammed with so many vehicles, cars, trucks, and vans.

"There she is!" a man shouted from across the road as he stood outside the motel.

A bright flash of light erupted once, twice, and before I could count how many more times, I realized Harper had stopped walking and shielded her face.

Vehicle doors began opening and slamming shut.

Men on foot with cameras and camcorders rushed toward us.

"Quick, my truck." I grabbed her free hand that wasn't shielding herself and hurried her to my truck.

I dug my keys out of my pocket as we rushed to the passenger side. I opened the door for her and slammed it shut as the men poured into the bar parking lot.

Who the hell were they? I didn't wait around to ask or find out.

I jogged around to the driver's side, climbed into the truck, and started the engine.

"Please get me out of here." Her voice quivered as she spoke.

She didn't need to tell me twice.

Yanking on my seatbelt, I put the truck into reverse, hightailing it out of the parking lot, my wheels squealing in the process.

"Thank you." Her words were soft. Her voice seemed fragile.

I left a trail of dust behind me as we drove away from the bar in a hurry. No one followed us, at least not yet. I took the mountain pass north. "Where do you want me to take you?"

Her motel had been a shitty dump. The place was known for bedbugs and not many visitors. How it stayed open was beyond me.

"Someplace quiet where they won't find me."

Who exactly were *they*?

Paparazzi?

I drove north on the mountain pass and headed for the restaurant. The place was quiet and deserted. There wouldn't be anyone stopping by or bothering us.

"Sure." I didn't push with questions. At least not yet.

Every so often, I glanced in the rearview mirror, making sure that we weren't being followed.

In the distance, headlights shined in my rearview mirror. I hit the gas harder, pushing up the mountain faster. Thankfully, the snow had recently melted, and while there had been some muddy days, the weather had been dry and sunny recently.

I turned off the mountain pass toward the restaurant and shut off the headlights.

"How can you see?" Harper asked, staring at the road in front of us.

I couldn't see a damned thing. I slowed to a crawl but didn't stop. I needed to be careful.

I'd driven this path thousands of times in the dark, but never without headlights. I inched forward, familiar with the path.

Trees surrounded us on both sides of the road, making it difficult to see anything in front of us. The new moon offered no light, but the trees would have hidden it anyhow.

I waited.

An engine roared behind us and passed the driveway.

Another minute, when I was confident the traveler couldn't see us, I flipped on my headlights and proceeded down the trail toward the restaurant.

Harper exhaled a heavy sigh.

"Don't worry. You're safe here." I pulled the truck up out front of the restaurant and shut off the engine. "Come on. Let's get you inside."

She followed out of the truck and behind me up the porch steps of the restaurant.

I unlocked the front door and flipped on the lights. I hurried to the shades, closing them, making sure that no one would see us inside, and while I didn't intend on hanging out downstairs, I didn't want to take any chances.

"Wow," Harper whispered. She stood by the front door and shut it after she stepped inside.

I closed another shade, the curtains darkened the building from the outside. "Make sure you lock the door."

Harper turned on her heels and secured the deadbolt before she stepped farther into the restaurant. "What happened here?"

"Long story," I said. With the last of the curtains shut, I glanced around, satisfied she wouldn't be seen.

With her eyebrow raised, she stared at me.

Was she waiting for me to elaborate? She wasn't the most forthcoming with the men chasing us with cameras. I assumed they were paparazzi, but I wasn't sure.

I'd never been chased by men with cameras, only men with guns.

She shrugged out of my coat and slowly let it slide off her shoulders before she held it out to me.

I took the coat from her grasp and carried it with me toward the staircase.

"Are you coming?" I called after her.

I didn't turn around.

The soft patter of her footsteps was her answer.

She followed me up the stairwell and into my apartment. Harper cleared her throat.

I flipped on the lights and made sure the curtains upstairs were shut too. I closed the living room blinds that peeked out to the parking lot of the restaurant. While I wasn't expecting visitors, I also didn't want to chance it. Clearly, she didn't want to be seen or found.

"Have a seat," I said and gestured toward the leather sofa.

She slunk down into the supple material. Slipping out of her shoes, she drew her legs up beside her body. Her eyes were heavy.

Had she been exhausted, or was it the alcohol that made her sleepy?

"Thank you." Her eyelids fluttered closed momentarily before they bounced back open. "You're probably wondering what all that was about earlier, at the motel."

I opened the wooden trunk my grandmother had given me and retrieved a throw blanket, offering it to her.

Harper's hand stretched out, clutching the cotton before she pulled it over her legs. She seemed to relax under the warmth of the blanket.

"You don't owe me an explanation," I said. I wasn't going to push her. If she wanted to tell me, she would.

Her eyelids fluttered closed again. This time she yawned and pulled the blanket higher toward her chin as she stretched out on the sofa.

I told her I'd grab a pillow to make her more comfortable if she wanted to crash here for the night.

"I do," Harper said, a half-mumble. Her words seemed to slur together as she spoke. "The paparazzi are always after me. Thank you, Lincoln. You're too kind."

"Happy to help," I said and let out a heavy sigh. I hadn't intended to invite her up to my place to sleep, but she was just about out already.

Attempting to be quiet, I strode down the hall and to the linen closet, retrieving a spare pillow. I brought it back out to the living room only to discover Harper softly snoring, stretched out, asleep on the sofa.

I bent down to her level, not wanting to startle her. "I brought you a pillow," I said in a soft, soothing tone, guiding her head up just a bit and the pillow under her neck to make sure that she was comfortable.

"Thank you," she mumbled.

I shut off the lights and quietly stalked to my bedroom.

My phone buzzed in my pocket, and I glanced down at the dozens of text messages that I'd missed from my friends, the guys at Eagle Tactical.

It would have to wait.

I'd answer them tomorrow morning when I knew more about what was going on, assuming she'd tell me.

Early the next morning, my phone buzzed beside me on the nightstand, waking me at the crack of dawn.

"Yeah. It's Lincoln," I said, answering the caller. I hadn't even noticed who had called on the caller I.D. since I'd been half-asleep when I answered the phone.

"I'm downstairs in your restaurant. Can you come down?"

"Jaxson?" What was he doing visiting with me on a Monday morning?

Did we have a new client? That was the only thing that made sense.

But why show up and not just call me?

"Yes, get dressed and come downstairs."

I ran a hand through my hair. "Yeah. I'll be down in a second." I ended the call and tossed my cell phone onto my mattress.

Stumbling around the bedroom in the dark, I grabbed a pair of jeans, a dark shirt, and socks and threw them on before I slipped on my shoes and quietly headed out of the bedroom and past the living room.

Harper was still sound asleep.

I didn't want to wake her. I hurried down the stairs, the bright light of the restaurant making my eyes burn.

Jaxson stood downstairs, leaning against the counter that had been pelted with dozens of bullets.

"Morning," Jaxson said. "I came up to visit but saw you had company."

I ran a hand through my tousled hair.

"Yeah. Busy night." I didn't want to elaborate, and while Jaxson may have thought something happened between me and the girl I left with at the bar, I wasn't going to confirm or deny his suspicions.

I don't kiss and tell.

"You could have just called," I said and folded my arms across my chest.

I needed coffee, but the brewer was shot to hell, and those little coffee pods didn't do justice.

"I texted you last night, but you didn't answer."

"Yeah, I was busy." I ran a hand through my hair and headed back to the kitchen to at least fetch a glass of water for myself. "You didn't drop by just to tell me you texted."

That wasn't at all like Jaxson. Something had come up, but I hadn't the slightest notion of what.

Jaxson followed me to the kitchen and stood in the doorway. "We have a new client. A Hollywood studio hired us as a security detail while they film a movie production over the next couple of weeks."

I lifted the glass of water to my lips and paused. "Paparazzi," I muttered under my breath.

No wonder the studio needed security. It wasn't from the townspeople of Breckenridge interfering with filming or harassing its stars.

"Yeah, probably," Jaxson said. "Mostly, they want us to keep bystanders away and make sure the stars feel safe. There's one other thing."

I finished the glass of water and placed it in the sink. "Of course, there is." There was always something else.

"The studio requested that one member of our team take on a security detail off-hours for the main movie star. I think you should be the one to handle the starlet. She's young, trouble, and you've already gotten to know her."

"What?" My head spun.

"Harper Madison. The girl upstairs in your apartment, she's the Hollywood starlet. The studio mentioned that she might not be on board with a bodyguard, but it's a requirement for the film to get financed and the insurance company to greenlight the picture. Apparently, she has a knack for getting into trouble."

Shit.

It was too early to hear this about Harper. "You don't say."

Jaxson stepped closer. "Listen, I wouldn't even ask you to do this, but I saw the way she looked at you, opened up to you, and I assume she trusts you."

"She's not going to trust me when she finds out I've been hired as her personal bodyguard," I said. She didn't seem the type to appreciate that I'd been hired to look out for her.

Maybe I was wrong, and she'd be ecstatic, but we had to keep things professional between us.

I didn't sleep with my colleagues or clients.

Jaxson exhaled a heavy breath, his jaw tight. "I suggest you don't tell her. Invite her out to dinner for tonight, after the film shoot, and tour her around town. Show her a good time but not too good of a time."

"We had a couple of drinks last night. That was it," I said.

I didn't go into detail about the men chasing her down with the cameras outside of her shitty motel room.

Did Jaxson need to hear about that? Maybe if he was her security detail, but he was putting me in charge.

"I know. I came upstairs and didn't figure a girl sleeping on your couch was someone you slept with. It's why I trust you with this security detail."

Great.

As much as I wanted it to be me, I also wasn't ready for the drama that would ensue. "You want me to be her bodyguard."

She was going to kill me.

I just had to make sure that she never found out that I'd been hired to protect her.

"Yes." Jaxson grew silent as we heard the upstairs door squeak and shut.

Harper was awake and on her way downstairs.

Jaxson stepped around the corner and into the kitchen and nodded for me to step out into the restaurant.

Her soft footsteps trampled over the wooden floorboards.

"Good morning," I said, greeting her.

She had cleaned up pretty well for sleeping on a sofa all night and having one too many drinks.

"Morning. Do you mind driving me back to the motel? I need to get my car."

"Sure." I dug into my pocket for my keys and led her outside, locking up behind myself.

I glanced once more in the direction of the kitchen where Jaxson had stashed himself.

I led Harper out to my truck. Beside it this morning, Ariella's sedan had been parked and abandoned.

"Whose vehicle is that?" Harper asked. She climbed into the front seat and glanced around.

Was she worried that it was more paparazzi out looking for her?

"Just one of the guys helping me fix up the restaurant." It wasn't a complete lie. Jaxson had mentioned how he wouldn't mind doing some renovations on the inside.

Why the hell had he taken Ariella's car?

I put the truck into reverse and headed back on the road we came in on last night.

Harper sat quietly, staring out the window. "Can I ask you something?"

"Sure." I had a feeling she was going to either way.

"What happened to your restaurant? Those bullet holes aren't for décor."

I snorted under my breath. "That's a new one. And no, they are one hundred percent real."

That story would take some time, and maybe it would buy me the opportunity to see her later tonight when I was working and keeping an eye on her.

"It's a long story. How about I tell you about it tonight over dinner?"

"I have to work, but I'll text you when I leave. It might be a little late," Harper said.

"That's fine." I contemplated digging out my cell phone and handing it to her to punch in her number, but I thought better of it. What if she read the texts about the studio security job that had been lined up with Eagle Tactical?

"Pull out your phone. I'll give you my number." I waited for her to retrieve her cell phone, and I recited my digits so that she'd be able to get ahold of me later.

A few minutes later, we were pulling up out front of the motel. The parking lot was nearly empty, unlike last night.

In the distance, I recognized Aiden's truck.

He was staking out the motel parking lot. At least Harper would be safe.

I needed to head home and shower. As long as I didn't have to be onset, then she'd never know I worked for Eagle Tactical.

CHAPTER FIVE

ARIELLA

I rubbed the sleep from my tired eyes and stumbled into the kitchen, the bright lights and wide-open blinds casting in the morning light.

I squinted.

My eyes didn't adjust fast enough and made it difficult to see.

My autonomic nervous system sucked. I was one of the unlucky few with a disorder that doctors struggled to understand.

"Are you okay?" Jaxson's warm voice met my ears as he wrapped his arms around my waist, steadying me.

My body melted into his embrace, his touch warm and inviting.

I didn't want to get ready for work.

"Just my vision." I could feel his look, the concern weighing heavily on both of us. "I'm fine. It's nothing."

The last thing I wanted was to worry him.

I wanted to climb back into bed, more specifically *his* bed, but we were careful. With Skylar visiting indefinitely and his little girl constantly inviting herself into the bedroom, I'd slept in the guest room more nights than I liked.

"Just your vision?" Jaxson repeated. "I don't like the sound of that." He backed me up several feet, cradling me against the cabinets.

His body trapped mine.

"Jaxson?"

He raised his right hand up to my eye level. "How many fingers am I holding up?" he asked.

My eyes had already adjusted by the time he'd trapped me against the counter, but I hadn't wanted to admit it.

I liked being pressed up tight against him, his guard down as he focused on me.

"Ariella?" He sounded worried that I hadn't answered him fast enough.

"Three fingers," I said. "My vision just takes a little longer to adjust than other people's does. Bright lights or going from a dark room to somewhere bright is difficult, and heaven help me if I go back to a dark room right after."

He brushed a strand of hair behind my ear, his touch stirring a desire he fueled within me.

"What happens then?" Jaxson asked. His fingers played in my hair and slid against my neck as he held me close.

I wanted to kiss him, but we had agreed to take things slow around Izzie and Skylar, not to mention we were hiding our relationship from our work colleagues, the guys at Eagle Tactical.

"I start seeing these weird shapes, and it makes me nauseous."

Skylar breezed into the kitchen, oblivious to the intimate moment between us. "I get those too. Auras are the worst. Well, technically, the migraines are the worst, but I can't stand when I get one of those visual trips," Skylar said.

Jaxson untangled his hand and pulled it away before he stepped back from within my personal space.

I whimpered in protest, and he locked eyes with me.

I hated that we had to play this game, a dance of what we could and couldn't do around others. I wanted to throw my arms around him, plant my lips on his, and not worry about who saw us or what they thought or felt. We were grown adults.

"Are you having an aura now?" Jaxson asked.

"No, I'm fine now. Thank you."

Skylar glared at me.

What had I done to piss her off? Was she ever planning on moving out of her brother's house?

"Any word from Mason?" I asked, trying desperately to change the subject.

Jaxson reached for his coffee and took a sip. "He's got a doctor's appointment this afternoon. He is hoping he gets the all clear from the doc and can come back into the office tomorrow."

I brushed past him for the cabinet that held the mugs and retrieved one for myself. "How likely is that?" I asked, pouring myself a steaming cup of coffee.

He'd been hit by two bullets. It took time to heal, but how much time did he need? "He seemed like he was doing well last night."

"It could go either way," Jaxson said. "I'll be glad to have him back, but yeah, he did seem like he was having a good time last night, which reminds me, I need to swing by Lincoln's place this morning before work."

"Oh?" I had no idea what he needed to discuss with him before work, but it wasn't any of my business. "Do you want me to get Izzie ready this morning and take her to daycare?" I asked. I'd picked her up a few times recently for him, so I'd become familiar with their routine.

"That would be really helpful," Jaxson said. He dropped a quick, chaste kiss to my cheek.

I froze, surprised by his gesture.

What if Izzie came running into the kitchen?

While we both knew that Skylar was aware of our relationship, we'd tried to be discreet around Isabella. Jaxson hadn't wanted to confuse his daughter and the fact I was already living under his roof… well, it wasn't helping matters, either.

"Can you secure her car seat in my vehicle?" I asked.

"I'll do you one better, take my truck today," Jaxson said.

"Are you sure?" He'd never offered for me to drive his truck before.

Didn't he worry about the Eagle Tactical guys saying something? Although they all knew I was living with Jaxson, that was because my house next door had burned down.

How long could that excuse last?

"I trust you with my daughter, Freckles. You can guarantee that she rates above my truck."

I took a long sip of my coffee. My cheeks felt hot under his stare.

"I need you to join me in the field today. Our newest client requires the entire team for their assignment," he said, sipping his coffee as he glanced at Skylar. It was clear he wasn't comfortable discussing specifics in front of her. "With Mason unavailable, I need you in the field instead of the office today."

I had so many questions, but he shook his head, silently telling me not to ask them right now. "Okay."

My stomach bubbled with nervousness.

What would I be required to do in the field? I wasn't a field agent, even with my time at the C.I.A.. I always stayed behind a desk or buried behind a computer in a hotel room.

"I'll be texting the team the meetup point. Just come by as soon as you're done dropping off Izzie at daycare."

My breath caught in my throat. "Sure."

Jaxson stepped closer.

Had he sensed my hesitation?

He rested a strong, warm hand on my upper arm. "You've got this, Freckles. I promise I wouldn't include you in the field assignment if I didn't believe you were ready for it."

I offered him a weak smile. "I appreciate it." Which was true, even though I felt sick at the thought of what I had to do, and I wasn't even sure what would be involved.

"You look like you're going to be sick," Jaxson muttered. With a heavy sigh, he grabbed my hand and pulled me into the bathroom, shutting the door.

"Jaxson?" What was he doing?

"Breathe," he said as his blue eyes stared right into mine.

I exhaled a heavy breath that I hadn't realized I'd been holding.

Jaxson clasped my hands tight, and I glanced down at our joined hands. Mine trembled. "You got this, Freckles." He held one hand tight and flipped on the bathroom fan with the other hand.

"Do I?" I asked, my voice squeaking. I grimaced and exhaled a long breath, trying to calm myself. "I'm not a field agent. I work well in an office, where there's stability and structure."

He wrapped his strong arms around my waist and pulled me tight against his body. "Just imagine that you're doing office work outside," Jaxson said.

His breath teased my neck, and his lips caressed my skin. Slowly, he dropped soft kisses just behind my ear.

He was my undoing—each and every time.

"You got this, Freckles," Jaxson said again.

I exhaled a heavy breath through my nose. My eyes shut, I nodded. "Give it to me. What's the assignment?"

He'd brought me into the bathroom to tell me, right? Out of earshot of Skylar, who had a big mouth.

"There's a film crew starting this morning for a movie. They're requesting a security team to monitor the production and make sure that no one uninvited breaches the set."

"That's it?" I breathed a sigh of relief. "Now I feel like an idiot."

"Don't," Jaxson said. "You can't help how you feel or how your body responds." He pulled me tight against him, one hand on my lower back, the other cradling my ass.

I smiled and leaned in, stealing a kiss, unsure when I'd get the opportunity again with him. Just the two of us, alone.

I'd never done security detail, but Jaxson needed an extra body, and while I didn't look the least bit threatening, I could at least make sure no one ran on set who didn't belong. Plus, I had a walkie-talkie, and I was to report to Jaxson anyone whom I deemed suspicious.

I wasn't expecting much to happen.

No one knew a film crew was scheduled in town, but people would talk when they noticed side roads were closed and the cast trailers parked out on the open field just off the main road.

The locals would come, curious about the production in a town of less than a thousand.

While I hadn't lived in Breckenridge for long, this was probably the most exciting thing to happen in the spring months, when skiing and snowboarding were closed for the season.

It was difficult to tear my gaze from Jaxson.

While he stood guard outside of the cast's trailer, specifically Harper Madison's, my responsibility was to make sure that the crew members all wore badges to easily be identified.

The job was easy for the most part, making sure no one snuck on set who didn't belong.

Did anyone even realize outside of the production crew that Harper Madison was in town?

She probably stayed under a fake name at whatever hotel she had checked into.

When the stars paused for lunch, I grabbed a quick bite to eat in my car, enjoying the solitude. I couldn't join Jaxson for lunch as much as I wanted to because we both couldn't afford to take an hour off at the same time.

Finishing a quick meal, I strode across the parking lot, back toward the set.

A sharp pinch struck my neck.

I reached up to rub away the pain, and my vision blurred. I opened my mouth to scream when I felt a hand cover my lips.

My body slumped, about to fall to the ground, when a set of arms lifted me into their embrace.

Darkness swept over me.

CHAPTER SIX

HARPER

I wanted a real home-cooked meal or at least something tasty, not the craft services deli spread that had been set out for the cast and crew to dine on during filming.

While I appreciated their effort, I wanted to steal an hour for myself away from the set.

I stepped out from my trailer, my purse on my shoulder, donning a pair of sunglasses.

I avoided the security team, a bunch of good-looking guys who were locals, former military, and they looked every bit ready to kick some ass.

If I hadn't met Lincoln the night before, I might have considered flirting with one of them, but truthfully, that was all an act.

How I wanted to be, not who I was as a person.

I snatched a baseball cap that had been abandoned on a nearby chair and tucked my long blonde hair under the cap, trying to disguise myself as best as I could.

No one seemed to notice me, dressed like everyone else. With their attention elsewhere, I slipped offset and out to the parking lot, a mowed field, for my rental car.

The hair on my arms stood on end.

A woman with long dark hair slumped over, and a gentleman caught her from behind and swooped her into his arms.

He carried her across the parking lot.

"Hey!" I shouted, rushing after the gentleman.

What the hell was going on?

Was she okay?

I didn't get a close enough glance to see if she was someone I knew from filming.

He carried her toward a white van. "Mind your own business," a gruff voice retorted.

He yanked open the back door of his vehicle.

I hurried after them and shoved my hand into my purse. I yanked out my hot pink can of mace and held it up, threatening the abductor.

Everything told me she was in danger, that whoever this guy was, he was out to hurt her.

"Let her go!" I screamed, hoping that someone would hear my shouts.

Where the hell was the security team who was hired to watch the set?

He wasn't the least bit gentle with the brunette as he tossed her into the back of the van.

The moment he turned around, I had my finger on the trigger of the mace, but he ripped it from my petite hands and backhanded me across the face.

My cheek stung, and my eyes burned with fear.

"Get in." He nodded toward the open back door where the young woman lay motionless.

Was she asleep?

Dead?

"No, I'm not going anywhere with you." I took a step back, unsure how to help the woman in the van. If I went with her, I'd be endangering my life.

I wasn't brave.

I wasn't fearless.

I was an actress, and while I could play a part, it involved lines and scripts. I couldn't play this part, not the one where I appeared strong.

He grabbed me by the waist and tossed me into the back of the van.

"No!" I shrieked and lunged at the man, my fingernails digging into his eyes and forcing him to stumble backward. I used the moment to my advantage and flung myself out of the van and past him, tripping over my feet.

I slammed into the grass, eating dirt.

"You bitch!" the perpetrator snarled and reached into the van.

I wasn't about to wait around to find out whether he drew a gun or something else at me.

I hurried to my feet and rushed between cars, ducking so that he couldn't see me. I kept low to the ground, listening for his footsteps or the heavy breaths that he took, panting for air.

As much as I wanted to help the woman in the van, the best thing I could do for her now was to get help.

If he had a gun, I would be outmatched.

I stayed low to the ground and hurried through the crowded parking lot back toward the production set.

Tires squealed and kicked up dirt as I lifted my head. The white van high-tailed it out of the parking lot.

I didn't bother needing to duck any longer or hide from the perpetrator.

I was free, but she wasn't.

CHAPTER SEVEN

JAXSON

Harper came running up to me, her cheeks red, the sunglasses she wore pushed back on her head, a baseball cap in her trembling hand.

"Help!" Harper came barreling back onset, glancing from one side of the set to the other, looking for someone.

I hurried over, unsure what was bothering her.

Had they run out of tiny sandwiches on the lunch table?

She looked frantic and panicked, but I couldn't even fathom what had gotten her quite so worked up. "What can I help you with?" I asked calmly, trying to ease whatever anxiety she was experiencing.

"He took her!" she gasped, with widened eyes as she pointed behind herself at the parking lot.

"Whoa, slow down. Can you tell me what you saw?" I gestured Aiden over.

I couldn't see Ariella or Declan from where I was positioned.

Aiden jogged over, sensing the urgency.

He didn't say a word, just listened.

"I was heading out to my car," Harper said, "and this guy, kinda big, taller than me, dark hair and dark eyes, was carrying a girl to his van, a white van. She was unconscious. At least I hope that's all it was and she wasn't dead."

I swallowed the lump forming in my throat. "Did you get a license plate?" I asked.

Harper shook her head no.

I hoped this wasn't a game or publicity stunt that she was trying to pull, but the quiver in her voice made me trust her.

"He tried to grab me too, so I fought back and ran," Harper said.

"Good." I exhaled a long slow breath. "Do you know the girl he took?"

She shook her head. "I didn't recognize her, but I'm not always great with remembering people. The girl had long dark hair. I'm sorry, I wish I could be of more help." Harper chewed on her bottom lip. "Can we do a roll call or something on set?"

"That's not a terrible idea," Aiden said. "There are no cameras on the parking lot."

"Did either of them have any distinguishing marks?" I asked, trying to jog her memory before it became even more clouded and faded with time.

"No. I don't remember anything special."

"What about facial hair?" I asked. "Was he wearing glasses? Any tattoos?"

"Definitely no glasses. I poked his eyes when I tried to get away. I don't remember any facial hair or tattoos."

"That's good," I said.

Aiden dug out his phone and called the local sheriff's department. We needed to report the abduction and hopefully get a team who could scour the area along with a helicopter in the sky to find the white van.

After he hung up, I met his stare. "Find Ariella. Have her and Declan set up a roster that we can go down name by name and find out who is unaccounted for."

"Who is Ariella?" Harper asked.

"One of us, part of the Eagle Tactical team," I said, not elaborating any further.

Harper's eyes widened as she pointed toward the parking lot. "Long dark hair, about the same size and build as me?"

I pulled my phone from my pocket.

"Do you have a picture of her?" she asked.

"Already on it," I said, unlocking my phone.

I opened the photos and scrolled through a few of Izzie before I landed on one with Ariella braiding Izzie's hair as they sat on the sofa together.

"Here." I held my breath, hoping it was anyone else who had been taken and not *her*.

Harper tapped the phone screen. "That definitely was the girl I saw carried into the van."

I flipped through my phone and opened a web browser before I typed in Benjamin Ryan.

Could he have shown up in Breckenridge?

He'd said on the news that he was going to reconnect with his wife, but I never expected this type of reunion.

Had he shown signs of violence in the past?

Ariella hadn't mentioned it to me. She had made it clear that it was over between them.

Had that been the reason why?

"What about this guy? Was he the one driving the van?" I showed Harper my phone screen with a picture of Benjamin Ryan. It hadn't been hard to dig up his mug shot.

Harper nodded. "You know who it is?" She seemed to breathe a sigh of relief. "That means you can help find her, right?"

"Yeah, I know of him. Never met the guy." I wasn't looking forward to meeting him now, either. "You should get back on set. I need to make a phone call and take care of some things."

"Okay," Harper said.

She seemed lighter on her feet, less stressed with the news that we knew who the missing girl was and who'd taken her.

I didn't feel the least bit better with the news that Ariella had been abducted by Benjamin.

Where the hell would he have taken her?

Had he drugged her?

She wouldn't have willingly gone with him. Harper had mentioned that Ariella had been unconscious.

I strode across the grassy field, away from the trailers and listening ears before dialing Lincoln.

"What's up?"

"Sorry to bother you. I wouldn't if it wasn't an absolute emergency, but I need you to get down here and cover my shift. Ariella's been taken."

The weight of a boulder nestled deep in my stomach, made it difficult to breathe.

"Slow down, Monroe," Lincoln said, referring to be my last name. "Are you sure she didn't just decide to go for a nice stroll?"

I shook my head, forgetting that Lincoln couldn't see me. Grimacing, I finally answered him, kicking a wayward stone tucked into the grass. "Harper saw her getting shoved into the back of a white van."

I couldn't just stand around but leaving while working a job. I couldn't do that until we had extra coverage.

What if Benjamin was a diversion?

"Shit. I'll head over there now. I'll call Mason while I'm on the way, see if he's done with his appointment and how he made out."

"Thanks." I hadn't wanted to bother Mason, but I was fairly confident that he'd want to know what was going on.

Sirens wailed in the distance. "The sheriff should be coming by any minute."

"Good. I'm still twenty minutes away. When the film shoot wraps up for the night, the rest of the team will swing by and help with the search. Keep us posted," Lincoln said.

"Will do." I ended the call and shoved the phone back into my pocket, relieved when I saw a squad car approach.

The sheriff put out an APB for the white van along with a notification that the abductor Benjamin Ryan should be considered armed and dangerous with a hostage.

I needed Aiden to do his magic with the computer, hacking into every record and account that Ben had, to locate where he might have taken Ariella.

Lincoln pulled into the lot and parked his truck. He hurried over. "Any news?"

"Nothing yet," I said as we hovered around the squad car.

"Does she have her phone with her?" Lincoln asked.

"If she does, it's off, and the battery has been pulled from the device. It's not pinging a signal when we try to access her phone." We had tried everything conventional. "Ben isn't the kind of guy to hold her for ransom."

Sheriff Nelson cleared his throat. "What makes you say that?"

"I did a background run on Ariella when she first moved here, for work," I said, clarifying that I hadn't done it for any other reason. I wasn't a creep. We'd been hired to look into her past for Blue Sky Resort. "That's how I found out her relation to Ben Ryan."

Rubbing the back of my neck, I still didn't like Ben, and that was before he'd abducted his ex-wife. He'd allegedly stolen money from hundreds of other unsuspecting individuals including me.

"The same Ben Ryan who was arrested and convicted of fraud?" Sheriff Nelson asked.

News traveled far and fast.

"Yeah, but he was released."

"On good behavior? What'd he serve, a year?"

"I doubt it. Something about new evidence and the charges being dropped. The conviction was overturned."

I hadn't read the specifics yet. I'd been busy with a toddler at home, and she stole the majority of my time when I wasn't at work.

"Hold on," he said as he answered his phone and stepped away for a moment.

I wanted to chase after him, find out what was being discussed, but what good would that do? "How's Harper?" Lincoln asked.

"She's fine. She's filming a scene," I said, gesturing toward the set. She was the last person on my mind right now.

Sheriff Nelson strode over to us. "We have a possible location. His phone may be off, but he used his credit card. He just checked into Blue Sky Resort."

Seriously?

Could he be any more of an idiot? At least that meant they hadn't traveled far.

"I'm calling for backup," the sheriff said, "and we're going in lights and sirens off. You want to ride with me or bring your truck?"

"I'll ride with you." I didn't want to admit that I didn't have the keys to my truck. I'd given them to Ariella earlier that morning. It was information the sheriff didn't need to have, but there'd be questions if I drove her car to the resort.

"Let us know what happens," Lincoln said. He patted me on the back before strolling onto the set.

I jumped into the passenger side of the squad car, and the sheriff jetted us out of the lot and onto the main road toward the resort.

My foot tapped against the floorboards, restless.

"We'll be there soon," he said. He flipped his lights on to hurry through traffic but left the siren off.

As we approached the last half mile, he turned off the lights and pulled into the parking lot with a half dozen other squad cars behind us.

We had to be careful.

The last time we all were here, there'd been a hostage situation, and while it had been different, I didn't want Ariella's life in jeopardy again.

"I should make you wait in the car," Sheriff Nelson said. He stepped outside, and I followed.

I had pissed him off the last time, storming in and saving Ariella and Hazel without thinking.

I'd been reckless, but I'd done what I had to do, and I held no regrets.

"Don't make me regret inviting you along."

CHAPTER EIGHT

ARIELLA

I blinked several times over and opened my eyes. My vision swam, and my stomach roiled.

"Good, you're awake."

I opened my mouth to announce that I was going to be sick when Ben brought me over a small trash can with a plastic throwaway shopping bag inside.

Was it that obvious?

I wiped the beads of sweat from my forehead and sat up. The room spun in the process.

I shut my eyes but clutched the small can before I heaved up my lunch from earlier.

What was he doing here?

Where was I? The sun hadn't set yet. What time was it?

Had Jaxson and the others realized I'd gone missing?

"You'll feel better soon," Ben said, his hand on my arm rubbing in soft motions, which made my stomach somersault.

I shrugged away from his touch. "Ben," I rasped, my voice rough, my mouth dry.

I wanted to get up, run away, and get the hell away from my ex-husband. I'd heard he'd been released from prison and that his conviction had been overturned. Apparently, Benjamin hadn't been responsible for stealing millions of dollars along with countless other financial crimes.

I hadn't known he was a kidnapper.

He was full of surprises.

I guess we both were.

It didn't matter to me whether he was guilty or not, I didn't want to be with him, and the fact he drugged me and dragged me to—wherever the hell we were—didn't make me change my mind.

Was I in a hotel room? The bedroom looked strangely familiar. A feeling of déjà vu wafted over me like fog.

Ben was an idiot. If he brought me to a hotel, then he would have had to use a credit card. The Eagle Tactical guys could track him and find me, hopefully before it was too late.

"Good, you're looking more awake already." He grabbed my arm and tied fabric around my wrist, pinning me to the bedpost.

"Ben." My voice hitched in warning as I struggled to keep my left arm away from him. I was still heavily sedated, making it nearly impossible for me to fight back. "Don't do this, please. Let me go."

I doubted I could run, even if I could get to my feet.

He huffed under his breath. "Let you go?" He climbed onto the mattress and straddled my body to keep me from fighting him.

Ben pinned my other arm down and tied me to the opposite bedpost. "I plan to have a little fun with you. After all, isn't that what you did with me? Pretending?"

"What are you talking about?" I shrugged away, trying to escape his putrid breath and his body that towered above mine.

My hands were bound, and while I had the use of my legs, I also was still far too weak to do much. Soon I would be completely at his mercy.

What did he plan to do with me?

Would he kill me?

He sunk his weight against mine, sitting down, pinning me further into the mattress. Ben leaned down, his breath hot against my ear, a knife in his left hand. If he thought he was arousing me, he was dead wrong.

He dragged the blade against my cheek as he drew blood.

I winced but didn't scream.

"You forgot to mention you were C.I.A.." Benjamin pulled back and stared down at me.

I didn't know what to say.

I never thought he'd find out.

"I finally figured out how to make you speechless. It's a real shame I had to learn the truth while I was in prison." He dragged the sharp tip of the blade down my neck and toward my cleavage.

This time he didn't draw blood, only scratched the surface.

My mouth felt like it was filled with cotton balls. I licked my lips. "Can I have some water?" Whatever he'd given me to sedate me had made me thirsty.

Maybe I could trick him into letting me get a drink of water or use the bathroom.

I wanted him off me.

He glanced me over. His eyes narrowed as he stared at me. "I don't think so."

"Please." My voice was soft as I pleaded with him.

He tore my blouse with the blade, leaving me at his mercy.

"Ben, please stop." I trembled from the cool air in the hotel room, my lacy crimson bra on display as he palmed the material. "Ben. Get off me."

"Do you really think you're in charge?" Ben growled.

I flinched but, because of the restraints, was unable to move any farther away. I squirmed to get away but he had a knife and I was bound to the bedposts.

"You want the truth." I stared at him, the sedative wearing off. My wrists hurt where he'd bound them above my head, spread out. "Release me, and I'll tell you everything."

"I didn't drag you here to lie to me!" Ben hopped off my frame and grabbed a clear crystal vase. He threw it across the room, and it shattered against the wall.

I took a slow and even breath. “You’re right,” I said. “I owe you the truth.” At least some semblance of what he believed to be true.

Would it be enough for him to let me go?

I doubted he’d set me free.

As the grogginess faded from my head, I recognized the room. We were in a hotel: Blue Sky Resort if I wasn’t mistaken.

I hated that damn place. It seemed like everything bad always happened there, and it wasn’t even a crappy motel.

Maybe they needed to hire their own security team.

“I’m waiting,” Ben said. He folded his arms across his chest.

My cheek stung but I had to ignore the pain if I wanted to get out of this alive. At least he wasn’t throwing anything across the room or at me.

He would when he found out the truth.

CHAPTER NINE

LINCOLN

"Lincoln!" Harper waved to me from across the set as I stood near the front entrance.

I'd been manning the entrance and exit for the past couple of hours since Jaxson rushed off with the sheriff.

I'd done my best to avoid Harper while she filmed the movie shoot.

Busted.

She jogged over. A huge grin lit up her face. "I thought I was supposed to text you when I got off work. Couldn't wait to see me?" Harper asked.

She looked lighter, carefree.

Work actually seemed to put her in a chipper mood, which I didn't mind. It meant she'd be easy to handle tonight, at least in the bodyguard respect. While I may have wanted to handle her in a different manner, that was off the table.

"You look great," I said, trying my best to change the subject.

If she hadn't realized I was with Eagle Tactical, I didn't want her to figure it out right now. After all, I wasn't allowed to tell her I was assigned as her personal bodyguard.

What if she figured it out on her own? I was pretty sure the contract was spelled out. I couldn't divulge it, even then, but I hadn't signed the contract. Jaxson Monroe had done that for the team.

"Thanks," Harper said, her cheeks slightly rosy as she blushed and chewed her bottom lip, glancing away. She tucked a strand of hair behind her ear. "We're actually done shooting for today."

"Good." I knew they were done; our shift technically was supposed to end fifteen minutes ago, but I wasn't leaving until I knew without a doubt that she was safe. "How about we head to dinner, and on the way back, we can swing by and get your car?"

Harper slipped her arm into mine. "That sounds fun. What do you have planned for us? I'm hoping it's somewhere low key. I'm not into the tabloids blowing up my phone or social media with the headline 'Harper lands another hottie.'"

I chuckled. "I don't know. That doesn't sound so bad." I leaned in close, my lips just beside her ear as we walked together toward my truck. "So, you think I'm hot?"

She swallowed and glanced away, quiet for a moment, lost in thought.

Was she thinking about the kidnapping?

She'd seen it earlier, been not only a witness to it but almost his next victim.

Harper hadn't said a word to me about it and while I wanted to ask her directly, I couldn't. Not without her knowing that I was hired by the studio.

I had to tread carefully. I liked her and didn't want to hurt her, either.

"Are you okay?" I asked.

"It's just..." she started and then stalled. Her mouth shut, and her stomach grumbled. Harper pointed at the door to my truck. "How about we grab dinner?"

She avoided talking about what happened.

I wanted to hear it from her, what she felt, how she was coping with it.

My guess was not very well.

Although she had done well on set, maybe I was wrong, and her way of dealing with the attack had been to throw herself into her job.

I knew all about that trick.

I unlocked the door and walked around to open it for her, offering her my hand to help her climb into the passenger seat. Once she was seated and her legs swung over in front of her, I shut the door and hurried around to the driver's side.

"How was your day?" Harper asked.

Avoidance.

Maybe I shouldn't have been quite so shocked that she was focusing on me and keeping the topic far from herself and what she'd witnessed and experienced today.

How would I get her to open up to me without confiding in her about myself?

"Let's see," I said, starting the truck's engine. "I had a nice, hot cup of coffee that no one stole." I glanced at her, and her eyes widened before she burst out laughing.

"Real smooth there, handsome."

I laughed under my breath; she'd caught me off guard with her compliment. "After my hot cup of coffee," I said, finishing my thought, "I relaxed until I was called into work unexpectedly."

Harper exhaled a loud breath. "That's a bummer. Enough about work. Can you take me someplace where we can see the stars? I live in the city, and there's always so much light pollution back home."

"Sure, we can do that after we grab a bite to eat. By then, the sun will have set." I knew just the place to take her that was remote and beautiful.

We finished dinner, and I drove up the mountain pass toward my place.

I passed the road for my home and kept heading north to a clearing that I knew would be abandoned.

"You really know how to pick a quiet spot. You don't plan on murdering me up here, right?" Harper joked.

I shut off the engine and stepped out into the darkness, leaving the headlights on for a minute while I grabbed a blanket from the backseat and laid it out to sit on. "Have a seat."

She stalked over to the blanket and sat down.

I killed the lights on the truck and came back in the darkness, having a seat beside her.

"This is nice," she said, lying down on the blanket. She stared up at the night sky, speckled with stars glittering in the distance.

I shifted to lie back down beside her. My knees bent as I stared up at the darkened oblivion. "It is," I said.

I let the silence envelop us, listening instead to the soft breaths that fell from her lips.

Several minutes passed as we stared up above us.

"I thought I might die today," Harper whispered. Her voice was soft but crystal clear.

I reached for her hand.

I wasn't supposed to get close to her. I wasn't supposed to have feelings for the client. I'd met her before we were hired, but did that matter?

I gave her hand a tentative squeeze.

She shifted onto her side and curled up against me.

I pulled her close, protecting and shielding her from the world around us.

"Do you want to talk about it?" I asked. I wasn't going to pry or force her to discuss what happened, but if she wanted to confide in me, I would be there for her.

She chewed her bottom lip, the moonlight casting a soft, blue glow over her features. "I guess you didn't hear about the abduction from the set today. A girl was taken from the parking lot. Apparently, she was with the security team who was hired by the movie studio."

I held my tongue, not wanting to give anything away. Instead, I held her and listened to what she had to say.

"On my way to lunch, I witnessed this guy carrying a girl to his van. It looked strange. It felt wrong. Everything about it, Lincoln. My stomach was in knots. She didn't move. She wasn't awake. For all I know, she's dead. He forced me into the van but I wouldn't go with him."

I couldn't remain quiet any longer. "But you fought him."

"I did," Harper said and nodded adamantly. "I gouged his eyes. I lunged at him and threw myself out of the van. I wanted to help the girl who was lying there, but I couldn't." Her voice cracked.

"You saved yourself, and there is nothing wrong with that," I said and pushed the long strands of her hair out of her face and behind her neck. My fingers danced over her skin. "You were brave, and by escaping, you were able to get help and notify law enforcement about what happened."

She let out a soft breath and rested her head on my shoulder. "Yeah. I never thought about it like that."

"Well, you should. You did good not going with him. Fighting him off probably saved your life."

While I understood who the culprit was, I didn't know what his motives were or if he was capable of murder.

Ben had taken Ariella for a reason, but Harper would have been a loose end.

He would have had no need to keep her alive.

Harper shivered in my arms. "How about we head back?" I suggested. I didn't have a jacket to loan her.

My job was to look out for her, and I was doing a terrible job of that if she was freezing in the forest.

"Just one more minute?" she whispered, her attention not the least bit on the night sky.

Her warm hand rested against my chest, and a moment later, she straddled me, and her mouth covered mine.

CHAPTER TEN

HARPER

I wasn't the kind of girl who kissed on a first date.

Well, technically, this was date number two with Lincoln. Even so, I wasn't even a three-date kind of girl.

I always took things slow.

Which no one ever would have believed, given the tabloid articles and pictures that surfaced.

The girl in those photographs wasn't me. Well, physically, yes, I was the one being photographed, but it wasn't who I was or wanted to become.

It wasn't me.

I'd been young, naive, and deceived.

With Lincoln, everything felt different. My heart pitter-pattered against my chest and soared the moment our lips met.

I leaned in first. I took the initiative, climbing above him.

His hands nestled at my waist. His fingers caressed my lower back, inching my shirt up slightly. The soft pads of his fingertips elicited a response that set my body on fire, wild and alive.

"Harper," he murmured.

I wanted to rock my hips into his, but I still had some semblance of self-control, even if it was only a tiny bit.

It faded fast.

I moaned as we kissed, and my tongue teased his lips apart, desiring further exploration.

I wanted him, and I was pretty sure he wanted me too.

"We can't," he said.

My eyes flashed open, and I pulled back.

Burned.

Why couldn't we? "Are you married?" I was an idiot, believing a nice, good-looking guy like him was still single and available.

"No. I'm not married," he said.

"Engaged?" I wasn't the kind of girl to break up a marriage or an engagement.

Throwing myself at Lincoln had been foolish.

I climbed off him, wrapped my arms around myself, and hurried to his truck.

I sat down in the front seat and waited for him to drive me back to the studio lot where I could pick up my car.

I never wanted to see him again.

He grabbed the blanket outside, folding it before he opened the back door of the truck, and tossed it inside haphazardly.

I yanked on the belt buckle and snapped it into place. Folding my arms across my chest, I stared out the side window, refusing to speak to him.

Lincoln opened the driver's side door, hopped in, but he didn't start the truck. Instead, we sat together in silence.

"I'm not married and I'm not engaged."

I no longer cared what he was or wasn't, for that matter. I shot him a nasty glare. "So, what, you're just not attracted to me? How does that make me feel any better?"

Lincoln let out an enormous sigh.

"What?" I wasn't sure I even wanted to know, but now that he'd made it clear the problem was me, I was livid.

He started the engine. "I'm attracted to you," Lincoln muttered under his breath. "My dick won't shut the hell up."

CHAPTER ELEVEN

JAXSON

The sheriff headed inside the resort first, speaking with the clerk at reception along with the security staff who appeared more like rent a cops than anything else. They were worthless and should have been fired.

Assuming she was in the suite, they were on the first floor, just down the hallway, but the clerk hadn't seen anyone matching either of their descriptions come through the front door.

That didn't mean anything. There were numerous entrances and exits for the resort.

If Ben was here, he wouldn't have waltzed in through the front door bringing an unconscious woman with him. It would have aroused suspicion.

Ben may have been a first-class asshole, but I doubted that he was a complete idiot.

Did he have a plan?

Did he intend to kidnap Ariella, force her to marry him again, or change her mind and win her back?

My stomach somersaulted at the thought of Ben putting his hands anywhere on her.

I'd kill him if he hurt her.

She was mine.

I should have protected her, kept an eye on her. It was no secret Ben had made it known that he was coming to find her. I just didn't have the slightest notion what it had meant.

Guilt swept over me.

I could have stopped this before it ever started.

I should have put a security detail on Ariella.

Though she'd have killed me if she'd have ever found out, it would have been worth her anger toward me, knowing that she'd have been safe.

Officers rushed guests back into their rooms as SWAT barreled down the hotel room door and burst inside.

I followed a few feet behind them, catching sight of Ariella tied up on the bed, her face bruised and cheek bloody. Her shirt was torn, her red, lacy bra exposed.

I untied her hands and she pulled her shirt closed, bunched together in her hands.

SWAT and the accompanying officers cleared the scene.

A broken window beside the bed held a trace of blood.

The curtain blew with the wind.

"He knew you were coming," Ariella whispered, her bottom lip trembling. "It isn't over."

Declan picked up Izzie from daycare.

It was late by the time we finished up for the night and headed home.

Ariella had to give her statement to the sheriff, and then we had to get a ride back to the lot to pick up my truck. She handed me the keys, but I kept hers.

I wasn't letting her drive back to the house. We'd drive into work tomorrow if she was up for it.

The sun began to go down beyond the horizon, but it wasn't dark yet.

Ariella remained silent as I drove us home.

Declan's car was parked out front. Skylar still wasn't home, but she was an adult. We'd yet to have a conversation, Skylar and me, about how long she planned on staying. She'd made it clear she wasn't leaving town, but I hadn't given her an open invitation to move in with me, either.

That was a conversation for another day. At this rate, another week.

Other things took priority, like protecting Ariella and finding Ben.

Ariella held an ice pack against her freshly bandaged cheek.

I parked the truck in the driveway and stepped out, coming around to help her out of the car.

She hadn't budged.

Ariella handed me the compress that was now warm. She stepped out, walking alongside me.

I wrapped an arm around her waist, keeping her close, protecting her.

The moment I approached the door, Declan threw it open and greeted us.

"Hey, glad you're all right," Declan said. He stepped aside, granting us entrance inside our home. "I just fed Izzie a snack."

I shut the door and locked it behind us.

Ariella hurried up the stairs without so much as a word.

"Mac and cheese!" Izzie exclaimed from the kitchen table. She hopped down from her booster seat and ran toward the door, sticky fingers and all. "Daddy!" Izzie held her arms into the air for me to pick her up.

I lifted her into my arms, giving her a bear hug.

Izzie scrunched her nose and nuzzled mine as she giggled wildly.

"Are you sure you didn't give her a plate of sugar with that macaroni and cheese?" I asked with a hearty laugh before I planted her feet firmly back on the ground.

My little toddler tore off for the kitchen table to finish her snack, which was more along the lines of dinner, but I wasn't going to argue semantics. I appreciated Declan's help.

"Nah, I just gave her a shot of liquor with her milk," Declan joked.

"Of course, you did." I kicked off my shoes and kept a watchful eye on the stairwell. Ariella hadn't come back downstairs.

Was she avoiding Declan and Izzie, or had she just gone up to take a shower and get cleaned up?

I hadn't heard the water start for the bath.

Declan lowered his voice. "How is she?" he asked, nodding toward the stairs.

"She hasn't said much since we found her at the hotel. The bastard snuck out the window of the first floor. It wasn't too difficult."

"Damn," Declan muttered. "So, he's still at large?"

I exhaled a heavy sigh. "Yes." I'd have to arm the alarm, just in case he decided to show up. I'd have done it the moment I came home, but I suspected Declan would take off soon.

"From what I saw, she looked pretty banged up," Declan said. He slipped on his shoes and grabbed a light jacket that he had brought with him.

I stood by the door, leaning against the material, my arms folded across my chest. "Yeah, he knocked her around pretty good, assaulted her, I'm not sure if anything else happened."

I ran a hand through my hair, frustrated that I hadn't gotten there sooner to protect her.

It was my fault that I hadn't put a detail on her and made sure she was safe from that monster.

"Don't beat yourself up over it," Declan said. "You couldn't have known what he was capable of. Ariella never told you. Right?"

With my lips tight, I glanced up at Declan. That didn't make me feel the least bit better. "Right."

I should have seen it coming.

It was my job to anticipate the unexpected, and it was no surprise that Benjamin Ryan had intended to show up looking for Ariella.

I had thought he'd come to win her back.

"I was going to head out, but maybe you should go and check on Ariella first," Declan said.

If I did that, we might never leave the bedroom. He had no idea that we were more than friends. "You go ahead. I can manage around here."

"Are you sure?" Declan asked.

"Yeah. Thanks for your offer." The last thing I needed was for him to witness something transpiring between the two of us, not that I figured Ariella and I would have sex tonight. But to say that was the last thing on my mind, would have been a lie.

"I'll see you tomorrow." Declan opened the front door and stepped outside.

I watched and waited until he got into his car to shut the door and lock it.

I armed the alarm.

Skylar still wasn't home yet, but she had her own code to shut it off.

"Daddy!" Izzie waved to get my attention, her fingers covered in bright orange goop.

"How about we take you upstairs and get you cleaned up?" I wasn't sure if Ariella was in the bathroom upstairs or not, but at the very least, I could wash up Izzie in the master bath.

"Where's Ariella?" Izzie asked. It was the first time that I'd heard Izzie say her name correctly. She was growing up so fast.

"She's upstairs. Ariella had a busy day today." I didn't want to worry Izzie or scare her. She didn't need to know what Ariella had been through. However, she was likely to have questions once she saw Ariella's bruises and abrasions on her face.

Izzie playfully stomped up the stairs, each step louder than the previous. I shook my head, smiling at how nice it was to be oblivious to the dangers of the outside world.

That wasn't entirely true, though. Izzie had been held hostage with Ariella in my home. It hadn't been a good day, and there had been nightmares that followed, another reason Ariella and I had to be careful about sharing a bed together.

I hated the distance that I'd been forced to put between us, hiding our relationship from Izzie, but how could I explain to my daughter that Ariella wasn't her mother and may never be a mom to her, but was a girl I liked a lot, including intimately? That wasn't a conversation to be held with a three-year-old.

I didn't know what the future held for Ariella and me. The fact we worked together and lived under the same roof complicated matters. More so, Ariella's past complicated matters. She'd lost a son.

Did she even want to be a mother to Izzie full-time?

"Ariella!" Izzie squealed, clomping up the last few steps before running down the hallway. The bathroom door was open, the light off.

I walked past my bedroom, and farther down the hallway was the guest bedroom where Ariella slept. Both doors were shut with no sign of her.

"Come on," I said and lifted Izzie into my arms, zooming her forward like an airplane, making sounds of a propeller with my lips before putting her down on the bathroom rug. I flipped on the light switch, and she stripped down while I ran the bathwater.

I gave Izzie a bath, cleaning the cheesy disaster that had managed to cake on her arms, fingers, and even in her hair.

Afterward, I dried her off, put her into her pajamas, fed her a healthy snack, and then read her a very short story before tucking her into bed. I turned on her nightlight and quietly exited her bedroom, my back to the hallway.

I bumped into Ariella.

"Sorry," she said, quick to apologize.

I reached for her hands as they dangled at her sides. "You have nothing to apologize for. How about we head downstairs and find something to eat?"

"I'm not hungry. I was just going to head to bed."

"You need to eat something. I'll see if I have any soup in the freezer." I led her down the stairs, my hand in hers, not letting her sneak off to bed.

She sat quietly at the table while I heated up some chicken noodle soup. "You really don't have to make that for me. I doubt I can eat much of anything."

I grabbed a soft ice pack from the freezer and wrapped a clean hand towel around it, bringing it up to her cheek.

She winced before I even touched her, and then when she must have realized I wasn't going to hurt her, she eased back.

I dropped a soft kiss on the top of her head before retreating back into the kitchen by the stove to check on dinner. I heated up some leftovers from yesterday because while Ariella may not have been starving, I was famished.

Thirty minutes later, and two bowls of soup eaten, she placed her spoon down.

"Wow, I ate more than I thought I would," she said.

"Good." I cleaned up the dishes and shut off the lights.

Skylar still wasn't home, and I hadn't gotten any texts from her. Maybe she had a boyfriend I didn't know about? "Have you heard from Skylar?" I asked, doubtful that Ariella knew anything more than I did, but they were both girls.

Didn't girls talk?

"No," Ariella said as she followed me to the sofa to sit. "It's not my day to watch her."

"I see you still have your sense of humor." I pulled her into my lap and grabbed the blanket off the back of the sofa, pulling it around us. "Can I do anything for you? Get you anything?"

"No, that feels nice," she whispered, her eyes closing as I wrapped my arms around her protectively.

"That was the point," I whispered into her ear, smiling, relieved that she let me hold her.

Her voice was soft, tentative. "I want to tell you what happened, but you have to promise not to be mad."

I couldn't do that, not if she meant that she didn't want me to be angry with Ben.

He'd drugged her, assaulted her, and who knows what else he'd have done if we hadn't shown up when we did.

"I have no reason to be upset with you." I wanted it made clear that my anger wasn't directed at her. "You didn't do anything wrong, Freckles."

"It's my fault. All of it."

CHAPTER TWELVE

LINCOLN

I drove Harper back to the studio to pick up her car.

Surprisingly, the studio hadn't asked us to keep watch overnight. The stars' trailers were locked up along with the film equipment.

I shut off the engine and climbed out, intending to walk her to her car. I wasn't going to leave her, and I needed to make sure she got back to the motel without any trouble.

After all, I was still her bodyguard while she was out of her motel room.

"You don't have to walk me to my car. Isn't that kind of cliché?" Harper asked.

"It's something a gentleman should always do," I said. I walked alongside her, a couple of short strides to her rental car.

The tension between us had mounted since my confession that she'd managed to turn me on.

She didn't appear disgusted by my remark, and while I'd wanted to hold my tongue, the truth of it was that she needed to hear it.

Harper had gotten the thought stuck inside her head that I wasn't interested in her or wasn't available, neither of which was true.

Approaching her car, I backed her against the door, my hands on her hips. My lips teased her neck, drinking her in, kissing her softly and slowly, wanting her to know that I desired every inch of her.

Her hands slid into my back pants pockets, pulling me closer. “Come inside with me.”

“We’re not teenagers anymore,” I said with a hearty laugh.

She had a small rental car. There was no way it would be comfortable having sex in there, not to mention the fact I was supposed to keep my hands to myself.

I failed miserably.

“I meant my movie trailer. I have the keys. It’s just you and me here.” Harper rocked her hips against mine. “I like you, Lincoln. I can’t say that about too many guys I’ve known.” She leaned in and planted a swift kiss to my lips. “Please don’t disappoint me.”

How could I say no to her? I wanted her.

She wanted me.

Why did things have to be so damned complicated?

I threaded my fingers into hers. “Lead the way,” I whispered.

CHAPTER THIRTEEN

HARPER

I thought he'd turn me down.

I was certain Lincoln would have made some lame excuse and leave me standing alone in the field, kicking up dirt as his truck tore away.

He wasn't like the other guys I'd been with, after only one thing: fame.

I hurried across the lot, my hand latched tight to Lincoln's as I pulled him with me to the studio trailer. I dug out my key and unlocked the door.

His hands were on my hips the entire time, his lips on my neck as he pushed my hair to the side.

"Lincoln," I moaned as he did things to my neck that made my body tremble and grow weak. I struggled to stand, thanks to him.

Glancing over my shoulder at him, I had to take a step back to open the trailer door, bumping up tighter against his body.

I could feel his excitement poking into me, the evidence of his arousal hard and promising of things to come.

With one of his large, firm hands planted on my hip, he guided me back as I opened the door before we fumbled inside, slipping out of our shoes.

I let go of him long enough to cross my arms over my waist and pull my shirt up and over my head, tossing it across the room.

Lincoln followed me, his lips back down against my neck, dipping into my cleavage, his hands at my waist keeping me close and tight as I fell back against the mattress.

He towered above, undoing the buttons on his shirt, taking his sweet time as he stared down at me, pausing for a moment after his shirt was unbuttoned.

"What is it?" I whispered, staring up at him.

Before he could answer me, I sat up and pushed his shirt over his arms. It fell to the floor in a heap.

I undid the button on his dark jeans, unzipping the material, my fingers grazing over his bulge.

Lincoln moaned as I touched him, and he pushed his jeans to the floor. The only remaining piece of fabric was his dark black boxers.

"You have too many clothes on," Lincoln said. His fingers caressed my back, and his mouth landed on mine.

He undid my bra, the material gliding down my arms, and I let the cotton undergarment fall to the floor beside the bed.

"Is that better?" I grinned. My eyes momentarily closed as his lips latched on, taking a taste, bringing me to new heights of pleasure as a wave of euphoria fell over me.

Lincoln's lips remained on my breast while his fingers deftly worked at undoing my pants. "Lift your hips," he instructed, and I did as told. He guided my pants off but left my black satin panties.

Thankfully, I'd packed my sexiest pair when I'd traveled. I never thought I'd be grateful to have brought them with me.

Lincoln was a dream come true, a real-life fantasy. Everything about him screamed sexy. My fingers grazed his chest, my palm rubbed over his bare skin, feeling over his muscles. I didn't want this moment to end.

His warm breath trailed a path of fervent kisses along my inner thigh, up toward my heated core.

I gasped and groaned as he kissed and touched me, discarding the last remaining ounce of clothing. His tongue did wonders, bringing me to new heights, dampness coating me, pulse-pounding, ready for him.

"You're so beautiful," he whispered, teasing me, tasting me, and making my body quiver under his touch.

My fingers clenched at the sheets, bunched into fists as my body responded to his ministrations, his tongue and fingers like magic in a way that I'd never quite experienced before.

There'd been others, but none quite so skilled or devoted in the bedroom. My lips parted, gasping for breath, already on the brink when he grabbed a condom from his wallet, opened the wrapper, and slid it on his length before he climbed back up my body.

I leaned forward, covering his mouth, my tongue pushing its way past his lips, hungry for more as he entered me. I moaned, starved, eager to please him. I bent my legs, drawing him deeper within me, eyes closed.

"Look at me," Lincoln commanded, his breathing heavy and raspy.

I struggled to open my eyes, but I gave him what he wanted. An eager moan fell from my lips. My head tipped back against the pillow, back arched as he filled me with each thrust. I was close, but I wanted him there with me, experiencing it together.

Lincoln grunted, and I clenched onto him, feeling him tinkering near the brink of oblivion.

I wrapped my legs around him, dragging him closer, my arms pulling him tight, needing every thrust as much as the last as I drew near.

He gave me what I needed, my body shuddering and pulsating as my heart pounded wildly against my chest, the sound deafening in my ears.

I awoke early the next morning. The light streamed in through the curtains of the trailer.

"I have to go," Lincoln whispered, dropping a soft kiss to my lips.

Moaning in protest, my eyes still shut, I reached out and grabbed his arm. "Don't go."

I didn't want him to run off like the others, never to hear from again.

He brushed a strand of hair behind my ear. "I'll pick you up tonight, after work, for dinner. Maybe we can do something fun?"

"I want to go rafting," I whispered, half-asleep. I'd never been, but I had heard while on set that the crew had plans to go on the river. Some were going tubing, others rafting downstream.

The bed dipped. Lincoln perched himself on the edge of the mattress.

I lazily opened my eyes, staring at him. Had I won? Was he going to stay a little while longer? I patted the bed beside me.

"It'll be too late in the evening to go rafting, but we can make a date of it on Saturday. If you don't already have plans," Lincoln said.

I rolled onto my side, pulling the blankets down slightly so he could get a glimpse of what he was missing by leaving. "Come back to bed," I said. "I'll make it worth your while."

Lincoln leaned down, his lips soft and sweet as he dropped a gentle kiss over my lips. "As much as I'd love to do that, I should get out of here before the crew starts showing up for work."

He was right, and as he pulled back to end the kiss, I groaned in protest. "Fine." I pulled the covers up around myself as I sat up, offering him a faint smile.

While I may have wanted him to stay in bed with me all day, we couldn't do that in the trailer.

Chuckling, he stood, fixing the buttons on his shirt. "I look forward to tonight."

After Lincoln left, I climbed in the shower, erasing any evidence that I'd had the most amazing and steamy sex of my life.

I didn't want to admit that my heart soared when I was around him.

Breckenridge was supposed to be temporary.

I had no intention of living in a small town in the middle of nowhere, but the thought of leaving hurt.

What did I have at home?

No one.

My house was nice, but it wasn't enough.

It had only been one night, one fabulous, earth-shattering night, but I couldn't let what happened between us change my plans or my life.

Lincoln wasn't about to upend his life and career because of a girl he just met.

Right?

I dressed quickly into my undergarments and a robe and hustled outside in flip-flops to the makeup trailer to finish getting ready.

I tripped over a stone and failed to catch myself in the process, stubbing my toe and then smacking my knee on the ground.

I grimaced and cursed under my breath.

"Are you okay?" Lincoln asked.

He bent down, offering me a hand to help me stand.

My eyes widened before I pulled back and stood without his assistance. "What are you still doing here?" I glanced over at him, noticing his change of clothes and the badge hung on a lanyard around his neck.

The lanyard in giant letters read *SECURITY*.

"Since when do you work here as security?"

CHAPTER FOURTEEN

LINCOLN

I had rushed home just before the sun came up. I hadn't wanted to leave Harper, but I had to get showered and dressed.

I didn't know if I was expected to work security detail today, but after what had transpired yesterday with Ariella, I didn't want to bother her or Jaxson.

I could come in this morning for my shift, and if I wasn't needed, I'd retire for the afternoon.

After yesterday, I expected that Jaxson would want the extra set of eyes on set to make sure everything went smoothly and everyone was all right.

It would be a long day, especially since I was still Harper's bodyguard, but that didn't feel like work.

Spending time with her, was something I wanted to do.

After showering and changing quickly at home, I grabbed a cup of coffee at the local shop, saying hello to Skylar. She scribbled her number on my coffee cup and told me that she hoped I'd call her.

I couldn't tell her I was dating Harper Madison.

Were we even dating?

What happened when the film shoot was complete, and Harper went back to sunny California?

Breckenridge was my life. I loved it here, the quiet solitude.

Los Angeles was nothing like our small town, a little piece of heaven.

Pulling up in the lot, I drove past a dark metallic blue sports car.

I parked my truck and stepped out, walking over toward the car, having a look at it from the outside.

"Can I help you?" a gentleman with a thick Italian accent asked. He was slightly rotund, with a sharp nose and a thick head of dark hair. It had to be dyed. It was almost too black for his age.

The parking lot was still mostly empty. I was early, but Eagle Tactical was expected to arrive on set before the entire cast and crew.

I pulled out my badge. The lanyard had the giant letters *SECURITY* along with my picture on the identification card.

"I'm with security. Can I help you?" I asked, turning the question on him.

He hadn't trespassed yet.

"No," he said. He shook his head and stalked toward his car. "I was just leaving."

I'd seen a photograph of Benjamin Ryan.

The mysterious man with the sports car wasn't Ben. I wasn't sure who he was, but I kept a close eye on Harper.

Harper had taken a pretty good fall, tripping over a rock and scraping her knee.

She'd barely been out of her trailer and certainly wasn't dressed for production.

Is that where she was heading when she fell?

"Let me help you," I said, ignoring her question about me being part of the security team for the film production. I didn't offer her just my hand.

Instead, I bent down and reached for her elbow as I helped her to her feet. She could scream at me all she wanted, but I doubted she would do it and make a scene.

She had a reputation to protect, and I suspected that she didn't want anyone to know that we'd slept together.

Though she did have a reputation, according to the studio and the tabloids, the truth was I didn't care what anyone else thought.

I'd spent time with her and gotten to know the real Harper Madison, and she wasn't like anything everyone claimed.

I'd heard the rumors. I chose to ignore them.

Her eyes tightened, and she pulled back. "I don't need your help," she said.

Harper stood and dusted her hands and knees off, the skin on her knee scraped with a small trace of blood that needed to be cleaned up but wouldn't require stitches.

"How about I take you to your trailer and find a first-aid kit?"

She snorted and stepped back. "Leave me alone."

I held up my hands in surrender. "I'm just trying to help."

"I don't want your help."

That was obvious. I held my tongue. There was no point in arguing with her when she was already mad at me. I knew it wouldn't go over well if she found out that I was her bodyguard.

Did she realize that I'd been hired to keep an eye on her off-set, or was she just mad that I was part of the Eagle Tactical team and ran security for the production?

Shit.

Did it matter?

She probably never wanted to see me again, and I had to keep an eye on her tonight. If I couldn't do it, I could ask Jaxson or one of the other guys, but she'd know they were hired as her bodyguard, and I doubted she'd be on board with the company.

Harper blew past me for her trailer.

I needed to give her space. If she wanted to be left alone, it wasn't my job to hover over her and help. I may have tried to protect her, clean up her skinned knee, and hug her, but she wasn't a little kid.

I had to respect that she probably wanted nothing to do with me.

Jaxson strolled over, his hands buried in his jacket. He nodded at me while glancing at Harper's trailer.

"Everything okay?"

"Couldn't be better. How's Ariella doing?" I asked. I hadn't seen her this morning and wanted desperately to talk about anything else. The least I could do was ask about her after what she'd been through yesterday.

His eyes narrowed, staring at me. He could probably see right through my facade, but he didn't say anything further about Harper. "She's recovering," Jaxson said. "I suggested she speak to a therapist but you know Ariella. She's tough and likes to think she can handle everything on her own."

"She's been through a lot," I said. That wasn't a bad idea, her seeking counseling. "Talking with someone could definitely help. And her ex-husband, Ben? Was he caught?"

I had hoped they had put the bastard behind bars.

"There's been no sign of him. Police have an A.P.B. out, but the sheriff hasn't reached out. He's out there, somewhere." Jaxson's brow furrowed.

"The police will find him."

"Yeah," Jaxson answered gruffly.

"What about Mason? How's he doing?" I asked.

"Mason's back in the office. The doctor told him he could do desk work for the next two weeks until he goes back again for another checkup."

It was good to hear that Mason was doing better. It was pretty tough to see what he'd been through and losing his uncle couldn't have been easy, either.

"Excuse me!" a young woman with strawberry-blonde hair rushed over to us.

"Yes, how can we help you?" I asked, glancing down at her badge, making sure that she belonged on the production set.

Her cheeks were pale, her eyes wide. "I can't find Harper Madison anywhere. The star of the movie, she's gone."

"She's in her trailer," I said, walking alongside the young blonde toward Harper's trailer, where things had been hot and steamy the night before.

I didn't enter.

I gave a firm, forceful knock.

"Ms. Madison," I said, not wanting anyone to know about the relationship between us.

There was no answer.

She was probably avoiding me.

Jaxson followed behind us. "Harper Madison. This is security," Jaxson said.

I stepped aside, and he gave another firm knock on the trailer door that was shut. "We're coming inside," he announced, opening the door.

It had been left unlocked, and Jaxson stepped inside first.

I followed behind, glancing around, but Harper was nowhere to be found. "Maybe she's on set or in makeup or hair," I suggested to the young woman.

"No. I'm the makeup artist, and she's late."

"How late?" I asked. I knocked on the bathroom door of the trailer and checked to find it empty. I didn't see her car keys or cell phone, but I wasn't sure that meant anything. I'd have to check the lot to see if her car was where she'd left it last night.

"Over an hour," the young woman said.

"I'm sure she hasn't gone far. Why don't you head back to your trailer, and we'll find her?" I said.

She retreated from the trailer, and I glanced at Jaxson, waiting until we were alone.

"What is it?" Jaxson asked.

"Harper was pissed when she found out that I'm working security for the film." I glanced out the back window of the trailer, over the sink, which led to the parking lot. There were too many vehicles to notice whether her car had been moved or not.

Jaxson's jaw was tight, his body stiff. "You think she fled?"

I didn't know her well enough to determine how she dealt with stress, or anger, for that matter. "Maybe. I hope that's all it is. There was a guy outside this morning in the parking lot with his Lotus Evora. A luxury car like that stands out."

"No kidding. I don't think I've ever seen one in Montana, let alone Breckenridge," Jaxson said. "Could it have been a studio executive?"

Anything was possible, but I didn't get that vibe when I looked at him. "That would be a relief if that's all it was, in which case, wouldn't he still be here?"

I headed out of the trailer and walked around past the ropes put up to the parking lot.

There was no sign of Harper's rental car or the luxurious sports car that I'd seen earlier. I pulled out my cell phone and dialed Mason. Since he was at the office, I asked him to track Harper's cell phone and call me back or text me her location.

A few minutes later, my phone buzzed with a text. "I know where she is," I said, glancing at Jaxson.

"How far away?" His expression was grim.

Pretty soon, other people would start noticing Harper wasn't on set too. She wasn't that far away, but she was near the river and appeared to be near an entry point with rafts available to the public for rent.

If she rented a raft and didn't have experience, I didn't want to think about what might happen to her.

It was spring thaw, which meant the river was high and the rapids dangerous.

CHAPTER FIFTEEN

HARPER

How dare he!

I stormed across the plowed field for my car and high-tailed it out of the lot. I rolled down the windows and belted out a scream, my hands gripping the steering wheel in tight fists.

"What a jerk!" I couldn't believe he tricked me into thinking he had shown up on set last night for me.

Is that all I'd been to him, just another assignment?

I hit the gas hard. My foot pressed tight on the pedal as I headed for the dusty mountain road.

I'd heard the stream last night when we'd been camping out under the stars. While I wanted nothing to do with Lincoln, the thought of rafting felt good, taking control, with no one else around for miles, in solitude.

The only problem was where the hell was I going to get a raft?

I raced up the mountain before I eventually pulled over on a gravel road and dug out my cell phone.

I had shitty service in the woods, and the internet was slow, but it worked.

I pulled up rental facilities and clicked on the information for a nearby location, letting GPS lead me where I needed to go.

Twenty minutes later, I had parked the car, paid for a rental raft, foregoing the opportunity to ride with a guide.

The attendant on duty went on and on about the danger of the river and his recommendation on hiring a guide.

It wasn't that I couldn't afford a guide, I preferred to be alone. Apparently, he had trouble grasping that fact.

Finally, he handed me the paperwork and I signed the legal waiver with a lot of jargon about injuries and death that I didn't bother to read thoroughly.

"Be sure to grab a helmet and life vest outside. Those items are hanging just on the other side of that wall."

"Thanks."

I headed outside, showed my receipt to the attendant on duty, and was handed a small raft, made to comfortably hold two guests, along with a paddle.

"Make sure you grab a helmet and vest," the gentleman said.

I pretended not to hear him. I carried the raft and placed it at the edge of the launch pad, a cement pathway that led to the river on a steep decline. I didn't see any boats, and the river was quiet, at least in terms of rentals.

It was, after all, a Tuesday morning, and I was probably their first customer for the day.

"Harper!" Lincoln's voice carried with the wind as I regrettably glanced back toward the voice.

He slammed the truck door shut and came jogging in my direction.

Oh hell, no.

He wasn't going to talk me out of this.

I pushed the raft farther into the water, my feet and knees getting wet as I made sure to push away from the cement. The last thing I wanted was for Lincoln to follow me.

I jumped onto the raft and used the paddle to hurry away from the river's edge. I didn't get far.

Lincoln chased after me, forging into the water, splashing, and then launching his body entirely in as he began swimming over toward me.

"Everything okay, ma'am?" the attendant shouted toward me.

I rolled my eyes at Lincoln. He wasn't going to hurt me, just annoy the hell out of me. "Yes, my boyfriend is just an idiot!" I shouted back at the gentleman.

Lincoln surfaced, his arms at the edge of the raft, holding on. I couldn't see the bottom of the river.

Was it deep?

"Boyfriend, huh?"

"Don't flatter yourself. I figured if I called you the guy I regrettably slept with, he might phone the cops. Do you want to climb on?" He'd probably do it without my permission, seeing as how he'd chased me downstream.

"I thought you'd never ask," Lincoln said. He hoisted himself onto the raft.

The boat swayed.

My eyes widened, and I pushed myself to the opposite side to keep the raft from tipping. "Careful!" I warned.

"Funny, I should be telling you that. No helmet. No life vest. And one paddle."

He knew just what to say, to get under my skin.

"Well, I wasn't expecting company."

"There's another rental unit a few miles downstream. We can grab the rest of the necessary gear as long as we're going rafting." Lincoln gestured at the paddle. "It's all yours."

"Gee, thanks. You're quite the gentleman, aren't you?" I mocked while attempting to paddle.

I couldn't reach both sides from where I sat.

We needed another paddle.

Lincoln grinned the entire time, pleased with the predicament.

I wanted to hate him, but that huge grin and his carefree attitude just made me almost relax.

"Are you having fun?" I still gave him hell. It was the least I could do considering what he put me through, not telling me the truth.

Had he ever intended on mentioning to me that he worked security for the production?

Did he think I wouldn't notice?

"I am, but I think it would be helpful if we carefully changed positions. I'll ride your back, and you take the lead."

I raised an eyebrow at his suggestion.

"The longer you stare at me with that come-hither look, the longer we'll be sitting on the river barely moving."

"It's not a come-hither look," I retorted.

We hadn't hit rapids yet, and I couldn't even see or hear them in the distance.

Slow and careful, we switched positions as I scooted around to the front center, and Lincoln sat behind me. "Of course, it's not," Lincoln said with a sly grin.

Thankfully, I was seated in front. At least he couldn't see the expression on my face.

We sat in silence for several minutes as I paddled from one side to the other, keeping us moving downstream in mostly the center. I avoided the rocks to the right and the tree root to the left of the riverbank.

The raft shifted slightly, and Lincoln's warm hands brushed the hair to the side of my neck.

With one hand, I gripped the raft and with the other, the handle of the paddle. "What are you doing?" I squeaked.

I hadn't intended to sound quite so unsure and not the least bit confident, but he'd caught me off-guard.

"Apologizing," his husky voice whispered into my ear, sending a shiver down my spine.

No way.

That wasn't going to cut it. "Sex isn't an apology," I said and glanced at him over my shoulder.

I contemplated smacking him upside the head with my paddle, but I didn't want to knock him overboard or risk him drowning.

The water was dark and deep.

I couldn't see the bottom.

Silence filled the void, and Lincoln pointed up ahead at the ramp and nearby rental station. It looked identical to the previous one that I'd just visited. "Pull up along the ramp," Lincoln said.

Yeah, I'd do that and drop his ass off.

"Sure." I paddled harder, wanting to get there quickly so I could dump him behind.

Lincoln jumped off, his feet getting wet. Not that it mattered. He was still pretty soaked from his earlier swim.

I waited by the entrance as he headed up the platform. The minute his feet were on solid ground, and he faced away from me to grab the gear, I paddled out.

It was a good two minutes before he turned around and noticed. "Harper!"

Snickering, I waved and gave him a salute before paddling downstream.

CHAPTER SIXTEEN

ARIELLA

The film had taken a pause. Without the lead actress, there wasn't much that could be done.

That was fine with me. I wasn't in the mood to work.

I wanted to curl up on the sofa with a carton of mint chocolate chip and eat away my feelings.

Jaxson stalked over toward me. He'd been watching me all day.

Mostly, I was grateful for the concern, but sometimes I just wanted my space too.

"I just got a text from Lincoln. He found Harper, and she's heading downriver," Jaxson said.

I didn't understand what he meant. "Downriver?" I hadn't lived in Breckenridge that long. I'd survived the winter, that was about it. Did we need to intervene? "Should we head out there and help?"

It didn't appear that filming would resume anytime soon.

"I think Lincoln's got this one handled. Harper's gone rafting, and he's the best guide I know," Jaxson said.

"Oh." That sounded kind of fun. "Maybe we should do that sometime? The three of us?" I suggested.

"The three of us," Jaxson repeated slowly. Was he trying to figure out who the third person I invited along with us? It wasn't Lincoln.

"Yes, it'd be nice to do something with you and Izzie." I liked spending time with them.

Was that a bad idea?

Did Jaxson have commitment issues?

We hadn't exactly told anyone about our relationship.

I wasn't looking for another husband. One had been enough, but I did want more with Jaxson.

He wasn't just a fling.

"You're quiet," Jaxson said.

"Just thinking."

"Uh oh," he teased and nudged me. "That can't be good."

I rolled my eyes and grabbed his arms, pinning them behind his back, my body pressed tight against his. I leaned up on my tiptoes to reach his ears. "Any chance you have handcuffs around here."

I needed to forget, to push the fear that crept in at night and held me hostage.

Jaxson raised an eyebrow. "Maybe, but they wouldn't be for me, Freckles."

I gulped and stared up into his calm blue eyes. He caught me off guard. I never expected him to admit that he had handcuffs. What else did he have or was it strictly for business' sake? He was former military and he worked security, but I'd never so much as seen his metal cuffs.

"You're blushing," Jaxson whispered into my ear.

My grip on his wrists wasn't that strong, and he broke free.

Grabbing my wrists, he spun me around, my hands pinned at my back, his body pressed against mine. With one hand, he held me tight, and with the other, he brushed the hair to one side of my neck, his breath caressing my skin.

"Have you ever used handcuffs in the bedroom?" he asked.

I glanced around, grateful no one paid either of us any attention.

"Have you?" I countered. A hint of nervousness struck my voice. Had he noticed?

He pulled me closer and around the corner on the opposite side of the trailer where we were out of sight of the handful of crew members who had stuck around. Most had left, and the director, twenty minutes earlier, had called it a wrap for the day.

"Are you okay?" he asked.

We were off the clock, but we hadn't left.

Jaxson insisted that we wait until we were the last to remain.

Like we were actually working and doing our jobs.

Someone could have driven off with one of the stars' trailers, and neither of us would have noticed.

I tipped my head upward, leaning in but not quite kissing him yet, letting the moment linger between us.

"I'm worried about you, Freckles."

I leaned into his touch, wrapping my arms around his neck, embracing him. He had no idea how much such a simple gesture had soothed me. "Me too," I whispered.

His breath tickled my neck as he spoke in a whisper. "I've been waiting to tell you this, but I made reservations for the spa. You and Hazel can spend the entire day tomorrow relaxing."

Visiting a spa sounded wonderful. "Hazel is coming with me?" That was a pleasant surprise.

"Yes, Hazel and Mason are getting under each other's skin, so we thought it would be a good idea to send the girls somewhere for a treat."

"Get us out of your hair?" I joked, laughing under my breath. "What about work?"

It was the middle of the week. I couldn't just blow off my job, even if Jaxson was my boss.

He leaned closer, his lips grazing my ear, and it sent a shudder down my spine.

Just being in his proximity, made my insides warm and toasty.

"I'm sure you can make it up to me in other ways," Jaxson said.

"If it involves handcuffs, then I'm the one securing you to the bed." While the thought just days ago would have been fun, being bold and adventurous, I wasn't ready to let my guard down after what happened with Ben at the hotel.

Smirking, he shook his head. "We'll see."

His hands caressed my waist as he tugged me closer.

I rested my hands on his chest, our bodies practically sandwiched together. While it wasn't particularly cool out, the slight chill of the wind was long forgotten, with his body heat warming me all over.

"I want you to spend the day unwinding, Freckles. You deserve it." He dropped a soft kiss to my cheek, and my eyelids fluttered shut.

I shifted slightly, leaning up on my tiptoes to taste his lips, wanting reassurances that whatever happened, we'd get through this together.

"I'm scared," I whispered, the words difficult to voice aloud.

I opened my eyes, feeling his steady gaze on me.

"I know," Jaxson said. "I won't let him touch you ever again."

It wasn't just the fact that Benjamin was still out there, waiting to make his move.

There was so much that I hadn't told Jaxson and when I did, would he ever look at me the same way again? I had intended to tell him last night, but I hadn't found the confidence, too afraid to come clean.

"I need to tell you something." My hands trembled against his chest, and I gripped his shirt, balling my hands into fists.

I leaned in, stealing another kiss, another taste, afraid that it might very well be the last.

CHAPTER SEVENTEEN

LINCOLN

That little spitfire!

Harper had snuck away the moment I had my back turned and been distracted.

She had no idea the danger of the rapids up ahead, especially this time of year.

A few cars were parked at the loading dock, but the one that stood out to me was the same one I'd seen earlier that morning, a shiny metallic blue Lotus. There was no way there were two of those vehicles in Breckenridge.

I exhaled a heavy breath.

Shit.

Where the hell was the Italian-looking guy who had driven the car? He wasn't outside.

Had he gone downriver already?

Would Harper run into him?

I hurried inside the small shop, but there was still no sign of him. "Busy morning?" I asked, trying to make small talk while fishing for information.

"Same as usual," the man behind the counter said. He spoke slowly, his movements not the least bit quick.

I yanked out my wallet. It was soaked along with my phone. Just great. "I'd like to rent a raft for one, please. Also, do you have any rope I can purchase?" I pulled out my credit card, not wanting to waste a beat.

The gentleman behind the counter leisurely strolled across the room to retrieve the rope. "Do you need six feet or twelve?"

"Six is fine." I didn't need a lot.

If I'd have had cash on me, it would have made the transaction a lot quicker. The moment he was nearly finished and handed me the receipt, I scribbled my signature and hurried out of the complex.

"Don't forget your helmet and life jacket."

I didn't let him finish his sentence. I'd heard it all before and knew the items were stored outside.

This wasn't my first rafting trip and hopefully wouldn't be my last. I hurried to the attendant and showed him my receipt.

While he grabbed the raft, I secured a helmet, the life jacket, and grabbed an extra set for Harper. She'd wear them before we hit the rapids.

I may not have felt I needed them, familiar with the river, but I wanted her to wear them. If I wasn't doing what I was asking her to do, she'd never listen to me.

I dropped the rope, helmet, and life jacket into the raft and launched the craft into the river.

The cool water felt good on my feet, and I climbed on, getting myself situated before I began paddling with a good hustle.

I needed to catch up to Harper.

I hurried downstream. At least I was moving in the same direction as the current.

The river forked up ahead, and I needed to get to her before she veered off in the wrong direction.

Eventually, the river came back together, but to the right held rougher rapids. For a novice, it was better to take the left side.

Did I need to worry about the mysterious man I'd spotted earlier that morning?

Was he out for a water adventure on the river or did he have something else in mind?

Had he known where Harper was or what she'd been doing?

I'd been able to track her with Mason's help. It hadn't been tough pinging her cell phone to the nearest tower, and then zeroing in on her location.

Had the Italian man done the same?

What did he want with Harper?

He didn't look like the type of guy who would be into water sports or go anywhere near a river.

I paddled hard and fast.

In the distance, I caught a glance at her raft. The fork was up ahead, and she headed toward the right.

Shit.

"Harper!" I shouted, hoping that she'd listen to my advice.

Her long blonde hair darted around as she glanced over her shoulder at me.

I paddled harder and faster, closing the gap between us. I honestly thought she'd try to outrun me. Instead, she put her paddle down in the raft and waited for me to approach.

My heart raced as I caught up to her, and as I came alongside her raft, I grabbed the rope and tied our rafts together at the handles.

A weak smile played on her lips. "I didn't think you'd follow me after I left your ass twice," Harper said.

"I'm persistent."

Harper laughed and shook her head. "You're something else."

Grinning, I secured a knot, keeping our rafts together. I handed her a helmet. "Put this on."

"And if I don't?"

"I won't let you go down the rougher rapids." The rafts were already nearing the right entrance of the fork, and it would take too much time to get to the opposite side. "Please."

She huffed under her breath and took the helmet from my hands, securing it on her head and clipping it under her chin.

I reached behind me for the life jacket. "This too, please."

At least I didn't have to hold her down and force her to wear it. I didn't think that would have gone over too well.

She'd have likely thrown me into the water.

"Fine. I can't afford to die out here. Too much paperwork for you, right?"

I swallowed the lump in my throat.

Had she known that I was hired as her bodyguard?

Did she realize the job went beyond just running security detail on set?

If she hadn't figured it out already, I couldn't risk her discovering the truth.

Already, she was pissed, but she'd hate me.

"It was a joke. Relax," Harper said. She secured the life jacket and reached for her paddle. "Are you going to untie us now?"

A huge grin crossed my face. There was no chance in hell that I was untying our rafts until I was confident that she was done for the day. She'd have to be out of the raft and on dry land. "You'd like that, wouldn't you?"

Her fingers grazed over the knot that I'd tied. She studied it for a long moment before giving up.

I wasn't sure whether she thought she couldn't untie it or just didn't care that much.

Maybe she didn't mind being stuck with me?

I had all day to convince her that she wasn't just an assignment.

The raft picked up speed as the current grew faster the closer we approached the rapids.

We'd been chatting and laughing, and I'd nearly missed the fact that we were drawing nearer to the rough waters ahead.

CHAPTER EIGHTEEN

JAXSON

Whatever Ariella wanted to tell me, it couldn't be that big of a deal. I knew she was former C.I.A., and not even her husband at the time had known about her job.

She had told me once that while he may not have been guilty of the financial crimes that he'd been convicted of, he certainly wasn't innocent, either.

I hadn't known what she'd meant until she'd been drugged and dragged by the monster into his van and held captive. Thankfully, we'd found her before he could have done any further damage or harm to her, but she was different.

Every time I reached out to touch her, embrace her, show her that I was there for her, I could feel her hesitate.

Maybe she didn't even realize that she was doing it, but I noticed.

"How about we have this conversation somewhere a little more private?" I suggested. "You want to take a walk?" If she was ready to talk about Ben, her ex-husband, then I was ready to listen.

Whether I could remain calm, was another obstacle that I'd have to face.

Her hand slid into mine as we walked alongside one another, away from the set toward the edge of the forest in the distance.

"I just—I don't want you to hate me when you hear the truth."

I could never hate her. I might be disappointed, but hate was a strong word.

"Let me guess. You married Benjamin because the C.I.A. advised you to do so?" I wasn't sure that was what she had intended to tell me, but it was a stab in the dark.

How far off was I?

"Not quite," Ariella said. Her hand fell from mine, and she folded her arms across her chest.

I stayed close, our bodies almost touching at our hips as we walked alongside one another.

I waited for her to elaborate, to tell me what had her so tied up in a knot that even Ben had managed to get to her.

"My ex-husband, Ben," she reiterated, "I didn't meet him by chance or by accident."

"You were staking him out," I said.

Her brow furrowed. "It wasn't like I was a field agent and was meant to go undercover. I was out having drinks with my team from the C.I.A., and while we were investigating Benjamin Ryan at the office, we ran into him at the bar. He kept staring at me and eventually came over and asked me to dance. It was obvious he liked me and wanted to get to know me."

"Bold." I shouldn't have been surprised by his move, considering what he'd done just yesterday.

"Yeah, I was hesitant, but turning him down, I was more afraid of what it might mean to the investigation. So, I danced with him, had a drink, and then he gave me his number. He told me the next move was mine."

That surprised me. I hadn't thought she'd have been the type to have willingly thrown herself into a burning building.

"I know what you're thinking, I did this to myself, but my boss insisted I call Ben."

My hands bunched into fists. I'd kill whoever her boss had been if I ran into him. "I never thought that, Freckles."

This wasn't in any way her fault. Even if she had made a poor choice in dating him, clearly, there had been something worth searching out.

She'd married him. It hadn't all been because of her boss. She must have loved him at one time.

Ariella started walking again, this time along the edge of the forest, as we reached the end of the open field. "Ben had been a gentleman, and the investigation hadn't turned up anything, so when he asked me out a second time, part of me wanted to see him again."

"But?" I had the sneaking suspicion that someone, namely her boss, pushed her toward Ben.

"But my boss insisted that if Benjamin Ryan wasn't involved in the human trafficking ring, then it had to be one of his colleagues or his friends, and they were shuttling women through the building where he lived."

My stomach sank at the thought of the danger that lurked. "Could it have just been a neighbor? Did Ben have an apartment or a condo someplace in New York?" I asked.

"That was what I thought, he lived in an apartment, but his phone records indicated his involvement. It turns out his brother, Richard, was living with him. He'd been in and out of prison and had friends over when I went back to his place after a few months of dating."

"What happened?" Clearly, she was still alive, relatively unharmed. Hell, she'd gone on to marry the guy.

Ariella shrugged her shoulders. "Nothing." She stopped walking and turned back toward the production set.

The trailers in the distance were small, and it was too difficult to see if everyone had left for the day or if any stragglers remained. Most had cleared out when we'd started our walk.

"You never told your supervisor?" I asked. I found that hard to believe. She didn't seem the type to betray the C.I.A. in favor of a man.

"I reported it, and his brother was arrested, but since Ben didn't seem to be involved and at the time I stupidly liked him, we continued dating. Honestly, a small part of me was relieved it was his brother, and the C.I.A. had been tracking the wrong guy. After the place was raided, Benjamin moved out, and all of it stayed behind. His brother, the drama, the investigation, it was in the past. As far as I knew, Ben and Richard never spoke again, and I never told Ben that I was the reason his brother went back to prison."

I took her hand in mine. "That was probably for the best. It wouldn't have gone over well and could have put your life in more danger."

"Yes, so instead, I married him. Grand idea," she quipped.

"We all make mistakes. We're allowed one really bad one," I teased.

She squeezed my hand. "Thanks. Ben hadn't realized I was with the C.I.A. until he was in prison. Someone told him. I have no idea if it was Richard or someone else. That's why he came here, and he blames me for all of it."

I pulled her tight into my arms, embracing her. "None of this is your fault."

Did she know that?

"We'll find Ben, and until he's located, you'll have one of the Eagle Tactical team watching your six."

"You're giving me a bodyguard?" Ariella smiled, laughing under her breath. "I should have expected that from you, but I did not see that coming."

"Well, you should have," I said.

For the most part, I planned on being her bodyguard and protector, but if I couldn't be around, then it would be one of the other guys I served with, men who had my back.

"Does that mean you'll be joining our lady's day tomorrow at the spa?" Her hands slipped under the back of my shirt, her fingers caressing my skin.

I wanted to be the one to give her a massage. Maybe we could do that tonight. Just the two of us? "How about I give you a little preview of your spa day at home?"

She pulled back slightly, her arms still wrapped around my waist as she stared up at me. "Hmmm," she said, mulling it over. "Will that massage lead to something else even more pleasurable because as tired as I am, I could get on board with that arrangement."

Leaning in, I dropped tender, featherlight kisses across her neck. "I wouldn't want to keep you awake."

"Oh, it would be worth it," Ariella said. One hand stayed pressed to my lower back, her other threaded through my hair.

Her touch felt wonderful, relaxing, hypnotic. I pulled her closer, growling into her ear. "Maybe we should take you home, get you undressed and ready for tomorrow's spa day."

I had other plans in mind that involved a full body massage and listening to her sweet moans and gasps as she pleaded for more.

CHAPTER NINETEEN

ARIELLA

The studio was pissed that Harper left for the day and filming was halted, but there wasn't anything we could do about it.

I headed home, and Jaxson stayed on my tail the entire time.

He planned to pick Izzie up before dinner but was letting her spend a little longer with her friends.

He was right. It was good for Izzie to have others to play with who were her age. She had no siblings, and I wasn't sure I could go through conceiving a child again. I'd lost my son, and to this day, it still haunted me.

I had worked through the grief, but seeing Ben had brought all those emotions and more, with memories resurfacing.

He hadn't always been the bad guy. At one time, I had loved him, but it felt like a lifetime ago.

Finally home, I sunk into the mattress, my head against the pillow, eyes closed, naked.

Jaxson's warmth and weight nestled against my hips, pressing me down farther into the bedsheets.

He lathered lotion on his hands, rubbing his palms together to warm his hands before he caressed my shoulders and down my back.

A soft sigh escaped past my lips.

Jaxson's hands were strong and firm, and his movements lulled me more toward slumber than anything else.

I had expected him to take the opportunity with the two of us alone to seduce me, but he surprised me. His hands massaged down my back in a soft, soothing motion.

My body drifted further toward slumber, relaxed and without a thought or care in the world.

His touch had a healing effect.

Jaxson lifted his hips off mine, and I moaned in protest.

"Do you want me to keep going?" he asked. His breath was soft and warm as he leaned closer, planting a kiss on my neck.

"Yes." It took every amount of measurable strength to answer him.

His lips were warm and soft against my skin. "Sleep, Freckles."

I opened my mouth to protest, but it took too much energy to answer.

His hands continued massaging over my bare skin as I drifted to sleep.

I had fallen asleep from the most amazing massage of my life. Jaxson had worked his magic, and it hadn't been remotely sexual like I had expected.

After dinner, we curled up on the sofa and watched a movie together once Izzie was tucked into bed. Skylar staggered in well past midnight, but neither of us said anything to her. She was a grown adult, but it was clear that she'd been out partying.

Jaxson gave me the day off, and Hazel was supposed to drop by in the morning at the house. We planned to grab breakfast together and then head to the spa.

I needed a day away from the world, a chance to unwind and not think about what happened with Ben.

The massage last night had lulled me into a peaceful slumber, free of nightmares.

While awake, I constantly glanced over my shoulder, waiting for Ben to reappear.

What I wouldn't give to feel calm and safe.

Jaxson was right.

I needed to speak with someone about it and maybe a therapist would help? As I exhaled a heavy sigh, a loud thud echoed outside.

My heart leaped and I jumped. I hurried to the window and glanced outside. I expected to see a car and had hoped Hazel was early.

No one was there.

My hands trembled.

I double checked to make sure the alarm was armed.

It wasn't Ben. He didn't know where I lived or how to find me. Even if he'd tracked me down to Breckenridge, there was no way he knew that I lived with Jaxson.

He shouldn't have even known we were an item and he hadn't mentioned it while I'd been held captive just a few days ago.

Maybe living with Jaxson indefinitely wasn't such a bad idea. With Jaxson, I felt safe and protected.

The truth was that I was afraid, fearful that if I spoke with a therapist, she'd try to convince me to move out, that a relationship with my boss was a terrible idea.

CHAPTER TWENTY

HARPER

I needed coffee, something strong with an extra jolt of caffeine. I'd spent last night at the shitty motel, alone. Lincoln and I had grabbed dinner and drinks at the nearby bar after we finished rafting.

He may have been hot, but he'd lied to me.

Lincoln worked security for the production set along with his buddies.

Maybe I shouldn't have been angry, but why hadn't he told me?

Had he known who I was when we had first stumbled into each other at the coffee shop?

Here I was again, in dire need of a shot of caffeine. On my way to the set, I stopped at the local coffee shop where I'd first run into Lincoln.

What were the odds I'd see him again today?

Probably pretty good, but that was when I got to the set. Thankfully, this morning he wasn't there.

I breathed a sigh of relief and headed straight to the register to give my order to the girl behind the counter. Her name tag read *Skylar*.

It was the same girl who had butchered my name the last time.

Wonderful.

"Harper?" An unfamiliar voice stepped up behind me in the line to order.

Finishing my order, I slid my credit card into the chip reader before glancing over my shoulder. "Yes?"

I didn't recognize the gentleman with short, military-cropped hair and wire-rimmed glasses. He wore blue jeans and a dress shirt and barely looked out of high school. "Charles Stone, I'm with the Hollywood Chronicle."

He pulled his lanyard with his PRESS credentials out of his jeans pocket.

Inwardly, I groaned.

"Do you have a minute?" he asked.

Behind him, the shop door opened and Lincoln headed inside.

Could this day get any worse?

"Are you stalking me?" I shot at Lincoln before returning my attention to the news reporter.

He wasn't a local.

The Hollywood Chronicle was an entertainment magazine based out of Los Angeles, which meant Lincoln wouldn't have recognized him. "Yes, join me, Charles. I'll grab us a table," I said a little too loudly, for Lincoln to hear.

I snatched my coffee from the counter and hurried to sit down.

Charles skipped the line and grabbed a chair.

Smart man.

He probably was worried I'd change my mind.

I also was on a time crunch, which he seemed to recognize. I sat across from Charles at the round table, one leg propped over the other, staring past him at Lincoln.

Lincoln scowled as he ordered, every so often, glancing back in my direction.

Was he jealous? I didn't want to make eye contact with him. I shifted my chair, hoping I could ignore him. Pretty soon, he'd have his coffee and leave, right?

No such luck.

He stood by the counter, waiting for his drink, watching me the entire time.

"Boyfriend?" Charles asked, glancing over his shoulder.

"Just someone from the set," I said and gestured for him to continue. "What would you like to know?"

Charles pulled out his phone. "Do you mind if I record our conversation?"

"Go ahead."

He opened an app and recorded an audio stream. "Thank you." He appeared young, perhaps bright, but also like I was his first assignment. "You're a long way from Hollywood," I said, surprised he'd chased me down in Breckenridge.

Charles laughed under his breath. "Yeah." He started his questions, asking me about the film, if I enjoyed the small town and what my dream role would be.

I kept my voice down to make sure it didn't carry throughout the coffee shop. Other than Charles and Lincoln, no one else here knew who I was. At least no one else had paid me any special attention. It was nice to be a nobody. I couldn't remember ever having that before.

"And one last question," Charles said, "do you mind if we take a photograph or two outside? I'd love to have a picture to go along with the article."

"How about you come to the set, and during lunch I'll give you that photo?"

I didn't want him snapping pictures of me without my hair and makeup done. I didn't look my best, and the last thing I wanted was to be interviewed in a Hollywood magazine looking like I'd just rolled out of bed, which was pretty much what I'd done.

I sipped the last of my coffee and stood, walking over and dumping the empty cup into the trash. I pushed open the glass door and headed outside.

Charles followed after me, phone in hand. "It's just one picture. We can always touch it up later," Charles said.

He lifted his phone and began snapping photos, ignoring my request.

I held my hand up in front of my face.

Asshole.

I'd been naïve to think that he'd actually do what I'd asked. He was probably one of the jerks who had staked out my hotel the first night that I'd been in town.

"I said no!"

"The lady asked you to leave her alone," Lincoln's gruff voice answered. His heavy footfalls clomped from behind.

I didn't need him to fight my battles, but he was quite a lot bigger and taller than Charles. Lincoln was every bit of a man.

"Fine!" Charles shoved his phone into his pocket. "I'm leaving. Already got the shot that I wanted anyhow."

Lincoln snarled at the man and stomped closer. "Give me your phone."

"No." Charles's bottom lip trembled.

Lincoln towered above Charles and grabbed him by the lapels of his shirt. "I wasn't asking."

I didn't have time to deal with Charles or Lincoln, for that matter. Already, I was running late, and after bailing yesterday, I needed to get to the set.

I hurried to my car, leaving the two of them to battle it out in the parking lot. I didn't think Lincoln would actually assault the idiot with the Hollywood Chronicle, but if he did, I wasn't going to intervene.

Hightailing it out of the parking lot, I made a sharp left and hurried toward the set.

My foot was lead on the gas, and as I rounded a bend in the road, a car was stopped on the main drag.

I slammed my foot on the brake, but it took too long. I plowed into the small four-door sedan.

Metal crunched on metal.

Shit.

CHAPTER TWENTY-ONE

ARIELLA

I felt like a stupid teenager, glancing out the window shades, waiting for Hazel to show up.

We weren't best friends, but I didn't know too many people in town, and small towns weren't easy for making friends, especially in winter.

Although winter was thankfully behind us, it didn't make it any easier to meet new people when I spent most of my days working and evenings with Jaxson and Izzie. I held no regrets.

Jaxson had already left for the day to go to the set of the film production. While I wanted him to play hooky with us, someone had to be the responsible one.

A pickup truck entered the driveway and pulled up out front of the house. Mason was behind the wheel.

Hazel climbed out and gave a wave before sauntering up to the front door.

I shut off the alarm and swung open the door before she had time to knock. "Are you ready?" I tried to hide the enthusiasm from my voice, but I was failing at it miserably.

"Yes, but it's taken me all morning to convince Mason not to follow us to the spa. He made me promise that I would call him when we check-in and again when we leave," Hazel said.

I'd have thought he was overprotective if it wasn't for the fact we'd both been kidnapped and taken against our will too many times recently. "Jaxson made me promise the same thing, plus he's tracking my phone."

"Oh, my gosh!" Hazel squealed. She threw her arms around me, greeting me with a proper hello.

Mason turned the truck around and headed out of the driveway and back down the mountain.

"Are you ready for a girls' day?" I armed the alarm and shut the door, locking it behind myself.

Hazel hurried to my car and waited by the passenger side door. It was clear she was as excited as I was to get out and have some fun.

In a matter of minutes, we were on our way. I sat behind the wheel, talking animatedly with Hazel. "You have to tell me everything about what's been going on in your life."

We'd been texting each other on occasion, but there was so much to catch up on. She had moved in with Mason after he'd been shot, and we hadn't spent any time alone to chat about what that had been like.

"My life has been surrounded by Mason, and that's it," Hazel said. "Imagine caring for Jaxson twenty-four-seven."

That didn't sound so terrible. "That much fun." She didn't sound like she had enjoyed it.

Mason was a handsome guy, and while I hadn't exactly gotten off on the right foot with him, it seemed the two of them shared a history together.

"Well, playing nurse, in the beginning, was fun, especially when he had me dress up in a sexy costume," Hazel said.

I glanced at her and caught her blushing as she stared out the window. "And?" I turned off the mountain pass and headed across the main road toward the spa.

"It's kind of hard to do anything when he's on bed rest and not allowed to engage in fun activities. It was torture playing nurse, not being able to do the things I wanted to do to him."

Giggling, I bit my bottom lip. "That isn't the case anymore, though. Right?" It had been weeks since he'd been shot, and the doctor had cleared him for desk duty.

"Well, we've had to take it slow," Hazel said. "I mean, I'm sure he wants to do more, and so do I, but he has needed time to heal."

"I understand."

"Do you? I know you think that you and Jaxson are a secret, but it's a really obvious secret. Like everyone in Breckenridge probably knows," Hazel said.

I gripped the steering wheel harder. "Please tell me you're joking."

Hazel stared at me as I focused on the road. "Am I wrong? Are you seriously telling me that the two of you are just friends?"

A deer leaped across the road, and I slammed on my brakes to keep from plowing into the creature.

The seatbelt locked in place from the abrupt stop.

Seconds later, we were thrown forward, metal ground together, as someone ran into us.

My heart hammered in my chest. "Are you okay?" I asked.

"Yeah."

I glanced in the rearview mirror. "Harper?" I whispered, unlocking the door.

I unbuckled my seatbelt and stepped out, surprised to see that she'd been the one who rammed into my car.

Hazel stepped out of the passenger side too. "Are you okay?" Hazel asked.

"Yeah, I'm fine." Just a bit shaken up, but relieved it was only Harper.

My first fear had been that Ben had found me.

Was that irrational? He was out there, somewhere.

Would I always be looking over my shoulder?

There were no recent hotel or other credit card receipts to

determine where he'd gone, no cell phone that we'd found and been able to track.

"I'm so sorry," Harper apologized. "I didn't see your car stopped around the bend."

A pickup truck slowed on its approach.

"Seriously?" Hazel muttered under her breath.

Was she grumbling about Harper hitting us or the approaching driver?

CHAPTER TWENTY-TWO

HARPER

"I'm sorry," I apologized again. "I didn't see you stopped. We can just exchange insurance and be on our way."

I stepped closer, getting a better look at the two young women I'd rear-ended. "You're the girl from the film set. The one who was taken."

I would never forget that moment.

It was forever ingrained in my mind.

The brunette exhaled a heavy sigh. "I should probably thank you for trying to stop Ben."

I hadn't succeeded, but at least she was alive. "I'm glad you're okay," I said.

She was all right, wasn't she?

She had a bandage on her cheek but otherwise looked all right.

A pickup truck slowed and pulled over behind us.

The two girls didn't look flustered, just angry. Was it because I hit their car? It was an accident. "Again, I'm sorry. I'll pay for the damage."

"Is everyone okay?" a gruff voice asked, his window rolled down.

"We're fine, Mason," Ariella said. "I can't believe you're following us!"

I reached into my pocket for my phone.

Did I need to call for help? Would Lincoln come if I called him?

"How about I give Hazel, Ariella, and you a lift? I can drop the girls off at the spa and drive you wherever you need to go." Mason said. "Pull your car over to the side of the road, and I'll give Declan's shop a call to get the cars towed and repaired."

Mine was a rental. "That isn't necessary." I didn't know this guy. The two girls did, but I wasn't climbing into his truck.

"Fine," Ariella grumbled. She moved her car and tossed Mason her car keys. The back of her vehicle had buckled from impact and had taken the brunt of the damage compared to my rental.

"Are you sure it's safe?" I asked, whispering my question to Ariella.

She was one of the security teams for the production set. If she trusted going with him, then it was okay.

Right?

"He's my boyfriend," Hazel said. "He'll take you wherever you need to go in town."

"You should come with us to the spa," Ariella said.

Gosh, that sounded perfect. However, I had a production to shoot. I couldn't bail two days in a row, even if I had been in a car accident. It didn't help that the crash had been my fault.

"I can't," I said.

"How about you come by after you're finished filming?" Ariella asked. "We have a girls' night in tonight."

"With wine!" Hazel added. It was clear she was excited and probably needed a break from whatever she did for a living.

Hell, I needed one too.

"You should come," Hazel said.

That sounded amazing. "Just the girls?" I'd miss spending the evening with Lincoln, but he was just a fling.

Wasn't he?

Besides, he had lied about working security on set. Some time apart wasn't a bad idea.

In a few short days, I'd be finished filming and back in Los Angeles.

"Yes," Ariella said. "I'll text you the information if you don't mind giving me your phone number."

I didn't want to admit the jealousy that seeped through my veins as Mason dropped me off at the set.

The director didn't look thrilled that I was late, again. He stormed toward me, and before he could blast me with being irresponsible or not caring about the role, I offered up an apology.

"I'm sorry," I said, quick to apologize on my way to makeup.

I didn't stop to make small talk or even offer up an excuse.

"Where the hell is your bodyguard?" the director fumed, stomping behind me.

I swallowed the lump buried in my throat. "Bodyguard?" I repeated.

My voice was hoarse. He'd caught me off-guard.

"I have a bodyguard?"

Is that why Lincoln had insisted on jumping into the damned river to go rafting with me? Even after I'd left him at the dock, he'd rented a raft and caught up with me.

I'd been fooled into thinking that he'd wanted to spend time with me.

That I'd meant something to him!

Tears threatened my vision.

The director scoffed under his breath. "Of course, you have someone watching your every move. Do you honestly believe the studio trusted you after the last incident when you worked for me?"

The sun beat down, and the air felt hot, suffocating.

"You don't know anything about me." I hurried into the makeup trailer and slammed the door shut behind myself, locking it.

The young woman, Melissa, sat on the bed. Her attention had been on her phone when I burst through the door. "Sorry I'm late. I rear-ended a car on my way in this morning."

Her eyes widened, and she stood. "Are you okay?" Her eyes raked over me.

Did I not look okay? "Fine, just a little off today."

It was hard not to be flustered from it, along with the argument from the director which didn't even take into account what I'd heard about Lincoln.

He was my bodyguard, wasn't he?

I'd seen him on set and off. Almost every night, he'd been with me since the moment that I had arrived in town.

Had that been planned?

My instincts told me to run, but without a car, I had no way of leaving. I slumped into the chair in front of the mirror, a scowl etched to my face as Melissa towered from above.

"Any chance I can borrow your car?"

CHAPTER TWENTY-THREE

LINCOLN

I'd snatched the bastard's phone and smashed it into a thousand tiny pieces on the ground before leaving the coffee shop.

How dare he take pictures of Harper when she explicitly asked him not to do so and even had invited him onto the set.

What a creep!

The twat had made me lose sight of Harper. I was supposed to keep an eye on her, even from a distance, but I had neglected to do that. Showing up at the coffee shop just moments behind her hadn't been a coincidence.

My phone had been set with an alarm to alert me when she'd been on the move.

I hurried toward the set, slowing the truck down, when I noticed her car and Ariella's both banged up on the side of the road.

I slammed my hand against the steering wheel. "Shit."

Where was she now?

Using my vehicle's hands-free device, I phoned Jaxson.

"Everything okay? Where are you?" Jaxson asked.

"Running late. Harper seems to have trouble follow her. I had to deal with a reporter, and I'm almost at the set, but I noticed two cars on the side of the road, and one of them was Harper's," I said. I didn't further elaborate, not wanting to worry Jaxson.

Had Ariella called him?

Where had the girls gone? Did a stranger pick them up?

"Harper just showed up a few minutes ago. The director seems pretty pissed. I should warn you. He let it slip about the studio hiring a bodyguard for her."

Why the hell had the director gone and done that? Was it to make my life miserable?

"Wonderful," I muttered under my breath. There was little chance Harper was going to let me spend the evening with her and keep an eye on her.

I wasn't concerned about her alone at the hotel. It was what trouble she might land herself in while on her own.

She had never just been an assignment. I wanted to spend time with her.

By now, word had begun to spread about a Hollywood starlet and film crew in the valley. The last thing I needed was Harper to have more press hounding her.

"Ariella called me on the way to the spa. She invited Harper over for a girls' night tonight."

Interesting. Since when had Harper made friends with Ariella? I hadn't seen them together except for the two cars abandoned on the side of the road. "Did Ariella mention anything about her car?"

"Yeah, Harper plowed into her when the girls stopped short from hitting a deer that ran across the road," Jaxson said.

He didn't seem angry with Harper about the accident. "Was everyone okay?"

I pulled into the parking lot of the production set and shut off the truck. I grabbed my phone as it switched from the speakers back to my cell phone.

"Just a little shaken up. Ariella and Hazel went to the spa as planned. Mason gave all of them a ride."

Climbing out of the truck, I breathed a sigh of relief. At least it wasn't Ben who had snatched the girls or forced them to go with him.

Most of the town's folk were friendly and would happily offer a lift, but there were a few people who had once lived off-grid who would have worried me.

The majority of those folks had died a few months ago in an ambush. There were a few people who mysteriously survived. Those were the guys who I worried about, the ones who had gotten away unscathed.

I slung my credentials around my neck. The lanyard swung as I strolled toward the set at a quickened pace. While I hadn't intended on being late, it wasn't in good form.

Catching sight of Jaxson, we ended the call, and I shoved my phone into my pocket. I kept an eye on Harper's trailer. I doubted she was in there. She was probably with hair and makeup or wardrobe getting ready.

From across the lawn a few strides away, the director had his phone plastered to his ear as he pounded on one of the trailers.

"You can kiss your career goodbye!" the director shouted.

The trailer door swung open, and Harper stomped down the steps.

Jaxson and I exchanged glances. We'd been hired to protect Harper and keep the set free from bystanders. But she didn't seem like she needed looking after right now.

She could take care of herself.

"Really?" she snorted and stormed up to face him. While she was shorter, she didn't look the least bit intimidated by him. "Maybe I should call your wife, tell her how you coerced me into taking nudes so I'd get my first lead role and then proceeded to share them with the tabloids?"

The director's face turned bright red. "You wanted to take those photographs."

"The hell I did!" Harper shouted. She didn't seem to care who heard her or what was said.

I waited for steam to shoot out of the director's ears. "When the studio fires you, don't come crawling back to me to help your career."

He stormed off and threw his clipboard onto the grass like a child having a temper tantrum.

Her hands balled into fists.

She turned on her heels and landed her gaze on me.

Shit.

CHAPTER TWENTY-FOUR

HARPER

The director was a grade-A asshole.

I'd dealt with him one too many times, and today I wasn't in the mood to button my lips and walk on eggshells.

Someone else could do that for him.

I didn't care if I got axed from the gig. It was a crummy acting job for a film that probably would have tanked anyway.

Lincoln watched me from across the set.

Had he seen the outburst between the director and me?

Great.

I ran a hand through my hair, not giving a crap about the production anymore. The director had stormed off, and I wasn't in the mood to put on a happy face and pretend to be someone I'm not.

Some days I could fall into the role, but after the accident this morning, my world felt upside down.

It didn't help to hear that Lincoln had been hired by the studio as my personal bodyguard.

He didn't hesitate in the slightest. Lincoln approached me, closing the distance between us.

How much had he heard from the director? I pinched the bridge of my nose. If he was here to give me a lecture on acting professional or some other crap, I wasn't in the mood.

"Are you all right?" Lincoln asked, his voice soft and calm yet firm.

"No." Nothing felt all right.

My world spun wildly out of control and while I may have been reckless and stupid yesterday, running off set during filming, today was a new day. I had vowed to take the job seriously and respect the time of the cast and crew.

Little good that had done.

The truth was I wanted to run, but I didn't have a car. It was on the side of the road. Maybe I should have driven it to the set. At least I would have had a vehicle to get around in still. However, I wasn't sure if it was safe to drive. The front end had quite a bit of damage.

The remaining cast members and crew began to pack up for the day, again. With the director gone, it meant another day without shooting.

"Want me to take you somewhere?" Lincoln asked.

Another security guard approached the two of us. "Everything all right?" he asked.

I glanced at his name badge: *Jaxson.* "You're Ariella's husband, right?"

He looked taken aback by the question. "I'm not her husband. We're just friends. Colleagues."

"Oh, my apologizes." I had thought they were together when she had called him while in Mason's truck and mentioned that he wasn't going to be home tonight during girls' night.

I was mistaken. "I misunderstood. Can you give me a lift to the spa where the girls are? I could use a me day."

I didn't want Lincoln to drive me anywhere and Melissa hadn't been willing to part with the keys to her car. Not that I blamed her, I wouldn't have given me the keys either after I'd smashed my rental.

Jaxson glanced at Lincoln before nodding. "Yes, of course. Follow me."

"Thank you." I left Lincoln standing there as I hurried out to the parking lot with Jaxson.

It wasn't that I didn't trust Lincoln, I did, but I was also seething inside for what he'd done.

He'd lied to me. He had every opportunity yesterday while we were rafting, or even the previous day, to come clean.

No, instead, he'd kept his dirty little secret.

"Everything okay?" Jaxson asked. He unlocked his truck, and I stepped around to the passenger side while he climbed in behind the wheel.

"Just peachy."

He laughed under his breath. "Gosh, you sound like my daughter."

"You have a kid?" Was Ariella the mother? That made sense, why they might have lived together.

He smiled, tightlipped, not answering my question. He seemed protective of his daughter. That wasn't such a bad trait.

Sighing, I glanced back at the studio as Jaxson pulled out of the parking lot. There was no sign of Lincoln. "Hey, can I ask you something?"

"Shoot," Jaxson said.

Had it been a coincidence that Lincoln had found me at the coffee shop earlier that morning? "If you had to find someone and track them down, how do you go about doing it?"

Jaxson turned the radio down and shifted in the driver's seat.

He glanced at me, eyebrow raised. He didn't answer my question.

"Hypothetically?"

Silence filled the truck.

"If you're wondering how Lincoln knew you were at the river, we traced your cell phone location."

It hadn't even occurred to me to ditch my phone.

I wouldn't make that same mistake.

I headed into the spa and made a reservation for a massage. I had twenty minutes until my appointment.

Glancing at my watch, I dug my phone out of my pocket and tossed it into the nearby trash. "Track me now," I muttered to myself.

Lincoln knew where I was, but he wouldn't know when I left or where I went afterward.

I doubted the production would continue. With the director pissed and threatening to contact the studio, I would be fired by morning.

I refused to grovel or beg for his forgiveness. He was the reason the studio forced a bodyguard on me, insisting that I couldn't be trusted. I didn't need protection. I wasn't helpless or a damsel in distress, damnit!

While I'd made mistakes and done things that I shouldn't have, on those rare occasions, I'd been drugged or coerced.

The sins of the past followed me like a shadow that I was unable to escape.

"Harper?"

"Ariella?" Hazel stood beside her. "I thought you both had spa appointments?" Were they done already?

"Our appointments got pushed back when we ran late this morning. They were really nice, giving us a later time. What are you doing here?" Ariella asked. "Did you decide to join us for a girls' day?"

I definitely needed to unwind. "Yes, you could say that."

"Do you want me to try to book us all together?" Ariella asked.

"Sure." I could use the company and a friendly face. "Thanks."

Ariella hurried to the receptionist and explained how the three of us were friends and asked if there was anything that could be done to put us all together for our appointments.

Every inch of my body ached.

The car accident had been to blame, and while it was entirely my fault, it didn't make everything hurt any less.

A blissful ninety minutes of a hottie giving me a full body massage had been quite a treat.

As angry as I was at Lincoln, the heat had dissipated, and I felt much more relaxed.

We all got facials after our full body massages and then manicures and pedicures.

While the morning had started off as a bust, at least the afternoon was definitely getting better. We finished at the spa, and Hazel called Mason to give us a lift back to Ariella's place.

Hazel shoved her phone into her pocket. "He'll be a little while. He's with Jaxson grabbing lunch. They suggested we grab a bite to eat too."

"Is there any place we can eat around here?" I asked. I wasn't familiar with the town.

"Follow us. We know this town inside and out," Ariella said.

They led me to a small café next door. The place seemed crowded for the middle of the week. We waited a few minutes to be seated and were escorted to a table.

Conversations around us clashed together, the noise in the restaurant rising with each other's voices. While it was difficult to hear Ariella and Hazel, it wasn't particularly hard to hear the gentleman one table over, situated behind me.

It seemed the restaurant had added an extra table and chairs to accommodate us, but leaving us very little room of our own.

"I'll offer you double your asking price," the gentleman said. He had an Italian accent, and I tried not to glance over my back to him. I felt like I was in his lap.

"And why would you do that, Enzo?" another male voice asked.

Enzo? I recognized that name.

No.

It couldn't be. I held my breath and refused to turn around to see if it was true.

Enzo Ricci.

The girls read over their menus. I pretended to be interested in mine as I listened to the conversation going on behind me. It was impossible not to hear whatever deal was being made between them.

Could Ariella and Hazel hear it too?

They didn't seem interested. Maybe they were too far away. The restaurant was loud and rather chaotic.

"I prefer to buy out my competition as opposed to other methods," Enzo said.

I swallowed the lump in my throat. The voice no longer just familiar, but I was certain that it was Enzo Ricci, my husband.

CHAPTER TWENTY-FIVE

ARIELLA

Harper held her menu up, oblivious to the fact that I'd tried getting her attention. The restaurant was crowded and busy, but she seemed distracted.

"I don't think she hears you," Hazel said.

I put my menu down, waiting for Harper to glance up.

She didn't budge in the slightest.

Our table was sandwiched into the café, giving very little elbow room, let alone space for privacy.

While I couldn't make out any distinct conversations, I noticed Jayden sitting at the table just behind Harper.

I hadn't met him firsthand, but I knew of him. Everyone in Breckenridge by now knew he was one of the few surviving off-gridders.

How had he survived the massacre from the Russian mob when they'd blown in and slaughtered everyone?

I didn't recognize the gentleman Jayden was with. I couldn't recall ever seeing him before in town. The mysterious man wore an expensive suit and was sharply dressed, obviously well off.

It stood out, with Jayden in his dark black jeans and a white t-shirt that hugged his chest. He was tall but not taller than the mysterious man who sat across from him.

"Harper," I said, trying again to steal away her attention from the menu.

She lowered the menu, her eyes wide, filled with trepidation.

"What is it?" I asked.

Had she forgotten her wallet or something? She looked terrified.

"I need to—" Harper stood and didn't finish her sentence. She grabbed her purse off her chair and high-tailed it out of the restaurant.

"Bathroom?" I guessed, glancing at Hazel. Maybe she could decrypt what I had missed. Where else had she gone off to?

Hazel sipped her glass of water. "You go check on her. I'll wait here."

"Thanks." I stood and hurried after Harper, trying to figure out what happened.

What had I missed?

Maybe she wasn't feeling well. I followed her into the bathroom.

Harper stood hovering over the sink, her hands on either side of the porcelain. The color had drained from her face.

"What's going on?" I asked.

"I heard his voice."

"Whose?" I asked, taking a step closer. I rested a hand on her back. Her body trembled.

"Enzo, my husband."

Shit.

Since when was she married? I ran a hand through my hair, surprised by the news. "You're married?" My voice squeaked, betraying me. Lincoln would be even more shocked than I was, and not happy about it.

I'd never heard about her marrying anyone, but then again, I did not read the tabloids or check out the gossip columns in the entertainment papers. I had heard of Harper Madison before her arrival in Breckenridge.

"I met him in Vegas during a film shoot. He was romantic,

charming, and I got really drunk. The rest is a blur, except that I woke up the next morning with his enormous diamond ring on my finger," Harper said.

"What did you do?"

"I ran. A few months ago, I saw a segment on television about the mafia and organized crime across America. Enzo was featured with his buddies, the same guys who had liquored me up that night."

"Shit," I cursed under my breath. The bathroom door swung open, and I froze, worried that Enzo might storm in and join us.

He didn't.

It was one of the waitresses. She headed for a stall.

Breathing a sigh of relief, I waited until the main door swung shut to speak. "We'll get through this. Mason is on the way. He won't let anything happen to you. Did Enzo see you?" It couldn't be a coincidence that he'd shown up in Breckenridge.

Harper rubbed her forehead and splashed cold water on her face. "No, I don't think so."

"That's good," I said. "I can head back to the table, get the check, and have Hazel meet us outside."

The waitress stepped out from the stall. "Are you okay?" she asked. "Do you need me to help?"

"I think we're okay," Harper said, offering a faint smile.

I texted Hazel to meet us outside, that we'd have to grab something to eat later, and then Mason to hurry, that we had a problem.

Hopefully, he'd make it before Enzo spotted us.

I stepped out of the bathroom first, making sure no one was waiting outside to snatch Harper. I had no idea whether Enzo was violent or not.

Had he come to Breckenridge to claim his wife and bring her home with him?

"Come on." I led her through the hallway and made a sharp right heading out of the restaurant. I glanced back toward the table, but it was too hard to see if Hazel had left already or if Enzo was still seated with Jayden.

What did Enzo and Jayden have in common? Why were they having lunch together?

We hurried out through the main exit and stood outside, catching up with Hazel.

"What's going on?" Hazel asked. "Are you okay?" Her attention was entirely on Harper.

Harper wrapped her arms around herself. "I just ran into someone who shouldn't be here."

She didn't elaborate.

Was she worried that if she told Hazel, Lincoln would eventually find out? I couldn't keep it a secret. It was too big, and Harper was in danger.

Wasn't she?

Mason pulled the truck up out front and unlocked the doors. "Are you guys okay?"

"We are now," Harper said. She yanked the back door open and hopped into the back seat. I climbed in beside her.

Were we seriously not going to talk about Enzo and the fact she'd married him? If it had been a moment of regret that she didn't remember, there were ways to fix it.

Divorce was the first option that crossed my mind.

What was she afraid of?

CHAPTER TWENTY-SIX

HARPER

Mason drove us to Ariella's house on the mountain.

I glanced every so often behind us, making sure that Enzo hadn't followed us.

Would he be waiting outside my hotel room tonight when I went home?

How long could I avoid him?

"Is anyone going to tell me why I had to rush over?" Mason asked.

"I don't know," Hazel said. She glanced out the side window. "Maybe Ariella or Harper can answer you."

"Thanks for that," Ariella huffed under her breath. "We saw someone we didn't want to converse with and thought it would be a good idea to leave."

Hazel shifted around in the front seat to face us. "Before we even ordered lunch? You're keeping secrets from me, and I don't like it."

Mason glanced up in the rearview mirror. His gaze landed on me. If I told him, wouldn't he tell all his buddies, and it would get back to Lincoln?

No, thank you.

"You're going to have to tell him," Ariella said. She nudged me with her elbow. "You can trust Mason."

"Right? So, he can go back and tell Lincoln?" I exhaled a loud sigh and folded my arms across my chest. "That's the last thing I need right now, more drama."

I wasn't talking to Lincoln right now. I'd just gotten over the fact that he worked security detail for the set, and today I'd discovered that he had been my bodyguard.

To say I was pissed at him, was an understatement. I couldn't even look at him without boiling over.

Had every night that we'd spent together, under the stars or shacked up in my trailer, been because of his job?

Ariella's voice was soft and quiet as she spoke. "Enzo is here for a reason."

I knew that. It was why my stomach was in knots, and I wanted nothing more than to go home.

I'd trashed my cell phone. I had no idea if the studio had contacted me to fire me.

Maybe I could lie low, hide out with Ariella for a few days, and just let this shit storm that brewed pass over.

Mason cleared his throat. "Does Enzo have a last name?" He didn't even pretend that he couldn't hear what was said between us.

"No." My jaw firm, I refused to give it up. If I did, then he'd find out the truth, that I was married to Enzo.

Mason pulled the vehicle up to the front of the house and turned off the engine. He climbed out with us, walking up to the front door.

Was he just making sure that we got inside, or was he planning on staying?

We followed up to the porch, and Ariella dug out her key. She unlocked the door and let us inside while she disarmed the alarm. "It's girls' night, which means you need to leave," Ariella said, pushing Mason out the door.

He took several strides backward but remained on the porch. "Set the alarm and don't answer the door for anyone," Mason said.

"Relax. Jaxson will be home late tonight. I promise not to let anything happen to your girlfriend," Ariella teased.

"Bye!" Hazel blew him a kiss and waved, giggling. "Shut the door!"

Ariella slammed the front door and armed the alarm.

I stood by the window, watching Mason retreat to his truck. "Is he really leaving?" I asked.

"He'd better," Hazel said, flipping on the lights, making herself at home. "Where's the wine?"

"How's Bear?" Ariella asked.

"Super cute and cuddly," Hazel said. "She's the dog we adopted from Mason's uncle when he died. She is honestly the cutest. I can't see how she doesn't like people. I swear all she does is lick me or cuddle me."

"Sounds like Mason," Ariella giggled, taking another sip of wine.

"Shut it!" Hazel's eyes narrowed as she glared at Ariella.

"What about you?" Ariella turned her attention to me.

"No pets," I said, answering a little too quickly, hoping the conversation was more along the lines of animals than boyfriends.

Hazel tilted her head back, finishing her glass of red wine. She grabbed the bottle and refilled her glass. "Anyone else?"

"I'm good." I didn't need a headache later or to be hungover. I was still on edge after spotting Enzo at the restaurant.

"Fill my glass," Ariella said, wiggling her glass in front of the wine bottle.

"You have to hold it still or I'll make a mess," Hazel said. "I can't pour into a glass that's all over the place."

"That's my tremor."

"No, it's you being drunk," Hazel said with a snort. "Nice try."

"Hey, I walk straighter when I'm drunk," Ariella retorted.

Hazel shook her head and rolled her eyes. "Do you see what I deal with?" She turned her attention back to Ariella. "No, you don't walk straighter when you're drunk. You just don't realize that you're falling over. It's quite amusing."

I sipped my drink, taking in the banter between the two of them. "How long have you two known each other?" I asked.

It seemed like they'd been friends forever.

"Not that long," Hazel answered. "We became friends through work." She lifted the glass to her lips.

Was she avoiding the question? I wasn't quite sure.

"We should toilet paper the neighbor's house!" Ariella squealed. Her eyes were wide and filled with excitement.

That sounded like a terrible idea. "We aren't supposed to leave the house," I said. Why did I get stuck being the responsible person?

"It's dark. What's going to happen in the dark?" Ariella giggled. She finished her glass. I'd only counted two. She mustn't have consumed alcohol very often, or she was a complete lightweight.

"Only murders and kidnappings," Hazel said with a straight face before she burst out laughing. She finished her second glass and poured a third. "Gosh, I need to get laid."

"What?" Ariella spun around on her heels. "Do you mean to tell me that you and Mason haven't done anything—"

Hazel stammered to the front door, pushed the curtains aside as she glanced outside. "I wanted to. You don't know how hard it is to play nurse and not do sexy things with Mason, but he had to heal, and doctor's orders were no sex. Too bad I was only a nurse and couldn't override the doctor's advice."

"Girl, what are you doing with us tonight?" I asked. "It's clear he wants you. I see you want him. Go to him, or since you don't have a car, call him."

"Yes, call him and have phone sex with him," Ariella said, giggling and clapping her hands.

"Oh my gosh! You two are troublemakers," Hazel muttered. She covered her face with her hands.

My stomach grumbled. "I'm hungry. We should order a pizza. Give me your phone." My purse sat at my feet, but I'd already tossed my phone. The decision was spontaneous and not without regret right now.

Hazel dropped her hand into her lap. "Why? You'll just call Mason and embarrass me."

"I won't, I swear." I saluted her.

"I think you're supposed to link pinkies," Ariella said. "Or you could just use my phone." She dug her smartphone out of her pocket. "Here."

Ariella unlocked her phone and handed it to me. "Any recommendations on where to call?" I asked. I didn't know any local pizza places.

After we narrowed down the restaurant and the type of pizza we wanted, I made the call and offered up my credit card to pay. I handed the phone back to Ariella to give the address.

Not even twenty minutes later, there was a firm knock at the door.

"That was quick!" I leaped up and hurried to answer the door.

Ariella shut off the alarm while I unlocked the door without so much as looking out the window or through the peephole which happened to be much too high for me.

A tall, burly gentleman with the same eyes and hair as Enzo towered above me. Time felt as though it stood still. A flash of recognition crossed my gaze. I pushed the door closed, but he shoved his foot inside and thrust it open hard, which forced me to stumble backward.

He flashed a glimpse of his gun holstered to him. "Don't touch that alarm," the stranger said with a thick Italian accent. "Back away slowly. Go, sit on the sofa with the other girl."

Ariella didn't turn around. She slowly shuffled back toward the couch, but never turned her back on him.

How did he find me? "Did Enzo send you?" I asked.

Why else was he here?

"You're coming with me," he said with a dark, sinister laugh.

He wanted me. I didn't need to put their lives in jeopardy.

He tilted his head, staring at me with his eyes of steel. "Isn't it awful running away from your husband? Enzo can take care of you, protect you."

"I'm not his wife," I scoffed at his notion of marriage. "We were in Vegas, and I was drunk, thanks to you and your buddies."

Had they drugged me too? The whole night was a blur.

Ariella stepped between the thug and me. "She's not going with you." She stood her ground. "You need to leave."

He backhanded Ariella across the face. "No one speaks to me in that tone," he growled. His top lip snarled, and the thug leaned in and grabbed Ariella's shirt. He yanked her close and held her tight. "A pretty girl like you, I'll bet you'd sell real quick."

Ariella slammed her fist upward into his jaw.

His eyes flinched, the only evidence of her assault on him. "Is that how you treat guests?" he asked. He unclenched his fist, letting Ariella free. He pushed her backward, forcing her to sit on the couch, as he had initially instructed her to do.

"You're not a guest," Ariella spat.

He thrust his gun from its holster, pointing it at Ariella's forehead. "Are you sure about that?"

I couldn't let anything happen to my new friends. "Please, I'll go with you, just whatever you do, don't hurt them."

He yanked me by the hair and dragged me outside. I didn't fight back. How could I without risking my new friends' lives?

He pulled out a set of metal handcuffs. "Hands behind your back!" he barked.

I did as instructed, and he snapped on the cuffs nice and tight. It dug into my flesh, piercing my skin.

He thrust open the back door and pointed for me to climb inside the car. I hurried inside, and he shoved a black bag over my head, making it impossible to see where he took me. He slammed the door shut.

Another door slam.

Within seconds, the car roared to life. He hit the gas, tearing away from the house.

Where was he taking me?

Would I ever see my friends again? What about my home? I had nothing with me. My purse was abandoned on the floor in Ariella's house, and my cell phone trashed hours earlier.

I needed help, and I didn't have the slightest clue what he wanted with me.

"Why are you doing this?" I asked, my voice tentative and afraid.

"Shut up!"

CHAPTER TWENTY-SEVEN

LINCOLN

"What do you mean, she's been taken? Who the hell grabbed her?" I paced the length of Jaxson's home, a lovely house, but at the moment, it felt small and confining.

The police were on the scene, taking Ariella and Hazel's statements.

Jaxson called me the moment he found out what had happened, when Ariella called him in tears.

She'd been sobbing about an intruder and another man named Enzo, and the rest had been hard to decipher until she had calmed down.

"I don't know his name, but he works for her husband," Hazel said a little too calmly.

My poker face was not doing me justice. "She's married?"

Why hadn't Harper told me that she was married to another man?

"It's clear the guy's a real winner," I muttered under my breath.

"Now's not the time," Jaxson said. He shot me a look of cool off or walk out. I wasn't leaving the scene. I needed to know every detail, whatever it took to find her, alive.

Ariella took a long, slow breath. "She didn't seem to know the man's name, but they kept talking about Enzo, her husband. It was clear she recognized the man who took her. Harper explained to me that she'd gotten married under false pretenses. She was in Vegas, inebriated, and by the sounds of it, maybe they'd even drugged her. She was scared of him, Lincoln."

My hands balled into fists at my side. "Bastards," I muttered. I'd kill anyone who ever harmed a hair on Harper's head.

Maybe she wasn't mine, but I wanted to protect her.

No, I *needed* to protect her. She needed someone to look out for her. She'd probably never had that in her entire life.

"There's something else you should know," Ariella said. She fiddled with her hands. "Enzo was at the restaurant this afternoon. That's why Harper panicked, but he wasn't alone."

"Who was with him?" Jaxson asked before I could say a word. "The man who came to the house and took her?"

"No, Jayden Scott," Ariella said.

The room spun. My jaw clenched, and I stopped pacing. "I'll kill him."

Jaxson turned toward me, his arms folded across his chest. "Go take a walk."

I opened my mouth to respond, but he pointed toward the door. I knew he was right, trying to protect me. I couldn't make threats like that in front of the sheriff. What if the bastard winded up dead?

Good!

I stormed out of the house and slammed the door behind myself. The ground crunched under my feet as I stomped over the gravel toward my truck. The night air was cool but not frigid.

Why had one of Enzo's goons shown up and taken her?

Why did Jayden have lunch with Enzo? I climbed into my truck and started the engine.

The front door of the house opened, and Jaxson stepped out and stood on the porch.

"Where are you going?" he shouted.

I didn't answer him. He knew me well enough to know where I was headed.

I needed to speak to Jayden.

I tore down the mountain at lightning speed and headed for Jayden's newest place of employment. If I was lucky, he was working a shift. If I wasn't, then I didn't know where I'd find him.

His house had been demolished with the off-gridders during the attack about six weeks ago. The land had been abandoned, and I hadn't heard of anyone living up there again.

He was out there somewhere, getting into who the hell knows what trouble.

The road was dry, which made for plenty of traction as I hurried to the bar. I slammed on the brakes, shut off the engine, and jumped out of the truck, rushing inside.

My feet thudded against the floor, ready for a fight. Jayden barely so much as paid me any attention on my entrance.

"I'm just saying, I know how to move merchandise," Ben said as he sat at the bar, nursing a beer, speaking to Jayden.

I'd recognize that scumbag anywhere.

What the hell was Ben still doing in Breckenridge? Were the authorities out looking for him? Although at the moment, they were all tied up at Jaxson's house dealing with Harper's disappearance. Had he known that?

"Benjamin Ryan," I said with a gruffness as I headed straight for the two most wanted men of Breckenridge and not for their charm or charisma.

Ben dug out a wad of cash and dropped it on the counter. He shot one look at me, eyes wide, and darted out the back door.

Fuck.

Do I chase him down or deal with Jayden?

I couldn't be in two places at once, and the rest of the Eagle Tactical team was busy. Grabbing my phone, I texted Jaxson to give him a heads up.

If he wanted to come down and string up Ben by the balls, then, by all means, I wanted him to have the opportunity.

Sighing, my choice had already been made up. Maybe I should have gone after Ben, since he was still a threat to Ariella, but I needed to find Harper. She was the one in danger right this moment.

"We need to talk." I thundered around behind the bar, closing in on Jayden's personal space.

He wasn't the least bit smaller or less intimidating than I was, but he knew I'd kick his ass. We'd served together as brothers overseas.

Over the last few years, we'd become estranged. He'd been tied up in some dirty shit with the off-gridders that hadn't ended well for him.

"I don't have anything to say," Jayden quipped.

Maybe it was time for him to clean up and shape up.

"Are you sure about that?" I stared him down. "You were seen having lunch with a gentleman by the name of Enzo."

Jayden shrugged, not denying the truth. "So I was, since when is having a meal a crime?"

"Did you consort with Enzo and his goons in a plan to kidnap Harper Madison?" I grabbed Jayden by his shirt lapels, demanding an answer.

"What? No. I don't know anything about that," Jayden said, shrugging me off him.

I let go, only because I believed him. "Did you happen to know that Harper was allegedly married to Enzo?"

He stepped back, putting distance between us. "Is that supposed to mean something to me? I don't care who he marries or what he does with the women he desires," Jayden said.

"You ought to care, because she's been abducted and forced to do God knows what against her will."

Jayden grabbed a rag from the bar and began shining the wood surface. "Maybe it wasn't against her will. Perhaps she liked it, or maybe, better yet, she wanted to go with him."

I launched forward and pummeled him with my fist. "You bastard!" With my fist, I gripped him by the back of the head and slammed his face against the edge of the bar.

"Okay! Okay!" Jayden shouted, his nose bloody.

I let go, not intending to kill him, just force him to tell me the truth. He owed me that much after all I did for him when we served together.

"I don't know where she is or who took her," Jayden said.

I raised my fist, and he held up a hand to indicate that he wasn't done.

"Enzo bought some land around here, under a pseudo corporation. He's expanding his enterprise and planning on finishing what the off-gridders started some time ago."

"And what is that, exactly?"

Jayden's jaw was tight. A flash of something crossed his face.

Was it fear?

"Not for me to say, but he might take your girl there. It's pretty remote, makes the off-gridders home look like paradise."

Damn. "Do you have an address?"

"Can't say I do, but I'm sure with your Eagle Tactical expertise and connections, you can figure it out."

"Does Enzo have a last name?" I asked.

"Ricci. His name is Enzo Ricci, but you didn't hear it from me."

CHAPTER TWENTY-EIGHT

HARPER

I found it difficult to breathe.

My heart hammered against my chest as I sat in the backseat, my hands bound behind my back. I couldn't free myself from the metal that dug into my skin.

Pleading with my captor wouldn't help, either. I didn't even know his name. I tried forcing the memory to surface from that night in Vegas. I'd definitely seen him before, but it was all an intense blur.

Why did Enzo want me?

Was it because I was his wife? A stupid piece of paper and words spoken had bound us together, but it could all be undone. Right?

That is, if he didn't have other plans for me.

Why was Enzo in Breckenridge? Why hadn't he tracked me down in Los Angeles or elsewhere?

Was it because there was less security on location than on the studio set?

None of it made sense.

He opened the windows of the car, the breeze loud as it whirled around me, the dark cloth making it impossible to see or feel against my face.

The car jolted as we hit a bump in the road. I wasn't buckled in and tossed around the backseat.

The driver slammed on the brakes, not helping matters, landing my face against the headrest before falling back onto my butt.

"Stay here," he grunted. He shut off the car, and the front door squeaked open and shut.

Silence.

I recognized Enzo's voice from the restaurant. "Where the fuck have you been?" Enzo demanded. His voice carried through the open window.

"I brought you a present in the backseat," he said. "Want to take a look?"

"I don't like surprises, Zan."

Zan's rough laugh sent a shudder down my spine. "I wouldn't call it a surprise, boss. She's your wife."

"Fuck!"

I swallowed the lump in my throat. My mouth dry.

"You really know how to ruin an operation," Enzo said. "You disappoint me, Zan. Do you know what I expect of men who disappoint me?"

Zan cleared his throat. "Boss, I just wanted to show my appreciation. Please, don't do this."

Was he begging?

"Bringing her here could destroy everything I've worked to achieve. I cannot have loose ends." Enzo's voice carried louder, more insistent, etched with not just disappointment but anger. His voice grew louder.

"Please," Zan begged. "I promise I'll get rid of her. No one has to know it was me."

"You idiot! She's my wife. The first place they'll check is here. They're going to be looking for me!" His voice boomed and carried through the car.

I shivered and pulled my body smaller, tighter, wanting to be invisible.

"You've disgraced the family."

"Please, Enzo. I beg of you, I have a wife and two daughters," Zan said, his voice trembling.

"Then do yourself the honorable task, or I will make sure they suffer with you."

What honorable task?

What did Enzo want Zan to do?

Was that a threat?

"Forgive me, Enzo," Zan said.

Bang!

A shudder rippled through my body.

I became one with the seat, curled up, and bent down, as I shoved my body onto the floor. Hidden.

It became harder to breathe beneath the darkened hood that covered my face. Each breath expelled from my lungs took two gulps of air to replace.

I began hyperventilating.

Heavy boots stomped over the ground. The sound came closer. The door squeaked on its hinges as it was opened.

I stayed curled up on the floor in a ball, my head bent down with the thick black bag over my head.

He yanked the material from over my face. It took no time for my eyes to adjust. It remained dark outside. I stumbled backward, moving to the opposite end of the car, away from him.

"*Tesero*, you need to come with me," Enzo said.

I shook my head. My name wasn't *Tesero*. I didn't even know what that word meant. It sounded Italian, and I didn't speak a word of Italian.

Enzo held out his hand for me.

How could I take it, even if I wanted to? My arms were behind my back, my hands cuffed.

He grabbed me by the arm and dragged me out of the car.

"Turn around," he demanded. "Face the car." I did as I was told.

How far could I run? It was difficult to see much in the darkness of night. The moon was obstructed from view, the thick clouds overhead. There weren't any nearby houses or porches with their lights on, except for the one just a few yards away.

We were in the middle of nowhere.

How long had we driven? It hadn't been that far.

Were we still in Breckenridge?

"Did you kill Zan?" I asked. I'd caught his name while the two men had been arguing about me.

His hands were rough, his fingers thick and warm. He undid the handcuffs. Was I free to go?

Enzo spun me around, trapped between him and the side of the car.

"That is none of your concern," Enzo said. His eyes were dark. "Come with me." He grabbed my arm and yanked me to follow him.

I wanted to run.

Where would I go? I had no phone, didn't know where I was or how to get away. How far was the next property? Darkness stretched on as far as I could see.

We stepped away from the car and toward the house.

Zan lay in a pool of his own blood, the metal of a gun glistening beneath the stars in his hand. Had he shot himself or had Enzo made it look like that on purpose?

"Keep walking." Enzo's clasp on my arm remained tight as he escorted me up the porch steps and inside his extravagant home.

"What do you want with me?" I asked. From what I'd heard, Enzo hadn't been behind my abduction, but why keep me? What did he intend to do with me now that I was here on his property, taken by his men?

"Relax, *Tesero*. I will have a cup of tea for you, and you will be on your way." Enzo escorted me into his home and shut the door behind us.

I trembled as I inched forward, my legs not wanting to cooperate. Hell, I didn't want to cooperate. "Let me go. Please, I won't tell anyone you were involved."

Was that what he was worried about?

The floors were made of gray and white swirled marble. My bare feet were cold over the slick material as he dragged me into what I presumed to be his office. A tall chair sat in the corner, his desk the centerpiece. "Have a seat," he said, pushing me into the dark blue velvet seat.

I collapsed into the chair, grateful his touch was no longer on my arm. There were no windows in his office. The door was the only way to escape. The room was dark with no decoration, only wallpaper that glistened from the desk lamp that remained on.

"Sit. Stay."

"I'm not a dog," I said.

"I'll be right back. Just sit tight." Enzo walked backward several strides before he slipped out the door.

I leaped from the chair and hurried toward the door. He'd locked me inside. Why had I sat there and done as he'd commanded?

Why had I followed him inside his home? I should have run when I had the opportunity.

Without an obvious way to escape, I hurried toward his desk. The mahogany was in pristine condition, the wood clean and well maintained. There were no papers left askew. I tried the drawers. Each one had been locked.

The door swung open, and Enzo stalked inside, a silver tray with two cups of tea in hand as he stared at me. "I thought I told you to sit and wait for me?"

"I don't take orders from you or anyone else."

Enzo stepped closer toward me.

I took a step back, away from his desk, wanting to keep my distance.

What did he want with me?

"I've already contacted the authorities."

"What? You did?" I didn't believe him.

Why would he do that? There was a dead body in his front yard.

Was he going to blame me for that man's death?

"They will be here soon to ask you questions. I think it would be wise for you to sit and have a drink while we wait. We could talk, get the opportunity to know a little about one another," Enzo said.

I didn't trust him, but he wasn't waving a gun at me or threatening me, either. That was at least a good sign.

"You called the police?" I asked. "Why would you do that?"

"So, they can see that I'm innocent. I took no part in your abduction. I'm not a monster."

He offered me the tea, placing the tray on the desk. "But you killed that man on your front lawn."

Enzo eyed his watch, his jaw tight. He lifted a cup, the china small and delicate, which looked almost rather comical in his large rough hands. "I don't know about you, but I could use some chamomile to calm down." He lifted the teacup to his lips and took a sip.

"Chamomile?" That was my favorite, especially when my nerves were shot. I approached the desk, the thick wood keeping a distance between us, which made me feel safe.

I lifted the delicate material to my lips, having a sip.

"Yes, it's my favorite. I don't drink tea that often, but when I do, I always prefer a cup of chamomile," he said.

Maybe he wasn't all bad? I smiled wistfully into the cup and took another sip. "Yes, mine too."

"I am sorry, Harper," Enzo said, calling me by name. Had he mistaken my name for *Tesero,* or had he bequeathed a pet name on me?

Sighing, I sipped the tea, the liquid hot but not burning my mouth. I swallowed the dark liquid, my body beginning to relax. Already, I felt better, calmer.

The china slipped out of my hands and crashed onto the floor at my feet. I opened my mouth to apologize, but no sound came out. My legs grew weak, my arms didn't cooperate, and as my body began to collapse to the ground, Enzo caught me before I hit the floor.

"Sleep now, *Tesero*." He kissed my forehead.

Inside, I screamed. I shouted. I begged for him to let me go.

I was paralyzed, and he held me in his arms, before my vision went dark.

CHAPTER TWENTY-NINE

LINCOLN

"Lincoln," I answered my phone. Seeing as how it was Jaxson, I took the call outside the bar. I didn't need Jayden overhearing anything and calling Enzo. I didn't trust Jayden.

"I just got word from Sheriff Nelson. He received notification that Harper Madison is at Enzo Ricci's residence."

I held my breath. "Do you have an address?"

"Yes." He relayed the address to me, and I climbed into my truck and high-tailed it across town to the property that Enzo had recently purchased.

The sheriff had already arrived on the scene. Jaxson waited with news to find out what I needed from him. I didn't trust that she was there and this wasn't a setup.

In front of the house, was the blue Lotus that I'd seen earlier in the week. There were a few other vehicles along with the sheriff's car outside.

I pulled out my flashlight and walked along the darkened path up toward the house. A body lay covered with a sheet.

Shit.

Was it Harper?

No one had warned me that she might be dead.

Had Enzo called to confess? I hadn't asked. I should have, but I'd been too afraid to hear the answer.

I bent down and held my breath. I pulled back the edge of the sheet to reveal a man with thick dark hair and a gunshot wound to the head.

It wasn't Harper.

I exhaled a relieved sigh and covered the body back up with the sheet.

"Lincoln!" the sheriff shouted at me from the front porch. "Use gloves or don't touch that damned body."

Shit. I knew that. I hadn't touched the corpse, but I should have been thinking more about it being an active crime scene.

Was the dead man the person who had grabbed Harper and taken her against her will? How was he connected to Enzo?

I hurried up the porch steps toward Sheriff Nelson. "Have you seen Harper yet?"

"Yes, the news media will be here any minute, and we need to get her out of here and to the nearest hospital before people start snapping pictures and trample the crime scene."

Who called the press? Had they gotten wind of her abduction? Had the news media been listening to the police scanner and discovered that she'd been found?

"I'll take her." I wasn't leaving her side.

I rushed past the sheriff and stammered in through the front door. "Harper?" I shouted, listening for her sweet voice.

What had Sheriff Nelson meant about needing to get her to the hospital? It was a two-hour drive, and he hadn't mentioned the local clinic, so it had to be pretty bad. Was she injured? What had they done to her?

"Lincoln?" Her soft voice carried through the corridor.

"She's this way," said an Italian man with a fancy suit and thick dark hair. I didn't know if he was Enzo or someone else, but I followed.

Harper sat in a tall blue chair in a darkened office. Bookshelves lined the walls at every corner. There were no windows, just a desk lamp that illuminated the dimly lit room. The overhead lights appeared off or not working.

"Are you okay?" I asked, bending down to her level.

"What am I doing here?" Harper asked me. Her eyes were glazed and squinty, her lips dry. Had she been drugged? "Enzo?" Her brow furrowed as she glanced from me to the Italian man hovering beside me. "I don't remember anything."

"I'm going to take you to the hospital," I said. I lifted her with ease into my arms and carried her through the corridor and outside.

The sheriff opened my passenger door, and I gently placed Harper into my truck, letting her sit in the front seat beside me.

"I'm tired," Harper said. She struggled to keep her eyes open.

"What did they give you?" I doubted she knew the answer, and I wanted to run back inside Enzo's and pound the shit out of him, but my focus needed to be on Harper.

She was here, alive, and I needed to get her help.

Harper didn't answer me.

"Stay with me," I said, worried she might fall unconscious. I didn't know if she'd wake up, go into a coma, or something even worse.

I reached for the seatbelt and buckled her into the seat, making sure she was secure. "I'm going to take her over to the hospital to get bloodwork done," I said to the sheriff. "See if you can find out what they gave her."

"I'll call you if I find anything," Sheriff Nelson said.

I hurried to the driver's side, hopped in, and tore out for the hospital. It was a long drive. I dialed Jaxson while on my way.

"Hey, any news?" Jaxson asked.

"I have Harper with me in the front seat. She looks like they gave her some type of drug. She seems heavily sedated, can't move around, and doesn't remember what happened. She seemed surprised to see Enzo when I showed up."

"Was Enzo in handcuffs? Did he confess to her kidnapping?" Jaxson asked.

My grip tightened on the steering wheel. "No, there was a dead man outside his house. I'm guessing Enzo's blaming Harper's disappearance and abduction on him."

"Bastard," Jaxson muttered. "We'll meet you at the hospital."

"That isn't necessary," I said, glancing beside me at Harper as she mumbled incoherently under her breath. She didn't seem fully awake or alert. "I can call you as soon as we hear anything further."

"Please, do that," Jaxson said. "I'll let the other guys know what's going on."

I hung up the phone and hit the gas harder, hurrying to the hospital. "Hang on, Harper."

CHAPTER THIRTY

HARPER

Beep. Beep. Beep.

The sound of machines pulled me from my reverie.

My eyes lazily opened as bright whiteness cascaded all around me. My vision hadn't focused yet. I felt tired, drugged.

A strong, warm hand gripped mine.

I froze.

"Harper?" Lincoln's soothing voice reached my ears. "Harper, it's me, Lincoln."

I let my eyelids drift shut, a faint smile on my lips. I should have been angry with him but all I felt was a warmth sense of calmness come over me.

"I know," I mumbled.

I was safe.

My memories fuzzy and faded, I couldn't remember any of it. Everything felt hazy behind a cloud that my mind refused to lift.

"Sleep," Lincoln whispered.

I did just that, let my body succumb to sleep.

I didn't know how long I slept or how long Lincoln's hand remained latched in mine. Time seemed not to exist.

My head began to grow less foggy, and as I came to, Lincoln lay in a chair pulled up beside the bed, his hand in mine, his eyes closed. Asleep.

I didn't want to wake him.

What was I doing here? I had an IV in my left hand. My right hand, Lincoln had clasped and even in sleep hadn't let go of.

I wanted to go home. Crawl into my warm bed and sleep for a week. Except I was far away from Los Angeles.

Did I need to worry that my husband would come back for me? He was the one responsible for having me taken, wasn't he?

"Harper?" Lincoln mumbled, his eyelids opened, staring at me. "You're awake." He rubbed the sleep from his eyes and sat up straighter. "Let me get the nurse."

I held his hand, my grip tightening. I didn't trust hospitals or doctors. I didn't trust too many people, but Lincoln, while maybe I was supposed to be mad at him, the anger had melted away. He was with me here now when it mattered.

"Don't," I said. I didn't want him to leave my bedside. "Aren't you supposed to be my bodyguard?"

Lincoln's brow furrowed, and he grimaced.

Had I said something wrong?

He reached for the call button and pressed it. "They need to examine you," Lincoln said.

"Why am I here? What happened?" I asked.

"What do you remember?" He stayed at my bedside, his hand in mine.

The curtain rattled as a nurse pulled it open. "Ms. Madison, I see that you're awake. That's good news. Let me page the doctor." She hurried out of the room, leaving the two of us alone.

"I was over at Ariella's house with Hazel. We ordered a pizza, and this guy showed up, dragged me out and down to his car. He handcuffed me, blindfolded me, and took me for a ride. The rest, I don't remember. What happened, Lincoln?" My voice hitched as I trembled beneath the covers.

I shivered. The room was icy, and the smell of antiseptic only made me cringe. "Did Enzo do something to me? Why am I in the hospital?" I didn't feel sick or hurt. I couldn't remember the incident. Was that why I was hooked up to machines. How long had I been here?

"Enzo reported your appearance to the police," Lincoln said.

That didn't make sense. "What?" Why would he do that?

"He called the sheriff's office. You don't remember anything else after you were put into the car?"

I shook my head no. All of it was a blackout. "We were in the car. I was in the back seat and nothing after that."

"The sheriff found the man who took you dead, Zan Marino. It appears that he committed suicide. He was found outside of Ricci's home with a self-inflicted gunshot wound to the head. The lab is testing Enzo for gunshot residue, but we're pretty sure Enzo will be clean."

"Zan killed himself?" That made even less sense to me. "Why abduct me and then bring me to Enzo only to kill himself?"

Lincoln squeezed my hand. With his other one, he brushed a strand of hair out of my face and behind my ear. "I'm pretty sure Enzo wasn't behind your abduction, but I think he ordered Zan to kill himself, or he made it look like Zan committed suicide."

"Who would do something like that?" I mean, I knew it was Enzo, but I didn't understand why. His motivation, what would possess another man to follow?

"Enzo's part of the crime syndicate."

"The Italian Mob." I had surmised as much from the articles that I'd discovered recently about his business and his practices, which were shady. The government had nothing on him, but that didn't mean they weren't watching him. Hopefully, they'd find something and put him behind bars.

"You didn't tell me you were married," Lincoln whispered, his gaze staring into mine.

The doctor stepped into the room, my chart in his hands. "It's good to see that you're awake and alert, Heather."

I swallowed nervously as he used my legal name, my real name.

No one called me by that, ever. Had they fished out my identification from my purse that I had left at Ariella's house?

He retrieved a penlight from his front pocket. "Follow the pen," the doctor instructed.

The doctor briefly examined me and then explained that the drugs were all out of my system and that I was free to leave. The bout of amnesia from the abduction may never return, but I shouldn't suffer any lasting effects from the drugs that had been forced into my body.

"The nurse will get the paperwork, and you're free to go," the doctor said. He headed out of the room, leaving Lincoln and me together.

Silence filled the small space. "I'll call a cab," I said. "You can head home." I didn't want to be a burden.

"It's a two-hour drive to Breckenridge, and there is likely to be press outside of your hotel. We'll be lucky if they're not outside the hospital when we leave," Lincoln said.

"Oh." Wonderful. Just what I wanted to deal with tonight.

"I'll take you back home. Well, to Breckenridge."

"Thanks," I said and sighed. I dropped his hand from mine. My fingers played over the white sheet, staring down at the cotton material.

Lincoln let the silence thicken like a cloud. The nurse eventually came back in, I signed the papers, got dressed with Lincoln waiting out in the hallway, and then he helped me down to his truck.

We had barely spoken two words since I was discharged.

Tension sizzled in the air between us like lightning, ready to strike.

"Here we are." Lincoln unlocked the truck, and I climbed inside, buckling myself. It was well past midnight.

"Are you sure you're okay to drive back tonight? Maybe we should get a hotel room?" I suggested. I didn't have anything to change into, but at least he wouldn't fall asleep behind the wheel.

Lincoln shut my door and stalked around to the driver's side. He climbed into the truck. "I'd rather sleep in my own bed tonight."

He started the truck.

"Okay."

More silence filled the vehicle as he pulled out of the hospital parking lot and drove us toward Breckenridge.

I stared out the side window. I should have been tired, but I wasn't. I felt more awake than I'd been in quite a long time.

Maybe it was the adrenaline, or perhaps something else? What had I been drugged with? Who had drugged me, Enzo or Zan? Did it matter?

I hated the silence.

It made me feel even more uncomfortable. I glanced at Lincoln as he stared at the road, both hands tight on the steering wheel. Was he mad at me?

"Are we going to talk about the fact you're married?" Lincoln asked. "Or that your husband runs the Italian Mafia?"

I licked my lips. "You know that saying what happens in Vegas stays in Vegas, well, getting married doesn't stay in Vegas."

"Is that supposed to be funny?" Lincoln shot.

I shrugged. "I guess not. I met him in Vegas. We danced together, got drunk, and somehow ended up at a wedding chapel marrying each other. I don't really remember much of it, just that I woke up with a really bad hangover the next day, and I had a diamond on my ring finger. I snuck out, vowed to forget about it, and move on. I didn't even know his name that morning."

"They let you marry him while you were intoxicated?" Lincoln fumed. "Didn't you need a marriage license that you get at a courthouse before going to the chapel?"

I gave a shrug. "Yes, but one of his buddies worked at the courthouse. He acted like he was doing us a favor."

"Maybe doing Enzo a favor. He certainly wasn't doing you one." Lincoln's grip tightened on the steering wheel.

I didn't want to be married to Enzo. Didn't Lincoln see that? "I called a lawyer to find out if the marriage was legally binding and because I was intoxicated at the time of the marriage, I can get the marriage annulled if Enzo is willing to, on the grounds that I wasn't capable of consenting or understanding what I was doing. If not, then we have to legally obtain a divorce. I hadn't spoken to him since Vegas. I didn't even know his name until a copy of the marriage certificate was sent to me."

"I'll get you that divorce if that's what you want," Lincoln said.

"It honestly is." I wanted nothing to do with Enzo, now or in the future. All ties between us, I wanted severed. "I'm sorry that I didn't tell you. It's not something I talk about, ever."

CHAPTER THIRTY-ONE

ARIELLA

Curled up in Jaxson's arms, in his bed, I'd found it difficult to sleep.

"You're still awake?" Jaxson whispered, his eyes open, the light from the nearby clock offering a hint of light in the darkened bedroom.

"Yes," I said and sighed. How was I going to sleep after today's events? Thankfully, Harper had been found, but I didn't feel better about her being taken and dragged away by a mafia thug.

Small towns were supposed to be safe.

Jaxson reached for his phone, glancing at the screen briefly. "Lincoln texted that they're on the way back from the hospital."

I exhaled a heavy sigh of relief. "She's okay?"

"I think so," Jaxson said.

Silence filled the room. His warm grip held me again at my waist, cuddling me to him. He smelled wonderful, and my body relaxed against him, but my mind wouldn't slow down.

"Hazel knows about us," I said.

"That's not a surprise. Lincoln saw us making out at the hospital," Jaxson reminded me.

"You're okay with people knowing about us?" Why were we continuing to hide our relationship? Little by little, our friends and colleagues had discovered what we'd been doing, sneaking around together.

We were two grown adults. Happy adults. Why did we have to hide it any longer?

He pulled me tighter, rolling us around so that I was on top. His hands slid under my pajama shirt, and he began rubbing my back in soft, soothing motions.

"I think by now everyone knows," Jaxson muttered with a laugh. "Hiding of it seems kind of pointless."

I rolled us around again, bringing him to lie above me, pinning me down. I liked when he was on top and took command, especially in the bedroom. I let my fingers dance along the rim of his boxers.

"What about Skylar and Izzie?" I asked, holding him tight against me. I didn't want him to pull away.

"Skylar is a grown woman. She's heard us having sex," Jaxson said with a laugh. "Seems silly to continue to hide it from her. Besides, she's hardly ever around. I like to be cautious around Izzie, but we're not friends with benefits. I love you."

"I love you too," I whispered. "Honestly, I've been worried. I know you wanted me to call that therapist, but I just can't do it. I hate opening up to strangers. It's hard enough for me to talk with you about my feelings. I keep worrying that they'll tell me to move out. That living with my boss and hiding our relationship is unhealthy."

"What?" Jaxson's brow furrowed. "I don't want you to leave, Ariella. If I haven't made that perfectly clear, this is your home, with Izzie and me. I hope we haven't made you feel unwelcome."

"Gosh, no. You've been wonderful. It's just sleeping in a different room, hiding our relationship. It makes me feel dirty."

"I never want you to feel that way, ever. From now on, you sleep with me in here," Jaxson said. "I like having you in my bed, knowing that you're safe."

"I like that too."

CHAPTER THIRTY-TWO

LINCOLN

I hadn't taken Harper back to her hotel room after the hospital. I didn't want to leave her alone.

She was right, I was her bodyguard, and she was my responsibility. I had taken her back to my place, let her crash on my bed, and I had contemplated the sofa, which would have been too small, when she let me join her.

I checked my phone early the following day. Jaxson had texted that the studio canceled the film shoot. I didn't know what that meant for Harper's career or if she'd be pissed or pleased by the news.

"Morning," she whispered. Her eyelids fluttered open as she lay on her side, staring at me.

"No work today, for either of us. It looks like the studio has put a hold on the production." Although there were a few things I wanted to do, I didn't have to run security detail on the set, which was a bonus considering what time we'd gotten into my place last night.

Harper rolled onto her back, staring up at the ceiling. "Good. I shouldn't have taken on the role, knowing I had to work for that asshat of a director."

"Well, if you hadn't, we never would have met." I doubted that she'd have found her way to Breckenridge on her own.

"True."

I rubbed the sleep from my eyes and climbed out of bed. "The workers will be here soon to work on the restaurant downstairs." There would be no chance of sleep with all the banging going on.

"What happened to your restaurant? Piss off someone? Are those real bullet holes?" Harper asked.

"Unfortunately, they are as real as they come. I did want to stop by Eagle Tactical this afternoon and find out if there's any word on Enzo and if he's being charged with murder or your abduction."

Harper remained quiet. Should I not have brought it up?

She sat up in bed, the blankets at her waist, her clothes from yesterday still on. "I should go back to the hotel, shower, and change."

"I'll drive you. Do you mind if I hop in the shower real fast?"

"Only if I can join you," she whispered.

I leaned in, capturing her lips with mine, wanting her to know that, yes, I wanted her. I hadn't stopped wanting her since we'd laid eyes on each other. I grabbed her hand and pulled her to her feet, leading her to the bathroom.

I flipped on the light and started the shower. I quickly undressed and discarded my clothes, leaving them on the floor.

Harper hesitated, but her eyes raked over my body, taking all of it in. She chewed on her bottom lip.

Did she like what she saw? Was she unable to stop staring at me? It felt good to be wanted. I needed to make her feel the way that she made me feel inside.

"Do you want a hand?" I offered and closed the distance between us, my hands on her hips. My fingers skimmed her sides and stomach as I inched the material up.

Harper lifted her arms into the air. I gently guided her shirt up and over. My fingers pinched the bra band, undoing the clasp in the back, letting the straps slide down her shoulders and flow to the floor.

Her lips looked warm and inviting. I leaned in, kissing her, tasting her, while my fingers went to work at her pants, pushing her slacks down along with her panties.

Wrapping my arms around her, I dragged her into the shower, under the spray, our bodies together, the heat caressing our skin.

Her hands explored my back and down to my ass. She gave it a firm slap.

I quirked an eyebrow, staring down at her. "Did you just spank me?"

She laughed and nodded, giving a wide grin as she did it again.

I grabbed her wrist and pinned her against the shower tile. Her nipples hardened, and my mouth fell hard onto hers as I slipped a hand between us, touching her.

She moaned and gasped in pleasure as I separated her folds, feeling over her wetness. I teased her pearl, her body shuddered, and her breathing only further intensified.

Her hand reached down between us, teasing my length, playing with the head, making my hips thrust. Oh God, she was killing me.

Closing the gap between us, I teased her entrance, the heat of the shower steaming up the bathroom. The room felt warm, sweltering, but I didn't care. Her cheeks were flushed, and a blush spread across her chest.

Swiftly, I entered her, driving deeper, harder, listening to her soft pleas in my ear.

"More." She wrapped her legs around me, pulling me closer.

I did as she instructed, burying myself inside her, every inch, until she and I were one.

Harper's head tipped back, and her moans grew louder and more insistent with need. I held her tight against me. One hand snaked between us to bring her over the edge.

She sounded close.

Harper tightened with each thrust.

She felt close.

I struggled to hang on.

"Please," Harper gasped, her eyes slamming shut, and her fingernails clinging to my shoulder, marking me. I was hers.

I withdrew, listening to her whimper in protest. I shut off the shower. So much for getting clean.

"Why did you stop?" Her breathing was raspy. She'd been on the edge, and I withdrew, teasing her.

"Because you deserve more than a shower fuck," I whispered into her ear, nibbling her skin.

She purred under my touch. I carried her out of the shower, back to the bed.

"I swear if you don't let me finish, I may just have to tie you up to the bedposts and have my way with you," Harper said.

A smirk crossed my lips. "Is that so? That doesn't sound bad at all." I guided her down to the mattress. My body hovered above hers, teasing her entrance.

"You're a fucking tease," Harper moaned. She grabbed my girth and forced me to lose all coherent thought as I entered her.

A huge smile etched across her face, pleased with her work.

Each thrust grew deeper, more intense and fulfilling, as I drew near.

I didn't want this moment to end. If the film shoot was done, then was Harper leaving?

I wanted to convince her to stay here for me.

My fingers slipped down, teasing her pearl. Her hands clutched the bedsheets, and her back arched off the mattress.

Her moans intensified, each more pronounced and sexier than the last. She gasped for air, her insides tightening on me, bringing me toward oblivion with her.

She shuddered and let go, panting hard, struggling to catch her breath.

I understood completely.

Several more thrusts, and I was there with her, drowning inside her warmth, breathing with her as one.

My heart pounded, and it was the only sound mixed with our

breathing that filled my ears. Slowly, I withdrew and rolled onto my back.

Hot and sweaty, I could use another shower.

CHAPTER THIRTY-THREE

HARPER

I packed my bags at the motel. The rental car awaited me outside. It was time to return to Los Angeles.

There was a sharp, resounding knock on the door.

"Just a sec!" I shouted. I zipped my bag and hurried to the door, glancing out the peephole before seeing Lincoln on the other side.

"Hey," he said, greeting me with a sly grin.

I couldn't hide the smile on my face, either. Earlier that morning, we'd spent a good half hour in the shower, not the very least bit bathing and then quite a while tangled in the sheets. I could have spent forever in bed with the man, but that wasn't a realistic possibility.

I had to return home. The film shoot was canceled. The director had resigned, and after the public news of my kidnapping, the studio put a firm hold on the production indefinitely.

At least the studio wasn't blaming me, but they felt I needed time to recover.

"Did you come to say goodbye?" I asked.

In his hands, he held a manila folder. "While you came back to the hotel to pack, I took it upon myself to have a word or two with Enzo."

My stomach somersaulted. "You did." What did that mean?

He stepped inside my hotel room and approached the desk. "Enzo will be out of your life forever. All you have to do is sign the papers." He pulled out the pages and laid them on the table for me to see.

"What are these?" I hesitated before I stepped forward, needing to read the contents. It was as thick as a book.

"Divorce papers. You and Enzo can go your separate ways."

What was he up to? I scoured the papers, reading as fast as I possibly could. "Enzo agreed to this?" I asked.

I stared at the pages. I was no lawyer, but it looked solid and acceptable for both parties. I would get none of Enzo's assets, and he would get none of mine. I would accept those terms. I didn't marry him for whatever wealth he had accumulated, and I sure as hell wasn't giving up anything of mine to him.

Flipping through page after page, it was long but appeared agreeable.

"How did you do this?" I asked as I lifted the pen from the desk and scribbled my signature.

"I had a few words with Enzo this morning. He already had the papers drawn up. It was as much his idea as mine."

That surprised me. "Do we need a witness?"

"No, but you will have to go before the county judge. As soon as you're ready, you can do so in any county or state together."

I groaned. The thought of seeing Enzo again made me want to vomit.

"I'll be with you the entire time," Lincoln said. "Ariella and Hazel offered to come too. They want to throw you a divorce party."

"Okay, but we're not ordering pizza. The last time we did that, Zan showed up." While I realized there was no relation between the pizza delivery service and the mafia arriving at the door, it still was an association that I wasn't ready to get past.

"So, you'll stay a little longer?" Lincoln asked, his eyes filled with hope. "A few more days?" Did he want me to stay indefinitely?

"Yes, I can do that, a few more days. You know, if you're really that upset about me leaving, you could come with me to Los Angeles."

Lincoln smiled, tightlipped. "Los Angeles is so—"

"Sunny?"

"I was going to say smoggy. Don't you love the outdoors? The quiet and beauty of nature. You can't go rafting down the river with a view like we have in Los Angeles."

Was he trying to convince me to stay? It wasn't that hard. I did love it up here. The thought of going home wasn't really making me that happy.

"No, I guess you can't," I said, glancing at my bag on the bed. "But the beaches, you have to admit that is a perk, even with the smog."

He laughed under his breath. "Maybe I should be more direct. Stay for me," Lincoln said, pulling me into his embrace.

I wrapped my arms around his neck and tilted my face up, my lips caressing his. "Won't you get tired of me?"

"I don't believe that's possible." He didn't so much as loosen his hold on me, his arms wrapped around my lower back.

"Are you asking me to move in with you?"

A huge smile spread across Lincoln's face. "I swear if you're teasing me, woman, I don't think I can take it."

My lips crushed his. "Do you see me laughing?" I would need to return to Los Angeles, if only to bring back some of my things.

EPILOGUE

JAXSON

Life felt almost too good. I waited for the ball to drop. Harper was safe and home from the hospital. Mason had been released from medical care and was back to his old self.

Ben was out there, somewhere, waiting to strike. It wasn't over. Would it ever be?

We'd yet to run into him again, but we would. It was only a matter of time.

The Eagle Tactical team was over, along with their girlfriends, for a cookout. We vowed to spend more time together having fun. We deserved it.

I sat on the back porch at my house, the view of the mountains always a beauty.

Izzie chased butterflies down on the grass by the garden where Ariella and Harper were busy planting flowers.

Harper rested a hand on her very pregnant belly. She and Lincoln were expecting their first child, and Izzie was probably as excited as they were, looking forward to a new playmate.

Bear plopped down next to me on the wooden deck, her tail wagging, bathing in the afternoon sun.

"Look at this," Hazel said, showing me her social media account. There were dozens of photos, but she scrolled to one in particular. "Skylar's got a boyfriend."

"Oh yeah? Let me see."

I'd barely seen Skylar. She'd been working long hours and out partying most nights.

Hazel handed me her phone. I nearly dropped the device when the picture staring back at me ripped my insides to pieces. Jayden had his arm around Skylar, a huge grin on both of their faces.

I clicked on Skylar's account, scrolled through a few photos until I landed on one that made my stomach drop to the floor. She held up her left hand, revealing a flashy diamond on her ring finger.

"When the hell did she get engaged?"

COVERT: JAYDEN

EAGLE TACTICAL BOOK FOUR

CHAPTER ONE

Skylar

The music blared over the speakers, making it difficult to hear myself think. Not that there was much to think about.

I downed a shot of tequila and then another.

"Bad day?" the bartender asked.

His first name was Jayden. I didn't get his last name, and I'd been coming to the bar a lot.

Mostly, to figure things out, which really meant hide from my brother and his girlfriend.

Jayden also wasn't a bad view to enjoy after work, imagining our bodies tangled together, hot and sweaty.

Too bad I didn't have the courage to invite him home. Then again, I didn't exactly have a home of my own.

The truth was that imagining him naked and the two of us wrapped up in the sheets was a welcome relief to my boring and inconsequential life.

"Something like that," I said under my breath.

While it wasn't a great day, working at the coffee shop was the only job I had been qualified for.

Besides, no one seemed to be hiring. Plus, I needed to save my money for a place of my own instead of blowing it on overpriced liquor, but it was easier to come here and stare at the hottie of a bartender.

There was something about him.

Dark and mysterious.

Tattoos covered his arms, which peeked out from under his black t-shirt. "Are those real?" I asked and gestured to the ink on his forearms.

I needed more friends.

My brother had a slew of tattoos, but I was unmarked and a blank slate. I couldn't tear my gaze away from Jayden's forearms.

"No, I spend every morning doodling with a permanent marker on my skin to impress the ladies," Jayden said.

Snarky.

I downed my shot and gestured for him to pour me another one.

He grabbed the bottle of tequila and poured the amber liquid into a shot glass. "You know, Skylar, you could just ask me out if you want to see me. You don't have to come to the bar every night after your shift."

My arms rested on the bar, and I leaned my head into my arms, face planted.

An uncomfortable groan spilled out past my lips.

"What's that?" Jayden asked, laughing under his breath. "Did I embarrass you?" He didn't sound the least bit apologetic.

I'd bet he flirted with all the female customers—anything for a bigger tip.

It probably worked too.

He was good-looking, albeit with a dark and mysterious vibe, and that look he shot me made my knees weak.

He was every bit a bad boy.

I didn't have to glance up to know he had a wide, smug grin across his face. With a heavy sigh, I lifted my head and stared up at him.

"Are you guys hiring?" I needed a job that paid enough so I could rent a place or buy something, eventually.

All my money went to car repairs, insurance, and liquor. Maybe I was staying out too much.

"Not the bar..." his voice trailed off.

That caught my attention. "But you know someplace that is?"

He reached for the empty shot glass and took it away, not refilling it with another drink. "Jayden?"

He glanced around before he leaned closer.

What was he worried about?

There were a few patrons in the bar, but it was loud and difficult to hear anything over the pulse-pounding music.

"Come with me out back." Jayden gestured to another one of the staff members that he was going for a break.

I followed Jayden through the darkened hallway and then out the rear exit of the bar.

The loud music seemed distant from behind the closed door. My ears rang.

"You know some place that's hiring?" I asked again, my voice louder than I intended.

His answer was a whisper, his voice quiet, his tone making it clear that we needed to be quiet about it. "I need a partner for an off-the-books type of job. It pays in cash."

I liked cash, especially if I could avoid claiming it with the government.

"What's the gig?" I asked. "I'm not going to be a drug mule." I'd seen enough movies to know that never ended well for the mule.

Besides, I had no intention of spending any time behind bars.

Jayden snorted under his breath. "Drugs aren't involved, but it's not any less dangerous."

"Okay." I could handle danger.

He stared at me with sharp eyes. He glanced me over from head to toe, twice. "You can't tell anyone about the job."

I pretended to lock my lips like I did as a kid. "Don't worry. It's not like I have friends around here."

"That includes your brother and his girlfriend," Jayden said.

I shifted the weight on my feet. “You know my brother?” That made me a bit uncomfortable.

What else did he know about me that I wasn’t aware of?

He gave a silent nod. “You live with him.”

“How the hell do you know that?” I pointed at his chest and poked him in the process.

He didn’t so much as flinch. “Your driver’s license has his address.”

Oh. He was right. I had changed my identification after I moved into town. “You know my brother.” It was more of a statement than anything else.

How did the two of them know one another? I’d never seen them converse, and Jaxson never mentioned Jayden.

Jayden didn’t elaborate further. “Can you keep a secret from him or not?”

“He doesn’t know I come here after work every day,” I said. That was a secret I kept from him. There were a dozen or so more.

“I’m serious, Skylar. If you work for me, no one can know. It’ll be a deep undercover operation.”

He sounded just like Jaxson when it came to his Eagle Tactical business. “Please, don’t tell me you work for my brother.” I wasn’t sure I could handle that news.

“No, and I can’t tell you who I work for, so do me a favor and don’t ask,” Jayden said.

“Okay.”

He must have been C.I.A. or some other agency. As long as I got paid on time, I could look the other way.

“What’s the job?” I asked. “What do you need me to do?”

“Marry me,” Jayden said.

I coughed, shocked by his proposition. “Excuse me? That’s crazy.”

He couldn’t be serious. I wasn’t marrying him for money or any other reason.

“Relax. It’s part of the assignment. I need you to post pictures of our engagement on your social media accounts,” Jayden said. “I’ll get you a ring. We’ll make it look official. We need to get my boss’ attention. He already doesn't trust me, and I need him to show an interest in you."

Okay, so maybe he wasn't C.I.A., and his boss was a bit shadier. Did he work for the mafia or a drug kingpin?

"You want your boss to hit on me because he thinks I'm engaged to you? What kind of bosshole is he?" I asked.

That was a terrible idea.

Jayden laughed under his breath and exhaled a heavy sigh. His eyes looked tired, with dark circles underneath. "I can't tell you anything more. Are you in or not?"

"Will I be risking my life?" I asked.

I had a feeling that whoever his boss was, it wasn't some top-notch guy.

He stalled for a moment before answering. Was he deciding whether to answer me honestly or not?

"Yes. I'll pay you a thousand a week."

If I was risking my life, I wanted more money. "I want double."

"Done," Jayden said a little too quickly.

Maybe I should have tripled it.

"Swing by my place tomorrow after you quit your job at the café. Say around ten o'clock in the morning. Give me your phone, and I'll put my address in it."

He tapped away at my phone screen, inputting his contact information before he handed me back my phone. "Remember, you can't tell anyone about this arrangement."

"I swear I won't."

Who would believe me, anyhow?

CHAPTER TWO

Jayden

I hadn't wanted to involve Skylar. Hell, I hadn't wanted to involve anyone else in my mess, but I needed a man on the inside. Or rather, in this case, a woman.

Could I trust the spunky little sister of my military brother? Jaxson and I had barely spoken to one another.

Well, that wasn't entirely true. He'd offered me a job with his team at Eagle Tactical.

I'd had no choice but to refuse.

Jaxson was completely unaware of my connection with Enzo Ricci. On occasion, I also worked alongside Sheriff Nelson and the tri-county task force, but even they didn't know my connection with Don Ricci.

Bringing Skylar into the job was against every protocol, but I needed her help.

My work went deeper than just bringing down the off-gridders. Nearly every last one of them was dead, except for Emma. She was now in prison, awaiting sentencing after pleading guilty.

Maybe I should have thanked the mafia for slaughtering my

enemy, the one I had to live with, sleep beside, and pretend to be one of, to gather their trust and intelligence.

It wasn't Don Ricci who had murdered the off-gridders. As the saying goes, the enemy of my enemy…

A firm knock resounded against the wooden door.

"Just a sec," I shouted and grabbed my Glock. I wasn't taking a chance, ever. I glanced through the peephole to see the five-foot-two beauty on the opposite side.

My hormones raged at one glance at her. Her shirt was cut with a low V, dipping into her cleavage, leaving little to the imagination.

Down, boy.

She was here for a job, not to fuck me.

That was too bad.

I unlocked the door and made sure she was alone.

I let her inside my apartment, and I shoved my Glock into the waistband of my pants.

The apartment was dark. I left the window shades closed to make sure no one could see inside.

Was I paranoid?

Yes, but for a good reason.

Skylar folded her arms across her chest. Her long locks fell across her face.

The longer I stared at her, the more irritated she looked.

"So, what's the job?" she asked.

I stalked across the room to a dresser drawer, yanked open the top handle, and pulled the drawer hard. I dug in between my socks and retrieved the tiny jewelry box. I tossed it at Skylar.

She fumbled with the box, nearly dropping the black velvet before flipping open the lid. "You were engaged?"

"Just something I keep around," I answered. That was all she was getting in the way of an explanation. "We need to spend the afternoon together, taking lots of pictures, making it look somewhat believable that we're happily engaged."

Skylar's brow furrowed. "Somewhat believable? You don't think I can do my part and act madly in love with you?"

I merely shrugged. "I haven't seen your acting skills. Besides, it's not me you have to convince."

She leaned against the bed and plopped down on the edge. "Are you going to tell me why I'm doing this? I would never have pegged you for the type who has to pay for a girlfriend to take home to your parents."

That's not what this was. Not in the slightest, but I held my tongue. "Don't worry. The entire arrangement is one hundred percent professional."

Skylar pursed her lips and patted the bed beside her. "It doesn't have to be."

Was she testing me? Enzo would expect some level of intimacy if we were seen together, but I didn't plan on that happening.

The truth was my plan was shitty at best. I needed Enzo to trust me, and he'd been offering me girls left and right, women he intended to auction off and sell to the highest bidder.

It disgusted me.

He wouldn't leave it alone, and I had lied to him, told him that I had a fiancée at home. Which meant I needed a girl who would have my back.

Emma was in prison.

There hadn't been anyone else since her, and even then, she had been a means to an end.

Another job. One that had turned complicated.

I don't usually sleep with my protégé, but with Emma, she'd been hot, fierce, and offered herself up to me.

I hadn't been able to say no. She had bewitched me.

"Well?" Skylar asked. "What's the gig? I strut around town showing off my flashy engagement ring?" She slid the diamond band onto her ring finger before she thrust out her cell phone.

I needed her to get close to Enzo. He still didn't trust me, not completely.

"It's more complicated than that. I need you to gather intel for me on Enzo Ricci."

"Excuse me?" Skylar pushed herself off the mattress. "Isn't that the shady billionaire who just moved into town?" Her voice raised an octave as she spoke. "Is he like a drug dealer or something? He kind of looks like he works for the mafia."

Apparently, word traveled fast.

"He's my boss. Already, he believes that I don't trust him. Which I don't. But that's beside the point. I need you to gather as much information from the girls he's holding. I'm looking for a girl named Lexa Clarke."

"Gather information. How, exactly, and who is Lexa Clarke?" Skylar asked.

This wasn't just a risky job. It was a lifestyle and not one that I wanted to commit myself to, but there'd been no other choice.

"You're going to accompany me to a party that Enzo is hosting at his home. He's already panicking because the shipment of girls that was due in was delayed."

"Delayed?"

The girls weren't exactly delayed. I had intercepted the shipment, having gained access to the manifest and released the girls into federal custody. Enzo didn't know it was me who had betrayed him. If he had, I would have already been dead.

I didn't want to worry Skylar or give her any intel that could be used against me later. The less she knew, the better.

"It doesn't matter about the girls. What matters is that you're going to join me at his home as my fiancée."

"I'm not following on how I'll be gathering information on the girls he's holding. Will they be at the party too?" Skylar asked.

"Doubtful. I'm sure he's holding them someplace at the compound on his property. Probably a basement or cellar."

"Let me guess. You want me to sneak around without getting caught?" Skylar asked.

"Yes. Dante will likely be guarding the access point, so you may need to flirt with Enzo's second in command, Dante."

"Second in command? What is he, mafia?"

I didn't answer. I wasn't about to lie to her. But yes, Enzo was the head of the Italian mob who owned most of the west coast and had branched outward. They dealt in smuggling guns, drugs, and girls.

Skylar exhaled a heavy sigh. "Wonderful."

"All you have to do is flirt with him if you get caught. He's a sucker. Easy to manipulate. Don't worry."

"Flirt with him? You're underselling the job." Skylar wasn't an idiot. Maybe I underestimated her.

"He's in over his head right now with the shipment of girls who have gone missing. Dante needs help. If you seem eager to please, he's desperate to keep Enzo happy. He'll easily betray me to get on Enzo's good side."

CHAPTER THREE

Skylar

I laughed at his ridiculous plan. "Are you insane?" He wanted me to sneak around a heavily guarded mafia fortress and flirt with the mob boss' second in command if I got caught?

"I know you're scared," Jayden said, "but once we get the intel we need from your wire, then we'll pull you out and shut down the entire operation."

It sounded too easy.

"What happens when they see the wire?"

I already knew the answer. They'd kill me.

He rested his hands on my shoulders as he stared at me, towering from above. "No one is going to find the wire. It won't be taped to you like in the movies. Our technology is better than that. I promise you'll be fine. In and out without a hiccup. You won't be at the party for more than a few hours."

A lot could go wrong in a couple of hours.

"Then why did I quit my day job if this is a one-week operation?" I asked.

He didn't answer me.

Exactly.

He knew that this was dangerous and went deeper than just attending a party.

We'd have to keep up the charade after the party too. How long would we pretend to be married?

Maybe Jayden wasn't risking his life, but I'd be putting myself straight into the hands of men who were monsters.

He may have wanted this to be over within the week, but a lot could go wrong.

I still didn't understand his crazy plan. "Why pretend to marry me? Are you really that desperate for a plus one to the party?"

I swallowed the lump that formed in my throat.

Jayden was a handsome guy and the thought of pretending to be married would have been fun if he'd invited me to a wedding or we pretended to be together to make an ex-girlfriend jealous.

This scenario was dangerous and it scared me.

"You'll be fine." His face showed no hint of emotion.

What was Jayden hiding from me?

"What benefit do you get out of us being engaged?" I asked, tilting my head to the side. There was more to it, something that I wasn't seeing.

Jayden laughed under his breath before he answered, "I've been trying to get Enzo to stop throwing women at me."

"Poor Jayden," I mocked. When he didn't so much as flinch at my remark, I leaned closer to him.

He wanted us to pretend to be engaged. Then we needed to pretend to like one another.

Maybe we needed to practice kissing too?

I was fully on board with making out with him. He was attractive and had a nice physique. It was clear that he worked out regularly.

I rested a hand on his chest and let it slide down to his belt buckle. "Who is Lexa Clarke? Is she your girlfriend?" I wanted to know who the girl was who needed saving.

Jayden cleared his throat. "What are you doing?"

"Shouldn't we know everything about one another? I mean, what happens if I get caught the minute we're inside Enzo's home and someone asks me about a birthmark or tattoo on your body?" My fingers unclasped his belt buckle.

He had a lot of tattoos on his arms. Where else did he have tattoos?

"That isn't going to happen," Jayden said, his voice rough and deep. He raised an eyebrow at me.

"And how do you know that?" I hadn't let go of him yet. "You're throwing me into danger. The least you can do is make sure that I'm fully prepared."

His lips descended hard and fast on mine, surprising me.

With one hand on his belt buckle, my other hand traveled up into his hair, pulling him closer and tighter against my body.

Everything inside of me ached with need.

I'd never felt this desperate before.

A moan spilled out past my lips as we kissed and he yanked me harder, closer, tighter.

There was a roughness to him that I'd never experienced.

I longed for more. I liked it a lot.

Jayden pulled back. "Fuck," he muttered and took another step away from me like I'd burned him.

He was hot and cold.

What the hell was going on with him?

"Who is Lexa Clarke?" I asked again, this time louder and with more insistence.

Is that why he stopped anything further from happening between us?

Was he in love with another woman?

I waited for Jayden to elaborate on why he wanted me to sneak around his boss' complex.

The heat and fire that he had beyond his gaze turned dark.

"She is my niece."

The weight of his words hit me like a ton of bricks. That was the last answer that I had expected.

"What?" I said, unsure I heard him correctly.

"Lexa is my niece. About eighteen months ago, I received a call that my brother and his family were in a horrible car accident. He'd taken the family off-roading on a camping trip, and their SUV had gone over the edge of a cliff. Lexa was the only survivor. According to the police report, she had been outside of the vehicle and had directed her father around the sharp turn when the tire hit a soft spot and slipped off the ledge of the road."

"Oh my gosh." I lifted my hand to my lips and covered my mouth for a brief moment.

Jayden ran a hand through his hair. "If that wasn't horrible enough, she never made it to Breckenridge. The police considered her a runaway as did DCFS. I did some investigating on my own, though, and tracked her whereabouts to a human trafficking ring that operated just outside of where she'd gone missing."

I slumped back onto the mattress. "That's terrible." That poor girl had lost her family and then was held against her will, with men probably doing horrible things to her.

Jayden's expression remained grim. "It is. She's just a child, barely fifteen. I haven't been able to track her any further than Enzo Ricci. Every trail leads directly to him. Hell, for all I know, she's already been bought and sold, but I can't give up. I won't give up. I refuse to leave her behind."

His eyes were glassy, his pupils dark, like two saucers. He exhaled a heavy breath as he paced the length of the apartment.

His place was small for someone who could afford to pay me two grand a week in cash. It was clear he was trying to keep a low profile. Working at the bar was probably a side gig to keep suspicions down.

"What do you need me to do?" I asked.

CHAPTER FOUR

ARIELLA

"Morning, Freckles." Jaxson pulled me tight against his body beneath the covers.

"Is it time to get up already?" I mumbled through heavy-lidded eyes.

Any minute, Izzie would come tearing through the bedroom door. If we were lucky, she wouldn't climb onto the mattress and start jumping on the bed.

She'd been a terror lately, and while I had thought I missed those years, boy, was I wrong.

Jaxson's warm breath caressed my skin as he kissed a soft trail of butterfly kisses against my neck and down my cleavage, dipping his head beneath the blankets.

I moaned, shifting on the bed to get comfortable but also knowing this was a bad idea. "Jaxson," I whispered, my voice raspy and filled with need.

"Shhh, we have to keep it down," he said, reminding me that we could get interrupted.

Buried beneath the covers, his lips made a warm path down my stomach and across my navel.

He didn't linger, going right for his intended target. He slid my panties down and trailed a slow path of warm kisses up my inner thigh to his intended destination.

I grew restless from his teasing and bit down on my bottom lip to keep from moaning as the bedroom door flew open.

Oh crap.

"Jaxson," I moaned, trying to tell him that his daughter was about to come barreling into the room.

His name was the only word that I'd been able to get out.

"Ariella!" Izzie squealed as she ran into our bedroom.

His tongue stopped working its magic, and I whimpered in protest.

Focus.

I needed to pay attention to his daughter and also scold Jaxson later for not having a lock on the bedroom door.

"Where's Daddy?"

Jaxson climbed out from beneath the covers, revealing himself to his daughter.

"Daddy!" Izzie climbed up onto the mattress without so much as an invitation. "What were you doing under there?"

His sly grin didn't help settle my heart. He made me breathless. My heart pounded wildly in my chest as I tried to calm down.

"Trying to sleep. Ariella makes all sorts of noises when she sleeps," Jaxson said.

"I do not!" I smacked his arm playfully. "You are full of lies."

Izzie glanced between us, her eyes narrow and sharp. She was the spitting image of her dad.

"Daddy doesn't lie," Izzie said and stood on the bed.

"Of course, she's going to side with you," I said, gesturing at Jaxson.

Jaxson grabbed Izzie by the waist and tackled her to the bed with tickles.

"Daddy!"

I laughed under my breath.

It was no wonder she loved running into the bedroom and jumping on the bed.

She always stole her daddy's attention.

"You're not a monkey." Jaxson reminded her. "No jumping on the bed."

Izzie thrashed and giggled before Jaxson let up. "Okay," she said with a loud sigh. She sounded just like her father.

I slid out of bed. My nightgown covered the fact my panties were buried somewhere beneath the bedsheets. I'd have to find them later.

"Any plans for this afternoon?" Jaxson asked, glancing at me as I headed toward the bathroom to brush my teeth.

"Harper invited me to take her shopping for maternity clothes and baby stuff. I think Hazel will be joining us too."

It was Sunday, which meant no work, and I was looking forward to unwinding with a girls' day.

Already, it was much needed with the added stress of knowing that my sister was planning on visiting.

I hadn't seen Delphine in months. She finally booked a flight and decided to come crash with Jaxson and me for a week at our place.

She'd insisted on coming to meet the man I was living with and wanted to make sure he wasn't anything like Ben.

"Also, Delphine is coming into town tonight. I'll have to pick her up at the airport around dinner."

"So, you want me to cook?" he said, teasing me.

Jaxson plopped himself at the edge of the bed while I brushed my teeth.

"Last night at the cookout, Hazel showed me her phone."

"Yeah?" I wasn't sure where he was going with his comment.

Izzie sat on his lap and traced her fingers over the tattoos that marked his skin. She seemed bored but was keeping herself entertained for the moment.

I began brushing my teeth and stepped out of the bathroom to listen to Jaxson.

"Skylar's engaged."

I nearly spit the toothpaste out of my mouth. I coughed and hurried back to the sink to spit.

"Are you sure?" I asked. Skylar hadn't so much as brought a boyfriend home since she moved in with her older brother.

"She posted it all over her social media account. I can't believe she didn't tell us!" Jaxson lifted Izzie into his arms and stood.

He headed toward the bathroom. Jaxson's footsteps were heavy against the floorboards as he paced the length of the room.

I finished brushing my teeth before stepping back into the room, leaning on the doorframe."

Obviously, it was a spur of the moment decision. Maybe she was worried about how you'd react?" I said.

Skylar and Jaxson hadn't been particularly close, at least from what I could surmise. There didn't appear to be any bad blood between them, but they weren't best friends, either. It was as if they had nothing in common except their parents.

"What's engaged?" Izzie asked. She wiggled in Jaxson's arms, wanting to be put down.

He planted her feet on the ground, and Izzie tore out of the room.

With a heavy sigh, he followed after his daughter, probably to discover what trouble she found her way into next.

I hadn't known Skylar that well. Even though she lived with us, I barely saw her. The glimpses that I'd gotten, she reminded me so much of Izzie with her carefree, snarky attitude.

Jaxson hurried down the stairs, and I followed a few steps behind, waiting until they were out of the bedroom to retrieve my panties from beneath the blankets.

A few minutes later, I joined the two of them in the kitchen. Jaxson was preparing breakfast while I came over to offer my assistance.

"What can I do to help?" I asked.

"I've got it," Jaxson said with a shrug. "Right now, it feels good to keep busy."

His jaw was tight. His eyes were narrow and filled with

determination as he measured each ingredient to put into the plastic bowl. This wasn't about making breakfast. Was it still about Skylar?

"I'm sure she intends to tell you," I said.

Jaxson huffed under his breath. "Doubtful. The post was from well over a week ago."

"Maybe she doesn't know how to tell you? You're her big brother. She could be intimidated," I said as I began putting yesterday's clean dishes away in the cabinet.

He shot me a look. "That's not it. I know my sister, and she's in over her head. She's marrying Jayden!"

"Who is Jayden?" Izzie asked.

"How about I take Izzie with me for a girls' day? We're just going to do a little shopping later this morning. It might give you time to stop by the café where your sister works and find out what's going on? Talk to her."

"Yeah, I'll do that." Jaxson exhaled a loud sigh as he mixed the batter for the pancakes. "Are you sure you're okay with all this baby shopping and planning a baby shower for Harper? Lincoln told me that you offered to throw her a party."

"Harper doesn't have any other friends here," I said, reminding Jaxson that she had upended her life from Los Angeles to live in Breckenridge with Lincoln.

Jaxson and Lincoln were buddies. I was doing this as much for Jaxson as I was for Harper.

I put the last of the dishes away in the cabinet and spun around to face him. "Besides, I like spending time with her."

"What about Hazel? She could do the baby shower. I'm sure if you ask her, she'd be happy to help facilitate things."

Jaxson turned the stove on.

"What is this really about?" I asked. I had a feeling it had little to do with the baby shower but something else.

He glanced at Izzie, stalling.

I doubted she even understood what we were discussing. "I'll be fine. You don't need to worry," I said.

Once the pan was hot, he poured the pancake batter into the skillet. "I'm sure you will, but is it a good idea? You lost a child."

Izzie's face scrunched up and she tugged on my arm. "Where did it go?"

"Where did what go?" I asked, glancing down at Izzie.

"Did you forget where you put it like I did with my stuffed ducky?"

I bent down and gave Izzie a swift hug and kiss on the cheek. I didn't want to elaborate on this conversation with her. She was bright, but far too young to be discussing the death of my son.

"How about we get you dressed while Daddy finishes cooking breakfast?" I asked, steering the conversation away from the topic.

Izzie slipped out of my grasp and tore up the back staircase.

"I'm worried about you," Jaxson said as I followed Izzie to the stairwell.

The last thing I wanted was to have a conversation about my deceased son. It was a memory that I always carried with me but didn't ever want to talk about with anyone. That included Jaxson.

CHAPTER FIVE

Skylar

It was a stupid plan, and I was an idiot for going along with it, but I needed the money. I also wasn't risk avert.

I threw myself into terrible situations all the time, but it usually involved sleazy men and too many drinks.

I wore a short, black sequin dress that Jayden had brought home in my size. I'd been staying over at his place the last few days since our fake engagement.

The dress fit nice and snug and hugged all my curves in just the right way.

How had he known my size?

I just couldn't quite reach the zipper.

I held the dress up around my torso. There were no straps.

"Zip me up in the back," I said as I gestured behind me to the open gown.

Jayden stared at me for a minute, his mouth agape.

I tilted my head to the side, smiling at him as he stared at the dress barely covering my assets.

"Did you hear me?" I asked, my voice softer. I could feel the heat creep into my cheeks. I had to be blushing.

"Wow, yes, hold your hair up," he instructed, grabbing a fistful of my hair and tugging. He pulled my neck to the side.

Jayden leaned closer.

His breath hovered over my exposed neck. A shiver coursed through my body.

Was he going to kiss me?

My gaze glanced up toward him.

Jayden leaned closer and whispered against my ear, "Grab your hair, and I'll zip your dress."

Right, the dress.

I'd already forgotten that was why he had nestled up behind me. I was ready to take the damned thing off and have my way with him on the mattress just a few feet from where we stood.

Why did he have this power over me?

I held up my tresses, keeping them out of the way as Jayden's fingers tugged the zipper slowly upward. His breath teased my skin in the process.

I shut my eyes, reveling in the feeling of being wanted.

Did he want me? Or was it just an act?

He had me believing it was real.

I wasn't the one he needed to convince that we were engaged.

His touch on me disappeared, and I felt an emptiness burn through me.

I spun around on my bare feet, staring up at him. Jayden was dressed sharply, in black slacks with a white button-down dress shirt. It was a far cry from his attire at the bar.

Was Jayden trying to impress Enzo tonight or someone else at the party?

"You clean up nice," I said, finding him irresistible as I glanced him over from head to toe.

"Me?" Jayden quirked a sly grin. "You look stunning." His eyes did another once over on my body, admiring my curves.

I would have felt overdressed if I hadn't seen how handsome Jayden looked. If he was uncomfortable, I couldn't tell.

"Big party?" I asked, surprised by the fancy gown. Why else would he have brought home the fancy dress?

"You might say that," Jayden said. He stalked over to his dresser and retrieved a silver heart locket. "The wire you need to wear."

"Jayden." My voice caught in my throat.

His gaze latched onto mine. "You can do this. I have faith in you."

Nervous didn't even begin to explain the feeling of dread that came over me. "Okay."

He kept his arm snug around my hip, introducing me to anyone and everyone at the party. "That's Enzo," Jayden whispered into my ear.

I plastered a smile to my face as one hand held a champagne flute and the other clung to my clutch.

I wasn't ready to sneak off and go in search for his niece or any other girls that Enzo might have detained.

Sipping the champagne, I hoped the bubbles would quell my nerves.

Enzo was a thicker individual than Jayden. Jayden was all muscle. Enzo, I suspected, had one too many jelly donuts. He had a sharp nose and a thick head of obviously dyed jet-black hair.

Enzo headed right for us, a stone-cold look of determination across his face.

Feeling his scrutinizing gaze, made me uncomfortable.

A part of me wanted to flee, to run out the front door before he so much as introduced himself, but I couldn't move. My feet were glued to the floor in my new shiny black stilettos.

"Jayden." Enzo's thick Italian accent permeated the ballroom. His voice bellowed beyond the music that played at the opposite end of the room.

A string quartet brought current melodies to life, vibrant and upbeat, but no one danced. Most of the crowd were men, certainly no younger than Jayden, a few were older with salt and pepper hair, everyone dressed sharply in a suit.

"Enzo." Jayden forced a smile as he clasped the other man's arm in a welcoming greeting. His other hand stayed tight around my waist. "I'd like you to meet my better half, Skylar."

Enzo lifted my hand to his lips and placed a kiss on the back of my hand. "It's lovely to make your acquaintance."

"The pleasure is all mine," I said, forcing a smile.

"I hope you both are enjoying the festivities this evening. I have a special treat for your fiancée this evening," Enzo said.

He retrieved a red ribbon and tied it up in my hair around the curls and elastic that had my hair partially up already.

How peculiar.

There was something about him that I couldn't read.

His expression sent butterflies to my stomach.

I refused to let my gaze wander as Enzo stared at me after securing the ribbon. "That's very kind of you, thank you," I said.

Enzo forced a smile before he took a step back and clapped his hands. "Gentleman," he announced.

The music came to a halt while he spoke. "It is my privilege to introduce you tonight to just a taste of what we have to offer."

The lights dimmed. A door from down the hall opened, and ladies dressed in lingerie wandered out onto the floor.

A dozen ladies, scantily clad, eyes glazed over, stood on display. A spotlight landed on them as they huddled together, clearly uncomfortable.

"Remember, if you'd like to sample the merchandise, it will cost you," Enzo said with a hearty laugh. "No woman tonight is off-market. If you see something you like, she's yours to own, tame, and do with as you see fit."

Glancing around the room, I realized there were no other women at the party other than the women being trafficked by Enzo Ricci—and me.

CHAPTER SIX

Jayden

Skylar clutched my arm. Her fingernails dug into my flesh.

I tried not to wince at the sudden pain. I rested my hand atop hers and glanced at her out of the corner of my eye.

While the plan had been to get her to sneak through the compound and gather information, I hadn't anticipated that Enzo would blatantly display the woman as if it were an auction.

Enzo stood just a few feet away.

A wicked grin crossed his features. He snapped his fingers. The music resumed, and the lights brightened the ballroom.

"I'm in charge, darling. Always have been. Always will be, especially while your fiancé works for me," Enzo said and stepped closer to Skylar.

His eyes raked over her body. His gaze stared at her cleavage and then down to the short skirt of the dress she wore. "Looks good on her, don't you think? I do know a thing about fashion."

"He picked this out for me?" Skylar's eyes widened, and her mouth dropped.

The color drained right out of her face.

"Yes, dear," Enzo said. "I wanted to make you the main attraction for this evening."

Enzo grabbed Skylar by the arm and whisked her across the room toward the other women huddled together, trembling in fright.

This was not what we had planned.

Where had Enzo found a dozen women for the event tonight?

The ladies who had been trafficked and intended for this evening had been intercepted. I'd delivered them straight to the feds.

Skylar glanced over her shoulder at me, silently begging me to save her.

CHAPTER SEVEN

Skylar

"Aren't you a beauty?" A dark-haired gentleman with a square jaw and the grayest eyes I'd ever seen looked at me as if I were standing naked, gawking. "I'll take her," he said and gestured at Enzo with two fingers.

"Excuse me?" I scoffed.

I wasn't here as one of his girls to be paraded around, or worse, as some form of entertainment.

While Jayden had wanted me to keep a low profile as his fiancée, this went beyond what even I was comfortable partaking in.

Enzo grabbed my jaw and yanked my face to meet his dark stare. "She's fiery and vibrant. A woman like this would ordinarily cost you double."

"Get off me!" I pushed away from him, only to feel a set of strong, forceful arms against my shoulders, keeping me in place.

Please, let it be Jayden.

I glanced over my shoulder.

It wasn't Jayden. He was being detained by two guards, with a third in quick pursuit to silence him or take him out. I wasn't sure which.

The music continued at a frenzied pace. The violins dropped quick and sharp notes that matched the pace of my racing heart.

Whatever Jayden shouted, couldn't be heard across the distance.

"She's stubborn, but I'm sure you are quite eager to tame and break her, Angelo," Enzo said, speaking about me as if I were a horse and not a person.

Unable to run, the giant behind me held me in place. He was monstrous with his thick hands and tight grip, towering a foot above me. In another life, he could have been a basketball player.

How had he ended up working for Don Ricci?

Hell, how had I been dragged into this mess for a few lousy dollars?

My life was worth more than a measly two grand.

"I'm not yours to have," I said, fighting the grip of the man who dug his fingers into my shoulders. He could have easily lifted and carried me out of the room. Maybe he would if I didn't settle down soon.

The other girls watched me squirm. None of them offered any help. They didn't try to run.

Did they realize they couldn't get away and it was of no use?

I wasn't willing to give up that easily, but it didn't appear as though Jayden was of any use.

Great.

"She is the starlet of the evening, our main showcase," Enzo reminded. "You can have her on one condition."

Angelo practically drooled at the invitation.

"And what might that be?" Angelo asked. He stepped closer, and I suppressed a shiver as his heavy scent of cologne that wreaked alcohol burned my nostrils.

Bile rose up in my throat. I held my hands in tight fists at my sides, my fingernails digging into my palms, leaving an indentation with the pain I felt. I did it to keep from crying.

Neither of these men deserved to witness the fear and trepidation that burned through me.

No, I wouldn't cower at either one of the bastards who thought I was nothing more than a piece of merchandise.

"I don't want you or your men anywhere near my turf. Our business is done."

Angelo folded his arms across his chest. "Who said anything about stepping on your land? You invited us here tonight; don't forget that, Enzo."

"Sir." A gentleman whom I didn't recognize approached Enzo and tapped him on the shoulder.

Enzo glanced at the other man who was a few inches shorter, but they had the same matching eyes, nose, and jawline and could have easily been brothers. "Yes, Dante?"

Dante. I recognized that name.

Jayden had told me that Dante was Enzo's second in command.

I tried not to feign too much interest in what the two men discussed.

They lowered their voices, and with the crescendo of the live band, it was difficult to hear.

Enzo gave a firm nod before Dante hurried through the crowd of people.

I couldn't quite see where he was going.

Had Jayden managed to fight off the guards? Was he bringing reinforcements?

Enzo cleared his throat. "My apologies for the interruption. As I was saying, our business, as I'm sure you're aware, is expanding, and we don't take kindly to other families betraying us. I have it on good authority that your Capo Sergio stole one of our shipments."

I tried not to act like I knew what the two men were conversing about.

But a stolen shipment?

I could only surmise that Enzo was referring to the women who had been trafficked.

If that was the case, then why had Jayden been removed by the guards and I was at the front and center with Enzo and Angelo?

What the hell was going on?

Angelo cocked an eyebrow. "Are you accusing my men of stealing from the Ricci Family? That's quite an accusation, Enzo."

"But not an accusation without merit. I tried to welcome you as a friend, invite you to do business with my family, but you come to my town and start moving in on my turf. Breckenridge isn't big enough for both of our families," Enzo threatened.

"The hell it isn't." Angelo huffed and shook his head.

Enzo's eyes narrowed, but he didn't speak. Not yet.

"I don't take kindly to threats. It doesn't matter if you're Don Ricci or a fucking capo." Angelo yanked my arm and thrust me out of the grip of Enzo's security giant.

I tried to pull myself from his clutches, but he didn't let go. Maybe without the surrounding guards, I could escape the moment he led me outside.

Was that a real possibility or wishful thinking?

I could take one man.

I was screwed if I had to fight an army.

Angelo's top lip snarled with disgust. "You make threats against me. I'm taking her as a promise to you, Don Ricci. We're not finished, not anywhere close."

"Stay out of Breckenridge," Enzo snapped. "And keep the bitch."

Angelo dragged me outside.

A half-dozen men followed us.

Were they with Angelo or guards for Enzo and escorting us off the property? I couldn't tell the men apart, but neither was there to save me.

Angelo led me toward his black SUV, waiting out front by the entrance of Enzo's mansion.

"Get off me!" I thrust myself away from him, kicking and clawing at him with my fingernails—anything to aid in my escape.

"Enough!" Angelo's voice bellowed as he backhanded me across the face, and his finger caught on my chain. He yanked the necklace off, letting it fall to the ground.

My cheek stung, and I tasted the metallic zing of blood on my lips.

"Get in!" Angelo ordered.

One of the guards who had escorted us outside opened the back door of the SUV.

I didn't budge. I wasn't willfully going to further endanger myself. "No," I said.

I wasn't going to bow down to anyone, mafia boss or otherwise.

This was my chance, my one and possibly the only opportunity to escape.

Angelo had climbed into the front seat of the vehicle and blatantly thought I would follow his orders.

I wasn't like those other girls.

Was I afraid?

Yes, but I would fight before I gave in to his demands.

I slipped past the guard who was a solid six-foot-two and hurried as fast as my feet would take me. I sprinted across the driveway and through the grass in stilettos—no easy task.

I headed for the tree line that led to the forest.

How far would I get before they'd catch me?

Would they stop if I made it home, or would they continue to hunt me down?

Bang!

CHAPTER EIGHT

Jayden

Fuck! That did not go as planned.

Enzo had been on to me, but I wasn't sure for how long.

Did he know that Skylar wasn't my fiancée? He'd made no indication that we weren't really together.

Why had he dragged my ass out of the party?

He hadn't executed me. If he believed I'd betrayed him, he would have murdered me in cold blood. Enzo wasn't a forgiving man.

Something had stopped him, but I wasn't sure as to what.

And Skylar was still inside, locked up amongst mobsters and perverts.

What would happen to her?

Two burly guards dragged me, kicking and screaming, out of Don Ricci's house. Neither had said a word to me about what the hell was going on.

They'd tossed me outside and waited until I got into my car and drove off the property before leaving me alone.

I couldn't leave Skylar with those men alone.

I'd gotten her into this mess. It was all my fault.

I drove away from Enzo's home, only out of force, but I didn't leave.

I pulled off the road at the turn, making sure that I had a good vantage point but that his men couldn't easily spot me.

Security cameras were situated outside the property. I couldn't sneak on without being seen, and while most of his security team was preoccupied with the party, there were still a number of guards keeping watch.

Which meant I needed another plan, one that was less conspicuous.

I could hide outside of the boss' house and wait for Angelo DeLuca to leave. Assuming Skylar was forced to leave with him, I could tail his vehicle as soon as he left.

But what if she was dragged down through the compound and led out another exit that I hadn't been privy to?

Or what if they left along with other vehicles, whether part of DeLuca's team or another guest of the party, and I couldn't determine which vehicle she was trapped inside?

A dozen different scenarios played out in my head. None of them ended well for Skylar.

And I had failed in finding my niece.

What chance did I have of rescuing Skylar?

I undid the top couple of buttons on my shirt. I was suffocating.

My phone buzzed in my pocket. Pulling it out, I glanced down at the text message from Dante.

I know you didn't leave. Meet me at the lookout. Ten minutes.

Was this a set up?

If Enzo wanted me dead, Dante would have taken the shot back at the house.

Why meet at the lookout?

I knew the location. It was where we picked up the shipment of girls. The ones who never made it the last time, which was odd considering the number of ladies forced to attend tonight's event.

Where the hell had they come from?

I glanced at the phone once more, considering my options. If I went, there was a chance that I'd miss Skylar, but if I stayed, who was to say that I'd even see her leaving?

Exhaling an unsteady breath, I texted back that I would be there and shoved my phone into my pocket.

I climbed into my vehicle and headed for the lookout point. It would take me every bit of ten minutes to get to where Dante wanted to meet.

CHAPTER NINE

Skylar

I was desperate to escape.

My stupid heels weren't helping me through the grass. I refused to glance behind me, worried that it might slow me down.

Bang!

A shot rang out and whizzed by my head.

"That was a warning shot," Angelo bellowed. "I don't ever miss."

Was he bluffing? He'd been close as hell to hitting me.

I had momentarily slowed down, tripping over my stupid heels.

That was all it took for his men to force me to the ground and frisk me.

Their hands wandered a little too long and close against my skin, under my skirt.

"Get off me!"

It took two guards, one at each side, to drag me to the black SUV.

"No!" I shouted and thrashed about, trying to break free.

"Do you want me to shoot you?" Angelo asked as he stood beside the car. Just moments ago, he'd been seated inside the front passenger seat.

Had he gotten out to shoot me? Was he a better shot than his men, or did he not trust them to do the job?

I slunk into the backseat.

Angelo held the door open for me. There wasn't much choice in the matter.

The two security goons refused to loosen their grip on me until I was in the vehicle.

Angelo slammed the door shut behind me. He climbed into the front seat and glanced back at me. "Don't try anything stupid."

He flashed his gun in my direction, his hand on the trigger.

"I'm just itching to pull it again."

My mouth felt dry. I pursed my lips but didn't say anything.

What could I say that would make him leave me the hell alone?

CHAPTER TEN

Jayden

Against my better judgment, I agreed to meet Dante.

Arriving at the lookout point, I recognized his vehicle.

I reached for my spare gun under the driver's seat and tucked it into my pants, beneath my jacket.

His driver sat in the car while Dante stepped out. His eyes raked over my body.

"Do you have a weapon?"

I wasn't coming unarmed, that's for sure.

"Do you?" I countered, turning the question on him. No doubt he was packing, and probably more than one gun if I knew any better.

"I didn't come here to shoot you," Dante said. He held up his hands in surrender as he drew nearer to me.

Enzo's men had already tossed me out of the party. I didn't want an ass-kicking to go along with it. "That's close enough." I didn't trust him or anyone who worked for Enzo Ricci.

"Your girl, Skylar, she's being used as a pawn for Enzo. He doesn't trust Angelo DeLuca, and neither do I," Dante said.

Why was he telling me this?

The sun beat down on the open expanse of land. From the overlook, there wasn't much to see but miles of forest down below.

Sweat trickled against my forehead from the oppressive heat of summer.

"You have to help me get her out of there. DeLuca will kill her."

Dante's brow tightened. "She'd be lucky if that's all the bastard did to her. Enzo believes that Angelo's stealing girls, skimming from our operation."

"Fuck." That was news to me.

I'd been responsible for ensuring the pickup went without issue.

Gino, Angelo's second, as well as Capo Sergio, had been my main contacts for DeLuca. Both men I'd had the privilege of dealing with were scumbags, but I hadn't even considered that they might not have delivered us the full shipment.

"You have evidence that DeLuca is keeping part of Enzo's delivery to himself?"

"If the boss had evidence, he'd have started a war with DeLuca. He sent your girl in undercover," Dante said.

Did Skylar have any idea what she was doing?

"No way." I didn't believe it. "You sent her in to get killed!"

What game was Dante playing? I didn't trust him in the slightest.

I'd have sworn, based on the fact they'd practically handed Skylar over to Angelo, that they'd been on to me.

Was I wrong?

Had that been a show for Angelo's sake?

"We need DeLuca to believe that we think you betrayed us. It's the only way we're going to find out who the real rat is, stealing Don Ricci's property." Dante took a step closer to me.

"Is she in on the arrangement?" I asked. "Does she know that she's working as a mole for Don Ricci?"

Dante laughed under his breath and gave a slight shrug. "Doubtful. If she did, she'd have told you, and you'd have inevitably stopped it from happening."

He wasn't wrong. There was no way I would have willingly gone along with the plan. It was suicide.

I grabbed Dante's suit and yanked him closer. "When Angelo suspects Skylar is a mole, he'll kill her. When that happens, I'm coming after you and Enzo."

Dante ignored my threat. "Women can be replaced. Don Ricci's been happy with the work you've done; don't disappoint him over some girl."

I drew my fist back and landed a sharp blow to Dante's cheek.

"Skylar is irreplaceable. You're going to help me get her out."

CHAPTER ELEVEN

JAXSON

I stormed into the bar with my fists clenched at my sides. My feet pounded against the floor. I didn't wait for an invitation as I tore around behind the bar, face-to-face with Jayden.

I grabbed him by the shirt lapels, giving him the opportunity to explain himself before I kicked his ass.

"When were you going to tell me that you've been screwing my sister?"

I hadn't quite meant for it to come out like that, so crude and condescending, but I was pissed.

They were engaged, and he hadn't so much as had the decency to show his face anywhere with my sister.

If I hadn't seen it on Skylar's stupid social media account, I wouldn't have even known she was engaged.

Did she not plan on telling me?

Shit.

Was she pregnant?

"Did you knock up my sister?" At least then he'd be doing the honorable thing, marrying her.

"Whoa!" Jayden shoved me backward, knocking my hands away

from his shirt and chest. "I didn't sleep with your sister. Chill out and keep your voice down."

His eyes flinched.

Anyone else wouldn't have seen it, but I'd been in combat with Jayden.

I knew that look anywhere.

What the hell had he gotten involved with? "What did you do?" I asked. I ran a hand through my hair.

"Don't worry about it," Jayden said. He turned his back to me.

Where the hell was Skylar?

I hadn't seen her in days.

Usually, she snuck inside late, well past midnight. I hadn't been thrilled with her behavior, but she wasn't my responsibility. Skylar was an adult. Though, sometimes I thought she could use a little growing up, still.

I couldn't just ignore the fact that they were engaged. "You're marrying my sister. If you didn't knock her up, then you have a lot of explaining to do."

I hadn't even known they'd been dating. Skylar had only been in Breckenridge for a short time.

How long had she known Jayden? Days? Weeks? I doubted that it could have been months.

"I'll come by your office in an hour. We shouldn't leave at the same time," Jayden said.

He'd never been particularly paranoid. "You think someone is watching you?"

"I know it."

I drove to the office and waited for Jayden to show up. It was a Sunday, so the guys had off, and I had the place to myself.

I wasn't sure that Jayden would stop by as promised, but the sound of a door slamming outside jarred me back to the present.

Jayden didn't so much as knock as he blew in through the front door. "We don't have long until they realize I shut off my phone and the GPS tracker on my vehicle."

"Who's following you?"

"That's not important," Jayden said. "Skylar's in trouble."

A knot formed in the pit of my stomach. That was not what I was expecting to hear.

I thought we came to the office to discuss the fact he was dating my sister and intended to marry her.

"What do you mean, she's in trouble?" He needed to elaborate. It was just the two of us. No one could overhear us like they could at the bar. "Explain yourself, now!" I snapped. He was testing my patience.

"She's with Angelo DeLuca."

"Who the hell is that?" I asked. "And why the hell is she with him?" I yanked my phone out of my pocket.

Was I supposed to recognize the guy's name, because I didn't?

"You can't call her. She doesn't have her phone on her. She left it at my place."

Jayden exhaled a heavy breath, ran a hand through his hair, and shuffled his feet toward the desk.

He looked nervous as hell as he handed me her cell phone.

"Shit." She wouldn't have gone anywhere without her stupid cell phone. She was tied to that thing like it was another limb. "What do you mean, she's with Angelo DeLuca? Who the hell is he?"

"DeLuca is a rival mob boss of Don Ricci. They've been doing business together, but Enzo believes DeLuca is stealing from him."

"What does any of that have to do with my little sister?" Skylar worked at a café. She had no dealings with the mob.

"Don Ricci sent Skylar in as a mole to find out what's been happening."

"What? Are you crazy? You'd better be joking." I stepped closer, closing the distance between us.

I was ready to pound the shit out of Jayden.

What the hell trouble had he gotten her involved with?

Jayden may not have been the cleanest guy, but it didn't seem right that he'd lead my little sister right into the hands of the enemy.

CHAPTER TWELVE

Jayden

I hadn't wanted to involve Jaxson. He was the biggest pain in my ass in existence. The truth was I hadn't forgiven him for kicking my ass at the Blue-Sky Resort when I'd been with the off-gridders and taking hostages.

I hadn't been on board with the plan, but the off-gridders had planned on going with or without me. At least I could make sure no one ended up dead. Plus, I had to keep Emma out of trouble. Little good that had done.

"Where the hell is my sister?"

"I don't know," I said and threw my arms up into the air. "That's what I'm trying to tell you. Angelo DeLuca has her."

"Tell me everything. Start from the beginning," Jaxson demanded.

I quickly recanted my plan and how Enzo had been one step ahead at the party, making Skylar the main attraction. "All I can surmise is the guy who I hired under me has been secretly working with Don DeLuca. Why else would the shipment details always match exactly?"

"Who's your associate? What's his name?" Jaxson rubbed his forehead. He looked pissed as shit.

Not that I blamed him. I'd royally fucked up.

"Benjamin something. I didn't catch his last name." He hadn't given it, and I wasn't asking.

The color left Jaxson's face. "Do you have his contact information or know how we can reach him?"

He wasn't answering his phone. "He's not responding to calls or texts." Not that I expected him to respond to me. I was on the outs, and it was any wonder they hadn't left me dead in a ditch somewhere.

"How long has Skylar been unaccounted for?" Jaxson asked.

"Seventy-two hours."

CHAPTER THIRTEEN

ARIELLA

Harper waddled through the mall. A hand rested on her very pregnant belly as she tried to keep up with us. "I need to pee again," she said.

Harper headed into the bathroom.

Hazel, Izzie, and I grabbed a seat on a nearby bench.

"Think we bought one of everything yet?" I asked Hazel, holding up the six bags of maternity and baby clothes for Harper.

Hazel plopped the bags that she'd been holding onto the floor at her feet. "Nah, I think she can still buy another boatload of onesies and receiving blankets. Do you think Lincoln is going to have a fit when he sees the bill?"

I doubted it. Harper had a lucrative movie career before abandoning it for Lincoln and motherhood. "He might freak out when he sees how much stuff a baby requires, but it's not like this all just happened. I mean, they bought a crib last month, and the guys helped put it together," I said.

That aside, it was still a surprise. Harper hadn't expected to get pregnant, and while she and Lincoln were excited to welcome a baby in a few weeks, it hadn't been planned.

"Can I ride the rocket?" Izzie pointed at the machine tucked into the corner of the mall.

I dug into my pocket to see if I had any quarters to feed the machine. "Sure. Can you watch the bags?" I didn't expect Hazel to abandon them and disappear, but I thought that I should still politely ask.

"Yes, go. Have fun!" She waved us off, and Izzie tore off toward the rocket.

I hurried after Izzie. She had already climbed into the seat and waited for me to feed the device.

I dropped several quarters in and watched as it came to life.

The rocket lit up and made several sounds before bouncing wildly, earning a fit of giggles from Izzie.

She was easy to entertain today.

Harper waddled down the hall from the bathroom and met up with Hazel by the bench. She waved at Izzie and me before she sat beside Hazel.

The two girls chatted animatedly, laughing and gossiping about who knows what.

I turned my attention back to Izzie, only to find her gone.

The rocket ended its jittering, and I poked around to the other side, relieved when I found her climb onto a motorcycle. "Again! More quarters?" Izzie asked.

The girl was going to give me a heart attack!

I dropped a few quarters into the motorcycle. The engine made an obnoxious grumble, and the headlights flashed a multitude of colors.

I glanced around the rocket to see Hazel and Harper still engrossed in their conversation.

"This is the last ride," I said to Izzie. "I'm all out of quarters."

She whined in protest and pouted her discontent.

"Psst!"

I glanced behind me.

"Skylar?" I hadn't spoken with her in a while. She'd gotten engaged in secret, and by the looks of it, she seemed to be in trouble.

Her hair looked dirty, her skin covered in filth, along with her clothes.

"I need you to come with me," Skylar said. She glanced behind herself at the side exit just a few feet away.

"Izzie, it's time to go." I couldn't leave her alone. I needed to get Hazel and Harper and let them know that something was going on with Skylar. However, I didn't have any idea what the hell it was at the moment.

"No, uh, just you," Skylar said.

"I can't leave her. What's going on, Skylar?" I asked, stepping closer.

"Please, it's a matter of life or death." She slipped out of my reach and tore out the side exit.

Fuck.

I grabbed Izzie and held her on my hip as I jogged toward the side exit.

I pushed open the door.

The bright sunlight momentarily blinded me.

"I'm sorry," Skylar's voice whispered from behind.

A white van parked outside the door. The back door slid open, and my breath caught in my throat when I saw Benjamin Ryan, my ex-husband, on the other side, a gun in his hand.

I reached behind me for the entrance to the mall, the door, my escape.

It was locked from the outside.

"Get in," Ben said, gesturing with the gun to follow his orders.

Slowly, I put Izzie down, planting her feet on the ground. "Run!" I shouted at her, praying that she listened and would go to get help.

I didn't want her tangled up in my mess.

What was Skylar doing with Ben? Since when had they become friends?

Izzie clutched to my side, unwilling to run to save herself.

He cocked off the safety of the gun and pointed it at the little brunette's head. "Get in, or she dies!"

CHAPTER FOURTEEN

Skylar

Running had seemed a grand idea, until the gunshot had gone off.

I didn't want to die.

Not today.

Escaping seemed the only option when faced with exploitation. Why had Enzo betrayed Jayden and me?

He'd handed me over to the enemy without a second thought.

My fingers grazed the ribbon that Enzo had tied into my hair. It had been a strange gesture. I yanked it hard, wanting no evidence of him on me.

The dress I wore, he gave me that too.

My stomach sunk. I was going to be sick.

I couldn't disrobe. I had nothing else to wear.

Had Enzo intentionally been trying to mark me?

Claim me? Show me that I belonged to him?

In the back of the SUV, I pulled my hair down, letting the long locks fall around my face. The bobby pins and clips, I dropped on the floor.

Inside the red ribbon, had been the tiniest message, meant only for my eyes.

Get information if you want to survive. You work for us now.

I was furious.

Had Jayden been in on the scheme, or had it been Don Ricci's idea? Jayden hadn't so much as mentioned it, and he had looked pretty shaken when he'd been detained and I'd been thrust in front of the crowd.

If I wanted to survive, I had to obey Don DeLuca's every command, at least until help arrived.

Would someone come and save me?

Jayden wasn't my fiancé, not really. We had pretended to be engaged to be married, and that had been short-lived. Sadly, it lasted longer than any of my real relationships.

Pathetic, I know.

Jayden's backup plan for me to flirt with Dante was moot. Angelo DeLuca had dragged me out of Enzo Ricci's home.

Angelo's fist gripped my neck, reminding me that if I didn't do as I was told, I was as good as dead.

I couldn't let anyone see the ribbon. I secured it back up into my hair, making sure that I'd dispose of it properly later. No one could find it. If they did, they'd think I was a spy.

I'd been alone, with only a cot, in a cold and moldy basement.

There were other girls. I'd seen them when I'd first been brought down to the basement, past their prison cells.

But I hadn't been able to talk to any of them.

The prison in DeLuca's basement had been quite large, and they brought me to another area, away from the girls who had been locked up together.

Why was I being detained?

Why did he keep me in the farther corner of his prison?

Cement walls and floors with iron wrought bars kept us contained. There was no way to escape, not without a key.

Every so often, I could hear the echo of female voices, but I couldn't hear what they said. It was as if Angelo DeLuca knew why I'd been given to him, and he was keeping me from ever fulfilling my secret mission.

Would Jayden come for me?

What about Enzo Ricci?

Heavy footfalls thumped over the floor.

I sat up, waiting to see who was coming in my direction. Was it help? I hadn't heard gunshots or any sound of fighting.

It didn't seem likely that Enzo would show up and Angelo would hand me over to him.

"Well, well, well," Angelo's voice carried into my cell as he rounded the corner. He dressed in slacks and a black button-down shirt. His black hair looked greasy as he slicked it back with too much gel. "Get up!" he commanded.

I stood, folded my arms across my chest, and hesitated as I gradually moved toward the cell door.

Was he going to let me go? He didn't seem the type to give a girl her freedom.

He leered in my direction, glancing every inch of me over. Was he undressing me mentally?

I was parched, and while my body trembled, I hoped that he didn't notice my fear. "What do you want with me?" I asked.

"Tsk. Tsk." Angelo shook his head, unapproving. "I ask the questions. You'll listen."

I wasn't loyal to Enzo or to Angelo. All I cared about was my survival.

The second set of footsteps descended farther down the corridor.

"We know you're the girlfriend of one of Enzo's associates. What I can't fathom is why Don Ricci gave you to us as a gift." Angelo unlocked the cell door and stepped inside, leaving the door ajar.

Could I push past him and make a break for it?

"Any thoughts?" Angelo asked.

The second set of footsteps grew nearer and rounded the corner. I didn't recognize the man. I'm not sure why I thought I might.

It wasn't Jayden. There weren't too many others I knew around here. I was still new to town.

Did Angelo know that about me? He already knew the same story that we'd fed to Enzo about our fake relationship.

Angelo stepped closer when I didn't answer.

I felt trapped, my back against the cold cement wall, leaving me nowhere to go.

Slowly, he lifted a hand. His index finger stroked my cheek. "You're a pretty girl. You might even pass for being honest." He laughed with a darkness that sent a shudder down my spine. "You can rot in this cell or come work for Ben. He needs an associate, and I need more girls."

Ben came to stand on the opposite side of the cell, his arms folded across his chest.

"Are you sure about this?" he asked Angelo.

"If she is intended as a rat, we'll have her working for us, and if she's not, then she'll be indebted to me. I'm giving her a taste of freedom. It comes at a cost," Angelo said.

His finger stroked my jaw before he grabbed my chin and yanked on my face hard, bringing my gaze staring into his cold, lifeless eyes.

I held my breath.

"Disobey any of my men, and they will put a bullet in your head. Then, we'll hunt down your pretty little boyfriend," Angelo said.

He released his tight grip on my face, and I breathed a sigh, though I didn't feel relieved, not yet. It was far from over.

"I want you back here by midnight with three girls. They'd better be young, fresh, and full of life." Angelo shot Ben a hard glare.

There was something unsaid between them.

A heaviness hung in the air.

Was it about me?

"Let's go," Ben grunted, and pointed at the hallway.

Wordlessly, I stepped out of the prison cell and followed Ben down the narrow hallway. I kept my head down. I didn't want to be here, and I sure as hell didn't want to get myself further involved in this mess.

I needed a plan, and I needed one fast.

Abduct three girls by midnight?

If I wasn't going to jail, I'd be going to Hell.

CHAPTER FIFTEEN

ARIELLA

Izzie clung to me. I held her tight, her arms wrapped around my chest as I reluctantly climbed into the back of the van.

While I was willing to risk my life, I wasn't willing to endanger Izzie.

I knew she was afraid, but I wished she'd have done as I asked and ran. At least she could have saved herself.

The back door, the exit we had been whisked out of, squeaked open.

Hazel and Harper stepped outside.

Shit.

I opened my mouth to scream, to warn them to run back inside and get help.

But it was too late.

"You!" Ben's eyes narrowed and he snarled at the two of them. "Get in!" he barked at both of them, waving a gun at Harper's pregnant belly.

Harper held up her hands. "Okay. Okay. Don't shoot us!" She waddled toward the white van. A look of fear crossed her face when she saw me in the back holding Izzie.

Did he know that Harper, Hazel, and I were friends? What did he want with them?

Hazel hesitated.

"Get in or I'll shoot the little girl." Ben whipped the gun around to point it at Izzie.

Hazel huffed under her breath but climbed into the back of the van, coming to sit beside me. She rested a hand on my leg as we all sat curled up on the floor.

Skylar climbed in with us before Ben slammed the van door shut.

A moment later, the engine roared to life. Where was he taking us? If he was after me, why involve everyone else?

"What the hell were you thinking?" I shot at Skylar as she sat on the floor across from us. Why was Skylar friends with Ben?

"I didn't have a choice," Skylar said, her eyes bent down on the metal floor of the truck.

Harper rested a hand over her pregnant belly. "Doesn't matter. We're in this situation now. What are we going to do about it?"

Ben couldn't hear us from the front seat as he drove.

I tried the door handle, not that I expected it to open. Even if it did, what would we do? Jump out of a moving van? We had a child and a pregnant woman, so that didn't seem the best plan.

I pulled out my cell phone from my pocket. Ben clearly wasn't versed in kidnappings. Thankfully, he hadn't learned much from the last time he'd abducted me.

"Where is he taking us?" I asked, staring at Skylar.

She sat with her legs crossed, gnawing on her bottom lip.

Great. Skylar wasn't going to help.

I pulled up Jaxson's number and tried calling him.

It rang and went to voicemail.

Seriously? What was he doing that was so important? Although he wouldn't have known we'd been tossed into the back of a van.

"Jaxson, your crazy ass sister got the four of us abducted by Benjamin Ryan. We're in the back of his white van and, according to GPS, heading northeast. I don't know how long we'll have our phones. Please call us."

"Daddy," Izzie said, reaching for my phone.

I hung up the call. "I'm sorry, sweetie, Daddy didn't pick up." I turned my phone on silent and shoved my phone into my fashionable boots.

Izzie trembled in my arms and clung to me even tighter, her hold making it hard to breathe.

Gently, I caressed her back, trying to ease her fears. The girl had been through enough already in her short lifetime.

Skylar stared at Izzie. "I'm sorry. It was never my choice to be here, either." Her gaze met my stare. "I know you think Ben is the monster. You probably think I'm one too, but you haven't even come close to discovering what *he's* capable of doing."

"Who?" I asked. If she wasn't referring to Ben, then who was behind our abduction. Who did Ben work for?

"Don DeLuca," Skylar whispered.

I'd barely heard her, and I certainly didn't recognize the name. She kept her stare averted.

Skylar wrung her hands together before she focused on her fingernails and picked away at the light pink nail polish.

"Is that name supposed to mean something to me?" I asked. I glanced at Hazel and Harper. Not that I expected them to recognize the name, but maybe they were aware of something I hadn't been knowledgeable about.

"Shit," Harper whispered.

"What?" I glanced at her. What did she know?

"DeLuca works for Don Ricci," Harper said. "Well, works for is a strong term. After I discovered Enzo's background, I did a little digging."

"Digging?" I asked.

"Yes, I hired a private investigator to find out who I was married to and why he'd been in Vegas. When I saw on the news that Enzo was wanted for a slew of crimes, I thought he was the only mob boss."

"Mob boss?" Hazel whispered. "If they know my last is Agron, they'll kill me." She pulled her knees to her chest, her eyes wide. I could feel her tremble beside me in the van.

Hazel's eldest brother was head of the Russian mob in Chicago, but he was dead. We hadn't kept up with who had risen in power, but Hazel was likely still a target of the Russian mafia. They'd left her alone after her betrothed, Franco Ivanov, had been arrested, but that didn't mean they weren't out for getting revenge if DeLuca had ties to Chicago.

"Turns out that Angelo DeLuca runs the Nevada and Southwest ring. They're enemies, at least they were. But Lincoln has been keeping tabs on Enzo. He doesn't trust that he'll leave me alone."

Maybe Lincoln was right, and Ben hadn't snatched the four of us because of me. That didn't make me feel the least bit better.

Could it have been because Don DeLuca was trying to get Don Enzo's attention with Harper? Did he think the baby was Enzo's?

"What do we do?" I asked, glancing from Harper to Skylar.

Skylar stared back down at the floor. "I can't help you. Don DeLuca expected three girls by midnight. I didn't have a choice," she whispered. Her voice sounded strained, like she was fighting back the tears.

I'd never seen Skylar cry. She'd been moody and difficult, emotional on a scale of bitchiness. But filled with concern, that wasn't a Skylar who I was familiar with seeing, ever.

The vehicle came to an abrupt halt.

The engine died.

Why were we stopped?

I wanted to grab my phone and glance at the GPS to determine our location, but the van door squeaked and slammed.

Ben was on the move.

Any second, he'd be opening the van door, and I couldn't risk him discovering my phone.

Ben jerked the handle and slid the van door open. "Out!" he demanded, waving his gun at us.

"I want to go home," Izzie said, clutching me tight.

Already, she was in my arms, but her hold on me didn't seem enough. "I know, baby girl." I wanted to go home, too.

I'd lay my life on the line to protect Izzie. She had become as much my daughter as she was Jaxson's.

CHAPTER SIXTEEN

JAXSON

How the hell had I missed her call?

I listened to it again and again. I could hear the fear in her voice, even as Ariella tried to be strong.

They'd gone to the mall. It had to have been where they'd been snatched.

We met up with mall security, a bunch of rent-a-cops, who showed us grainy black and white surveillance footage of the abduction.

Skylar was with them, and Ben definitely had a gun that he pointed at my little girl.

I was going to kill him.

Mason and Lincoln stood at both sides of me, watching the video too. Their girlfriends' lives were on the line, just like my daughters and Ariella's.

It took everything in me not to beat the hell out of Jayden.

He'd caused this mess.

"Call Declan," I rattled off orders. "Have him start pulling surveillance and footage for where Ben might have taken them. Ariella said they were heading northeast. I want Aiden to track her phone. Hell, track all their phones, see if anyone pings a signal. Who the hell is Ben working for?"

"If Skylar is with them, I know who has the girls. They're with Angelo DeLuca," Jayden said.

"DeLuca, as in the crime boss from Vegas? What the hell is he doing in Breckenridge?" I spun around on my heel, coming face-to-face with Jayden, demanding an answer. Suddenly, the name clicked with me.

Lincoln towered over Jayden. "I've been asking myself the same question about Don DeLuca. What is he doing in town? I've had suspicions about him and Enzo. A man like DeLuca doesn't just show up for a nice little vacation in the middle of nowhere," Lincoln said.

Lincoln was right.

DeLuca was up to no good.

"Think it's a turf war?" I asked. Lincoln knew more about the mafia than I did.

I was well aware of his side project in digging into dirt on Enzo Ricci. As much as I wasn't keen on it, I didn't think his private investigative work was the reason that the girls had been snatched.

But I didn't like coincidences.

"No," Lincoln shook his head. "I have it on good authority that they're doing business together."

Fuck. That was news to me.

It wasn't bad enough Enzo Ricci had moved into Breckenridge, but now we had to deal with Angelo DeLuca as well? "What kind of business?" I shot a glance back at Jayden. "You know what this is about, don't you?"

He had kept quiet for far too long.

I was ready to get my hands dirty and torture the bastard if it meant finding my daughter and getting her and the girls back.

Jayden took a step back in the small confines of the mall security room.

I cleared my throat. The mall security officers didn't need any more intel than we'd already provided them.

"How about we take it outside?" I asked. It wasn't a question.

The guys headed out of the mall security office and through the double doors outside.

"Listen." Jayden held up his arms in surrender.

He was probably worried we'd all pound the shit out of him.

It certainly crossed my mind, but he was far more useful to us alive and unharmed.

"I didn't mean for any of this to happen. You have to know that I wouldn't ever get involved in hurting a pregnant woman or a kid," Jayden said with insistence. "I want to help. Let me talk to Enzo and see if we can get DeLuca to turn over the girls and the kid."

Mason's scowl hadn't left his face. "Do you honestly think putting Enzo in the middle of this is going to help anyone? We don't need to get indebted to a mobster. We'll handle it Eagle Tactical style," Mason said.

"If you mean we go in guns blazing and blow-up DeLuca's compound, I'm all for it," Lincoln said.

I had no objections. We needed to act quickly.

I headed outside for the truck, the guys falling in step just behind me. Our weapons and tactical gear were all back at the Eagle Tactical office.

Besides, we needed blueprints or some type of schematics so that we weren't going in blind.

It would take time to devise a foolproof plan, a commodity that we didn't have a lot of considering what we were up against.

We hightailed it back to the office where Declan and Aiden were busy doing research, trying to track the girls' phones and getting us access to security footage inside DeLuca's compound.

Lucy, the receptionist, jumped up the moment we came inside. "I'm so sorry. I just heard what happened," she said, following us down the hall. "If there's anything I can do to help. I know how much your daughter means to you, sir."

I exhaled a heavy breath. It wasn't just Izzie missing, although she was at the forefront of my mind.

Ariella had also been taken, and given her medical condition, I wasn't too keen on her being detained by a mobster. Not that I was happy any of the girls had been abducted at gunpoint.

"That's appreciated, Lucy," I said.

I recognized that she wanted to help. It was why she wasn't hidden behind her desk and was actually taking an active role in what we did for a living.

But I couldn't involve her or put her life at risk. She wasn't former military. Lucy had no tactical training. She was well versed in answering the phone, making appointments, and keeping the office stocked.

I probably sounded like an ungrateful ass. Yes, I was grateful for Lucy's offer to help, but I wasn't going to risk her life to save the girls.

In all honesty, there was nothing that she could do.

"Guys," Aiden's voice carried through the hall.

I hurried with a brisk pace to his office and poked my head inside. "You got something?" I hoped he wasn't just telling us hello.

My heart was like a jackhammer, pounding against the torn pavement. I felt on edge, ready to scream and unleash a fury that I hadn't known I harbored until today.

My baby girl was in danger.

Ariella was in danger.

The two people in the world who mattered the most to me could die today.

It wasn't a thought I could handle or a reality I was ready to live with.

"I got a ping off one of the phones, Ariella's," Aiden said. "It was brief and only lasted a second, but we've got the vicinity narrowed down."

Declan carried his laptop into the office and joined us, along with Mason and Lincoln.

"Jayden's convinced they're being held at Angelo DeLuca's compound," I said. I caught him up to speed with what he and Declan had missed.

Jayden hung out in the hallway, his arms folded. He appeared remorseful but uncomfortable. Probably because we were prepared to string him up by the balls if anything happened to any of the girls who had been kidnapped.

"You should see this," Declan said. He had hacked into surveillance footage for DeLuca's residence, which also happened to be the location of his compound.

He tapped the screen and zoomed in, cleaning up some of the video surveillance footage.

A little girl tore up the wooden staircase alone. "That's Izzie!"

Had she gotten away from the men?

Why was she running upstairs and not out the door?

"We need to move, now!" I couldn't watch and witness something horrific happen to my daughter.

I whisked out of the room for the door. "Call me as soon as you have something concrete!"

Jayden took off after me. "I'm coming with you. I got your families into this mess. I'll get them out of it."

I shot him a glance. I didn't know what he had planned, but we were likely going to need a distraction. For all I cared, Jayden could be the bait.

CHAPTER SEVENTEEN

Skylar

I never had a plan, not when Don DeLuca demanded that I help his associate nab three girls by midnight.

Running might have been the better option, but I wasn't one to flee. Besides, where would I have gone that wouldn't have wound up with me shot dead and tossed into the forest?

Ben had insisted we do the kidnapping at the mall.

He was an idiot.

I couldn't believe he wanted us to grab three girls while on camera. Was he trying to get us caught? Maybe he wanted me tossed in jail, and he planned on driving away, leaving my ass behind.

I put nothing past him.

We weren't friends.

I didn't even like the bastard.

Would Jayden come for me? I doubted that I'd happen to run into him. That was too big of a coincidence, and I didn't so much as have my cell phone on me that he could track.

I'd done as instructed, stalked into the mall and, upon seeing Ariella, I had hoped that I could involve her, if only for her help.

Having lived with her and Jaxson for the past few months, I knew her secret. Ariella had once been a C.I.A. operative. Well, I knew she worked for the C.I.A.

I wasn't exactly sure what she did, but if anyone had training and could get us out of this mess, Ariella was smart, cunning, and had been through enough hostage situations that she had to be prepared this time.

Right?

Boy, was I wrong.

Fuck me.

I still couldn't get over the fact Izzie came chasing after us.

Don't get me wrong. I hate kids. I plan never to have any, but she's my niece, and as much as she's a snotty toddler, she's also my kin.

Why couldn't she have listened to Ariella when she told her to run?

I should have done something.

I could have fought Ben, helped her get away, and aid in my own escape, too.

But I'd been foolish and selfish. The truth was I was afraid that Ben would kill me, or worse, the little girl he'd pointed the gun at.

And so I'd done what I'd been told, sheepishly climbed into the van and prayed that one day Ariella and Jaxson would find it in their hearts to forgive me.

Today, wasn't going to be that day.

"Get out!" Ben shouted at us, waving his gun.

This time he wasn't alone.

He'd parked the van by the back entrance of the compound, and DeLuca's men held their guns, reminding us to obey their commands.

No one wanted to climb out of the van first, least of all me.

The girls didn't budge, and I'd been here long enough to know that if we didn't follow their instruction, there would be consequences.

Exhaling a loud huff, I climbed out of the van first and, without so much as looking, could hear the commotion behind me as the other girls followed.

"Follow me," Ben said and led us in through the metal door and down the stairs toward the basement. "Not you. You stay here," he instructed Skylar.

"Where are you taking her?" Ariella asked.

Did she still care about me after what I'd done?

Her glance toward me was brief as she clutched Izzie tight to her chest, holding the little girl in her arms. Maybe I imagined it, but she didn't look angry like I would have expected.

Was it disappointment? Perhaps sadness.

Or I just didn't want to see that she hated me. That was as much a real possibility.

"That's none of your concern," Ben said.

"Who's the kid? We haven't been apart long enough for her to be yours," Ben said.

He reached for Izzie, prying her from Ariella's grip.

"No!" Ariella shifted her body, protecting my niece from his grabby hands.

"What do you want with her?" I asked. "She's just a kid."

I didn't know what Ben planned to do with the girls, but I suspected it wasn't good. I'd seen the handful of women in the basement, and from what I'd gathered previously from Jayden, they were being trafficked.

"Fine. You want her. She's your responsibility," Ben said as he shoved Izzie into my arms.

Shit.

What did I know about kids?

Izzie's eyes filled with tears and her bottom lip trembled before the dam broke. "I want my Daddy!" Izzie wailed, squirming in my arms.

She didn't want me to hold her, not that I blamed her. We weren't best friends. She probably knew I wasn't keen on her, and she obviously was making it clear she didn't want to be stuck with me, either.

"You're going to be fine," Ariella said, gently rubbing Izzie's back. "Skylar isn't going to let anything happen to you. Isn't that right?"

The look she shot me sent a shiver down my spine.

"Yes, that's right. You're safe with me," I said, holding Izzie on my hip.

I wanted to put her down. I wasn't used to holding a kid, let alone thirty or maybe forty pounds that had latched itself around my neck and hips.

The kid had no intention of loosening her grasp on me.

"You'll protect her, at all costs," Ariella said and leaned in close to my ear. "Or so help me, I will hunt you down and make you suffer Jaxson's wrath."

Ariella was right. I feared my older brother far more than I feared her.

CHAPTER EIGHTEEN

ARIELLA

Jaxson was going to kill me.

The scum-sucking vermin had snatched Izzie right out of my arms and handed her over to Skylar.

Jaxson's sister didn't look the least bit pleased to have to take charge of the little girl.

Ben led Skylar away from us, up another set of stairs and out of sight.

"Momma!" Izzie screamed.

Was she calling for me?

I hated the fact that Ben was up there with Izzie and Skylar. Anyone else, and I'd have been afraid but not like this. I knew what Ben was capable of.

He was a monster.

Ben had abducted me, threatened me, held me captive, and would have killed me if given a chance.

My heart ached and my stomach sank.

Was he going to hurt Izzie to get back at me for what I'd done all those years ago?

I may not have been Izzie's biological mother, but I was the only mother Izzie had known. Emma, her biological mother, was out of the picture, in prison. She hadn't wanted her daughter and had intended on giving her up for adoption.

"Move!" a man I didn't recognize commanded. He had thick, bushy eyebrows and short, dark curly hair.

He led Hazel, Harper, and me down a set of stairs, a gun poised at us to remind us that he was in charge.

"Hurry up!" the man commanded as we stepped down into the dim basement.

Row after row of prison cells lined the underground compound. To the right, several women were locked inside one of the cells.

He unlocked the second prison cell, and the iron-clad door squeaked open as he swung the door outward.

"Get in," he said, gesturing with his gun for us to do as he instructed.

I glanced over my shoulder at Hazel and Harper in the rear. Behind them, two guards stood armed with semi-automatic weapons.

There were too many of them, and Harper was pregnant. I couldn't fight them without risking too much.

I hesitated before I did as I was told. I stepped into the prison cell. Hazel followed just a few steps behind me.

"Please, sir," Harper said, a hand on her oversized belly. There was no hiding the fact that she was pregnant from these men.

She stood at the entrance to our cell but hadn't stepped inside yet.

"Move!" he shouted and shoved Harper in past the iron gates.

She stumbled forward, tripping over her swollen feet.

I rushed forward and reached out to catch Harper and keep her from falling onto the ground. We needed to get out of this situation unscathed.

He stood blocking the exit, but he hadn't yet shut the metal doors, locking us inside.

"Give me your phones."

Hazel and Harper slowly dug into their pockets, retrieving their devices.

I didn't budge from where I stood on the cement floor. "Mine fell out when we were picked up," I said, doing my best to lie. I refused to back down, my eyes staring into his.

If I so much as flinched, he might see through the charade.

His eyes narrowed as his eyes raked over my body. "I don't believe you. Strip down."

"I swear, I don't have my phone." I held up my hands in surrender. "You can search me," I said. I hoped that would suffice.

I didn't want to strip down, least of all for him.

Thankfully, Skylar had already been shuffled away or she might have given up the location of my cell phone.

She was the last person I trusted, well, her and Ben.

Were they working together, or had she gotten herself involved inadvertently? They weren't keeping her in prison with us.

The man with the bushy eyebrows stepped toward me.

His breath smelled of stale coffee, and he wreaked of day-old cigarette smoke. "Arms out," he commanded.

I held out my arms while he patted me down a little too intimately. With one hand, his fingers cupped my breasts, fondling them in the process before he shoved his hand inside the waistband of my jeans.

"Please, stop." My voice caught in my throat.

Bile rose to my lips. I swallowed down the burning liquid and pinched my eyes shut.

He lifted his hand with the gun, placing the barrel against my forehead. "I give the orders. Don't ever forget that."

His fingers grazed over my panties.

My stomach flopped and my body trembled.

He yanked his hand out of my pants.

"Turn around."

Was it over?

His hand did the same dance over my buttocks, inside the waistband of my jeans, before he withdrew his hand away and lowered the gun.

A moment later, he stalked to the door, stepped out, and closed the iron bars. The metal squeaked as he latched the lock.

Once he was gone, out of sight, I collapsed onto the cold cement floor.

I didn't feel cold.

My body was numb from the inside, and the tremors took over every ounce of my existence. I sat with my legs pulled up to my chest, shaking uncontrollably.

Hazel bent down and rested a hand on my back.

"We'll figure this out," she said, her voice soft and comforting.

I nodded solemnly and glanced toward the hallway. There were no guards standing in wait. Perhaps because we were behind bars, they no longer considered us a threat.

With a quick glance around the room, I recognized no surveillance equipment. There were no signs of cameras and recording devices, although I wasn't sure if they were listening to us.

I'd have to be careful.

Slowly, I withdrew my cell phone from my boot.

I lifted my finger to my lips, warning the other girls in the next cell over not to say anything as they watched us with a fierce intensity.

Would they betray us?

We were all in this together, right? Unless one of them had been like Skylar, hired by the mob to kidnap women.

Was that what happened with Skylar, or had I gotten it all wrong? Did it matter? She'd led us into the hands of the mob. And for what purpose?

I retrieved my cell phone from my boot and glanced at the signal.

No service.

That was strange.

Just about everywhere that I'd been in, Breckenridge had cell service. While the signal might not have been strong in the mountains, there had been plenty of cell towers.

They were probably blocking the signal. But if I could just get outside with my phone, then I could reach Jaxson and he could track me.

That was an unrealistic expectation.

Why would they let me outside?

And if I could get outside, I'd sure as hell run far and fast. I wasn't going to stick around to make a call.

Hopefully, Jaxson was able to locate the signal before we were tossed into the compound.

"Nothing," I said and shoved my phone back into my boot. As long as they'd already searched me, hopefully, they wouldn't go looking again for the device.

Gunfire erupted in the distance.

Was that Jaxson and the team coming to rescue us?

The lights flickered in the basement, and the three of us sat huddled together on the floor.

"We move the girls, now!" Ben's voice echoed as he hurried down the basement stairs.

Behind him, a half-dozen men with guns ushered us out of the prison cells and to follow them outside.

Hazel and I quickly stood and helped Harper to her feet.

"She stays," the man with the bushy eyebrows said, pointing at Harper.

"Are you sure?" Ben asked the other man. "We could get double for her."

"These men don't want babies. They want sex. I'll make some calls, see if we can find a buyer outside of our usual channels."

"No," I said and stepped in front of Harper.

Was I helping her or making things worse by leaving her behind with these monsters?

I wanted to protect Harper, but I felt the barrel of Ben's gun against my head. I heard the click of the safety being turned off.

"Don't tempt me, sweetheart," he said, his breath against my ear as he leaned in and grabbed my arm.

CHAPTER NINETEEN

Jayden

I'd sworn to myself that I'd never work with the guys from Eagle Tactical.

Why?

Because I already owed them my life.

We'd served together in the military. Jaxson had pulled my ass out from behind enemy lines while I'd been shot, bleeding to death.

I should have died.

He should have left me to die.

Thanking him seemed inadequate after he risked his life, bullets flying at him. He'd been reckless but selfless.

I wasn't deserving.

He threw himself on the line. He could have died, and I owed him.

What did I do when we returned home?

I kept my distance.

I might have owed Jaxson my life, but I wasn't going to risk his, not when my niece's life was on the line. He'd already done more for me than I deserved. I couldn't involve him. It was my burden to bear.

He had a kid, a daughter at home. It was no secret that he was a single father.

I wouldn't risk his daughter not growing up with a father, alone in the world.

And so, every time he offered me a gig with Eagle Tactical, I turned him down. It wasn't out of pride. Though he probably thought that was the reason. It's what I made him believe so that I could protect him.

Because deep down, he was still my brother.

Family protected each other.

And now I'd torn his family apart.

I walked the final distance up toward the gate and pressed the buzzer of the wrought-iron gates that protected the property of Don DeLuca.

It was the last place I wanted to be, but Don Ricci had made sure that I got what was coming to me.

Betrayal tasted bitter.

I bite down on my tongue, shoving down any and all emotion that showed conflict. I was doing this to save Skylar.

And I owed Jaxson my life.

"We're even," I said quietly into the microphone that I wore in secret. After this, I no longer owed Jaxson or any of my brothers anything ever again.

"We'll see about that. Head down, be quiet. Quit attracting attention to yourself," Jaxson said.

He was right.

I had to play this carefully. Talking to myself, or rather Jaxson, was going to get me killed.

I didn't want to die. Definitely not today.

I stalked up to the gate and pressed the buzzer. From above, I could spot a guard, gun poised at the tower, ready to shoot.

Hopefully, Don DeLuca didn't shoot first and ask questions later.

"Yes?" A heavy male voice answered the buzz. "Can I help you?"

"My name is Jayden Scott. I'd like to speak with your boss, Angelo DeLuca," I said.

"Don DeLuca isn't taking guests," the voice on the other side of the intercom answered.

"I have information for him regarding Enzo Ricci." I didn't elaborate further.

The lock on the gate clicked, and the iron fence separated, allowing me access to enter.

I stepped forward and walked the length of the driveway up toward DeLuca's compound.

It took every ounce of strength not to glance to my left and right, where, in the distance, Jaxson and his team snuck onto the premises.

Bang!

I ducked, hearing a bullet whiz by my head.

What the hell? Who was shooting at me? Eagle Tactical or DeLuca's men?

The sound of gunfire erupted all around me.

"I'm under heavy fire," Mason's voice filled my earpiece.

"On it," Jaxson answered, changing positions. I watched as he tore across the yard by the hedges that sat against the wrought-iron gate.

He shot off several rounds, taking out the guy who had been shooting at Mason.

Gunshots erupted from all around. I was a giant target with no place for cover at my current position.

I rushed to the front entrance as I pulled my pistol from its holster at my hip.

"I'm heading inside," I announced to the team.

"No, I'm going through the west entrance," Lincoln said as he scaled the building and climbed up to the balcony. "They'll expect us to come in the front door."

We had gone over the plan, with Lincoln sneaking up the ivy on the side of the property. I was supposed to waltz through the front door, invited.

It seemed the plan had changed.

"Jayden, your cover's been blown. Stay outside with Mason. I'm heading in with Lincoln to find and recover the girls," Jaxson said.

I kept my position, shooting at DeLuca's men as they headed for the front door. I wasn't letting them step outside.

Gunfire erupted at every position all around us.

From inside, shots were fired.

What the hell was going on in there?

CHAPTER TWENTY

ARIELLA

Ben yanked me forward and out of the cell, in line behind the other girls who were in the next prison cell beside us.

We hadn't said much to them.

The sound of gunfire grew louder and nearer.

Was it Jaxson?

Had the guys from Eagle Tactical come to save us?

I wanted to stay, to fight, to see if we could stall and help aid in our rescue, but with the gun against my skin and Ben trigger happy, I was out of options.

We were marched up the back stairwell, the same way that we came in. Ushered outside, I glanced at Hazel and hoped that she had the same idea I had.

Now was the time to fight.

I thrust my elbow at Ben, landing a blow to his stomach and then his face, feeling his nose crack under my fist.

The other girls gasped and stood frozen.

They didn't fight.

They didn't run.

They stood there, trembling out of fear.

I couldn't count on them to help.

Where was Jaxson?

The gunfire erupted on the opposite side of the compound. Several additional shots were inside.

Was Harper all right? What about Izzie?

Ben grabbed me by the hair and dragged me the remainder of the distance to the van. He tossed me inside, and the other girls silently followed.

"Move!"

Hazel climbed in last. Her bottom lip trembled as she came to sit beside me, cuddling up against me.

Ben slammed the van door shut and the engine roared to life. The vehicle jolted forward as we were whisked off the premises.

Where the hell were they taking us?

CHAPTER TWENTY-ONE

JAXSON

I climbed the trellis of ivy up the side of the compound.

We had to move quickly.

Lincoln was already upstairs, staking out the place, making sure we were clear.

Gunfire erupted as I breached the window and threw myself inside. I couldn't shoot. I could barely cover myself as I flung my body through the small space.

Lincoln covered me.

Two men of DeLuca's lay in a pool of their own blood, dead.

"We need to move," Lincoln said.

I leaped to my feet, gun poised and ready to go. The tactical gear weighed us down and had made it a little more uncomfortable to climb the ivy and whisk me in through the window.

"On it," I answered. I followed behind Lincoln as he had already scoped out the room and made sure it was safe where we'd entered.

Together, we exited the small bedroom and flanked into the hallway.

"Upstairs!" a gruff voice shouted.

Several pairs of boots trampled up the steps in haste.

"Reinforcements," I muttered under my breath to Lincoln.

We positioned ourselves around the edge of the banister, careful not to be seen. As DeLuca's men tore up the stairs, shooting blindly, we landed shot after shot at their heads for a kill shot.

We didn't come to take prisoners. We were here on a search and recovery mission.

Anyone standing in our way was the enemy.

The compound was at least two stories. I suspected there also might have been a basement. The girls could have been kept anywhere.

Room to room, we searched the premises, just the two of us. The majority of the rooms upstairs were empty.

Additional gunshots erupted outside.

"We need to move," I said. We had to hurry. It wouldn't be long until more men tore up the stairs looking for us. We'd shot down the half-dozen soldiers who had come for retribution.

Lincoln opened door after door, and I went with him, gun drawn, prepared to take out anyone who stood in the way of finding our families.

Yanking the door open, I stared at Izzie as she sat at a child's table with Skylar and a teen girl having a tea party.

"Daddy!" Izzie shouted. She leaped out of her chair. The tiny wooden seat fell to the floor as she rushed across the room.

"Don't move," DeLuca's voice echoed from behind.

I heard the click of the safety being turned off as I felt the barrel of the gun at the back of my head.

CHAPTER TWENTY-TWO

ARIELLA

"You okay?" I whispered to Hazel.

We sat huddled together in the back of a van. Darkness surrounded us.

There were more than just the two of us. Nearly a dozen women had been crammed inside the back of the white van, the same vehicle we were brought in with, just a short while ago.

"No," Hazel muttered. "None of this is okay."

I knew that.

"We'll get out of this alive," I said.

"How?" Hazel asked. "As sex slaves? I'd rather take a bullet to my head."

"Don't talk like that," I said. "We do what we have to for survival. We can fight these men. As far as I can tell, there's only one driving us. When we get to wherever they're taking us, we fight."

"That won't work," another girl said. I didn't recognize her voice. It was raspy and thick. She sounded parched. "You fight, you get tied up, beaten, raped, the list goes on. The men, they all take turns, and we all have to watch."

"How long have you been with these men?" I asked.

I wasn't sure I wanted to know, but it was clear she'd been around for a while to witness what transpired when the prisoners fought back.

"Not long, a few weeks. Some of the girls have been shuffled between families. Bought, used, and sold like garbage. That's how they treat us, and you're lucky if their interest is sexual and not masochistic," she said.

A shiver ran through me.

"Being forced to marry Franco Ivanov, suddenly sounds like a picnic," Hazel muttered.

I wrapped an arm around her shoulder, trying to reassure her as best I could that we would get out of this alive.

I just wasn't sure how.

With a gun poised at your temple, there's no way to fight back.

Two men stood guard outside of the van. One held a gun at our heads while we climbed out of the vehicle, the other secured a collar to each of our necks.

A third guard waited just a few feet away, a black remote in his palm.

"No one's going to fight back?" he asked with a chuckle and tilted his head. "That's too bad." He pressed down on the button, forcing a jolt of electricity to run through all of our bodies at the same time.

I fell to the ground. My eyes squeezed shut.

Everything inside of me ached like lightning burned through my veins. I gasped for breath. My heart hammered in my chest.

The electricity lasted only a few seconds, but it felt like forever.

"There will be no insubordination," the man said, "or you all will suffer the price."

We were connected. All of us, forced to endure torture together.

The collars were their method of control. There was no way to escape.

CHAPTER TWENTY-THREE

JAXSON

"Don't shoot, Angelo," I said, holding my hands up.

"It's Don DeLuca to you," Angelo said.

"I'm on it," Mason said through the earpiece.

Good, he'd gotten the message that we were in trouble and needed additional backup.

I hoped he'd come in time.

Lincoln refused to lower his gun as he pointed it across the room at Angelo. He closed the distance as he stepped forward.

"Don't hurt him!" Skylar jumped up from her seat at the table, where she'd been having tea with Izzie and the teen girl.

"What are you doing?" Don DeLuca's eyes narrowed as he studied the young woman.

"Izzie, come here," Skylar said, holding out her arms, trying to protect my daughter from DeLuca.

My daughter's eyes watered as she glanced from Skylar and then back to me. Her bottom lip trembled.

"Go with Skylar," I said, trying desperately to protect my baby girl.

It was clear Izzie wasn't sure what to do.

I needed to protect her, and it was difficult with the barrel of a gun against the back of my head.

"Time's up," Mason's voice echoed from behind DeLuca as he stood in the hallway. "You'll let them go, or I'll end your inconsequential life."

"Shoot me," DeLuca said. "Do you honestly think it's over? Your girls, they're gone."

Skylar grabbed Izzie and pulled her safely out of harm's way, behind her legs, shielding her from danger.

Mason yanked a pair of metal handcuffs from his belt loop and thrust DeLuca's hands behind his back, securing his wrists in place.

"What do you mean, they're gone?" Lincoln seethed.

Izzie rushed past Skylar for me, arms raised.

I pulled her into my arms, cuddling her for only a moment. I wanted to relish the moment, reassure her that everything was fine and she was safe, but we weren't home.

There could have been countless other men ready to take aim.

I was just hoping Izzie was no longer in danger.

Where were the others?

Where were Ariella, Hazel, and Harper?

With DeLuca detained, we searched the compound, shooting anyone garnishing a weapon.

Most of his men fled. The few who had stayed, we'd gunned down. They hadn't given us another option.

With our guns raised, we headed down the stairs for the basement.

DeLuca accompanied us, arms bound behind his back with metal cuffs. Skylar, Izzie, and the teenage girl stood with Mason, keeping guard, protecting them in case Angelo tried anything stupid.

"There's no one down here. I'm telling you, the girls are gone," DeLuca said.

He didn't appear the least bit apologetic or contrite.

"How about we see for ourselves?" I led the way, gun drawn, making sure there were no more men brandishing weapons.

"Help!" Harper's voice carried from down in the basement.

"Harper?" Lincoln hurried past me for the prison cell, as I made sure there were no other guards hidden in the basement lockup.

The hallway twisted and turned.

The overhead fluorescent bulbs flickered and sizzled.

I glanced past the empty prison cells and reached the end before turning around to come back and join them.

Lincoln grabbed a pair of keys that hung on the opposite wall and unlocked the metal door. He helped Harper to her feet, examining her with a quick gaze. "Here, let me help you up." He offered her his hand.

"I told you they left," DeLuca said. "They're not coming back to the facility. At least the girls aren't." He quirked a sly grin.

My stomach flopped, and I lurched forward, yanking him by his hair, my gun poised at his chin, pointed upward.

"Where did you send them?"

Ariella and Hazel were still out there and, by now, could be anywhere.

I tapped my earpiece, connecting me to Declan and Aiden who were back at the office.

"I need eyes in the sky. We've got Harper, Skylar, and Izzie, but Hazel and Ariella have been taken off the property."

I cocked the safety off on my gun. "You'll tell me where you're taking the girls."

"We came into the compound in a white van," Skylar said.

"We're looking for a white van," I reiterated to Aiden and Declan.

Aiden was a guru with computers, satellite surveillance, and hacking anything and everything, including top-secret government servers. I trusted that he could get us eyes on the van.

"Any idea what direction they headed?" Declan asked.

"Lincoln, take the girls outside. Call in for an ambulance if Harper needs to get checked out," I said.

I didn't want Izzie or the others to witness what I was willing to do to find Ariella.

"Jaxson." Lincoln's voice held a hint of warning. "We've got DeLuca. Why don't we hand him over to the authorities? We could use their assistance in tracking the other girls down."

Of course, Lincoln would want to contact the local sheriff's department, now that we had Harper and she was safe.

I couldn't risk their interference and ruining our operation. We trained for this type of situation and had far more experience than the local Breckenridge sheriff's department.

"Not an option," I said gruffly. "We're doing this on our own."

"What about DeLuca?" Lincoln asked, glancing at him.

"I'll get the information out of him."

While there were some lines I wasn't willing to cross, when it involved my family and my friends, I'd do whatever it took to save them.

CHAPTER TWENTY-FOUR

Jayden

I stood guard out front of the compound.

While I wanted to be inside and helping rescue Skylar and the others, I also recognized that someone had to stand guard and keep a lookout.

If DeLuca's men intended to flee, I wasn't going to let that happen.

The gunfire inside had silenced after quite some time.

I'd have been worried if I hadn't been connected via an earpiece and could hear the conversation amongst the men of Eagle Tactical.

Lincoln stepped outside first, through the front door.

I lowered my gun, careful not to shoot him.

Skylar followed, holding Izzie's hand.

Exhaling a sigh of relief, I was grateful that they were both all right. "I'm glad you're safe," I said.

Skylar dropped Izzie's hand and threw back her fist, landing a blow to my face.

"You bastard!" Skylar shouted at me.

Okay, maybe I deserved that. While I hadn't known what Enzo

would have done, I shouldn't have ever involved her in my mess. I'd been selfish and irresponsible in bringing a civilian on board.

"You're right. I'm an asshole," I said.

She cocked an eyebrow.

Had she expected me to fight back?

I rubbed my cheek. It stung like hell, but I'd survive. It was nothing an ice pack and a couple of aspirin couldn't cure.

Were my eyes playing tricks on me? Behind Skylar, a young brunette hesitated. Her pale blue eyes stared back at me.

"Lexa!" I shouted to my niece and rushed forward, past Izzie and Skylar.

Lexa threw her arms around my neck. "Uncle Jayden," she whispered before the sobs wreaked havoc on her body.

I caught her in my arms, not letting her collapse to the ground.

"Are you okay?" It was a terrible question, the stupidest that I could have asked, and yet here I was, asking it anyhow.

"We should get the girls into the truck," Lincoln said. "We don't want to be standing out here in case DeLuca brings in rcinforcements."

"Affirmative."

Lincoln was good at taking charge and commanding a team. I followed his lead.

Skylar held Izzie's hand and followed behind Lincoln as I wrapped an arm around Lexa, escorting her across the lawn, past the open gate and to the other side, just beyond the road where the truck was parked.

"What about Daddy?" Izzie asked.

"Yeah? Where's Jaxson and Mason?" I asked.

I'd heard briefly over the transmission that they'd stayed behind to interrogate DeLuca. I didn't know what they were capable of outside of a war zone.

Then, again, when one's family was in danger, it meant war.

I'd been down that path looking for Lexa.

"Getting information," Lincoln said. He didn't further elaborate.

We rushed to the vehicle and threw open the back door, letting the girls inside first. Izzie climbed into the back seat with Skylar on one side and Lexa on the opposite.

"I want my daddy," Izzie said. She had trouble sitting still in the backseat.

The kid probably needed a car seat, which was in Jaxson's truck.

"How about we play a game?" Skylar said. "I spy with my little eye something yellow."

"The sun!" Izzie squealed.

Skylar laughed. "Yes, your turn."

Lexa reached for my arm as I stood just outside the truck at the door, keeping watch.

"What's going to happen to me? I mean now that my parents are gone," Lexa asked, her bottom lip trembled.

"You'll come and stay with me," I said.

I had every intention of bringing her home with me. While I might not have known anything about raising a teenager, I wasn't going to send her to foster care or let someone else get their slimy paws on her.

Lexa reached out and wrapped her arms around me for a hug.

She sobbed into my chest.

I wasn't used to girls crying, let alone kids. Well, she was fifteen, not exactly a kid, but still, she needed a role model. And I was the last person on the planet who Lexa should be looking up to.

"I've got you," I said, patting her back as I held her. "I won't let anyone hurt you ever again."

Skylar glanced in my direction. A frown line etched to her brow. She opened her mouth but quickly shut it.

Smiling, Skylar returned her attention back to Izzie and their little game.

"I spy, Daddy!" Izzie squealed. She pointed to Jaxson as he and Mason hurried toward the truck. His hands were covered in blood, his pants just as dirty.

I didn't dare ask what the hell they'd done to DeLuca. The bastard deserved everything he had come to him.

Jaxson was the first to approach the truck. He wiped his filthy hands on his pants, as if that would erase the memories and the bloodshed.

"There's an auction at midnight," Jaxson said. "We need to be there. I've got the GPS coordinates in my phone."

"What about DeLuca?" I asked. "Do we need to worry about him warning his men?"

Mason exhaled a heavy breath. "He's not talking."

CHAPTER TWENTY-FIVE

ARIELLA

I expected to be tossed into a cellar or a basement, behind metal bars on a dingy surface that made me fear my life.

The electric collar pinched my skin. But the men who abducted us brought us inside a home, though it felt more like a fortress.

From the outside, it was heavily guarded, more so than even the last place we'd been taken. While the last prison had been a holding cell, literally keeping us until we reached our next destination, this prison was completely different.

The lights were dimmed as we entered. It took a few moments for my eyes to adjust.

I followed the other girls, keeping close together as the men shoved us forward and through the long hallway and up the staircase.

A dark red carpet led a path up the stairs. My boots sank into the plush material.

Was Jaxson able to track us?

I had to believe that he would come for us, rescue us. It was only a matter of time before we got out of this mess.

A guard opened the door to the right, and we were all ushered inside before the door slammed behind us.

A woman in her mid-seventies stepped out of the shadows, dressed in a pink satin robe. "Come closer," she said, gesturing for us to approach.

When we shuffled slowly, she dug out a small handheld device, the same black remote that the guard had used earlier to shock all of us.

She pressed down on the button, forcing a jolt of pain to sear my neck.

I was doubled over in pain.

Fire burned my skin as I shuddered and fell to my knees. My hands instinctively reached for the collar, but I couldn't remove it.

"I'm Diamond, and remember, ladies, that I do not ask twice," the woman said, a stern expression crossed her face.

Was that even her real name, Diamond?

Had she been one of us once in her life, or was she running the operation?

She held not an ounce of empathy.

We hurried closer, afraid to be zapped again by the madwoman with the remote.

"Very good," Diamond said with a glint in her eye. "You will find this all will go by so quickly and painlessly if you follow my orders the first time."

She paused for a moment and paced slowly, the window behind her. It held cast iron bars, locking us inside.

I imagined the door was locked behind us too. I didn't try to make a break for freedom. It wasn't going to come so easily, not with dozens of armed guards in and around the premises.

"Tonight, you girls will be the most fabulous and precious guests for the evening event. Like me, a diamond, you must shine, sparkle, and gleam. I expect each of you to bathe quickly. After which you will be dressed, and we will do your makeup and hair. Do I hear any objections?" she asked, revealing the black button in her palm.

No one spoke.

"Perfect. Do not be shy. You are the jewels of the evening and, as such, will be passed around to be examined, touched, and thoroughly inspected."

My stomach flopped.

We weren't jewels.

We were people.

And while I appreciated that at least she wasn't calling us sex slaves, that's what we were, being sold into slavery. Any way you diced it, this woman was sick.

The woman pointed at me. "You'll be the first, darling. What is your name?"

I stared at her, unsure of what to say.

She humphed under her breath. "Well, I don't have all day."

"Ariella," I whispered, afraid Diamond might zap me with her twitchy fingers.

Her eyes squinted as she stared at me. Her hand jerked out to grab my jaw as she examined my face from side to side. "That's no good. From this night forward, you are Jade. Now, hurry and get washed up. You need to be presentable for this evening's auction."

I didn't move. My feet were frozen in place.

"Quickly, we haven't got all day," Diamond said.

She snapped her fingers. Thank heavens she didn't press the damned buzzer again.

I hurried across the room to where a guard stood and pointed at the open door.

It led to a connected bathroom with several individual shower stalls. I felt like I was back in college, a lifetime ago.

Hazel was right behind me a few feet. "Apparently, I look like Violet. Why she couldn't let me be Hazel is beyond me," she muttered.

I quirked a grin at her. "She loves purple."

Now wasn't the time to let our guard down. We needed to bide our time but be careful. I needed to strip down, but I wasn't looking forward to bathing around these monsters.

A guard stood at the entrance to the bathroom. There were partitions for each stall, but no curtain and certainly no privacy.

"Do we have to leave this on when we shower?" I asked, pointing at the collar. "I don't want to get zapped from the water."

"The only one zapping you is Madam Diamond herself or one of the ranking guards," the uniformed guard said.

I exhaled a heavy breath but didn't budge from my position in the stall. I'd yet to disrobe.

"Clock's ticking. You have five minutes in here. If you're not sparkly clean at that point, you can bet that necklace will light up like Christmas."

Wonderful.

Slowly, I disrobed, leaving my phone buried inside my boot. What other choice did I have?

It wasn't just a threat. I'd felt the sting of electricity and sure as hell didn't want to feel it again. I'd follow their orders to survive. I just needed to give Jaxson and the Eagle Tactical team a little more time.

They were coming for us, and even if there was a cell phone jammer like the last place, they had to have caught the signal when we were outside or in the van.

I held on to that bit of hope while I stepped forward and turned on the shower spray.

While I couldn't see Hazel because of the frosted tinted partition between us, I could hear her shuffle around as she undressed.

The shower spray warmed, and I stepped under. It was like a rainstorm, pouring down and soaking me from head to toe.

I let the water envelop me as I became one with the shower. I wanted to wash away the filth, the trauma that I'd already endured, but I knew that was foolish.

How could I relax when I was further from being safe?

"Two-minute warning, Jade," the guard said.

Against the wall, was a dispenser for soap and shampoo.

I hurried to clean up the stench that surrounded me. The dirt that covered me was an invisible layer created by Ben and others, like the men standing guard and Diamond with the remote ready to cause pain to anyone she deemed unworthy.

Suds covered me, and just as quickly as the rain shower soaked me, it was over.

The shower shut off without my approval.

The guard shucked a gray towel in my direction. "Dry off and drop your clothes in that bin." He pointed at a giant garbage can by the exit of the bathroom.

Shit, my phone was buried in my shoes.

Well, at least it would stay on unnoticed. I wouldn't be able to secure it on me without being seen. Even with just a towel, the guard hadn't so much as looked away.

Privacy was apparently not in his vocabulary.

I wanted to offer a smartass remark about him taking a picture or if he'd never seen a naked woman before, but I held my tongue. I didn't want to feel Diamond's wrath or force it on the group of girls.

They'd come to hate me if I was the only one fighting back and we all were suffering the consequences.

One of Diamond's assistants, her name was Iris, dressed me in a black satin negligee with thin straps that revealed too much cleavage and barely covered my ass.

I felt naked.

That was probably the point.

They hadn't let me put my panties back on, so I kept pulling down the hem of the dress only to have it show more of my breasts.

Wonderful. I was going to be on display for a bunch of pervy men.

My hands trembled, and I tucked them into my arms, folding them across my chest, trying to at least keep some semblance of modesty.

I wasn't the least bit comfortable. And while that should have been the last concern given the men with guns and the collar on my neck, it still was unsettling.

Iris fixed my hair up in curls, pinning part of it up while leaving some long locks in the back.

She did my makeup too, paying extra attention to my eyes and lips.

There wasn't a mirror. I had no idea how I looked, but based on the other girls' appearances, they were going a little too heavy with the eyeliner and lipstick.

I hardly ever wore makeup anyhow, and when I did, it was a little gloss or colored balm for my lips. This felt like overkill.

It had grown dark hours ago.

My stomach grumbled.

The guards had brought in pizza for them to eat, but we weren't given anything more than water.

Were they trying to starve us? Force us into obedience?

We were already following their every command.

The lights dimmed and flickered.

Hazel and I exchanged a brief glance.

"Girls!" Diamond clapped her hands, getting our attention. "It is time to unveil you to our guests. You are to use only the name we've given you tonight. There are cameras everywhere inside and outside of the property. If we so much as suspect any betrayal, you will be punished along with your sisters," Diamond said.

She had us all line up with Hazel and me last in line. I wasn't in any hurry to meet the men downstairs. They were probably men like Ben, wanting to get their dirty hands on us.

Diamond let the other girls step out into the hallway. She stepped in the way of the line, preventing me from walking out before Hazel.

"You two aren't like the other girls," Diamond said. She stepped closer. Her eyes raked over us which sent a chill down my spine.

My hands trembled, but I tried not to let her see.

Hazel and I remained silent.

"Doesn't matter your pasts, backgrounds, what you did to deserve this life," Diamond said. "I shall give you each one piece of advice and use it wisely. Entertain these men tonight, and you may find yourself like me, bathed in fortune."

She reached into her pocket and pulled out a gold bracelet. She grabbed my arm and slipped the metal over my arm, locking it into place. "We will be listening to every word that you speak, Jade," Diamond said.

I swallowed the lump in my throat.

Diamond retrieved a second bracelet and snapped it onto Hazel's wrist.

"Now go. Let the festivities commence," Diamond said. She stepped aside, letting us catch up with the girls as they headed down the stairwell barefoot.

CHAPTER TWENTY-SIX

JAXSON

Heading back to Eagle Tactical, I parked the truck out front.

Mason climbed out first and headed inside to talk to Declan and Aiden. He wanted to know what was going on with Hazel and if they had any new intel since the last time we checked in with them a few minutes earlier.

Lincoln pulled up beside me and killed the engine. "I'm going to swing by the local clinic and have them take a look at Harper."

"I'm fine!" Harper said, waving her hand dismissively at him.

He shot her a look. "You might be, but I need to know our baby is fine too."

Lexa and Jayden climbed out of the backseat. They'd driven back with Lincoln.

"Do you mind if we tag along? Lexa should probably have a doctor examine her."

"I'm fine, Uncle Jayden," Lexa said, rolling her eyes. "I just want to go home, take a hot bubble bath, and relax."

Jayden stalled, probably waiting for one of us to interject.

I unbuckled Izzie from the backseat of my truck and opened the main door. I paused, exhaling a heavy sigh.

I wasn't sure when to do this, to break it to Skylar that her invitation to stay with me was retracted. Now seemed as good a time as any.

"Skylar, you need to find someplace else to crash. You're not coming home with us except to pack your bags."

Skylar's eyes widened. "We're family, Jaxson. You can't kick me out."

"The hell I can't!" My voice grew louder as I spoke. "You just had my daughter and my girlfriend kidnapped. If it were up to me, I never want to see you again." I refused to lower my gaze.

She needed to know what she'd done hurt. It went beyond betrayal. She'd cut my heart and made me bleed.

"I have work to do. We still need to track down Hazel and Ariella. I expect you to clean out your shit and be gone when I get home tonight."

Skylar shoved her hands into her jeans. "If that's what you want."

"I don't trust you, and as long as you're keeping company with him," I said and pointed at Jayden, "you're not welcome in my home."

She opened her mouth to say something, but just as quickly shut it.

Good. I didn't want to hear her lame excuses to justify what she'd done.

I stormed inside the building, leaving Skylar outside without a ride. Jayden or Lincoln could help her if they were so inclined.

It was doubtful that Lincoln would offer Skylar any help.

While they'd been chummy months ago, before he'd fallen for Harper, she'd betrayed him just like she'd betrayed me.

Izzie sat at the table where Ariella worked. We'd moved the computer and given Izzie a pencil and a handful of colored pens to doodle with on some blank computer paper.

We weren't prepared for a kid in the office. I didn't have crayons or a coloring book, and while I usually kept those things in a spare bag in the truck, I didn't have it on hand today.

I hadn't planned on going on an excursion.

"Tell me you have something," I said to Aiden.

He tapped away diligently at his keyboard.

Mason stood on the opposite side, arms folded across his chest, his expression solemn, his jaw tight.

"I've got a recent location for Ariella's cell phone, which matches the location that DeLuca gave us," Aiden said.

He scribbled down the information on a piece of paper and handed it to me.

"Thanks," I said gruffly.

"You can't go dressed like that to the auction," Declan said as he waltzed into the office, a fresh cup of coffee in hand. He sipped his mug and stood in the doorjamb.

"What's wrong with the way I'm dressed?" I asked and glanced down at my attire. My dark blue jeans had a streak of blood, and my shirt didn't look any better.

He wasn't wrong. "You have anything I can borrow?" I doubted they kept spare clothes at the office. "Or am I taking the clothes off your back?" I asked.

"You can't go into the auction," Jayden said.

I glanced behind me as he hurried in to catch up with us. Skylar stood by the door, waiting inside, and Lexa kept her company.

"And why the hell not?" I asked.

If anyone was going to rescue Ariella, it was going to be me.

Mason could come too. He'd want to rescue Hazel, and I wasn't going to stop him. Just like I knew he wouldn't stop me.

We were in this together.

"We don't know who is running the auction," Jayden said. "It could be anyone, and you're a prominent name in Breckenridge."

"Everyone knows we work for Eagle Tactical," Mason muttered. "So, what, we just let the girls get bought by some scumbags and then have to mount two rescue missions?" He shook his head and stormed toward Jayden.

"Hey! I'm just trying to help!" Jayden threw his arms up in surrender. "If you want to go and get turned away at the door, then by all means, show up. But if you want someone who can get in and get the girls out, then you need me."

I didn't like whatever plan Jayden had in mind. He was the reason Ariella and Hazel were still missing.

I glanced at the clock on the wall. Time wasn't on our side.

While we could create fake identities and even put on a disguise, it was too risky. These types of events were by invitation only.

"You can get an invitation?" I sized up Jayden.

Jayden nodded eagerly. He was trying too hard. "I know the guy running the auction, Capo Sergio. He's part of DeLuca's family," Jayden said.

Was he trying to make up for what he'd done, or was he hiding something from us?

What choice was there but to trust him?

My phone buzzed in my pocket. Could it be Ariella? I didn't recognize the phone number.

"Hello?" I answered the caller.

"Hi, is this Jaxson?"

"Yes." I felt the guys' eyes on me as I took a step out of the room and stared at Izzie as she quietly colored. She'd managed to get ink all over her hands and on the desk.

"It's Delphine. Ariella was supposed to pick me up from the airport, but she isn't answering her phone."

CHAPTER TWENTY-SEVEN

Jayden

She'd spotted me before I'd even managed to lay eyes on her.

I'd yet to see Ariella, but Hazel sauntered her way over to me, giving me an overly seductive smile.

I tried to play it cool and calm.

Capo Sergio stood beside me. "See anything you like, my man?" he asked, patting me on the back. "You can take her home for the right price."

I cleared my throat. "And what price is that, exactly?" I looked her up and down. I needed to pretend that I was deciding whether she was of interest to me.

"It's a silent auction and cash only. Don't forget that," Sergio said and wagged his finger at me. "I tell you, these girls get hotter, the longer we keep them locked up."

It took everything in me not to slug Capo Sergio. He was the one running this operation, and while I intended to bring it down, I couldn't do it alone.

Wearing a wire had been a discussion, and then turning the information over to the authorities. But I couldn't risk getting caught.

Already, I'd been treading water, barely surviving, between Enzo throwing me out in the cold and handing my fake fiancée over to DeLuca's men.

Sergio probably trusted me as much as I trusted him.

"You can take her for a test drive," Sergio said and gestured with his index finger toward the private rooms. "There is, of course, a fee, but you know how these things are. Anything goes. Nothing is off-limits."

"Good. I'd hate to pay for tainted merchandise," I said. It took everything in me not to vomit, hearing the words leave my lips.

I grabbed Hazel by the hips and pulled her against me. "How much for an hour with her?"

"Twenty minutes, tops. Other prospective buyers should get an opportunity with her too," Sergio said. "Four hundred for twenty minutes."

"Fuck me," I muttered and pulled out four one hundred-dollar bills.

My hand latched onto Hazel's wrist, and I dragged her with a force of intensity toward the private suite and slammed the door behind us.

I wasn't an idiot. There were cameras everywhere. Were there cameras in the private room?

I didn't see any, but that didn't mean anything.

"I'm Violet," Hazel said. Her voice trembled as she took a step back from me.

My eyes tightened as I studied her.

She and the other girls all had black collars around their necks, secured with a metal lock that buckled into place. On her arm, she wore a gold bangle, and she tapped on the bracelet repeatedly as she glanced past me.

Hazel tugged on her bottom lip, bringing it between her teeth, not saying anything further.

"Violet," I said, using the name she'd given me. If she wanted me to know her name wasn't Hazel while we were alone, then she probably thought the men were listening to us.

"Do you understand that I bought your time for the next twenty minutes?" My expression remained cold and dark as I pulled her arm with the bracelet toward me. My fingers fiddled with the bangle while my gaze stayed locked on her eyes.

"Yes, I understand," Hazel said. She stepped closer and climbed onto my lap.

Perhaps she thought they were watching us too?

I didn't think she'd want to be anywhere near me otherwise.

"Suppose I'm interested in buying more than one girl. Is there anyone else who might hold my interest as much as you?" I asked. "I like brunettes with long hair, soulful eyes, with a bit of spark." I had to be careful that no one could decode what we said and make sense of it.

"I, yes, perhaps Jade might be to your liking," Hazel said.

"Good." I smiled, tightlipped.

It'd be a lie to say that I was surprised they required the girls to use different names.

"Tell me, Violet, why might I choose to buy you when I could have any woman in this place?" I asked only because I knew they listened.

She opened her mouth and quickly shut it.

I raised an eyebrow, waiting for her to answer.

Hazel exhaled a heavy breath and leaned closer. Her fingers raked through my hair as her lips reached my ear, whispering so that only I could hear her. "Because if you don't, Mason will hunt you down and kill you."

She wasn't wrong.

I had several thousand dollars in cash, most of it on me, but a few grand had been hidden in the truck outside.

I'd been concerned that if all the cash was on me, I could get some of it lifted.

The truth was I had no idea how much it would cost, what a

silent auction for a person went for. It wasn't like I could ask someone.

Capo Sergio stood in the center of the room. The lights dimmed, as he had a microphone in his left hand.

"The final moment of the evening you all have been patiently waiting for, the winners of the silent auction," Sergio said.

A wayward smile reached his lips. He received a stack of notecards from an older woman I didn't recognize, dressed in a glittery gold gown that shined like a chandelier under the lights.

"Thank you," Sergio said to her.

The girls were lined up against the wall, and he gestured for the first girl to join him.

"Our first prize of the evening, Ruby, will be going home with Rafael. You may pay me or bring the funds to Diamond to claim your prize." He gestured toward the woman in the gold gown.

Ruby walked to the opposite side of the room beside Diamond.

The young redhead, Ruby, looked downright frightened as she stood waiting for Rafael to complete his transaction.

If I could have saved every girl tonight, I would have, but that wasn't why I came to the auction. I was here for Ariella and Hazel, or rather Jade and Violet.

The auction continued, girl after girl, transaction after transaction.

My stomach flopped as I watched the girls leave, forced to go with a stranger—most of the men, I didn't recognize. However, a few were DeLuca's crew and hadn't been at the compound from what I'd seen earlier in the day.

If they had, I'd have been dead by now.

Thankfully, my cover hadn't been blown.

Did they know Angelo DeLuca was dead? I doubted it was the end of the DeLuca family. Another boss would rise up in his place. Would it be Gino, his second in command?

"Next up this evening, we have Violet. Violet, please step forward," Sergio said as she hesitated to do as told.

She stepped up to the stage and held her breath.

She wasn't the only one. What if I hadn't bid enough to take her home with me? I didn't have any idea how much it cost, and I had to split the amount between Ariella and Hazel.

What if I couldn't afford either one of them?

"Violet, you will be going home this evening with Jayden."

I breathed a sigh of relief. One down.

She crossed the room and headed over toward Diamond, where I was to make the final payment for her to accompany me home.

"And last of the evening, our rare gem, Jade."

I'd barely seen Ariella all night. Had different men bought her time? Had someone else held a firm interest in her?

Capo Sergio glanced down at the card in his hand and shoved it into his back pocket. "Jade will be coming home with me."

CHAPTER TWENTY-EIGHT

JAXSON

"What do you mean, you only got one girl out? We gave you enough money to pay for both Ariella and Hazel."

This could not be happening!

The room spun, and I pinched my eyes shut.

While I was relieved Hazel was safe and reuniting with Mason any minute now, I was sick to my stomach thinking about what would happen to Ariella.

I shouldn't have gone home. Aiden and Declan talked me into taking Izzie home.

I should never have left Jayden to handle the operation.

"Capo Sergio, the bastard who runs the auction, he kept Jade, I mean Ariella, for himself. It didn't matter how much money I threw at him. He intended to keep her."

"Damnit!" I slammed my fist on the kitchen table.

Izzie was asleep upstairs, tucked into bed.

I winced. Hopefully, I didn't just wake her up.

I listened but didn't hear any noises coming from upstairs.

Good. I exhaled a heavy sigh. "I need everything on Capo Sergio. Does he live at the place this auction occurred?" We needed to know where he would take Ariella.

"No, he's got a house on a lot of land, just outside of town." Jayden paused as if he was holding his tongue, keeping something from me.

"If you know where he lives, then we go tonight." I wasn't going to wait for daylight to rescue her.

"No."

"What do you mean no?" I asked.

This had been all his fault.

Jayden didn't have to come. Hell, if he wanted to stay home and play house with Skylar or whatever, he could do that. I just needed to know where Sergio lived so that I could plan a rescue mission to retrieve Ariella.

"Sergio is sick," Jayden said and stalled for a minute.

"I don't have all day." I was growing impatient with Jayden.

"He makes what happened to the off-gridders look like a picnic."

Most of the off-gridders had been murdered in cold blood by the Russian mafia months ago. Jayden and Emma were the only two survivors, as far as I knew.

Last I heard, Emma had been hauled off in handcuffs and plead guilty to a half dozen charges.

I was surprised Jayden hadn't been behind bars with her. After all, he'd been one of the gunmen at the hostage takeover at Blue Sky Resort. Emma had been the brains behind the operation, but Jayden wasn't so innocent, either.

He had a dark past, but I was beginning to understand and unravel it because it all led back to his family, finding his niece Lexa.

"What are you suggesting?" I asked.

I valued Jayden's opinion, especially in regard to Sergio and the DeLuca family. He had far more knowledge about the mafia than I ever did. I'd done all that I could to avoid them.

"Sergio isn't going to touch your girl tonight. He always comes home after one of these parties, gets drunk, and passes out."

"And you know this because?"

Could I trust that he wouldn't lay a hand on Ariella? How

confident was Jayden? I couldn't stare him in the eyes over the phone. I had to trust him, and my gut said he was honest.

"I've been invited over after a party or two," Jayden confessed. "Ariella isn't the first girl he's brought home. I should have realized that he might pick her. She's definitely his type. But I assure you, he won't touch her until tomorrow, and by the end of the week, it'll all be over."

My stomach dropped.

"Why's that?"

"He sends them on a hunt before the next auction. I've never known a girl to escape."

CHAPTER TWENTY-NINE

Jayden

I shouldn't have told Jaxson about the hunt. He'd never let me go home tonight, climb into bed, and get a few hours of shut-eye.

"You're telling me he's going to send Ariella out into what, the mountains, and hunt her down for sport?"

My mouth was dry. My eyes were blurred.

I'd already dropped Hazel off with Mason and was on my way home.

"That's right. He's a bastard, Capo Sergio, but he's never done it before fucking the hell out of the women he buys. So, you have about a week until he grows tired of the same girl and wants a new plaything."

"I can't—there's no way I can sit still and listen to this. What's the address?"

While it was a question, I knew without a doubt that Jaxson wasn't asking. He was demanding I tell him where Sergio lived.

My eyes blurred and burned. I wanted to get a few hours of sleep before the sun came up.

"You're not going alone," I said.

It was a minimum of a two-man rescue job. Someone had to kill Sergio and another rescue Ariella.

Sergio wasn't going to open his front door to Jaxson. I was the one he'd trust, the one he'd let inside his house.

Jaxson could sneak in and help Ariella escape while I distracted Sergio.

If only it were that simple.

"I don't care whether you come with me or not, but I'm not leaving Ariella there another minute," Jaxson said.

"What about your kid?" I tried throwing the Daddy card at him. It was all I had left to try to stop him from doing this tonight.

"Leave my little girl out of it!" Jaxson bellowed into the phone.

"Okay. Okay. I just meant you couldn't honestly leave a little kid like that home alone."

"She's not alone. I've got one of the guys here and Ariella's sister. Not that it's any of your concern," Jaxson spat.

Sleep was a commodity that I wasn't getting any of. Just like sex lately.

"Do you have a pen and paper? I'll give you the address. Then I need to call my house and check on Lexa."

"It's the middle of the night," Jaxson said. "Let the poor girl sleep."

Yeah. Now I understood how he felt.

I relayed the address and directions to him and then agreed to head straight there as long as he brought me a cup of coffee. I didn't care whether he brewed it at home or had a bottle of iced coffee in his fridge that he brought with him. I just needed an extra jolt of caffeine to keep me awake.

We were going on a rescue mission to get Ariella back, and I didn't want to fall asleep before my head hit the pillow.

CHAPTER THIRTY

ARIELLA

I should have been grateful the collar and bracelet were removed. Sergio may have stolen me for himself, but he didn't have any intention of sending pulse-pounding electricity through my neck.

Maybe he wasn't a sadist?

I still didn't trust him.

He'd locked me in the backseat of his black SUV, shoved a bag over my head, and drove us all of about twenty minutes.

The terrain had been rough. The ride was quite bumpy. I didn't feel like we'd stayed on any main roads.

I doubted that Sergio was concerned about being seen.

He must have lived off the beaten path. It wasn't quite off-grid, per se. I suspected there was electricity and all the finer things that money could buy.

I wasn't wrong.

"Let's go," Sergio said, his voice rough and thick. His words slurred just a bit as he grabbed me by the arm and thrust me out of the backseat.

"I can't see anything," I said, reminding him I had a bag over my head. It was difficult not to trip over the rocky terrain. He didn't have a paved driveway, or if he did, he'd opted not to use it.

"That's the point," he said.

Grass and stones grazed my bare feet.

I missed my leather boots even more, not to mention my cell phone that had been tucked away. I loved those shoes and had even splurged on them because I thought they looked fantastic with a pair of jeans.

I doubted I'd ever get them back, and breaking a new pair in was hell on my feet.

How would Jaxson ever find me?

"Step up," Sergio instructed.

I took a careful step up to feel warm wood under my toes.

Was it a porch?

It didn't creak, but it probably wasn't old or rickety, either. Sergio was a mobster and was probably rolling in dough. At least that's how I imagined it, especially after running the auction. He was clearly in charge, or else someone would have intervened when he'd decided to take me home.

I could hear the jingle of keys and the clank of metal as he shoved the key into the lock.

We would be heading inside soon.

What if I took off on foot? My hands weren't bound behind my back. I could toss off the bag over my head and run.

How far would I get?

Did he have his gun handy? I was sure he had a weapon, and he'd probably shoot me the first opportunity that he had, especially since I didn't cost him a cent.

The door squeaked on its hinge as he opened the front entrance. Well, I assumed it was the front entrance.

My heart pounded like a boat that smashed against rocks in a storm. Sweat covered me, but I knew it wasn't hot outside.

My stomach somersaulted.

At that moment, I had to act. And so I ran.

I yanked off the cloth that covered my face in my pursuit of freedom. I stumbled down the porch step, but it didn't stop me from the beginning of the chase.

I took off as fast as my legs would take me. My calves burned, but I didn't care. I refused to slow down or cower to Sergio, or any man who thought he could own me.

I was not a piece of property.

It was still dark outside, and my feet tore over the rough gravel of the thick forest.

I wished more than anything I had on my boots—something to protect the bottoms of my feet. I ran over branches and leaves, thistles, and rocks.

Everything that littered the forest floor was crunched beneath my weight as I made a beeline away from the property.

I had no idea where I was headed, only that I needed to get help.

I hadn't so much as turned around or slowed to glance back at Sergio.

He hadn't chased me, and during that brief moment, I found it strange and almost unsettling, I couldn't slow down.

I wasn't going to give him time to catch up to me if he intended to put running shoes on or change clothes. I didn't have the slightest idea why he let me run, but I wasn't going to second guess the decision.

Sure, there were bears in the woods. Grizzlies. The meanest and most deadly creatures. Possibly wolves too. I wasn't quite sure about all the wild beasts in the forest.

I hadn't lived in Breckenridge that long, and I sure didn't grow up around here.

I couldn't think about what lay beyond the forest, sleeping, or foraging for food. The only way to survive had been to escape.

Was I free?

My chest ached with a screaming intensity that made my eyes burn and tear.

Slowing down would get me killed.

I'd felt this pain before, like my chest was being crushed. Agony.

I didn't slow. I wasn't dying. It wasn't a heart attack. Sure, I had issues that made my heart quite literally skip a beat. Thanks to tachycardia and the autonomic dysfunction I was plagued with, it felt like hell.

But it wouldn't actually kill me.

Right?

I'd made sure to take my medication twice a day. I'd been religious with the routine, never missing a dose because when I did, it would tear me down, disrupting my life even the next day.

While I'd missed a dose, it wouldn't have been the end of the world if I hadn't been in fight-or-flight mode. Running for my life wasn't helping alleviate any of my symptoms.

Beyond anything, I wished I had my phone to call Jaxson.

Wincing, I remembered Delphine was coming into town tonight.

Shit.

Would she forgive me for not picking her up at the airport? We were finally reconnecting, and I'd ditched her ass.

That's what she'd say.

I could already hear her nagging tone and a look of disapproval.

Refusing to slow, I kept running through the forest. Would I reach a road, a house, some sign of civilization?

Breckenridge might have been a small town, but I'd end up there eventually, right?

What if I was headed in the wrong direction?

The world around me spun as I ran. The trees swayed, and I gripped the rough bark of one, holding myself up.

Gasping for breath, I couldn't afford to slow down.

In the distance, tires crunched on gravel.

I couldn't ascertain whether the vehicle headed toward Sergio's house or away from it. I didn't think I'd gotten turned around, but the forest seemed to extend onward forever.

Who would be coming to visit Sergio in the middle of the night?

No one.

And while I wanted to believe it was Jaxson, he probably had no idea where I was or how to find me.

Had Jayden even intended on securing my freedom, or only

Hazel's? I knew there was bad blood between the two brothers, but I didn't know how bad it went.

A shotgun fired from behind, and I threw myself on the forest floor.

I hadn't heard footsteps. He'd been quiet. Unless he'd driven close by and aimed through the window of the vehicle?

I ran farther from the road, through the forest, until I ran straight into a metal fence that towered above me.

I was trapped.

CHAPTER THIRTY-ONE

JAXSON

She was out there all alone, and I was the only one who could save her.

Jayden and I pulled up outside Sergio's house. The door had been left open, the house abandoned.

While I'd expected a slew of men guarding his home like Angelo had, the fact was Sergio wasn't a mob boss. At least not yet.

I didn't know who would take Angelo's place, probably Gino, his second in command, but wars had been fought for far less amongst such men.

Jayden unholstered his gun as we quickly searched the house and the perimeter.

"They couldn't have gone far," I said. I stopped and bent down, picking up a dark cotton hood.

Jayden glanced at the material in my fist. "Think she ran?" he asked.

"Like hell I do."

Ariella was a fighter, and she'd do everything in her power to stay alive. If that meant a chance at escaping, I knew she'd take it.

I exhaled a nervous breath. I was scared for her.

She'd been through hell in a single day and was probably tired, exhausted, and I didn't even want to consider the ramifications it meant on her health.

Would she be able to run and escape?

I knew I was fit, and I'd probably be tired after being dragged around, tossed from one compound to the next, and sold at a slave auction. The trauma she'd endured alone was staggering, and thinking Sergio was still after her. To say I was worried, was an understatement.

The bastard wasn't going to give up. Not easily.

Neither would Ariella. She'd fight until the bitter end.

"We need to spread out, find her before it's too late." I unholstered my gun from my hip.

The forest extended as far as I could see, with a winding gravel road that I'd traveled in on. I hadn't spotted her cross the road, and frankly, she could be anywhere.

A shotgun rang out in the distance.

"She's got to be that way," I gestured, hearing the shotgun.

"He's hunting her, has to be," Jayden muttered under his breath.

"Or chasing her because she ran away from him."

It was as much the fact she tried to flee that resulted in Sergio hunting her down with a shotgun.

Either way, she was in danger, and I needed to find her before Sergio.

"Do you think he's got sight of her?" I didn't slow down as I popped the latch of my truck. I unzipped my tactical gear bag and retrieved a set of night vision goggles. It was the only way to find them in the dark.

While she probably hadn't been careful in her escape, examining shrubbery and broken branches would take too long. Hopefully, they hadn't gotten too far ahead.

I tossed a second pair at Jayden.

"We need to find Ariella before Sergio gets to her."

"It may be too late," Jayden said.

I wasn't accepting defeat. We'd only heard one shot. There was no scream from Ariella. No sound of victory from Sergio.

I geared up with a bulletproof vest and let Jayden help himself to any additional equipment of mine that was left over.

I grabbed a second pistol, tucking it into my boots, and a semi-automatic that I secured around my shoulder.

I wasn't taking any chances.

I jogged into the darkness, my feet not the least bit silent as my boots smashed leaves and stomped on branches.

Maybe I would get Sergio's attention and he'd leave Ariella alone.

That was my hope.

Would it go according to plan? Probably not.

At least he knew someone else was in the forest trailing him.

He wasn't alone, and neither was Ariella.

Jayden kept close behind me. It only took him a minute to catch up, and he was on my heel.

"Fan out?" he asked.

It was only the two of us.

"No. If he's got the gear, we don't want him to see both of us," I said. While I didn't want to get shot, I was also willing to die to make sure that Ariella was safe, and if that meant Jayden was getting to her in time, so be it.

I glanced down at the ground, seeing a broken branch—a sign they'd come this way through the forest.

"Keep moving," I said in a hushed whisper. The sound carried through the forest. Sound always traveled farther at night, and while I tried to keep my voice down, my feet weren't exactly quiet.

"Anything?" Jayden asked.

"Nada." I hadn't spotted any signs of life. I should have brought gear with me to detect heat signatures, but that was back at the Eagle Tactical office.

We didn't have time to call for reinforcements or request additional gear.

Ariella's life was on the line, and at any moment, Sergio could find her, shoot her, or worse, kill us and drag her back to be his sex slave.

Bile rose to my throat at the disgusting thought of what he would do to her.

My Ariella.

I'd sooner die than let him lay a hand on her.

A second shot rang out.

This time it was pointed in our direction and whizzed by, piercing a nearby tree.

The googles revealed no one to me. I held up my arm, indicating to Jayden to hold up.

Sergio had to be hiding.

Was he hidden behind a tree?

Where else could he be? I didn't see anything else, no sign of him. No sign of movement.

My eyes narrowed and twitched as I spotted the long end of the shotgun.

"Duck." I reached behind me for Jayden and threw him down on the ground with me.

Sergio had spotted us.

CHAPTER THIRTY-TWO

Jayden

Heavy footsteps pounded over the ground as Sergio rushed in our direction. Jaxson had saved my life.

Shit.

It wouldn't matter now. Any moment, he'd discover us lying on the forest floor. We had to think and move fast.

I glanced at my comrade for only a split second, and he gave off a quick nod.

He had the same idea.

We had to split up.

"I'll find her. You take care of him," Jaxson seethed.

He wasn't the least bit quiet. Did he not know how to whisper?

Did we want to give up our location to Sergio? I sure as hell didn't want him to locate us.

I took in a deep breath.

It was now or never. Jaxson had crawled away on the ground, low to the shrubs and branches, out of sight, before I spotted him leaping to his feet and running for Ariella.

Had he spotted her?

I couldn't see anything but Sergio coming right for me.

I reached for my gun, only to find the trigger jammed.

Great. Jaxson had given me a weapon that was useless.

I dropped the gun and used my fists to push the shotgun farther from me as he aimed it at my chest. I spun the weapon around, hearing the snap of his trigger finger.

Sergio dropped the gun and lunged for me. His hands fell around my neck. His grip was tight, making it hard to breathe.

I kneed him in the crotch as we rolled around on the hard surface, sticks and broken branches stabbing at us.

"You fucking bastard!" I spit as I spoke and used my thumbs to jab Sergio in the eyes.

He screamed and momentarily released his hold on my throat, long enough that I could take in a deep breath and drink in the air.

It didn't last long. He grabbed my gun that had been jammed and pulled the trigger outward, not pointing it at me.

"I'm the bastard?" he scoffed. "You come into my home and take one of my girls. Then proceed to fight me?"

Was he trying to shoot Jaxson? Had he found Ariella yet?

I couldn't see them. My focus was entirely on my own survival and stopping Sergio.

"I paid for her, fair and square." It sickened me even to think about the fact that we'd practically funded the mob by giving them money.

What other choice did we have?

At that moment, it had been the right course of action to save Hazel. If only I had been able to do the same for Ariella, we wouldn't be out here at night, wrestling for our lives.

Sergio hadn't used his dominant hand. I'd made sure to break that finger, but he held the gun in his opposite hand, continually putting pressure on the gun and trigger until it finally fired.

Shit.

Sergio's sinister laugh echoed through the forest. He rolled away from me, shooting into the darkness of night, blanketing the forest with bullet after bullet in every direction.

I could hear a high-pitched scream, female.

It had to be Ariella.

Had she been shot?

I shouldn't have ever given Sergio the opportunity to get the gun. This was my fault.

Everything was my fault. I'd caused this, and while I'd only gotten involved with Enzo and Angelo to find my niece, everyone's blood was on my hands.

I was as guilty as the mob.

CHAPTER THIRTY-THREE

ARIELLA

With my back against the metal fence, I glanced up at the barbed wire.

There was no way to scale the fence without getting hurt. I had no shoes, was wearing a scantily clad nightie, and no underwear.

It was like asking to mutilate myself.

A shot pierced through the air.

Sergio.

Maybe climbing the fence wasn't the worst idea ever.

A grumble roared in the distance.

Hell, was that a bear? No, bears didn't come out at night, right?

I had no idea if they were nocturnal. Only that I'd never seen one, minus the zoo, and I never wanted to be up close with one, either.

I skirted the fence, keeping my fingers against the metal in hopes that I'd find a break, a tear, some way to run and escape.

I tried to make myself as quiet as possible. The shotgun that had pierced through the air hadn't hit me.

Had Sergio intended it as a warning shot?

I had expected him to yell, to scream, to indicate that he wanted me to return home with him or else he'd kill me.

The silence was the only answer that followed.

I swallowed the lump that formed in my throat. Was I afraid?

Yes, I was terrified.

But I couldn't stand still.

I refused to wait to be shot or beaten, raped, or tortured by a monster.

Keeping the metal fence at my back was risky. It indicated the property line. At least I assumed that was why it existed, but it also trapped me if he drew nearer.

"Tsk. Tsk." Sergio's voice rang out in the distance.

My stomach clenched, and I froze.

Maybe he could hear my footsteps. If I didn't move, would he be unable to find me? I remained perfectly still with the calm of night.

I held my breath and listened to the sound of the wind that whipped the leaves and lapped at the trees, causing them to sway.

I, too, felt my body sway. Not from the wind, but from the exhaustion. I wanted to curl up, lie down, and sleep for a week.

My adrenaline had other ideas.

Trembling hands didn't cease to slow, but at least he couldn't hear my hands. My entire body was racked with tremors. Soon, he'd hear the rattle of the fence.

I pushed myself away from the metal.

I needed to seek shelter.

Was there a cave nearby? Perhaps a tree or large rock where I could slip away, hidden and unseen.

Did Sergio know the woods by heart? Did he frequent the area often?

This was his home, his land. I had to assume he knew every inch of the forest.

His footsteps trod away. He hurried in the opposite direction.

Where was he going? Had he given up?

I exhaled a nervous breath and kept still for another solid minute before I quietly headed toward the road. At least, that was the direction I thought I was going.

Earlier, there'd been the sound of a vehicle, traffic, which meant there were others nearby.

I needed to search whoever it was out and seek their help. Hopefully, they weren't friends with Sergio, his posse.

Time seemed to stand still. A shotgun blasted in the opposite direction.

Had Jaxson and the team come to rescue me?

I heard a scuffle in the distance. Shit.

Tears threatened my vision. I kept moving. I couldn't slow down.

I quickened my pace through the forest. My legs burned. My feet throbbed and were bloodied raw, but I didn't slow down.

What if Sergio shot whoever had come to help? What if there was no one to find me? No one to save me.

I needed to save myself.

I hurried as fast as I could. I pushed away from the fence line and kept my pace, refusing to slow down even though my feet were raw and torn with cuts and scrapes.

A hand covered my mouth.

I opened my mouth to scream and bite down on the assailant.

"Shhh, it's me, Freckles." Jaxson's warm whisper reached my ears.

I'd never been so relieved to hear that nickname or feel his body nestled tight behind me.

My body trembled, and the tears sobbed out of me like a river.

"Take a breath," Jaxson said, his voice soft and reassuring. "Jayden's with Sergio. It's not over yet."

It wasn't the time to rejoice.

Bullets flew through the air. Jaxson forced me quickly to the ground, shielding my body, lying above me, as gunfire erupted from one direction.

"Well, we know where Sergio is," Jaxson said. "I need to get you out of here and help Jayden. Can you stay down?"

"Don't leave me," I whispered. I'd never sounded so helpless in my life.

I didn't want to be helpless. I wanted to be brave, but I was afraid.

"Who else is with you?" The other members of Eagle Tactical had to be out there and could help.

"It's just Jayden and me."

I whimpered in protest. I didn't want anything to happen to him.

He unfastened his vest. "Here, put this on."

"What? No." I couldn't take it. He had a daughter at home. I had, well, I had me. That was it.

"You're wearing it. Don't argue with me," Jaxson said, his voice firm. He had already made up his mind, and I wasn't going to convince him, no matter how hard I tried.

The truth was I didn't try very hard.

I was terrified, and Sergio wanted me dead.

He probably wanted Jaxson and Jayden dead too, but those guys were former special forces. They had military training. I had nothing.

I lay cowered on the ground, and Jaxson was quick to help me secure the vest.

He was risking his life for me.

"Wait," I whispered, pulling him tight and close. My lips crashed against his.

If this was goodbye, I didn't want it to be without him knowing how I feel.

"I love you," I breathed against his lips.

Jaxson pulled back and cocked a sideways grin. "Yeah? I know. I love you too, Freckles." His lips devoured me one more time before he pulled back. "Stay here and stay down. I need to know where to find you. Don't move. No matter what. Okay?"

I nodded in understanding and watched as he took off, disappearing into the night to save Jayden and stop Sergio from killing all of us.

CHAPTER THIRTY-FOUR

JAXSON

Leaving her had been devastating, but I trusted that she'd be safe. She had my Kevlar vest, and I handed her a pistol before leaving her alone.

I wasn't going to let anything happen to Ariella ever again.

Well, at least not tonight.

I may not have been able to protect her from every little thing in the world, but I could keep her safe from Sergio and the mob.

I headed opposite the road several meters before closing in on Sergio and Jayden. I didn't want Sergio to know about my previous position.

Protecting Ariella was everything.

I hurried, not making myself too silent.

Go ahead, buddy, come at me.

He hadn't fired another shot in a few minutes, which either meant he was out of bullets or Jayden had restrained him.

There was a scuffle as I drew nearer.

Jayden and Sergio wrestled on the ground, throwing punches at one another.

That, I could handle.

With my steel-toed boots, I kicked Sergio while he was down on the ground, nailing him in the back of the neck. I grabbed him by the hair and ripped him off Jayden with one hand. My other gun was positioned at his neck.

I tilted the gun up under his chin.

"You get a kick out of abducting, selling, and raping women?"

It wasn't a rhetorical question.

He huffed and shrugged, probably trying to get out of my grasp.

I didn't let him go.

Jayden stood, dusted his pants off, and reached for the gun that was on the ground, the one that had fired several rounds at Ariella and me minutes earlier.

"Are you just going to stand there threatening or finish the job?" Jayden asked.

"Call the authorities," I said.

Jayden shook his head. "He doesn't deserve a cell and three meals a day."

"That's not up to us." I wasn't a murderer.

At least I didn't want to be one. I'd crossed the line with Angelo DeLuca. My interrogation methods had gone too far, and I had to live with what I'd done. DeLuca was a monster, same as Sergio, but killing them didn't make me the good guy.

"The hell it isn't!" Jayden lifted the gun and pointed it at Sergio's head. "Tell me why I shouldn't blast his ass to pieces?"

Sergio snickered as he stared at Jayden. "You don't have it in you."

CHAPTER THIRTY-FIVE

ARIELLA

I trembled as I lay against the grass. I'd have covered myself with branches if that had been possible.

Gunfire erupted in the distance.

My eyes slammed shut.

Silently, I prayed Jaxson was safe and that he was all right.

The Kevlar vest felt tight, constricting. I gasped for breath, finding it impossible to breathe, like I was suffocating.

Footsteps hurried through the grass in my direction.

I'd only heard one bullet.

Who'd been shot?

Was Jaxson safe?

What about Jayden?

My eyes remained shut, afraid that Sergio had survived and was gunning me down next.

Worried that he might see the whites of my eyes glinting in the moonlight, I buried my head. My hair fell around my face.

Fear didn't begin to explain the horror that flowed through my veins and pumped adrenaline to my heart.

Heavy footsteps smacked the ground.

Whoever it was didn't attempt to conceal their identity.

Why would they? It was over for them. Was it over for me?

The hurried steps came closer. "You're okay." Jaxson's voice was music to my ears, and I glanced up, making sure what I saw was real.

"I heard a gunshot." My bottom lip trembled.

Jaxson bent down and guided me to my feet. His arm stayed secure around me, his gaze glancing me over.

The adrenaline didn't cease to exist any more than it had minutes earlier. My body was racked with shivers, tremors that encompassed me from head to toe.

It wasn't a seizure. No, this was normal when the spikes of norepinephrine beat me at my own game: life.

His brow furrowed. "Jayden, give me a hand." Jaxson handed Jayden the gun that had been slung over his shoulder earlier.

Jaxson lifted me into his arms, cradling me.

"What are you doing?" I asked. I didn't fight him. I wrapped my arms around his neck as he carried me, his arms tucked under my legs.

He didn't appear to struggle in the least, but I couldn't have been easy to carry through the forest.

"You're not wearing shoes, you're visibly shaking, and I can't, in good conscience, let you walk back to the truck. It's at least a mile away," Jaxson said.

Jayden walked ahead of us a few feet. Whether he was giving us our privacy or keeping to himself, I didn't know and didn't care.

"Thank you," I whispered, exhaling a soft breath. My head leaned against his chest.

I drank in his scent, his warmth, and the comfort that he offered me.

While the tremors didn't cease, just being in his embrace was enough to bring a calmness to my emotional state, while my physical one, I still wrestled with.

"After I get you into my truck, I'm taking you to the hospital to get looked over and make sure you're all right."

Why did he have to be the sensible adult? “Jaxson,” I whined. “I just want to go home.”

While I knew he was looking out for my wellbeing, I didn’t like hospitals.

However, I didn’t know anyone who did. Even so, I would have preferred to go home, climb under the warm covers and curl up with him while I fell asleep.

“I know, and you will after you get checked out,” he insisted. “Don’t argue with me.”

He was using that tone, the same one he used when he spoke to Izzie, and he wouldn’t let her get her way.

I appreciated his protectiveness, even if I didn’t want to go to the hospital. Emergency room visits were never quick. “Can’t we just go to the clinic in town?” I countered.

Jaxson wouldn’t have it. He insisted on driving me the two hours to the hospital. However, it was more like an hour and ten minutes since we were partially on the way and he drove at lightning speed.

I found it difficult to sleep. The gurney was hard and uncomfortable. The doctors had run a ridiculous number of tests.

We waited for the results.

Jaxson sat beside me, his eyelids heavy as he struggled to stay awake.

“You can shut your eyes,” I mumbled.

“Not until we’re home,” Jaxson said.

I exhaled a heavy sigh. And when would that be? The sun was coming up already. It had been when we arrived at the hospital.

“Who’s watching Izzie?” I yawned as I lay on the cot. Jaxson’s hand nestled in mine.

The tremors had slowed but not fully subsided with the second bag of I.V. fluids.

We were waiting for a number of tests to come back. The doctors wanted to ensure that I wasn't drugged or facing any other issues before prescribing me my regular regimen.

"Declan's staying at the house with Izzie."

"What about Delphine? Oh my gosh, she flew in last night. I was supposed to pick her up!"

"I know," Jaxson said. He squeezed my hand gently. "She called me when she couldn't get ahold of you. I told her to take a cab and that I'd pay for the ride to my place. I also sent Declan over to let her in and put Izzie to bed. He decided to crash for the night at our place, which worked out for me."

My eyelids fluttered closed for a brief moment.

"Thank you," I whispered and opened my eyes. I struggled to stay awake. I didn't want to sleep. Not here. Not now.

"Just rest." He patted my shoulder with his other hand.

Easier said than done. The bright fluorescent overhead lights hummed with each passing second. Time felt as though it stood still. But at least I was safe.

The doctor didn't so much as knock as he pulled back the curtain and stepped into the room. "I have good news. Both of you are doing fine."

"Both of us?" What was he talking about? I glanced at Jaxson.

"Yes, you and the baby." The doctor paused. "You didn't know you were pregnant?"

"No. I mean, I didn't think I could be after the last time." I exhaled a nervous breath.

"Well, you are both healthy. However, I suggest that you see an obstetrician soon. I am concerned that one of the medications that you told us you're taking can cause issues and is not recommended to continue while pregnant. In the meantime, I'm going to give you a prescription to help lower your heart rate, but you should remain on bed rest until you see the doctor treating you for autonomic dysfunction."

"Okay," I whispered.

We were pregnant. Jaxson and I were going to have a baby.

CHAPTER THIRTY-SIX

Skylar

Jayden hadn't exactly invited me to stay with him, but I hadn't given him another option. He was the reason my brother wasn't talking to me and had kicked me out of his house.

Well, it had been a bit of my fault too, but I still needed a place to crash.

While Lincoln took Harper to get checked out, Declan eventually dropped Jayden's niece and me off at Jayden's apartment.

I was familiar with the place and gave Lexa the briefest tour before showing her the guest room.

Which meant that I was crashing in Jayden's room, whether he wanted me to or not.

I had a few things at his place already stashed away for our fake relationship arrangement. A handful of photos, some clothes, even a pillowcase on the bed, just in case his boss had shown up at the apartment to meet me unannounced.

Thankfully, that hadn't happened, although I'd dreamt of it, had nightmares of a faceless man tearing down the door and interrogating me.

And that was before I was forced to go with Angelo DeLuca and help Ben kidnap the girls.

How could I ever live with myself for what I'd done?

Would Jaxson ever forgive me? What about Ariella and Izzie?

Lexa headed straight to bed. I couldn't blame her. I was exhausted too.

I slipped into one of Jayden's t-shirts that fell just above the knee.

It smelled uniquely of him, strong and musky with a hint of sawdust. I'd never seen him work a saw, but I hadn't spent that much time with him.

I'd been angry with him, blamed him for what happened, but he went and risked his life to save Hazel and Ariella.

Maybe he wasn't the bad guy, just the bad boy.

I climbed under the covers. Everything smelled of Jayden.

The scent was overwhelming. My eyes burned as I sobbed into the pillow.

I hated myself, what I'd done, what I'd become to save myself.

How would I make it up to my family, my friends?

It was impossible to sleep. I tossed and turned. Without my phone, I didn't have the slightest idea when Jayden would come home or if he'd come home alive.

What if the auction took a turn for the worse?

The night dragged on, and daylight finally shined through the curtains. Just as I started to drift to sleep from exhaustion, the bedroom door opened, and I was startled awake.

"Jayden?" I mumbled and rubbed the sleep from my eyes.

"It's all over," he said, his voice rough and thick.

"Hazel and Ariella, are they okay?" I asked as I sat up in bed. I pulled the surrounding covers tight into my fists.

"Hazel, I rescued from the auction. Jaxson and I had to go after Capo Sergio and retrieve Ariella. She's on the way to the hospital, but I think she's all right." He stripped down, not seeming to care that I was in his bed.

His shoes were first left on the floor as he removed his shirt and tossed it into the nearby hamper. Jayden unzipped his pants and tossed those in the bin along with his boxers.

I tried not to stare.

He didn't seem to care in the least. He stalked across the room for the bathroom and flipped on the light.

My eyes burned, and I squinted as he left the door open. "I'm going to shower. I need to rid myself of all this filth. Did you get washed up already?" Jayden asked.

"I uh, no." I had been too tired, too broken to do anything but wallow in self-pity. "I probably should have."

"You want to get cleaned up with me? Share a shower? Conserve water together."

I rubbed my tired eyes and shifted on the mattress, tossing my legs over the side. I swayed for a second before stepping forward, following him into the bathroom.

"That's my girl," Jayden said and quirked a sideways grin. "I'm so sorry about what happened."

"Shhh," I said, silencing him with my finger to his lips.

He kicked the door shut with his foot and backed me up against it, bringing my hands up above my head.

"I've wanted to do this with you since you first walked into the bar," Jayden whispered.

He didn't kiss me. Just stared at me. Was he teasing me on purpose?

"What are you waiting for?" I asked, trying to catch my breath.

"Permission," Jayden said, his voice raspy and low. "Unlike those men, I won't take what isn't mine."

"I want to be yours," I confessed.

Was that what he wanted to hear?

His lips descended hard on mine, our mouths crashing together, tongues dueling for control.

He kept me pinned to the door, his body pressed tight, naked.

The only thing between us was the shirt that I wore.

"You're going to have to take this off if you plan on showering," Jayden said, eyeing my shirt.

I chuckled, my arms still pinned against the door above my head.

"Kind of hard to do without the use of my arms. Maybe you should undress me," I said.

Jayden growled. His desire poked at me. He moved my hands together, one hand holding me firm, the other guiding my shirt inch by inch up. His touch was warm and gentle, far more tender than I had anticipated.

His lips teased my ear, sending a shudder through my body as I grew antsy with need.

"I'm so sorry," he whispered into my ear. Soft kisses danced over my neck as he dropped his tight hold on my wrists, freeing me. "I shouldn't have risked your life." His eyes bore into mine.

"We both made mistakes," I admitted, meeting his stare. We would have to live with those consequences. Right now, I just needed to feel alive and loved.

I leaned forward, and our lips collided once again. I didn't want to hear his apologies. I wanted to feel his admiration and his care.

"I need to forget," I whispered against his lips and gently tugged on his bottom lip with my teeth. "Please, make the pain go away."

Jayden opened his mouth and expelled a soft sigh. Was he going to tell me that he didn't know how?

As quickly as the look of darkness and sadness crossed his face, it was gone.

His mouth descended onto mine, and he removed the last barrier between us, tossing the shirt to the floor. Jayden scooped me up into his arms and put me down to sit at the edge of the bathroom sink.

He retrieved a condom from the drawer, ripped it open, and unraveled it before his gaze met mine.

"Are you sure?"

"Yes," I said. My hand reached for him, stroking him, touching him, proving to him that I wanted this with him.

I'd been through hell today, but the other girls, the ones who were supposed to be my friends, had been through so much worse. Jayden didn't have to tell me what he'd witnessed to see the pain and anguish behind that steel gaze.

His warmth filled me, fueled me, and made me forget the pain and ache that had been darkening my heart.

I wrapped my legs around him and pulled him deeper and tighter with each thrust. My fingers dug into his shoulder, marking him.

Jayden grunted and he pulled out, running a hand through his hair. His eyes looked distraught.

"Are you seriously going to tease me to death?" Why the hell had he stopped?

"This was not how I wanted our first time to be," he rasped, meeting my stare. "You deserve better."

"I'm not sure about that." I laughed darkly. I stared at him, my gaze unwavering. My fingers trailed a delicate path down his chest. "Please, I just want to feel something other than regret, and with you, I could never regret this."

Jayden's lips came down hard on mine. "I've imagined fucking you in the bar for the past several months," he whispered. "But you deserve the royal treatment. Wine, dinner, and lots of foreplay."

"That sounds nice for next time. Tonight, I don't care that it's in the bathroom or if it were in the bar. I just want to listen to you moan and hear you scream my name."

"Bossy." Jayden laughed. His fingers tangled in my hair as he brought my lips down to his, clinging to me, our kisses fiery and feisty as he entered me again.

I moaned in pleasure. I wanted him to know that he made me feel good, and I didn't want him to have any further second thoughts.

There would be no regrets tonight, at least not between the two of us.

My eyes slammed shut as the sensation grew, building and intensifying.

"Come for me, Skylar," he whispered into my ear.

I tightened around him, my insides pulsating. Already, I was so close, teetering on edge. My toes curled, and I listened as he grew near.

Everything felt like fireworks exploding around me as I trembled in his embrace, gasping for breath as we both came undone.

"Shower?" he mumbled as he slid out and tossed the condom into the trash.

I laughed under my breath. That was why I'd joined him in the bathroom. I slid off the counter, my legs like jelly.

Jayden steadied me, his hands on my hips. "Are you okay?"

I nodded, staring up at him. "Perfect."

CHAPTER THIRTY-SEVEN

ARIELLA

I'd fallen asleep in the truck on the way home from the hospital.

I didn't know how Jaxson had managed to stay awake.

The truck pulled to a soft halt, but it stirred me awake. "We home?" I yawned and rubbed the sleep from my eyes.

"Yes," Jaxson said. He shut off the engine and climbed out, coming around to help me out and carry me through the front door.

My feet were bandaged and sore as hell from the chase through the forest, but I would survive. Besides, that was the least of my worries.

I was pregnant, and not only did I have to look after myself, now I had to think about the little boy or girl growing inside of me.

Crippling fear was an understatement of how I felt.

Jaxson carried me inside, sat me down on the sofa and shut off the alarm before he locked the house up. "Do you want to head right to bed, or are you hungry?"

I could barely keep my eyes open. "Sleep sounds wonderful. I can just crash on the couch." I shifted to stretch out.

"Izzie will be up soon," Jaxson reminded me. "How about I take you up to bed and tuck you in?"

"What about you?" I didn't want to be away from him. I knew it was probably a combination of the hormones and the trauma of what I'd been through, but I was feeling incredibly needy.

I hated the way I felt, like I didn't want ever to be alone again.

"I'm exhausted. I'll climb into bed as soon as I let Declan know we're home. Okay?"

"You're home," Delphine said, a warm smile on her face. "I'm glad you're okay. Your boyfriend's friend told me what happened. Declan, is it?"

My boyfriend.

I smiled faintly at my sister calling Jaxson that term. We hadn't used labels.

"Yeah, sorry I missed you at the airport."

Delphine waved her hand dismissively. "It's not a big deal. I mean, with what you went through, don't even think about it." She scooted closer to me on the sofa. "Is it true that Ben was behind your abduction?"

I exhaled a heavy sigh. I wasn't sure I was ready to talk about it, but it seemed Declan had looped her in on what he knew at the time.

I didn't blame him. He had to tell her something, and it was better she knew the truth.

At least then she wouldn't hate me for not showing up when I promised to give her a ride.

"It's okay if you don't want to talk about it," Delphine said. She stood and headed to the kitchen. "I'm going to grab myself a cup of coffee. Do you want some?"

"I can't," I said. I had to watch everything that elevated my heart rate, even more so with the pregnancy.

"Oh, that's right." Delphine assumed it had been because of my health condition. She'd been blessed with great genes.

Not me.

We still hadn't told anyone about the baby. I didn't want to jinx it.

"I'm glad you flew here. It's good to see you," I said. Things still felt strained, but at least she was trying. I felt like I'd been the only one trying since Ben's initial arrest over a year ago.

Delphine wrapped an arm around me, giving me a much-needed and long-awaited hug. "Sis, there is nowhere else I'd rather be. I'm sorry I listened to my stupid husband. I should have ditched his ass and flown out here sooner."

I laughed under my breath. "It's all right. Love makes us do stupid things."

"Tell me about it," Delphine said with a grin.

"What made you decide to come out here now, after all this time?" I asked. It couldn't just be that she realized Ben was a jerk.

Delphine's smile faded from her lips. "The truth is that your boyfriend called me."

"What?" My stomach sank.

Why would Jaxson do that?

"He called to tell me about how, a few months ago, you'd been kidnapped by Ben, and he asked me to come and see you. I should have come sooner."

I wanted to be angry with Jaxson for interfering, but I understood what he was doing. His intentions were good, but I wasn't happy about him going behind my back.

"I can't believe he called you," I said.

"He wouldn't have had to call me if you'd told me that Ben had abducted you," Delphine said. "I just wish that you trusted me. We're family, and I know that I haven't always been there for you. I'm sorry."

"It's in the past." I wanted to forgive her and move on. She was here now, and that was what mattered, right?

We were finally reconnecting.

"Is Ben in prison again?" Delphine asked. "Did they catch him? Declan was explaining that Ben had been part of the human trafficking ring."

"Jaxson and the team are tracking him down as we speak."

Her brow creased. "They'll catch him, right?"

I'd never feel safe until he was arrested and behind bars.

CHAPTER THIRTY-EIGHT

Jayden

I wasn't thrilled with being back here without a weapon.

Jaxson had insisted I wear an earpiece and a wire that relayed everything I said to the Eagle Tactical team.

They wanted to nail Enzo Ricci and, more importantly, find Benjamin Ryan.

Stalking up to the front door of Enzo's luxurious mansion, I stood in front of the door, palm raised.

I gave a firm knock and waited.

Silence was the only response I received.

"Don Ricci?" I knocked again and rang the doorbell.

Still no answer.

I stepped off the porch and glanced through the window. The lights were off. There was no sign of anyone inside.

Three cars were parked in front of the property, but the car I knew he drove regularly, the electric blue Evora Lotus, was nowhere in sight.

"He's not here," I said to Jaxson and the team.

They had sent me on a mission but weren't far, listening to the wire from their truck. They were on standby, should I require backup.

"You have other connections to the Ricci family. Call them." Jaxson's tone was firm and sent a shudder down my spine.

"Yeah, on it."

I exhaled a heavy sigh and dug my cell phone from my pocket. I scrolled through my phone and stopped when I landed on Dante Ricci's name.

He was Enzo's second.

We'd done business together, and he'd been the one to inform me what had been going on when Enzo had tossed me out of the party and taken possession of Skylar.

My blood was boiling just thinking about the way they'd treated her and me, like pawns.

Dante picked up on the first ring.

"Didn't expect to hear from you," Dante said.

"I need to see you." I didn't want to do this over the phone.

I waited for a beat. Silence filled the phone line.

"Dante?"

Had he hung up?

"I'll come to the bar," Dante said. "Twenty minutes."

It would take me twenty-five to get to the bar where I worked. I hung up the call and hurried toward my vehicle.

"Dante is having me meet him at the bar," I said. There was only one bar in Breckenridge.

"We're heading there now," Lincoln responded into the communication device.

"Great," I muttered. That's just what I needed, the entire Eagle Tactical team and the mafia coming head-to-head.

My foot was like lead on the pedal, flying through the gravel roads, kicking up stones and dirt in a cloud of dust behind me.

I hurried toward the bar. I shouldn't have been surprised that Dante wanted to meet me there. It was, after all, their turf.

Dante owned the bar, laundered money through it, and that had been how he'd gained power with Enzo, earning his trust as his second.

What happened to Enzo?

Was he at the bar with Dante right now? Had that been why they'd asked me to join them?

I pulled up out front and shut off the engine. Exhaling a heavy breath, I checked the glove compartment for a weapon.

I shoved the Glock into the waistband of my pants before I stepped out and headed for the front door of the bar.

The hinges on the heavy wood squeaked as I yanked it open.

In the corner booth, the darkest part of the bar, Dante sat his back to the wall, his gaze on the door.

Jaxson and Lincoln sat at the bar, both of them with a drink in their hands, but they didn't appear to be throwing any back.

The place was mostly empty.

Dante had been waiting for me.

How long had he been here?

Dante nursed a cold bottle of beer. His fingers stroked the glass. "Nice of you to join me," he said.

I climbed into the booth and sat opposite of him. I wasn't comfortable with my back to the door. My stomach sunk from the feeling that someone could come up from behind and I wouldn't see them.

But Jaxson and Lincoln were a few feet away. They'd have my back.

At least I hoped they'd have my back. I hadn't exactly had theirs lately.

I was trying to make amends and do right by them.

"Enzo didn't answer his door," I said.

Dante shrugged and sipped his beer. "I suppose he's not home."

Well, that was cryptic.

"I have questions," I said. "For starters, you all betrayed me, snatching my fiancée and handing her over to the enemy."

Dante held up a hand. "Was she really your fiancée?"

Had he seen through the charade?

"Where's Benjamin Ryan?" I asked, ignoring Dante's question and changing the subject.

"You mean the rat," Dante muttered under his breath. "You tell me. You hired him." Dante's eyes tightened and flinched.

"You know where he is," I said and leaned forward. "Tell me, and I'll keep you out of this mess that Enzo and Angelo dug for themselves."

He took another swig of his beer. "They dug their graves. I always told Enzo not to deal with Angelo. You can't ever trust another don, but Enzo was all brass and no brains."

Was?

Did he realize that he spoke about him in the past tense?

"Enzo's dead?" I asked.

Dante didn't answer my question. At least not directly.

"He made his bed and is lying in it."

"What about Ben?" I asked. "He betrayed the Ricci Family. That doesn't come without a cost."

Dante finished his beer and gestured the bartender over for a second. He waited until we were alone again before speaking.

"Do you know that Enzo suspected that you were the traitor?" Dante asked.

I held my tongue, not wanting to reveal that Enzo was right. I had betrayed him to save those girls, but I hadn't been the only one. Ben had betrayed all of us.

"If I was, would I be coming to you?" I asked. "Seems like suicide."

"Truth is I never liked Enzo's recent business dealings." He huffed and shook his head. His top lip snarled with disgust. "I'm no saint by any means, but things are going to start cleaning up around here, and you can guarantee that DeLuca's men will be driven out of town."

Was that a threat?

"You're the new don," I said, letting the realization dawn on me that Dante had taken over the Ricci Family. Not only was he second, but he also had Enzo's men behind him, an army that supported him.

"You're lucky I like you," Dante said. "But I don't trust you to be an associate anymore. That was Enzo who wanted to hire you. You can come and have a drink on me, but you need to find another place of employment."

That was fine with me.

"We're not going to let you steal any more women or children." I wanted it made clear that I wasn't going to allow him to hurt anyone else in Breckenridge.

Dante laughed under his breath. "As I stated earlier, I wasn't a fan of Enzo's business practices and have no intention of continuing his games. I have other matters that have captured my interest that I don't care to discuss with you."

He took another swig from his beer before putting the bottle down forcefully against the table. "Your fiancée, or whatever she is, I have no desire for her. As long as she keeps my name out of her mouth, you can rest assured that my men will leave you alone."

"Is that a threat?" If Skylar testified against Dante, was he going to endanger her life?

Dante smiled. "The way I see it, I've done nothing wrong. Enzo snatched your fiancée, and you hired Ben. My hands are clean."

"Where is Ben?" I'd come here to locate Benjamin Ryan, and I hadn't gotten the slightest detail on where to track him down.

"You tell me; he betrayed the Ricci Family for the DeLuca Family. Rats end up dead, but I didn't kill him. He wasn't massacred in the bloodshed?"

I opened my mouth but shut it just as quickly. Ben was dirty, but I wasn't a saint, either. How I'd managed to avoid jail and turn my life around was a miracle.

"If I get my hands on Ben, he's a dead man. Then again, maybe I should thank him. With Don DeLuca out of the picture, Sergio dead, and his guards mopped all over the compound, my newest enemy is Angelo's second, Gino, and he's too old to be on the front lines. It's like being don was just handed to me. And in a matter of time, the DeLucas will be under my control. I'm guessing I have you and your pretty little team to thank for that?"

Dante held up a beer to say 'cheers' to Jaxson and Lincoln as they sat at the bar.

"The best part is I've got my sights on Gino's daughter, Nicole. That hot little piece of ass, I'm going to get my hands on her and ruin her."

CHAPTER THIRTY-NINE

ARIELLA

I still couldn't believe the doctor at the hospital. He had to have been wrong.

Pregnant?

How was I pregnant? I mean, yes, we hadn't been one hundred percent careful, but I was assured that I couldn't get pregnant again.

My last, and only, pregnancy with my son had been difficult. He'd been born early and hadn't survived life outside of N.I.C.U.

Worry filled every ounce of me, and while Jaxson had accompanied me to an obstetrician, neurologist, and midwife, they all confirmed that I was doing well, had adjusted the medication I was on, and assured me that the baby was in good health according to every test they'd run.

Bed rest wasn't a requirement as long as I was taking it easy, not undergoing too much stress, and my heart rate was within the normal perimeters.

The doctors also assured Jaxson and me that we could have sex, as long as we were careful not to do anything too strenuous, and recommended a bed, anything to keep me seated or lying down.

My cheeks had flamed with embarrassment. But Jaxson had

seemed like he was mentally taking notes at the appointments, learning what he could and couldn't do with his pregnant girlfriend.

Jaxson insisted I monitor my heart rate constantly, which wasn't complicated with a smartwatch. He was more than just a tad overprotective, but I appreciated his concern.

Besides, he wasn't the only one worried about the health of the baby.

How could I not have fears after the last time I'd been pregnant? The good news was that the chronic symptoms that plagued me were minimal in my second trimester. Being pregnant had at least temporarily made me feel better.

I could get around easier without my heart rate skyrocketing when I stood. My stomach, while in knots, had been over concern for our little one and not from the adrenaline spikes that I had been accustomed to.

As we curled up in bed together, Jaxson's hand grazed my growing belly. While I hadn't felt our little pumpkin yet, it was only a matter of time.

I rolled onto my back, and Jaxson lifted the hem of my shirt, dropping soft kisses over my belly. "I've never seen you so eager to kiss my stomach," I teased.

His long, dark lashes fluttered as he smiled up at me. "I will have to rectify that, Freckles." His touch was soft and light and made my stomach feel like a thousand butterflies.

My eyes widened, realizing it wasn't my nerves or his touch exciting me. Well, it did that too. But it was the baby.

"Oh my gosh! Did you feel that?" I asked, staring into Jaxson's gaze.

"The baby likes my attention."

"What sane person wouldn't?" I asked. My fingers tangled in Jaxson's hair, caressing his scalp. "I'm almost afraid to admit it, but I like being pregnant."

Jaxson stared up at me. His breath hovered against my stomach. His hand rested over the small bump. "It suits you," he said. "The saying is true that a pregnant woman glows."

I rolled my eyes and scrunched my nose. "I'm not sure I believe that," I said, laughing. "But you should know, my symptoms that I'm accustomed to—the heart rate issues, nausea, all the chronic bad stuff, seem better. Like being pregnant healed me. I mean, it's probably crazy and nonsense, but if I always felt this good, I'd be happy always to be pregnant."

He quirked a grin. "So, we're going to have a herd of little Monroes running around here?"

I smacked his arm. "They're not cattle!" Shaking my head, laughing, it felt good not to have to hide our relationship or the fact that he was the father of my little pumpkin.

"Platoon?" he grinned. "I can have my own little Eagle Tactical army."

"You are horrible!" I pointed my finger at him. "You're not teaching our boys or girls any military training. They're children."

Jaxson leaned in and planted a soft kiss on my forehead. "I know that. I meant when they're older. Not just boys, but grown men. So, like when they're thirteen."

"Oh, brother," I muttered.

His fingers tickled my hips as he inched my shirt higher, disrobing me of my clothes.

"Another added benefit." He grinned, admiring my round breasts. "I could get used to keeping you pregnant and barefoot in the kitchen."

"You'd better be teasing!" I swatted at him, and he grabbed my wrist and pinned me down on the mattress.

"Maybe we should try to make another brother or sister," Jaxson teased.

I rolled my eyes. "You know it doesn't work like that. You can't get a pregnant woman knocked up."

"Really?" He quirked his head to the side with a laugh. "Are you sure? I think we need to test that theory."

His breath teased my lips apart. I wanted more. His fingers were caressing me, undressing my pajama shorts and panties.

"When did you become a scientist?" I joked, continuing our

playful banter. For the first time in a long time, I felt free, safe, and unconditionally loved.

My fingers pushed at his boxers. I tugged them down his hips and felt the bed shift as he kicked the cotton material to the floor. "Didn't you get the memo? The boys at Eagle Tactical and I are all—"

"Stop right there." I held up a hand. "I don't know where this is going, but you're the only one testing that theory with me."

Jaxson grinned. His cheeks reddened. "That's not what I was suggesting!"

"Good, because I want only one man for the rest of my life." The confession spilled out before I'd even realized what I'd said.

He felt that way too about me, right?

"Good, because that's exactly what I want. You and Izzie. The two girls who vie for my attention."

"Yeah, well, that's totally different. Izzie can have your attention." The grin spread across my face as my fingers trailed soft, featherlight touches over his chest and down toward what I had my sights on. "I get your body."

"So that's all I'm worth to you, sex?" Jaxson asked. He laughed, not sounding the least bit upset or mad.

"Well, that's not all you're worth. Your mind is sexy too." I grinned up at him. "Come here and kiss me already."

His lips descended on mine, his breath warm and comforting, his body making my insides ache with his soft caress and gentle kisses. He was an expert in making me restless and full of need.

We rolled around in bed, each of us vying for control. Warm, strong hands caressed every inch of my skin, setting me ablaze.

I couldn't take much more of his teasing. My hand moved down to stroke him, touch him, and guide him inside my warmth.

I needed him like I needed air to breathe. "Please," I whispered, wanting this dance between us to quicken.

I'd never felt quite so desperate in my life, desiring something so much that I thought I might die if I didn't have it.

His eyes were bright and wide. His mouth covered mine as I moaned.

We had to be quiet.

Izzie was in bed, and we definitely did not want to wake her.

His warmth filled me, and his hands clasped mine as he slowly began moving, savoring each moment together.

"God, you're going to kill me," I muttered.

Sweat coated my skin.

My heart pounded against my chest, but it felt good.

Satisfying.

"More," I grunted.

Maybe it was the hormones and the fact that I was pregnant, but I couldn't seem to get enough of Jaxson. My fingernails grazed over his back and down to his bottom, pulling him tighter, claiming him for me.

His pace quickened, sensing my urgency and need.

Everything inside of me ached.

My heated core trembled and throbbed as he filled me, fueled me, and satisfied me.

Toes curled, I clung to him with eyes closed as fireworks danced over my vision. Gasping for breath, panting hard and held him tight as he came undone with me.

He was quick to roll off and pull me against him. "I don't want to squish you or hurt the baby."

"You won't," I said with a soft laugh. "Our little pumpkin is well protected." I gently patted the slight bulge of my stomach.

Curled against Jaxson, my fingers danced in his hair, my eyes never leaving his. "Your sister, Skylar, wants to throw me a baby shower. Well, us."

"No."

"Come on. She's trying to make amends," I said.

His eyes twitched. "What she did, it's unforgivable."

He was one stubborn man. I'd give him that. "Yes, but she's trying to do better. She's your sister. Didn't you forgive Jayden?" I asked.

"That's different."

Jaxson had offered Jayden a spot with the Eagle Tactical team. I'd been surprised that he'd invited him to join them and even more shocked to learn that Jayden had accepted the offer.

"How?" I asked.

"I expected Jayden to betray me."

I sat up slightly in bed. My fingers paused in his hair. "You are so full of shit." I grabbed the pillow and smacked him playfully with it.

"You did not just hit me with a pillow."

"Oh, I did," I countered. "And you can't hit your pregnant wi—girlfriend back."

Jaxson grabbed me by the hips and tucked me under him, straddling me. His hands tickled my hips. "That's not what you were going to say."

I kept my mouth shut. My eyes were wide, and I was trying desperately not to laugh too loud and wake Izzie next door.

"You don't know what I was going to say," I countered.

Jaxson's hands stalled on my hips. "Is that so? It sounded quite a bit like you were about to refer to yourself as my pregnant wife."

His gaze bored into mine.

Shit.

He went there.

He said what I was desperately trying not to say and that had slipped out inadvertently. It just felt natural, far more familiar, and better than when I'd been married the first time around.

I had sworn I'd never remarry. And I'd meant it until I met Jaxson.

We were having a pumpkin together.

I could still hear Jaxson's voice in my head. The first words he'd said when I'd referred to the baby as pumpkin. *You've got to be kidding me!* He'd come to understand it was a coping mechanism and a way to discuss the baby without me fretting that I'd jinx it.

He'd gone along with it because he was Jaxson Monroe, and he'd do anything for those he loved.

"Well?" Jaxson smiled. He stared down at me, waiting for my answer.

"I didn't hear you propose," I countered.

Two could play at that game.

"I'm not going to."

The smile fell from my face.

Wow. He went there.

I tried to slip from his embrace, but he wouldn't let me.

Tears threatened my vision. The room felt hot, stuffy. "Let me up," I gasped. I needed to move, get out of bed, run to the bathroom.

And do what?

Cry?

Hide?

I felt like a fool.

"Ariella, look at me."

My bottom lip trembled, and he guided my chin to meet his stare.

"I'm not going to propose to you until I know you'll say yes."

"What?" Had I heard him correctly?

I blinked back the tears. Now I felt like a mess. An even bigger one that I had moments earlier when I thought he said he'd never want to marry me.

"I want it to be a big, fancy ordeal, and I'm not going to have you blow my ego and say no." Jaxson grinned as he stared down at me.

I wiped the single tear that had fallen down my face.

I was a mess. A pregnant, hormonal mess. Which was Jaxson's fault. But even so, he'd been sweet and kind, and I'd jumped to conclusions.

"I'll marry you on one condition," I said, staring up at him through glistening eyes.

He stared and waited for me to continue.

"You make amends with Skylar."

Jaxson whined like a child as he straddled my hips. "Aww, come on. After what she did to you and Izzie? How am I supposed to forgive her?"

"She's trying. Maybe baby steps," I said. "She's your family, and I know she was selfish and put all of our lives at stake, but I've come to forgive her."

"Really? You don't hate her in the slightest bit?" Jaxson asked.

I wasn't going to lie to him. "Oh, I'm still mad at her, but I'm working through my anger. You've forgiven Jayden. It's time for you to make amends with Skylar."

He exhaled loudly through his nose. "I don't know, Freckles. You're asking an awful lot of me."

I laughed at the absurdity of the situation. "And marrying you will be a picnic?" I grinned up at him.

"Damn right, it will be. I'll be your knight in shining armor," Jaxson said. "I'll sweep you off your feet and carry you over the threshold."

"Yeah, right, before knocking my head into a wall. I've seen the movies. No thanks."

Jaxson leaned down. His lips grazed mine. "How about I think about it?"

"What? Marrying me?"

"No, silly. Forgiving Skylar," Jaxson said. "I definitely want to marry you."

"Good, because she's hosting the baby shower. She'll be over next Saturday. You can work things out with her."

A part of me still hated Skylar for what she'd done, but I understood she'd been coerced into helping Ben, or Angelo DeLuca would have sold her as part of the slave auction. Her life depended on it, and while she hadn't intended to kidnap anyone but me, hoping that I would be able to save the two of us, her plan had imploded.

At least that's the story she gave me when we sat at the coffee shop to talk.

"Fine, but if she so much as looks at you the wrong way, she's gone," Jaxson said.

"Good." I leaned over and planted my lips on his. "I'd expect nothing less from the man I love."

EPILOGUE

JAXSON

Everything had fallen into place. Ariella had delivered a healthy baby girl whom we named Olivia Monroe.

Izzie had been ecstatic to have a baby sister but hadn't quite understood why she couldn't play tea party or push her on the swings just yet.

Harper had been blessed with a surprise, twins. The doctors had been shocked to discover in the third trimester that there had been a second baby, a boy hiding behind his sister.

Harper was thrilled by the news.

Lincoln hid his initial panic well, and by the time the twins were born, they handled it together like a pro.

It also helped that Harper still had residual royalties from her film career, and they could afford to hire a nanny to help out with the twins.

A firm knock echoed through the front door.

"Just a second!" I called out, holding little Olivia in my arms. She was cuter than any pumpkin that I'd ever laid eyes on.

I glanced through the peephole, surprised to see Sheriff Nelson on the opposite side.

I turned off the alarm and unlocked the front door, greeting him. "Sheriff, I didn't expect to see you," I said.

"I wanted to bring you the news in person."

It had better be good news. I couldn't handle anything terrible. "Yes?" I asked. My mouth was dry, parched.

"Is this your little one?" Sheriff Nelson asked, cooing at Olivia.

"Sure is. Sheriff Nelson, please tell me it's good news that you have."

"It is." He nodded firmly. "We tracked down Ben Ryan last night. We received a tip from an anonymous source and discovered him nailed to a wall with his own nail gun."

I did my best to look surprised.

"Wow."

I hadn't told Ariella that the boys and I had located Ben last night, played with him a bit, and then called in the local police to make sure that he survived to stand trial.

"You don't look that surprised," Sheriff Nelson said.

"No, I am. I'm relieved that it will finally be over." I bounced Olivia as she started fussing in my arms.

Had my newborn daughter sensed my frustration and anger with Ben? I hadn't wanted to worry Ariella; it had been why I hadn't told her that we'd tracked him down to a shed that he was living in, next door to us.

He'd taken up residence in the shed on her old property.

Had he been stalking us?

Waiting for the moment to snatch our children or hurt my fiancée? I refused to stand still and wait for him to ruin our lives, again.

"He's been arrested and charged with kidnapping, child endangerment, attempted murder, trafficking women across state lines, the list goes on," the sheriff said.

"I'm just glad you guys finally nailed the guy."

The sheriff's eyebrow twitched. "I really hope you weren't involved, Monroe."

"I'm sure you asked Ben and he told you the truth."

Sheriff Nelson rolled his eyes. "Like they always do. Anyway, I've already spoken with Skylar Monroe, Hazel Agron, and Harper Madison. They've all agreed to testify against Benjamin Ryan. Your wife, Ariella Monroe, was kidnapped twice by Ben. Her testimony would go a long way to help keep him locked up indefinitely."

"I'll do it," Ariella said as she came around the corner from the hallway into the living room.

I hadn't heard her sneak in.

Shit.

Had she heard how he'd been found, nailed to the wall?

"Are you sure?" I glanced back at Ariella.

"Yes, I need to make sure that he never sees a day outside of prison again."

I'd be there for Ariella every step of the way. "Okay. What about Enzo Ricci?" I asked the sheriff. "Has there been any word about him?"

While I'd had to give a statement along with the Eagle Tactical guys about Angelo and Sergio DeLuca, Enzo had been involved. He'd handed my sister over to Angelo without her consent and triggered this train wreck of circumstances.

"He's gone. Missing, as far as we can tell. Left town, and no one's seen or heard from him. At least no one's talking. We suspect foul play. It's possible one of DeLuca's men crossed him and killed him, but we've recovered no body, and there's been no apparent crime scene."

"He's still out there," Ariella said. She folded her arms across his chest.

"I wouldn't lose any sleep over it. He knows the local sheriff and the feds are looking for him. If he's smart, he left town, flown to another country that doesn't have extradition. The feds flagged his passport, but a guy like him, he doesn't fly commercial."

Based on the conversation Jayden had with Dante, I suspected Enzo was dead.

The mafia knew how to cover up and destroy evidence.

No one would find Enzo, ever.

"And the human trafficking ring?" I asked. We'd handed over the information that we had obtained, and the eyewitness testimony from Ariella, Hazel, and Jayden was enough to put the DeLuca Family out of business.

Dante Ricci was still out there, but he'd sworn that he'd taken his business ventures in a different direction.

Olivia began fussing, and Ariella stepped in, taking her from my arms to feed her.

"No more shipments are coming in and out of Breckenridge. We've got feds keeping a watch on Gino DeLuca and Dante Ricci. If either of them so much as slips up and they will, just give it time, we'll be on their asses."

"Thank you," I said, relieved to hear that it finally would all behind us.

The mafia probably still laundered money, sold drugs or weapons, but at least it wasn't people.

I walked the sheriff out and secured the door behind him, turning the alarm back on. You could never be too safe.

"Are you sure you want to testify against Ben?" I asked.

Ariella sat on the sofa feeding our baby girl who was cradled in her arms.

"I don't see another choice. I need to keep my family safe, and the best way to do that is to lock that bastard behind bars."

Izzie jumped down the steps, two at a time, hopping like a kangaroo before hurrying over to sit next to her baby sister.

"Momma, what's a bastard?" Izzie asked.

Shit.

Some things never changed.

Thank you for reading Covert: Jayden. I hope you've enjoyed the entire Eagle Tactical series.

Want to see more of Dante and the Ricci Family?

Secret Vow, the first book in the Mafia Marriages series, is hotter and darker, but each book will deliver a happily ever after!

There will even be a special appearance from one of the main characters in the Eagle Tactical series. But don't worry, I promise not to destroy their happy ending.

She wants her freedom, and all I want is her...

Nicole DeLuca, she's the daughter of the biggest crime boss on the west coast. Did I mention that her father, Gino DeLuca, is my enemy?

I slept with Nikki, and I can't for the life of me forget about her. I've been keeping tabs on her, making sure no other men come anywhere near her.

I'll chase them away like the beast that I am to protect her.

Like a caged bird, she's desperate for freedom. Nikki sneaks out only to get snatched and sold as a bride.

Even in the darkest room, the dirtiest corner of the world, I recognize her. She's my little dove.

I buy her. Own her. Save her.

Except she doesn't see it that way...

She wants her freedom, and all I want is her and that baby.

One-click Secret Vow now!

And sign up for my newsletter to find out about new releases, giveaways, and freebies: www.authorwillowfox.com/subscribe

I appreciate your help in spreading the word, including telling a friend. Reviews help readers find books! Please leave a review on your favorite book site.

GIVEAWAYS, FREE BOOKS, AND MORE GOODIES

I hope you enjoyed the Eagle Tactical Collection and were satisfied with the happily ever after for Jaxson, Ariella, and the Eagle Tactical team.

While this is my first series as Willow Fox, I've been published professionally since 2013.

Sign up for my Willow Fox newsletter

If you enjoyed the series, please take a moment to leave a review. Reviews helps other readers discover my books.

Not sure what to write? That's okay. It doesn't have to be long. You can share how you discovered my book; was it a recommendation by a friend or a book club? Let readers know who your favorite character is or what you'd like to see happen next. Do you normally read HEA? How are you feeling about the HFN? (I hope satisfied but I promise I will be delivering a HEA at the end of the series!)

Thank you for reading! I hope you'll consider joining my mailing list for free books, promotions, giveaways, and new release news.

ABOUT THE AUTHOR

Willow Fox has loved writing since she was in high school (many ages ago). Her small town romances are reflective of living in a small town in rural America.

Whether she's writing romance or sitting outside by the bonfire reading a good book, Willow loves the magic of the written word.

She dreams of being swept off her feet and hopes to do that to her readers!

Visit her website at:

https://authorwillowfox.com

ALSO BY WILLOW FOX

Eagle Tactical Series

Expose: Jaxson

Stealth: Mason

Conceal: Lincoln

Covert: Jayden

Truce: Declan

Mafia Marriages

Secret Vow

Captive Vow

Savage Vow

Unwilling Vow

Ruthless Vow

Bratva Brothers

Brutal Boss

Wicked Boss

Possessive Boss

Obsessive Boss

Dangerous Boss

Bossy Single Dad Series

Billionaire Grump

Mountain Grump

Bachelor Grump

Faking it with the Billionaire

Looking for kinkier books? Try these spicy stories written under the name Allison West.

Boxsets

Academy of Littles

Western Daddies Collection

Obey Daddy Collection

The Alpha Collection

Western Daddies

Her Billionaire Daddy

Her Cowboy Daddy

Her Outlaw Daddy

Her Forbidden Daddy

Standalone Romances

The Victorian Shift

Jailed Little Jade

Prefer a sweeter romance with action and adventure? Check out these titles under the name Ruth Silver.

Aberrant Series

Love Forbidden

Secrets Forbidden

Magic Forbidden

Escape Forbidden

Refuge Forbidden

Boxsets

Gem Apocalypse

Nightblood

Royal Reaper

Royal Deception

Standalones

Stolen Art

www.ingramcontent.com/pod-product-compliance
Lightning Source LLC
LaVergne TN
LVHW090543110826
845146LV00001B/2

* 9 7 9 8 8 8 6 3 7 1 9 1 8 *